THE
JUDGMENT

Previous novels by the author

The Prosecution
The Defense

D.W. BUFFA

THE JUDGMENT

WARNER BOOKS

A Time Warner Company

Copyright © 2001 by D. W. Buffa
All rights reserved.

Warner Books, Inc., 1271 Avenue of the Americas, New York, NY 10020

Visit our Web site at www.twbookmark.com

A Time Warner Company

Printed in the United States of America

First Printing: May 2001

10 9 8 7 6 5 4 3 2 1

Library of Congress Cataloging-in-Publication Data
Buffa, Dudley W.
    The judgment / by D. W. Buffa.
      p. cm.
    ISBN 0-446-52737-8
    1. Trials (Murder)—Fiction. 2. Judges—Fiction. I. Title.

PS3552.U3739 J8 2001
813'.54—dc21   00-060013

For My Father
Harold David Buffa
Who always told stories I never wanted to end

Acknowledgments

Wendy Sherman, my agent, gave me all the support and encouragement of a friend. Rob McMahon, my editor, showed me how to write the book I wanted to write. In ways only she can know, my wife, Kathryn Martin, made me believe that it was something worth doing.

THE
JUDGMENT

One

I have spent years defending some of the worst people who ever lived, but the most evil man I ever knew was never once accused of a crime. Nothing, not even curiosity, could have made me attend his funeral had he died in his sleep or been killed in an accident, but Calvin Jeffries had been murdered, and I felt an obligation as someone who practiced in the criminal courts to attend the services of the only trial judge to become the victim of a homicide.

Surrounded by strangers, I sat in the crowded church and listened to the eulogy of someone I had never met. There were words about justice and public service and dedication and honor and goodwill, words about family and friends and how much the honorable Judge Jeffries would be missed, words which made everyone feel better because the lie is so much more comfortable than the truth.

At the end, when there was nothing left to say, the widow of Calvin Jeffries placed a rose on top of his flag-draped coffin, waited until the pallbearers were ready, and then, turning around, walked at the head of the procession as it moved down the aisle. Even the light that streamed through the stained glass windows failed to penetrate the heavy black veil that covered her face, and I wondered as she passed by me what emotions were masked behind it.

Outside, under a harsh blue sky, the mourners watched while the coffin was lifted into the back of a sleek, shiny hearse. The judge's widow was helped into the first of a half dozen waiting limousines and, moments later, with two police motorcycles leading the way, the cortege began the long slow journey to the cemetery.

The bitter March wind stung the side of my face and watered my eyes. I pulled my topcoat close around my throat and began to jostle my way down the church steps. I was in a hurry to get away. Now that it was over, I wanted to forget all about the late lamented Calvin Jeffries.

As I turned up the sidewalk, I almost ran into Harper Bryce. "Any comment you'd care to make, Mr. Antonelli?" he asked.

Bryce, who had covered the courthouse as a newspaper reporter longer than I had practiced law, was standing in front of me. His tie flapped outside his buttoned jacket and his eyes squinted into the wind, each gust stronger than the one before. I made no reply other than to shake my head, and we trudged up the street without exchanging a word until he asked me if I wanted to stop somewhere for a drink.

"It's a little early, isn't it?"

On the next block, in one of the old buildings with the date of its construction embedded in stone above the entrance, a bar and grill was just opening its doors. We ordered at the empty bar and carried our drinks to a wooden table next to a dusty brick wall covered with the autographed pictures of people once famous or important and now long forgotten.

With a slow, heavy breath, Harper drew the chair as close as his expansive stomach would allow, hunched his sloping shoulders forward, and rested his arms on the edge of the table.

"Here's to Judge Jeffries," he said as he lifted his glass. When he finished, he cocked his head, waiting for me to explain why I had not joined him. "Most people liked him," he reminded me.

I nodded and then took a drink, wincing as it burned its way down my throat.

"Whatever you thought of him, you have to give him credit," Harper went on. The words came a few at a time, punctuated by the wheezing sound of his breath as his chest heaved up and down like a bellows. "He wrote most of the law—most of the procedural law—in this state. He had a brilliant legal mind. You have to give him that."

The liquor had reached my stomach, and I remembered I had not had anything to eat.

"You have to give him that," Harper was still insisting as I got up from the table. At the bar, I exchanged the drink for a cup of coffee and ordered bacon and eggs.

"I'm having breakfast," I told him as I sat down. "You want something?"

He started to shake his head, then changed his mind. "I'll have the same thing," he yelled across the empty room.

"Don't you think he had a brilliant legal mind?" Harper asked, curious why I seemed so reluctant to agree.

"You want me to tell you about the first time I ever met him?" I asked, surprised at how clearly I remembered what until that moment I had not thought about in years. "That isn't exactly right," I corrected myself. "I didn't really meet him. I appeared in front of him, in a trial—not even a real trial—a trial on stipulated facts."

It had happened years ago, at the beginning of my career, and it was as if I had just walked out of that courtroom. Harper gave me a quizzical look as I laughed at how angry it still made me.

"You know what a stipulated facts trial is? It's a plea bargain that allows the defendant to appeal a legal issue that is in dispute. That's what we were doing. I had not been practicing more than six months, and I had this kid charged with stealing a car. I tried to get his confession thrown out, but I lost on that. The deputy D.A. was one of the good ones. He thought it was a close call, and that an appellate court should decide."

Harper never forgot he was a reporter. "Was Jeffries the judge who denied your motion?"

"No, another judge had done that. Jeffries wasn't the one who might get overturned on appeal. He didn't have any stake in what happened one way or the other. At least not that way," I added.

I lifted the cup with both hands and sipped the black coffee, remembering the way Jeffries had looked that day, his pug-fingered hands folded in front of him, waiting for me to begin. He was still in his thirties, but his wavy hair, which ran in a straight line from his brow, was already silver smooth.

"McDonald—that was the name of the deputy D.A.—recited the facts of the case. The defendant—I've forgotten his name— was standing right next to me, his hands cuffed in front of him. He had broken into the home of his former girlfriend, taken her keys, and stolen her car. It was simple, straightforward, nothing to it. McDonald finished, and Jeffries turned to me. 'Does the defendant agree with this rendition of the facts?' he asked. The kid nodded and I said yes out loud for the record. It was the first stipulated facts trial I had done, but McDonald had done dozens of them. It was all routine.

"Jeffries drew himself up and looked right at McDonald. 'Very well. Based on these facts, I find the defendant not guilty.'

"Not guilty! It was impossible. But there it was. Jeffries kept looking at McDonald, daring him to open his mouth."

I raised my eyes until I met Harper's gaze. "So far as I know, I'm the only defense lawyer who ever won a stipulated facts trial, and I only won it because Jeffries was so utterly corrupt."

"Your client bought him off?"

"My client didn't have anything to do with it. It was worse than bribery. It was power. Earlier that same week, McDonald had been late for a court appearance. Jeffries, who was never on time himself, was in a rage. He told him no one was ever late to his courtroom. And he meant it."

The bartender brought breakfast, and Harper began to cut the eggs with his knife and fork. "Everyone always said he ran a tight courtroom," he remarked as he lifted the fork to his mouth.

"And everyone said Captain Bligh ran a tight ship," I replied as I started to eat. The eggs were runny and the bacon was charred. After a couple of bites I shoved the plate aside and forgot about food. My mind was filling with images of things that had happened, the oldest of them crowding out the others, as if clarity came only after a memory had been buried for years.

"The next time I saw Jeffries was about a month later. I had a case that had to be set for trial. Jeffries liked to do these things in chambers. When he got to my case, he leaned back in his chair, a big smile on his face, and said, 'Tell your client if he pleads guilty, he'll get probation, but if he goes to trial, he goes to prison.'"

I looked at Harper as I cradled the warm coffee mug in my hands. "I was young, new, more interested in saying something smart than doing something wise. I couldn't let it go. 'Even if he's acquitted?' God, you should have been there. The room was full of lawyers. Everyone was laughing, everyone but Jeffries. He stared at me with cold-eyed suspicion, and then, without a word, went on to the next case."

Harper mopped up a liquid yellow yolk with a piece of toast and stuffed it into his mouth. With a paper napkin he wiped his lips, and asked, "What did Jeffries do to get even?"

"Even?" I replied with a rueful laugh. "That was never good enough for Jeffries, not by half."

The door opened and I shuddered as a gust of cold air struck the back of my neck. An old man in a tweed jacket and a woman bent over a cane took a table on the other side of the room.

"A few weeks later I had a case on the criminal docket, and Jeffries was on the bench. My client was in custody and all we are going to do is enter a not guilty plea. It isn't going to take more than two minutes. All the in-custody arraignments were set for eight-thirty. I was there at eight twenty-five. Jeffries was ten minutes late. He's late so often he doesn't bother to apologize. Court begins when he gets there; lawyers can wait.

"Usually the deputy D.A. calls the cases on the docket, but not in Jeffries's courtroom, not that day. Jeffries called them himself, called them alphabetically, all except my client. When he came to him, he skipped to the next name on the list and took everyone after that in order, all the way through until he had finished with them all. I had sat there for three and a half hours, and it was now five minutes before noon and my client was the only one left. Jeffries got up from the bench and went to lunch."

Harper seemed amused by it. If it had happened to someone else, or if it had been the only time it had happened to me, I might have found something humorous in it as well.

"So he made you wait until after lunch?"

"He came back in the afternoon, and without so much as a glance in my direction announced that because the civil calendar was unusually crowded, any criminal matters left over from the morning would be taken up the next day."

"Judicial discretion," Harper remarked with a wry expression. His eyes grew distant, as if he was starting to remember other occasions on which he had witnessed other judges inflicting injury on lawyers they did not like. "It was a long time ago," he said, coming back to himself. "Why does it still bother you so much?"

"It probably wouldn't, if it had been the end of things," I explained. "But it was just the beginning."

Another blast of cold air hit the back of my neck. A slightly built middle-aged man with slick black hair held the door while a taller, broad-shouldered man with snow white hair and wintry blue eyes passed in front of him. As soon as they saw us, they headed for our table.

"Hello, Joseph," the old man said softly as I stood up. Nearly seventy, Asa Bartram still practiced law. He came in late every morning and left early every afternoon, but he never missed a day. The other attorneys in the firm he had started before most of them were born parked in the underground garage, but Asa, who owned the building, parked his Cadillac on the street in front, directly under a NO PARKING sign that always kept his space vacant.

"You know Jonah," he said to me as he turned and shook hands with Harper. Small, dark-eyed, with a nervous twitch that locked his left eye into a permanent squint, Jonah Micronitis paid no attention to me. He pulled out a chair for the older man and waited until he sat down. "How are you," he said finally, with a quick, cursory nod as he moved to the other side of the table and took the fourth chair for himself.

Harper and I exchanged a brief glance as Micronitis leaned across and asked Asa what he wanted. Rubbing his large raw-boned hands together, the old man thought about it for a moment. "Just coffee." Micronitis nodded once, and lifted up his head. His eyes darted toward the bartender. "Coffee," he called out in a peremptory tone.

"Were you at the funeral?" Asa asked.

"Yes, I was."

He was a large man, with a high forehead and prominent cheekbones, who despite his age held himself rigid and alert. He looked at me, his white bushy eyebrows drawn together, his blue eyes sparkling, enjoying a private joke. "It's always good to outlive your enemies," he said finally.

Too impatient to wait, Micronitis went to the bar to get the coffee himself. He brought back two cups and set one in front of Asa.

I tried to be diplomatic. "I didn't view Jeffries as an enemy. We just never quite got along."

There was nothing hostile in the way he looked at me. His eyes remained friendly, if a little distant, but my answer had plainly amused him. "Jonah," he said without moving his eyes, "how would you describe the way Judge Jeffries felt about Antonelli?"

Slipping back into his chair, Micronitis glanced first at me, then at Bartram. A smirk shot across his small, tight-lipped mouth. "Hatred, pure and simple." His voice, a flat, slightly nasal monotone, carried no more emotion than if he had been asked for the time.

This reply seemed to add to the old man's amusement. "It's rather more of a challenge not to speak ill of the dead when it turns out the dead speak so ill of the living, isn't it?"

I shrugged it off and tried to turn the conversation in a different direction. "As I say, for some reason we just never got along. But you were quite good friends with him, weren't you?"

He took his eyes off me and stirred the cup of coffee on the table in front of him. He put the spoon down on the saucer, lifted the cup to his mouth, and, out of habit, blew on it before he drank. The loose, mottled skin on his throat throbbed as he swallowed.

"We went to law school together. The class of . . ." His voice trailed off, and at the first sign of uncertainty, Micronitis, always waiting to help, supplied the year. "Calvin didn't want to go to law school," Bartram continued, glancing at Harper, then at me, certain we would find this not only surprising but interesting as well. "Calvin wanted to be a doctor. He applied to medical school, and they were eager to have him. As well they might. Calvin had a brilliant mind. But when he told them that he had to work part-time while he was going to school—he had to help support his mother—they wouldn't let him in. They told him medical school was too difficult, that no one could get through if they were working at a job, even one that was part-time . . ."

"You never wanted to be the defense attorney in a medical malpractice case in his courtroom," Micronitis interjected. His eyes glistening, he slowly drew his index finger across his throat. "Hated doctors."

Bartram, his mind focused on what he wanted to say, had not stopped talking. "We started out together, opened our own office. We almost starved to death. Not that Calvin would have noticed. He never cared anything for the business side of the law. Always left all of that to me. He was too busy, reading cases, sitting in court listening to other lawyers make their arguments. He used to get in his car and drive down to Salem just so he could watch oral arguments in front of the Oregon Supreme Court."

Grasping the handle of the cup between his thumb and the gnarled knuckle of his forefinger, Bartram lifted it to his mouth, staring straight ahead as he drank.

"He should never have been a lawyer. He didn't have the temperament for it. You have to treat people with respect. You have to at least pretend that a client might have something to say worth listening to. You have to defer, with a show of good grace, to anything a judge decides to say. Calvin couldn't do it." As soon as he said it, he took it back. "No, that's not true. He could do it—and he did it—at least with judges, but he hated it, every minute of it. He thought it was all too demeaning."

He paused, a blank look on his face, as if he had lost the thread of his thought.

"All too demeaning," Micronitis reminded him.

The thin film of vague ambiguity dissolved, and Bartram's eyes came back into focus. "Calvin Jeffries," he said like someone recalling the name of a long-lost friend, "was blessed—or perhaps I should say cursed—with a really remarkable capacity to take in both sides of a question almost simultaneously." A shrewd glint entered his pale eyes. "I suppose I should have said 'to see the flaws' in both sides of an argument. He had the most analytical mind I ever saw."

He hesitated, just for a moment, and Micronitis opened his mouth. With a shake of his head that was more like a quick shudder, the old man cut him off. "There was something quite destructive about it, this way he had of demolishing every argument he heard. It became an obsession with him. He was so intent on showing everyone that they did not measure up, that he sometimes completely lost sight of the difference between better and worse. With that restless mind of his, everything was reduced to the absolute equality of imperfection."

This moment of lucidity seemed to exhaust his critical faculties. His head sagged down and as he fumbled with his coffee cup his hand trembled for a moment before he was able to bring it back under control.

"Well," he said, looking around the table, "for someone who wasn't interested in money, he did all right." His eyes landed on Micronitis. "Thanks to us, he was pretty well off, wasn't he."

You could almost see the electrons racing around the agile brain of Jonah Micronitis as he calculated, no doubt to the last dollar and cent, the net worth of Asa Bartram's deceased friend. "Quite a wealthy man." He caught the meaning of the look that passed between Harper and myself. "It all started years ago," he explained. "Before I joined the firm. Asa always had an eye for investments. He put the judge into some things—real estate, mainly—that didn't cost that much at the time."

With a grim laugh, the old man interjected: "But whoever killed him didn't get any of it. One thing you could always count on about Calvin—he never had enough money on him to pick up a check."

"The killer was probably after the car," Harper suggested. "That's where he was stabbed, right next to his car in the courthouse parking structure."

Wincing, Asa dropped his eyes. "Terrible thing, terrible thing," he muttered. "Just left there to die like that, and then somehow managed to drag himself back to his office. Must have crawled part of the way."

Micronitis checked his watch. "We better get going," he said.

Asa gave no sign he had heard. Instead, he raised his head and grinned at me. "Jonah was right. Calvin really hated you."

Laying my hand on his forearm, I looked into his aging eyes. "And do you hate me, too, Asa?" I asked gently.

He was startled at first, but then he realized I was not asking him about me at all. "No, of course not," he replied, patting my hand. "Calvin hated everybody." A shudder seemed to pass through him, and his mouth twisted into a grimace. He stared down at the table, shaking his head. Then he stopped, placed both hands on the arms of his chair, and drew himself up to his full height. "He was the most brilliant man and the meanest son of a bitch I ever knew. I made him rich, and he made me feel like he was doing me a favor by letting me do it."

"Then why did you?" Harper asked.

Asa did not understand. "Why did I what?"

Harper never had a chance to answer. Before the second word was out of the old man's mouth, Micronitis had already begun to explain. "Why did you make him rich if he treated you like that?"

With a toss of his head, Asa snorted. "Wish I knew. I just did it, that's all." He paused, his dim eyes twinkling with a thought that had just come to him. "It was like a marriage. After a while you settle into a kind of routine, and later on you can't remember why. I handled the business end of things when we started out together. It became one of the things I did, and I kept doing it after he went on the bench."

With his elbows on the table, he wrapped one hand over the other and rested his chin on top. His eyelids were closed into narrow slits and a shrewd smile played at the corners of his wide mouth.

"Once you did something for Calvin Jeffries, it stopped being a favor and became an expectation. He never thanked me, not once in all those years." Folding his arms across his chest, he sank back in his chair. "I don't think he even liked me," he said, pressing his lips together as he pondered the meaning of what he had received for all his trouble. Brightening, he turned his head until his eyes met mine. "He didn't like me, but he hated you."

Micronitis could hardly contain himself. "Yes, he really hated you," he said, his voice a cheerful echo.

I turned away from Asa and looked at Micronitis. "Do you know why he hated me?" I asked, irritated.

His eyes darted from mine to Asa and back again. He fidgeted around in his chair. The side of his mouth began to twitch. "No," he finally admitted. "I just know that he did."

Finished with his breakfast, Harper set his empty plate to the side. "Do you know why?" he asked, looking right at me.

"It was the Larkin case," Asa explained. Harper turned his head, waiting to hear more. "The Larkin case made our friend here famous," he said, nodding toward me. "Every lawyer who ever became famous became famous because of one case. The Larkin case was yours, wasn't it?"

Harper's eyes flashed. "I remember now. It was years ago. I couldn't cover it. I'd already been assigned to a murder trial that was scheduled at the same time." Harper thought of something. "Wasn't that the case the judge threw you in jail for contempt?" Then he realized what had happened. "Ah," he said, suddenly subdued, "Jeffries."

For a moment, no one said anything. Then, turning to Asa, Harper asked, "What was it about the case that made him hate Antonelli so much?"

Furrowing his brow, he tried to remember. Finally, he shook his head. "I don't really know. I never paid much attention to what went on in the courthouse. All I know," he said, repeating himself, "is that it was the Larkin case." He smiled apologetically at Harper and looked at me. "Tell us what happened, Joe. The Larkin trial."

Micronitis started to object. He tapped his fingernail on the glass crystal of his wristwatch, trying to remind Asa that there was somewhere he was supposed to be.

"Go ahead, Joe," Asa insisted. "I've always wanted to hear about it."

Harper endorsed the suggestion. "I've always wanted to hear about it, too." He stole a quick, sideways glance at Micronitis, then added, "And take your time. Don't leave anything out."

TWO

The Larkin case. As soon as I was reminded of it, I remembered everything, all of it; the way the women who worked in the courthouse went out of their way to let me know what an awful thing she had done; the rigid certainty that she was guilty; the vexation that whatever sentence she was given would be less than she deserved. Perhaps part of it was because she looked so much like they did, a plain, scarcely noticeable woman who seldom wore makeup and thought nothing of wearing the same dress two days in a row. Most of it of course was because her husband had already confessed to having done with their daughter what she was accused of having done with their son.

That was perhaps the most intriguing thing of all, and even now I cannot pretend to understand why the reaction against her was so much more ferocious than it was against him. He had been having sex with his own daughter for three and a half years. Not his stepdaughter, his own flesh and blood. It is difficult to imagine anyone doing anything worse, yet from the time his wife was first accused of having sexual relations with their young son, she became a monster of depravity and he became, well—nothing. He was a part of the background, a bit player, someone who had done something unspeakable, but something no different than the unforgivable acts of a thousand other men. The blame that attached to what he had done to his daughter had, as it were, been diffused by the frequency with which such things had been done before. Edward Larkin was a sexual predator who would be dealt with in the normal course of the criminal law; what Janet Larkin had done was beyond anyone's experience. No mother had sex with her son; it was an unnatural act outside the boundaries of not only every convention but every instinct. It was the ultimate taboo, and for that reason it had to be true. It was not the kind of thing someone, especially a child, would just invent.

I got the case for no other reason than that it was my turn. I was still doing court-appointed work, and when Janet Larkin was called for arraignment and announced she could not afford to hire a lawyer of her own, my name was next on the list. It is strange how often the most important things that happen to us are matters of chance, and how often we don't understand it at the time. I certainly did not. When I went to the district attorney's office to pick up the discovery in the case, the clerk, a tall woman in her late forties with long dangling brightly colored earrings, suggested I come up with a reason to get out of it.

"Have you heard about the book?" she asked, shaking her head in disgust. "It talks about having kids in the same bed with their parents. That's really sick," she added, as she turned away.

Just as I got to the door, Spencer Goldman grabbed my arm. Short, with a bristling brown mustache and wiry hair, he talked the way he moved, in sudden, explosive bursts.

"There's not going to be any deal in this case," he announced with ill-disguised hostility. There was a look of triumph in his eyes, as if he were certain that he had just inflicted a mortal wound. We had had cases together before, and he knew I was not shy about going to trial. I took every case I could to trial— that was the whole reason I became a lawyer: to try cases. He was not trying to scare me; he was trying to show me just how confident he was that Janet Larkin was guilty and that he was going to be able to prove it. There was something else as well, a sense of moral outrage about what had happened. Others, of course, had the same feeling, but I believe that he felt it perhaps more than anyone else.

"It was his case," Asa suggested by way of explanation.

"It was more than that. It was personal. Not between him and me," I added quickly. "Between him and the boy. He believed him, believed every word of the story the boy had told. Goldman didn't have any doubt—none—and it was, really, the most extraordinary story you've ever heard." Pausing, I stared down at the table, remembering the look of defiance on Goldman's face when he told me he knew the boy was telling the truth. "I suppose we believe what we want to believe, or what we think we're supposed to believe. Whatever the reason, he believed him, and he came to believe that the only chance the boy had to recover from the awful thing that had been done to him was to let him know that everyone believed him. The mother had to admit what she had done, or there had to be a trial to prove to the world that she had done it. He wanted to punish the mother, all right, but he mainly wanted to save the child." I shook my head. "The child! He was smarter than anyone else involved in the case. There was no question he was his father's son.

"Perhaps the most important thing to understand is that Edward Larkin, the father, never got caught. He had been abusing his daughter for years, and no one knew. The girl never told a soul. Once, it is true, she tried to tell someone—a girl she went to school with—but she pretended she was talking about someone else. She could not bring herself to admit the truth. It was a secret, and it might very well have remained a secret, if her father had not decided to talk about it himself.

"Try to imagine, if you can, what happened to Edward Larkin. For years he had been having sexual relations with his own daughter. I can't tell you that he felt guilt, or remorse, or had any kind of regret about it at all. I can't even tell you he thought it was wrong. Of course he had to have known that other people thought it was wrong; he had to have known that it was the kind of thing people get into very serious trouble about. It is certain that he never breathed a word about it to anyone. Then, one day—or so he claimed—he saw a television show, a discussion about incest, and he decided he had to talk to somebody. I don't know. It may be true. It's easier to admit you've done something when it's something other people do. And it's easier still, if it's something that can be considered a disease, something that isn't your fault, something that can be cured. He began to see a psychologist, and the psychologist convinced him that he had to see the police.

"Larkin told them everything. Charges were filed, but because he had come forward voluntarily, and because he was already in therapy, he pled guilty to one count of sexual abuse and was placed on probation. And because he was in therapy, the rest of that family had to go as well. Obviously, the girl needed help, and the mother, who had just learned what her husband had been doing with her daughter, needed it as well. The boy, it was thought, required counseling to help him cope with what had happened to everyone else.

"Gerald Larkin was eleven years old, and all of a sudden his whole world had been destroyed. Before anyone else could tell him what had happened, his father told him, though precisely what he told him no one ever really knew. But it would have been natural for the father to suggest that what he had done was not all that serious, or all that blameworthy, to spare his son as much pain as he possibly could and to tell him that at some point everything would be back to normal.

"Two months after he began seeing a counselor, the boy revealed that at the same time his father had been abusing his sister, his mother had been abusing him. He did not bring it all out at once. At first he remembered only being touched by someone's hands. Then, gradually, under the questioning of the therapist, he was able to recall more of what had happened until, finally, he had a clear recollection of everything. His mother, he insisted, had repeatedly forced him to have sexual intercourse.

"Everyone believed him, the psychologist, the police, the district attorney's office. It explained certain things. How could the father have been doing these things with the daughter without the mother knowing anything about it? The answer of course was that the mother did know, but did not care. You can see why everyone thought she was a monster. And then, of course, it seemed to explain the meaning of that book. It was nothing more than the simple proposition that it was better to let children crawl into bed with their parents when they felt afraid or insecure, than force them to stay in their own room alone. Whether that is good advice or not, I would not know, but there was nothing sinister in what it intended to teach. You could not tell that to anyone who had only heard about it, however. As far as they were concerned, it was a manual of depravity, written by the devil himself, instead of something you could find in any bookstore.

"Everyone knew she was guilty, and her continued insistence that she was not seemed only to prove her contempt for decent behavior. Not satisfied with ruining her son's life by repeated acts of incest, she was determined to make him a public spectacle by dragging him through the indignities of a jury trial. Janet Larkin inspired something close to universal hatred, and because I was her attorney, much of it was directed at me. Nearly every day a new batch of letters was delivered to my office expressing in language laced with obscenity the moral outrage of their anonymous authors. Even people I knew began to look the other way when they passed me in a hallway of the courthouse. I decided that in the best interest of my client I had no choice but to ask that the trial be moved as far away from Portland as possible. I filed a motion for a change of venue. It was the first major mistake I made.

"I was of course a lot younger then, and it was early in my career. Still, it's hard to believe I was ever that naive. Jeffries was already the presiding circuit court judge, and he could have had the case assigned to any judge he wanted. He assigned it to himself. He wanted that case, and he was not about to let it go. The motion never had a chance, but the price I paid for filing it had nothing to do with that.

"Someone once said that chance rules the universe. I don't know if that is true or not, but I do know that there are occasions on which it can completely change your life, and this, like the fact I was given the case in the first place, was one of them. I drafted the motion and then put it in final form. Normally, I would have had it sent to the court by registered mail or simply dropped it off at the clerk's office. But I was in a hurry. I wanted a hearing on it as soon as possible. I did not want to wait while it was sent through all the usual bureaucratic channels. I took it directly to Jeffries's office.

"No one was there. The outer office, where his judicial assistant had her desk, was deserted. It was not quite one o'clock, and assuming that she was probably on her way back from lunch, I took a chair and waited. Not ten seconds later, the door to Jeffries's chambers opened, and she emerged from the darkness inside. Barefoot and disheveled, she was pinning her hair up in back when she caught sight of me out of the corner of her eye. Flushed with embarrassment, she froze in her tracks. I walked from the chair straight to her desk, pretending that I had noticed nothing out of the ordinary. Laying the motion down in front of her, I gave a brief, formal explanation of what it was. She glanced at the document and, without breaking her silence, looked back at me, a question in her eyes, not whether I knew what she had been doing—no, she was certain of that—but whether I was someone who was likely to talk.

"'I'd like to have a hearing on this as soon as the judge has time on his calendar,' I said, maintaining the fiction that there was nothing in my mind but the motion I had come to deliver.

"'Is someone out there?' I heard Jeffries call as I turned and left.

"There are few things that make us feel more vulnerable than the suspicion that someone knows something about us we don't want them to know. It was not a feeling that Jeffries enjoyed, and the first chance he had he let me know that it was within his power to give me that same feeling a dozen times over. It happened during the first day of trial.

"The motion for a change of venue was denied. There was no hearing, no oral argument, nothing, just a two-sentence order that read: 'Defendant has moved for a change of venue. Defendant's motion is denied.' The trial started a few weeks later, on a Thursday afternoon. As soon as Jeffries took the bench, I renewed my motion.

"'That motion was denied,' he replied.

"I was incorrigible, and worse yet, rather proud of it. 'If it had not been denied,' I retorted, 'there would not be much point in renewing it, would there?'

"Jeffries stared hard at me. 'Denied again.'

"'Why don't we have a hearing on it first,' I suggested with an arrogance that not even my youth could excuse. 'That way, after you have listened to the arguments on the motion, you might be able to accompany your ruling with a reason.'

"Raising his head, he twisted it slightly to the side as he studied me intently. He took a slow, deep breath, and as he did so his nostrils flared and the corners of his mouth turned downward. For a long time, he did not speak a word.

"'You will do well to remember, Mr. Antonelli,' he said finally, 'that you are here to try your case, not my patience.' His voice, never deep, was more high-pitched than I had heard it before, as if only by an effort could he keep it from becoming a shriek. 'And, yes, Mr. Antonelli,' he went on, 'I do provide a reason when I rule on a motion, but only when the reason isn't obvious on the face of it, and only when the lawyer who filed it might actually be able to understand it.'

"There was nothing I could do. I had gone too far as it was. Retreating behind a mask of rigid formality, I played the lawyer, hiding my resentment while I nodded my acquiescence in every harsh word he lavished upon me. 'Thank you, your honor,' I said when he was finished, mindful that of all the tyrannies ever established on earth, a courtroom is the only one in which abuse is always to be followed by an expression of appreciation.

"I thought that this was the end of it, but it was only the beginning. I had barely begun questioning the first juror on voir dire when he was on me again.

"'That question is not germane to whether or not this person is qualified to be a fair and impartial juror,' he instructed me. I had asked the woman what grades her children were in. 'The juror questionnaire tells you how many children she has and how old they are. That's all you need to know about them.'

"It was the same with the next question, and the one after that. Nothing I asked was right; everything I asked was wrong. He interrupted me so often that I started to hesitate halfway through a question, waiting for him to do it again. He was making me look awkward, indecisive, someone who did not know what he was doing. He was making me look like a fool in front of the very people who had to trust me if I was going to have any chance to win. And he was doing it on purpose. Somehow, despite his constant badgering, his incessant corrections, I kept going. Then I asked the eighth juror the question I should have been asking all of them, the question I've asked every juror in every criminal case I've tried since: 'Even if you're convinced the defendant is probably guilty, will you still vote to return a verdict of not guilty if the state fails to prove that guilt beyond a reasonable doubt?'

"Jeffries practically jumped out of his chair. 'That question is not permissible. You are not allowed to ask a juror how they might vote on the ultimate issue in the case. You will not ask that question again, Mr. Antonelli. Not of this juror, nor of any other juror. Understand?'

"It was late on the second day, Friday, and I had been beaten on long enough. I turned back to the same juror, and more slowly than I had before, asked the same question again.

"'This will be a good time to end for the day,' Jeffries announced before an answer could be given. 'We'll resume Monday morning at nine-thirty.'

"He waited until the last prospective juror left the courtroom. His eyes were cold as ice. 'You were told not to do that. I told you that question was not allowable, and yet you immediately asked it again. You deliberately flouted the authority of this court, and I have no alternative but to hold you in contempt.'

"I had expected it, and if the truth be told, had almost looked forward to it. I was in contempt, not of the court, however, but of him and the way he was trying to destroy my ability to put on a defense. I stared back at him and kept my silence.

"'I sentence you to three days in jail.' He nodded toward the bailiff to take me away. 'You can be released Monday morning, in time for the trial,' he added as he gathered up his books and papers from the bench.

"'Your honor,' I replied, trying to stop myself from screaming, 'you can charge me with contempt, but I can't be put in jail for it—not under these circumstances—unless I'm found guilty after a trial.'

"He knew I was right, and we both knew it did not matter. The bailiff had his hand on my arm, warning me under his breath not to say another word, while Jeffries rose from the bench and disappeared into chambers.

"'He would have added more time,' the bailiff explained. 'I've seen him do it often enough before. You look cross-eyed at him, he throws the book at you.'

"I was delivered to the county jail and learned what it was like to become one of those who no longer exist. They took my wallet, my watch, my car keys, everything I had in my pockets, and looked at me like I was crazy when I asked if I could keep my briefcase. Apparently concerned that I might use my tie either to strangle someone or hang myself, they made me give it to them. Then they took my fingerprints, grabbing each hand and pushing down on it as they rolled each fingertip onto the paper sheet. When that was done, I stood on a taped line, looking straight ahead into the camera, and then with a quarter turn, gave them my profile. They now had my prints, my photograph, and all the possessions I had brought with me. Most important of all, they had me, and I did not like it one bit.

"I was a model of diplomacy and tact. When they finished processing me, one of the deputies grabbed my shoulder and shoved me ahead. I caught my balance and turned on him.

" 'You lay a hand on me again, you son of a bitch, and I'll have you in court for the rest of your natural life.'

"He was a large, bulky man, with small fat hands. I would never have believed he could move as fast as he did. Before I knew what was happening, my face was flat against the cinder block wall and both my arms were pinned behind my back. I felt the cold metal around my wrists and then the clicking noise as he locked the handcuffs tight.

" 'You're not in court now, counselor,' the deputy reminded me. He grabbed the same shoulder he had before and with one hard push sent me flying. He walked at a steady pace, and each time he caught up with me did it again until we reached a windowless metal door. I braced myself when he opened it, ready for the push that would send me tumbling inside. Instead, he turned me around, and unfastened the handcuffs.

" 'Nothing personal,' he said.

"He had that kind of stupid grin that you imagine on the face of the schoolyard bully after he has just flattened some scrawny little kid with thick glasses and a stutter who can't hit back. It was the first time I had ever actually seen that look. A coward from the cradle, I had learned to avoid that kind of trouble. I suppose it was the fear of being found out for what I really was that made me do what I did next. With both hands, I shoved him in the chest as hard as I could. He did not move, not so much as an inch. I might just as well have tried to move the wall. He stared at me, a blank look on his face, as if he did not quite comprehend what I was doing. Then, in an instant, the heel of his hand came up under my jaw and I was knocked backward into the cell, and the door slammed shut behind me. I was locked in a room, six feet by four, the only furnishing a wooden bench suspended from the wall on two metal chains. There was no window, no source of light, except a single dim light bulb that hung high overhead inside a wire mesh screen.

"Without any means to measure it, time came to a stop. After I had been there for what I knew could only have been a few minutes, I felt as if I had been sitting there, staring into nothingness, for hours. I stood up and started to pace back and forth, three small steps each way, counting out loud. It gave me a strange sense of satisfaction, the sound of my voice tolling off the passage of time, tangible proof that I was not imprisoned in a permanent present. It was a way of protecting myself against the fear that had already begun to gnaw at the edge of my conscious mind, the incipient panic at being shut away in a small confined space, the sense of terror that had always accompanied the thought of being buried alive.

"After a while I stopped counting and began to concentrate on the trial. I tried to think about what I was going to say in my opening statement after we finished selecting the jury. I sat down on the hard bench, and studied as carefully as I could the remembered faces of the jurors with whom I had already talked, and thought about which ones I should keep and which ones I should let go. There was a sound at the door. It swung open and a different guard motioned for me to follow him down another corridor. I asked him for the time. I had been in the cell for less than fifteen minutes.

"I assumed he was taking me to eat, or perhaps to change into the clothing of an inmate. He stopped, opened a door, and I found myself squinting into a glaring light. I was on a kind of stage, standing next to four or five other men in front of a wall with odd markings on it. From somewhere in the darkness on the other side of the light, a voice told us to turn to the left. Then I knew. I was in a lineup.

"As soon as I realized where I was and what they were doing,

I became convinced they were looking for someone who had committed either murder or rape, and that their witness would mistakenly pick me. I was certain of it, and I tried to look like someone else. I rolled my shoulders forward, until I was as bent over as someone who does stoop labor in the fields. I dropped my head and let my chin sag down onto my chest. I knew nothing about the crime and yet I thought I had something to hide. When it was over, and along with the others I was led out of the room, I almost felt as if I had gotten away with something.

"Instead of taking me back to the small cell, I was led down another corridor and put in what we used to call the tank. It was a large room, perhaps thirty feet by twenty, with benches on each of the four walls. On one side, two dirt-covered windows, so high up you could not reach them, much less see out of them, let in a gray, dismal light. Thirty or forty men were crowded together inside. Most were hunched over, staring down at the cement floor, or leaning back against the wall, their hands lying listlessly at their sides, or locked around an upraised knee, gazing straight ahead, an absent look in their eyes. Several were lying on the floor, arms crossed in front of them, sleeping off a drunk. The air was stagnant with the fetid smell of urine and sweat. Stepping carefully over the bodies on the floor, I found a place on the bench directly under the window. As my eyes adjusted to the light, I made out the figure of a man crouching low in the corner. It took me a minute before I realized that his pants were down around his ankles and he was squatting over the one toilet everyone was supposed to share. I turned away, disgusted. Then, convinced I must have been wrong, I looked again. He was sitting there, black hair matted down on his head, with a thick neck and huge fleshy arms, masturbating. In an instant, I was on my feet, moving across the room. Stumbling over the body of a drunk who woke up just long enough to swing his arm at my legs, I made it to the door and banged on it as hard as I could.

"'How long are you going to keep me in here?' I demanded when the guard opened the peephole.

" 'Be quiet,' he shouted back as he closed it in my face.

"I beat on the door again, yelling for the guard to come back, though I knew it was nothing more than an empty gesture of defiance. No one was going to help me, and the only thing I could do for myself was accept my situation without further complaint.

"I spent that weekend—three nights that seemed like three years—surrounded by drunks, derelicts, people who could barely function, men who had lost the capacity to distinguish between what happened forty years ago, before they had become addicts and alcoholics, and what was happening right in front of their eyes. They were the victims of their own self-inflicted madness.

"On the bench next to me, a bleary-eyed old man scratched the gray stubble on his cheek, trying to remember where he was. He opened his toothless mouth and, glancing up at me, began to talk in a rapid senseless monotone. At best, I could make out every third or fourth word as he rambled along, stopping every so often to ask, in a sudden burst of lucidity, 'Don't you see?' He would wait until I gave some sign, a nod, a shrug, a smile, something that showed him that I understood, that I sympathized with what he was telling me, before he lost himself again in his own incoherence.

"He babbled on and on, stopping every once in a while to see if I was still listening, an endless monologue that had meaning only for himself. Gradually, his voice grew fainter, as if he was slowly drifting away. 'Don't you see?' he asked, suddenly alert. Then, without waiting for my response, he closed his eyes and a moment later began to snore. His shoulder slid up against my chest until the back of his head, greasy gray hair matted to his whitish skull, was directly below my chin. Careful not to let him fall, I got to my feet and left him slumped on the hard wooden bench, a harmless old man who, when he was not crawling into a bottle, was being shoved into a cell. I found myself wondering what stories he thought he was telling me in that torrent of unintelligible speech.

"I found a place on the other side of the cell, as far away as I could get from the stench that emanated from that shit-splattered toilet. The windows high above were black with the night and the dim gray yellow illumination from the single electric bulb lent a spectral quality to things that even in the clear light of day would have been troubling enough. How was it possible that human beings could of their own volition have been reduced to this? How was it possible that the only thing we could think to do about it was to take them, throw them in jail for a few days or a few weeks, and then put them back out on the street to do the same thing all over again? That old man I had left lying on the bench somewhere in the darkness would spend the rest of his life either drunk or locked up and no one seemed to think a thing about it. That was the first time that I began to think that the law itself could be the worst crime of all.

"I became aware that I was being watched. A few feet away from me, sitting straight with his back against the cement wall and his hands extended to his knees, a gaunt figure was staring at me. As soon as he saw me look, he came over and without a word sat down next to me the same way he had been sitting before.

"'Thank you for coming, Mr. Steelhammer,' he said, his eyes focused straight ahead.

"Ignoring him, I started to move away. 'We have an appointment, Mr. Steelhammer,' he said, turning his head toward me. 'I've been waiting for you since yesterday when my wife called you.'

"I shook my head to let him know he was making a mistake.

"'You're my lawyer,' he insisted. 'The trial starts tomorrow.'

"'I'm not Mr. Steelhammer. I'm not your lawyer.'

"'Just a minute,' he said, quite serious. 'I'll ask my wife.' Squinting his eyes, he started moving his lips, noiselessly, like someone forming the words they are reading from a book held right in front of them. His lips stopped moving, and his eyes opened wide. 'Yes, now I understand.' His gaze raced from one side to the other.

Then he leaned over and whispered, 'She told me that you didn't want to use your real name in here. What shall I call you?'

"'You just talked to your wife?' I asked. 'Where is she?'

"'In Rome. She's a nun,' he replied. 'She's the Pope's daughter,' he added, eager to share this proof of his own importance.

"Madness has a logic of its own, and there was nothing to be gained by insisting on the rules of reason that every normal person follows without a conscious thought.

"'I'm not your lawyer. I was sent here to make sure you were all right. Mr. Steelhammer will come tomorrow, or perhaps the day after. In the meantime,' I cautioned him as if it were a matter of the gravest importance, 'you are not to talk to anyone about this.' He followed every word with obedient eyes. 'Silence is the key,' I insisted.

"'Silence is the key,' he repeated, nodding to himself. Without another word, he went back to his place on the bench, stretched his hands out to his knees, and, perfectly content, started once again the endless wait for someone who would never come.

"If I slept at all that night, it was only for a few minutes at a time. Chased by nightmares, men cried out like children, lonely and afraid, or woke up with a start, screaming obscenities or throwing wild punches at anyone they thought had disturbed their rest.

"I stayed in that holding tank—that dungeon—all weekend long, living a slow-motion death. They never moved me to a cell of my own; they never let me shower or change my clothes. Monday morning they let me go, but not until nine o'clock when, as the jailer reminded me when he gave me back my briefcase, I had only thirty minutes to get to court.

"'Why wasn't I let out two hours ago? That's the normal time, isn't it? Seven o'clock?'

"He was reluctant to answer, but finally relented. 'It wasn't up to me,' he explained as he emptied out the contents of a manila envelope. I picked up my keys and then my wallet. 'Judge Jeffries signed the order.' He hesitated, a question in his eyes. 'You're not really going to go to court like that, are you?'

"I had not shaved since early Friday morning. I had not brushed my teeth or even washed my face and hands. My hair felt like it was alive, infested with a million microscopic organisms on a feeding frenzy. I itched everywhere. My suit was in ruins, rumpled, wrinkled, soiled with sweat and God knows what else. My black wing tip shoes were dirty and scuffed. One of them was discolored with a stain left when one of those drunks sitting next to me had urinated down his leg.

"The more he looked at me, the more sympathetic the deputy became. He offered to help. 'I've got some things in the back. A razor, an extra toothbrush.'

"'Thanks,' I said, as I turned to go, 'but I think I owe it to the judge to let him see me the way I am.'"

Three

A drink in his hand, Harper Bryce let his eye wander across the bar and grill. A few more people had come in while we talked, a blast of late winter wind announcing each new arrival, and it was now almost half full. It was one of those places that stay in business for years, seldom empty but never crowded. The dishes had been cleared from the table, and the coffee had gone cold, but no one felt any pressure to leave. We could sit there all day if we wanted, talking among ourselves, and no one would think twice about it.

Pushing up the sleeve of his shirt just far enough to steal a glance at his watch, Jonah Micronitis started to say something, another reminder that it was getting late and there were things they had to do. Time was money, and money, for Jonah Micronitis, had always been everything. Asa Bartram ignored him. With a slight movement of his head, and an even less discernible movement of his hand, he stopped him from making a sound.

"Did you really go to court, Calvin's court, like that?" Asa asked, encouraging me to go on. His arms, folded together, rested on the table. A faint smile flickered at the corners of his broad mouth. There was a look of nostalgia in his aging eyes, as if he had been reminded of some indiscretion of his own, some act of defiance which he had grown too prudent to commit, but on which he still looked back with pride.

"I did not even stop at the men's room to comb my hair and wash my face. I was furious. I don't think I had ever felt quite so righteous in my life."

Asa knew exactly what I meant. "Having nothing left to lose is a kind of liberation, isn't it?"

"You would have thought I was leading a slave rebellion. Three days in that place, and in some ways I had become more demented than any of the poor souls I found there. I could have killed Jeffries and gone to my execution convinced that I was entirely justified for what I had done. I didn't kill him, of course, but when he took his place on the bench I tried to murder him with a stare. I need not have bothered; he damn near died when he saw what I looked like.

"I was sitting at the counsel table, pretending there was nothing out of the ordinary, one leg crossed over the other, my left arm trailing over the back of my chair. With my thumb and forefinger, I stroked my chin like some elegantly dressed fop, bored to tears with everyone around him. Mrs. Larkin, sitting in the chair next to me, did not know what to make of it. The deputy district attorney, who had been reading his file, lifted his head, like an animal which has just caught a scent. Jurors shifted uneasily in their chairs, nudging each other to make certain they were all seeing the same thing.

"'Mr. Antonelli!' Jeffries shouted, his face red with rage.

"I had already turned to the same juror I had been talking to on Friday. 'Thank you, your honor,' I said without looking back. 'Now tell me,' I went on as if time had stood still, 'even if you're convinced the defendant is probably guilty, will you still vote to return a verdict of not guilty if the state fails to prove that guilt beyond a reasonable doubt?'

"I'll never forget the look on that juror's face. The poor woman did not know what to do. She was willing to answer my question, but afraid to open her mouth.

"'Mr. Antonelli!' Jeffries was screaming from the bench.

"With a speed that surprised even myself, I shot to my feet. 'Will you stop interrupting me!' I shouted back at him. 'I've earned the right to ask that question!'

"I don't know that I've ever seen anyone that angry. 'Do you know who you're talking to, counselor?' he asked, clenching his teeth so hard his whole face seemed to tremble.

"I had always had a fondness for the kind of English barrister we used to read about in the old novels, the ones who could stand there, hand on hip, and with only a slight change of inflection destroy an opponent with a single well-turned phrase. I don't know where I got it—it must have been something I had read. I certainly did not make it up myself, but all of a sudden I remembered, and before I knew what I was doing, the words just came out.

"'Your honor, I'm not sure. Because, you see, I'm like a Buddhist in front of his idol: I know you are ugly, but I feel you are great.'

"The jury, the bailiff, the clerk—everyone in the courtroom—froze, and every eye turned to see what Jeffries would do.

"I had called him ugly and I had called him great. He could not contest the one without contesting the other. He stared hard at me, but behind those piercing eyes he was gaining control of himself, quickly calculating what he could safely do. Folding his hands together, he lowered his head and pursed his lips. When he looked up again, he nodded slowly, a thoughtful expression on his face.

"'That was very good, Mr. Antonelli,' he said in a quiet, reassuring voice. There was an almost audible sigh of relief from around the courtroom. 'Very good, indeed,' he added before he turned to the jury. 'Mr. Antonelli,' he informed them with a solemn smile, 'has obviously been under a great deal of stress. I'm sure that with a good night's sleep he'll be back to his normal self. In the interest of everyone concerned, I think it would be better if we recessed now and started again tomorrow morning.'

"I went straight home, threw my clothes into a pile on the bathroom floor, and took a long hot shower. When I was finished, I crawled into bed, languishing in the pure luxury of clean sheets. I slept all day and got up only long enough to have something for dinner before I went back to bed. The next morning, wearing a fresh shirt and a new suit, I sat at the counsel table and as if I had never laid eyes on her before began questioning that same juror.

"'At the end of this trial, after you have heard all the evidence, if you believe that the defendant is probably guilty, but you also believe that the state has not proven it beyond a reasonable doubt, will you return a verdict of not guilty?'

"Instinctively, her eyes flew toward the bench. Jeffries was hunched over, reading something. 'Yes,' she replied, her eyes coming back to me.

"We moved rapidly through voir dire, and by the end of the morning had a jury. That afternoon we made our opening statements and the next day the prosecution called its first witness, Edward Larkin.

"He could have been anyone, the father of the kid down the block, the husband of a woman you work with, a pleasant-looking, well-dressed man, someone you would chat comfortably with while you stood together waiting for a bus. He spoke about the sexual relationship with his daughter as if he were a psychologist describing something that one of his patients had done. That was what you had to understand about him: He had learned to analyze his past behavior with almost clinical detachment. Yes, he had for years been having sexual intercourse with his own daughter. Yes, he understood this was something he should not have done. But now he was in counseling, where he was learning how to deal with his problem. Remarkable how a few words can change the way we think. His problem! Suddenly, it becomes something private, his own possession, something that ultimately does not concern anyone else, except insofar as the people affected by his behavior can help him with his problem. He is no longer the subject who has inflicted an unforgivable wrong that must be punished as an example to others, but an object for the professional attention of those trained to deal with his particular disease. He testified at the trial of his wife as if he had been called as an expert witness on a case that had nothing whatever to do with him.

"He admitted everything; he gave no indication that he was embarrassed, much less ashamed, of anything. In response to the questions put to him, he described the way he had several times each week left the room he shared with his wife and gone down the hall to his daughter's room. Though he said he always waited until his wife was asleep, he said it in a way that suggested he could not always have been sure.

"The prosecution tried to make certain no one missed the point. 'Then, it's quite possible, isn't it,' Spencer Goldman asked, 'that during the years this was going on, your wife became aware of what you were doing with your daughter?'

"It was a call for speculation if there ever was one, and I was on my feet shouting my objection before he was finished with the question. But if I had thought that Jeffries was through with me, I quickly learned just how wrong I could be.

"'Overruled!' he barked, motioning for me to sit down.

"'Your honor,' I insisted, still on my feet, 'he's—'

"'He's eliciting testimony that the mother must have known what the father was doing,' Jeffries interjected. He gave me a sharp look. 'And he's doing that to demonstrate that the mother herself must have had something to hide. Isn't that correct, Mr. Goldman?'

"I stood there, speechless. There was no precedent for this. The judge had become the prosecutor, and I was the one he was after.

"'Isn't that correct, Mr. Goldman,' he asked again, his eyes still locked on mine.

"Astonished at what Jeffries had done, Goldman had difficulty getting the words out. 'Yes, your honor,' he said finally.

" 'Objection, your honor,' I said, forcing myself into an even-tempered voice.

"He thought I was repeating the same one. 'I've already ruled,' he said, turning away.

" 'I'm objecting to the comment of the court. It was gratuitous, and irrelevant, and completely prejudicial. I ask that the court withdraw it and instruct the jury to ignore it.'

" 'You what!' he blustered. Then, aware that a packed courtroom was watching, he stopped himself before he said or did something he might later regret. 'You made an objection, Mr. Antonelli. I ruled on it. You made it again. I gave you the reasons for my ruling.'

" 'The reasons for your ruling, your honor?' I shot back. 'Or the reasons why you think the jury should convict?'

"He was livid. It was written all over him. But we were now on a public stage.

" 'I hope you're not questioning the integrity of this court, Mr. Antonelli,' he said, with an ominous glance.

" 'Far be it from me, your honor,' I replied with a quick, aggravating smile, 'to deprive anyone of the right to hope.'

"If he had had a gun, I think he would have killed me. Instead, all he could do was try to ignore it. He shook his head as if I wasn't worth his trouble and invited Goldman to continue his examination of the witness.

"When it was my turn, I attacked. 'You never saw your wife do anything with your son, did you?' I asked before I was halfway out of my chair.

"He was unflappable. 'No,' he said without expression.

" 'Your wife never admitted to you that she had ever done anything improper with your son, did she?'

" 'No.'

" 'You never saw or heard anything from anyone that led you to believe that anything improper was going on, did you?'

" 'No.'

"I stood in front of the counsel table and let my gaze wander from the witness to the bench. 'And despite what was suggested earlier, your wife, Janet Larkin, never said or did anything that made you think she had any suspicions at all about what you were doing with your daughter, did she?'

"His head down, Jeffries pretended to be busy, though he knew full well that my eye was on him and not the witness.

"'So any suggestions about what your wife must have known, about what your wife must have been hiding, are nothing more than speculation. Isn't that right?'

"Jeffries snapped his head up, an angry expression on his face. Before he could say anything, I took a step toward the witness and asked, 'Isn't it true, Mr. Larkin, that your son never said anything about any of this until he came to live with you?'

"He started to answer, but I talked right over him as I moved another step closer. 'And isn't it true, Mr. Larkin, that your daughter isn't the only child of yours with whom you wanted to have a sexual relationship?'

"Jeffries raised his gavel; Goldman shot out of his chair; the noise from the crowd was deafening. I never heard what Goldman said or the sound the gavel must have made. The jurors, who by hearing it so often had almost forgotten what Larkin had done with his daughter, were stunned by the enormity of what they had now been told he had wanted to do with his son. The only one who seemed unaffected by what I had charged was Edward Larkin himself. He sat on the witness chair, hands folded together, waiting impassively, as if all this commotion had nothing to do with him.

"Jeffries did not know any better than I did the objection Goldman had made. It did not matter. Over the dying tumult, he struck his gavel and shouted, 'Sustained.'

"'Do you deny that you told your daughter that you had fantasies about your son?' I asked so rapidly one word ran into the other.

"'Objection.' Goldman was on his feet again, waving his arms like someone trying to stop a train.

"'Sustained,' Jeffries ruled, beside himself.

"'Do you deny having fantasies—sexual fantasies—about your son?'

"Jeffries sustained the objection before Goldman could finish making it. I spun away from the witness. 'Grounds?' I demanded to know as if it was my right. For an instant, Jeffries was at a loss for words. He was not used to anyone, much less a young lawyer, talking back.

"'Relevance, your honor,' Goldman managed to interject.

"'But it is relevant, your honor. It goes to the credibility of the witness.'

"Glowering, Jeffries told me to move on to something else. 'The objection has been sustained.'

"'Tell me, Mr. Larkin,' I said, turning back to the witness, 'when you testified that your son told you that his mother had forced him to have sexual intercourse with her, did he explain why he had never said a word of this until he started living with you?'

"Larkin shook his head. 'It only came out after he started therapy.'

"'Then tell us this, Mr. Larkin. Until your son told this story, you never once suspected anything like this was going on, did you?'

"'No, I didn't.'

"'And wouldn't you of all people have been alert to any sign that something like this was going on?'

"Goldman objected, and Goldman's objections now practically sustained themselves. Without so much as a glance in Jeffries's direction, I waved my hand, as if to signal how boring they had both become, and asked the next question.

"If I could pick a moment when my life changed, this was it. I don't mean the next question I asked. I'm not sure I even remember what it was. I mean this time, this point in the trial, when without quite realizing it I had taken that one decisive step that decides forever who you are. Everything up until then had been training, instinct, the combination of things that lets you react, lets you adjust to everything that is going on around you. I had been practicing for about three years, and I was good at it—at least I had thought I was. I hardly ever lost, and that was the way everyone else seemed to measure things—did you win or did you lose. But now, really for the first time, I knew what I was doing. I was conscious of myself, of the effect I had, of the way everyone else involved in that trial was reacting to me. It was not ego, though I'm sure there was plenty of that; it was something more. I could not have explained it then, and I probably can't explain it now, but I understood what everyone was doing and why. I understood the reason for things. I learned to trust myself in that trial and not care what anyone else might think. It was either that, or let Jeffries help the prosecution convict a woman who had never done anything wrong of the worst crime with which any mother could ever be charged.

"Finally finished with Edward Larkin, the prosecution called the boy's psychologist, who had believed and reported what he had been told. Then they called the police officer who had reported, and claimed to believe, what the boy had said.

"'How old are you?' I asked the officer on cross.

"'Thirty-eight,' he answered.

"'And are you married?'

"When he said he was, I asked if he had children. He had three and was obviously quite proud of it. I picked up my copy of his report off the table and turned to the page I wanted. 'You wrote this?' I held it up at arm's length, a bewildered smile on my face.

"He was not sure where I was going. 'Yes,' he answered.

"I looked at him a moment longer, as if I was not sure whether I should believe him. 'I see,' I said, as I brought the document close enough to be read. After a few moments, I looked up. 'You wrote this part? "According to the boy, the sexual intercourse with his mother usually lasted one and a half to two hours."' I lifted my hands, and shrugged. 'Between one and a half and two hours?' I asked skeptically.

"He seemed not to understand the question. 'Didn't it strike you as—what shall we say?—unusual?'

"'That's what the boy said,' the officer replied as if that had been my question.

"I looked at the jury and let my gaze settle for a moment on each of the men. 'Between one and a half and two hours.' I repeated the phrase like an awestruck spectator.

"'Do you have a question, Mr. Antonelli?' Jeffries snarled.

"'Oh, I think I do, your honor,' I said cheerfully as I walked back to the counsel table. 'But not of this witness.'

"It was an amazing thing, the way everyone had been drawn into that boy's story. All of us understand how something like a rape can take place. We can understand how someone, driven by the same impulses and desires that drive us all, can become so twisted, so violent, that he attacks a woman. It is much more difficult to understand how anyone can attack a child, and next to impossible to imagine how a mother could do anything like this to her own son. And that, I'm convinced, is what gave his story a strange kind of credibility. It was so utterly bizarre, so far beyond the range of anyone's experience, everyone was afraid to express any doubt about what the boy had said. The only way they could distance themselves from an act so completely obscene was to denounce it, and the only way they could do that was to believe that it had really happened.

"The boy was the prosecution's star witness, and from the moment he took the stand, Spencer Goldman treated him like a victim. And Goldman believed it, believed it with a passion. He looked upon himself as the boy's protector. When I asked for the chance to interview my client's son before trial, Goldman turned me down flat. 'He doesn't want to talk to you,' he told me as if I was the one who had been accused of abuse.

"Gerald Larkin was poised—too poised—for his age. He sat straight, with his hands in his lap and his legs close together. He waited for each question Goldman asked, and then, without a moment's pause, produced his answers, answers that were direct, to the point, not a word out of place. And each time he did it, he looked at the jury. He described the ways his mother had aroused him in bed the way any other child might have described what he had done at camp. We are supposed to like children, but I did not like him. I had believed his mother nearly from the moment I met her; I knew he was lying with the first answer he gave. All he was asked was to state his name and spell his last for the record. The way he did it told me everything I needed to know. Here he was, a child claiming that his own mother had sexually abused him, not once, not twice, but on numberless occasions over a number of years, and he walked into court like he owned the place. A child who has been sexually abused does not like to talk about it, and he will never look you in the eye when he does. Gerald Larkin was like an actor taking center stage.

"On cross, I asked him if he remembered talking to the officer and whether everything he had said to him was true. He looked me right in the eye and said it was.

"'You say that the first time this happened you were living in the house on Roanoke Avenue. Is that right?'

"He was never hesitant. 'Yes.'

"'I see.' Stroking my chin, I stared down at the floor. 'Are you sure?' I asked, lifting my eyes. 'Absolutely sure?'

"'Yes.'

"'Your family moved from that house to the one over on Arlington Street, right?'

"'Yes.'

"'That happened when you were just starting the first grade, when you were seven years old, correct?'

"He did not grasp the significance of this. 'Yes,' he replied.

"'So you're telling us that you were seven years old when you began to have sexual intercourse with your mother. Is that what you're telling us?'

"His gaze never wavered. 'Yes.'

"'And it went on until you moved out of the house with your

mother and sister and into the apartment with your father. Is that what you're telling us?'

" 'Yes.'

"I was standing a few feet in front of him. Turning away, I walked over to the jury box and put my hands on the railing. 'And you told the officer that each time this happened, it lasted for one and a half to two hours, didn't you?' One by one I looked into the eyes of the jurors. 'And did it always last that long— one and a half to two hours—right from the beginning?'

" 'Yes,' I heard him answer.

" 'When you were seven years old,' I added, searching the last juror's eyes.

"I went back to my chair and sat down next to the boy's mother. He could look me in the eye, and he could look the prosecutor in the eye; he could even look at all twelve adults in the jury box when he answered a question; but he would not, and I dare say could not, look at her.

"Shoving the chair back from the table, I bent forward, my elbows on my knees, and looked up at him. 'What is it you really want?' For the first time, he hesitated, and in that moment, watching his eyes, I saw a glimmer of doubt, as if he now realized that things might not work out the way he had thought they would. 'When your father left,' I asked, more sympathetically, 'did he tell you that one day things would be like they were before?'

"He looked down at his hands. 'Yes.'

" 'When your father left, they told you it was because of things he had done with your sister?' He did not answer, he just nodded. 'What you'd really like, more than anything, is for everyone to be back together, and for everything to be like it was, isn't that right?'

"He raised his head high enough to see me. 'Yes.'

" 'Is that the reason you said these things about your mother, because if there wasn't any difference between them, if everyone thought they had both done the same thing, your father could come home again?'

"I thought for a moment he was going to answer. I think he wanted to. But things had gone too far, and whether because he thought it would be a betrayal of his father, or the simple fear of what might happen to him if he did, he could not bring himself to admit the lie."

Four

━━━━━━━━━━━━

Why didn't it end right there?" Asa Bartram inquired. Meditating on his own question, he furrowed his brow, a troubled look in his pale blue eyes. "You must have made the motion. It's almost always denied, but still, in a case like that, after what the boy said . . ." His voice trailed off as another thought came to mind. "Calvin denied it, didn't he? But why?" An instant after he asked, his eyes flashed and he began to nod his head. "He thought there was still a chance you could lose, didn't he?"

Asa knew his old friend well, and he was right. The boy could have admitted on the stand he had made the whole thing up and Jeffries would still have denied a motion for acquittal at the end of the prosecution's case. But that was not what happened.

"I didn't make the motion," I admitted.

Asa thought I was making a joke. "Everybody makes that motion. You have to make that motion."

"Ineffective assistance of counsel," Jonah Micronitis observed, as if he had actually spent time in a courtroom.

Harper Bryce was laughing to himself. "And then the defendant—if she lost—would get a new trial."

With a blank expression, Micronitis stared at Bryce and then looked at Asa for an explanation.

Asa appraised me with a shrewd eye. "Is that the reason you didn't make the motion?"

I wanted to say that it was, but at the time I was not thinking that far ahead. The only thought in my mind then was simple defiance.

"As soon as the prosecution rested its case, I was on my feet, calling the first witness for the defense.

"'Mr. Antonelli,' Jeffries interjected. 'Isn't there something you wish to take up with the court first?'

"It had become a war between us, and I was not about to give him the satisfaction of ruling against me again. 'No, your honor, there is not,' I replied. At that moment, all I could think about was getting Janet Larkin onto the witness stand. She had waited a long time for the chance to reply directly to the awful things that had been said about her and the terrible thing she was accused of doing. She deserved to have it.

"That was the only thing I knew I could do for her, give her that chance. Even after all these years, I don't think I ever had a case where anyone was put in a worse position. In a lot of ways, it is easier to be convicted of something than just accused of it. If the truth be told, it was easier to be Edward Larkin than Janet Larkin. He did something, he admitted it, and it became a tangible fact, something to be dealt with, something that gave a sort of definition to everything else. She was accused, and there was nothing she could do. She was helpless, impotent. Guilt clings to no one the way it does to the innocent. Imagine the shock of it. If you did something, something wrong, and you are caught, there is no surprise when you hear yourself accused. But when you did not do it, when you never would have thought about doing it, it eats you alive. You feel guilty. You think everyone who looks at you, everyone you pass on the street, is thinking of nothing else but this thing you supposedly did. The whole world is watching you, convinced you did it. Your friends—the ones who still come around—tell you they believe you, but you're not sure they really do; you're not sure they don't look upon themselves as victims, caught between their obligation to you and the embarrassment they start to feel every time they come near you. No one believes you, and you begin to wonder whether you should believe yourself. Could you have done this thing, and then, because it was such an awful thing to do, blacked it out as if it had never happened? You don't really believe that, but you have to admit that, impossible as it seems, it could conceivably be true. Does anyone really know when they first begin to go mad?

"Janet Larkin had been living with thoughts like these for nearly a year. It was a miracle that she had any sanity left. When I called her name as the first witness for the defense, she had the look of someone not quite awake, not quite certain that this was not still part of a bad dream.

"She did everything wrong. When she answered a question, she looked at me instead of at the jury. When she denied that she had ever done anything improper with her son, she spoke in a timid, quiet voice that instead of carrying the kind of outrage you might expect from someone wrongfully accused, made her sound as if she herself was not quite sure.

"At first, she would not answer the question. I had to put it to her directly. 'Mrs. Larkin, did you at any time have sexual intercourse or sexual relations of any kind with your son, Gerald Larkin?'

"The courtroom was mobbed. The benches were crowded tight. Without objection from Jeffries, those who could not find a seat had been allowed to stand along the wall at the back. All those eyes staring at her frightened her, and from the moment she took the stand she refused to look anywhere except at me. Until, that is, I asked her that question. A look of utter hopelessness came into her eyes. Her shoulders sagged forward and she gazed down at her hands. She began to rub them together as if she was trying to wash them clean. It was only when I repeated the question that she stopped and looked up again.

"'No,' she said, shaking her head back and forth. Her sad eyes were wide open. 'I never hurt my children.'

"I had to remove any possible ambiguity. 'You never had sexual intercourse with your son?'

"She bit her lip and a shudder passed through her. 'No.'

"I took her back through all of it, what her husband had done to her daughter and when she had first learned about it. I had her describe what she did to help her daughter and how she tried to help her son.

"'He told me one day that he didn't think his father should have to live alone. I told him he could visit, but he needed to live at home.'

"'After he made this accusation, he was taken out of your home and allowed to live with his father, correct?'

"We went on like that for hours, explaining everything that had happened until, finally, we were at the end of it, and I had only one question left to ask.

"'You think it's your fault, don't you? What happened to your daughter, and then what happened to your son to make him tell a story like this?'

"I do not know how much time or how many different days we had spent together, going over every detail of her married life, but we had never talked about this. Not once. I asked it now because suddenly it seemed the only question that made sense. She looked at me as if I had just betrayed a secret. Her mouth began to quiver and tears came into her eyes. She had to force herself to answer.

"'Yes, I do. I should have known,' she said as she buried her face in her hands. 'It's my fault. I should have known.'

"Because he had believed the boy from the beginning, Spencer Goldman had no sympathy for the boy's mother.

"'Are you trying to tell us that your husband was having sex with your daughter, that it went on for years right under your nose, and you knew nothing about it?'

"His manner was cold, caustic, and he threw questions at her so fast that she had barely started to answer one before he was shouting the next. Each time he did it, I objected, and each time

I objected, Jeffries overruled it. We went back and forth, like puppets in a Punch and Judy show. 'Objection.' 'Overruled.' 'Objection.' 'Overruled.' Finally, I bounced up one last time and instead of objecting, said, 'Perhaps your honor would like to lend Mr. Goldman your gavel so he can save us the trouble of a trial and just beat a confession out of her?'

"You have never seen such a wrathful look. 'Do you want to be held in contempt a second time?'

"'At least that would be a ruling we could both agree on, your honor,' I replied with studied indifference.

"There was really nothing he could do. No matter what he said, he was not going to hold me in contempt and have me dragged out of the courtroom. We were too far along in the trial, and besides that, there were too many people watching. Jeffries abused his power too often not to understand that it was best done in private. His only reply, at least for the moment, was a withering glance just before he turned his attention back to the prosecution. 'Please continue, Mr. Goldman.'

"I continued to object, not because I thought there was any chance that any of them would be sustained, but simply to give Janet Larkin time to collect herself. Goldman never could break her down. She answered every question and she told the truth. That was all she had left. Her husband had taken everything else. He had taken her daughter, and he had taken her son, and not just taken them, but in different ways stolen their innocence and destroyed them.

"Afraid of making a mistake, aware that hundreds of eyes were watching her, she formed each word of each answer with the deliberate care of a mother teaching a child the first letters of the alphabet. Goldman, always ready with the next question, could barely contain himself. When he tried to hurry her along, she ignored him; when he tried to interrupt, she went right on talking as if she had forgotten he was there. He kept after her, asking the same thing over and over again, trying to get her to admit what he knew she had done, or to change her testimony so he could use the inconsistency against her. He hurled questions at her with incredible ferocity. He would have stoned her to death if he had been able. It had no effect. She sat there like a glass-eyed automaton, going back to the beginning of the answer to repeat it all over again. Frustrated beyond measure, Goldman finally gave up.

"'You can deny it from now until kingdom come, Mrs. Larkin, but we both know you raped your son!'

"With the sound of that accusation ringing in the air, Goldman shot one more glance at the accused and then turned away.

"'The defense calls Amy Larkin,' I announced before Goldman had reached his chair. Until the last minute, I did not know if Janet Larkin's daughter would show up. She had said she might not. She knew how important it was to her mother's defense—I had left her in no doubt on that score—but she had let me know it was her decision to make and that she was not going to be forced into anything. I had her served with a subpoena and it did not make any difference. If she decided she was not going to testify, there was nothing anyone could do about it. She was willful, but she was not defiant. She did not question the authority that could drag her in front of a judge and put her in jail for contempt. It was not that at all. She just was not going to do anything she did not want to do. Not anymore.

"I have not seen her since her mother's trial, and I never tried to find out what happened to her after it was over. Perhaps I did not want to know. Perhaps I preferred the comfort of an illusion, the vague hope that somehow everything had turned out well. All I know for sure is though she was wise beyond her years, it was not the kind of wisdom that was conducive to what we think of as happiness.

"It never occurred to me that I was doing anything wrong. She was a witness—a crucial witness as far as I was concerned—and she had to testify. If anyone had suggested that I was doing something as obscene as what her father had done, I would have dismissed it as the ignorant comment of someone who knew nothing about the conduct of a criminal trial. But they would have been right. All the unspeakable things that had been done to her had been done to her in private; they were a shameful secret that she had never been able to share with another human being. By confessing, her father had betrayed her twice. He had violated the primal obligation of a parent, and then told the world what he had done. Called to testify on behalf of her mother, she was compelled to tell hundreds of strangers what she had for years concealed from people she might have trusted with her life. What business did I have—what business did anyone have—doing that to her?

"I was not thinking of any of that then. All I cared about was that she was actually there, inside the courtroom, holding up her hand as she listened to the clerk recite the oath.

"She did not seem the least bit nervous, but how many witnesses ever do? They sit there with their hearts racing and their minds filled with a thousand fears, wondering if they will be able to open their mouths when it is time to answer and whether anything will come out if they do. But on the outside they look completely composed, as if this was something they do every day. We are all actors, wearing the mask we think the world wants to see.

"I led with the question that was at the heart of the prosecution's case. 'During the time it was going on, did your mother know you were having sex with your father?'

"She shook her head emphatically. 'No. I'd never allow him in my room if my mother was still awake.'

"I was struck by her choice of words. 'You wouldn't allow him in your room?'

"'I made him promise me that she'd never find out. I didn't want her to be hurt.'

"She was sixteen years old, and she talked like a woman who had been having an affair with her best friend's husband.

"'How can you be sure that she didn't find out?'

"She dismissed it out of hand. 'She wouldn't have kept something like that to herself. She would have done something.'

"I turned toward the jury. 'The prosecutor claims she didn't do anything about it because she was having the same kind of relationship with your brother your father was having with you.'

"'That's a joke,' she said. Her voice was filled with scorn. 'Gerald and my mother! He's just trying to get back at everyone.'

"Goldman was on his feet. 'Objection. Move to strike.'

"Jeffries did not hesitate. 'Sustained,' he thundered. 'The jury will disregard the witness's last remark.'

"His voice was still echoing off the courtroom walls when I asked, 'And did your brother ever once so much as suggest to you that something improper was going on with his mother?'

"'No, never. I told you. He's just trying to get back at everyone.'

"Jeffries did not wait to hear the objection Goldman was rising to make. He leaned toward the witness stand. 'Young lady, I know you've been through a lot. But your testimony has to be confined to things you saw or heard. You can't speculate about what someone might or might not have been doing or why they may have said something. Do you understand?' he asked firmly.

"She was not like any sixteen-year-old girl you've ever seen. Age meant nothing to her. 'I understand,' she replied. 'I'm not speculating about anything. Gerald told me he was going to get back at everyone.'

"There was a dead silence. His eyes still on her, Jeffries drew back, a scowl on his face. 'Did it ever occur to you that he wanted to get "back at everyone," as you put it, because of what was done to him?'

"She did not back down. 'Nothing was done to him,' she insisted.

"'Do you have any more questions of this witness, Mr. Antonelli?' Jeffries asked, eager to get her off his hands.

"Nodding, I gazed down at the floor, reluctant to begin the series of questions that I knew would be unlike anything anyone in that courtroom had ever heard, questions the answers to which might shatter the last illusions we had about who we were and what we could trust.

"'Amy, how old were you when your father first started to do things with you?'

"'Eleven,' she replied without hesitation. 'That's when he started to touch me. I was twelve the first time we actually had intercourse.'

"She was sixteen years old, with hair that, depending on the light, looked brown or blond, and with just enough freckles on her face so that even in a dress she had the fresh-scrubbed look of a tomboy who could outrun any kid in her class.

"'When this first started,' I asked, 'why didn't you tell your mother? Why didn't you ask her to make him stop?'

"'He was my father,' she explained. 'He told me it was the way he could show me how much he loved me. He told me it had to be our secret.'

"'That wasn't the only reason though, was it?'

"Her eyes were fixed on mine, and she did not open her mouth. We had been over all of this before. We both knew what she was going to say. She kept looking at me, and then I realized what she was doing. She was waiting for me, waiting until she was sure I was ready. She had seen it the first time she told me, the stunned disbelief, the awkward embarrassment, and she did not want that to happen to me again. It had become second nature to treat adults like children. I smiled at her and repeated the question.

"'That wasn't the only reason, was it?'

"'No. The real reason is that I didn't want it to stop. I liked it. That's what everyone forgets. Sex feels good.'

"It was so deathly quiet in that courtroom that I swear you could have heard a heartbeat if you had been able to take your eyes off this woman-child on the witness stand.

"'But despite that, there were times when you wanted it to stop, weren't there?'

"She hesitated, and beneath that air of worldly self-confidence there was the first glimpse of doubt. No, not doubt, certainty. She knew that it was wrong, and she knew—or she thought she knew—she could have stopped it.

"'Yes,' she said, looking down at her close-clipped schoolgirl hands. 'Sometimes I'd ask him not to.'

"It was like trespassing on evil, asking those questions. I had the strange sensation of engaging in some utterly depraved private vice.

"'What would he do, when you asked him not to?'

"She lifted her head, a lost look in her eyes. 'He'd leave.'

"We were in the dark, just the two of us, falling down a bottomless black hole. 'What would happen then?'

"'He'd come back.'

"'And then?'

"'And then he'd sit on the edge of the bed and tell me that he knew I really wanted to, and that it was all right because a lot of people did the same thing; and he'd tell me that he really loved me and that there was nothing to worry about because it was always going to be our secret. And he'd tell me that he'd never do anything I didn't want him to.'

"'And then?'

"'And then I'd do what he wanted.'

"'But only after he made you believe it was really what you wanted?'

"'Yes.'

"'You thought it was wrong?'

"With a gesture almost identical to the one her mother had used, she bit her lip and nodded. 'Yes.'

"'But he told you it was all right?'

"Again she nodded. 'Yes.'

"It was in some ways worse than murder, worse than what we normally think of as rape. He never took her by force; he did something far worse. He made her the accomplice of her own destruction. He made her think herself guilty of her own defilement. He taught her pleasure. That is how he stole her innocence. He made her want what she believed only he could give her. He corrupted her, his own flesh and blood, and so far as I could tell, never gave it a second thought. All the therapy in the world was not going to change it. Everyone in that family was seeing a psychologist—two of them testified at the trial—but they knew nothing about what had really happened to that girl. They droned on forever about 'dysfunctional relationships,' and they described the coping mechanisms by which everyone could eventually learn how to adjust to what had happened, but they had nothing to say about the human soul or the evil of incest. Not one word. There was madness in all of this; madness in what the father had done; madness in what these self-proclaimed experts in human behavior had done or rather failed to do. I am not a religious man, but I tell you without hesitation that you will find more wisdom in the book of Genesis than in all their scholarly texts. The girl had been forced to eat of the tree of knowledge by her own father, forced to leave the Garden of Eden and the unquestioning innocence of childhood. Even worse, she was made to believe that it was her fault, that she was the one who had committed the original sin.

"She certainly believed that her knowledge of what her father really was made her responsible for what happened to her brother.

" 'Did your father ever do or say anything that made you think he might do something to Gerald?'

" 'He told me that sometimes he'd find himself getting aroused.'

" 'By Gerald?'

" 'Yes.'

" 'And do you remember what you said to him about that?'

" 'I told him if he ever did anything to Gerald, I'd tell mother what he'd been doing with me. He promised he never would.'

" 'Did you believe him?'

"She did not answer, not directly. 'I tried to take care of Gerald. I spent a lot of time with him. I took him places, even when my friends didn't want to have a little kid along. I let him know every way I could that he could talk to me about anything he wanted, that I wasn't just his sister, but his best friend. I told him that parents didn't always understand what kids were going through.'

" 'Did Gerald ever say anything that made you think he was doing what he now says he was doing with his mother?'

" 'No, of course not. He told me everything, and he never said anything like this until . . .'

" 'Until?'

"She rubbed the corner of her eye, and then, grasping the arms of the chair, sat straight up, her mouth pressed into a rigid straight line. 'Until he went to live with my father.' With a thin, bitter smile, she added, 'My father is very good at seducing children and getting them to believe whatever he wants them to believe.' Her eyes moved to her mother, sitting in the chair next to mine, as if she wanted to make sure she was all right. It was the look of a parent checking on a child.

"Goldman was no fool. Most of his cross-examination was short, to the point, and done with a show of reluctance.

" 'After all the terrible things that have happened, it must be good to know you can count on your mother's support.'

"She was too smart. She did not say anything. She watched him, waiting for a question.

"Goldman flashed an ingratiating smile. 'You know what it's like, don't you? Not being able to tell anyone, even your own mother, about something that has been done to you?'

"He should have known better, but despite everything he had heard, he still thought he was dealing with someone too young, too inexperienced, to know that questions often have meanings beyond the things they ask.

" 'I couldn't tell my mother,' she replied, fixing him with a withering stare, 'because it would have hurt her beyond anything anyone could have done. But Gerald could have told me—would have told me—because why would he think it would hurt me?'

"Goldman did not take his eyes off her, but his whole body tensed as he felt himself come under the watchful scrutiny of everyone in the courtroom. He tried to bury her answer beneath another question, but she was too quick for him.

"'I watched out for him. Gerald knew I wouldn't let anything happen to him. And nothing did—not until they let him go live with my father!'

"Goldman's face was screwed up tighter than a drum. 'You'd lie to protect your mother, wouldn't you?'

"It's the question that never works, and I've heard it a thousand times.

"'I don't have to,' Amy calmly answered."

I stopped and looked around at the three men gathered at the table with me. Harper, who had been staring into his empty glass, glanced up. Micronitis tapped the crystal of his watch to remind Asa that they were already late. The old man paid no attention. He took his hands, which had been folded together under his chin, and spread them open, large, soft, and pink, like the smooth surface of a baby's belly.

"What happened then?" he asked in a quiet, sympathetic voice. Micronitis pulled his sleeve down over his watch and sank back into his chair.

I could see it in my mind, feel it in my soul, all the pulse-pounding, heart-stopping rhetoric I threw at that jury of strangers, all those years ago, when I stopped doing the things that were expected and started doing what something deep inside my own conscience told me to do.

"I quoted Euripides," I said out loud, surprised when I heard myself say it. "During closing."

Micronitis blinked and then moved forward, resting his elbows on the table. The sullen worried look on his face was replaced with an expression of immediate interest.

"What was the quote?" he asked, an eager, expectant smile on his small, pinched mouth.

I remembered not only the quote, but whole sections of a closing argument that had taken nearly two hours. I had worked on it for days, written it out longhand, written it and rewritten it, read it over so often that it echoed in my brain when I tried to sleep; I read it and rehearsed it so many times that it lost all familiarity and began to seem like something I had never seen before. I was certain I would not remember a word of it when I stood up to give it, and determined that even if that happened I would not read anything from the written page, not in front of a jury and a crowded courtroom. No, this had to appear spontaneous, something I believed in so much that the words came of their own accord. In a real sense, they did. When I began to talk to that jury I forgot all about what I had written, rehearsed, and tried to remember. I forgot it all, and did not forget a word. I had learned it so well that it had become a part of me, something that had gone deeper than my conscious mind. It now had all the force of passion.

The passion was gone, and only the words were left. To repeat them now, without the fire, without the righteous belief in what they meant, seemed awkward and even embarrassing.

Asa saw my hesitation. "Go ahead," he urged. "You'll be the only one who might laugh."

"'Oh where is the noble fear of modesty, or the strength of virtue, now that blasphemy is in power and men have put justice behind them, and there is no law but lawlessness and none join—'"

Micronitis finished it for me. "'And none join in fear of the Gods.' *Iphigeneia at Aulis*. You really said that in court?" he asked, looking at me with a new respect.

Dragging his finger back and forth across his lower lip, Asa studied me for a moment. "That was Antonelli's secret," he said, with that same shrewd look in his pale blue eyes. There was a wistful tone in his voice, the nostalgia of regret. "Lawyers make the mistake of thinking they have to explain everything to jurors in the simplest possible terms. So they talk down to them, like they're children. Antonelli always talked to them like there was at least one person on the jury who knew more about the case than he did. He talked to them the way you would talk if you were standing in front of the twelve most serious-minded people on the face of the planet. That's why you always won, isn't it? Because you understood that people don't have to be smart themselves to recognize intelligence."

I shook my head and shrugged, as if it were something about which I had never given a thought.

"I think Jeffries probably had a different interpretation."

Asa was too old, and too clear-sighted, to indulge in a lie, even the kind we pass off in polite conversation as a concern for the feelings of other people.

"He thought you were a dangerous person, that you could persuade jurors to do things they shouldn't, that you corrupted the system."

Harper Bryce's eyes widened as he looked at Asa and then at me. "How many times did you try cases in front of him?" he asked.

Asa answered for me. "Just that one time. The Larkin case." He turned back to me. "How long was the jury out?"

"Twenty-five minutes."

Harper's stomach knocked against the edge of the table as he laughed. "No wonder he thought you corrupted the system. But why was that the only time you ever tried a case in his courtroom?"

Asa had known Jeffries most of his life, and he had known me through my whole career. The story had become as much his as mine.

"It was the case that made Antonelli famous, and part of it was because of what Calvin had done. He threw him in jail for contempt; he took the side of the prosecution every time there was an objection. You heard what he said to the girl when she testified—about how if her brother wanted to get back at people it was because of what his mother had done. About the only thing he didn't do was tell the jury they were supposed to convict. Calvin had gone too far. It might not have mattered if Antonelli had lost, but Antonelli won, and that made it look like

Calvin had lost. That was one thing Calvin could never forgive. He always had to win. Antonelli would have been a fool to try another case in front of him."

Shoving back from the table, Asa stood up. "Well, he's gone now," he said. "He had a brilliant mind, one of the best legal minds I've ever encountered. It's too bad he didn't have more use for other people." He glanced at his watch. "Why didn't you tell me it was getting so late?" he asked, darting a glance at Micronitis before he looked back at me and winked.

After he was gone, Harper bent closer, a wry expression on his face. "Maybe that explains why Jeffries hated you, but why do you still hate him? He threw you in jail for a couple of days, but he was doing you a favor. That's all anyone talked about, how you showed up in court right from the county jail, looking like some wino off the streets, and asked the same damn question all over again. You became a legend because of what he did. And even if you weren't as smart as I think you are, it happened too many years ago to still carry a grudge."

He watched me for a moment before he said, "It wasn't the Larkin case at all, was it? There was something else, some other reason why you can't stop hating him, even now, after he's dead."

Five

As soon as I saw her leading the funeral party out of the church, her face hidden behind the widow's black veil, I knew I had to see him. I had always meant to. God knows, I had thought about it often enough, especially when it first happened, when everything fell apart, but there always seemed to be something else I had to do, another case, another trial, something that got in the way. I kept promising myself I would do it, and after a while the promise itself became enough to assure me of my own good intentions. Finally, I managed to put it out of my mind altogether, but then, every so often, I would hear a name that reminded me of his and would convince myself again that this time I would really do it.

If I did not do it now, I never would. It was not just because Jeffries was dead and that Elliott Winston had once been married to his widow. If I did not see him now I would never get over my own sense of guilt, the feeling that what happened to him was in some measure my fault. It was not really my fault, of course; I had nothing to do with it, at least not directly. But I still blamed myself for not seeing what was going on before it was too late. I knew better than almost anyone what Calvin Jeffries was capable of doing.

I think I liked Elliott Winston because he reminded me of the way I had been at the beginning, when I was young, and enthusiastic, and convinced of the importance of what I was doing. I suppose that is not quite true. I had only looked innocent: Elliott really was. Maybe that is why I liked him so much: He reminded me of something I wished I had been.

No one wanted to hire him, at least no one in the firm of which I was then one of the senior partners. There was nothing personal about it. Elliott had clerked for me the summer before his last year of law school. Everyone liked him, and everyone thought he would become a very good lawyer, but Elliott had not gone to one of the nation's best law schools, and that, for most of the twelve partners who had gathered in the conference room, was an insurmountable objection.

"Elliott Winston wants to be a criminal defense lawyer," I tried to explain. "That's what I do, and I've never once had a client—or a judge, for that matter—ask me where I went to law school."

"You went to Harvard," one of the partners remarked.

"And when I graduated I knew less about practicing law than anyone who went to night school. I certainly knew less than Elliott."

"Perhaps," the partner replied, furrowing his brow, "but Harvard trained you to think like a lawyer."

I looked at him, a wry smile on my face. "Which side of this argument are you on?"

No one thought it funny. They had all gone to the best schools, and they had all graduated in the top tenth, or the top fifth, or in the top two or three of their class. It was who they were, part of a hierarchy, a legal aristocracy bent on preserving its identity by a rigid policy of exclusion.

Pointing at the stack of résumés on the table, I challenged them. "Find me one person in there who will be a better lawyer—a better criminal defense lawyer—than Elliott Winston."

"There isn't one person there who did not graduate from one of the top law schools in the country."

"That wasn't my question," I insisted.

"We have a reputation to maintain," another partner objected.

I wanted to say, "A reputation as a place where everyone sits around telling each other how great they were before they were admitted to the bar!" I seized instead on what he had said and pretended to agree.

"That's exactly what I'm trying to do, maintain the reputation of the firm as the place everyone wants to go because we hire only the best. I think I know something about what it takes to be a criminal defense lawyer. I've been through all those résumés," I said, nodding toward the stack. "They're very impressive, but there isn't one of them I'd take ahead of this kid. I know him. I know what he can do. He worked for me. He's the best clerk I ever had. He put in longer hours, had more initiative, more energy, and more imagination—more of the things that can't be taught in a classroom—than most of the associates we already have."

I was at my persuasive best, and it had no effect whatsoever. Elliott Winston had not gone to Harvard or Yale, or Stanford or Michigan, or any of the other places whose prestige would apparently be threatened by his presence. On the vote, he was rejected ten to one. Michael Ryan, who had started the firm and built it from nothing, had not said a word and did not vote. Fidgeting constantly with his hands, always grinding his teeth, Ryan watched everything with a kind of malevolent stare.

"We brought Antonelli into the firm because we needed someone who could do criminal law. He wants to hire Winston as an associate. I think it should be his call." His eyes darted down first one side of the table, then the other. "Anybody disagree?" No one looked back at him. "All right, then. Elliott is hired. Let's move on to something else." Every partner had a vote; Ryan had the only one that counted.

Elliott could not believe it. After I told him a second time, he made me repeat it again just to be sure.

"I didn't think I had a chance," he cried. "They never hire

anyone who didn't go to one of the best law schools in the country. Wait till I tell my wife!" he exclaimed before he hung up the telephone.

At the time I doubt I even noticed that his reaction seemed to prove me wrong and the other partners right. There were people impressed with where they had gone to law school. But then, Elliott was young, and one of the hazards of youth is to be impressed with all the wrong things for all the wrong reasons.

Though they never came out and admitted they had been wrong, there was not one among the partners who had voted against him who would not, six months later, have voted for him. Of all the associates we hired that year, Elliott was everyone's favorite. He made them all feel important. There was nothing disingenuous about it. He thought they were important. They had gone to the great law schools in the country; he had never spent more than two days at a time outside the state. Whenever he had the chance, he asked them what it had been like, going to a place he had only dreamed about. For all their sanctimonious insistence that the best lawyers were the ones who kept their clients out of court and their own names out of the newspapers, the only thing they liked more than talking about themselves was having an audience that listened to every word as if it were the revelations of a prophet. When we gathered in the conference room to make the final decisions on the next year's crop of associates, there was a great deal of grumbling about the failure of the hiring committee to find any more like Elliott Winston.

I never saw anyone work harder. He was always the first one there in the morning and almost always the last one there at night. If I came in on a weekend, I usually found him in the law library, his feet stretched out over the arm of the chair next to him, a thick volume of the *Oregon Reporter* open in his lap. He did anything you asked, whether it was to run down the street to file a motion with the court clerk or research the latest opinion of the United States Supreme Court, and he did it with such cheerful eagerness he made you think you had done him a favor.

In a way I suppose it must have seemed to him as if we had. For all the incredibly long hours he put in, they were not any longer, and they were certainly more interesting, than what he had done working the night shift in a warehouse while he was going to law school during the day. With a wife and two small children it was the only way he could go at all. It would have been better for him, better for his children, better even for her, if he had never tried, or, if he had to try, had given it up as more than he could do. How easy it is to say that now, as if anyone could have known what was going to happen.

I still don't know why it happened. There was nothing inevitable, nothing preordained about it. He might have spent an entire career and except for an occasional courtroom appearance never become acquainted with Calvin Jeffries. He would not have met him at all had it not been for his wife.

Sometimes on a Saturday, when he knew there would not be anyone around, Elliott would bring his two children with him to the office. The boy was then about five and his sister four. They were remarkably well behaved. They would sit at the conference table, drawing on the back of the discarded pleading paper their father had pulled out of the bins, keeping perfect silence while he studied the advance sheets on the latest appellate court decisions. The first time I saw them there, he explained that their mother, a nurse, had sometimes to work on weekends. I learned later that she was employed at a small hospital in Gresham, just east of Portland. The administrator was one of Calvin Jeffries's few close friends.

That is how it all started, how they all met, how the circle of those three lives came to intersect. That was all I knew, and I only knew that because Elliott mentioned one Monday that he had had dinner with "Judge Jeffries" that weekend. He must have seen the look of confusion in my eyes. "My wife knows him. Not very well," he added. "He comes by the hospital once in a while. The head administrator is a good friend of his."

I was curious. "So he invited you to dinner?"

"No, not quite like that. The administrator—Byron Adams is his name—invited us. There were maybe ten people. He told Jean he thought I might enjoy meeting the judge." He thought it had been an uncommonly thoughtful thing to do.

"And did you?"

"Did I what?" he asked, a blank look on his face.

"Enjoy meeting Jeffries?"

"He was great," he replied, gushing with enthusiasm. "He told me anytime I had a question I should just drop by. Anytime, he said."

The smile on his face dissolved. He hesitated, as if he was not sure he should say what a moment before he had been eager to share. I was certain from his expression that it was something Jeffries had said about me. "Go ahead," I told him. "It's all right. I don't mind."

"He told me about the time he had to throw you in jail for contempt."

The way he said it made it sound like a schoolyard prank, something that was worth all the trouble it got you into as a kid because it was such a great story to tell when you were all grown up.

"Is that what he said? He *had* to throw me in jail for contempt?"

Elliott was too glad that he had not done anything wrong in telling me what Jeffries had said to pay any attention to the tone with which I had said it.

"Did he tell you about the trial?" I asked.

"No," he replied. "What kind of trial was it?"

I started to tell him, then thought better of it. Why should he have to take sides in a war that had nothing to do with him?

"Doesn't matter," I said, dismissing it as something of no importance.

As he turned to go, I heard myself say, "Be careful around Jeffries." He glanced at me over his shoulder, expecting an explanation. I just shook my head.

"Be careful." What could that have meant to him, young, idealistic, a lawyer who believed he could help people, thrown together with a legendary judge who had taken a personal interest in him. First a firm that never took anyone who was not from one of the best schools, now a judge who would not give the time of day to the best known attorneys in the city. Elliott Winston was on top of the world. He was indestructible and all I could think to say was "be careful." He must have thought I was out of my mind.

He might have been right. He worked hard, as hard as any associate I had ever seen, but he also had a life outside the law. He had two healthy, gorgeous children and a beautiful wife, and his career was off to a better start than he could ever have imagined. I was not married, had never had children, and while I knew hundreds of people I could think of only two or three I really regarded as friends. Surrounded by the anonymous faces of courtroom crowds, I spent my days doing everything I could to become the closest acquaintance of the twelve new strangers that made up the next jury I had to persuade. I went home each night to an empty house and only on rare occasions thought there was anything wrong. Young and affable, bright and decently ambitious, Elliott Winston was living the American dream, while I lived alone, still searching for something I could never quite define. Had I known that one of us would one day find himself making this drive, I would have thought it much more likely to be he.

Elliott would not have waited nearly so long to do it. He always moved quickly, without hesitation, without any of those second, qualifying thoughts that cowards call prudence and use to excuse their failure to act at all. It was one of the advantages of having lived a blameless life. He never had to question his own motives or examine his own conscience. He could do whatever he decided to do and know that he was doing the right thing. Perhaps it was more likely after all that, as between the two of us, I would be going to see him instead of the other way around.

I had meant it when I promised myself I would go to see him, but my calendar was full. There was a trial that lasted a full week instead of the three days for which it had been scheduled. There was a brief to research and write on a complicated issue on which no two courts had been able to agree, and I had only a few days left to do it. There were a dozen trials I was supposed to be getting ready for, and a dozen more after that. There were a thousand things to do and no time in which to do them. I had a million reasons not to go and I kept inventing more. I was afraid of what I would find, afraid of what I would feel. I gave myself a deadline of the last day of March and tried to convince myself that waiting until then was an orderly way to proceed instead of just another excuse for delay. On the morning of the thirty-first, I got in my car and began the drive, telling myself that I could always change my mind and turn back.

It was the second week of spring and it was as cold as any day we had that winter. Slate gray clouds ran across an angry sky, fleeing in front of a towering black thunderhead. The rain began to fall, light at first, then a hard, relentless downpour. Then, suddenly, it stopped, and there was nothing, not a sound, not a breath of wind, only an eerie half-lit calm. A single quarter-inch piece of ice rattled off the windshield, then another one, and then another, and the hail hit like machine gun fire. Cars swerved across the freeway as drivers turned on their lights and put on their brakes, and some of them tried to pull off onto the shoulder. It was over in a matter of minutes. A shaft of sunlight broke through and gave a silky sheen to the wet surface of the road. Across the valley to the west, the low-lying hills of the coastal range were covered with clouds. Before I had driven another five miles, the sky had turned black again.

Half an hour later I turned off at the third Salem exit and stopped at the traffic light. Across the street, an old man with weathered skin squinted straight ahead as he shuffled toward the entrance of a pancake house. A step behind him, a plump woman with short, iron gray hair gestured with her hand, talking rapidly.

He held the door open for her, a blank expression on his face, nodding as she passed in front of him.

I drove through a section of small wood frame houses built in the 1950s and 1960s, single-story houses bunched close together, with green grass lawns in front and square fenced yards in back. When they were new, children could ride their bicycles in the street and no one thought about locking their doors at night. Now there was too much traffic and everyone locked everything they owned. Finally, I reached Center Street and found what I was looking for.

You did not need to know the date it was built; you knew as soon as you saw it that this was something out of the nineteenth century. There must have been a certain pride of construction when it was finished, a belief that something spectacular had been achieved. It is hard to imagine what old buildings looked like when they were new. Even when a fortune has been spent on their restoration, it is like seeing a very old woman dressed in expensive clothes: She may look elegant, but she will never look young. The photographs that were taken of it at the time are old themselves, grainy black and white shots of stone and marble and brick, an enormous public building rising up in the middle of a place where, as yet, scarcely anyone lived. And always and everywhere, the people whose pictures were taken, staring into the camera, somber, sullen, as if each of them carried in their souls the secret of their own damnation. You could see the same thing in courtrooms all over the state, old enlarged photographs showing the early settlers, with grim faces and dead eyes, standing near the covered wagons that had brought them across the prairies and over the mountains. The women look meaner than the men, and the men look demented; the children look as old as their parents, and their parents look like they have already died.

My imagination was too much at work. Everything here reminded me of death, or things worse than death. Lining the street, large leafless elms, grotesque black shadows set against a hard leaden sky, looked as if they had been torn out of the earth and set upside down so their roots would wither and die in the harsh arctic air. But more than anything else, it was the building itself that gave me this awful sense of emptiness and despair, this sense that nothing had any meaning. It ran along the edge of the street, not more than twenty feet away, for the equivalent of two city blocks, a three-story brick fortress with a metal roof joined together with pinched, overlapping seams, like the old buildings of Paris. The yellow paint had in places faded white and in others peeled away, leaving behind bare bricks bruised with splotches of brownish purple covered with moss and mold. Supported by heavy three-sided braces, rotting wooden eaves extended the roof out over the walls. In vertical rows, narrow windows, some of them six feet tall and not more than a foot and a half wide, let in the outside light through a dozen small wood-framed glass panes.

At the far end, below a grass-covered knoll, I turned into the long circular drive. There were two street signs at the entrance, one for each of the narrow paved roads that bridged off from one another. Bluebird Lane and Blue Jay Lane. At the top, a third road led down the other side, through a cluster of tall firs, past two tennis courts laid out end to end and separated by a rusting chain link fence. The nets were frayed and one of them sagged to within a foot of the playing surface. Large puddles of water had collected in the hollows of the cracked cement. The road, little more than a pathway, disappeared into another clump of trees and came out a little farther on at a row of clapboard houses with dormer windows. The road was called Bobolink Way. I wondered who had given each of these small streets the name of a bird and what must have been going through their minds.

I parked at the top of the knoll in front of the entrance to the three-story brick building I had just come around. Unlike the rest of it, this part, which was four stories instead of three, had been newly painted, a vibrant yellow trimmed in harvest brown. At the top was a cupola with four false windows. Whether they had been painted over or whether there had always been wooden panels there instead of glass, I could not tell. The roof above the cupola was shaped into a narrow spike, and on top of that was a flagpole with a round orb on top. Freshly painted, the roof was already leaching rust.

Closing the car door, I took one last look up. A pigeon sat on top of the flagpole. Then, eager to get out of the weather, it flew off. For a moment I thought about getting back in the car and driving back home.

I stood in front of the steps, which were covered by an ornate iron canopy, and read the sign posted discreetly next to the entrance. Cascade Hall. It had a nice, northwestern ring about it. I turned around and headed across the parking lot to the building on the other side, built, by the look of it, in the middle of the twentieth century when the only criterion for a public building was how much it was going to cost. This one, a brick rectangle with square glass windows and linoleum floors, must have come in under budget. I checked to make sure I was in the right place. Siskiyou Hall. It was the administration building where I had my appointment.

As I started up the steps, I stumbled, a sharp pain in my leg. I caught my balance and the pain vanished as quickly as it had come. It had been years since that leg had bothered me. It seemed a strange coincidence that it should happen now. I paused in front of the door and read the neatly painted letters. Even after all this time, it was still hard to believe that Elliott Winston was a patient in the Oregon State Hospital for the criminally insane.

Six

Dr. Friedman was going to be a few minutes late. I sat down on a cushioned chair and thumbed through a computer magazine, glanced at the beginning of an article claiming that the printed page was about to become an anachronism, and tossed it aside, wondering if the editor had caught the irony. I heard a voice. "Mr. Antonelli?"

I turned around and found myself under the firm, clear-eyed gaze of a man in his early forties with thick brown hair and a round, perfectly symmetrical face. He was wearing a tweed sports jacket and had a clipboard tucked under his arm. After we shook hands, Dr. Friedman led me back to his office and gestured vaguely toward the two armless chairs in front of his government-issue metal desk. There were two steel bookcases, one on the wall next to where I sat and a smaller one that covered the wall below the window behind the desk.

"Dr. Friedman, I—"

He had begun to concentrate on the page on top of the clipboard. He looked up and, with a brisk smile, raised his hand. "I'll be with you in just a minute," he said as he went back to what he was reading.

I tried not to be angry and made a conscious effort to relax.

He flipped over one page and began reading the next. A moment later he went to the next one, and then, apparently satisfied with what he had seen, nodded twice and shoved the clipboard to the side. Leaning back in the swivel chair, he crossed his ankle over his knee and with his hands began to rotate a pencil he held in his lap.

"How can I help you, Mr. Antonelli? You're here to see one of our patients, correct?"

"Elliott Winston."

"Elliott. Yes, I know." The pencil was going back and forth a quarter turn each way. His eyes, now that they were on me, never left.

"Is there a problem?" I asked, wondering why I had to see him before I could see Elliott.

"Why don't you tell me?"

Friedman's voice was a warm monotone, and it was starting to make me feel uneasy. And it was not just his voice. He was a trained observer, always looking for symptoms of abnormality, and whether he was aware of it or not, he was studying me with the same clinical detachment with which I imagined he regularly diagnosed the various forms of psychosis.

"I'm not sure it's really a problem," I remarked. I looked out the window over his shoulder. "But when I was very young I used to have two dreams every night. In one of them I killed my father; in the other I slept with my mother." My eyes came back to him. "But that's just a normal part of growing up, isn't it?"

For half a second he believed me, and even when he knew I was kidding, he was not quite prepared to laugh. It was my turn to study him.

"There's something I've always wanted to ask."

"Yes?" he replied carefully.

"You know that old line about if you speak to God, you're okay, but if God speaks to you, you're not?"

He hesitated, not sure where I might be going with this. "Yes," he said, dragging out the word.

"What about the person who decides he must be God, because every time he prays he finds he's talking to himself?"

His eyebrows shot straight up. "That's quite good. I'll have to remember that one. But, after all, it amounts to the same thing, doesn't it? Whether God talks to him or he thinks he's God and he's talking to himself. In both cases he's clearly delusional."

"Insane?"

He shrugged. "Yes, of course."

"That leaves us with an interesting problem, doesn't it? Either Moses lied when he claimed God gave him the tablets with the Ten Commandments written on them, or he was delusional—insane according to your diagnosis. The result of course is that the entire moral and legal framework of the western world either rests on a falsehood or is part of an insane delusion. Which do you think it is?"

"I shouldn't like to think it was either, Mr. Antonelli," he said in that practiced, well-modulated voice of his. "We're talking about the kind of mental disease that affects normal people, ordinary human beings. We're talking about the kind of thing that happened to Elliott Winston," he added, trying to steer the conversation back to safer ground.

"Does Elliott talk to God?" I asked, curious.

Pursing his lips, Friedman narrowed his eyes and peered into the distance. Once again, he began to spin the pencil back and forth between his fingers.

"You mean, does God talk to him," he said. His eyes came back around. "The answer is, I'm not quite sure I know. Sometimes he hears voices, all right, but whose voices . . . ?" The question hung in the silence, unanswered and, from the doubtful expression on his face, I assumed unanswerable.

A look of hopeful encouragement entered his eyes. "As long as he stays on his medication everything seems to be all right."

He reached forward and grabbed a file from a metal holder on the front corner of the desk. Hunched over the open folder, he drew his index finger from the top to the bottom of the page and then, shaking his head, turned to the next one.

"When he first came here, they had him on some pretty dreadful stuff. Thorazine, mainly." He closed the file. "Well, it was twelve years ago, and that's what was available," he tried to explain. "You have to remember, he was considered quite violent. Not to put too fine a point on it, they kept him pretty well doped up. Have you ever seen anyone on heavy dosages of that stuff?" he asked, a distasteful expression on his face. "They're like zombies. They can barely function. I wouldn't have done it, even if he were violent—and, by the way, I have my doubts about that. I don't have any doubt he was mentally ill—he still is—but since he's been my patient—a little over three years now—I've not seen any evidence of a disposition toward violent behavior.

"He was initially diagnosed as a paranoid schizophrenic. That was the diagnosis made before he got here, when it was decided that he was suffering from a mental disease and was committed to the state hospital instead of being dealt with in the normal fashion by the criminal justice system. 'Guilty, but insane.' That is the operative phrase," he started to explain. "Oh, I'm sorry," he quickly apologized. "You're a lawyer, aren't you? You probably know all about this sort of thing, don't you?"

I remembered the man who sat next to me for a while that first night I was serving my sentence for contempt, the one who thought I was working undercover to help him because the voice in his head told him that was why I was there.

"I know a little about it," I replied. I did not tell him what had happened to me in jail; I told him instead about what I had seen in court.

The rain had started to fall, a steady downpour of gray depression, streaking the window and twisting the view of the things seen through it into strange, monstrous shapes.

"I did commitment cases for a while. The standard was whether they were a danger to others or a danger to themselves. We would gather around a table, sometimes in a conference room, sometimes around the counsel table in the courtroom. Whoever was making the claim that there should be a commitment would give their reasons. And then, because the statute required two doctors, and because you could never find two physicians willing to spend an hour of their time for the small amount that was paid, there would usually be a young general practitioner and a psychologist."

Friedman had retreated somewhere behind his eyes. He was listening to me the way someone listens to a radio or a television set in the background while they read the newspaper or carry on a conversation with someone else.

"What I learned right away," I went on, gazing right at him, "is that the doctors never asked the right questions."

You could almost hear the slick, sliding sound of a single thin transparent film dropping away from the lenses of his eyes.

"So I decided I'd do it. My client said he heard three voices in his head all the time. That was all the doctors needed to hear. The judge asked me if I had any questions. 'These voices you hear. Do you know who they are?' He looked at me, his face all lit up. 'Yes,' he said eagerly, grateful that someone had finally asked. 'Linda Ronstadt, Roy Orbison, and Conway Twitty.'"

I was back under Friedman's clinical gaze. "That's very amusing. But what difference did it make whose voices he heard? He was hearing voices, after all."

"That's what one of the doctors said. And then I pointed out to the doctor that while I couldn't say I ever heard the other two, I heard Linda Ronstadt singing in my head fairly often and that I would frankly be surprised if he hadn't heard the same thing. And to tell you the truth, depending on the song, there were times when I could not get her voice out of my head at all. Even right now, sitting right here, if I concentrate, I can hear her. I mean, once it starts, you just can't get 'I've been cheated, been mistreated' to stop, can you? Now, tell me, Dr. Friedman, am I going to get to see Elliott Winston or do I have to have myself committed and become a patient first?"

For a moment I thought he was going to take it under advisement. "No," he said, blinking rapidly, a nervous smile rushing across his face. "Elliott wants to see you. That's what concerns me." He immediately qualified it. "Not concerns me, interests me. You see, Mr. Antonelli, you're the first visitor he's ever had."

He waited for my reaction. I had the feeling he was trying to find out whether I knew something about what had happened to Elliott before he was committed, something that would tell him more about his patient than he already knew.

With a civil smile I expressed a polite doubt. "He has children, parents, relatives, and a great many friends. Surely, some of them must have come to see him?"

Stroking his chin, he gave me a measured look. "I should have said you're the first person he has allowed to come. Others have tried, though no one now for a long time. You're the only one he wanted to see. He's quite eager, actually. Why do you think that is?"

I turned the question back on Friedman. "What reason did he give?"

"He said you were a partner in the law firm where he worked, that you had given him the job, that for a long time he had thought he wanted to be just like you." He paused. "I'm sure he meant what he said, but I'm also quite sure that that isn't the real reason he wants to see you," he added candidly. "There's something else. Perhaps it's the same reason you want to see him." He put it to me directly. "You've never come before, Mr. Antonelli. Why now?"

There was not a trace of reproval in his voice, no suggestion that I had done something wrong by waiting this long. It was simply a question put to me by someone who I understood was trying to help.

"I always wanted to," I explained. "I always thought I should. About a month after he first came here, I started to drive down. I hadn't called ahead. I just decided to come. Halfway here I changed my mind. I told myself I needed to make an appointment before I came, but that was just an excuse."

He moved his head, just a slight turn to the right, enough to create the impression that while his left eye kept me under surveillance, his other eye was drawing back, as if there was something else it needed to see.

"I've always felt a certain responsibility for what happened."

"For what happened?" His voice was calm, reassuring, full of reasonable encouragement.

"Yes. I saw it all happen, each step. But I didn't understand what it meant, not until the end, when it was too late. I should have known. I should have done something before it ever got to that point, though I'm not sure, even now, what I could have done."

Friedman did not say anything. He did not ask me to explain. He sat there, watching, waiting for me to go on.

"Have you ever read Sallust?" When he did not answer, I explained: "One of the Roman historians."

"Oh," he replied, laughing softly, the willing admission of his ignorance. "But you must have. I've always envied people who read serious things. Perhaps someday. When there is more time." He smiled and waited.

"I had not read him either, not until about a year ago. And it reminded me, or rather it explained, because it described what I'm almost certain someone did to Elliott Winston. Sallust talks about what he calls the conversion of the zealous and the innocent to a criminal conspiracy. First, they have you tell an innocent lie, a white lie, something that can't possibly hurt anyone and may even help someone. Then, they bring you around to more substantial lies. You had lied before, and after all, this is only a difference of degree."

Friedman, the passive observer, was listening intently, caught up in the insidious logic of evil.

"Once they get you to tell lies like these, lies that have consequences, lies that if discovered can get you into trouble, serious trouble, then it is not so difficult to lead you into acts of violence. Not against anybody, you understand, but against somebody who has done something terribly wrong, an enemy, someone who is part of a conspiracy, a conspiracy directed at all the things you believe in. But then, after it's been done, you discover that it was done to the wrong person, someone falsely accused. You've made a terrible mistake, and it has to be covered up. You have to protect your reputation, but you can't do it alone. They tell you, these friends of yours who taught you how to lie, who convinced you to commit a violent act, that everyone makes mistakes. They tell you, these friends of yours, that they'll do everything that has to be done to make sure no one ever finds out what you did. After all, friends have to protect one another. Then, finally, when they do something you never would have dreamed of doing, something that was not the result of some tragic mistake, they come to you and remind you, these friends of yours, how they protected you when you needed them."

Friedman stared at me. "Someone did that to him?"

"I think so. There was no violence. That came later, after he broke down. But before that, yes, I think so. I think he was taken, step by step, from one thing to the next, until he finally realized he had become someone he did not want to be and he did not know what to do about it."

"Who would have done a thing like that? How could anyone have done a thing like that? He was a lawyer, after all. He must have known when he was being asked to do something that was wrong."

How childlike, how trusting, we all are outside the narrow, limited range of our own experience! Dr. Friedman, the student of human behavior, actually believed that the law was a rigid system of unbreakable rules. I began to feel more confident in my own analysis.

"There was a judge," I began to explain. "A much older man."

Friedman nodded emphatically. "His parents were divorced when he was a very young child. He was raised by his mother.

He seldom saw his father. Elliott was always drawn to older men as sources of guidance, inspiration. He was drawn to you that way. You were the older, successful attorney, the model of what he wanted to become. But not only that, of course. He needed someone he admired to give him encouragement and approval. He would have been dependent—extremely dependent—on anyone who could give him that. And a judge—yes, well, that is the source of the most important kind of approval for a lawyer, isn't it?"

I thought he was wrong about the way Elliott viewed me and almost certain he was right about the way he had become attached to Jeffries.

"And you think this judge abused Elliott's trust?"

It was a question only someone who had never known Calvin Jeffries could have asked.

"It's like I told you, there were things that at the time did not seem like much."

As I said this I began to doubt whether they would seem any more important now. Maybe I had read too much into them.

"A short time after they first became acquainted, Elliott missed a deadline. Or at least he was told he had missed a deadline. It seems odd. He was always very well organized. When you practice law," I explained parenthetically, "there are time limits on everything. Ten days to file this, twenty days to respond to that, everything has a schedule, and if you fail to meet it the consequences can be lethal: You lose the motion, you pay costs to the other side, you lose the case. Elliott knew that. When he told me what had happened he looked like death itself. But when I saw him the next day, he had that embarrassed, grateful look of someone who has just been saved from his own stupidity. The judge, he informed me, had simply instructed his clerk to backdate the document. So far as anyone would ever know, Elliott had done everything right."

Dr. Friedman rocked back and forth in his chair, pressing together the tips of his outstretched fingers. "The rules were relaxed because of who he was, because the relationship between

them was more than just that of lawyer and judge. And the relationship was even closer now because they had done something
together that they had to keep secret. I see. Yes."

"A few months later, it happened again, or rather, it happened
again and I knew it. I don't know how often it may have happened in between. He was working on a motion, and he came
into my office to talk to me about it. The issue was interesting,
and the more we talked, the more I thought he was on to something, that he actually had a chance, if not to win at the trial
court level, to take it up to the appellate courts and help make
some new law. We talked for a couple of hours, and at the end
he thanked me and told me I had given him some new ideas he
wanted to pursue. I asked him when his brief was due. He told
me it was due the next morning, but he thought he would work
on it through the weekend and get it in on Monday. I must have
looked alarmed, because he just laughed and assured me there
was nothing to worry about. 'They always give me a few more
days, if I need them.'

" 'But you can't do that,' I blurted out, angry that he could so
blithely dismiss the obligation to follow the rules.

" 'Why not?' he asked. 'It doesn't hurt anyone.' That was his
answer, and I remember how struck I was, not so much by what
he said, as by the almost cynical indifference with which he said
it. It was as if the rules had been made for other people, people
who did not know how things really worked, people, he seemed
to believe, who could not be trusted to do the right thing on
their own. There was something else—I still can't quite put my
finger on it—but something that told me that he thought I was
one of those people, too.

"I didn't see him quite so much after that. He was an associate
in the firm, and I probably saw him several times every day, but
we did not talk, not the way we had before. But if you had asked
me at the time whether there had been any change in our relations, I probably would not have thought so. It was impercepti-
ble, one of those things that happen and you don't become aware

of it until, suddenly, one day, you realize that everything has changed. And with Elliott, of course, there was no question of when that day came."

Friedman knew what I meant, or thought he did. "The day of the shooting."

"No," I said, shaking my head. "The shooting happened later. It would not have happened at all if any of us had had a whit of intelligence about us. Think of it. We see it all the time, but when it happens to one of our own, it's the last thing we think of. Elliott was tired, overworked, and he had a breakdown, so of course it must have been stress. Give him some time off, get him into counseling; everything will be fine. No one wanted to be the first to say: Elliott Winston is insane and needs to be in a hospital.

"The twelve jurors on the case he was trying that day would not have hesitated to say so. He had just finished the direct examination of a witness for the defense. He sat down, scratching at something on the back of his wrist. As the prosecutor began to ask his first, preliminary question on cross, the scratching grew more rapid, more intense. Jurors started to look. Elliott was tearing at his skin, digging into it, drawing blood. A juror screamed and as everyone turned to look, Elliott shot out of his chair, stabbing the air with his hand, the fingernails glistening red with his own blood, shouting at his own witness, 'You're part of it, aren't you? I saw the way you were looking at the prosecutor. I saw the two of you giving each other messages with your eyes!' He wheeled around and began to challenge the jury. 'And I've seen the way you look at him, and the way you look at each other!' He turned to the judge, one of the most fair-minded men on the bench. 'Don't think I don't know what's going on here! What's the case number?' he demanded.

"That stopped everyone cold. No one had any idea what he meant. 'It's the number of the year I was born,' he announced as if it proved everything. 'You're in it, too, aren't you?'

"A long time after it happened, months after the shooting in fact, I read the transcript, trying to figure out what had happened. I could not believe it. The day before, he seemed as normal as anyone else."

"That isn't surprising," Friedman assured me. "It's a classic case. Acute schizophrenia, the sudden onset of symptoms in a person who until that point appears to be functioning quite well. The delusions you describe are exactly what you would expect. There is a sudden, perhaps slight change in the chemistry of the brain. That is all it takes, I'm afraid. It is usually precipitated by precisely the kind of crisis you described, some kind of emotional trauma from which they can see no way of escape."

The doctor got up from his chair. "We better go. Elliott is waiting."

The rain was pounding down, exploding on the pavement when it hit. Thunder rumbled in the distance, and the sky was lit up with lightning. Pulling our coats over our heads, we ducked down and jogged across the parking lot to the hospital on the other side.

"Tell me," Friedman asked once we were inside. "You obviously have a great interest in what happened to Elliott. You read the transcript because you wanted to know what happened at the time of the first episode—what you call his breakdown. What do you know about the shooting, the crime for which he was committed?"

I stopped and looked at him, searching his eyes until I was certain he really did not know. Then I turned and we started to walk again down the long gray corridor.

"I'm the one he shot," I explained.

Seven

The voice of the doctor was speaking his name, but I was looking at the face of someone I did not know. It had been twelve
years, but the changes I saw had not been produced by time alone.
The Elliott Winston I knew had been quick, alert, easygoing, and
always affable; the man standing in front of me waiting for Dr.
Friedman to unlock the heavy gauge wire screen was tense, expectant, impatient. He was wearing an old suit that was too tight
for him. Buttoned in front, the lapels bowed out from his chest.
A solid-color tie was off center at his throat, and one of the collar points of his soiled white shirt bent up. His hands were clasped
behind his back and his feet were spread the width of his shoulders. Though I was just a few feet away from him, he stared
straight ahead as if there was no one else around.

We stepped inside, and Friedman rolled the gate shut behind
us. Elliott did not move. He stood there, erect, immobile, locked
in that rigid stare.

"Elliott," Friedman said in a calm, unhurried voice, "you remember Joseph Antonelli, don't you?"

There was no reaction, no movement of any kind, not even a
slight flutter of the lashes over his eyes. I wondered if he had
slipped into a catatonic state where he could not hear anything.

"He does this sometimes," Friedman explained. "When he's thinking about something." With a hopeless shrug, he added, "I've seen him do it for hours. When it happens, I'm afraid there really isn't—"

He never finished. Elliott had turned toward me and extended his hand. "Joseph Antonelli. I knew you'd come one day."

I took his hand, and then, when I saw his face, had to force myself not to let go. He was looking at me with such enormous concentration that I thought his eyes would burn right through me. There was a power about him that was extraordinary.

"It was good of you to bring Mr. Antonelli," he said, looking over my shoulder. "Thank you, Dr. Friedman."

He said it the way someone might address a subordinate, not with a tone of command, but with that benevolence which underscores the distance between the one who bestows it and the one who receives it. No doubt used to the strange eccentricities of his patient, Friedman seemed not to mind. He signaled a white-coated orderly who was standing at the far end of the large, open ward.

"Mr. Antonelli will be visiting with Elliott for a while," he said when the orderly drew near. "Make sure he has anything he needs."

After Friedman had gone, Elliott and I sat down at a square wooden table in front of a wire-covered window at the side of the room. Farther down, in the corner, three patients, dressed in white short-sleeve V-neck tops and baggy drawstring trousers, were sitting in a semicircle on plastic chairs. One of them, one leg folded under the other, held a magazine in his hands, turning it around and around, upside down, then right side up, over and over again. Another one, short, balding, with thick, stubby fingers, kept throwing out one or the other of his hands, clutching at the air, and then, bringing it back in, slowly opening his fist to see what he had caught. The third scarcely moved at all. He slumped forward, eyes glazed, mumbling to himself.

Elliott caught me looking. "Watch this," he whispered.

"Chester!" The mumbling stopped, and the third man lifted his head, a bewildered expression on his face.

"What is 3,182 times 5,997?"

The third man blinked, then answered, "19,082,454," and then blinked again.

"I'll ask him something difficult this time," Winston remarked under his breath. "Chester," he called out. "What is 8.105698 times 10.00787?"

Chester blinked. "81.120771." And then blinked once more.

"Chester, who is the president of the United States?"

This time he did not blink. He smiled, a foolish, heartbreaking smile. "George Washington."

"Very good," Elliott remarked with a glance of approval. "Now, if Lincoln freed the slaves, what did Washington do?"

"Freed the cherry trees," he answered with a childlike grin.

"Thank you, Chester," Elliott said in the same supremely confident voice with which he had dismissed Dr. Friedman.

"Chester was a high school history teacher," he explained. "In the other world."

"The other world? You mean, before he was sick, in the real world?"

This last phrase seemed to bother him. A dark look swept across his visage. "The other world," he insisted. His mood switched again. "And I think that is the way he taught it, too," he said, laughing. Abruptly, the laughter stopped. "That's not true. In the other world he taught history the way they all teach history, and he could not balance his checkbook. Then, when he became sane, he forgot all the names and dates and all the other unimportant things they cram their heads full of, and as soon as his mind was clear he knew everything about numbers."

He looked at me for a moment. "You don't believe me. Go ahead, ask him anything you want, any combination, any calculation. He can do it in his head instantaneously. I should know. I've been trying to catch him in a mistake for years."

"How would you know if he did?" I asked without thinking.

He felt sorry for me. "Didn't you notice? He only makes a mistake when he doesn't blink."

I was wrong. He did not feel sorry for me, not the way I had thought. He was playing with me. I could see it in his eyes.

"It's true though, isn't it?" he asked. "Whenever the answer is right, he blinks before he gives it. Isn't that a perfect example of reasoning from effect back to cause?"

I did not know what to say. There really was nothing I could say. I tried to change the subject. "You've changed a lot, Elliott. I'm not sure I would have recognized you."

A smile passed quickly over his face. "You didn't recognize me. You thought I was someone else." He seemed to be enjoying some small private joke. "It must be the mustache. I didn't have one when you knew me. I had a beard, too," he admitted with what I thought was a rueful expression. "And my hair was long. I'm afraid there were people in here who began to think I looked a little like Jesus Christ. Jesus Christ! Can you imagine! Then the next thing you know, some of these people started to think I *was* Jesus Christ. That might not have been too bad. At least that way I could have saved Christianity from itself. But there was someone here—not right here, but over in one of the other wards—who really believed he was Jesus Christ. He might have been for all I know," he added, his eyes feverish with delight. "I did not want anyone to have to start questioning his own identity because of me, so I got rid of it—the beard—cut my hair short, and almost got rid of the mustache, too, but I changed my mind—or my mind changed me. Either way, I kept it. How have you been?"

It was difficult to know whether to be more astonished at the rapid-fire lucidity of his speech or the manner in which he had just brought it to a dead stop.

"I've been very well myself," he said before I could think of what to say or how, now that I was finally face-to-face with him, I should say it. He seemed to sense every doubt, every hesitation, every slight uncertainty. "I mean it," he continued, speaking now in a quiet, smooth-flowing voice. "I'm much better off here."

My eyes darted around the drab-colored room, taking in the cheap furniture, and the dull finished floor, and the painted pipes that hung on metal braces as they passed under the ceiling; the sleepy-eyed orderly reading an out-of-date magazine; the three patients at the other table, barely aware of each other's existence, a fourth inmate I had not noticed before moving like a sleepwalker down the corridor that connected the day room to the rest of the ward.

His eyes were waiting for me. "I wrote you a letter once. A long time ago."

"I never got it."

"I never sent it. I knew what I wanted to say. I had finally understood what had happened—all of it—everything. My mind was thinking quite clearly, more clearly than it ever had. In an instant I could see all there was to see. I could take it all in, all of it, all of the relationships, all the subtle nuances, every shade of meaning," he explained. His eyes were glistening. "But then, when I sat down and started to write, it all disappeared—everything— and all I could remember was that I had lost something I had thought was unforgettable. This was not the last time this happened. Finally, I gave up trying to write anything down. Nothing ever sounded the way I meant it, or was really what I wanted to say."

As I listened I began to smile. He was describing what I had so often experienced myself: the inability to connect the thought with the word.

"But that isn't—" I blurted out before I realized what I was saying.

"Isn't a sign of insanity?" he said, raising an eyebrow. "What is?" The wry expression that had taken possession of his features faded away. "In any event, I could not write it the way I wanted to write it."

"What did you want to write me about?"

His eyes seemed to lose a little of their intensity, as if he were turning inward on himself. When I repeated the question, he became even more introspective, staring down at the table with the troubled aspect of someone searching for the answer to a riddle. Finally, he lifted his head, but instead of looking at me, he stared straight ahead.

"When I tried to kill . . ." His mouth hung open and his body began to tense. Then it started, a shrill, staccato stutter, one word rushing after the other in a mindless, rhyming speech. "Kill . . . thrill . . . will . . . ill . . ." His face became rigid, and then began to quiver as if it was on the verge of blowing itself apart. His eyes became enormous hollow black voids. ". . . chill . . . till . . . dill . . . quill." He gasped the words, each one requiring more effort than the one before. Then, as if it had never happened, the life came back into his eyes, the expression returned to his face. "I wanted to write to you about the time I tried to kill you," he said in a voice completely normal.

Whether he was unaware of what he had just done, or had become so accustomed to it that he assumed it was taken for granted by everyone with whom he came in contact, he mistook my silence as a sign that I was not entirely comfortable with the subject of my own attempted murder. That is what he had been charged with, and that was the reason he had been sent here, to the forensic ward of the state hospital, diagnosed as a paranoid schizophrenic, clearly a danger to others and probably a danger to himself.

"I would have, too, if you hadn't wrestled the gun away from me." He said it with a kind of gay indifference, the way someone might explain how they would have won the last set of a tennis match if you had not made a ridiculously lucky return of serve right at the end.

I had been waiting for a long time to tell him he was wrong. "I don't believe you ever intended to kill me or anyone else. You were sick, Elliott. You didn't know what you were doing. You came into the building that day, started walking up and down the hallways, screaming all those unintelligible threats no one could understand. Then you came into my office and you started waving that gun around. The truth is, if I had just talked to you, calmed you down, instead of going after the gun, it never would have gone off and I wouldn't have been hit in the leg and we could have gotten you the help you needed. Listen to me. I had never had anyone point a gun at me before. It scared me, more than I had ever been scared in my life. I didn't think, I just reacted. I should have known better, and I'm sorry for that. I know you never meant to hurt me."

I had put off saying this for twelve years, even though I had known at some level of my subconscious mind that it would lift a great weight off my shoulders when I did. Elliott reached across the table and, as if he wanted to console me for what I had been through, laid his hand on my shoulder. A moment later, he pulled it away. "You were sleeping with my wife," he said, his eyes flashing.

"I hardly knew your wife," I sputtered, suddenly defensive. "Whatever made you think . . . ? Who made you think . . . ?"

A detached, faintly ironic smile on his lips, he watched me, amused at the vehemence with which I denied something I had never done.

"I know you weren't," he said, nodding his assurance of the truth of it. "But I thought so then, and it was a long time before I realized I had been wrong. Even after the divorce, I didn't know what had really been going on. What else was she going to do? I was in here. You couldn't expect her to stay married to a lunatic—a criminal lunatic—could you? It was only after she remarried that things fell into place. It was only then, at the very end, so to speak, that I understood what had happened, all of it, even the beginning. I'm not saying that they planned it all out," he added, with a quick, rueful glance. "They couldn't have known what would happen to me. Though it would not have made any difference to them if they had."

His head sunk down between his shoulders and his eyes focused on a spot just below my chin. "You warned me about him. Do you remember?"

"Jeffries?"

His eyes narrowed even more. "I used to think he was evil. I was wrong. He was just indecent. People who are evil do interesting things. There wasn't anything interesting about Jeffries." Slowly, without any movement of his head, his eyes climbed up my face until they met my own.

"Did you know Jeffries was dead?" I asked.

He raised his head and his eyes flared open. "Death and betrayal, the fortunate circumstances of my life."

"The fortunate circumstances of your life?" I asked, confused.

With a quick movement of his hand, and a strange, triumphant look in his eyes, he started to wave my question away.

"I can't really explain. All I can tell you is that sometimes the only way you can deal with what happens to you is not just to accept it, but make it your own."

He seemed to regret that he had said as much as he had, though he had not said nearly enough to make his meaning—if there was a meaning—intelligible to me.

"I don't have any interest in thinking of myself as a victim," he said. His eyes darted across to the other table. "Will you stop turning that damn magazine around!" he demanded in a high-pitched scream that set my teeth on edge. Without so much as a glance to see where the shouting had come from, the inmate stopped the constant rotation and held the magazine perfectly still, directly in front of his eyes. It was upside down.

"So Jeffries is dead!" he remarked in a civil tone, looking at me as if he had never in his life so much as thought about raising his voice.

It had all happened so quickly, and had been so isolated from what he had been like just before and then immediately after, that I was forced again to wonder whether he was himself always aware of what he was doing.

"How did he die?"

"You really don't know? It was the front-page story in the news-papers for weeks."

"I let my subscription lapse," he said dryly.

He might not have access to the papers, but a television set, sitting on a plywood platform halfway up the wall, was flickering in the far corner of the day room.

"I never watch," he said, surprised that anyone might ever think he would. "Tell me how he died," he insisted with avid curiosity.

"He was murdered, stabbed to death, late at night, outside his office, on his way to his car."

Nodding thoughtfully, he asked, "Have they changed the def-inition of homicide? The unlawful killing of a human being?"

"No, it's always been that."

"Then it wasn't a homicide, it was not a murder." He said it as if I would immediately understand and could not possibly dis-agree with his conclusion.

"You mean," I suggested tentatively, "that it wasn't unlawful because there must have been some form of justification? Self-defense, for example?"

"No, I mean it can't have been a homicide because homicide's the unlawful killing of a human being and whatever else Calvin Jeffries might have been, he was certainly not a human being. No, it was not murder."

I did not know what to say, or even, for that matter, what to think.

"Shall I tell you what they did, the late lamented Calvin Jef-fries and my always blameless wife, Jean?"

He turned his head, as if he had just heard someone call out to him. "Jeffries is dead," he said to no one. The corners of his mouth pulled back until the tendons of his neck were stretched taut. Then it started again, that insane rhythmic repetition, like the harsh clang of a rusty bell rung from the belfry of a distant church. "Jeffries is dead . . . wed . . . bed . . . fed." He was staring straight ahead, his eyes as vacant as the conscious mind behind them. "Red . . . bled . . . med." He was choking on the words, as if he had lost the instinct for taking a breath, and in the confusion of his panic had thought he was supposed to push it out instead of bring it in.

It stopped and the memory of it stopped as well. "Jeffries is dead," he said, each syllable pronounced with glittering clarity. "Murdered. And they say there are no happy endings. Shall I tell you what they did to me, the great judge and the loving wife?"

He glanced away, a wistful expression in his deep-set eyes, the look sometimes seen on the face of men much older than Elliott Winston, the look they get when they begin to think back, not just to their vanished youth, but to the way they saw the world when they were still that young.

"I believed in him. I believed in them both. I worshipped Jeffries. It was an honor to be in the same room with him. He knew everything. He could do anything. There was nothing about the law he did not know." He looked at me, an eager glint in his eye. "Do you know that he wrote most of the procedural law we use?" Again he turned away. "He told me how he did that and why and he told me a lot of other things that had happened when he was a young lawyer like I was, trying to make a name for himself. We used to spend long evenings, sometimes the four of us—Jeffries, his wife, Adele, Jean, and me—but more often just the three of us. His wife was an invalid." A strange, almost sinister smile crawled over his mouth. "An invalid! She was an addict."

I had met Adele Jeffries only on the rare occasion when I happened to run into her husband at some social event. She was supposed to be five or six years older and she looked every bit of it. Instead of hiding, makeup seemed to heighten the effect of the deep lines that crossed her forehead and creased the sagging skin on her cheeks. Her eyes, however, were lively and alert, the somewhat amused observer of her own sad deterioration. There had been rumors about her for years, the kind of soft-spoken, gently insinuated suggestion that became an indelible part of the way everyone thought about her. No one could actually explain what it was she was supposed to have done, but everyone knew that she was not quite right, and that besides drinking too much she required fairly constant medication.

"Poor Adele," Elliott was saying. "I'll bet there wasn't a doctor in Portland who didn't at one time or another get one of her famous phone calls. I kind of liked her," he added as an aside, "even though I knew she had to be crazy." Catching the irony of what had just slipped out, his eyes darted away and then darted back, while he shrugged his shoulders and threw up his hands.

"She really was," he insisted, growing more serious. "She'd go right down the Yellow Pages—under 'Physicians.' I saw her do it one day. She sat on a stool in the kitchen, moving that wrinkled finger down the list, crunching up her eyes to make the name come into focus. As soon as someone answered the phone, she'd clear her throat and with as much formality, as much solemnity as if she were introducing the president of the United States, announce that 'Mrs. Judge Jeffries'—that's what she called herself— was calling for Dr. Dolittle or Dr. Whomever. They'd always put her through. And then she would do it again, announce she was Mrs. Judge Jeffries and ask if the doctor would kindly be good enough to order a refill of her prescription for Percodan or Demerol or any one of the other two dozen pain-killing, mind-numbing, nerve-deadening, brain-altering, mood-elevating, awareness-closing pharmaceuticals she was taking by the handful morning, noon, and long into the literal and proverbial night."

Elliott was panting hard, glaring at me as if the addiction of Mrs. Judge Jeffries had been somehow my fault. Then, suddenly, his head snapped back and he started to laugh. "There was nothing wrong with her. There never was. She had some minor ailment, twisted her ankle, something like that, years before. She told me once, during one of her brief interludes of sobriety. After that, every time she had a pain somewhere, just a twinge of discomfort, Jeffries would give her something, just for the pain. Eventually, she was hooked—couldn't live without her pills, that and the booze. Jeffries didn't mind. He encouraged her. Why deal with pain? It was a way of getting rid of her. She was always there, but she wasn't there at all. He married her for her money. Now she's in a nursing home somewhere. She probably doesn't know where she is. Jeffries worked everything out. He had her declared incompetent while they were still married, put everything of hers in a trust, and named himself trustee. I told you he knew everything about the law."

Elliott opened his eyes wide and took a deep breath, and then let it out, a look of disgust on his face. "You know who he had draw up the papers? You know who he asked to handle the whole thing?"

I did not want to believe it and I knew it had to be true. "You did that?"

"I didn't want to. I really didn't. I told him I thought she was all right, that perhaps if she saw a doctor he could get her to stop drinking, to stop taking all that pain medication. He told me every doctor he talked to told him the same thing, that it was too late, that the damage was permanent, that she needed constant round-the-clock care.

"It still didn't seem right to me. He insisted he knew a lot more about his wife than I did and that he was surprised and, yes, disappointed—more disappointed than he could say—that I would refuse the favor he had asked. Had I forgotten all the favors he had done for me, the way he had actually broken the law when I had missed a filing deadline or needed extra time to finish something? Then he told me what he had never told me before. He told me that he had sometimes ruled on motions in my favor just because he believed I always wanted to do the right thing, and that if anyone ever found out, if he ever let slip what he had done, he'd be in a lot of trouble and so would I. We had to trust each other, he said. Surely, I didn't believe that he could possibly want to do anything that wasn't in the best interest of his own wife? I couldn't possibly know how painful this was for him, and how the only way he thought he could get through it was knowing it was being taken care of by someone that both of them, he and Adele, had come to think of as a son."

He gritted his teeth and his eyes fairly started out of their sockets. "At the hearing, she sat next to me, docile, unprotesting, until the very end. She leaned over, that vacant smile still on her face, and as clear as a bell said to me, 'You helped him get rid of me, but I'm not the only one he wants to get rid of!' And then she started to laugh, this hideous, bloodcurdling laugh that rolled on and on, louder and louder, till I had to put my hands over my ears, for fear that ghastly sound would crack my head. Sometimes, if I'm not careful, I see her face in my sleep and I hear that voice again, that dismal warning I failed to heed. At the time, of course, all I did was watch them take her away, that awful laughter shrieking through the courthouse. The only thought I had was that Jeffries had been right after all, that there was too much damage, that there was nothing to be done but put her away in a place where she could get the constant care she needed.

"She had tried to warn me, but even then I still believed in Jeffries. How could I not?" he asked with a shrewd glance. "I had just helped him get rid of his wife. Everyone wants to believe that what they're doing has a justification. I'm sure Jeffries thought he was justified."

Elliott was quick, preternaturally so, and he caught immediately the slight glimmer of doubt in my eyes.

"Of course he did. At each step, over all the years he had lived with her. Think of it! She has a slight accident; she's in pain; the medication works. She stops complaining. He would have noticed that right away. Finally! Relief from her constant, and for him, mindless talk. After that, every time she mentioned pain—the medication. He could always get it. He knew people. He knew doctors. He knew—oh, yes, how well he knew—the doctor who ran the hospital where my dear, loving, loyal wife, Jean, was working.

"That's how they met. That's how it all began. Innocent at

first. It usually is, isn't it? Innocent, I mean. For all the loathsome, filthy thoughts that began to creep into their minds, like worms eating away at a corpse, or, more likely, the spiral-shaped vermin that infest the syphilitic, they were on the outside nothing but a couple of civilized, compassionate people, concerned, both of them, with the welfare of the great man's wife. I didn't notice it at the time," he added confidentially, "but thinking back on it I'm almost certain there was a peculiar odor—a kind of stench—whenever I was with the two of them together." He paused. "You think I'm making that up, that it's just my imagination?" he asked with a stern sideways glance. "Don't they say that when two people are attracted to each other there is a certain chemistry between them? Didn't you ever mix chemicals together when you were a child to see what the worst smell was you could make?

"But you're right," he admitted, waving his hand back and forth in front of his face. "At the time, I noticed nothing." There was a slightly astonished look on his face. "There was nothing to notice. We were always talking about the law, and she was always asking about his wife. The first time I noticed anything was one night when we were having dinner, the three of us. His wife was—well, you know—'not feeling well.' Jean had to leave before we had coffee. She had the late shift at the hospital. After she was gone, Jeffries seemed to draw into himself, as if there was something that was bothering him. Finally, after I urged him to speak, he asked if Jean was working some kind of double shift. When I told him she was not, that she was working nights all week, he looked distressed. He had been out at the hospital that afternoon, he explained, to visit his friend, the doctor who ran the place. He had seen Jean walking down a corridor too far away for him either to catch her eye or say hello, but he was certain it was she.

"I dismissed it as best I could. 'She was probably called in for some kind of emergency. That happens once in a while.' He pretended to agree, but I could see he did not believe it."

Elliott bent his head forward and rubbed the back of his neck. "It's a fairly shrewd tactic, don't you think? Suggest to someone that his wife may be up to something improper? You become the last person he'll ever suspect as the one she's doing it with. Jeffries was, after all, a truly brilliant man." He hesitated before he added, "At least I thought so then." His eyes sparkled with malice. "I was thirty-three years old when I came here, the same age as Christ when he died. Do you know the best thing ever said about Christ?" For a brief moment he was seized by a look of uncertainty. "Said about him, or did I make it up? It doesn't matter." His face brightened. "'If Christ had lived, he would have changed his mind.' That's what happened to me, you see. I lived, and I changed my mind. I believed in him, I thought he could do nothing wrong. Then, when I realized what he had done, how utterly corrupt he was, I understood how my own life had been nothing but a lie." His eyes flashed, and a smile darted across his mouth. "There are certain advantages in losing your mind."

Eight

Chester, the patient who could do anything with numbers and nothing at all with simple historical facts, was standing in front of our table, trembling from head to toe.

"Elliott," he said, gulping a breath, "I have to go to the bathroom. What should I do?" Closing his mouth, he pulled his upper lip all the way down over the lower one.

Elliott placed his hand on Chester's shoulder and, remarkably, the trembling stopped. "It will be all right," he said in a calm, soothing voice. He nodded toward the orderly, now reading a tattered paperback, at the other end of the room. "Mr. Charles always takes you, remember? Just go tell him you have to go."

He removed his hand from his shoulder, and the trembling started once more. Gently, he put it back, and again it stopped. "Don't you believe me?" he asked, peering into his eyes.

"Yes," he insisted, "but I'm scared."

"You're not scared of Mr. Charles, are you?" Elliott asked evenly. "He always takes good care of you."

"I'm scared I'll go in my pants," he replied in a childlike voice. He looked down at the floor, too embarrassed to meet Elliott's gaze.

"Look at me," Elliott instructed. Dutifully, Chester raised his eyes. "It's all right. It won't happen. I promise. Now, go tell Mr. Charles what you have to do." Elliott patted him on the shoulder and then took his hand away for good. The trembling did not come back.

"Thank you, Elliott," he said as he turned to go. He had taken perhaps three steps, when he stopped and yelled at the top of his lungs: "Mr. Charles, I have to take a piss now!"

I watched the orderly look over the top of his book and then slowly get to his feet. "He seems harmless enough," I remarked. "Why is he here?"

"Too much history," Elliott explained. I waited for the rest of it, but that was all he offered.

"Too much history? I don't understand."

"Yes, exactly. Too much history," he mused. "He spent so much time reading about it, the past finally became his whole reality. If he had been studying something like the history of music, he might have walked around telling everyone he was Beethoven. He was studying the Vietnam War and he decided one day that he was in the war, and that he was surrounded by the Vietcong. He wrapped a bandanna around his forehead, covered his face with grease, and hid on the steam pipes that ran through the underground garage of the apartment building where he lived. No one knows how long he was there, clutching the bayonet he had picked up at some army surplus store. He might have been there for days, waiting for the Vietcong to come. They came all right, wearing a business suit and carrying a briefcase. Chester thought he was a scout sent ahead to get his exact location. He jumped down from the pipes above that poor fellow's car—turned out he was an insurance salesman—slashed his throat, and left him to bleed to death while he went running through the garage looking for more. But you're right. He's harmless. He wouldn't hurt a fly. Not in here, anyway."

Several more patients had wandered in, taking their places on the molded plastic chairs scattered around the large day room. They moved slowly when they walked and, apart from an occasional twitch or a sudden jerk, barely moved at all while they sat. They did not speak, and the silence hung heavy in the air, broken only by a short-lived moan or a sob quickly suppressed. It made me think of an old train station, or a bus station late at night, places where strangers wait in crowded solitude the endless hours until it is their time to go.

"They get tired late in the day," Elliott explained. "The medication has that effect."

Elliott did not seem tired at all. If anything, he had become more energetic, and more intense, the longer I was there. I thought it might be because of the excitement he must have felt at having a visitor from the outside. I started to get to my feet.

"Perhaps I should be going. We can continue this another time."

He seized my wrist and held it fast. "No," he insisted. "There's no reason for you to go. I haven't told you yet why I thought you were having an affair with my wife. Don't you want to know?"

I sat down again and he let go of my arm. "It isn't true," I said, wondering why I felt compelled to repeat the denial. Was it because the idea had once crossed my mind, and I felt guilty for the thought if not the deed?

The look he gave me was uncanny. While his eyes bored in on me, trying to reach the back of my skull, they seemed at the same time to dart all around. It was like watching a solar eclipse. In the middle was a deep, dark, impenetrable point, that for the moment at least stayed fixed, surrounded by a dazzling fireworks of dancing, flying light.

"I saw you talking with her once at a party. She was always doing that, talking to the most attractive men. She liked to know that men, attractive men, found her attractive. It was important to her. It was part of the way she defined herself: a woman who was attractive to men."

I remembered her all right, sleek, proud, and willful, with golden brown hair and dark, bottomless eyes. Her gaze never left you while she talked, and she drew you so far into her, made you feel so much a favorite, that you almost failed to notice how her eyes moved restlessly around the room when it was her turn to listen. You could not help but notice her hands, long bony knuckled fingers that looked like they were waiting to snatch at something, to close tight around something, to grab at whatever they could get. I did not like her, and that might have made me want her even more, had she not been married to an associate in my firm for whom I felt a certain responsibility.

"She was a very attractive woman," I heard myself saying.

"She knew you thought so. After that party she used to tease me about it. She'd tell me how much she liked older men." He sensed my reaction before I was quite conscious that I had one. "You were about the same age then, I am now," he remarked. "She said that if she ever decided to be unfaithful it would probably be with someone like you."

Vanity, not hope, is the last thing to die. Why otherwise would I have tried to get the assurance of someone clinically insane that more than a dozen years earlier I was still young.

"Someone older?" I asked, lifting an eyebrow.

Elliott was not thinking of me. "She was always ambitious. I wanted to be a teacher; she wanted me to be a lawyer. She convinced me that I should, told me how great she thought I'd be, told me how much she believed in me. And I believed what she said, because I believed in her." He looked at me for a moment, pondering something he had clearly thought about before. "I was always defined by what other people thought, people I trusted, people I believed in. Isn't that what everyone does—think of themselves in terms of what other people think they are or think they should be? The danger of course is that you find out one day that you can't believe in them anymore, that there is nothing you can believe in anymore, that everything you believed before was based on a lie. Then you don't know who you are. You're alone, by yourself, without anything to go back to and without anything to look forward to."

A sly, cynical grin stole across his mouth. "So they put people like me in an asylum, because, after all, what happened to me could only have been some kind of aberration, a mental disease, a mental defect. But, fortunately, a condition that can be cured, or at least controlled, with the right regimen of therapy and medication. Controlled! Do you know what they mean? Unquestioning obedience, docile acceptance. You agree with everything anyone tells you, do whatever they tell you to do, believe everything they tell you to believe. You become as crazy as everyone else out there. You don't have to believe in God, but you damn well better believe in golf!"

"What?" I asked, startled less by what he had said than by the fanatical look that had entered his eyes. "Golf?"

He looked at me like I was crazy. "Yes, golf. Recreation is good; getting along with other people is good. Taking life as a game. It's good. Not getting upset at the insanity of the world. That's good. Everyone believes in golf."

His eyes became wilder, and his head began to swing from side to side. "Jean liked golf, and tennis, and swimming, and horseback riding." He stopped, a shadow of doubt in his overheated eyes. "I think she drew the line at bowling. Not that she had anything against the game itself, you understand. Jean believed in games. She just didn't think the right sort of people played that particular game. Bowling at one end of the scale, chess at the other. Too intellectual, she thought. Whatever else she was, she was always upwardly mobile. As a matter of fact, I think . . ."

It happened again, that same terrifying seizure that took possession of him like some demonic force, shaking his body like a limp rag while he tried desperately to find the one key rhyming word that would open the lock and let him go free.

"I think . . . blink . . . ink . . . wink . . ." His eyes bulged out, his face turned red. "Stink . . . chink . . . mink . . . fink."

It was over. The life came back into his eyes, his skin became pale again, and from the tone of his voice you would have thought you were talking to a completely normal man.

"What were we talking about?" he asked, as if he had just for a moment forgotten what he was saying. "Oh, yes," he said as soon as I reminded him. "Jean. She wanted success, and when she met Jeffries and realized how much he wanted her, I don't think she thought about resisting. I was still several years away from the possibility of a partnership. Why would she wait for something she could have right away?" He looked at me, a whimsical expression in his eyes. "In your world—the sane world— isn't instant gratification what everyone wants?

"Of course I didn't know anything about it at the time. I still thought Jeffries was my friend. I had proof of it. Of all the people he knew, of all the lawyers he could have asked, I was the one he chose when he had to have his wife declared incompetent. And after that happened, after he was all alone, we spent even more time together than we had before."

Elliott now seemed perfectly calm, almost relaxed, as if we were trading gossip about someone we had once both known.

"What made you think she was having an affair with me?" I asked.

"She started to lie to me. She came home two hours after her shift ended and told me it was because someone on the next shift called in sick. But because I was worried, I had called the hospital and been told she had left at the normal time. She fumbled for some excuse, something about it happening at the last minute and the switchboard did not know anything about it. I believed her. But things like that started to happen more and more often. Each time she had an excuse. Each time I believed her, or tried to. My questioning became more intense, more frantic, and she began to replace explanation with analysis. She was worried about me, she insisted. I was imagining things; I was in danger of becoming paranoid. Finally, after she had come in late and made up some story that made no sense at all, I came right out and accused her of having an affair.

" 'And just who am I supposed to be having an affair with?'

"She looked at me with such disdain, such contempt. I had been in love with her from the first moment I ever saw her. We were married six months after we met. I was never in love with anyone but her. And the way she looked at me! It felt like someone had torn my insides out. I wanted to die, right there and then; I just wanted to stop breathing.

"'I can't live like this,' she told me. 'I need to get away for a few days. I need time to think.'

"She went away for three days, all weekend. Monday morning she called from the hospital to talk to the kids. She said she would be home for dinner. Later that day, during a break in a trial, I went to see Jeffries. I needed someone to talk to and he was the only person I could trust with something like this.

"I can see it all quite clearly now: Jeffries sitting behind his desk, looking up at me from over his glasses. 'I must have just missed you Saturday,' he said. I didn't know what he was talking about. 'Over at the coast, at Salishan, at the bar conference. I saw Jean in the hotel lobby, talking to Antonelli. They must have been waiting for you. I couldn't stay. I was with some other people.'

"I'm not quite sure what happened after that. I don't remember anything about that afternoon in trial, only that all I could think about was getting home, seeing Jean, trying to convince myself that she could convince me none of it was true. When I got home, she was not there and neither were the children. A few minutes later, the doorbell rang and when I answered a stranger handed me a summons. Jean had filed for divorce."

His elbow on the table, Elliott rested his cheekbone against his thumb and the corner of his forehead against his index finger. He sat there, lost in contemplation.

"The next day," he said presently, an absent expression on his face, "I had the breakdown. I was in court, in the middle of that trial, when it happened. That's what they told me, anyway. I don't really remember."

His eyes came back into focus. "That's why I came to kill you. It was the only thing I could think about, killing you because of what you had done to me." A cryptic smile floated over his mouth. "I'm sure Jeffries was disappointed when I didn't. He was always telling me things about you, how you would do anything to win, and how one day it was all going to catch up with you. He told me you were the most amoral person he had ever known, and that if he had to do it over again he would have made you serve thirty days for contempt instead of three. Then someone else would have had to take over the defense in that case he said you should never have won."

He remembered something else. "He told me once that there were people in the firm who had not wanted to bring you in, who didn't want you there, people he knew, people who would be delighted if I was the only criminal defense attorney in the firm. You see what he was doing. He never missed a chance to stir something up, to create resentment, to make me think that without you around I'd have everything I wanted. You were the senior partner, the lawyer with the great reputation, and then, on top of everything else, you were the one who was taking away my wife."

Elliott smiled again, that same enigmatic look that suggested that there was always something else, some deeper meaning beneath the literal meaning of what he said. His fingers brushed across his mustache, over and over again, each time faster than the time before, and then, abruptly, stopped.

"Maybe Jeffries really did know I'd have a breakdown and what would happen if I did."

It was easy to be carried along by what he said. Not only was there a sort of logic about it all, but, like most things exotic, Elliot exerted a strange kind of attraction. The longer I stayed there, the more difficult it was to remember that I was sitting at a table inside an insane asylum talking to a mental patient.

"There is an obvious question, Elliott," I said with a self-conscious smile. "Forget what Jeffries said about me. Why go through all this deception? Why didn't your wife just simply file for the divorce? Why make you think I was involved?"

He answered without the slightest hesitation, as if there could not possibly be any doubt about what the truth really was. "They couldn't afford the scandal. Judges weren't supposed to be sleeping with the wives of the lawyers who practiced in front of them. It would have made it more difficult to get the other thing they wanted. Jeffries did not just want my wife, he wanted my children. He'd never had any of his own."

Elliott reported this as if it was not only a self-evident fact, but one that had nothing directly to do with him. It was the way he described nearly everything that had happened before his breakdown. I had of course heard people talk about themselves with a certain detachment, passing judgment on their own behavior, but never anything like this. There was a break in time for Elliott, as definite as the way we divide all of history into what came before and what came after Christ. When he talked about things that happened before his commitment, there was no connection between what he was now and what he had been then. The old Elliott was dead, and, as near as I could tell, the new Elliott did not miss him at all.

Elliott's eyes glistened with laughter. "If all this sounds a little paranoid—well, I am, a little paranoid, that is. That's what they tell me, anyway. Of course, that's what they tell everyone here. Paranoid schizophrenia. They always try to give it a little twist, something that makes it sound like they really know what they're talking about. Type I or Type II, delusions of this or delusions of that, acute or not so acute. And they always say it with such gravity, such enormous seriousness, and with the same somber, slow-moving gestures, the head bent forward, the hands behind the back, the stooped shoulder. You would think they were in church, getting ready to take communion. Paranoid schizophrenia." His eyes turned hard and his voice was filled with contempt. "They cover their ignorance with that phrase. It gives them a sense of power. They're the ones who are really sick."

At the end of the room, the orderly got to his feet and stretched his arms. All around, the patients began to stir.

"Time for class," Elliott explained. The contempt had vanished. His manner was almost playful. "Staff call it group therapy; we call it class. There are several different classes. My personal favorite is 'medication management.' We learn about the symptoms of our illness and how to manage them." His eyes filled with mirth and he shut them partway to keep from laughing out loud. "Think of it," he said in a hoarse whisper. "You explain to someone that he's a paranoid schizophrenic. Then, as if this was all news to him, you explain the symptoms to look for. You tell him that these symptoms can be kept under control by medication, and that the trick is to take the medication in the prescribed dosage at the precise moment that you first detect the symptom. In other words, you explain to him that he's crazy, and then you tell him all the perfectly reasonable things he can do not to show it."

There seemed never to be any gradual transition between his moods. It was one thing, then it was another. He had been cheerful and ironic; now he seemed completely serious.

"The strange part is that it seems to work. Some people become quite good at it. They learn to deal with their disease, to control it, and even perhaps to use it. Some of them, I think, even learn how to hide behind it."

I did not know what he meant by this last remark. "Hide behind it?"

The cheerful glint came back to his eye. "Everyone learns how to tell people what they want to hear—or to see what they want to see—don't they?"

I started to ask him something else, but his glance suddenly darted away and his face lost all expression. Before I could turn around to see what had brought this about, he was on his feet, standing still. The wire gate was rattling as Dr. Friedman opened the lock with his key.

There was something I had to know, though I could not have said then why I needed to know it. Perhaps it was just a feeling, or perhaps it was something more than that, a sense that there was more to this story than what he had told me.

"Elliott," I said, taking him by the arm, "who represented you when you went to court? Who was the lawyer that handled your case?"

Dr. Friedman had come through the gate and was waiting a few feet away. Elliott looked at me and shrugged. "I don't remember. Someone Jeffries found."

We said goodbye and I turned to go. "Joseph," he called out. It was the only time he had used my first name. "Would you do me a favor?"

"Of course," I replied.

He reached inside his suit coat, and when he did I realized it was probably the same suit he had worn the last time he had been in court, the day he was sent to the state hospital. He handed me an envelope and asked if I would deliver it to his children. It seemed an odd request.

"You don't want to just put it in the mail?"

"I can't. I don't know where they live. I don't even know their names."

I was not certain I had heard him right. "You don't know their names?" It was too late. He had already started to walk away.

"Do you know what he meant by that?" I asked Dr. Friedman as we made our way out. I glanced at the envelope. The word "Children" was written on the front, and nothing else, not a name, not an address, nothing but that one word.

"I think so," Friedman explained. "Quite some time ago—before I was here—his children were apparently adopted by his wife's new husband."

"But that's impossible," I protested. "That can only be done with the parents' consent." Then it hit me. "Oh, my God. Of course! How stupid of me not to think of it."

"What?"

"They went to court—his wife and her new husband—and the court took away his parental rights. In the eyes of the law, he doesn't have any children. That's what he meant when he said he doesn't know their names. He doesn't know them—or rather he doesn't want to know them—by their new last name: Jeffries."

Friedman nodded politely. "Yes, I suppose that's possible," he said in a neutral voice. "It's hard to know with Elliott. He's a difficult case—interesting, but difficult."

We had reached the glass door at the entrance. Friedman started to push it open then, with his hand still on it, hunched his shoulders forward, bent his head, and stared down at the linoleum floor. "Elliott is a paranoid schizophrenic," he said in a somber tone, as he raised his eyes. "Why are you smiling?" he asked, baffled at my reaction.

I had not been aware of it. "Sorry," I said, a little embarrassed. "It was something Elliott said."

He took my explanation at face value. He was used to people who had a number of things going on in their mind at the same time.

"As I was saying, he's a paranoid schizophrenic, and unlike some patients with this illness who exhibit only a few symptoms, Elliott seems to experience a great many of them."

"Is one of them getting caught in a word and then repeating words that rhyme?"

"Yes. 'Clanging.' Something happens in the brain, the wrong message gets sent, and instead of the sequence of words to complete the thought, it sort of reverses itself, and it is the word that in some sense has to be completed. That is a fairly common symptom, and, quite frankly, not a very serious one. Elliott has much more serious problems. Sometimes he does not talk for days. He withdraws into himself and when that happens there is no reaching him. You saw the way he looked when you first arrived, that trancelike stare. But then, other times, he'll start talking, fast, furious, and half the time it doesn't make any sense at all, or the words are run so close together you can't tell if it does or not. Then, at other times, he's completely rational and remarkably intelligent."

Friedman paused and searched my eyes. "Is he anything like the way you remembered him?"

I had to think about it. He was not the same at all, but now that I had seen him, a dozen years older, an inmate in a hospital for the criminally insane; now that I had a better idea of what had happened to him, I wondered if what I had remembered about him had not been more the work of my own imagination than anything that had ever been real.

Nine

The rain had stopped, but the clouds were still so dark that though it was only three o'clock in the afternoon day had already turned to night. On the street below the hospital the headlights of the cars that passed cast an eerie yellow glow in the gloomy mist. At the end of the lane that led from the parking lot, someone darted out of the shadows. I slammed on the brakes. His face twisted into angry contortions, he waved his fist at me and shouted a silent curse. I wondered if he was a patient, or just someone normal giving vent to his rage.

I thought about Elliott Winston while I drove back to Portland, and I thought about him during the next several days, every time something I heard or something I read ignited in my head a burst of similar-sounding words. Once, at lunch with another lawyer, I did it out loud. I said the word "eating," and then heard myself say, "greeting . . . meeting . . . beating."

"Don't you ever do that?" I asked, rather amused at what I had just done. "Listen to the sound of words, rhyme them together?" He said he did not, and I wondered whether to believe him. One thought led to another. "It's the basic principle of poetry, isn't it? The sound, the rhyme?" I thought of something else. "Before things were written down, it was a way to help people remember what had been said."

He did not disagree, but he also did not really care. We were there to discuss a question of law, and there was very little room for poetry in that.

For the next several weeks there was not much room for much of anything. I was in one trial after another, and I might not have thought about Elliott at all, had the search for the killer of Calvin Jeffries not remained front-page news. Whenever I was reminded of that murder, something about Elliott, a remark, a gesture, his astonishing piercing stare, flashed in front of me. The two of them, one dead, the other alive but living in a world of his own, had become permanently linked in my mind, a Janus-faced image of good and evil, reason and madness, with my own sympathies fully engaged on the side of insanity.

Perhaps not with all forms of insanity, I told myself as I dressed for a dinner I had no desire to attend. I had gone to his funeral out of a sense of obligation. The murder of a judge, even a judge like Jeffries, was an attack on the law, and the law, despite all my disappointments and disillusions, was the only thing in which I still believed. I was like a priest who had lost faith in the Church but who, perhaps for that reason, clung closer to God.

I had to go to the funeral, but I did not have to go to this. It was a mystery to me why I had ever agreed. Probably it was nothing more than a vague desire to watch one of the ways in which we try to improve the future by telling lies about the past. A picture of Calvin Jeffries had already been hung in the courthouse; his bust would now occupy a niche somewhere in the wall of the law school library. He would become the latest in a long line of supposedly brilliant and honorable jurists to have a professorship, a chair, endowed in his name. He had left the money for it, three quarters of a million, in his will, and no one, especially not the law school, was inclined to look too closely into where it might have come from. Some of it, of course, had come from the money which with the assistance of Elliott Winston he had stolen from his first wife. It did not matter. No one cared about the past. The important thing was this truly wonderful act of public-spirited generosity. Nor did anyone seem to think it at all extraordinary that he had required as a condition of the gift that it be called the Calvin Jeffries Chair of Criminal Procedure. Vanity is not always the last thing to die: Sometimes it does not die at all.

His large pink face beaming, Harper Bryce waved to me from a table in the second row below the dais. Apologizing as I bumped my way through the clogged passageways between tables, I found my place at the last empty chair, right next to Harper. He was standing up, surveying the crowd.

"Full house," he said. "Must be seven, eight hundred people." A jaundiced grin cut across his face. "First the funeral, now this. Jeffries can really turn them out."

I followed his eyes out across the ballroom, filled with well-dressed men and expensively dressed women, women with glittering smiles and bright-colored jewels. There was noise everywhere, glasses tinkling, shoes shuffling, chairs moving, and voices, hundreds of them, all talking at once, a deafening, unintelligible din, roaring in your ears like a thousand thoughts clamoring for your undivided attention. Then, above it all, a sound at first like a flight of Canadian geese, then like a single blast from a fat schoolboy's tuba. I turned around. Harper Bryce, his face buried in a white linen handkerchief, was blowing his nose.

"Every damn April," he groused, a look of disgust on his face. He folded the handkerchief and put it back in the breast pocket of his dark blue suit.

We were sitting at a table paid for by Harper's newspaper. The publisher, Otto Rothstein, and his wife, Samantha, were seated on Harper's left. Rothstein was short, stocky, with a thick neck, and hard, relentless eyes. He looked right at you when he talked, as if he were always trying to size you up. His wife was all legs and arms, with a concave chest and nothing at all where her hips should have been. She had large, mocking eyes, and the bored smile of a woman who could always think of a place she would rather be. When you were with her it was hard not to share her feeling.

The new editor of the paper, Archie Bailey, cheerful, unassuming, and, according to Harper, one of the smartest newspapermen he had ever met, was there with his wife, Rhoda, seven months pregnant with their first child. After I said hello to them both, I was introduced to an older, gray-haired man with a craggy forehead, heavy eyebrows, and a long, straight nose. Dark olive-colored skin stretched tight from his round cheekbones to his narrow, dimpled chin.

"Cesare Orsini," Harper said, suddenly quite formal. As I leaned across the table and shook his soft, pliable hand, Harper added, "Professor Orsini teaches at the University of Bologna. He's the leading expert on Italian Renaissance literature. He's here to give a series of lectures the paper is helping to sponsor."

"Mr. Bryce overstates my qualification," the professor remarked, an amused gleam in his eyes. "I'm just an old man who likes to read things written by people who died a long time ago. It makes me feel young." His English was impeccable, with only a trace of an accent.

Next to Orsini was an attractive woman with quiet eyes and shoulder-length brown hair. She had the athletic look of someone who spent a lot of time on a golf course or a tennis court. Lisa Laughlin, Harper explained, was the editor of the society page.

"It's a great pleasure to meet you," I said. There was something about her, something about the way she looked at me, that made me stop.

"It's all right, Mr. Antonelli," she said, laughing.

I tried to figure out why she was laughing, and I had the odd sense that it was something I should know.

"Joseph," I said.

This only made her laugh more. "Joseph? Yes, of course," she said as the laughter died away. "But, you see, Joseph, when I was thirteen and had a crush on you so bad it hurt, everyone called you Joe. Except my sister, who I hated, who called you Joey."

I still did not know, and she took pity on my ignorance. "My maiden name was Frazier."

I could have fallen through the floor. Suddenly I was eighteen again, with a butch haircut, two gray stripes on the sleeve of my red letterman sweater, wearing saddle shoes and peg pants, the captain of the high school football team, with a cocky smile but so pathetically self-conscious that I would not wear a short-sleeve shirt on the hottest day of the year because I thought I was skinny and that everyone would laugh. And then Jennifer Frazier, the best-looking girl in school, which meant the best-looking girl in the world, said she'd go out with me and I became a novitiate in the fine art of romantic failure.

I remembered it as if it had all just happened. We went to a party, and while everyone else ate and drank and talked, we stayed in the darkened corner of another room, dancing together as if the night was forever. She was tall and thin, with wide, almond-shaped eyes that changed color with the light, through several shades of brown, and, when everything was just right, to yellow. She was gorgeous, and I was in love before I kissed her and doomed when I did. When I took her home, sometime after midnight, she lingered in my arms and with a bittersweet look I never forgot, told me that she would ask me to spend the night, but her mother wouldn't like it. After Jennifer, I didn't think I could ever fall in love again.

It took me a long time to get over Jennifer Frazier, and now that I was looking at her grown-up little sister and felt the blood rushing to my face and a surge of awkward embarrassment, I knew that I never really had.

"You were just a little kid," I heard myself say. "A little kid with pigtails and rubber bands, braces on your teeth, a little, skinny kid who liked to play with frogs. You told me you hated boys."

She smiled at me, and nodded. "And I haven't changed a bit," she said. "And neither have you."

Under the throbbing din, dozens of white-coated waiters, their eyes darting from large pewter-colored trays to the place on the table where they had to set the next dish, bustled around the cavernous room. At the end of a forgettable meal of lukewarm food, the dishes were removed and coffee was served.

Slowly tapping his fingers on the tablecloth, Professor Orsini seemed to be lost in thought. When he raised his eyes and found me watching, his cheeks flushed, as if he had been caught doing something he should not.

"I was just thinking about the Borgias," he explained. His dark brown eyes sparkled and he began to gesture with his hands. "It has been said of them that they came into the world as a declaration of war against morality through incest and adultery."

Everyone at the table stopped what they were doing. Orsini glanced from one to the other. "One of the Borgias became Pope, Alexander VI. His son, named, like myself, Cesare," he remarked with a cunning smile, "was the one Machiavelli so much admired—or at least seemed to admire. Yes, yes, I know," he said quickly. "It is unfortunate, but true. The Pope was not always so holy. He also had a daughter, Lucrezia, who was not so good, either." With a sigh he opened his hands in a gesture of supplication. "She had relations with several of her own family. Today, of course, the Borgias would be considered quite a dysfunctional family and no doubt required to undergo a lengthy process of psychological counseling. On the other hand, they did some truly amazing things. It is an interesting question, don't you think, Mr. Antonelli? I mean the connection, or perhaps I should say the tension, between conventional morality and the willingness to take great risks, to invent what Machiavelli called new modes and orders?"

He let the question hang in the air for just an instant, and then, turning away from me, went back to what he had been saying.

"You Americans come to a dinner like this, where a prominent political figure is going to make a speech, and you enjoy yourselves immensely. In my country—in Florence in particular—no one ever wanted to be invited to dine with the Borgias. It was always dangerous to refuse and sometimes fatal to accept." Narrowing his eyes, he looked down at the table and shook his head. "At least I had always thought that was a great difference between Italy then and America now," he said, lifting his gaze. "But after eating this dinner, I'm no longer quite so sure!"

"You have nothing to worry about, Professor," Rothstein's wife assured him with a cadaverous grin. "In this country we don't poison people, we shoot them."

"Or stab them," Harper added, an offhand allusion to what had happened to Calvin Jeffries.

Running a protective hand over the expanding stomach that sheltered her unborn child, Archie Bailey's wife lowered her eyes. With a shudder she shook her head in dismal silence.

Immediately, Harper regretted what he had done, but before he could apologize Otto Rothstein asked a question.

"What do you hear about the investigation? Have they got anything at all?"

Harper started to say something, then closed his mouth and wrinkled his nose. He twitched it back and forth, and then, with a hissing noise, drew in three short breaths of air. It did not work. Pulling out his handkerchief, he blew his nose.

"No, nothing," he said, sniffing. "They've got every cop in the state working on it, and so far they don't have a thing." Folding the handkerchief, he paused, a shrewd look in his reddened eyes. "Or if they do, they're not talking about it. They're under a lot of pressure. It's the biggest case any of them has ever worked on."

Rothstein furrowed his brow. "It's been almost two months. We've kept it on the front page about as long as we can. If they don't do something soon, it'll be back in the Metro section." He stopped and looked at me. "What do you think? You know something about criminal behavior. What do you think happened? Did somebody plan to kill him?"

"The only reason anyone thinks that is because of who the victim was. If it was anyone else—someone whose name was never in the papers—there would be no reason to think it was anything other than a random killing, a robbery gone bad."

Rothstein liked to argue. He liked to draw people out. If you agreed with anything he said, he would change his position just to see if you were willing to stand your own ground.

"People are murdered on purpose all the time. Most of them aren't famous."

"That's right. But if you plan to kill someone, you don't usually plan to do it with a knife. Too many things can go wrong. You have to get too close; the victim has a chance to fight; you may not be able to get it done without doing it more than once."

I darted a glance at the Baileys. They were talking together and not paying any attention to us.

"Jeffries didn't die right away. He almost made it back to his office. If he'd had a cell phone on him, he could have called 911. If he'd had a gun, he could have taken a shot. A lot of things could have happened, any one of which might have saved his life or captured his killer. If someone did set out to kill him, they probably would have used a gun." I shrugged my shoulders. "Having said that, I have to admit that most killers aren't the smartest people in the world. It's possible someone wanted Jeffries dead and just decided that was as good a time to do it as any other, especially if they were on something."

"If they're not very smart," Samantha Rothstein wanted to know, "why is it so difficult to catch them?"

"If it wasn't planned, if it was random, if there isn't any direct physical evidence—fingerprints, DNA—then there is nothing to tie the killer to the victim. That's the most difficult case to solve, and when they are solved it's almost always because the killer tells someone what they've done."

Orsini had been following every word. "Tell me, Mr. Antonelli, have you never come across someone of great intelligence who committed murder?"

No one had ever asked me that before. I searched his eyes, wondering if it was just curiosity or if there was something else behind his question.

"No, I haven't. But, then, I only meet the ones who have been caught. Cesare Borgia, if I remember correctly, died in his bed."

Orsini's eyes flared open and then narrowed down until he was looking at me from behind half-shut lids. "He was the unusual case, though I think not unique in this respect. I believe, Mr. Antonelli, that there are always three kinds of people: those who obey the law; those who break it and are punished; and those, like a Borgia, who follow a law all their own and try to impose it on others." After a brief pause, he added, "By the way, the Borgias liked knives. They do their work in silence."

The lights dimmed and static noise ripped through the ballroom as someone switched on a microphone.

If Jeffries had died in his sleep of natural causes, another judge would have been the most likely candidate to extol his virtues and ignore his vices in a public tribute. The manner of his death had brought him a posthumous fame, and instead of someone who had known him, the governor had seized on the chance to honor the memory of a man he was not certain he had ever actually met.

William Jackson Collins had won election to a first term in a race so close that only after a recount was the result made official. Two years later nearly everyone thought he was unbeatable. He never told the truth and he did not seem to mind that even those who agreed with him thought he was a liar. He gave his word to anyone who asked for it and then, when he broke it, explained it all away with distinctions so difficult to follow that it was easier just to forget about it. Then he would do it all over again, and no matter how many times he had lied to you before, when he looked at you with those large round boyish eyes, you just knew that this time he was telling you the truth. Deep down, however, you would have been disappointed if he had, because every instinct told you that he had only lied to you in the first place because he could not bring himself to say anything that might lose you as a friend. Everyone who knew him expected him to seek higher office.

When he rose to speak, Collins did what every politician does, the same ritual litany which, one way or the other, tells an audience how great they are and how glad he is to be there. I glanced at my watch, wishing he would speed it up. With a gracious, deferential smile, he nodded toward Jeffries's widow, sitting three places down the dais, and made the obligatory remarks about her loss. By the earnest expression on his face it was a loss which had been felt by no one more than himself.

I slipped my shirt cuff away from my watch, decided it must have stopped, and started to wind it before I remembered it was a quartz. When I looked up, Collins was staring down at the podium. The shy, bashful smile had dissolved. He raised his eyes and stood straight up. His head began to move slowly from side to side, taking in the crowd. He began to speak, stabbing the air for emphasis, his voice rising and falling in a mesmerizing staccato. The murder of Calvin Jeffries was more than the murder of a single human being, bad as that was. It was more than the murder of a distinguished judge. It was nothing less than the attempted murder of reason itself. The law was the anchor of civilization, the only thing that separated us from the worst kind of barbarism, the only thing that kept us safe and kept us free. The law protected us all, and we all had a moral obligation to protect the law.

I looked around the ballroom. Every face was lifted toward Collins, every eye fixed on him, as he led them from one emotion to another, building on their excitement until they had to explode. At the end, when it was over, he stood there, a triumphant smile on his face, waving into the tumultuous darkness, the center of every thought and every feeling. He had given a speech about the law and about reason, and had for the moment deprived his audience of their senses. I watched the way he kept waving at the crowd as if he could not bear the thought of being left alone without them. Suddenly I remembered the last time I had seen eyes burn with so much fire. It was when I found Elliott Winston waiting for me, at the state hospital, locked in a catatonic gaze.

The end of the governor's speech was the end of the evening. As the house lights went on, the vast ballroom swarmed with noise. As I was saying goodbye to Harper, I glanced across at the podium where a crowd had gathered around the governor. Jeffries's widow was standing at his side. I had forgotten about the letter. It was the only thing Elliott had asked me to do, and it was still sitting in the desk drawer where I had put it. I promised myself to take care of it first thing Monday morning.

Lisa Laughlin touched my arm. "It was nice to see you, after all these years. By the way," she added, as she turned to go, "Jennifer moved back a few months ago." She said something else, but the crowd had swept her too far away and I could not hear what it was.

Outside, a damp gray mist hung in the cool night air. A long line of limousines jammed the street in front of the hotel. Women in slinky evening gowns that trailed below their fashionable furs chattered with each other, or stood alone, distant and impassive, while they waited for their rides. Harried-looking men were waving their arms and yelling at their drivers, as if that would make things move faster. In the middle of it all, his head held high, a whistle firmly between his teeth, a man was holding up one hand to force cars to stop, while he used the other to wave the traffic through. Wearing a frayed, filthy brown coat, and tattered, moth-holed woolen gloves, his greasy hair flew in all directions as, oblivious of everything else, he listened intently to the voice inside his head telling him what to do.

I stood at the edge of the sidewalk, the collar of my blue cashmere topcoat pulled close to my throat, watching this strange apparition with its empty eyes and mechanical motions. Over and over again, the screeching whistle, the arm thrust out, the other arm moving underneath it in a wide sweeping curve. Had he been dressed in a police officer's uniform, everyone would have done exactly as he ordered and been grateful he was there. Dressed as he was, they simply looked away, as if, in a parody of his own madness, by not seeing him he would somehow cease to exist.

The cold cut through me like a knife. I stuffed my hands into the overcoat pockets and walked away. I had left my car in the garage at my office, a few blocks away. After I passed the courthouse, I cut diagonally across the narrow park on the other side. Reflected through the cold, dense air, the dim nighttime lights from the surrounding buildings covered it with an ash white haze. I felt a shooting pain in my left leg and had to stop. It had not bothered me for years, and now it seemed to bother me all the time. A few seconds later and the pain had gone. I tested the leg a few careful steps, and then, just as I started to resume my normal pace, I saw them, looming out of the mist just in front of me. Two men with matted gray hair and tangled gray beards, knit caps pulled down over their ears, one in front and one behind a metal shopping cart, both of them staring straight ahead, like the lookout and the pilot of a sailing ship gliding silently through the fog-shrouded sea, were stopped next to a trash can. Without a word, without a gesture, the one in back waited while the one in front lifted the lid and reached inside. He removed a single aluminum can, placed it on the concrete walkway, straightened up, pulled the cart forward, and stopped again. Without a word, without a glance, the other one, the shadow of the first, placed his foot on the can and crushed it flat. Bending down, he picked it up and placed it inside the basket. There was no wasted motion, no loss of time; they were the perfect expression of the soulless efficiency that had, at the end, left these two lost survivors to wander through the city, searching for a few cents' worth of waste. I watched them as they moved on to the next trash can, where they repeated the same silent motions. Then I lost them as they slipped away into the vast impenetrable night.

I rode the elevator down to the underground garage where I had left my car. Harsh yellow overhead light illuminated the center pavement and projected the shadow of anything that moved on the cold concrete walls. With the smell of damp cement in my nostrils, I listened to my footsteps echo back at me, a sharp staccato noise. Or was it an echo? I stopped, stood still, listening to the echo fade away. Nothing. I took another step, and stopped again. There seemed to be a second sound, following close upon the first. I turned around, searching the distance behind me. There was no one there, at least no one I could see. I moved quickly to my car and locked it from the inside as I started the engine. I glanced in the rearview mirror and began to back out. As I put the car into drive, I glanced again into the mirror. Two wild malevolent eyes were staring at me. Someone was in the back seat, directly behind me. My head snapped around. It was empty. They were behind the car, not in it. I shoved my foot down on the accelerator, grabbed the wheel with both hands, and took one last look in the rearview mirror. There was nothing; the garage was empty. But someone had been there, I was sure of it. I had seen him with my own eyes.

By the time I drove out onto the street, I was not sure what I had seen, and began to think I had just imagined the whole thing. The mind does strange things while the sun still sleeps.

Ten

It was nearly ten o'clock before I opened my eyes. For a few
minutes I lay there wondering if I could fall back to sleep. Finally, I dragged myself out of bed and stumbled, bleary-eyed, into
the bathroom. I stood in front of the toilet, staring down at the
bowl, watching the ripples spread in the water until I was finished. Then I stepped into the shower and slowly changed the
water temperature from hot to warm to as cold as I could stand
it. When I was younger and drank too much, I did it to get sober;
now I just did it to force myself to wake up.

I threw on a dark blue T-shirt and a pair of jeans and walked
barefoot to the kitchen and made a cup of coffee. I was almost
finished with the Sunday paper when the doorbell rang. No one
had buzzed from the gate at the bottom of the drive, and I was
not expecting anyone. Annoyed at the intrusion, I opened the
door.

"Yes?" I demanded irritably.

A woman, tall, willowy, with black hair and wide sloping eyes,
was standing in front of me. She was wearing a yellow dress, with
a white sweater thrown around her shoulders. Her chin was tilted
back at an angle, and a half-mocking smile played on her mouth.

I knew that look and, though it must in some ways have changed in all the years that had passed, I knew that face.

"Yes?" I asked again, starting to smile.

"Have you forgotten me, Joey?" she said, teasing me with her eyes. She pronounced my name in a soft, low, lilting voice, as if she did not want to let go. It was the same way she had said it on her front porch, sometime after midnight about a hundred years before, when we were both just kids and I was in love with her the way I would never be in love with anyone again.

We looked at each other, not quite certain what to say. Her gaze drifted away, and all her bright, shiny confidence seemed ready to turn and run. I put my arm around her waist and her arm encircled my neck, and for a minute we clung to each other.

"I saw your sister last night, and she told me that . . ."

"She called me late last night," Jennifer explained as we stepped back from each other. "A friend of hers, someone she works with— Harper something—told her where you lived."

"Come in, come in," I said, stepping aside.

"How did you get through the gate?" I asked as she looked around the living room.

"It was wide open."

Then I remembered. "I forgot to lock it last night when I got home."

It was a lie. I had not forgotten. I did not lock it because, afraid of what might be lurking in the shadows, I did not want to get out of the car. I had not seen her in years and I still did not want her to know that I was capable of courage only if I thought someone was watching.

She walked around the living room as if she had been there before and was making certain that everything was still the way she remembered it. With her hand trailing behind her, barely touching the spines of the books that lined the shelves, she moved the length of the bookcase that covered one wall. When she reached the end, she looked back.

"Remember I told you that you were too serious for me? You

always knew exactly what you wanted to do. You always had such great plans. I didn't think much beyond the next weekend." She laughed, softly, and her mouth twisted down at the corners, tender and sad. "Maybe if I had been more like you, things would have been different."

As soon as she said it, she shook her head, embarrassed, and laughed again. "I didn't come here to complain about my life. Honest. I came to ask if you'd like to go for a ride. Like old times," she added.

It would not have occurred to me to say no, but I felt somehow awkward and stupid, like someone who does not know quite how they are supposed to act. I could not know how much she had changed, and I could only wonder how different I was from the way she must have remembered me.

"Where would you like to go?" I asked, sounding stiff and formal and every bit the pompous fool.

She looked at me again with that same half-mocking smile, that look that had always told me that she knew more about me than I ever would myself.

"Does it matter?"

"No," I admitted with a laugh. "Doesn't matter at all."

I changed as quickly as I could into a pair of slacks and an oxford shirt. When I came back downstairs she had left the living room and found her way into the library. She was standing on her tiptoes, gazing up at a row of books on the top shelf bound in green and gold leather.

"The collected works of Francis Bacon," she said when she became aware of my presence. "Have you really read all of this?"

I leaned against the door, my arms folded across my chest, and shook my head. "Not only have I not read them, they don't really even belong to me. They were given to me, along with the house. A judge, the kindest, most intelligent man I ever knew, left it to me when he died. I think he thought I might be able to learn something."

She smiled at me from across the room. "And have you—learned anything?"

"Yes," I replied. "Marry the first girl you fall in love with. Nothing is ever as good as that."

Outside, on the front steps of the porch, she let her eye wander across the green grass lawn and the flower gardens filled with azaleas and beyond that to a stand of fir trees at the fence.

"Reminds me of that song," she said, as she stood next to her car, her hand on the door. She wrinkled her nose and tossed her head. "The fool who lives on the hill."

"The old fool who lives on the hill," I said as I climbed into her shiny black Porsche convertible.

"Nice car," I remarked with deliberate understatement.

She reached into the console between the red leather seats and pulled out a pair of dark glasses. "Married badly, divorced well," she remarked as she put them on.

She started the engine, then turned to me, an innocent mischievous smile on her face, as she unfastened the ribbon with which she had tied her hair. "Ready?"

Leaning against the passenger door, my arms folded loosely, I shrugged. "Sure, why not?"

As soon as I said it, she ducked her head, jammed her foot down on the accelerator, and threw it into gear. I grabbed the side of the seat with one hand and braced myself against the dashboard with the other. The car hurtled down the drive and onto the street. Her long black hair was flying back around her face and over her shoulders, the wind whipping it into long twisted tangles. Her eyes were fastened on the road in front of her. She drove with one hand on the wheel and the other on the gearshift knob. Darting in and out of traffic without bothering to signal or even to look, she left it to everyone else to get out of the way.

Leaning toward her, I shouted above the whining roar of the engine, "You're still the worst driver I've ever seen!"

She slid the dark glasses down to the tip of her nose and glanced across at me. "You forget," she yelled back, "I used to drive like this!" Clutching the wheel with both hands, she closed her eyes and laughed as if it was the most fun she had had in years.

I grabbed the wheel away from her and held it steady. The speedometer was edging past ninety. "I was only kidding. You were always a great driver."

"Remember the MG? British racing green? You didn't mind the way I drove then."

"When I was eighteen I thought I'd live forever." I started to laugh. "Of course in those days I thought forever meant forty-five at the outside."

"I liked that MG," she said, looking straight ahead, her head held high. "It was safe." She darted her eyes at me and then looked back at the road. "It didn't have a back seat."

We drove to the coast and followed the highway south as it curved through dark forested headlands and high rocky cliffs beaten smooth by the sea. We crawled through oceanside towns, waiting at crosswalks for the tourists and day-trippers eager to see the huckster shops filled with candy and myrtlewood carvings or to visit the coffee shops and ice cream parlors on the other side of the street. The April sun beat down through the cloudless sky, drying against our skin the cool salt air. As we drove on, I closed my eyes and slouched down until my head was resting against the top of the seat. The breeze that blew by us had a chill to it, but the sun was warm on my face and I felt as drowsy as the boy I had once been, when I slept with a blanket pulled up under my chin while my feet stuck out the other end.

We barely spoke. We had not even talked about where we were going. I could not count the number of times we had come here, to the coast, on a weekend day, stopping wherever we felt like it, and seldom the same place twice. We had always come in her car, and Jennifer always drove. She loved it and never got tired of it, the sheer, hypnotic thrill of taking a car high around a corner and then flat out through a straight stretch of road. I used to watch her, the constant, fluid motion of her hands and arms and wrists, the fixed determined look in her eyes, the way she laughed when she had taken the machine right to the edge of what it could do. In the shared silence of those day-long drives, I had felt closer to her than I had ever felt to anyone before, or ever felt again.

Jennifer pulled off the road onto a promontory high above the sea, and parked the car in front of a restaurant that had been there as long as I could remember. It was a long, low-lying wooden frame building that looked like a roadhouse, the kind you once saw in movies where long-legged women sat at the corner of the bar, staring through languid, half-closed eyes into the cigarette smoke that danced slowly into the air with every provocative breath they took.

We found a booth next to a window that overlooked a small cove. Down below, on the rock-covered inlet, waving their arms in the air, children ran into the water and then, when it was up to their knees, tumbled back to shore.

"Do you remember this place?" Jennifer asked as she studied the menu. "We stopped here the first time we came to the coast together." She glanced at me over the top of the menu. Her dark glasses were on the table. The lines at the edges of her eyes, barely noticeable before, spread out and deepened as she smiled. "It hasn't changed, has it?"

I followed her gaze around the busy dining room. A man in his early thirties was sitting at a table with his blond wife and their three blond children, talking to someone on his cell phone. One of his children was playing with a handheld video game. At the far end of the restaurant, next to the steps that led up to the bar, a bearded, heavyset man was sitting alone, drinking coffee, his plump fingers tapping slowly on the keyboard of a slim laptop computer.

"The restaurant hasn't changed," I replied.

"Neither has the menu," she said, inspecting the cracked plastic surface of the art deco cover.

The waitress, a woman in her late forties with a cupid mouth and a quick smile, took a short yellow pencil out of her graying blond hair and jotted down our order on a green paper notebook, the kind that wind up stuck on a spindle next to the cash register. I watched her walk away. "I think she waited on us last time. I remember her. A cute blond high school kid."

My eyes came back to Jennifer. "Your sister said you moved back a few months ago. She's really the society editor? It's hard to believe. I don't think I ever saw her in a dress." I was going off in all directions at once. I stopped and shrugged helplessly. "Why didn't you call me?" I asked quietly.

"Do you know how long it's been? I couldn't even be sure you still remembered me. If Lisa hadn't called last night and told me that she had seen you, and told me that you lived alone, I don't know if I ever would have . . ."

"You don't believe for a minute that I could have forgotten you. I was in love with you. I was always in love with you."

The waitress brought our food, and for a while we talked about nothing but the mundane details of everyday life, like two old friends who had never been more than a few months apart.

"Why didn't you ever get married?" she asked, pushing her dish aside. She had barely touched her food.

I tried to make a joke out of it. "You ruined me for other women."

"No, really," she said, searching my eyes.

"In a way, it's true. I never had that same feeling again. Not for a long time. Just a few years ago," I said, gazing out the window. The sea stretched out in the distance and then, at the far horizon, dropped off into the sky. "There was someone I wanted to marry."

"What happened?" she asked sympathetically.

"Nothing," I said, turning back to her. "She wasn't in love with me. We lived together for a while, and then she left."

I did not want to talk about it, not even with her. "What about you?"

This time, she looked away and watched the children play on the beach.

"Remember the summer after your first year in college, the summer after I graduated from high school? Remember that August, the night before I was leaving for Europe, when we stayed up until three o'clock in the morning, talking about what we wanted to do?"

She was still watching out the window, a distant look in her eyes. "Remember when you asked me to marry you? Remember what I said?"

"That you weren't ready for that yet, but that maybe someday, when you were older . . ."

"Yes, but then you remember the letter I wrote you the next day, just before I left, the letter—"

"What letter? I never got a letter."

Her eyes seemed to freeze, and then, slowly, she turned away from the window. "The letter I left at your house. The letter I gave to your mother to give to you."

"She never— What did it say? What did you write to me?"

"That you were right, that there was no reason to wait, that I was in love with you, that we should get married just like you said."

"I never got it," I said, shaking my head in disbelief. "She never gave it to me. Why would she have done that?"

We both knew the answer. My mother had tried to control everything I ever did. It was one of the reasons I had decided to go so far away to school.

"She thought I'd ruin your life. She expected you to do great things."

"That was her all right. She was always trying to run my life, but I still can't believe that she—!" I stopped myself and laughed derisively. I knew it was true, and despite that I had still felt this strange irrational compulsion to say something in my mother's defense. "I believe it. It's exactly what she would have done. And it worked, didn't it? I never got the letter. All I knew when I left you that night was that you said you would think about what we talked about. I never heard from you again. I went back to school and I didn't come home again until the summer after my senior year, the summer before I started law school. You know why I didn't come home? Because I knew if I did, I'd try to see you again, and I knew—I thought I knew—that would just make things worse."

We were looking at each other and thinking of ourselves, all the ephemeral events of our lives, wondering how much different things might have been, astonished to discover that everything that had happened had been a kind of fiction that began with a lie.

"Maybe your mother was right," Jennifer said. "I might have ruined your life. I was selfish, self-absorbed, and sometimes even cruel. And we were so young! If we'd gotten married, how long do you think it would have lasted? And then what would have happened?"

I felt again inside me the vast emptiness of that next year away at school, the awful sense that nothing mattered anymore and that I had become the unwilling spectator of my own meaningless life.

"It would have lasted," I said, certain it was true because everything else had been so false.

She smiled and touched my hand. "It's nice that you still think that."

The waitress cleared away the dishes and brought coffee. It was after two and only a few people were left in the restaurant. The sunlight slanted through the window and I twisted around against the corner of the booth to avoid the glare.

"That's the way you always used to sit. You never sat up straight. You always slouched like that, and you'd look at me with those big brown eyes of yours, always sulking about something." She hesitated, as if there was something she wanted to tell me, but was not sure she should. "I fell in love with someone once because he had eyes like yours, brown eyes that seemed to look right through me."

"Is he the one you married?"

It took a moment for her to remember that we knew next to nothing about the way we had lived our lives. "No. I was married at the time, but not to him. I met him at a country club dinner. Some friends of ours from college had invited us. They brought along a friend of theirs who was visiting from Chicago. He had your eyes. I think I fell in love with him before they finished introducing us . . ." Her voice trailed off, and she gazed out the window at the ocean lying motionless under the sun.

"We danced together," she said, still staring out the window. "We were in the middle of the dance floor." She took one last look and then turned back to me. "One moment we were dancing, and the next moment, while everyone was dancing all around us, we stopped, stopped still, right in the middle of the dance, and he said, 'Leave with me, now, right now. Let's just walk off the dance floor and never come back.'"

She looked at me as if she had just made a confession and was waiting for me to pass judgment.

"Did you want to? Leave with him, and never come back?"

"More than anything."

"Why didn't you?"

"Because I felt sorry for my husband, because I'd never loved him."

"Never loved him?" I asked, confused. "Then why did you marry him in the first place?"

"Because he raped me," she said simply. "You know how it used to be in those days. Everyone used to drink too much and then use it as an excuse for things they wanted to do anyway. It wasn't really rape, not in the way we usually mean it. We'd been to a fraternity party and we had both had a lot to drink. We were parked in his car, necking, that's all. Then he tried to do more than that, and I told him not to, and when he wouldn't quit, I shoved him away from me and told him to take me back."

She lowered her eyes, and with a wistful look slowly stirred the cup with a spoon. "He didn't take me back," she said as she lifted the cup to her mouth, holding it with both hands. She sipped the coffee and then placed the cup back in the saucer. "Anyway, I got pregnant and we got married. That's how it worked in those days, remember?" she asked, a faint, reluctant trace of defiance flashing for just a moment through her eyes.

"Why didn't you—?"

"Have an abortion? I'd done that once already. I wasn't going to do it again." Her eyes flared again, followed closely by a sad, apologetic smile. "It was a long time ago, Joey. We were just kids."

We left the restaurant and found a bench at the edge of the cliff, next to a wooden staircase that led down to the beach. Above the low roar of the ocean, we listened to the shouts of the children playing and tried not to think too much about what might have been. After a while we got back in the car and drove along the shore, like two aimless wanderers with no place to call home.

"We lived in Los Angeles, until four years ago, when we got a divorce, and he moved back to Seattle. My son, Andrew, is a producer. Television shows. He's done very well. I'm a grand-mother, for God's sakes. Twice. A boy and a girl, eight and six."

It was what every parent wanted to think, that their child had done well. My parents had thought it about me, and I guessed Jennifer's parents had thought the same thing about her. It was, I imagined, one of those instincts that must come with having a child of your own, the capacity to limit your memory to what was only seen in the best possible light.

"Did you ever see him again?"

Her eyes stayed on the road. "The man at the country club?" She wrinkled her nose. "The man!" She laughed, struck by how incongruous it all seemed now. "He couldn't have been more than twenty-five or twenty-six. He was just a boy. And I was only twenty-four, just a girl." The smile lingered a moment longer, then faded away. "Yes," she said finally. "I mean, no. I never saw him again. He called me, left me his number. In case I ever changed my mind, he said. I kept it for a while, then I threw it away. If I'd kept it any longer, I would have changed my mind."

On the way back, we stopped and watched the sun slide down the sky and dissolve into a liquid orange fire that spread out across the horizon as it pulled down the darkness over the edge of the sea. And then we left, the lights of the Porsche slashing the night as we followed the narrow road that cut through the coastal range and took us back to the city.

"Want to have dinner tomorrow night?" I asked, as casually as I could, when she dropped me off at the house.

"Call me tomorrow." She leaned over and kissed me on the side of my face. I watched her drive away, and thought about all the years I had missed, all the things that might have been.

When I got inside, I picked up the telephone and dialed the number. No one answered but I let it ring anyway. Finally, she picked it up, and I heard her frail voice.

"It's me, Joseph," I said brusquely.

"Oh, hello, dear. I was asleep. Is everything all right?"

I had forgotten the three-hour time difference between here and North Carolina where my mother lived with her second husband in a retirement community.

"Do you remember Jennifer Frazier?" I asked. The anger that had been building inside me was suddenly replaced by a feeling of helpless fatigue.

"No," she said, "I don't think so. Was she a friend of yours?"

"It doesn't matter," I said quietly. "I just called to see if you were okay. Sorry I forgot how late it is there."

My mother had kept Jennifer's letter and changed two lives forever, and had dismissed it from her mind as a matter of no great consequence. It was probably better that she did not remember. She would still have insisted that she had been right.

Eleven

I heard it on the radio the next morning on my way to the office. The police had made an arrest in the murder of Judge Calvin Jeffries. According to a police department spokesman, no other details, not even the name of the suspect, would be released until a formal press conference, tentatively scheduled for five o'clock in the afternoon.

The timing was anything but accidental. I had seen it often enough before, the brief preliminary announcement, followed by a day-long wait; the rumors started and then denied in a way that made it seem certain they were true; the frenetic race among reporters to be the first one to get the story right before there was any story to tell; and then, finally, the press conference itself scheduled at the time when the local television news shows would have no choice but to carry it live. The chief of police, the head of the state police, the lead investigator, everyone who had played a prominent part in the search for the killer, would stand in front of the camera, surrounded by every politician who could bluff or cajole his way onto the stage, and explain in muted monotones the highly efficient way in which they had developed and explored thousands of different leads and how all their painstaking patience had finally paid off. It was the law enforcement equivalent of a military parade. Watching it, everyone felt safe, secure, protected by a well-trained and well-equipped force of dedicated men and women. They caught a killer and called it a victory; someone had been murdered and no one even wondered whether that might not have been a defeat.

My investigator, Howard Flynn, was waiting for me when I arrived at the office, hidden behind a section of the newspaper. "Come in, Howard," I said without stopping.

Squeezed tight between the arms of a straight-back chair, Flynn shoved himself up and followed behind me. While I settled into the leather chair behind my desk, Flynn, breathing heavily, lowered himself into the blue wingback chair directly in front. He looked like an aging bouncer in one of those bars where the drinks are watered and the customers too drunk to care. Over six feet tall, and well over two hundred thirty pounds, the skin at the back of his short, squat neck lay in taut, thick folds, as if a hangman had decided that a single rope could never hold him. His face was blotched like a red rash. Reddish brown hair, graying at the sides, swept back from a flat forehead in a series of small, sharp waves. He was wearing what he always wore, a brown plaid sports coat and a solid brown tie. The left collar of his starched white shirt curled up at the tip, and the thread on the top button had begun to unravel. Without a word he pulled out a pack of Camels and lit one up.

"You quit drinking," I remarked as I glanced through the stack of papers my secretary had left on my desk. "Don't you think it's time you quit that, too?"

"And make the same mistake twice?" Flynn asked in a gruff voice. He took a long drag, and then added, as if it was the end of all argument on the subject, "I'm Catholic."

Each excuse he offered became more bizarre. "What?" I asked, astonished. "What do you mean? The reason you don't quit is because you're Catholic?"

He shrugged. "I'm Catholic. That means I believe in the hereafter." He paused as if this was some fine point of theology. "And that means that I'm not some goddamn health nut who doesn't care about anything except how nice and pink his goddamn lungs are."

Knitting my brow, I shook my head and studied him through half-closed eyes. "You really should have been a priest. With that kind of logic you might have become a cardinal."

A faint smile formed on his heavy mouth. "Listen. I became a lawyer. How much more Jesuitical can you be than that?"

We exchanged a glance, a silent acknowledgment of what we both understood and never talked about.

Flynn looked away, the cigarette dangling in his pudgy fingers as he stared out the window. In the distance across the river the snow on the peak of Mt. Hood shimmered a rosy pink in the early morning sun.

"Actually, I was going to be a priest once. My mother wanted me to." He caught my reaction out of the corner of his eye. "No, really," he insisted. "I'm not making it up. I was an altar boy. True story. For almost a year." He raised his hand to his face and sucked on the cigarette that was stuck between his fingers like a nail driven through a board. "Then the goddamn priest decided he liked me."

I thought I knew what he meant. "Liked you?"

"Yeah. He tried to put his hands on me. I never went back. My mother never quite got over it."

"What the priest did?"

"No. I never told her about that. It would have destroyed her. She was about as devout as they come."

Leaning forward, I searched his tired, red-rimmed eyes. "You never told her? Not even later on?"

The single strand of smoke twisting up from the burning cigarette spread out into a slow-turning gray-marbled haze. Flynn stared into it, lost in the shapeless shifting design of something that had no plan, no purpose, nothing but the free-working forces of chance. With one last drag, he blew what was left of it straight ahead, watching it like it was a river running into the sea.

"No," he said finally, looking back at me. "What good would it have done?"

"Some people would tell you that things like this have to be brought out into the open; that you have to talk about things that happened to you as a child if you're going to get on with your life."

Pursing his dry lips, Flynn nodded thoughtfully. "Shows you what the fuck they know, doesn't it?" A jaundiced smile crawled onto his mouth as he rolled his wrists over and opened his thick-fingered hands. "I mean, I just talked about it with you, and I hate to tell you, but I don't feel any different about it now than I did before. Besides, you're forgetting something. For a priest, the guy wasn't that bad-looking."

Shaking my head, I turned my chair until it was at a right angle to the desk. My eye caught the small clock I kept on the corner. It was just seven-thirty.

"What are you doing here, anyway? You were supposed to come by this afternoon."

I had known Flynn for years, and he had never once been on time. If he showed up within an hour either side of when he said, he thought you had nothing to complain about. Any later than that, he would shrug his shoulders and look at you with those ruined eyes that seemed to chronicle centuries of destruction and offer the same excuse he was giving me now.

"I've been in the program more than fifteen years. I do what they tell me. I take it one day at a time. But sometimes I have a little trouble keeping track of the hours."

It did not make any sense at all, and I knew exactly what he meant.

"Tell me something," I said, my eyes fixed on him as I tilted my head back and to the side. "How come I haven't fired you?"

"Probably because you never hired me."

"You sure?"

"No, not really. I started doing this kind of work sometime after they kicked me out of the law, but before I stopped drinking."

"Well, I must have hired you then."

He shrugged. "Maybe. Or maybe I just showed up one day. Why? You want to fire me now?"

I hesitated, as if I wanted to think it over. "No," I said finally. "You'd probably sue me, and the way I remember it, you were a pretty good lawyer."

The grin faded from his face. He bent his head and slowly worked his jaw back and forth. "Not bad, I guess," he said, looking up, and then quickly changed the subject. "I finished everything on those two cases."

He reached down and opened the black briefcase he had set on the floor next to him. The stitching on the leather handles was frayed and one of the hinges was loose. He handed me two neatly marked file folders, containing the results of the investigations he had done on cases, both of which were still months away from trial. I was more interested in what he thought about the arrest in the Jeffries murder. He had not heard about it, and when I told him, he had no reaction. I wondered if it was because, deep down, he had hoped that whoever had killed Jeffries would not get caught. It was a sentiment I could not entirely be sure I had not harbored myself, somewhere in the deep recesses of my soul. It was an evil, fugitive thought, the kind no one would admit, but one that would have been infinitely more excusable in Flynn's case than in mine. Without wanting to, Jeffries had helped make my name as a lawyer; he had made certain Flynn would never practice law again.

"You didn't hear anything about who they were looking at?" I asked, anxious for the latest rumor. "No idea who it might be?"

He studied his hands, held in his lap, then raised his head, searched my eyes for a second, and looked away. When he looked back, there was a glint in his eye, whether of malice or amusement I could not tell.

"If I was still drinking," he remarked with wry sarcasm, "I would have suspected myself." With an effort, he shoved himself up and sat erect in the chair. "No, that's not true. Well, it might have been true then. Not now," he added, shaking his head like someone trying to free himself of a bad memory. "He did me a favor."

"Did you a favor?" I asked, incredulous and a little irritated. "Because he's dead, you think you're supposed to forgive him—just forget about it? After what he did?"

Flynn put his arms on the edge of the desk and bent forward. "What exactly would you suggest I do? Go out to the cemetery and kick a little dirt on his grave? It was fifteen—no, sixteen—years ago. You weren't there. Do you have any idea how drunk I was or what I said to him?"

He could not help himself. As the memory of what he had done, what he had said, came back, he remembered it all, and there was still a part of him that was glad he had done it.

"I got so damn tired of being put down by him, and the way he used to interrupt me to correct something I'd said, sometimes just the way I had pronounced a word. The bastard was relentless. He enjoyed it. You should have seen his eyes. You remember those eyes? The way they cut right through you. And that smug little thin-lipped smile of his. And all you could do was stand there and say: 'Yes, your honor. No, your honor.' It was like standing in front of your father after he had just beat the hell out of you with his belt and agreeing that you did something wrong and deserved everything you got. I couldn't take it anymore." He paused, clenched his teeth, and shook his head. "I couldn't take anything anymore," he said, a bitter look in his eyes. "Not one more thing. I tied one on. God, was I drunk! And I marched into his courtroom and called him every name in the book and then some. Hell, I don't even remember most of what I called him." He laughed helplessly. "But I'll never forget that look on his face. 'Who do you think you're talking to?' he demanded. His face was all flushed. His eyes were popping right out of his head."

Flynn thought of something. "You know how when you're drunk—really drunk—there's a place inside your head, the place where you watch yourself make an idiot of yourself and think it's really kind of funny? Well, as soon as I heard Jeffries say that—

'Who do you think you're talking to?'—I had a whole speech ready, but the only part of it that came out was, 'I have the privilege, your honor, to be addressing the biggest asshole in the western world.' I think I even bowed."

"You did bow," I said. Flynn looked at me, a quizzical expression on his face. "That became part of the legend," I explained. "It was the first thing the two deputy sheriffs who dragged you out of there told everyone. 'Called Jeffries an asshole and then he bowed.' That's the way the story got handed down. After that, for months, every time a lawyer had to appear in front of Jeffries, as soon as he finished, as soon as he said 'Thank you, your honor' and turned to leave, he'd whisper to the lawyer who was coming up next, 'And then he bowed,' just to see if he could make him laugh while Jeffries was watching."

"And all this time I thought my short-lived legal career had been a failure," Flynn drawled as he got to his feet. He stood in front of the desk, a pensive expression on his face. "The police came to see me about this."

I could scarcely believe it. "His murder?"

"Yeah. Just routine stuff. But they knew all about what happened. They knew I'd been disbarred and that it was because of Jeffries."

"How would they have known about that?"

"With all the pressure they were under, they must have looked at every case he ever had anything to do with. And besides, I was a legend, remember? As soon as they started asking around the courthouse about who might have held a grudge, who might have wanted to kill him, my name was bound to come up."

"They never talked to me," I objected.

"Maybe you should sue them for defamation."

"So what did they want to know? Where you were that night?" I asked. I was smiling because I knew where he was nearly every night.

"Yeah. I told them I was at an AA meeting. Stupid cop—he

was young—asks me if I'm an alcoholic. I say no, I just go there because it's the only place left I can still smoke."

His eye wandered around the room, surveying the gold-sealed diplomas and the framed degrees; the hundreds of uniform cloth-covered volumes that contained thousands of appellate court decisions; the thick treatises on criminal procedure and the law of evidence and the endless updated alphabetized manuals on the criminal law; all the books every lawyer owns and seldom takes the time to read.

"I liked being a lawyer," he said, thoughtfully. He took a deep breath and let out a long, soulful sigh. Glancing back at me, he flashed an apologetic smile. "But Jeffries was right. I had no business being one. Not like that."

"You needed help, that's all. You shouldn't even have been suspended. You should have been put into a residential treatment program. That's what anyone else would have done."

Flynn was not convinced. "Sometimes you have to hit bottom. I'm serious. Jeffries did me a favor. The law was all I had left, and when that was taken away . . ." As the thought finished itself, he remembered something else. "I once wrote him a letter of apology. It was part of the treatment. You were supposed to write to everyone that had been hurt by your drinking. I wrote to Jeffries, read the letter out loud in front of everyone in my group. I meant it, too. Every word of it. I was really sorry."

I got up from behind the desk and walked him out to the elevator. "Did Jeffries ever write back?"

Flynn laid his hand on my shoulder. "I wrote it so I would feel bad, not so he'd feel good. I never sent it to him," he said with a wry grin. "Screw him."

It reminded me of the letter that was still sitting in my desk drawer, the one I had forgotten to mail.

"Why don't you take the case," Flynn said as the elevator arrived.

I did not know what he was talking about. "What case?" I asked as he stepped inside.

"The case of whoever they charge with killing Jeffries," he replied, holding the door open with his hand. "Whoever did it probably had a pretty good excuse."

A few minutes later, at precisely eight o'clock, my secretary, Helen Lundgren, hung her coat in the closet and with her usual efficiency entered my office with both hands full. "Finished with those?" she asked, nodding her forehead toward the stack of files she had left at the end of the day on Friday. Before I could answer, she dropped another manila folder in front of me. "This is the one you need for court this morning. *State v. Anderson*. Motion Calendar. Nine-thirty." Her left hand now free, she placed it on my arm so I would not move while she set a steaming cup of coffee down on the desk next to the file.

She moved all around me, arranging files, issuing instructions, a bare-bones skeleton of a woman, with sharp pointed elbows and razor thin legs, a shrill high-pitched voice and dark black eyes that were always darting from one thing to another, as if she could never quite decide which emergency to handle first. I told her I needed to send a letter, and before I had finished the sentence, she was on the other side of the desk, perched on the edge of the chair, a pencil held at attention just above the steno pad open on her bony knees.

I handed her the envelope that had been entrusted to me by Elliott Winston and asked her to find the home address for Calvin Jeffries and send it on to his wife. Then I dictated a short note explaining the circumstances under which I had received it, and added at the end a few words expressing my condolences for her loss.

Helen's blue-veined hand flew across the page. "Anything else?" she asked as she snapped the notebook shut and rose from the chair. With the question still echoing in the air, she turned and walked rapidly back to her desk.

"No, I guess not," I said to the vacant chair.

When it was time to leave, I found her hunched over the keyboard of her computer, peering intently at the monitor while her red-lacquered fingers added new language to an old form.

"I'm going to court," I announced, my hand on the doorknob.

A furtive smile creased the corners of her mouth. "It's a little chilly out. Better take your coat," she said dryly, her eyes fixed on the screen.

I started to open the door and she stopped typing. "Would you drop this in the mail slot next to the elevator?" She handed me a large envelope. "It's what you wanted me to send to Mrs. Jeffries."

Television trucks were parked on both sides of the park that separated the county courthouse from the police department, waiting for any news they could get from either the police or the district attorney's office. There had been an arrest, but nothing had been said about an indictment. Every journalist in town had a question they were dying to ask, and they were willing to ask it of anyone they could get to answer. One reporter, microphone in hand, stood on the sidewalk at the courthouse entrance and asked anyone who happened to walk past what they thought about the news that the killer of Calvin Jeffries had been arrested. He stopped a young blue-eyed blonde, so attractive that everyone around stopped to watch. Gazing down at her, he adjusted his tie and asked what she thought should happen to the killer of Judge Jeffries.

"Who?" she asked with a glittering blank smile that for a moment made him forget the question.

"Cut," he said, shaking his head, as he let the microphone dangle down from the cord he held in his hands.

Inside, journalists prowled the hallways, talking to bailiffs, court clerks, anyone they knew who might know something they did not. On the second floor, as I was making my way to the courtroom at the end of the hall where the presiding circuit court judge took care of all the preliminary motions made before a case was set for trial, Harper Bryce caught up with me. Before he could ask me anything, I held up my hands.

"It's not true, Harper. They did not arrest me; I'm not out on bail; and I don't think I'm even a suspect." I looked first one way, then the other. "But off the record, just between you and me, I did it. I swore I'd get even with him, and I did."

He rolled his eyes. "You're in a strange mood. I wasn't going to ask you about the Jeffries killing. I know who killed him. I mean, I know who they arrested," he said, remembering the supposed sensibilities of defense lawyers to the distinction between guilt and accusation.

"You know?" I asked, just as we reached the courtroom.

"You have something in there?" he asked, nodding toward the door. My hand was already on the handle. "Is it going to take long?"

"What I've got won't take more than two or three minutes. Depends on how long I have to wait."

We went in together and sat in the back row. At the front, Quincy Griswald, who had taken Jeffries's place as presiding circuit court judge, was trying to control his temper. Griswald had nothing like the brilliance of his predecessor, and the knowledge that he could never dominate a judicial proceeding through the sheer force of his intellect had gnawed at him like a worm that was slowly and painfully eating him alive.

"What's your name?" he asked peremptorily, a contemptuous sneer on his haggard face.

The young assistant district attorney froze in mid-sentence, hesitated long enough to be sure he meant it, and then, with a slightly bewildered look in her eyes, replied, "Cassandra Loescher, your honor."

"I ask that," he remarked, his voice dripping with sarcasm, "because I thought we had better start with something you might actually know."

She stared at him in a way that made it obvious that this was not the first time she had been subject to his abuse. Dropping on the table in front of her the brief she had just begun to read, she hunched her broad shoulders, planted her feet wide apart, and put her hands on her hips. "I always look forward to the opportunity to learn," she said with cool detachment.

Narrowing his eyes, Griswald cast a sharp glance at this self-assured show of defiance. "Then learn this," he said in a voice full of menace. "Once I've made a ruling, that's the end of it. The answer was no when you first filed this last week and it is no again today. There is not going to be a continuance. Trial begins tomorrow morning, as scheduled."

She recognized her mistake. With a deferential smile she tried to appeal to his better nature. "But, your honor, this is an unusually complicated case, involving three different defendants, and Mrs. Hall, who has been in charge since the first arrest nearly a year ago, is still in the hospital, and—"

Griswald stopped her dead. "Prosecutors are incapacitated all the time. Some of them even practice law that way. Somebody else can take her place." With a backward flick of his hand, he waved her off, as he looked down at his copy of the docket, ready to call the next case.

She took a deep breath and pulled herself up to her full height. "As I was saying, your honor, the state renews its motion for a continuance on the ground and for the reason that—"

Griswald bolted forward, jabbing his finger into the air. "How many times do I have to say no? Now get out of here," he yelled at the top of his voice, "before I have the bailiff throw you out!"

The blood rushed to her face. "Yes, your honor," she said through tight-clenched teeth. Trembling with rage, she grabbed the brief from the table and threw him a wrathful glance. She raised her chin like a flag of battle. "Thank you, your honor," she said, and then turned on her heel and marched out of the courtroom.

I leaned toward Harper. "What was it the governor said the other night? The law has only reason to protect it?"

While Harper rolled his eyes, I started toward the counsel table in front. Griswald had just called my case.

"Yes, Mr. Antonelli?" Griswald asked as he jotted a note on a file.

I waited until he looked up and then, with a shrug, tossed my head slightly to the side. "You're never going to believe this, your honor, but—"

"How much of a continuance do you need?"

"A month. We have a problem with a witness. The state doesn't oppose the motion," I reported.

He nodded once. "The case will be continued one month per defense counsel's motion," he announced, passing the file over to the clerk.

As soon as we were outside the courtroom, Harper badgered me for an explanation.

"It's simple. Griswald started out as a deputy district attorney. There weren't as many of them then, and they didn't get paid nearly as much as they are now. So he thinks they're underworked and overpaid and that none of them are as good as he was. He never misses a chance to make life difficult for them, especially if they're as young as that one was. Why? Did you think there was some interesting legal distinction between the two cases? You've been around as long as I have. Do you think if there had been a distinction like that, Griswald would have known it? He hasn't read a law book since law school, and he probably didn't read one then, either," I grumbled. "He probably cheated his way through."

I had gotten so caught up in what I was saying about the new presiding circuit court judge, I had forgotten that Harper was going to tell me who had killed the old one.

"Who did they arrest?" I asked, turning so we were face-to-face. "Who murdered Calvin Jeffries?"

Twelve

You could almost feel the simultaneous movement of a hundred thousand hands reaching for the remote control to change channels. In love with death, Americans could mourn collectively for victims they never knew when schoolchildren were slaughtered by classmates and that event became the central preoccupation of the national news. They would become overnight experts in every dull detail of a trial reported at second hand when someone famous was charged with murder. Calvin Jeffries, however, had been killed by someone no one had ever heard of, a man without a name, one of the anonymous hordes of homeless that, like other unpleasant facts of life, we train ourselves not to see.

The air had gone out of the balloon. For eight long weeks, the police had been under enormous pressure to make an arrest. It had reached the point where editorial writers had started to call for an investigation of the investigation. Quick to anticipate the ephemeral moods of the electorate, politicians lined up for the chance to offer their own assessments of who should be blamed and what should be done. The governor—belatedly, in the eyes of some—suggested it might be wise to bring in the FBI. Inside the investigation itself, where double shifts and weekends had become the normal work schedule, nerves were frayed and tempers were on edge as everyone wondered whose careers would be sacrificed next as part of the ongoing cost of catching a killer.

Now the killer had been caught, and suddenly it no longer seemed that important. It was written on their faces as they stared straight into the vacant eye of the television camera, describing the arrest. After all the endless stories about possible conspiracies, hidden motives, and rumored revelations about powerful people, stories that seemed to make sense out of the murder of a prominent public official, it turned out not to have had anything to do with money, power, or sex. It was a random act of violence, committed by a poor pathetic human being who would not have known Calvin Jeffries from the proverbial man in the moon. Despite a long recitation of facts and figures purporting to show how incredibly exhaustive the investigation had been, the police were forced to admit that a single anonymous phone call had told them where the killer could be found.

His name, or at least the name he gave them, was Jacob Whittaker. They were using his fingerprints to get a positive identification. Whatever his real name turned out to be, there was no doubt he was the killer. They had found the knife, and the suspect, after all the proper warnings about his right to a lawyer and his right to remain silent, had made a full confession.

My legs were stretched out over the corner of my desk, one ankle crossed over the other, watching on the small television set I kept on a shelf in my office the murder of Calvin Jeffries become yesterday's news. When the police finished their statement, the questions asked by reporters were all ordinary, routine; questions about whether blood was found on the knife and what kind of tests were going to be run if there was; questions about the condition of the prisoner and the time and place of his formal arraignment. After each answer, there was a dead silence before someone could think of what to ask next. The same reporters who had struggled into front-row seats, convinced this was only the beginning of one of the biggest stories they would ever have the chance to cover, were sitting back, an ankle crossed over a knee, an arm thrown over a chair, following what was said with a shrug and a yawn, and only occasionally jotting down a note to use in what would undoubtedly be the last front-page mention of a story that was now without interest.

With the droning sound of another question fading into the background, the anchorwoman appeared on screen and, with a cursory five-second summation of what everyone had just seen, turned to the other day's news. The murder of Calvin Jeffries had now been relegated to the vast obscurity of a homicide finally solved and quickly forgotten.

I flicked the button on the remote control. Helen stuck her head in the doorway to say good night. "Someone named Jennifer called to tell you that it was not too late if you wanted to have dinner." Helen arched her painted black eyebrows. "Well?" she asked when I did not say anything. "Are you going to have dinner with her or not?"

"I was waiting for you to tell me."

Her mouth turned down at the corners. "It's after five, and after five you can do whatever you like." She thought of something as she turned to go. "Just make sure you're here on time in the morning."

"Thank you," I said after I heard the outer door shut behind her.

I picked up the phone to call Jennifer, started to dial, and then hung up. I had been fretting about it all day. I still did not know what I wanted to say. One minute I was certain I wanted to see her again; the next minute I was not sure about anything. It had taken me years to get over her. There had been times, especially that first year, when I was certain there was nothing else to live for. Sometimes I think the only thing that kept me alive was the knowledge that I would not have to live forever. It gave me a kind of detachment about myself, and I became, as it were, an observer of my own desperation. Eventually, the pain went away, but what had happened had changed me forever. I understood, and I accepted, what I was, a permanent stranger, someone who passes through other people's lives without leaving a mark.

I picked up the telephone again, and saw myself back in college at a pay phone, dropping in quarters, deciding as the last coin rattled in that I could not do it. I told myself it was a matter of pride, but knew it was because I was too scared to hear her voice again, afraid of how much it would hurt if I did, especially because I knew what she would say. I did hear her voice, once. It was just before Christmas, and the snow was falling thick and heavy outside in the freezing night air. She answered the phone, and I listened to her say hello, and then I listened to her voice go quiet, and then I heard her say my name, like a question, and then I hung up. I went back to my dormitory room and lay on the bed and hoped I would fall asleep and never wake up.

I dialed the number and, when she answered, felt for just an instant that same fear of being hurt again.

"Joey?" she asked, when I did not respond.

I stared down at the desk. "Yes," I said, clearing my throat. "It's me. Do you still want to have dinner?"

We met at an obscure little restaurant on the west side of town and spent the next two hours trying to remember who we had been. She asked about law school and about being a lawyer, and I found I was talking about things that happened years apart as if they had taken place at the same time. I asked her about what she had done after she got married and she was talking about her life as a fashion designer before I knew she had once lived in New York. We would start on one thing and come back to another. The history of our lives became a vast circle which could be traced from any place you cared to begin.

"I called my mother after you dropped me off last night."

She looked alarmed. "You shouldn't have done that." Reaching across the table, she wrapped her hand around my wrist. "What good would it do?"

"I was angry, but as soon as I heard her voice, I knew she would not remember. She would not have remembered a week after she did it," I added. "Do you know how often I had to listen to her tell me she only wanted the best for me?"

She drew her hand away from my wrist and placed it in her lap.

"I think that's one of the reasons I became a lawyer. She wanted me to be a doctor."

"Like your father."

"No, not like him. She didn't want me to become a general practitioner who loved being a doctor. She wanted me to be someone she could think of as successful, a surgeon, the chief of staff of a hospital. My mother didn't know a damn thing about medicine, but she could take one look around a country club dance floor and know immediately where each couple stood on the social scale."

A woman who had grandchildren was sitting across from me, and I was telling her things about myself that I had never told anyone. I leaned over my plate and lifted my fork to my mouth, and then put it down before it reached my lips.

"The worst part is how much like her I am."

She looked at me with those wonderful oval-shaped eyes that had once inspired so many romantic thoughts and erotic dreams, and a moment later began to laugh.

"I have a very hard time imagining you at a country club dance. And I don't believe for a minute that you ever gave a thought to someone's social standing or even if they had any. You didn't even like to dance," she said, taunting me with her eyes.

"I remember I liked to dance with you," I said, grinning.

The color deepened in her cheeks. "That wasn't dancing. We were just necking, standing up." She dared me to deny it, but I just looked at her as if I had no idea what she was talking about. "You still do that, don't you?" she asked, a glimmer in her eye. "You get that look, that really extraordinarily larcenous expression on your face, like a thief announcing at the door that you've come to rob them blind, and it all seems so honest no one thinks twice about trusting you completely. That's right, isn't it?"

I issued every false-faced denial I could think of that would let her know that I hoped she was right about me and that I was still the boy she remembered.

"I remind myself of my mother sometimes when I hear myself giving advice to a client. I never have any doubt that I'm right." It was too flippant, and it was not true. "No, it's when I catch myself going crazy because something isn't quite perfect. Everything always had to be just right for her. Nothing out of place; nothing that might cause a complete stranger to notice you for the wrong reasons. Sit straight, walk straight, pronounce each word properly, always be polite, never lose your temper. I can still feel her fingers picking away a piece of lint from my slacks, or pushing a strand of hair back from my forehead. She was always fussing over me. She still does it." I caught myself. With an embarrassed laugh, I tried to explain.

"She came out last summer. She stayed a week. Every morning when I got up," I admitted with a sheepish grin, "I made my bed, put everything away, made damn certain my room was all cleaned up before I went downstairs for breakfast." With a frown, I added, "She still wants to know when I'm getting married."

There was something I wanted to know, something I wanted to hear her talk about, but I sensed a reluctance on her part to discuss it. Finally, over coffee, I asked.

"Why did you come back here? What happened?"

A brief smile flitted over her mouth and then disappeared. Her eyes looked away and then peered into mine, and then looked away again. She bit her lip, tried to smile, but could not. For a long time she stared down at her hands, and when she finally raised her eyes there was a distance there that I had not seen before.

"Seven years ago I got sick, very sick. I couldn't do anything. I couldn't work, I couldn't function." She sighed and then turned her face up to me with the kind of trusting smile that once made me feel we were the only two people alive. "I had a breakdown. I was in a hospital for months. I'm a manic-depressive. I used to sit in my room for days, staring at the walls. Sometimes I couldn't even get myself dressed. For a long time I thought I was just depressed, the way everyone gets depressed about things once in a while. But then I started to have these strange thoughts, things that did not make sense, delusions really. I thought people were following me. If someone looked at me on the street, I thought they were letting me know they were watching me. I thought things that were said on television were secret messages being sent to me."

She saw the look in my eye and, instinctively, reached across and ran her hand over the side of my face. "I'm all right now. When they finally figured out what it was, a chemical imbalance in the brain, they put me on lithium."

A thoughtful expression on her face, she sipped some coffee and then, very slowly, put the cup back in the saucer. With her middle finger she traced the edge all the way around to the beginning.

"I got a divorce four years ago. I told you that I'd felt sorry for him—because I never loved him. And I never did, not the way you think you will, not the way I loved you; but we had a child together—it doesn't matter why we had a child—and we had a life together. It hurt—it hurt a lot. He did what he could, he handled it the best way he knew how, and I think he always thought it was somehow his fault—that I got sick like that—but it made him as crazy as I was. It really did. He was depressed, and angry, and nothing seemed to be going right in his life, either, and . . . Well, that's what happened. I went crazy and now I'm better, and I was married and now I'm not." Struggling with herself, she managed to force a smile. "See how much trouble I would have been."

It was like seeing her again for the very first time, and falling even more in love with her than I had before. There was no place else I wanted to be, no one else I wanted to be with, nothing else I wanted except to do whatever I could to make sure she was never afraid or unhappy again.

She took my hand when we left the restaurant and walked to the end of the block where she had parked her car. The night was cool and clear and there was no one else on the street. I pulled her toward me, and felt her free hand slip around my neck. We kissed the way I think we must have kissed the very first time, a brief, awkward trembling touch, and then she snuggled against my shoulder and I felt her warm breath on my neck and the smell of her hair was like the morning breeze that floats through the window when you are only half awake.

"I have to go," she whispered.

"It's early," I said. I held on to her hand as she let go of my neck.

"I told you I had an early flight tomorrow." She kissed the side of my face, and we walked the last few steps to her car. I would not let go of her hand. She fumbled with her key ring until she found the one she needed. Laughing, she managed to unlock the door, and as soon as she did I pulled her back into my arms.

"Wouldn't you like to go somewhere and dance?"

She was still laughing, softly. "I'd love to, but not tonight."

I let go of her and held the car door open while she got in. "How long are you going to be gone?"

She switched on the ignition and turned on the headlights. With one hand on the convertible top and the other on the window of the door, I watched her buckle herself in. She looked up and tugged playfully on my tie. "Just a week. I'll call as soon as I get back."

"Don't you think it's a little curious that even now, at our age, you still have to leave me because of your mother?"

At first she did not understand, but then it came back to her and her eyes gleamed with that same schoolgirl seduction she had used on me that night on the doorstep of her parents' home. Then it was gone, and I bent down and we kissed each other on the side of the face like the two old friends we were. As I watched her drive off, I felt empty and alone, and the self-sufficiency of my solitary life suddenly seemed pretentious and false.

It was still early and the last place I wanted to be was in that strange place I called home. For a long time I wandered aimlessly through the streets, in a neighborhood I did not know. My leg began to hurt, and I thought it was funny, because I thought it must be psychosomatic. That leg had not bothered me in years. The bullet had passed right through, without doing any real damage at all. There was no reason for it to hurt now.

Everything seemed to be conspiring to bring back the past; more than that, to make the past seem more real than the present. I kept switching back and forth, looking back at the past and then going back to the very beginning of things, when I first fell in love with Jennifer, when I first started to despise Calvin Jeffries, when Elliott pointed that gun in my face; going back to the beginning to then watch the way things happened, watching them as if I were seeing them for the first time, like someone who had been given the gift of clairvoyance and could see the future and everything that was going to happen.

The leg hurt like crazy. I passed the open door of a crowded restaurant full of friendly noise. I went inside and found one last place at the bar. The bartender removed a crumpled napkin and a glass of melting ice, wiped the bar with one pass of a towel, and then flung it over his shoulder. He looked at me just long enough to let me know he was ready for the answer to the question he did not need to ask.

"Scotch and soda," I said in a whispered shout.

I laid a twenty-dollar bill on the bar and watched the bartender take it with one hand while he set the drink in front of me with the other. While the bartender rang up the sale on a refurbished bronze cash register just a few feet away, I was hunched over the bar, running my fingers along the base of the glass. He stacked the change in front of me, and with the same silent question took another order from someone else. Lifting my eyes, I caught a glimpse of myself in the mirror on the other side of the bar. All around me people seemed to be having a good time, talking, telling stories, making jokes, and laughing every chance they got. I was older than most of them, and much older than some. I felt out of place and alone.

After I finished the drink, I ordered another, and then one after that. It had been a long time since I had come to a bar by myself and done nothing but drink. I had almost forgotten the wonderful self-indulgence of self-pity, the free fall into the full enjoyment of every felt emotion, the pure untrammeled luxury of caring nothing for what might happen next, the fervent belief that you could tell the world to go screw itself in one breath and have everyone love you in the next. I had another drink, and another, and I was almost there, the lucid madness of intoxication.

I saw my reflection in the mirror, and I seemed older than I had just a few minutes before, and everyone crowded all around seemed even younger. It used to make me pause, the sight of a middle-aged man, drinking alone at a bar, when I was still young and certain nothing like that would ever happen to me. Looking down at the half-finished drink in front of me, I shoved it away with the back of my hand.

I reached inside my coat and pulled out my brown leather wallet and thumbed through the bills until I found another twenty. With my hand on the bar, I swung off the stool and stood up.

"There a phone here?" I asked above the din as I picked up the change and counted out a tip.

The telephone was in the back, just outside the door to the rest rooms. "It's me," I said gruffly into the receiver. My head was leaning against the wall and I was staring straight down at my shoes. They needed a shine. "I'm in a bar. I've had too much to drink. You think you could come?"

Fifteen minutes later, Howard Flynn found me at a table in the corner, drinking a cup of black coffee. "Thanks," I said, somewhat embarrassed. "Order something. I'll buy dinner."

He settled into the chair opposite and shook his head. "Hell, I thought you called because you wanted someone to get drunk with."

I peered at his heavy-jowled, impassive face and tried to smile. "Tell me something. How long was it before you figured out that AA didn't stand for 'anytime, anywhere'?"

"It was one of my life's bigger disappointments," he said with a grin. His thick upper arms bulged inside the white dress shirt he was wearing buttoned at the wrists and open at the collar. "You did good," he said in his slow, methodical way.

"I did good? Why? Because I came here and started to get drunk?"

"Because you didn't get drunk. Not all the way. And because you had sense enough to know you couldn't get home by yourself." He looked at me through half-closed eyes. "Besides, it isn't like you went into a liquor store and got yourself a bottle of Thunderbird."

My head was spinning. I lifted the coffee cup with both hands to make sure I would not spill it.

"How many guys have you seen in the gutter drinking Chivas Regal out of a paper bag?"

"It's where you end up, not where you start," I replied.

With a show of impatience, Flynn waved his large, puffy red hand. "You sure you've never been in AA? You've got all the answers down pat. Listen. I didn't come down here to hold your goddamn hand. I came down here because you sounded like if you were left alone you might just keep drinking, maybe all night, maybe longer. I'm here to see you don't. Okay? Now, finish your coffee and let's get the hell out of here." His heavy-lidded eyes moved from one end of the teeming bar to the other. "I can't stand to be around people when they're having such a good time."

Flynn pushed back his chair, stood up, and waited for me to come. We shouldered our way through the boisterous crowd, past the bartender with his starched white shirt and black bow tie filling the glasses and emptying the pockets of everyone who lined up for the chance to feel even better than they did already.

Outside, Flynn put his burly arm around my shoulder. "I meant what I said. Don't get down on yourself. You did good. You knew when to stop."

Flynn drove me home. He held the bottom of the steering wheel with three fingers of his left hand while his right arm was draped over the back of the seat. Each time the car hit a bump, it vibrated like a hard board plank dropped twenty feet onto a concrete floor. He did not seem to notice as the shocks dissipated in the round folds of muscle around his neck. I was not so fortunate. Each time it happened, I doubled over a little farther and wondered how long the queasy feeling in my stomach would last.

"You know why I drive this car, don't you?" he asked in the apparent belief that an explanation would make me feel better. "It isn't just because I don't want to spend the money on a new one."

I knew the reason. I had heard it one time or another from every recovering alcoholic I had known. It was part of the list, the twelve steps to sobriety.

"It's because it's good for my humility," he said, his eyes fixed on the road.

It was just a word, but the sound of it, repeated so often, had become part of a secular scripture, but one that seemed without either context or depth. There was something trancelike about the way it was used, like the mumblings of a catechism in a language no one understood. There was something depressing about it, a reminder of how empty things were when something as simple as this was deemed sufficient. Or was it a form of snobbery, a kind of intellectual condescension on my part? I had called Flynn not only because I knew I should not drive, but because I did not want to be alone. Those supposedly simpleminded formulae he followed like they were his personal Ten Commandments had made him into the kind of man who would come out in the middle of the night to help someone else stay out of the bottle that once nearly destroyed his life.

"Of course, humility is kind of relative," he was saying. "We've got a guy in our group who got up at the last meeting and reported that he thought it was pretty humble on his part when he got rid of his Mercedes and got a Lincoln instead. Well, whatever works."

He drove on, and the spinning inside my head began to slow down, and my eyes became heavier and heavier until I could barely keep them open. We were almost there. The gate at the bottom of the drive loomed out of the darkness.

"It's too bad about that guy who killed Jeffries," I heard him say. He said something else, something that made me want to ask a question, but I could not find the words. And then, though I tried to listen, I could not make sense out of anything Flynn was saying. A moment later, I could not hear anything at all, except a voice somewhere inside my own head telling me something was wrong.

Thirteen

With a start, I sat up in bed, peering into the darkness, wondering whether I was really awake, surrounded by a dream that seemed more real than any daytime thought. The smooth, naked body of the girl I had just married, curled around me as she slept, a soft, unworried smile floating on her mouth, the warm breath of life flowing through her like a mysterious gift. I closed my eyes and tried to reach her one last time before she faded into the morbid gray light of dawn.

I lay back down and felt as if I had fallen into the sea. The twisted sheets were drenched with slick cold sweat. Throwing off the covers, I swung my legs over the side of the bed and stood up. My head was throbbing. I put my hand on it to make it stop, but my hair was wringing wet, and I pulled it away. With slow careful steps I moved across the familiar room until I reached the bathroom door. I found the switch on the wall and squinted into a blinding glare. A few minutes later, I plodded back into the bedroom and opened the shutters to let in the late morning light.

After a shower I threw on a white terry cloth robe and wandered downstairs to the kitchen. The smell of fresh-brewed coffee wafted through the air. I tried to remember if I had set the coffeemaker on automatic the night before, but I could not remember that or anything else. My head still hurt and my eyes felt like sandpaper.

Hunched over the kitchen table, reading the morning paper as if he had all the time in the world and no better way to spend it, was Howard Flynn. Without looking up, he extended his arm toward the coffeemaker on the counter. "I made the coffee," he said, as he turned the page.

I poured myself a cup and sat down on the other side of the table. Through an open window I heard the sound of a woodpecker hammering its beak against an oak tree in the backyard. Cradling the cup in both hands, I sipped on the steaming black coffee and tried to figure out what Flynn was doing here.

Folding up the paper, Flynn neatly arranged each sheet in the section until it was exactly the way it had been when he brought it in.

"Anything interesting?" I asked when he finished.

"On page three," he said, shoving the paper across to me. "They left out most of the details."

He could tell I did not know what he was talking about. "You all right?" he asked, grinning. "I brought you home, in case you don't remember."

It started to come back. I remembered the bar, and I remembered bouncing around in Flynn's car, but that was all.

"I managed to get you upstairs," he explained. "We left your car downtown. I thought you might need a ride in this morning."

Reaching into his shirt pocket, Flynn pulled out a small tin case. He opened it with a flick of his thumbnail and removed an oblong-shaped green pill. In one fluid motion, without using either hand for support, he rose straight up from the chair. His weight on the balls of his feet, he walked in the pigeon-toed fashion of someone once trained to make each movement as efficient as possible. He tossed what was left of the coffee into the sink and filled the cup with water.

"Take a look at page three," he said as he put the pill in his mouth. He took a drink of water, then threw his head back and swallowed hard. "Would have been interesting to know why he did it," he added. Staring out the window, he wiped his mouth with the back of his hand. Resting his other hand on the sink, he turned and looked directly at me. "If he did it."

I had that vague feeling you get when someone tells you something you think you should know. I picked up the paper and turned to page three. My eye drifted across the stories above the fold, and then, in the bottom right corner, I found it. The story was not very long, four column inches at most, the short report of a suicide.

When I glanced up, Flynn was looking down at the floor, his left hand gripping tight on to the edge of the sink. He was clenching his jaw so hard, the muscles rippled down the side of his face.

"Are you all right?"

He managed to nod once, and then, lifting his head, took a deep breath and seemed to relax. "Yeah. Nothing," he said with an expression that was part grin, part grimace. He tapped his right hand against his chest. "Little angina, that's all." Gesturing toward the newspaper, he asked, "What do you think?" Before I could answer, he added, "It's all a little too easy, isn't it? They find the guy who killed Jeffries, and he still has the knife he did it with. Instead of denying it, he gives them a full confession— doesn't even bother to ask for a lawyer—and then, as if he hadn't been helpful enough, he kills himself in his cell before he had spent so much as a single night in jail."

Suddenly it came back to me. "You told me about this last night, didn't you?"

"It was on the eleven o'clock news. He killed himself sometime around eight-thirty or nine. That's all they reported last night, and they don't say much more about it in the papers, either. All they say is that he killed himself. They don't say how."

"He hung himself," I guessed.

Flynn came back to the table and sat down. Leaning forward on his arms, he twisted his mouth first to one side, then the other. "I talked to a few people." He lowered his eyes and with his finger traced an invisible line back and forth in front of him. "Never saw a suicide like this. He gets on the top bunk in the cell. There was a guy in the cell opposite. He wasn't paying much attention. Then the metal bunk started to shake, making a lot of noise, and he started swearing at the guy, telling him to knock it off. The guy is standing on top of the bunk, jumping up and down on it. The other guy can't believe it, and he starts to say something, but the next thing he knows the guy has jumped."

"Jumped?" I asked blankly.

"He jumped off, head first, smashed his head on the concrete floor. But the thing is, he didn't just jump, he held his hands behind his back, held them while he threw himself head first onto the floor. How could anyone do that, hold your hands like that and not let go? Wouldn't you throw your hands out at the last minute, try to break your fall? And why would he want to kill himself like that, anyway? Why didn't he just hang himself? Easy enough to do. Make a noose out of your shirt, your pants; that's the way most jail suicides happen. Never heard of anyone doing this. It's strange. The whole thing is strange, if you ask me."

I poured myself a second cup of coffee. Across the yard a bushy-tailed squirrel launched itself in full flight from the oak tree that hung over the spiked fence to the top of the umbrella that covered a glass table at the end of the brick patio. It slid down the blue canvas, regained its balance just before it reached the edge, leaped onto a chaise lounge, then scurried across the lawn and out of view.

"What is so strange about it?" I turned around, the cup in my hand, and waited until Flynn lifted his eyes. "You have a random killing by someone who was probably demented or stoned out of his mind, he gets caught, and he decides to do away with himself instead of spending the next ten or twelve years in a cell waiting for his own execution? I admit that the way he killed himself wasn't exactly normal, but—"

"It wasn't random," Flynn interjected.

"What?"

"It wasn't random," he repeated. "I told you, I talked to a few people. He confessed. He knew who he killed."

"Then it must have been revenge. Jeffries must have put him in prison at some point, right?"

Flynn shrugged his shoulders. The lines in his forehead deepened. He reached in his pocket, pulled out a rumpled cigarette pack, and wiggled his index finger inside the opening. With a disgusted look, he crushed the empty pack in his hand and shoved it back in his pocket.

"Don't know. He wouldn't say why he did it. Jeffries must have done something that made him want to kill him. It would have been interesting to know what it was, and now we never will."

"No?"

He shook his head. "The investigation is over. It'll be a while before they get the DNA results on the blood left on the knife, but it'll belong to Jeffries," he said with complete assurance. "They have the knife, and they have the confession, and, as if that wasn't enough, they have the suicide. People don't go around killing themselves for something they didn't do. No question, the guy did it. Now he's dead. Case closed."

Late that afternoon, after I caught up on all the work that, as Helen repeatedly reminded me, I should have done that morning, I called Harper Bryce to see if he knew anything more than what Flynn had found out. Harper had heard none of the details of the suicide and knew nothing about what the killer had said. When I told him that it had not been a random killing, that the killer had intended to murder Jeffries, he expressed regret at the suicide, because, as he put it, "the trial might have been worth watching after all."

It only seemed callous. Harper's professional appraisal was exactly right. The murder of Calvin Jeffries had riveted the public's attention because of who he was and because of the mystery surrounding the circumstances of his death. But once the killer had been caught and it appeared to have been a random act of violence committed by someone desperate enough to kill for a few dollars, it became for all practical purposes indistinguishable from any one of the thousands of accidental deaths that happen every year. Drunk drivers killed people they did not know, and people without names who lived on the street might at any moment decide to stick a knife in someone who did not give them what they asked for. It was one of the unfortunate facts of city life, and while it was always to be condemned, it held none of the same fascination as the deliberate, purposeful, intentional murder of someone you had a reason to want dead. That was what made people read newspapers and follow trials, not that someone had been killed, but that someone had actually taken that last, irrevocable step, and, in that ancient phrase, "with malice afore-thought," taken someone's life. I agreed with Harper: It would have been an interesting trial. And now there would never be one.

There was a story in the next day's paper about yet another political scandal, but there was nothing about the murder of Calvin Jeffries. There were stories about the state of the economy and stories about what was happening on the other side of the world, but there was not so much as a line about the suicide of his killer. There were new things to read about, new things to talk about, and a day or two later the only people who thought about Calvin Jeffries anymore were the people who had actually known him, and perhaps not all of them.

Friday morning, Helen was waiting for me. "Judge Pritchard's office just called," she said, following me into my office.

"Let me guess," I said as I sat down. "They want to reschedule the Burnett motion."

She perched on the edge of the chair opposite, clutching in her hand a stack of telephone messages scribbled on pink paper.

"He's going to be out of town on Wednesday. They want to reset it for Tuesday the following week at two o'clock. Your schedule is clear."

"Did you tell them my schedule was clear?"

"No, I said I'd have to check with you."

"Good. Call them back. Tell Pritchard's clerk that I don't have anything open for weeks; tell them that this damn thing has been reset twice before; tell them that the defendant has a right to have his motion heard; and then tell them that if the judge wanted to have Wednesdays off, he should have become a god-damn doctor!"

Nothing I did, nothing I said, ever made the slightest impression on her. "Right," she drawled, making a note to call the clerk and ask very politely whether there might be some way to fit it in anytime at all next week.

"What else do you have?" I asked, gazing out the window.

The telephone rang. "I'll get it," Helen said as she got to her feet.

"Take it here," I said, handing the receiver to her as I pressed the flashing light on the console.

The telephone pressed to her ear, the fingers of her other hand fidgeted with the curled cord. "Law offices of Joseph Antonelli," she announced in a voice that managed to be both friendly and pressed for time. "I'm afraid Mr. Antonelli is in conference and can't be disturbed." It was the standard all-purpose lie, told so often she could have passed a polygraph each time she told it.

Glancing through the stack of messages she had placed on the desk in front of me, I did not notice at first when she began to scribble on a scrap of paper.

"Yes, I understand," she said. "Is there any message you'd care to leave?" Reaching across, she waved the paper under my nose. "Could you hold for just a moment?"

I read the name she had written down. It took me a moment before I was certain who she was. Helen handed me the phone and, shutting the door behind her, left me alone. I sat straight up and plopped both elbows on the desk.

"This is Joseph Antonelli," I said with all the formality I could summon. "What can I do for you?"

My head moved back and forth with the rhythm of what I

heard. "Yes," I replied, "I'd be glad to do that. Six o'clock would be fine."

I looked around until I found a pen. "Would you give me that again. Yes, I know where it is," I said as I wrote down the address. "I'll see you at six. Thank you for calling, Mrs. Jeffries."

I do not know why I agreed to see her. Perhaps it was nothing more than the desire to see for myself how she lived and what she was really like. Perhaps it was something else, an instinct that told me there was more to her husband's death than I knew.

The address she had given me was on the West Side, just minutes from downtown, a tall apartment building constructed sometime before the Second World War. It was something of a landmark and one of the city's most expensive places to live.

A heavyset man with a pockmarked face and slow-moving eyes was sitting behind a small wooden desk just inside the high-ceilinged lobby. I waited while he lifted a black telephone receiver that looked like it had been in use since the day the building opened and announced, "A Mr. Antonelli is here." He nodded silently and then hung up. "Sixteenth floor." He pointed a stubby finger across the gray marble floor to the walnut-paneled wall on the other side. "The elevator is just around the corner."

There was only one elevator. I pushed the tarnished brass button and heard a buzzer echo high above. The elevator rattled ponderously down the shaft and thudded to a stop. The door creaked open and an old man in a coat that hung off his hollow shoulders and a dress shirt two sizes too large for his shriveled throat stood with his pale white hand on the lever. "Floor?" he gasped. My hands folded in front of me, I leaned against the back of the mirrored, gold-leaf compartment. With a teeth-clenching groan, the ancient elevator began a tedious ascent to the top floor.

Two doors faced each other across the landing. On the wall opposite the elevator, a large blue vase filled with fresh-cut yellow chrysanthemums stood on a narrow, granite-topped table in front of a gilt-edged mirror. The flowers looked too perfect, and

I touched one of them to make certain they were real. I started to pull the piece of paper out of my pocket to check the apartment number when the door to 16A swung open.

I had seen her at a distance at the dinner, and I had seen her picture in the newspapers after Jeffries's murder, but the way she looked now reminded me more of the way I remembered her when she was still a young woman married to her first husband. She was wearing black tights, a black turtleneck sweater that clung to her ribs and fell halfway down to her knees, and a pair of unremarkable flat shoes. Her shiny brown hair was pulled back around her head and tied in a ponytail.

She extended her hand, stiff-armed, straight out from her shoulder. "Thank you for coming, Mr. Antonelli." Her voice seemed forced and artificial. As soon as we had shaken hands, she stepped away from the door. "Please come in."

The apartment was an oriental masterpiece. Hand-knotted rugs, blood red and midnight blue, littered the hardwood floor. Teak and mahogany cabinets, filled with delicate porcelain vases, lined the walls. In the corner of the large living room, a five-foot ivory sculpture of a Mandarin clasped in its tapered fingers a parchment scroll.

She gestured toward a light blue sofa opposite the window. "Can I get you something?" she asked as she removed the stopper from a crystal glass decanter that, along with several others, stood on a silver tray on the coffee table.

"No, nothing, thank you." Whatever she was drinking, the only thing she mixed it with was a little ice.

She sat down, and a moment later sprang back to her feet and began tapping her fingers on the top of a bamboo chair. She was tall, and quite thin, but she had fairly wide shoulders and extremely long fingers with large, misshapen knuckles. They were the hands you would expect to see on a migrant worker, a woman who was bent over all day long in the fields, pulling things out of the ground, or standing on her tiptoes in an orchard, picking fruit out of the trees. They were constantly in motion, closing, opening, grabbing, letting go, or, as she was doing now, drumming them in quick bursts with staccatolike speed, before they suddenly stopped what they were doing and started doing something else.

Staring straight ahead, her fingers still tapping on the hard surface of the chair, she took a quick gulp of whatever she was drinking and then sat down again.

"Are you sure I can't get you something?" she asked. She held the drink in both hands, while her wrists rested on her knees, which were pressed tight together. Her eyes jumped from side to side and then settled on the squat, black-lacquered Chinese coffee table.

"I'm sorry," she said abruptly, looking up. "Did I ask you if you wanted anything?"

"Nothing, thank you." Leaning forward, I began to draw an invisible figure on the table's hard gleaming surface. "I was very sorry about what happened to your husband, Mrs. Jeffries," I began tentatively. "If there's anything I can do . . ."

Her eyes flashed with the kind of contempt lavished on fools. "Do you think I'm an idiot? Do you think I don't know what's going on?"

Pressing her lips together until they lost what little color they had, she leaped to her feet, and then, after she took another drink, began to walk up and down the room.

"What I want to know is why you're doing this. I know you hated my husband. And yes, I remember you, Mr. Antonelli, from years ago, when I was married to Elliott and he first joined your firm. I can understand why you might feel sorry for him, locked up the way he is. But Elliott is crazy. He's insane. Why you would help him try to torment me, after what I've had to go through, is really quite beyond me, Mr. Antonelli, and I think you owe me an explanation."

I started to get up. "Perhaps I should go. I really don't know what to say."

She searched my eyes and then lowered her gaze. "No, don't

go," she said after she took a deep breath. "I'm sorry. I jumped to conclusions."

She sat down again and, though her glass was not even half empty, reached for the decanter. When she finished filling the glass, she looked up at me. "Do you know what was in that letter you sent me?"

"I have no idea what was in it," I answered. "I sent it to you for the reasons I stated in the cover note I sent with it."

She began to drum her fingers on the edge of the coffee table, but slowly, easily, without any of the rigid, metallic abruptness of before.

"You really don't know, then?"

"All I know is that I went to see him. I had been meaning to do it for a long time, years, really, ever since that day . . ."

"When he tried to kill you."

"I don't think he wanted to kill me at all, Mrs. Jeffries. If I hadn't tried to wrestle the gun away from him, I don't think he would have pulled the trigger."

With a shrewd, cold-eyed glance, she assured me I was wrong. "He would have killed you and never given it a second thought. I knew Elliott. He was crazy, Mr. Antonelli," she said, drumming her fingers faster. "After he had the breakdown, after what he did in court that day, he blamed everything on you. It was an obsession with him. He thought you were trying to destroy him. He thought—"

"I was sleeping with his wife."

The drumming stopped. She raised her chin. "I told you. He had become completely paranoid. You're lucky you're alive."

"Perhaps. But tell me, why would he have thought you were having an affair with me? Why would he have thought you were having an affair at all?"

Her long, crooked fingers stirred back into motion, slowly, noiselessly. "Things were never very good with us, Mr. Antonelli. Elliott was always difficult, demanding. He was under enormous pressure. He always thought he had something to prove because he had not gone to one of the best schools. He blamed me for that. He was always telling me how much easier things would have been for him if he didn't have a wife and children slowing him down."

I did not believe her. "He worshipped those kids, and I must tell you, I always had the impression that he worshipped you as well."

"Why? Because he had my photograph in his office and every so often he'd bring the kids with him when he went into work on a Saturday or a Sunday? It was about the only time they ever saw him." A look of disdain passed over her face. "Don't misunderstand me. I'm not saying Elliott didn't love the children. I think he even loved me—for a while. But whenever things didn't go quite right—and for Elliott everything always had to be exactly right—he had to blame it on someone else."

She still had not answered my question. "But why did he think you were having an affair with me?"

She stared hard at me for a moment, and then, reaching for her glass, got back on her feet and began prowling the room. She seemed to grow more agitated with each step she took. The ice was banging against the glass and when the clear gold liquid sloshed over the top and dripped onto her hand, she seemed not to notice.

"Have you ever known anyone who went crazy, Mr. Antonelli? Have you ever lived with anyone who was completely—and I mean completely—irrational?"

She tried to calm herself. Instead of pacing back and forth, she leaned against the chair, and when that did not help, she stood in the middle of the room, one foot crossed over the other, then, a moment later, one turned out to the side.

"The worst part is trying to hang on to your own sanity. What happened that day in court—when they had to bring him home— had been building for months. He had already started to talk about conspiracies. He kept telling me how each seemingly innocent thing that happened was really a part of it. Do you know what is really crazy? How much of it makes sense. Elliott would say to me: 'Just for the moment, assume I'm right.' He was always asking me to do that. He would wear me down. Then I'd listen to him, and, if you assumed he was right, that there was a conspiracy against him, then everything he said was perfectly logical. A woman pushing her grocery cart behind him when he stopped on his way home to pick up a loaf of bread was following him; a camera he noticed on the back seat of a parked car was put there on purpose to let him know he was under surveillance. Everything fit, because, once you agreed that there really was a conspiracy, anything that happened could be explained as being a part of it, and, more importantly, became one more thing that proved he was right."

With a pensive expression, she sipped on her drink, as she thought about what had happened, or what she wanted me to think had happened.

"I wouldn't do it," she said as she looked at me again. "I wouldn't assume—not even for just a moment—that he was right, that there was this terrible conspiracy against him. I was afraid that if I did that he would never get better and I might go insane right along with him. Because, you see, if I had said yes, it makes perfect sense, it all ties together, then I would not have any ground left to stand on, no way to tell what was real and what was not. Insanity is insidious, Mr. Antonelli. It invites you in, and then it closes the door behind you, and after a while your eyes adjust to the darkness and then you don't think it's dark anymore."

She moved next to the window and stared out across the flickering lights of the city and the great flowing river, toward the mountain where the snow glowed blue and purple and gold as the sun slipped away into the night.

"My refusal was seen as a betrayal, and that betrayal, in Elliott's diseased mind, could only mean that I was part of the conspiracy as well. Not just part of it, either. No, I was the one who had started it all."

She turned around, just far enough to see me. There was a sense of weariness about her, as if nothing much mattered anymore, a sense that everything that was going to happen in her life had now taken place.

"I didn't know then how sick he really was. It all seemed like a bad dream, like something that wasn't really happening. Sometimes when I went to bed I could almost convince myself that when I woke up in the morning everything would be just the way it had been before. Other times I thought he was having a bad dream, and if I just grabbed him and shook him as hard as I could, he'd wake up and be normal again. I just could not believe it was really happening."

She sat in the bamboo chair and put the glass down on the table. Folding her arms together, she leaned back, stretched out her legs, and crossed one ankle over the other.

"You could almost hear a clicking noise when he put each piece of the conspiracy together. Once he decided that I was the one who had started it, there had to be a reason. And of course there could be only one reason: There had to be another man."

Her voice was quiet, controlled, as if she were telling a story about someone else.

"You cannot imagine the depths of his anger and hatred. He was screaming at me like I had never heard anyone scream before. I started screaming back. It was self-defense, that's the only way I can explain it. He was accusing me of everything imaginable, terrible things, obscene things, and I was screaming back, taunting him with everything he said about me, telling him it was all true, laughing about it. He was hurting me, worse than I'd ever been hurt before, and at that moment I was every bit as crazy as he was. And that's when I said it, that's when I told him, that, yes, of course he was right, I was out to destroy him, I had done everything he said I had done, I was having an affair, I was sleeping with another man, I was sleeping with his great good friend, Joseph Antonelli."

"But why?" I asked, astonished at what she had done.

"Because I wanted to hurt him back. He idolized you. He wanted to be just like you. And because I never thought he'd believe it. I thought it would show him how insane it all was, that it was all in his mind, and that he needed help. But instead it just convinced him he was right."

Watching her tell me with apparent sincerity a story that exonerated her of any blame for what had happened to her first husband, I wondered whether it was the truth or whether, after years of subtle reinterpretation, she had gradually come to believe it had happened just the way she said it had. If she was a woman who was perfectly willing to lie, she was also a woman who would never admit, not even, or perhaps especially, to herself, that she was a liar.

"You have no idea how awful I felt when Elliott tried to kill you. I kept telling him it wasn't true. I had not been having an affair. I didn't even know you. Despite everything that had happened up till then, I never thought he was capable of anything like that."

She looked at me with eyes searching for sympathy. If I had never known Elliott, or perhaps if I had never known Calvin Jeffries, I might have given it.

"Elliott still thinks you were having an affair, but with Judge Jeffries."

Her eyes turned cold. "Did you think I didn't know that? As soon as Calvin and I were married, Elliott started sending letters, weird, scary letters, accusing me of it and threatening to get even. After a while I started sending them back, unopened. That's why he asked you to deliver that letter. It wasn't because he didn't have the address. It was because he knew I wouldn't open it, and because he knew I'd never let the children read it." She paused, her lips trembling. Slowly and methodically she began to beat her fingers on the arm of the chair. "Do you know what he wrote? What he wanted the children to read? 'Your mother is a whore, and now you're orphans twice.' That's what he wrote, Mr. Antonelli. That's the sort of thing he wants to tell his children.

That's the reason I never allowed them to see him. That's the reason why I sent them away to private school: So he wouldn't have any way of finding them."

"So it isn't true?" I asked as I got to my feet. "You weren't having an affair with him?"

"Of course not," she said as she walked me to the door. "Calvin was like a father to me. He treated Elliott like a son. He tried to help him every way he could. When Elliott got sick, Calvin did everything he could. He knew what it was like for me. He had gone through something of the same thing with his wife. I don't know what I would have done without him. If it hadn't been for him, Elliott would have gone to prison for trying to kill you. Calvin made sure he was sent to the state hospital where he could get help."

We were at the door. "Judge Jeffries had him sent to the state hospital?"

"He didn't do it himself," she said as she opened the door. "But he made sure it was done."

I said goodbye and turned to go. "It didn't do any good, though," she said. "Elliott still hates me and he's still insane. If I didn't know he was locked up in that place I'd swear he killed Calvin just to get even with me."

"They have the killer, Mrs. Jeffries," I said, looking back.

She nodded twice. "The one who killed himself? Are you sure, Mr. Antonelli? Are you sure someone like that murdered my husband?"

Fourteen

I read it in the newspaper the next morning, a front-page story under the byline of Harper Bryce. Another judge had been murdered. While I had been talking to the widow of Calvin Jeffries, Quincy Griswald, the new presiding circuit court judge, had been killed in a murder that was in all important respects virtually identical to the one before. Like Jeffries, Griswald had been stabbed to death, and, like Jeffries, Griswald had been killed in the parking structure where both of them had kept their cars. Jeffries had managed to crawl back to his office; Griswald had been found dead in the garage, slumped down next to the door of his late-model Buick.

I took the paper with me when I went into the office later that morning. Saturdays were the days I tried to get caught up with my cases. As I drove past the courthouse on my way in, I noticed that the flag had again been lowered to half-mast. No judge had ever been murdered in Oregon and now, in the space of little more than two months, two had been killed, both of them the presiding circuit court judge at the time of their death. I remembered what Jeffries's widow had said, the doubt that someone like her husband's confessed killer could really have done it. If he had not been found, and if he had not confessed, the immediate assumption would have been that both judges, Jeffries and Griswald, had been killed by the same person. But the killer of Calvin Jeffries had been found, and he had confessed, and then, as if that was not sufficient to prove his guilt, he had taken his own life. Yet I still could not get out of my mind the thought that this had to be more than sheer coincidence.

I reached Howard Flynn at home. "You're not calling me from a bar, are you?" he asked in his usual gruff manner.

"Do you know if the police have gotten the DNA results yet?"

"From the knife the guy used to kill Jeffries? No, I haven't heard. It'll be a match, though. It'll be Jeffries's blood." There was a brief silence and at the other end of the line I could hear Flynn's labored breath. "You must have read the paper this morning. The guy that killed Jeffries is dead. This is someone else."

I stared out the window, watching the leaden gray sky grow darker. "What if it isn't a match?"

Flynn preferred to deal with tangible facts. "Then you have an interesting situation. But the Griswald killing sounds like a copycat to me. Some guy has a grudge because Griswald sent him away. He heard about what someone did to Jeffries and he figures he'll do the same thing. These aren't original thinkers we're dealing with here."

"What did they ever find out about him, the one who confessed to the Jeffries murder? Did Jeffries send him to prison?"

"I don't know," Flynn replied. "Do you want me to find out?"

None of it had anything to do with me. I was not defending anyone who had any connection with either the murder of Calvin Jeffries or the killing of Quincy Griswald. Besides, I had asked Flynn for quite enough already. Still, there was something missing in all this and I wanted to know what it was.

"If you can do it without too much trouble, then yes, I'd like to know what you can find out."

After I hung up, I tried to reach Harper Bryce. He was not at the paper, and he was not at home. I left a message on his voice mail and turned my attention to the cases on which I was supposed to be working.

I began reviewing the police reports in an armed robbery case set for trial the next week. Three lines after I started, I found myself searching my memory for anything that would tie the two murders together. They were both presiding circuit court judges at the time of their death. If someone were trying to make a statement about the judiciary, or about the legal system altogether, killing two chief judges would certainly be one way to do it.

With a conscious effort I went back to the reports. Then I remembered, what after all was only obvious, that Jeffries and Griswald were both trial court judges who regularly imposed punishment on violent offenders. But every trial court judge did that, and none of the others had been killed. I looked down and found the place where I had left off, read a few words more, and looked up. There was a difference. Jeffries, because he thought he was so much smarter than everyone else, Griswald, because he was afraid he was not, would go out of their way to let a prisoner know how much they thought he deserved what he was going to get and how much they were going to enjoy giving it to him. They were both easy to hate.

I shook my head in a futile attempt to clear it, read down to the end of the first page of the report, and then turned to the next. The words went out of focus. One murder might be explained because of a sentence one of them had given, but what were the odds that the same man would be sentenced to two different terms in prison, one by Jeffries, one by Griswald, and only decide after he had served the second one that both judges deserved to die. And even if it were possible, there was no way to explain the confession. Flynn had to be right. The only conceivable connection between the two crimes was that the first had inspired someone else to commit the second.

I put it all out of mind, at least long enough to finish reading the police reports. There was more work to be done after that, but I could not concentrate on anything for more than a few minutes at a time. I got up from the desk, told myself that it was almost time for lunch anyway, and headed out the door.

The zinc-colored sky was crisscrossed with turbulent black clouds and there was a hush in the clean damp springtime air. I felt a light sprinkle on my face and quickened my step. I was only a few blocks from where I wanted to go, but then, a moment later, the rain began to pound down, beating on the pavement in hard fast bursts, like shrapnel from an exploding shell. People with umbrellas struggled to get them open. A woman, one hand holding down her skirt, whirled past me. I fell into the open doorway of a small corner grocery and waited for the rain to let up. The worst of it passed in a few minutes, and, staying close to the buildings, I moved on.

I spotted the bookstore on the other side of the street half a block away. Dodging the traffic, I jogged across and spent a moment in front of the window examining the sets of used books on display. In front of a clothbound set of the collected works of Pushkin, a place card listed a price which no longer seemed quite as expensive as when it had first been posted several years before. A bell rang when I opened the framed glass door.

Anatoly Chicherin was sitting on a plain wooden chair behind the front counter. Long rows of unpainted bookshelves stretched down both sides of three narrow passageways that led toward the back. The air was stagnant, heavy with the stale dust of books that had been left to molder nearly as long as the dead bones of their mainly forgotten authors.

Five foot six, with an owlish full face and a small flabby mouth, Anatoly Chicherin wore glasses so thick that, seen through their distorted refraction, his eyes seemed to bulge right out of his head.

He looked up at the sound of the bell with a smile on his face. With surprising agility for someone his age, he leaped to his feet and came around the counter to greet me.

"You're a little early," he said in a voice that when you first heard it made you think it must have come from someone else.

It was resonant, rich, a voice that seemed to come from somewhere deep inside the earth.

Chicherin turned the sign that hung in the glass door so it read CLOSED instead of OPEN, and then pulled down a shade smudged with hundreds of his own fingerprints.

"This will give us a little longer for the game," he said. "I have the board all set up."

He led me past two rows of Russian-titled volumes toward the dimly lit storage room in back. The Cyrillic script on the spines looked to my ignorant eye like English letters seen backward through a mirror.

Two straight-back wooden chairs faced each other across a small square wooden table with a chessboard in the middle. Flecked with the minuscule remains of a dozen dead insects, a single light bulb, suspended by a cloth-covered cord, hung down from the grease-covered ceiling. When Chicherin shut the door, shadows like black curtains fell over the walls.

On the front corner of an unremarkable metal desk, next to a pile of dog-eared journals, was a dented electric teakettle, which Chicherin proceeded to plug into the wall.

"It will just take a few minutes," he said as he sat down opposite me. Rubbing his hands together, he glanced avidly at the chess pieces. "Shall we start, or shall we wait for the tea?"

"Let's wait for the tea," I replied, barely suppressing a grin. "I like to delay defeat as long as I can."

"We've only been playing for six months. Did you expect to win so soon?"

"I lose every time we play, and we've played enough that I know we could keep playing for years and I'd never be able to beat you."

With a laborious groan, as if something dead were being forced against its will to come back to life, the teakettle began to sizzle and then, a moment later, began to boil.

"You shouldn't think like that," he said while he poured the boiling water into a porcelain teapot. "You're much better now than when we started." He put the teapot on the side of the table and then brought us each a cup and saucer. "It needs to steep for a few minutes," he said as he sat down.

Magnified out of all proportion by the thick-lens glasses perched on the bridge of his small snub nose, his eyes seemed to draw me toward him.

"You just need to slow down a little. You see a move and you take it. But sometimes, when you focus in like that, when you concentrate on what seems to be the main line of attack, you fail to see what is coming at you from the side, so to speak. Now," he said as he poured the tea, "let's begin."

It was over almost before the tea was cool enough to drink, another in my unbroken string of defeats.

"Much better," he remarked as he swept the remaining pieces into a cigar box and folded up the board. Reaching for the teapot, he filled my cup and then his own. Holding the saucer in his hand, he sipped the tea, his eyes focused on me. "Now, tell me, what do you think about this business of a second judge being murdered? Is there perhaps a connection?"

My own suspicions suddenly seemed groundless and I found myself telling Chicherin what Flynn had told me. "The first one may have given the idea to someone else to do the second. Beyond that, no. The man who murdered Judge Jeffries confessed and then killed himself, so it can't be the same person responsible for both."

I said it as if it was simply self-evident, but his instincts were too good: He detected my doubt. "You're not completely convinced that the man who confessed was telling the truth?"

"I'm not sure," I admitted. "There's no reason to doubt it. He didn't just confess, he committed suicide. Why would he have done that if he had confessed to something he had not done?"

His eyes on me, Chicherin ran his finger back and forth over his lower lip. "My father could have given you an answer to that," he said presently. "He once confessed to a crime he didn't commit."

"In Russia?" I asked, meeting his gaze. "What was the crime?"

A faraway look came into his eyes and his mouth twisted to the side. His head began slowly to move from side to side, and I was left with the feeling that there was not much in the past that he wanted to remember. "Treason," he replied, as he sipped more tea. "Treason against the Revolution. My father was part of the generation that came of age during the October Revolution of 1917, the generation that believed in Lenin and thought the Communist Party was history's chosen instrument." A shrewd smile crossed Chicherin's small moist mouth. "Communism was the religion of the intellectuals. They believed in it the way a true Catholic believes in the Church, without question or condition.

"The problem, of course, was that when Lenin died, Stalin took over, and Stalin was interested only in people who were loyal to him. He got rid of everyone who had come into positions of power under Lenin. Stalin was very shrewd. Instead of having them shot, which might have made martyrs of them, he accused them of crimes against the Soviet Union; he said they had spied for the capitalist powers that had sent troops to defeat the Red Army after the October Revolution. The charges were false, but most of the people accused, confessed, including Bukharin, the most famous of those put on trial. In open court Bukharin confessed to things he had never done."

Bending forward, Chicherin looked at me intently and struck the table three times with his knuckles. "He didn't confess to avoid his own death. He knew that once he made that confession, the only thing left was his execution. His confession was suicide. He didn't do it to save his life. He did it because he believed that without that confession his life would have no meaning.

"Bukharin believed—they all believed—in the infallibility of the Communist Party. The party was in the service of history, and history," Chicherin said with a rueful look, "was the one true God. If they denied the party, they would be denying the only God they had. Bukharin was put in the following position: He believed in the party, but the party insisted on his guilt. The only way he could deny his guilt was to deny that the party was right. But how could the party—how could God—be wrong? Bukharin chose to remain a believer. He confessed and he was sentenced to death."

Chicherin leaned against the back of the armless chair and folded his arms across his chest. He lowered his eyes, and placed one hand on the back of his neck. For a long time he stared down at the floor, a brooding look on his mouth. Finally, he tilted his head to the side far enough to cast a sideways glance at me. "Have you never represented someone who confessed to something he did not do because of something he believed in?" he asked.

"I've had a few cases where someone made a false confession, but it was always to protect someone else. I've never had one where someone did it because of something they believed in."

Removing his glasses, Chicherin closed his eyes and grasped the bridge of his nose. "I'm sorry," he said when he opened his eyes. There was a trace of weariness in his voice. "What you said made me think of how the world has changed. You find it perfectly reasonable that someone would be willing to take the blame for something they didn't do to protect someone they loved. I remember the time when millions of people were in love with an idea, a cause, and were willing to die for it, Communism, democracy, Fascism, whatever it was, that was larger than themselves. First God died, then Fascism, then Communism, and now what is there left to die for? Has the world become less insane, or perhaps more so?"

He pursed his lips and nodded slowly. Then he sat straight up and put on his glasses.

"The people who prosecuted my father were able to use both of these things, the cause he believed in and the people he loved."

"What happened to him?" I asked after Chicherin fell into another long silence.

He turned up the palms of his hands. "He confessed to everything; he would have confessed to anything. He had a wife and a child. It was the only way to protect my mother and me from Siberia or worse."

"I'm sorry," I said sympathetically.

Chicherin smiled. "It was a long time ago. I was a small boy. I didn't know what happened until years later. My mother never told me. She said he had been killed in an accident."

Finishing his tea, Chicherin sprang to his feet. "There's something I should give you, something I think you should read."

When he opened the door, the dim light from the shop dissolved the shadows that had draped the walls. I followed him as he moved briskly through the stacks. He lifted the shade on the front door and turned the sign around to announce that he was once again open for business.

With his back to me, he searched the shelves of a bookcase behind the counter. Most of the books had slips of paper sticking out the top, the name of the buyers who had ordered them or, sometimes, the address where they were to be sent. On more than one occasion he had explained to me that most of the money he made came from the rare or out-of-print books for which collectors were willing to pay substantial amounts. His own specialty was Russian-language first editions.

"Here it is," he announced, tapping with his outstretched finger the spine of a small volume on the shelf second from the top. He moved the stepladder into position and pulled it out. "*The Possessed*, by Dostoyevsky. Have you read it?" he asked as he handed it to me across the counter.

"I've read *The Brothers Karamazov* and *Crime and Punishment*, but no, I haven't read this. I may have started it once."

As if seized by a sudden impulse, his head gave a slight jerk. A moment later, a thin smile dashed across his mouth.

"In a certain way," he said, "this is a companion to *Crime and Punishment*. Raskolnikov kills the old woman with an axe because he wants her money and because he believes in nothing that would stop him. He has rejected all morality, all religion; he is a nihilist, someone for whom nothing can be more important than himself. *The Possessed*, on the other hand, is an account of what can happen when people like this band together, and decide to destroy not just one human being, but everything, because they believe in nothing except the supreme importance of replacing everything with something of their own creation. They believe they can create a better world, because they don't believe in the one that exists."

I was still thinking of the confessed killer of Calvin Jeffries, trying to make it fit into what Chicherin was telling me. "How does that explain someone who confesses to a crime he did not do and then commits suicide?"

"It's what Bukharin did; it's what my father did," he reminded me. "This book," he went on, nodding toward the volume in my hand, "has some extraordinary things about the way in which people who no longer believe in religion or morality, who feel betrayed by those beliefs, have nothing left but the desire to destroy everything connected with them. Dostoyevsky understands the emptiness of the soul; but he thinks it can only be filled again by a belief in a Christian God. Anything else is nihilism. And, who knows, perhaps it is, but the same thing that leads some people to Dostoyevsky's God leads others to believe in other things, things for which they are sometimes willing to die."

Chicherin sat down on the chair behind the counter and sighed. Removing his glasses, he blew his breath on them until they clouded over and then wiped them clean on the arm of his gray long-sleeve shirt.

"Consider Dostoyevsky himself. He had the unique experience of being a witness to his own execution. Arrested in his youth for radical activity with organizations advocating a socialist society, he was sentenced to death. He was lined up against a wall and blindfolded. He could hear the order being given to the execution squad to raise their rifles, then the order to take aim. In the stillness of that early morning he could hear the sound of the rifles being cocked."

Chicherin looked at me. "What do you think must have passed

through his mind? Do you think it was what people so often say about the last few seconds before you're about to die: that his whole life passed in front of his eyes?" He folded his arms and crossed his legs and began to rock back and forth. "There was a time in my life when I used to think about that: what it would be like, waiting for your own execution." He gave me a reassuring glance. "I was in Russia then, and it was never anything imminent, just an occasional possibility. But when I did think about it, and when I've thought about what Dostoyevsky went through and some of the things he later wrote, I think it's more likely that it would seem as if your whole life had been nothing—had no meaning at all—except as the prelude to this one moment, this last moment you'll ever know."

He looked down at his pale hands, pondering another thought. "It's fascinating, isn't it?" he asked, tilting his head toward me. "The way someone who knows he will be executed stands and waits, as if, even at that last moment, he cares for nothing so much as how he looks and what others—the people who are about to take his life—will think of him. He doesn't fall on his knees— at least not very often—he doesn't grovel, try to beg for mercy. He may have thought himself a coward all his life, but now, when there is no alternative but death, he looks it calmly in the eye. Who knows what it is? Courage, defiance, or nothing more than good manners, the belief that this is how he is supposed to act, no different in principle than knowing what to say to your host when you take your leave. Even in death we don't want to make a bad impression." A look of disgust spread over his face. "My father of course was not given this opportunity. They shot him in his prison cell, in the back of the head."

He stared straight ahead for a moment and then his expression changed again. When he looked at me, his eyes, or what I could see of them through those thick lenses, seemed cheerful and alive.

"I've sometimes wondered what my father thought about, when he felt the cold hard steel of the revolver push against the back of his head. Did he think about my mother, about me? Did he try to let us know his last thought was for us? And what of Bukharin—was his last thought for that revolution he loved so much he was willing to tell the world he had betrayed it?

"The rifles were cocked and aimed, and the only order left was the order to fire. Dostoyevsky knew that the next word spoken would be the last word he would ever hear. It never came. There was no order to fire. The prisoners stood there, blindfolded, their hands tied behind their backs, waiting, wondering, trying not to let themselves begin to hope. Then, gradually, they knew that it was over, that there would be no execution, that they had been put out there to teach them what it would be like if they were ever sentenced to death again. Some of them went mad; the rest went to Siberia. Dostoyevsky became a deeply religious man. Instead of revolution, he now believed in the importance and the power of redemption."

Scratching his chin, Chicherin opened a drawer and took out a ragged sheet of stationery. With slow, tedious strokes he guided the blunt point of the dark blue fountain pen back and forth across the page.

"The crucial thing to notice about Dostoyevsky," he remarked as he wrote, "is this astonishing capacity to believe, this need to believe in something that made sense of the world."

When he finished, he removed the cap from the end of the barrel and slid it down the nib until it clicked into place. He folded the sheet in half and, gesturing for the book I was holding in my hand, placed it inside and then handed it back.

As we shook hands, he nodded again toward the book. "All I'm suggesting is that it is by no means impossible that someone could confess to something they did not do and then commit suicide. It is not impossible at all."

It was only when I was a few blocks away that I remembered the sheet of paper Chicherin had placed inside the book. I thought he had given me the book on loan, but when I read what he had written I knew he had made me a gift of it.

"For Joseph Antonelli, who has learned that sooner or later everyone has to lose. From his good friend, Anatoly Chicherin."

There was a sudden chill in the air. I put the sheet of paper back inside the book and hurried down the street.

Fifteen

oward Flynn might be early, but he was never on time. I knew that as well as I knew anything, but when he asked me to meet him outside my building at two-fifteen it never occurred to me that I could be late. It was now two-thirty and there was still no sign of him.

Loosening my tie, I unbuttoned my shirt collar while I searched up and down the sidewalk. The sky was a harsh white glare and the air had the smell of something burning. It was the first hot day of the year, the day that made you believe that this might be the year when you did not have to endure yet another month of rain before the clear dry days of summer came to stay. I kept watching the sidewalk, hoping by an act of will to make Flynn appear. I concentrated so hard I could almost see him, his red face dripping with sweat as he lumbered up the street.

"Over here," someone yelled.

Absently, I turned around. Flynn was in his car, stopped in the middle of traffic, waving at me while the drivers behind him leaned on their horns.

"You were supposed to meet me in front," I complained after I tumbled in.

"This is the front," he muttered between his teeth as he bolted through a red light. He swerved just in time to miss a car that had started through the intersection when the light changed. "Learn to drive!" he shouted when the driver of the car shook his fist.

"Your window is up," I reminded him, rolling my eyes. "He can't hear you. You're wasting your breath."

With both hands on top of the wheel and his eyes focused straight ahead, Flynn slowed down, content to follow the traffic ahead of him. A jaded smile flickered at the edges of his mouth. "It doesn't matter he can't hear me. That's not the point."

I knew that look and the twisted logic that usually accompanied it. "Well, then, what is the point?"

"The point is, I can hear me. And, frankly, I thought I sounded pretty good. What did you think?" he asked with a sideways glance. "I could have given him the finger, but, hell, everybody does that these days. I could have screamed an obscenity, but everybody does that, too. Besides, those things just show anger. I was trying to be helpful," he explained. "I said, 'Learn to drive.' It was my civic duty and I did it," he said with mocking pride. "And just what the hell have you done for your country lately, counselor?" he asked with a ruddy grin.

Ignoring him, I stared out the window at the passing buildings. "Where we going anyway?"

"There's someone I want you to meet. He was one of the lead investigators in the Jeffries murder. He interviewed the guy who did it. He heard his confession."

Flynn had told me when he called that there was someone who knew something about the murder of Calvin Jeffries that I ought to hear. He had not told me it was a cop.

"But I know about the confession," I said, trying not to sound as agitated as I felt. "The only thing I don't know is whether the confession was true, and I won't know that until I know the results of the DNA test."

"I forgot to tell you. The blood on the knife belonged to Jeffries."

"The DNA results prove it? Then that's it. You were right. Whoever killed Griswald was a copycat."

"That's why I thought you might want to talk to this fellow. It may not be that simple after all."

"It wasn't a copycat killing?"

His eyes on the road, Flynn shook his head. "No. I still think that's what happened. It's the Jeffries murder that isn't so simple."

We had left the city and were going south on the freeway. "Why aren't we meeting him at the police station?"

He let go of the wheel with his right hand and rubbed his shoulder while he moved his head from side to side, stretching out the muscles in his neck. "He didn't want to have to explain what he was doing having a private conversation with a defense attorney."

I was pretty certain I knew the answer, but I asked anyway. "How do you happen to know him?"

Flynn shrugged. "Meetings."

That was how Flynn had met most of the people he knew, the meetings he attended sometimes seven nights a week where alcoholics took turns telling the stories of their addiction. It was surprising how many lawyers, judges, and cops went to those meetings. Or perhaps it was not surprising at all. Most of the people I met, after you got to know them, had problems of their own, whether it was alcohol or drugs, errant children or unfaithful wives. Madness comes in all shapes and sizes.

A few minutes later we were off the freeway, winding along a narrow blacktop road. Large brightly painted wooden signs propped up from behind by long two-by-fours announced one new development after another. Two-story houses in various stages of construction with wood shake roofs and massive stone fronts stood so close together that each seemed to trespass on the other. They were everywhere, on both sides of the road and as far ahead as the eye could see, new houses for new families, with enough bedrooms for each of the children and enough garage space for all of the cars. There was something vaguely depressing about the sameness of it all, which only deepened my growing sense of annoyance.

"This isn't something you could have told me?" I asked as the car hit another teeth-rattling bump.

"What are you complaining about? Don't you think it's a nice day for a ride in the country?"

"I'm not involved in the Jeffries case." I winced as soon as I said it. I was not involved, but neither was he, and I was the one who had asked him to find out what he could. Flynn paid no attention to what I had said, and I felt even worse. "Sorry," I mumbled.

We passed the last development with its dozen red banners flying from a dozen white-painted poles, and followed the road as it curved under the branches of an oak tree and then out into an open field. A half mile farther on, Flynn turned into a dirt driveway that ran down to a small ranch-style house near a river at the back of a fenced five acres.

At the end of the driveway, opposite the house, inside a small corral next to a two-stall barn, someone was rubbing down a spirited chestnut-colored horse. In his early forties, with short black hair parted on the side, the man was dressed in dark jeans and boots. He was not very tall, but he was muscular across his shoulders and upper arms. When he heard the car, he patted the nose of the horse and then, stepping back, slapped his open hand on its flank. The horse snorted, tossed its head, and bounded away, dust flying up behind its hooves. Shutting the gate to the corral behind him, Flynn's friend waited while we got out of the car.

I recognized him right away. When Flynn started to introduce us, I stopped him. "Detective Stewart and I are old friends."

"But it's probably the first time we've ever shaken hands," he remarked pleasantly. He moved slowly and spoke quietly and had about him a certain understated authority that made you think he was someone you could trust.

"We've been in a few trials together," I explained to Flynn.

"A few I'd rather not remember," Stewart remarked, chuckling to himself. "Let's get something to drink," he said as he slapped me on the shoulder.

We sat at a wooden picnic table in front of the house, drinking lemonade. A breeze stirred the branches of the oak tree overhead, and shadows ran back and forth across our hands as we talked about the way things had changed and tried to remember the first trial in which he had been a witness for the prosecution and I had been the attorney for the defense. After a few minutes there was a long silence. I looked across the table at Stewart and waited.

"Howard tells me you're interested in the Jeffries case."

"Yes, but I'm not sure why," I admitted.

Stewart laughed. "If he'd thrown me in jail for contempt, I'd be interested in his murder."

Was there anyone who did not know what Jeffries had done to me? Stewart read my eyes. "Everyone thought Jeffries was a hero when he did that."

"I didn't."

"Every cop," he explained, though he knew he did not have to. I understood the way cops—most cops—thought about defense lawyers. "Every cop who had not spent much time in his courtroom," he added. He looked at me with a knowing smile and then shook his head. "I used to feel sorry for the lawyers. He had to have been the meanest man alive. That's what makes his murder so difficult to understand."

"I should have thought it was the other way around," I said without thinking. He was not speaking about the fact Jeffries had been killed but, as I now realized, something else altogether.

"With all the people who hated him and no doubt wished him dead, it seems a little strange that the one who killed him had no reason to hate him at all." He pondered the meaning of what he had just said and then added, "At least no reason we could find."

"Are you saying it was random after all, a robbery gone bad?"

He hesitated and then shook his head. "No, it wasn't random.

He meant to kill Jeffries." Again he hesitated. "He meant to kill someone, anyway. He was waiting in the parking garage, hiding behind Jeffries's car."

We were sitting in the mid-afternoon sun, the scent of hay and horses in the air, swatting away an occasional fat fly, but our conversation still fell back into the old habits of lawyers and witnesses: I broke everything he said into new questions I wanted to ask. "He was hiding behind Jeffries's car. Did he know it was Jeffries's car?"

"I don't know. It might have been a coincidence. At that hour there were only a few other cars there. He might have been hiding there, waiting for Jeffries; or he might have been hiding there, waiting for the first person to show up."

"That was the section though where only court staff were allowed to park, right?"

Stewart nodded. "He wanted to kill someone connected with the court, and from a couple things he said, I'm pretty sure he wanted to kill a judge. But whether he intended to kill Jeffries in particular . . ." His voice trailed off, and he gazed across at the small corral where his horse was munching on a bucket of oats. "He had no reason to kill Jeffries," he said presently.

"Jeffries had never sent him to prison?" I asked, repeating the assumption that had seemed to explain everything.

"No, and if he was ever inside Jeffries's courtroom it was not as a defendant. That much we know for sure."

"But he confessed. He didn't say whether he intended to kill him?"

"He said he meant to kill who he killed." Stewart watched me, waiting to see if I took it as literally as he meant it. "That's what he said, almost verbatim. 'I meant to kill who I killed.' He must have said it a half dozen times before I started to wonder if he had any idea who the victim was." With his index finger, Stewart drew a face in the condensation that had formed on the glass pitcher filled with lemonade and ice. "I don't think he did it," Stewart said, as he carefully retraced the circle he had drawn.

"But you just said he intended to kill someone, whether it was Jeffries or not."

His finger stopped moving and he looked up. "No, I think he did it, all right."

"You think he did it, but you don't think he did it?"

He followed his finger as it began to move again, broadening the outline of the face he had drawn until it disappeared. "That's exactly right," he said, as he picked up the pitcher and refilled our glasses. "He did it, but he didn't do it." When he finished pouring, he put the pitcher to the side, out of reach. "Everything fits. There's no question that Whittaker killed Judge Jeffries. None at all. We found him and he confessed. He described every detail of what he had done: where he was; how he held the knife; how he waited until Jeffries opened the door to his car; how he slipped up behind him and grabbed him around the throat while he plunged the knife into his gut. The way he described it was like watching a movie: You could see everything, just the way it happened."

Stewart raised his eyebrows. "It was like he was watching, too; watching himself, observing everything, making sure he did not miss any part of it. He talked about the way the knife went into Jeffries's stomach, straight to the hilt, as if he had been standing in front, watching it happen, instead of holding on to Jeffries from behind. He told us details only the killer could have known. It was not just what he said, either: He had the knife. He did not even try to hide it. Hide it! He had not even tried to wipe it clean! He was found living under the Morrison Street Bridge, one of the homeless. He was surrounded. There was no way for him to get away. But he acted like he was expecting us. There were a dozen cops, weapons drawn, every one of them trained on him, or rather trained on a group of four or five homeless men sitting around a small fire they had built to keep warm. Any one of them could have matched the description we had been given by an anonymous informant. You know what he did—as soon as his name was called out? He stood up, raised his arms, and . . .

smiled. Smiled! Can you believe it? It was as if he had been waiting for someone to find him—not like a fugitive, but like somebody who got lost in the woods waiting for a rescue party. As
soon as they had the handcuffs on him, he told them where to
find the knife. They had not asked him anything. He just nodded his head toward a greasy bedroll a few feet away. 'The knife
is in there.' Just like that. It's the only piece of evidence that can
link him to the crime and he gives it up without being asked."

Flynn, who since we sat down had listened in silence, had a
question. "If he was that eager to be helpful, why didn't he just
turn himself in?"

"I don't know, Howard. Nothing about him made much sense.
Maybe it was part of the game."

"The game?" I asked.

He acknowledged the question with a nod as a way of post-
poning an answer. Once he started following a train of thought
he did not want to lose it. Flynn had the same habit, born, I suppose, out of the fear that unless they concentrated on one thing
at a time they might forget something important, the way they
had forgotten things when all they thought about was the next
drink and the one after that.

"Everything fit. He had the knife—his fingerprints were the
only ones on it. The blood—and we know it for certain now—
belonged to Jeffries. And he described things about the crime no
one else could have known."

"And then he killed himself," I interjected.

Stewart gave me a strange look. "If you believe what the junkie
in the cell across from him said."

"What are you suggesting? That he didn't kill himself? That
someone else . . . ?"

He was careful. "I'm not suggesting anything. But all we know
for sure is that he was found in his cell with the top of his skull
caved in, and the only eyewitness is a barely literate drug addict
who couldn't remember the last time he told the truth about anything."

"Are you saying you think the police, or someone—?"

He held up both hands and turned his face to the side. "I'm not saying anything, but it's a real strange way to kill yourself." He drew his jaw back and made a clicking noise as he tapped his teeth together. "Why I should find anything about this case stranger than anything else is a kind of mystery in itself," he said, thinking out loud. He leaned forward, resting his folded arms on the table. "I've interviewed thousands of suspects, listened to hundreds of confessions, but this was different. There was no remorse. I don't mean just about what he had done, killed another human being. There was no remorse, no regret, about anything: not about getting caught, not about being locked up, not about what he had to know was going to happen to him. I've sometimes wondered whether—if he really did kill himself—he had already decided to do that while he was talking to me. He was—or at least he seemed—completely indifferent to everything. No, that's not right. He was not indifferent, not the way we normally mean it. He was pleased. Yes, that's right: pleased, satisfied—more than content, almost serene.

"I asked him why he had done it, and he said: 'I really can't say.' He said it each time I asked, always that same phrase: 'I really can't say.' But the meaning seemed to change. It was not clear whether he did not know why he had done it, or—and I know this must sound incredible, but it is what I started to think at the time—he knew exactly why he had done it, but for some reason thought that he was not supposed to tell.

"As soon as I understood that his words could be taken in two different senses, I realized that he was aware that the phrase had a double meaning and that he had chosen it deliberately. I began to watch him more closely. At first I thought he was playing a game with us, laughing at us. There were two other investigators in the room, and we took turns asking him questions. His basic expression never changed, that same look of self-contentment, the look of someone who knows something you do not—something so incredibly important that he actually feels sorry that he can't tell you what it is, something he knows you'll never figure out on your own."

Biting his lip, Stewart narrowed his eyes and shook his head, struggling to catch hold of a thought so elusive that it slipped farther away each time he was sure he had it. With one last shake of his head, he gave up. "I'd seen that look before." Turning his shoulders, he waved his arm toward the oak trees scattered over the open space around us. "My wife loved it out here. Twenty years ago, this was the country. There wasn't anything else, just trees and green grass, and the river. You could ride your horse for miles and not see a house or a car. It was a wonderful place to live, a great place to raise kids." He exchanged a glance with Flynn. "Then I started drinking. The more I drank, the more involved she became with her church. I became a drunk; she became a born-again Christian. That's when I first saw that look, on my wife's face, a kind of light in her eyes. Whether it's peace or joy, I don't know; but whatever it is, it's there, it's real, and it used to make me crazy."

He clenched his teeth, mortified by the thought of what he had once been like. "I did some pretty bad things," he said presently. "But I think I could have killed her and with her last breath she would have forgiven me. That's what made me crazy, this absolute certainty she had that she knew the truth and felt sorry for me because I did not. That was kind of the look he had."

He stopped, and in the same way he had before, bit his lip, shook his head, and narrowed his eyes. "You know how most of these people are, the ones who wind up in the system: dull, sullen, lethargic, only roused to rage. He was not like that at all. He moved around a lot, animated, lively. His eyes never stayed still: They jumped all around. His face was full of expressions, all of them colored by that same look of—what shall I call it?—cheerfulness? It seems a strange thing to call the look on the face of a murderer, but that's what it was. He had no regret about what he had done and no fear at all about what was going to happen to him. In that sense at least he was like someone born again, all his sins washed away, and heaven waiting with open arms." Stewart searched my eyes. "The difference is that I'm convinced he did not think what he had done to Jeffries was a sin. I believe he thought he had done something commendable, something he was supposed to do. And I'll tell you something else," he said, raising his chin. "If he had not died in jail, he never would have been convicted of murder in a court of law."

It was irrational. There was no logic to it. None of it made sense. I reminded him of what he had just finished telling me: The police had a confession and all the physical evidence a prosecutor would need.

Stewart's eyes had an inner light of their own. There was something he had not told me yet. I remembered what he had said at the beginning, that seemingly paradoxical remark about being both guilty and not guilty at the same time.

Flynn shifted his gaze from me to his friend. "Tell him about the other murder."

"The other murder?" I asked.

Stewart nodded. "This wasn't the first time he killed someone; Jeffries wasn't his first victim."

I was confused. This seemed to supply the very motive Stewart claimed he had not been able to find. "Are you sure—absolutely sure—that Jeffries wasn't the judge who sent him to prison for the first murder?"

Stewart looked at me without expression. "He never went to prison," he said evenly.

"He murdered someone, and he never went to prison?" I asked skeptically.

"When he was eighteen, he killed his father. The father was a drunk," he said, exchanging another glance with Flynn. "Whenever he got really drunk he used his wife—the boy's mother—as a punching bag. He put her in the hospital a couple of times. One night, the boy came home, found him kicking the hell out of her—literally kicking the hell out of her—and he killed him.

He didn't just kill him, either. He did to his father what his father had been doing to her, just beat the hell out of him. And then, when he had him down on the floor, barely conscious, he started kicking in his face. By the time he was through there was nothing left.

"They charged him with manslaughter and they did a psychiatric. Something had broken inside him, whether because of what he had seen his father doing to his mother, or because of what he had done to his father—who knows? Whatever the cause, he wasn't competent to stand trial."

I knew what had happened next. "And so they shipped him off to the state hospital. When did he get out?"

"A few weeks before the murder. He escaped. It would have all come out of course. But when he died in jail, there didn't seem to be any point in telling anyone that Jeffries had been murdered by a mental patient."

"How many people know about this?" I asked.

"Just a couple of us. We didn't know anything about him when he was picked up. By the time we ran his prints and were able to check his records, he was already dead. The investigation was over."

"But you're sure it was him? He couldn't have confessed to something he didn't do? The physical evidence could have been planted, and if he was that far out of his head . . ."

"No," he said emphatically. "He described how he killed him. Only the killer knew that. We never released those details."

"Jeffries was stabbed to death," I said, repeating what everyone knew from the published reports.

"Stabbed him, then disemboweled him."

I could not believe it. "You're telling me that Jeffries somehow managed to crawl back to his office with his intestines hanging out?"

We finished what was left of the lemonade and said goodbye. As we drove off, I turned around and watched Stewart stroke the nose of his horse and then lead him into the barn.

"What happened to his wife?" I asked Flynn as we jolted down the dirt drive and onto the main road.

"I don't know. She left him a long time ago. Took the kids and moved away. He stopped drinking after that."

We drove past the same new development we had come by before, and the same brightly painted signs, some of them with pictures of happy-faced families about to take possession of their share of the American dream.

"Tell me," I said as Flynn stared ahead at the road. "Do you think Elliott Winston would appreciate the irony that after what Calvin Jeffries did to him, the great judge was murdered by a mental patient?"

Sixteen

The death of Quincy Griswald had in a certain sense been the unfortunate imitation of his life. He had spent years under the intellectual dominance of Calvin Jeffries, constantly reminded of his own shortcomings as a judge, never allowed to forget the distinctly second-rate qualities of his mind. Finally freed of the burden of this invidious comparison, he was murdered barely two months after Jeffries was killed. If the order had been reversed, and Griswald had been murdered while Jeffries was still alive, the search for his killer would have been the one conducted with intense public scrutiny and a relentless demand for immediate results. Instead, though no one was willing to come right out and say it, after one judge had been murdered there was nothing unique about the murder of another. Even in the manner of his own murder, Quincy Griswald had not been able to escape the enveloping shadow of Calvin Jeffries.

The press treated it as a copycat killing, and I had no reason to disagree. Both had been killed the same way, or rather both had been killed the way the police had told everyone Jeffries had been killed. Both had been stabbed to death, but Jeffries had also been eviscerated. The crimes were too much alike for the similarity to be coincidental, and too different to support a suggestion that the two together had been the work of co-conspirators taking turns in a private war against the judiciary. It seemed clear that whoever had killed Griswald had read about the murder of Jeffries and decided for reasons of his own to do the same thing.

There were no more stories about possible conspiracies, none of the vague allusions to powerful enemies that had been made during the investigation of the first murder of a state court judge. The public could breathe easily. Quincy Griswald had been killed by someone without originality, and Calvin Jeffries by a man of no consequence. It might as well have been a random act of violence, which, because it could happen to anyone, was no more to be feared than any other chance event. It might have been a little more disconcerting had the public been told that Jeffries had been murdered by a mental patient who had murdered once before. It might have raised a question about how he had managed to escape. It might have raised a question about how many of the homeless men who slept in the alleyways and under the bridges, how many of these ruined creatures whose presence among us we tried so hard to ignore, had at one time or another been institutionalized because of a mental disease or, a question even more uncomfortable, should be institutionalized now instead of left free to wander the streets without proper care or, for that matter, any care at all.

In only one place did the murder of Quincy Griswald have a more dramatic effect than the murder of Calvin Jeffries. So long as only one judge had been murdered, it was an exception, an extraordinary event that, precisely because it was extraordinary, required no serious alteration in the way things were done inside the courthouse where he had worked and where he had been killed. The murder of a second judge meant that no one could feel safe. Almost overnight, the parking structure was fenced off with a steel screen and only people with the proper official identification were allowed to go in or out. Security inside the courthouse was tightened as well. Everyone who entered had to empty their pockets, open their briefcases, and pass through metal-detecting devices. Uniformed guards roamed the corridors, and floors where the public had no business were sealed off. Now, for the first time, when a stranger walked into a courtroom, everyone noticed. You could see it in their eyes, that sudden, barely concealed fear, the fear that it might be Quincy Griswald's killer come back for more.

There were other, more subtle changes. The clerk who checked my name off the list of those who had a matter before the court that morning actually looked at me and said hello. When a deputy sheriff brought my client, shackled at the ankles and wrists, into the courtroom, he seemed to move more slowly, as if time was no longer quite so pressing. The deputy district attorney who was there to argue the state's position on my motion to suppress nodded politely when I took my place at the counsel table. When the judge invited me to begin, his voice was calm, subdued, a bare whisper in the somber stillness of the room.

It was a straight legal argument on a disputed point in the Byzantine case law on search and seizure, and as I went through it, summarizing what I had written in my ten-page brief, I knew the judge would rule against me, and I knew he knew it, too. The defense made the motion; the state opposed the motion; the judge, after both sides had filed their written briefs and made their oral arguments, denied the motion. That was how you set into motion the legal machinery by which one day, perhaps five or six years from now, the Supreme Court of the United States would decide that the existing law, or the way in which that law had been interpreted, was in some respect invalid. It was what held the whole thing together, this knowledge that whether you practiced in downtown New York or in some dusty, windblown town in the high desert of eastern Oregon, no one had the power of final judgment. You could appeal and appeal again, appeal until you finally had the chance, a chance that might come once in your life, to argue a case in front of the nine justices of the only court from which there could be no appeal.

If you were serious about your work, if you were serious about yourself, you wrote every brief, and you made every oral argument as if you were already there, in front of the Supreme Court itself. You stood in an empty courtroom, in front of a judge you sometimes suspected had not bothered to so much as glance at the written brief you had submitted, a judge who might be a friend or an enemy, someone you might play cards with in your spare time, and you always began, "May it please the court."

It went like clockwork. I argued, the state argued, and I argued again. The judge had no questions he wanted to ask and, passing the file to his clerk, announced in a cool, deliberate manner that, in the phrase uttered so often it had become engraved in my mind, "Having listened to the arguments of counsel, and having been advised of the premises, the court finds that the defendant has failed to show why the evidence alluded to should be suppressed. The motion is therefore denied."

Gathering up my papers, I dropped them into my briefcase, and then, putting it behind me, turned to go. It was like stepping into a hole. The weight that was supposed to be at the end of my hand was not there. Half the leather handle had ripped away from the briefcase and was dangling from my hand like a fallen climber clinging to a rope. Reaching down, I scooped it up and with my hand around the bottom held it next to my side.

"You were very good, Mr. Joseph Antonelli."

I knew who it was before I looked, the voice I used to listen to in the middle of the night when I was still young, the voice that could now make me remember things I thought I had forgotten. Sitting alone at the end of the spectators' bench closest to the door, Jennifer laughed at the surprised expression I had not been able to hide.

"What are you doing here?" I asked as she began to walk toward me. Holding her hands in front of her, staring down at her shoes, a mirthful look on her face, she slid first one foot, then the other ahead. I watched her come, wondering at the mischief going on in her mind. "When did you get back?"

"A couple of days ago," she said, looking up. As soon as she saw me, her expression changed. "What is it? Why do you have that funny look on your face?" she asked, cocking her head.

"I was thinking about the agonies of self-doubt and suspicion I would have gone through—that I used to go through—when you went away somewhere and I didn't hear from you the moment you got back."

She wrapped her fingers around my arm and gently squeezed. Then she let go and the catlike grin again spread over her mouth and her eyes began their cheerful dance. "Did I ever tell you that before you ever asked me out, before you even knew I was alive, I was dreaming about you and about the things that would happen, things I would do that would make you notice me, make you want to be with me and love me the way I already knew I was going to love you?" Her hand was on my sleeve again, and as she pressed her fingers tight, she tossed her head.

"And did I ever tell you that I was doing exactly the same thing, dreaming about what I would do to make you want to be with me, fall in love with me as desperately as I was in love with you?" I asked.

The door on the side opened and the clerk bustled in to collect something she had left on her desk.

"How did you know I was here?" I asked as we left the courtroom.

"I called your office and your secretary told me you were in court this morning. I thought it would be fun to watch."

I shifted the briefcase to the other arm and held the door for her.

"It was interesting. You seemed so serious. It was you, and it wasn't you. It's funny. I used to think about what you'd be like when you were older, and then, watching you, I kept thinking about what you were like when you were younger." Trying to keep hold of the thought, she stopped and turned to me. "I see you the way you were, and when I do, I start to see you the way you've become. Does that make sense? To see you both ways at once, as if all the time between then and now vanished? That you've always been both what you are and what you were?"

We stood outside in the late morning light, not quite certain what to do next.

"I'm parked down the street," she said.

"I don't have to go back to the office for a while." After an awkward pause, I added, "I mean if you have time."

Aimlessly, we wandered down the street. My hand brushed against hers, and once or twice she touched my sleeve, gently tugging it to emphasize something she said. We passed a café, noticed it was largely deserted, and without a word about what we were doing, turned around, went inside, and took a booth at the back. A stoop-shouldered, blunt-eyed waitress, her mouth twitching at the side while she listened, took our brief order. Soundlessly, her eyes locked in a petrified stare, she brought two sand-colored mugs and a grease-stained coffeepot. Setting the mugs together at the edge of the table, she filled them full and, taking the pot away, left them there.

I crossed my eyes and made a face as I shoved one cup toward Jennifer and dragged the other one toward me. She started to laugh, then covered her mouth with her hand. I took a drink and then put it down. It had a stale bitter taste and I wanted to take it back and ask for a fresh pot. Jennifer put her hand on my wrist. "It's all right," she said after she had taken a sip. "It isn't that bad."

I shook my head in disagreement, pushed the cup out of my way, and leaned forward on my elbows. "How was your mother?"

"Fine. I told her I'd seen you." She paused, amused at something that had been said. "I told her about our first date—what I said to you when you brought me home." Her eyes stayed on me while she turned her head slightly to the side. "She said that the next time I wanted to invite you to spend the night, I didn't need to ask." Her eyes flashed for just an instant, and then she looked down and stirred cream into the coal black coffee. "And what have you been doing while I was gone?"

"Not too much. I got so drunk the night we had dinner and you had to go home early that I had to call for help. Howard Flynn—there's a story—took me home and put me to bed and came back the next morning to take me to work."

"You got drunk?" she asked, a look of alarm in her eyes.

"Close enough. First time in a long time."

"But why?"

Somewhere below the surface of my conscious mind I knew the answer, but I was not ready to put it into words, and I was not sure I ever would. After all this time—a lifetime—Jennifer was back, and things I thought were dead had come back to life. At least I thought they had, or was I just imagining that nothing had really changed, that I still loved her because of the way I had loved her then, all those years ago, when I thought I would never see her again and was convinced that my life was as good as over? That night at dinner I thought I was falling in love with her the way I had the first time, but then, after she was gone, I began to wonder how much of it was because of what had happened before, how much of it was because it seemed somehow finally to make sense out of things and to give some meaning to a broken heart. If we had just met, two middle-aged strangers, would there have been any real attraction at all, or would we have just enjoyed each other's company and not been terribly worried whether we ever saw each other again? I did not want to talk about it. Things were all too tangled up.

"I didn't intend to get drunk," I said with a shrug. "It just happened."

Jennifer looked at me, searching my eyes, a gentle, sympathetic smile floating over her wide mouth.

"It's all right, Joey. You don't have to be in love with me."

The thought, spoken out loud, spoken by her, that I might not be in love with her anymore, gave me a strange, empty feeling, as if I were losing her again, the way I had lost her before.

"No," I insisted vehemently, "that's not it. I am in love with you. It's just that I don't quite understand it."

For a while we did not say anything. We sat there, seeing each other the way we used to be, the way no one else had ever seen us, and realized as we did that whatever else had happened there was something about us both that had not changed at all.

I began to talk, but not about us. I told her instead about the things I had done while she was away. I told her about my visit with the widow of Calvin Jeffries and what Calvin Jeffries had done with her help to Elliott Winston.

"He's been in the state hospital for twelve years?" she asked, horrified. "I told you what happened to me. I was in the hospital, but for only six months, and it wasn't a state hospital—an asylum for the criminally insane—it was a private clinic where everyone is very discreet and everyone has a private room." She shook her head. "Twelve years! In a place like that!

"You start to change," she went on, talking in a clear, calm voice. "Even when you're there for just a relatively short period of time. You don't notice it, not at first, and perhaps if you stay there for a long time you never notice it. You have your particular problem, the problem that brought you there, but everyone around you—all the other patients—have problems, too. There is not as much difference between you and the others as there is on the outside. Everyone has a mental illness, and you begin to see that as the normal state of things."

No matter how hard I tried, I still saw her the way she had been. It was almost impossible for me to think of her hospitalized for depression. Instead of trying to go further into what she had said, instead of inquiring into what she understood as the ambiguous meaning of normality, I denied that she had ever been seriously ill.

"But you're fine now. Elliott Winston, on the other hand, will probably never be well."

She started to say something, seemed to think better of it, and withdrew behind a polite smile. She sipped on her coffee for a while and then asked me how I had spent the weekend.

"Nothing unusual. I went into the office Saturday morning,

then played chess with a Russian émigré whose father was executed by Stalin in the name of history."

She was not sure whether I was telling the truth or not.

"Anatoly Chicherin runs a bookstore. He convinced me to play chess with him, though I don't know why: I could play him for a hundred years and never win."

"His father was killed by Stalin?"

I leaned against the wall and pulled my knee onto the bench seat. "The irony is that Anatoly became a state prosecutor. He left when the Soviet Union self-destructed. He likes to talk about criminal cases. That's how we became friends. He's fascinated by the way we do it here." I tapped my fingers on the table, watching the way she kept her eyes on me. "He thinks we're crazy. He says everyone here wants to win; no one cares about justice. He insists he never charged anyone unless he was absolutely certain they were guilty. Imagine! Inside the most corrupt system in the world, and he would not think of charging anyone if he thought there was a chance they were innocent."

I was showing off, talking about things on a grand scale, though I knew all the time that it had no effect because it made no difference. Talk, be silent, say something halfway interesting, or make a fool out of myself, the way she looked at me would not change.

"Saturday was the first time he told me about his father. We were talking about the Jeffries murder. A second judge—Quincy Griswald—was killed Friday night, and I thought there was a chance that the same person might have done both."

"You don't think so now?"

"No. The one they arrested for the Jeffries murder did it, but for a while I wasn't sure. I was trying to understand how someone might commit suicide over something he didn't do. That's what led Anatoly to tell me about his father."

I looked down at the table and then slowly raised my eyes. "You look at me the same way you used to."

Her face brightened. "Good. Tell me about his father."

I stretched my leg out, pulled up my other knee and grasped it with both hands. "His father believed in Communism. He also wanted to protect his family. He was accused of treason. It was a lie. But he confessed, though he knew it was a death sentence. In effect, he committed suicide, and he did it because of what he believed and who he wanted to protect."

I turned my head toward her and then, a moment later, sat up and leaned forward. "An Arab terrorist drives a truck full of explosives into a building and blows himself up and we think he's crazy, but he thinks he's dying for Allah and is going to paradise. How many Christians were burned at the stake during the Inquisition because other Christians thought they were heretics? Atheists died for the Communist Party because they believed they were acting on behalf of the new god, history. We think all of them were crazy, but what do we believe in? What are we willing to die for?"

"A mother will die for her children," she said simply.

I was sure she was right. It probably explained why every religion had been founded by a man.

Jennifer reached inside her purse and removed an orange plastic bottle. With the kind of precision that comes with habit, she unscrewed the cap, tapped a single white capsule into the palm of her hand, put it into her mouth, and washed it down with water from her glass. As soon as she swallowed, the cap was back on the bottle and the bottle back in her purse.

"Lithium," she explained. "I forgot to take it this morning."

I wondered if she had, or if she had decided to wait to see my reaction. It was not that long ago that someone suffering severe depression was put away, and spent the rest of their days staring at a wall, without the will to move or the power to speak. Now you took a pill and wondered whether people believed it was no different than taking insulin for diabetes, or whether, deep down, they thought you would never be quite right.

Outside, she took my hand as we walked up the sidewalk, headed for her car. She seemed relaxed, perfectly at ease, almost girlish. Tossing her head to the side, she teased me about the briefcase I was cradling under my arm. "Did anyone ever tell you," she said, reaching in front of me to tap the cracked leather, "that you could probably use a new one?"

"It's the only one I've ever had," I replied. "We've been through a lot together."

Her large wide eyes, painted yellow by the high arching sun, did their light-footed dance, mocking my stiff-legged attachment to what I was used to. "Yes," she said, "but you've survived it."

"It can be repaired," I tried to insist, but she only laughed. Holding hands, we walked along, blending in with the faceless parade, just another middle-aged couple, not worth the attention of anyone else, an anonymous part of a great swirling mass.

"Here," she said in a soft, husky voice, that seemed always on the verge of laughter.

"Where?" I asked dimly, startled out of a daydream of my own. I gawked at the buildings around us, wondering if she meant one of them or something else.

"Here," she repeated, laughing at the confusion in my eyes. "My car. It's in here."

We were standing at the front entrance of a parking garage. A horn blared and we stepped out of the way as a frizzy blonde steered a brown Lexus into the street.

"I'll drop you at the office if you like."

I could have walked there in less time than it was going to take to get the car out of the garage. "That would be great," I replied.

We found the Porsche and I watched, fascinated, as she drove down the narrow spiral chute that led out to the street. Her eyes, glazed with the thrill of it, stayed fixed on a spot immediately ahead of the car, while her mouth moved with the soundless rhythm of someone talking to herself.

"Is it still your intention to die like Isadora Duncan, your scarf caught in the spokes of your Bugatti?" I asked dryly when she passed through the last curve and was slowing to a stop at the ticket taker's window.

"No," she said as she paid the bill. "That was a schoolgirl fantasy. Now I'm all grown up." She darted a glance to her left and then turned right out of the garage. "I want to die in bed," she said as she sped through an intersection to beat the light. "Of overexertion."

She parked across the street from my building. Leaning against the window, she smiled. "I'm glad I came today. I liked watching you in court."

I opened the door and started to get out. "Would you like to have dinner tonight?" I asked, turning back to her.

She smiled, and I knew the answer, and more than that I knew that the answer would now always be the same.

I watched her drive off, the tires squealing as she raced down the street, her hand trailing out the window, waving one last goodbye. As I jogged across the street, I remembered what it was like, years ago, when I was a teenage kid and I could run forever and never get tired and could not imagine that I ever would.

Helen was waiting for me when I walked into the office. She marched right behind me, clutching a wad of phone messages in her hand. "Before we do anything else," I said as I dropped into my chair, "could you do me a favor?" I opened the briefcase, removed everything in it, and handed it to her. "Could you take this somewhere and have it repaired. All it needs is some new stitching where the handle fell off."

She looked at the briefcase, then looked at me. "You sure you don't want to get a new one?"

"Anything important?" I asked.

"There's one from Howard Flynn," she said, handing me the stack.

Flynn answered on the first ring. "Stewart called about an hour ago. He said you might be interested. They made an arrest in the Griswald murder."

"It was good of him to call," I said, wondering why he had

gone to the trouble. If it were not already public information, it would be by the end of the day.

"That isn't the reason," Flynn went on. "He thought you'd be interested because the guy they arrested was another mental patient."

Seventeen

John Smith, for that is the name by which I first came to know him, suffered from a serious mental defect, but there was no record that he had ever been a patient in a mental hospital. It would have been surprising if there had. John Smith did not exist. There was no record of him anywhere; there was no record he had even been born. He had been found under a bridge, the same one where the killer of Calvin Jeffries had been found, living in the cardboard squalor of a homeless camp. When the police arrived, he was sitting on his haunches, digging in the dirt with the steel point of the knife that turned out to be the weapon used to murder Quincy Griswald. When the police, guns drawn, demanded he surrender it, he stood up, clutched it to his chest, and repeated over and over again the single word "Mine." He did not resist when they took it away from him, but as soon as it was out of his grasp he began to cry.

They brought him to the police station and he said the same thing all over again when they asked him if the knife was his. When they asked him if he had used it to murder Quincy Griswald, he still mumbled that same word. They told him he would feel better if he admitted what he had done, and there was not a sign that he understood what they meant. It was only when they asked him where he had gotten the knife that there was a spark of recognition in his eyes and that he made something like a clear response. "Billy," he said. That was all. Just that single one-word name. No last name, no description of what this unknown person looked like, nothing about where he gave it to him or why.

The police had found the suspect exactly where an anonymous caller had told them they would find the killer, and they had the murder weapon. They did not have a confession, but they quickly convinced themselves that they did not need one and that, in any event, their suspect was too far out of his mind to give one that could stand up in court. What had not been quite so obvious in the case of the killer of Calvin Jeffries was impossible to ignore in the case of the killer of Quincy Griswald: He was homeless and he was crazy. He did not confess, because he could not remember. He could not remember anything, not even his own name. That he remembered the name, and apparently nothing else, about the person who had supposedly given him the knife was the kind of inconsistency that only served to underscore the irrational workings of whatever mind he had left. The only one who had any serious doubt about his guilt was Detective Stewart, and he kept his own counsel. He told only Flynn, and he asked Flynn to tell me.

The next night I waited in my car across the street from a single-story brick building next to a warehouse on the east side of the river. A few minutes past ten the door opened, and through a yellow haze Flynn and Stewart made their way out of the crowded smoke-filled room. Puffing on cigarettes, they climbed into Flynn's car and, signaling me to follow, drove off.

We stopped a couple of blocks away and went into a tavern. A couple of old men and one old woman were hunched over the bar. At the pool table in front, a woman with dishwater blond hair and vapid blue eyes chalked a cue stick while a man with a smug mouth and oily black hair racked the billiard balls for another game. The place reeked with the dead smell of stale beer and nicotine. We took one of the two booths in back and ordered coffee.

"This place is awful," I said to Flynn.

He exchanged a glance with Stewart, sitting next to him. "We always come here after a meeting." His head moved from side to side on his thick neck, the way someone who used to fight follows the action in the ring. "In case we forget what a glamorous life we gave up."

"I wouldn't have come here drunk," I replied.

"Depends how long you'd been drunk," he said with the assurance of someone who knew what he was talking about. "Once I found myself wearing a three-piece suit, sitting in the dirt talking to some guys at a construction site. It was Monday morning and the last thing I remembered was Friday night. You would have come in here if you were drunk. You would have been camped out on the doorstep waiting for them to open, grateful to get out of the daylight and back into the dark."

Just as I lifted the cup to my mouth a loud, cracking noise struck my ear with such force that I ducked my head and put the cup down on the table. "What!"

"Bitch!" shouted a surly voice from the front.

Flynn shook his head and rolled his eyes. He looked at Stewart. "Didn't I do it last time?"

Stewart shrugged. "You're closer."

"Christ," Flynn muttered as he got up from his place at the end of the booth.

I leaned around and followed him with my eyes as he walked pigeon-toed toward the pool table. With his hand on her throat, the pool player had his partner up against the wall, screaming obscenities in her face, while he brandished his pool stick with his free hand.

"Let her go. Put the stick down," Flynn ordered in an irritated voice.

His hand still on her throat, the man turned and, with his lips pulled back in a murderous grin, snarled incredulously, "You gonna do something about it, old man?"

"I'm going to bust your ass, is what I'm going to do about it."

In a single motion, he threw the woman to the side and with

both hands swung the stick as hard as he could. Flynn had already taken a half step forward, and with one hand caught the stick in midair. With a quick downward turn of his wrist he twisted it behind the back of the other man until it dropped on the floor, and then grabbed him by the shoulder and the seat of his pants. With two quick steps he threw him as hard as he could head first into the door. For an instant, he lay there, motionless, and I thought Flynn had killed him. Then he began to stir, and a moment later got to his knees.

"What are you trying to do—kill him?" the woman yelled as she shoved Flynn out of the way and dropped down on one knee, putting her arm around the shoulder of her boyfriend, who a moment earlier had been ready to crush her windpipe.

Straightening his jacket, Flynn came back to the table. "Didn't that door used to swing open?" he asked as he slid in next to Stewart.

"You're a credit to the nobility of the Irish race," I said. "Still rescuing damsels in distress."

He dropped his chin and raised his eyes. "She didn't look like any damsel to me. I should have stayed out of it."

Stewart laughed. "No, you did the right thing. If you hadn't stopped it, she would have killed him."

"What were they arguing about, anyway?" I asked.

Holding the cup with both hands, Flynn sipped his coffee. "I don't know. Maybe she finished off his beer while he was making a shot." His face had a wry expression. "That can be a really serious thing, leaving a drunk without anything to drink."

My leg began to hurt again. I reached down and rubbed it with the heel of my hand. The sharp, stabbing pain subsided, replaced by a dull throbbing ache. Soon there was nothing left of it, and I could only wonder how much of it was real, and how much of it was in my mind, a figment of an imagination over which I was beginning to think I had little, if any, control.

"Tell me about this John Smith," I said, looking at Stewart. "You're not convinced he's the one who killed Griswald?"

"I'm convinced he did not." He paused before he added, "It's just a feeling. I don't have any proof."

"Like the feeling you had about Whittaker?"

"Not quite. I knew Whittaker killed Jeffries; I just couldn't figure out why. I still don't know. Whittaker was crazy and, remember, he had killed before. There was no question that he was capable of murder. I don't think John Smith—or whatever his name really is—could hurt anyone." He thought about what he had just said. "Maybe if he was backed into a corner, or maybe if he was scared—maybe then. But I just don't think it's possible that he would lie in wait for someone and then use a knife on him," he said, shaking his head.

Though he seemed certain of himself, it was clear from his expression that there was something else, something about which he was not nearly so confident.

"It's not my case," he explained. "But ever since Jeffries's killer killed himself—if that's what he did," he said, suggesting once again the possibility that it might not have been suicide at all, "I keep wondering what made him do it. When I heard an arrest had been made in the second murder, and that everything seemed to be the same: an anonymous call; the suspect another homeless man living under the same bridge; the murder weapon a knife and the knife still in his possession, I wanted to find out if there might be some other connection between the two murders or the two killers. That's why, when they brought him in, I sat in on the interview."

Stewart slowly rubbed one thumb over the other. Long deep lines creased his forehead. His eyebrows were knit close together. Something had left a bad taste in his mouth.

"They brought him into the interrogation room and sat him down in a chair. It had been raining. He was soaking wet, and his shoes and the bottoms of his pants were caked in mud. He was filthy. Forget about when he had last had a bath; God knows the last time he had changed his clothes. He had on an old olive-colored overcoat, torn, tattered, ripped; underneath that, a sweater with more moth holes than wool. His hair was down to his shoulders and he had a scraggly beard."

He shuddered as a look of disgust passed over his face. "I could not tell exactly how old he was, but he was young, probably still in his twenties, and he had what I can only describe as innocent eyes. When you looked at him and he looked back, it seemed as if he wanted you to tell him what to do, that it would not occur to him that there was any reason not to trust you. He seemed helpless.

"That's when I noticed—when he looked at me with those childlike eyes. At first I thought it was because he had gotten all wet. His hair was plastered to his head and his beard was stuck to his face when they first brought him in. He was starting to dry out, and his hair and his beard extended farther out from his head, from his face. Then I realized—we all realized: His head, his beard, were crawling with lice, with disgusting vermin. I could only imagine—I did not want to imagine!—what was living on the other side of his clothing. It was like watching an eruption: They were coming from everywhere, and still he looked at us the same way he had before, without emotion, without any sign that he was even aware that he was being eaten alive by this unspeakable infestation. The awful thing is, I don't think he was aware of it; I think he was used to it, the way you or I might be used to a little dirt under our nails if we were out in the garden."

"What did you do?" I asked, amazed at what he had seen.

"We had all seen it at once; and we all reacted the same way. We jumped up from the table, afraid that some of those things had already had time to get on us. No one wanted to touch him, and we gestured like a bunch of panicked fools, pointing toward the door. They managed to get him out of there and down the hall to the shower. When they got him undressed, they burned all his clothes. They got him deloused and they shaved his beard and cut his hair. But before that, when they saw him naked, they got the doctor. He had scars all over his legs and his buttocks.

They were cigarette burns, the doctor said, and they had probably been there since he was a child.

"The next day he was interviewed again."

"Without a lawyer?" I asked.

Stewart raised his head. "That's right. He was told he had a right to one," he added, anticipating my next question. "Well, not told, exactly." His eyes seemed to open wider, while his gaze turned inward. "They read it to him from the card we all carry, read it to him in a flat monotonous voice. Then, at the end, the detective put down the card, bent toward him, and put his hand on the suspect's arm. 'Or do you want to just talk to me?' He asked that question like he was talking to a friend. It's an old technique."

"And he didn't want a lawyer?"

A scathing look came into his eyes. "He didn't know what a lawyer was! We should have known it from the beginning—the way he talked, the look in his eyes. Without the beard, without those filthy clothes, you had to know what he was. It was not just his eyes anymore. You could see it in the way his mouth sagged to one side, the clumsy, awkward way it moved when he gave his one- or two-word answers to a question, the way the words seemed to drag out: rough, slurred, without any definable end. Our suspect—the one arraigned this morning for the murder of Judge Griswald—is retarded. God knows just how retarded! There aren't any records. He doesn't have an identity. If he was ever tested we don't know about it."

With narrowed eyes, Stewart studied me for a moment, and then looked down at his hands and again began to rub one thumb over the other. "This is a travesty," he said without looking up. "And there's nothing I can do about it. Everything was done by the book. He had the weapon; his prints are all over it; and he was living under the bridge." With his head bent over his hands, he raised his eyes. "It's the similarity. A homeless man with mental problems murdered Jeffries with a knife. Griswald is murdered with a knife, and a homeless man with mental problems of his

222 ᐬ **D. W. Buffa**

own has it. He doesn't confess, but that doesn't matter because you can tell yourself that he's so far out of it he might not even remember what he did. Besides, that's someone else's problem. The police did their job. They found the evidence and they made an arrest. They read him his rights and they brought him to court. That's the way the system is supposed to work, right? The lawyers will sort it all out."

"Nothing to worry about," Flynn remarked as he rubbed the back of his thick neck. With a droll look, he added: "He'll have the finest defense lawyer the public defender's office can spare. They'll probably plead him to two murders instead of one just to get rid of it."

I leaned my head against the back of the booth, slowly shifting my gaze from Flynn to Stewart and back again. It was a setup and they knew I had finally caught on.

"All we're asking," Flynn said as his co-conspirator concentrated on the spoon with which he began to stir his coffee, "is that you think about it."

"Think about it?" I asked, with a laugh. "You don't want me to think about it. You want me to do it."

Flynn never backed down. "What do you have to lose? Why do you practice law, if it isn't to take a case like this? The kid's retarded, for Christ sake; and when he was growing up some son of a bitch tortured him just for kicks. You imagine? . . . A child, retarded, somebody tortures him!" Hunching forward, Flynn hit the table hard three straight times with his stubby fingers. "He lives under a bridge; he's got things crawling all over him. If you're not going to help someone like that, who the hell are you going to help?"

Stewart was glued to the coffee cup, mesmerized by the movement of the spoon. "I'll help," he said. Reversing direction, he began to stir counterclockwise. "I'll get you everything we've got." His hand stopped moving, and for an instant he seemed to tense. "On both investigations," he said, looking straight at me.

"Aren't you taking something of a chance?"

He shook his head. "So what? Let me tell you something: I was one of the people in charge of the Jeffries investigation. There was too much pressure, too many people with too much to lose. As soon as Whittaker confessed, as soon as he was dead: That was all anyone needed to end it. No one wanted to go farther; no one wanted to hear about it anymore. We know who did it. What difference did it really make why he did it? Well, I still want to know. Maybe there's a connection between the two murders. Maybe Griswald wasn't a copycat killing. The only way we'll ever know is to catch the killer. This kid didn't do it. See for yourself. You tell me if you think he could have killed someone."

I did not agree to take the case; I did not even agree to see for myself, as Stewart had put it, whether John Smith was capable of murder. I did agree to talk with whoever in the public defender's office had been assigned the case; and two days later, when I finally had a break in my calendar, I dropped by a few minutes before noon.

With the telephone cradled between her chin and shoulder, the receptionist glanced up at me while she continued filing her nails. "Hang on a second," she said into the receiver. "Which case was that?" she asked, reaching for a thin gray three-ring binder.

She was young, not more than nineteen or twenty, with long brown hair and eyes that never stayed still. On the counter in front of her, a straw smudged with red lipstick stuck out of an ice-filled container of Pepsi-Cola. When I told her the name of the defendant, she hesitated just long enough to decide that I was serious. Her eye followed her finger down a handwritten list of cases and the lawyers assigned to them.

"You'd think they'd put all this in the computer," she remarked, making a face. Her finger came to a stop. "William Taylor," she said, looking up. She flapped her hand in the air and picked up the phone with the other. "Third door on the left."

I went down a corridor, passing between same-size cubicles

identically furnished. Sitting in his shirtsleeves, his tie pulled down from his throat, William Taylor wadded up a piece of paper, leaned back and took careful aim at a wastebasket next to a file cabinet on the other side of the small room. It hit the edge and bounced onto the floor. With a sigh, he got up from behind his metal desk and picked it up. I was standing in the doorway, just a few feet away, but I might as well have been invisible. He went back to his chair, leaned back the same way he had before and tried again, with the same result.

"Mr. Taylor?" I said when he bent down to pick it up.

He did not look at me. "Yeah?" he said as he resumed his position and got ready to throw.

"Do you have a minute?" I asked patiently.

The paper wad ricocheted off the side of the file cabinet into the basket. It did nothing to improve his mood. He looked at me with sullen, insolent eyes. "Depends," he replied as he opened his desk drawer and began to rummage through it.

In his early thirties, he was tall and lean, with fine brown hair and a pale complexion. He had the dour look of a moralist, someone who could never bring himself to admit there was a second side to anything about which he had a firm conviction. He was the kind of lawyer who became apoplectic about the death penalty, but seldom cared that much about any particular case.

I decided to start over. "My name is Joseph Antonelli. I'm interested in a case you're handling. The defendant's name is John Smith."

He kept searching through the drawer. "I know who you are. Why are you interested?" Whatever he was looking for—if he was looking for anything—he gave up. "You don't represent the indigent."

I had been standing in his doorway the whole time, deliberately ignored. He stretched out his arm and waved his hand toward the chair in front of his desk, a reluctant invitation to sit down. I did not move. "No, thanks. I don't want to take any more of your time than I have to. What can you tell me about John Smith?"

The harsh tone of my voice got his attention, but that was all it got. "I can't discuss a client," he said, as if I should have known better than to ask.

"Look, Mr. . . ." I twisted my head around until I could see the place where his name was printed on the door. "Mr. Taylor. I just want to know whether this is a case you're going to take to trial."

He was not going to answer me until I answered him. "Why are you interested?" he asked in a voice filled with fatigue.

"Because I've been asked to take the case."

"I thought he was homeless."

"He has a few friends," was my vague reply.

"He has a few friends? He's homeless and he has a few friends that can afford to hire you?"

I had had enough of this. "Have we met? Is there some reason you don't like me, or is this just the way you talk to everyone?"

It did not faze him. He shrugged and looked away. A short while later, he sat up, pulled a file out of a metal holder on the corner of his desk, and glanced at the first page inside. "We entered a plea of not guilty," he said as he closed it. "It won't get to trial, though. We ordered a psychiatric. He's not competent to stand trial," he said with assurance. Sitting back, he crossed his ankle over his knee and laced his fingers together behind his neck. "Good thing he's a loon," he said with a cynical glance. "It's the only thing that can save him from the death penalty."

"You think he did it, then?"

"Probably," he said with indifference. "It doesn't matter. As I said, we're getting a psychiatric. There won't be a trial. He can't assist in his own defense," he said, using the phrase that provides one of the standards by which a court decides upon the mental competency of a defendant.

Without waiting for another invitation, I sat down in the chair in front of him. "You know what will happen to him then, don't you?"

His eyes flashed. "I handle more cases in a week than you do in a year. You think I don't know what will happen? What should happen. He isn't responsible. He has a mental disease. He should be hospitalized, not put in a cell on death row!"

"Have you talked to him?"

"John Smith? You can't talk to him. That's my point. He doesn't understand anything. He has no idea what's going on."

"He knew enough to tell the cops that someone gave him the knife."

Taylor just looked at me, and I knew then that he did not know anything about it. The police had apparently not bothered to include that little detail in their report.

"You didn't know that, did you?"

"It doesn't change anything. He isn't competent."

"And he isn't guilty. Do you really think an innocent man should be locked up in a hospital because of something he didn't do?"

"He isn't competent," he repeated. "And all the evidence is against him. If he went to trial, he'd be found guilty. Don't you think he'd be better off in a hospital? Even if he wasn't found guilty, what does he have to go back to? More nights under a bridge?"

I got up from the chair and looked down at Taylor, wondering whether, if that was the choice, he might not be right after all.

"The innocent are supposed to go free," I said. "If he needs help, there are other ways to get it."

Before he had a chance to ask me what they were, I heard myself announce a decision I did not know I had made. "I'm taking the case. I'll have my office send over the substitution order." I paused. "If that's all right with you, that is."

Even if he had wanted to keep the case, he could not. The public defender could only represent clients who could not get an attorney of their own. But he was glad to get rid of this one.

Taylor did not mind losing—public defenders were used to it. What he did mind, what he could not bear to face, was the possibility that someone he was representing might be sentenced to death when they could have spent the rest of their life in the relative comfort of the safe white sheets of an insane asylum bed. It was a risk he would not have run for himself; it was a risk he thought me mad to run for anyone else.

Eighteen

Jennifer refused to think there was any risk at all; and even if there was, she did not see that there was any choice. "If he didn't do it . . ." she said, letting the thought finish itself as she searched my eyes.

We were at the restaurant bar, waiting for a table. She was sitting on a leather stool, one long leg crossed over the other, the hem of her black dress just above her knee. I was standing, wedged in tight by the crowd that pressed two and three deep all around us. She said something, but the noise was so loud I could not hear. I bent closer, and as I did her soft, pliable hand slipped into mine. Her eyes were laughing.

"When was the last time you lost a case?"

I started to reply, forgot what I was going to say, and, unaccountably, felt my face grow hot.

"You're blushing. That's perfect," she said, gently squeezing my hand.

"No, I'm not," I replied, trying to shrug it off. "I just looked down the front of your dress and got all excited."

She wrinkled her nose and tossed her head. "You're such a liar. Why can't you just admit it? You blushed."

She watched me out of the corner of her eye as she lifted the thin-stemmed glass of wine to her mouth and drank. We had lived our separate lives and she still knew me better than anyone ever had.

"Was I a liar then?" I asked, pretending that it was too long ago and that I had forgotten half of what had happened.

Sliding off the stool, she took my arm. The waiter was beckoning from across the room. "Every time I said don't, and you said you wouldn't?" she whispered in my ear.

The waiter pulled out her chair, and I settled into the one across the small table for two. As he handed her a menu, I said, as if it were nothing more than a casual remark, "Then we were both lying, weren't we?"

She thanked the waiter and opened the menu. "I used to wonder why it took you so long to figure that out." Her eyes came up until they met mine. "You're doing it again," she said with an innocent stare. "Your face is turning red."

The waiter returned and took our order. Jennifer sipped on her wine, a pensive look in her eyes. "What is he like?" She put down the glass. "You saw him today in jail?"

I began to tell her again how I had decided to take the case as soon as I discovered how little the public defender was going to do. She was not listening.

"I used to think that would happen to me," Jennifer said. She was looking right at me, but she had turned in on herself. "I thought I was going to become like the people who walk around with vacant eyes pushing their shopping carts with all their belongings stacked on top, the people who sleep under blankets made out of cardboard boxes." Gradually, her eyes came back into focus. "How long has he been like that: homeless?" she asked.

"You really thought that could happen to you?" I asked, a trace of skepticism in my voice.

"You think people are born homeless?"

"I'm beginning to think John Smith may have been," I said almost as an aside. "No, I don't think people are born homeless. But I don't think many of them started out as members of the upper middle class, either. Most of them are alcoholics, addicts, people suffering serious mental disease, people who should be in hospitals."

"Like John Smith?"

I shook my head. "He isn't delusional; he doesn't hear voices . . ."

"I heard voices," she said matter-of-factly. "Perhaps not in quite the way you mean. I thought things that were said by people I didn't know—things said by people on television, for example—had a special meaning meant only for me."

I started to explain what I thought was the difference. "Don't," she said, laying her left hand on my wrist. "You can make all the distinctions you want—but what it really comes down to is you don't want to believe I was ever that sick . . ." Raising her head she turned first one way, then the other. "Look around," she said when her eyes came back to mine. "Tell me what you see."

The restaurant was filled to capacity, with dozens of people crowded around the bar. Men wore ties and women sparkled.

"Everything depends on how you look, how you dress, what kind of car you drive, what kind of house you own. That's how we decide about people, that's how we decide about ourselves: whether we're successful or not, whether we know what's going on or not, whether we're crazy or not."

She stared at me a moment longer, challenging me to disagree. Then, suddenly aware of her own intensity, she became embarrassed. "I'm sorry," she said, laughing quietly at herself. "I didn't mean to go on like that."

"It's my fault," I replied. "I shouldn't have been so quick to dismiss what you were saying. But it's hard for me to think of you like that . . ."

"Mentally ill," she added for me.

The waiter began to serve dinner, and for a while we talked only of inconsequential things. It did not really matter what we talked about. The sound of her voice was all I cared about. It was the sound of home, the place you wanted to come back to, the place where no matter how long you had been away, you were always welcome, and always wanted.

"You still haven't told me," she said halfway through dinner. I didn't know what she meant. "About the boy: John Smith. What's he like?"

It made me smile. Most of the people who appeared as defendants in the criminal courts were men in their twenties, but for Jennifer, anyone that age was still a boy.

"Remember how we used to feel when someone older—someone our parents' age—called us boys or girls? One of the things I've learned is that each generation thinks the one it follows must have been born ancient and incompetent, and the one that comes behind it will die young and inexperienced."

Jennifer bent forward, a birdlike look of astonishment on her face. "And one of the things I've learned is that each generation thinks it invented sex." She paused, an impish glow in her large bronze-colored eyes. "I happen to know, however, that sex was actually invented late one August night in the back seat of somebody's old Chevy while Johnny Mathis was singing 'Chances Are' on the car radio." She paused again and broke into a dazzling white smile. "And I have a witness—unless he's forgotten."

"I remember the car," I said vaguely.

She raised her eyes and opened her mouth and taunted me with her smile. "I can understand if you've forgotten. It was over almost before it started."

I turned up my hands. "Before that night, it always had ended before it started—in a manner of speaking."

"I knew I was the first," she said with a show of triumph. Then, as we looked at each other, surrounded by strangers but somehow alone, the bright, glittering grin slowly dissolved into a sad-eyed bittersweet smile.

"I wish you had been the last," I whispered with a sigh.

"Me, too," she said, a lost look in her eyes. "We would have had a good life, I think. I know I would have been happy married to you. Do you think . . . ?"

She was the only thing in my life that had ever made sense. I could almost feel what it would have been like sitting here with her, in one of the most expensive restaurants in town, on her birthday, or our anniversary, or just because, no matter how long we had been married she would always be the best-looking woman I knew.

I looked at her a moment longer before I said anything. "You know the answer to that better than I do," I said finally.

She stared down at her hands and then forced herself to smile. "Now," she insisted as she sat straight up and pretended everything was all right, "tell me about John Smith."

I hesitated. I did not really want to talk about John Smith. I wanted to talk about us. She shook her head. "Tell me."

I hesitated again, this time because I was not quite sure how to begin.

"He makes you want to believe in the essential goodness of human beings."

She tilted her head. "Don't you?"

"Believe we're born innocent and only become corrupted by civilization? No. I think there are a lot of people born evil. I think Calvin Jeffries was like that. Jeffries had a brilliant mind and was perhaps the worst human being I ever knew. John Smith suffers from some kind of retardation and he wouldn't hurt a soul. His parents—whoever they were—didn't want him, and whoever had him as a child tortured him—deliberate, unspeakable acts— that had to have caused incredible physical pain."

I started to describe what had been done to him—what from the scars left on his body we could tell had been done to him— but I caught myself in time. "He was treated like an animal," I instead remarked. "Have you ever known anyone who did that: mistreated an animal? Sometimes the animal becomes vicious; other times they become scared, quick to shy. Hard to know why there's that difference: Maybe it's just their nature. John Smith is like that: frightened of everyone, scared of his own shadow, and yet, at the same time, just dying for an act of kindness. He looks at you with orphan eyes, the eager look of an innocent boy—you're right about that: He is a boy—a boy who wants someone to take him home. It hurts even more when you think about what they did to him. You have to know that they made him think it was his fault, made him believe that it was because he had not done what he was supposed to do. How hard he must have tried to understand what he was supposed to do; how difficult it must have been to comprehend the meaning of the names they must have called him."

"Then you've decided for sure," Jennifer said. "You're going to defend him?"

At first I thought I was hearing the unfamiliar voice of my own conscience; then I remembered that the words echoing in my mind were simply a variation on what Howard Flynn had told me to my face. "If I don't help him, what good am I?"

It was the kind of sentiment Jennifer was certain to approve, and among the other things that seemed not to have changed through all the years of her absence was how much I wanted her approval. When I was eighteen, or nineteen, or twenty-one, or twenty-two, I would have said those words, words that someone had said to me first, and, in her presence, believed they told the truth about myself. I would have been Clarence Darrow or Don Quixote or both of them together, anything I thought she might want me to be.

"Howard Flynn told me that," I admitted. "He tries to be my conscience."

She put her coffee cup down and touched her mouth with a white linen napkin. "You're not taking this case because someone else thinks you should. You're taking it because you think you should."

I handed the waiter a credit card and when he had gone I looked back into Jennifer's waiting eyes. "I'm taking it because that kid in the public defender's office was an embarrassment." I was trying to sound tough and cynical and I failed so miserably I started to laugh. "I'm taking the damn case because of you."

"Because of me?"

"Yes. I knew what you'd think of me if I didn't."

For a long time she looked at me without saying anything. "Did you really?" she asked finally.

I tried to be completely truthful. "I think I might have," I admitted, as I helped her out of her chair.

Outside, in the misty night air, she held my arm with both hands as we walked down the street. Her high heel shoes tapped lightly on the sidewalk, and our breath blew like white transparent clouds into the darkness. Our foreheads bent close together, we turned the corner to the street where we had parked the car, and then, suddenly, without any warning, a metal shopping cart appeared out of nowhere and nearly ran us down. My hand shot out in front just in time to grab it. Pulling Jennifer behind me, I swung around to the side while the cart passed in front of us. An old woman—or what looked like an old woman— was shoving it along as if nothing had happened, as if she had not seen us at all.

The old woman was wearing a torn overcoat and a green wool scarf. Her face was fat and red, with tiny slits for eyes and a pudgy, off-center nose. A red wool knit cap was pulled down below her ears and what looked like dirty cloth bandages were wrapped around her hands in a way that covered her palms and left her fingers free. Her mouth hung open and as she passed by you could hear a harsh rasping noise with every breath she took. A tooth was missing in front, and just above her lip three long white hairs grew out of a mole. The cart was loaded with bulging black plastic garbage bags, but whether they were the sum total of her earthly possessions, or debris she had found to trade or sell, there was no way to know. The back wheels were broken and wobbled sideways as the cart rattled into the night.

I took Jennifer by the hand and turned to go, but she was frozen to the spot. Then, before I could do anything, she let go of my hand and started running. When I caught up to her, she was standing next to the homeless woman who had almost run us over. Jennifer dug in her purse and handed the woman a fist-ful of money. There was no sign of recognition in the woman's eyes; her expression remained dull, blank, without comprehen-sion. Jennifer reached down and put the money inside the over-coat pocket and stood aside and watched her go.

"You have a good heart," I said as we walked to the car.

She looked up at me. "No. Just bad memories."

The engine was running by the time I got around to the pas-senger side, and the Porsche was moving away from the curb be-fore I had the door shut.

"What do you think they talk about?" she asked, her eyes fixed on the road. "They move along the streets like they're in a trance. Have you ever watched them?" she asked, darting a glance at me. "They seem to stick together, don't they? You'd see them sitting on the sidewalks, or in an alleyway, or in a park, all huddled to-gether. It's like a community of their own—maybe a country of their own. What do you suppose they tell each other?"

Both hands were on the wheel, her head was up, her eyes vi-brant, excited, with almost too much life in them, as if what had made them that way was itself not quite normal.

"Wouldn't it be interesting if there was a whole civilization all around us, right in front of our eyes, and we didn't even know it—like a kind of parallel universe that is there and yet isn't there?"

She cranked down the window and lifted her face to the rush of cool night air. It seemed to sweep away all the feverish ex-citement, all the anxious care. A dreamlike smile floated across the long curve of her sad gentle mouth.

"Want some music?" she asked as she turned on the radio. As soon as she heard it, the smile on her face started to dance and her eyes began to come alive again. Then she was laughing, the way she had laughed when she was still a girl and did not yet know what it was like to be unhappy. She was laughing, and I knew why.

"You just happened to turn on the radio to Johnny Mathis singing 'Chances Are'?"

She reached down between the seats. "I cheated a little," she admitted as she pulled out a plastic CD holder. The laughter faded into the night and the sparkle in her eyes became a warm, luminous glow.

"It's Saturday night," I said, as she turned onto the street that ran along the river at the edge of the city. "What would you like to do?"

"Nothing," she said, a wistful look in her eyes. "Be with you. What would you like to do?"

"Marry you."

She did not look around to see me and there was no change in her expression, nothing, except a slight quiver at the corner of her mouth.

"I love you, Joey. I always have. I always will."

That was all she said. She did not say yes, and she did not say no, and when she reached for my hand it did not seem to matter.

She lived in a condominium on the edge of the river less than half a mile from town. As soon as we shut the door behind us, she was in my arms. She kissed me on the mouth and then, keeping hold of my hand, led me into the living room. She turned on some music and kicked off her shoes. We went onto the balcony and watched the lights of the city reflected in the black water of the river and listened to the thousand sounds drumming in the glass and steel darkness. Closing the sliding glass door, we went back into the living room and with both her arms around my neck we began to dance. We moved slowly to the rhythm of the music and then more slowly still.

"It's like the first time," she said in a muffled voice as she lifted her face to mine.

I slept late into the morning and for a few minutes after I woke up thought I was still asleep. At first I did not know where I was, and then, when I remembered, wondered if I had been left there alone. I found my clothes draped neatly over the arm of an up-holstered chair in the corner of the bedroom and put on my pants. Then I slipped on my white dress shirt, fastened one button and rolled up the sleeves. In the bathroom, I washed my face and tried to do something with my hair. With my shirttails hanging down behind me, I walked barefoot out to the living room and through gauze curtains saw Jennifer sitting on the balcony.

Leaning against the sliding glass door, I squinted into the bright yellow sunlight. "What are you reading?" I asked.

She put the paperback novel down next to her coffee cup on the black metal table, got up from the deck chair, and kissed me on the side of my face. "I'll get you some coffee," she said, laughing at the way I looked.

I stood there, in my rumpled shirt and wrinkled pants, bleary-eyed and unshaven, watching her as she walked away, clean and fresh, in a white silk T-shirt and a pair of cuffed shorts that flared out above her thin knees. When she disappeared into the kitchen, I went out onto the balcony and sat down on the other green-cushioned wooden chair. I picked up the book she had been reading and looked at the cover. A woman with a low-cut dress was laid out in a half faint, held around her slim waist by a muscle-bound bodybuilder with hair longer than hers.

"I'll bet you can't find anything like that in that library of yours at home," she said as she handed me a cup of coffee.

"Is it any good?"

She laughed. "That? Of course not. But I'm afraid I don't read much of anything that is. I just do it to escape." She sat down on the edge of her chair, her knees close together. She could not stop laughing. "I'm sorry. But you look like someone who got caught sneaking out of someone's hotel room."

She stood up, took the cup away from me, and held out her hand. "Come on," she commanded. "Get the rest of your things. I'm going to take you home so you can change clothes and we can go somewhere."

"Where?" I asked, stumbling along behind her.

"Anywhere. It doesn't matter. It's a gorgeous day. We'll just go."

She drove me home and waited in the library while I changed. When I came back, she was sitting in a chair with her glasses on, peering intently at the open page of a leather-bound book. "So if we were married," she said, looking up, "we would sit in here every night, and while I read some of my trashy novels you'd be reading . . ." She thumbed back to the title page. "*The History of Italy* by Francesco Guicciardini."

"I have to read that sort of thing," I explained as I took her by the hand. "I spent too much time in school chasing girls."

"You caught a few, too, from what I heard."

"Lies, all lies."

We climbed into her car, and she switched on the ignition. "Yes," she said just as she pushed on the accelerator and we shot down the driveway and out the open gate at the bottom.

"Yes?" I asked, my hand braced against the dashboard.

"I'll marry you."

"When?"

"In a year—if you still want to."

From the moment weeks before, when she showed up on my doorstep and after an interval of a lifetime had gone on another drive to the coast, what I wanted or did not want had disappeared as questions I could no longer ask. I had never lived with anyone for longer than a few months at a time, and had been hurt so badly the last time it had never entered my mind that I would ever do it again. And then Jennifer showed up on my doorstep, and before we had reached the coast I had known that nothing any longer was a matter of choice. We were going there again. The top was down and the wind raced past us as she drove ahead of the sun, speeding toward the western sea. I folded my arms in front of me, and sank back against the leather seat and closed my eyes, and I knew better than I had ever known anything before that I belonged to her and she belonged to me. We were nothing more than different parts of the same person. We might as well have been married at birth.

Nineteen

I t was simply a matter of chance. Any one of a dozen different deputy district attorneys might have been assigned to the case of *State v. John Smith*. Despite all the publicity, despite the editorials insisting that the district attorney himself should handle the first murder trial in which the victim was a sitting circuit court judge, it was treated like any other homicide. Whether the victim was one of the homeless found butchered behind the garbage cans in an alleyway, or a member of the state judiciary found stabbed to death next to his car, the bureaucratic machinery of the criminal justice system treated everyone with the same rigid equality of death. Cases within the same category were assigned in a strict rotation among the deputies within that division. Without a second thought, an anonymous clerk entered the name Cassandra Loescher and with that simple act made her famous.

When the district attorney announced that Cassandra Loescher would prosecute the killer of Judge Quincy Griswald he lavished such praise on her qualifications that it would have been hard not to believe that she had been his personal choice. With the wide-eyed sincerity that had helped get him elected, he insisted she was one of the most experienced, best-trained prosecutors in his office. Leaning toward the cameras, a confident smile on his suntanned face, he called her "a tough, smart lawyer who knows her way around a courtroom," as if it might have entered anyone's mind that she did not. A quick, furtive glance at a three-by-five card was followed by the observation that "there are not more than three or four prosecutors in the whole state who could match her 96 percent conviction rate." Turning to the somewhat bewildered woman next to him, he shook her hand and, with one last smile and one last wave to the circle of reporters crowding the corridor, vanished into his office.

Blinking into the TV lights, Cassandra Loescher was left alone to listen to herself repeat the same vapid generalities she was too intelligent not to have once ridiculed in the mouth of someone else. It was always interesting, the way the words we mock in others no longer seem insincere when we use them ourselves. She meant it when she said she was determined to bring this killer to justice; she meant it when she said she had the greatest faith in the world that a jury would do the right thing. She was now so convinced of the importance of a guilty verdict in the case against John Smith that she had probably forgotten the day when, while I watched, she had tried to trade insults with Quincy Griswald and then stalked out of his courtroom, wishing him dead.

The look she had given him then was the look she was giving me now. She was annoyed she had in effect to repeat the arraignment with a new attorney, and even more irritated that it had not started on time. It was scheduled for ten o'clock; it was now seven minutes after. She sat at one of the two tables reserved for counsel, tapping her fingers and clicking her teeth, listening to the murmurs of the handful of reporters and spectators scattered over the hard wooden benches that ran across the low-ceilinged room behind us.

The clerk took two steps inside, stopped and stamped her foot. "All rise," she announced.

His black robe trailing behind him, Judge Morris Bingham

walked briskly into the room where in the course of a long tenure on the bench he had heard nearly every complaint and every excuse suffering could create or duplicity could invent. In his mid-fifties, with blue eyes that were lively and alert, Bingham had only a tinge of gray in his close-cut brown hair. Though he was not in any serious sense a legal scholar, he had a clear mind and the kind of sound judgment that builds on its own experience. No one—not even the criminal defendants he had sometimes to sentence to long terms of imprisonment—had ever complained that he had treated them unfairly. He was civil, sometimes to a fault, but his impeccable manners, an honest reflection of his basically decent character, also provided him a barrier against any closer contact. Lawyers who practiced before him loved him without knowing him; judges who worked with him did not like him because he had no interest in knowing them.

There was no wasted motion in what he did, and no sense that he worried about time. He sat down, folded his hands together on the bench in front of him, leaned forward, and turned to the deputy district attorney. With nothing more than an expectant look, he let her know what he wanted.

"We're here in the matter of *State v. John Smith,* your honor."

He glanced at the deputy sheriff standing next to the door at the side. The deputy understood. His eyes still on the judge, he opened the door and called the name of the prisoner. When John Smith appeared in the doorway, the deputy put his hand on his arm and led him across the front of the courtroom.

Shackled with chains, the young man—the boy—known only as John Smith shuffled across the floor, his wrists held together in front of his waist, his head bobbing slowly up and down. As he drew closer, he stared at me with a puzzled expression. I had spent an hour with him late Friday afternoon, just three days before, but I was not sure he remembered who I was.

The deputy guided him to a spot next to me and then stepped back to a place in front of the wooden railing a few feet behind. Bingham looked at me and raised his eyebrows.

"Your honor, for the record my name is Joseph Antonelli. I have agreed to undertake the representation of the defendant known as John Smith. Mr. Smith, as the court is aware, has previously been arraigned on an indictment charging him with the crime of murder in the first degree. At the time of that arraignment, Mr. Smith was represented by the public defender's office. A not guilty plea was entered, defense counsel filed a motion for a psychiatric examination to determine if Mr. Smith was in fact competent to stand trial, and the case was assigned to this court for all further proceedings."

This was one of those routine appearances which, though most lawyers hated them as a waste of their time, were among my favorite things to do. I was like an actor who has only five lines, but knows that they are as important as any lines in the play. I stood with my shoulders straight and my hands held behind my back, bent slightly forward at the waist, my feet spread wide apart. I spoke each sentence rapidly, snapped off the last word, paused long enough for the word to echo back, and then did it again.

"I have filed with the court a substitution order, signed by both previous counsel and myself. With the approval of the court, I wish to begin my representation of Mr. Smith by asking that the motion for a psychiatric examination be withdrawn. The defendant has no desire to avoid trial of this case on the merits. The defendant, your honor, wishes to establish once and for all that he is innocent and that whoever killed the honorable Judge Quincy Griswald is still at large and—"

Morris Bingham raised his chin, and with that single gesture cut me off. I had begun to play to the reporters and he was not going to allow it. His gaze lingered a moment longer, and I thought I detected something close to a smile. Then he looked over at Cassandra Loescher, who already knew the question and had no doubt about her answer.

"The state has no objection," she replied as soon as he lifted his eyebrow.

With a quick, abbreviated smile and an even quicker nod, Bingham sat up, glanced inside the case file, closed it, and nodded once more. "Mr. Smith," he said, leaning forward.

There was no response, none that I could hear. I looked to the side and was surprised to find John Smith looking up at the bench, waiting for what the judge was going to say next.

"Do you understand what we're doing here today?"

Smith said nothing, but he seemed completely attentive. More than that, he seemed drawn to the judge in a way I had not seen before. Perhaps it was the sound of Bingham's voice: soft, quiet, the sound of someone you could trust, the sound of someone who would never hurt you.

"Mr. Antonelli has indicated that he wants to be your lawyer. Do you want him to be your lawyer, Mr. Smith?"

I moved a quarter turn away to watch more clearly, hoping he would do something, make some sign so that we could satisfy at least the minimal requirement that the defendant know that he has been charged with a crime and that he has a right to an attorney. To my astonishment, he answered out loud, a single three-letter word that seemed to stretch out forever between the beginning and the end, a long, quivering cry that until it was over you were not sure he would have the strength to finish. It was like the first full word spoken by a child, who then wants to see if he got it right.

Biting on his lip, Bingham stared at him, and then stared hard at me, as if there was something he would have liked to know.

"Very well," he said presently. "The order previously entered for a psychiatric examination of the defendant is withdrawn. Is there anything else, Mr. Antonelli?"

"Yes, your honor. I would ask that the defendant be released on his own recognizance."

Startled out of a reverie, Cassandra Loescher shot up from her chair. "Your honor," she sputtered, barely able to contain herself. "The defendant is charged with capital murder. Even if he wasn't, he has no job, no family, no ties to the community. For that matter, your honor," she said, putting her hand on her hip, "he doesn't even have a name. The police called him John Smith because they had to call him something. They ran his prints: Nothing came back. There are no records of any kind. We don't know who he is, and if he were let out there would be no way to find him." Glancing across to where I stood, she added caustically, "Perhaps Mr. Antonelli can tell the court who his client is. Someone hired him to represent him."

I waited until Bingham's eyes left her and came to me. "The terms under which I have agreed to represent Mr. Smith are a private matter between myself and my client."

Bingham did not need to be told what he already knew. Without expression, he waited for more.

"The court will notice that Ms. Loescher did not say that Mr. Smith has a criminal record. She did not say that Mr. Smith has a history of violence. We may not know who he is, but if he had a criminal record—if he had ever been arrested—Ms. Loescher would have known that, because his fingerprints would have told her that. We have, your honor, a man without a name; a man, as nearly as I can tell, without much in the way of a memory; someone who has almost certainly never hurt another human being, now charged with a crime to which he has pled not guilty, held in confinement for something he did not do."

Bingham threw out his hands and spread open his fingers, tilted his head and looked at me, waiting. I answered his unspoken question with the same sort of gesture. "I know," I agreed. "I just wanted to point out the unfairness of it all."

"In light of the seriousness of the charge . . . without a stable home . . . someone to take responsibility . . . the defendant will remain in custody," he said reluctantly. "Trial will be set for . . ." He looked down at the clerk and waited until she found the next available date on his calendar.

"I'll see you later today," I said to my client, carefully pronouncing the words as the deputy put his hand on John Smith's shoulder and led him away.

Howard Flynn was waiting for me in the corridor, a solemn expression on his rough-edged mouth. I started to ask him why he had not come inside. Then I remembered.

"It still bothers you, doesn't it?" I asked as we walked toward the elevator.

"Not sure why it should," he replied, shaking his head. "I come here often enough."

There were other people in the elevator and we rode down in silence. Outside, the late morning sun, filtered through the thick-leafed trees, scattered a yellowish haze over the sidewalk in the courthouse park. We sat down on a bench across from a bronze statue turned dark green with age, honoring the dead of the First World War.

"What have you been able to find out?" I asked.

With his feet spread wide apart, Flynn rested his elbows on his thighs. "Nothing," he said glumly. "Not a damn thing. It's like the kid never existed. I've pretty well used up every inside contact I've got. The cops don't know who he is. Social Services doesn't have anything." He sat up, pushed his elbows over the top of the bench behind him, and, tilting back his head, searched the heavens for an answer. "The adoption agencies don't have anything. There's only one thing left I can think of. You ever hear of a psychologist named Clifford Fox? He testified for the prosecution in a case you had a couple of years ago."

"That son of a bitch?" I cried, as I pulled my knee onto the bench and turned to face Flynn directly. "Specializes in so-called repressed memories; testified that my client's niece had remembered fifteen years later that her uncle had abused her as a child. The jury didn't believe it," I reminded him.

Flynn's chest heaved up as he snorted. "Yeah, you'd be the last guy to convince a jury to acquit someone guilty." His eyes half shut, he slowly shook his head. "Doesn't matter. Listen to me. Whatever he said at that trial, he was telling the truth, at least what he thought was the truth. He doesn't lie." He paused long enough to form the gruff smile that usually introduced one of his brief commentaries on human weakness. "At least when he's sober—and he hasn't had a drink in years."

I should have known. Flynn had friends everywhere, and every one of them was an alcoholic.

"What are you suggesting? What can he do that will help us find out something about John Smith? I don't think we're dealing with a repressed memory, do you?"

Flynn's mouth twisted to the side. "All I know is that the only person who knows anything about John Smith is John Smith. You're wrong about Fox. He doesn't specialize in repressed memory; he specializes in handicapped children. If anyone can reach inside that kid's mind, he can."

I checked my watch. "I have to get back to the office," I said as I got to my feet. "I have to see John Smith this afternoon. You need to meet him anyway. Come along. Then we'll decide about your friend, the psychologist."

Before I turned to go, I looked at Flynn and laughed. "First Stewart, now Fox? If we're not careful we're going to have a defense team made up of every drunk in the city."

He stared at me from behind hooded eyes. A wry, rueful grin creased his mouth. "Could do a lot worse," he said with a shrug.

When I walked into the office, Helen handed me a large, heavy manila envelope. "It just came," she explained. "It's the list of Judge Griswald's cases."

I told her to hold my calls and began to examine, caption by caption, all the criminal matters that had ever come before the honorable Quincy Griswald. There were thousands of them—trials, hearings, every conceivable kind of case—stretching back through the long years of his service on the bench. I must have gone through hundreds of pages, each of them listing line by line the name of a defendant and the crime with which he had been charged. There was nothing there, nothing that could either supply a motive as to why he had been killed or offer so much as a hint as to who might have killed him. I stayed at it for hours, and there were still hundreds more pages to go. I began to read faster, skimming the words as I traced my finger down each page. I was in such a hurry to finish that I flew right past it, and only realized what I had seen when I was halfway down the next page. Turning back, I stared at it for a long time, wondering why I had not put it all together before.

I had worked straight through lunch and far into the afternoon and had lost all track of time.

"Call Court Records and ask them to order up from the archives the court file from *State v. Elliott Winston*," I said to Helen on my way out the door. "It's an old case—about twelve years ago— Quincy Griswald was the judge. I don't have a case number. Then call the state hospital and tell Dr. Friedman I'd like to see him as soon as possible."

Twenty

When I told Flynn what I had found, and what I thought, he looked at me as if I were the one who should be in the state hospital. "What are you suggesting: that Elliott Winston killed Jeffries and then Griswald?"

"No," I objected. "I'm not suggesting that at all. I'm saying that the two murders seem to be connected somehow. All I know for sure is that Jeffries managed to drive Elliott over the brink, and Griswald was the judge who sent him away."

"To the state hospital," Flynn reminded me. "Not to prison. The guy tried to kill you. Griswald did him a favor."

"Did he?" I wondered aloud. "Elliott didn't have a criminal record. He thought I was having an affair with his wife, and I would have testified that he only meant to scare me. The gun went off during a struggle. Even if he had been sentenced to prison—instead of probation—he would have been out years ago."

Unconvinced, Flynn shook his head. "Griswald was just doing his job. He didn't have any choice. When someone gets sent to the state hospital, it's all according to the statute."

We were standing in front of the county jail, a few minutes past four in the afternoon, waiting to see John Smith. The trees in the park across the street cast their shadows on the sidewalk as the sun slipped down the western sky. With a purse slung over her shoulder and a child clutching each hand, a stocky young woman, her legs stuffed into her jeans, hurried down the steps.

"Doesn't matter anyway," Flynn went on, narrowing his eyes. "We already know who murdered Jeffries." I was not sure we knew that, or anything else. "All right," he said, beginning to get exasperated, "let's say we don't know who killed Jeffries; let's say we ignore the confession, the suicide, everything. Elliott Winston is locked up tight in the forensic ward of the state hospital. It sounds like a pretty good alibi to me."

"I told you," I said more sharply than I intended, "I'm not suggesting Elliott killed anyone. I'm not suggesting he had anything to do with it."

He stared at me, a puzzled expression on his face. "Then what are you suggesting?"

I was not quite sure. I had that helpless feeling of grasping at something vague and indefinable, something you thought for a moment you understood, but that suddenly, as soon as you have to explain it, vanishes from view.

"I don't know," I admitted, still trying to think of what it was. "You're right. Elliott couldn't have done it, but it doesn't seem possible that it's all just a coincidence."

Flynn peered down at his shoes and stroked his chin. "What else could it be?" he asked, raising his eyes until our gazes met.

"The one who confessed to killing Jeffries—the one who killed himself—was a mental patient."

"And?"

"And it would be interesting to know if Elliott knew him."

"The hospital has hundreds of patients. But even if he knew him, so what?"

"Then we have another coincidence, don't we?"

Flynn put his hand on my shoulder as we began to walk toward the front entrance. "All you have then is that a mental patient who once knew someone who got killed happened to know another mental patient who happened to kill him. Go to the hospital; talk to the doctor—talk to Elliott: Find out everything you can about Jacob Whittaker. Maybe there is a connection between the death of Jeffries and the death of Griswald; maybe there is a connection between the two killers . . . But Elliott Winston? If you didn't know what Jeffries had done to him—if you didn't know what his wife had done to him—you wouldn't even be thinking about it."

He was right of course, and at least on a conscious level I knew it. I put aside all my vague imaginings and dim suspicions and tried instead to concentrate on the reason we were there.

"Did the psychologist agree to see Smith?" I asked as we got to the door.

"He will," Flynn replied confidently. "I haven't called him yet. I wanted to see what we could do first."

We could not do much. John Smith was brought into the small, windowless conference room. His head hung down between his shoulders and swayed from side to side, while his eyes, glazed over, remained fixed on the same point. The jailer walked him to the table where Flynn and I sat waiting, helped him into the chair, then knelt down beside him and removed the handcuffs. Powerfully built, with a square jaw and broad straight shoulders, the deputy gently patted him on the back.

"You'll be all right here," he said in a soft voice. "This is your lawyer, Mr. Antonelli. He was in court with you today. Remember?"

The head stopped moving. A shy smile started onto his mouth and then floated away. He looked at me a moment longer and then, as he lowered his eyes, his head drooped down and began to sway slowly first to one side, then the other.

I spoke to him in the tone of voice I would have used with a child. "John, this is Mr. Flynn. He's going to help us with your case. Would you like to say hello?"

If he heard, he gave no sign of it. His head swung like a pendulum, a long, looping motion that when it reached full extension at one end, hesitated for just an instant, and then fell away, speeding backward through the same trajectory until, at the other end, it stopped again.

Flynn seemed to grow nervous. Though it was against the rules, the guard had gone. He pulled a cigarette out of his pocket and with his thumb flipped open the cover of a matchbook. It was barely audible, but at the sound of it, John Smith's head froze. I turned to Flynn, but it was too late. He struck the match, and as it burst into flame, John Smith jumped away, knocking over the metal folding chair. "No!" he cried. "No! No fire! Don't hurt! Don't hurt!" he screamed. He sank down in the far corner of the room, as far away as he could get, his arms crossed in front of his face, cowering with fear.

Flynn was on his feet, the unlit cigarette stuck in his mouth, the burning match still held in his hand. "I'm sorry," he said, trying to appear calm. He took the cigarette out of his mouth. "See? I was just going to light this. I wasn't going to hurt you." Cautiously, he took a step forward. The boy—and he was only that— drew his knees farther up and tightened his arms around them. Flynn took another step forward and went down on one knee. He held the match in front of him. "Look," he said. "I'll put it out."

Words meant nothing. At the sight of that match, he screamed, "No, please no!"

Flynn held it there, the flame grown larger, and then slowly closed his thumb and forefinger around it and crushed it out. It must have hurt, but you could not tell it from the expression on Flynn's face. The boy's eyes widened in amazement and the shaking began to stop.

"I'm sorry," Flynn repeated. He got to his feet and reached down to help him up. The boy watched him but kept gripping his knees.

"That's all right," Flynn told him in a quiet voice. "Take your time. Come on your own when you're ready," he said as he straightened up. "No one is going to hurt you. We're going to try to help you."

Smith's eyes followed Flynn as he came back to the table, and stayed on him even when he stood up, picked up the chair, and sat down on it.

I have seen people, gifted in ways I could only imagine, communicate with dogs and cats and even horses, but until now I had never seen anyone do something like that with another human being. Howard Flynn sat across the table from that unfortunate soul and something passed between them, some ineffable thing that made the boy respond—not with words or even a gesture—just a look, but a look which, had you seen it, you would never forget. It was the look of someone who has no knowledge—no conscious knowledge—of himself, the look of someone who has not, like the rest of us, permanently divorced himself from the world around him. Clear your mind of every thought, rid yourself of every felt emotion, every seeming instinct of fear, until all that is left is that essential part of yourself that is yourself, and you will begin to understand what happened. The unspoken word, the thought that is silent even to itself—the thought that does not need expression to know what it is—that was the communication that was taking place right in front of my eyes.

"What can you tell us about Billy?" Flynn asked finally.

"Friend," was the one-word answer.

"Billy gave you the knife?"

Smith nodded, and Flynn asked, "Where did Billy go?"

"Away. Billy went away."

"Where did he go?"

"Away."

"But where away?"

"River."

I glanced at Flynn, but he was concentrating too hard to notice. With his arms folded together on the table, he leaned forward, cocked his head, and smiled. "What is your name?" he asked simply.

The boy smiled back. "Danny."

"What's your last name, Danny?"

It was so still in that room I thought I could hear my own heartbeat. Without any change of expression, he looked at Flynn and said, "Danny."

Flynn nodded patiently. "Danny is your first name. You have another name, too. My first name is Howard."

"Howard," the boy repeated.

"That's right. My first name is Howard. My last name is Flynn. Your first name is Danny. Your last name is?"

There was a flash of recognition in his eyes, the look someone gets when they first realize that something is not where it is supposed to be and that they might have lost it. He shook his head. "Danny," he said again. It was the only name he knew, and perhaps the only name he had.

For half an hour I watched, an interested observer, while Howard Flynn did his best to learn where Danny had come from and what he knew about the man who had given him the knife. Flynn was as gentle, as patient, as it was possible to be, but it made no difference: Danny seemed to know nothing about his past. As innocent as the child he was, he lived in the moment, a moment that for him had no beginning and no end. He remembered me, and he remembered we had been together in a room, but he could not have said whether it had happened that morning or a year ago. When Flynn had lit that match, it did not just remind him of when he had been burned all over his body with a cigarette: It was the same event. Time did not exist. Everything that happened—everything that happened to him— was now.

Though none of our other questions had been answered, we had gotten his name, and that at least was a start. We had gotten something else as well: the knowledge that this was a case we had to win. It was always more difficult to defend someone you were certain was innocent: You could not comfort yourself with the thought that justice had been done if you lost. But this was worse. Danny was not just innocent, he was helpless. We were all he had. It hit Flynn harder than it hit me. When we left he was as angry as I had ever seen him.

"They should hang people like that!" he growled as we made our way to the front entrance. "And I don't mean by the neck, either!"

I thought I knew whom he meant, but just to be sure, I asked, "The people who burned him with cigarettes?"

"Yeah," he muttered under his breath. His arm shot straight out in front of him and hit the door with such force I was afraid his hand was going to go right through the glass. At almost the same spot where we had stood talking together before, he stopped still. "Forget about that son of a bitch Jeffries. Forget about the guy who killed him," he said, shaking his head impatiently. "Forget about whether he might have known Elliott Winston. Forget about the state hospital. Unless we find out who gave the kid the knife, we haven't got anything." He paused and stared hard at me. "You have to find out, and there's only one way left to do it."

People were swarming all around us. It was a few minutes past five and the sidewalks were filling up as civil servants walked quickly to the parking lots where they had left their cars or headed a few blocks across town to catch the light rail.

"You think the psychologist can get more out of him than you did?"

Flynn nodded, but his mind was on something else. "He'll learn some things from him. He may learn quite a lot." He worked his jaw back and forth, then he stopped and scratched his chin, a distant look in his eye. "He won't learn that, though. The kid doesn't know."

"Then who?"

His eyes came back into focus. "The people he lived with."

"Under the bridge?"

"Exactly."

"Well," I said skeptically, "we can try. But half of them are probably mentals and the rest are probably addicts or drunks."

On the other hand, we had nothing to lose. "All right," I agreed, "if you think it's worth the chance. When do you want to go?"

For the first time since we had left the jail, Flynn seemed to relax. He greeted my question as if I had just broken my own world record for stupidity. It was all he could do not to roll his eyes or laugh in my face. "Sure, why not? Let's just go down there right now, two guys in coats and ties."

Now I realized what he had in mind—or I thought I did. "You want to go undercover: pretend you're one of the homeless—one of them?"

"No," he said, looking away as he dragged out the sound. "Not exactly."

For a few moments we did not say anything, and then I knew. "You want me . . . ?"

"I can't do it," he said, turning to me. Earnestly, he shook his head. "I can't. I can't spend three or four nights—I can't even spend one night—by myself with people who are drinking. I'm sorry. I couldn't do it." He looked down at the sidewalk and sighed. "But I will if you want," he said, lifting his head.

He meant it, and I knew it, and I could never let it happen. "All right," I said with a rueful glance, "I'll do it. But only after the psychologist sees Danny."

"He'll do it first thing tomorrow."

"You said you hadn't talked to him yet."

"I haven't," he replied as if that was an answer. "This will be a great experience for you," he said cheerfully. We turned and began to walk and he again put his arm around my shoulder. "You remember that time Jeffries put you in jail for the weekend? Look at it like that: You might not like it much, but think of all the stories you'll have to tell."

I thought about that after I left him at the corner and headed back to the office: not what it would be like to pass myself off as one of the homeless, but what it had been like spending three nights in the county jail. Three nights—and I had never forgotten it! One weekend all those years ago, and as vivid as if it had happened last week or the week before. Three nights! How many nights are there in twelve years, the length of time Elliott Winston had already spent locked up in an asylum for the criminally insane? I could list the numbers and make a rough estimate of the result, but I could not do the multiplication, not in my head, not without a calculator or at least a pencil and paper. If I had been at the state hospital I could have asked Elliott's friend, the former high school history teacher somehow given the gift for mathematics by his own insanity.

Somewhere behind me a voice called my name. I stopped and turned around, but I did not see anyone I recognized among the crowd of faces that moved past me on the sidewalk. The voice called again, but I still could not find who it was.

"Here," Jennifer said, laughing. She was sitting in her car, parked at the curb just a few feet away. The top was down. "You looked like you were in a trance. Have you been sleepwalking?"

"No," I replied, embarrassed. I took a step toward the car, then stopped and looked back over my shoulder. We were directly in front of my building. If she had not called out to me, I might have walked right past it.

"You told me to pick you up in front at quarter past five," she said as I got in. "Did you forget?"

"No, I didn't forget. I was thinking about something." As we drove off, I remembered the look—that trancelike look—Elliott had on his face when I first saw him at the hospital. "You ever do that?" I asked her. "Think about something and forget where you are?"

Jennifer glanced across at me, a puzzled expression on her face.

"I don't mean when you were sick," I said, touching the back of her neck. But I realized that that was exactly what I meant. "Is that what it's like—you don't know where you are?"

She looked straight ahead, steering through the downtown traffic. Dressed in a white short-sleeve blouse and a green and blue cotton skirt, she looked young and pretty, eighteen years old all over again, and both of us certain that nothing bad could ever happen. A faint smile flickered across her mouth. She lifted her head and bit her lip; and then she turned to me and her eyes seemed to beg forgiveness. "I can't," she murmured.

She stared ahead at the road, and with a quick turn of her wrist shifted down to the next gear and gunned the car through a yellow light at the intersection just before the bridge.

I tried to get her mind off the past. "We're passing over my new home," I said brightly.

She passed the back of her hand over her eyes and cleared her throat. "What?" she asked, forcing herself to smile.

"Yeah, it's true," I said with a cocky grin. "It's my new home. Right down there," I added, jabbing my finger in front of her. "Under the bridge. It's Flynn's idea."

Jennifer listened intently while I explained what I was going to do and why there did not seem to be any other choice. I was not quite prepared for her response. Instead of trying to talk me out of it; instead of telling me how much she was going to worry about me; instead of reminding me that I was a lawyer and not a private detective; she thought it was a perfectly wonderful idea and tried to invite herself along.

"If you just suddenly show up—I don't care how much of a homeless person you make yourself look—you're still a stranger and they're not going to trust you. But if there are two of us—a homeless couple—that makes sense. It happens all the time. You see couples holding up cardboard signs saying they'll work for food. We could be like that," she said eagerly.

On the other side of the bridge, her eyes darting all around, she merged into the freeway traffic and then crossed over into the lane that, a little farther on, connected to the highway that led east along the Columbia.

It was out of the question. She was not going with me. "It's too dangerous," I said quietly, and then started to laugh at the way I sounded, all self-assured and protective, as if it had been my idea instead of Flynn's.

She waited until I stopped. "So you rather I went alone?"

"Flynn told me I had to do it. By the way, where are we going?"

"Oh, I don't know. I thought maybe we could drive out along the river, maybe go a ways into the gorge."

We drove along the shore of the great slow-moving river as it cut its way through the tree-covered cliffs of the gorge, changing color from gray to silver and then, finally, as the sun slanted in the stillness of dusk across the far edge of the horizon, a deep purple mixed with gold. The river ran forever, through the rough red rocks of the high windblown desert; through wheat fields that flowed under a yellow sun and cloudless skies and clear starry nights in places where a tree had never grown; through high mountains that had risen from the earth thousands of years after the river had already begun to run out to the sea; through the flatlands and low-lying hills where another river joined and where a city had been built and a handful of generations had lived their lives and died their deaths. Always changing and always the same, the river carried us back and carried us forward, and gave us the feeling that though we could never quite put it into words, we knew something important, something that had value.

We stopped at a restaurant with a view of a narrow steel suspension bridge and the green black hills of Washington on the other side. We ate hamburgers that came in red plastic baskets covered with white wax paper and slapped ketchup over the French fries and drank Cokes out of Coke glasses with straws. Every few minutes, Jennifer would reach across and wipe my mouth with her paper napkin.

"You sure you want to do this? Get married in a year?"

Holding it with both hands, her teeth had just sunk into the hamburger. "Why?" she asked, almost choking as she swallowed hard and tried not to laugh. "Are you having second thoughts?"

"Second thoughts? I haven't had first thoughts. I've been in love with you all my life, but until you came back I didn't think about it very often. It's like breathing. Most of the time you don't know you're doing it."

Her hands were in her lap under the table, and she was looking up at me, making fun of me with her eyes, while she drank Coke through a straw. She finished what little was left in the glass and kept sucking on it, laughing with her eyes at the sound she made, waiting to see my reaction. I signaled the waitress to bring her a new one.

"Got a quarter?" Jennifer asked. I found one in my pocket and she went to the old-fashioned jukebox that stood against the wall on the other side. I watched her tap her foot as she searched for something she wanted to hear. She came back to the table and held out her hand. I looked around, hesitant. "Come on," she insisted.

" 'Chances Are'?" I asked, laughing quietly as we began to dance on the linoleum floor in front of the jukebox.

We moved together to the music, a few steps one way and a few steps back. She let go of my hand and wrapped both arms around my neck, and both of mine went around her waist. At a booth a few feet away, two teenage boys nudged each other. The girls they were with first scolded them with their eyes so they wouldn't laugh and then, because they were young and sentimental and still dreamed that love could last, turned and watched themselves.

When it was over, Jennifer went to the cash register, got change for a dollar, and played it again. She wanted to do it a third time, but I pulled her away and we went back to our table and she drank some more Coke and teased me again with her wide laughing eyes.

"It wasn't like breathing for me," she said, peering down at the glass as she twisted the straw through crushed ice. "I thought about you much more often than that. I thought about you a lot when I was in the hospital." She raised her eyes until her gaze met mine. "I tried to think of why I was there. They told me it was because of some chemical imbalance in the brain, that it was something physical, that it could happen to anyone. But it didn't happen to anyone: It happened to me—and I kept thinking maybe it wouldn't have happened if my life had been different, if I'd been married to someone I was in love with. How could I have been depressed if I had been happy?" She paused and, reaching across the table, ran her fingertips down the side of my face. "I kept thinking I wouldn't be there, in that awful place, if I'd been married to you."

Slowly, her head came up straight and she sat perfectly erect, and perfectly still. "Is that what you want, Joey?" she asked, measuring each word. "After all this time. Are you sure that's what you want—just to be with me?"

I nodded toward her nearly empty glass. "Drink your Coke. We have to get out of here. It's a long drive home."

I waited until she bent her head over the glass and took the tip of the straw in her mouth.

"I'm going to ask you this just once. Will you marry me? Not next year, or next month. Just, will you marry me?"

Her eyes still on the glass, she began to smile. Then she looked up.

"Yes."

That is all that was said, all that had to be said. We sat there for a few more minutes while she finished her Coke and I wondered why marriage, as opposed to simply living together, had assumed such an importance in my mind. We were past the age when marriage meant children. Perhaps it was a way to show defiance to the long years we had been apart. I suppose it would also put a period to the sentence that would seem to strangers to explain our lives: "We fell in love, and then we were married."

Jennifer finished her Coke, and I helped her up from the table. "We can always tell people we had a very long engagement," she said with a smile. Suddenly, her head shuddered and her eyes flashed with pain. She gripped my hand with all her strength. "I'm all right," she said, trying to apologize. "I'm just tired, and it hit me kind of fast."

By the time we got to the car, she seemed fine, but when I insisted on driving she did not object. As we drove through the darkness, she curled up beside me and was fast asleep before we had gone more than a mile.

The next morning, Helen, as usual, followed me into my office, a high-heeled tap dance accompanied by shouted instructions about what I was supposed to be doing.

"I finally reached Dr. Friedman's office down at the state hospital. He's out of town this week and won't be back until Monday. I said we'd call back." Helen looked at her notebook and found the next item on her list. "The records clerk called from the courthouse. The file on the Elliott Winston case came over from Archives. You can look at it anytime you want." Her eyes went back to the notebook.

"I'm getting married, Helen."

"Somebody named . . . ?" She looked up, puzzled, and for a moment searched my eyes. The tiny lines at the corners of her eyes and the lines at the corners of her mouth seemed to fade away. She dropped into the chair and put her hand on her heart. "Really?" she asked. Her eyes sparkled and a huge grin spread across her face. "To the girl you wanted to marry, years ago, the one you went to high school with?"

I could not remember ever having told her about that, but it did not surprise me that she knew. She started to say something and then, changing her mind, came around the desk and kissed me on the cheek. There was an awkward silence, and then, because that kiss had said everything there was to say, she offered a few words of congratulations and I replied with a few words of thanks.

"I have a lot to do today," I said finally. "I don't know if I'll have a chance to see that file or not. Would you call the records clerk back and ask if they would hang on to it for a while."

A few minutes later, I heard Helen on the phone. There was one thing I could find out without going to the courthouse and reading it in the file. I picked up the line and asked the records clerk to tell me the name of the attorney who had represented

Elliott Winston. She told me and I asked once more to make sure I had heard her right, and one more time after that because I still did not believe it.

"But Asa Bartram never practiced criminal law in his life," I said, as if this was something the clerk would either know or have reason to care about.

"Sorry," I said, more baffled than ever by what had happened, and more certain than ever that it was somehow the answer to everything.

Twenty-one

Now that we were to be married, Jennifer moved in with me and we spent five days alone together, trying not to talk too much about the things we had missed. Middle-aged, all the glamour gone, we spent the passion we had left and learned the gentler sentiments of love.

Early the next Sunday evening we left the house I would never again live in alone and drove down the long sloping driveway, through the open iron gate to the street below. She could not stop laughing.

"You look just awful!"

"This is how I earn my living," I said, deadpan. "The law is a noble profession."

"Try going to court looking like that."

"I did—once," I replied.

She nodded. "The time you went to jail. I wasn't there to see it, but—trust me—you look a lot worse now. You'll probably get picked up by the police and put in jail again."

She drove me into town and dropped me off on a dark corner next to a small park, a block away from a mission where the homeless could sometimes get a meal and a bed.

"Are you going to be warm enough?" she asked as I opened

the door. "There's a chill in the air. It's going to get cold tonight." She stared at me with large, melancholy eyes. "Look at you! We haven't even lived together a week, and you don't shave, you dress like a bum, and you make up the most outrageous excuse any woman ever heard about why you have to spend the night away from home."

"You going to be all right?" I asked as I leaned over to kiss her goodbye.

She held me for a long time, laughing quietly about how rough my face felt with its scraggly five-day growth, teasing me that I smelled too good to pass for homeless. When she was certain I did not want to go, she pretended she did not mind and with one last kiss let me leave. With my hands shoved into the pockets of an old, ragged, oversize wool coat, I watched her drive away and then, when she was gone, turned around and walked slowly into the night.

There was at first a feeling of adventure, like someone starting out on a voyage, when danger and hardship still seem like a romance, and hunger and thirst are things you talk about on a full stomach. I was doing this to find out what I could about who had killed Quincy Griswald and then given the murder weapon to someone who would not be able to explain where it had come from. But deep down I also wanted to know what it was like to live like this: homeless and abandoned, surrounded by things you could not have and people who, when they saw you coming, would cross the street to get away.

It was not yet completely dark. A man and a woman coming from the opposite direction saw me and moved as far away on the sidewalk as they could. I went right for them and held out my hand.

"Spare change?" I asked in a harsh, rasping voice. My head rolled to the side and my chin sagged down to my chest. "Haven't had anything to eat all day," I said, pleading with my eyes.

He did what I probably would have done. He put his arm around her and tried to shelter her with his shoulder. She was pretty and well dressed, and as they hurried past she looked at me with loathing and disgust.

I had gotten away with it and I felt a thrill of exhilaration. "All right," I yelled after them in my normal voice, "if you don't have any change, how about the keys to the BMW?"

The man shot a glance at me over his shoulder and then quickened his step, afraid I might follow.

I crossed the street to the mission and studied the dead eyes of the men who were sprawled against the front brick wall near the entrance, waiting for it to open, as I walked past them and turned the corner. Cheap hotels with dirty windows and dimly lit bars with shadows sliding slowly across the floor; hookers in short tight dresses and junkies with vapid smug smiles and pock-marked faces; fat men with fat wallets ready to buy a good time, and haggard tired women no one wanted trying to forget they had no one waiting at home: This was the world I now entered instead of my own.

In an alleyway behind an adult bookstore I rummaged through the trash cans and watched the people who came in and out the back entrance, and realized I had become invisible. A girl in a black leather miniskirt led a short, paunchy man out the door, watched with calculating eyes while he counted out the money, tucked it in her bra, and then got down on her knees in front of him and did what she had been paid for. When she finished, she watched him walk nervously down the alley toward the side-walk, and then turned to me, searching through the garbage less than ten feet away.

"I'll bet you wish you could have some," she said with a smirk, and then disappeared inside.

I had just bent down to look inside the next garbage can when, suddenly, I went flying over it, and landed in a heap on the other side, buried under the trash that collapsed on top of me. Twisting around, I pulled my head up, tried to get to my feet, and was shoved back. A hulking wreck of a human being, with stinking breath and a slobbering mouth that looked like it bred corruption, was waving his arm at me and pointing a finger at his chest.

"This is yours?" I asked, as I scrambled sideways to get beyond his reach. "Yours?" I asked, nodding. I kept moving, and kept repeating the same question, letting him know that my trespass was entirely inadvertent. "Sorry," I said when I was far enough away from him to risk struggling to my feet. I backed down the alley, apologizing, and then, when I was safe, turned around and walked away as quickly as I could.

Late that night I made my way to the Morrison Street Bridge. I dragged a few rotting pieces of cardboard I found under the bushes, and crawled underneath this makeshift blanket. The ground was hard, cold, jagged with rocks, and each time I turned over there were only a few moments of relief before I started to hurt in a new place. I hardly slept at all that night, and never for very long. Though I could not clearly see more than a few of them when I first arrived, I could sense that there were breathing bodies scattered all around. Years had passed, but the memory I had of the nights spent in the county jail was still vivid in my mind. This was not like that. No one cried out; no one moaned or whimpered or cursed; no one made a noise, nothing, except the heavy rolling sound of people who were sleeping in their own beds, the only ones they knew.

I did not think I had slept at all, but when I opened my eyes the sun was out and the traffic on the bridge overhead was deafening. My mouth felt like glue and my teeth hurt. I climbed out from under the cardboard blanket and looked around. Down at the edge of the river, two men stood side by side, urinating. Off to the side, sitting on his haunches, another man soaked his shirt and then wrung it out with his hands. On the shadows next to the concrete pilings, four men were gathered around a small fire, warming their hands while water boiled in a blue aluminum pot. No one moved aside to let me in, and I stood a few feet away. The one who had been doing his laundry in the river came back, carrying his shirt in his hand.

"Let him in," he said as he sat down in the circle. "Come on," he insisted when at first I did not move. They made room, and I joined them. No one said anything, and looking at them, dull-eyed and lethargic, I wondered how many knew how.

"It's the best coffee in town," the man said, urging me to drink it. My eye darted to the river behind him. He shook his head. "The water came from a fountain. I fill my canteen."

I wondered if, with that careless glance, I had given myself away. With a blank look, as if I had no idea why he thought he had to explain something so obvious, I tried to cover my mistake. My eye still on him, I took a drink, and almost gagged on the rancid taste. He watched me for a moment longer, and then, smiling to himself, lowered his gaze.

No one said anything, not to me, not to anyone. They sat in a circle, drinking that awful brew, made, I discovered later, from the used coffee grinds found in the garbage behind one of my favorite restaurants. Then, a few minutes later, as if by some silent signal that passed my notice, they got to their feet and, without a word, drifted off in different directions.

The one who had given me the cup lingered behind. "You coming back tonight?" he asked.

I let him know with a look that it was none of his business what I did. If he thought my belligerence a threat, he did not show it. He reached inside his overcoat pocket and brought out a half-pint bottle of whiskey and offered it to me.

"Suit yourself," he said when I refused. Removing the cap, he took a short swig and wiped his mouth with the back of his tattered, greasy sleeve. "Helps keep the coffee down," he explained as he shoved the bottle back in his pocket.

I started to walk away. "You can come with me, if you want," he said. I stopped and looked back. He had already turned and was heading along a path that led under the bridge and came up on the other side. I followed behind and when we reached the top, he moved a bush aside and pulled out a rusty shopping cart heaped with black garbage bags stuffed full. Craning his neck, he squinted up at the glaring white sky. His lips pressed tight together, he moved his mouth back and forth while he made up his mind. Opening the bag on top, he dug out an olive green army camouflage jacket. He took off the overcoat, rolled it into a ball, and shoved it as far down in the basket as it would go and then put on the jacket.

We worked our way through town, stopping at every trash basket. A division of labor soon developed between master and apprentice: I pushed the cart, and each time we halted, he did a thorough search, deciding what was useless and what had value. He always found something, a bottle, a can, something that could be turned into cash. When we reached the park behind the courthouse, I remembered the two men I had seen there late at night, doing what we were doing now, my own life somehow prefigured in that dreamlike apparition from the past.

On the sidewalk outside the courthouse entrance, afraid I might be recognized, I left my newfound friend and partner to rummage through the wire mesh trash baskets alone. I stood off to the side, next to a lamppost at the curb, watching people I knew at least vaguely going in and out the doors. Hunching my shoulders, I pulled the flaps of the cap I was wearing farther down over my ears. I ran my fingers over my beard and felt a little more confident that at least at a distance no one would know it was me.

He finished with the one basket and looked around to see where I was. I was about to catch up with him when someone bumped into me from behind. Instinctively, I turned around, and found myself face-to-face with Cassandra Loescher, the deputy district attorney who was prosecuting the case. She had been talking to someone, not paying attention to where she was going, and when she knocked into me had spilled the paper coffee cup she was carrying in her hand.

"Damn it!" she cried, holding the cup out in front of her. She started to apologize, but as soon as she saw me all she could think about was getting away. I reached out to help, but she dropped the cup on the sidewalk and walked rapidly up the courthouse steps.

Emboldened, I took a position next to the steps, held out my filthy hand, and studied the various ways in which the people I asked for money averted their gaze and tried to avoid making an answer. Two otherwise fair-minded judges treated me with open contempt, one of them complaining loudly to the other that it was bad enough this sort of thing went on in the public park and disgraceful that it was allowed in front of a public building. Defense lawyers sneered and turned away when I asked them if they could help one of the indigent. Harper Bryce, his reporter's notebook sticking out of his suit coat pocket, ambled past me, on his way to cover yet another trial. He stopped, turned back, reached into his pants pocket, gave me all the change he had, and without once looking at me, disappeared inside. I opened my hand, counted seventy-eight cents, and felt like a wealthy man.

I caught up with my nameless friend and his shopping cart a block away and, while he searched through a basket, stood ready to push when it was time to move on to the next one. All day long we did this, drifting from one street to the next, taking what no one wanted, until the cart groaned under a mountain of debris and I had to lean my shoulder into it to keep it going. I never did know what he did with it. At a corner near the mission, he took over control of the cart, and made me wait while he pushed it down an alleyway. When he came back a few minutes later, he had emptied the cart of everything we had picked up during the day. He took out of his pocket an old coin purse and gave me three one-dollar bills, the wages of a scavenger's helper. He snapped the purse shut and put it in his pocket, and from the same place pulled out the half-pint bottle. Thrusting it toward me, he held it still until I shook my head and then, with his head thrown back, guzzled a mouthful. He smacked his lips while he screwed the cap on and slipped the flat bottle back into his coat pocket.

We made our way through back streets and alleyways to the

bridge, pushing the cart ahead of us, staring into the distance in a dull-witted daze. I had lived homeless only a night and a day and already the edge seemed to be off all existence. My senses were numbed and the only things that had meaning were the simple necessities of survival. Homeless, I was learning, meant more than not having a place of your own: It meant having nothing of your own—no friends, no family, no one you could talk to, no one you could trust. I could go home whenever I wanted, and I could only wonder at how it must feel to know that you could not.

"How long have you been doing this?" I asked when he finished hiding the cart in the bushes on the side of the bridge.

He studied me, suspicion in his eyes. "Long enough." He turned and walked down the path that led under the bridge, the dull echo of the traffic throbbing overhead.

The pieces of cardboard I had used as a bed and a blanket were still where I had left them, and so strong is the instinct for possession, I felt a sense of relief that no one had taken what I now considered my own. There was no one else around, and after he had gone down to the edge of the river, where he took off his shoes and washed out his socks, he climbed barefoot back to where I was sitting. He lowered himself down beside me, wrapped his arms around his knees, and watched the slow-moving brown water flow past.

"Are you an undercover cop?" he asked in a flat voice that seemed not to care one way or the other.

He had guessed wrong, but the fact that he had guessed at all told me that I had failed. "No," I replied.

"When you came here last night, the others wanted to roll you."

"Roll me?"

"Yeah. Whack you over the head, take whatever you had. I told them they better not, that you might be a cop."

I looked down at my shoes. A beetle was crawling across the toe and down the other side. The gravel gave way and it tumbled over on its back, legs flailing helplessly in the air. With a flick of my fingernail I flipped it right side up and watched it scramble to safety.

"When you live on the streets you know better than to show up some place for the first time after dark." He reached in his pocket for the whiskey bottle. "And besides that, you don't move right: You're too quick, too nimble. You're not one of us." He took a drink and offered it to me.

I took it from him, wiped the opening with the heel of my hand, and put it up to my mouth. It ran down my throat like fire and acid, and for a moment I thought it had burned away my larynx and left me without the power of speech. A second surge scalded my nostrils and flamed out of my ears.

"Thanks," I said, gritting my teeth as I handed the bottle back to him. "And thanks for last night. But I'm not an undercover cop. Why would a cop come here?" I asked, poking at the dirt.

"You're not a cop? Why are your clothes so new?"

"Why don't you mind your own damn business," I said, pretending to be angry. "You didn't want to tell me how long you'd lived like this, but I'm supposed to tell you? Who the hell are you, anyway?"

He made no reply. Instead, he passed the bottle back to me. I had no choice, not if I wanted to keep him there, talking. I took another drink, and this time it did not burn quite so much.

"They come once in a while, looking for drugs. They came a week ago, a whole bunch of them, just swooped in on us. We weren't doing nothing. They took away a guy because he had a knife. They said he killed somebody with it. They're all nuts." He scratched the side of his face and took the bottle out of my hands. There was not much left in it, and he finished that with one last gulp. "Have to get more tonight," he said matter-of-factly.

A couple of other homeless men appeared at the far side of the bridge and wandered down to the riverbank. "You better not stay here tonight," he warned me. "Better move on. Find another place."

"I'll stay here if I want," I insisted, tossing a contemptuous look at the pair down at the river. "The guy with the knife didn't kill anyone?" I asked, trying to sound indifferent.

He tapped the side of his head. "Feebleminded. We looked after him, best we could. It wasn't even his knife."

Looking out across the river, I picked up a rock and sent it sailing into the water. I picked up another one. "So whose knife was it?" I asked as I sent it on its way.

There was no answer, and I looked back over my shoulder. He was watching me, a grotesque grin on his face. "You sure you're not a cop?"

I found another rock. "Go screw yourself," I grunted as I let it fly. I looked back at him and waited.

"A little guy with crazy eyes. He stayed here a couple of days— started getting real friendly with the feebleminded kid. We caught him one night. He had the kid's pants down and he was—you know—trying to do things to him. We sent him on his way."

"Sent him on his way?"

"Yeah, we threw him in the river," he explained.

"What happened to him—after you threw him in the river?"

He looked at me and then shrugged. "Don't know. Didn't see him get out."

I fought back the panic that swelled up inside me. Whoever had given Danny the knife had disappeared and was probably dead. We did not even know his name, and the only witness I had that he had ever existed was a homeless drunk who had probably killed him.

"We were pretty tired of that jerk anyway," I heard him saying. "Always going around mumbling to himself, and then every time he had to take a leak coming up to me to ask if it was all right. I'm telling you: The guy was nuts. He was nuts; the cops are nuts; everybody's nuts. I gotta go get another bottle," he said without a pause. He struggled to his feet. "You want to come?"

I walked with him to a liquor store and told him before he went in that I wanted him to get me something, too. I put a few folded-up bills in his hand and said I would wait outside. As I walked away, I wondered what he would end up buying when he discovered that I had given him a couple of twenties instead of a couple of ones.

Though it called itself a city, Portland, or at least that part of it that had stayed on the same side of the river, was no larger than a New York neighborhood. You could walk from one end of it to the other in less than twenty minutes. I was at Howard Flynn's place in less than ten.

The curtains were open, but it was dark inside. Flynn lived alone and never went out, except to an AA meeting or when one of his friends called for help. I climbed the steep stairs to the unlighted front door and for the first time all day suddenly felt tired. I leaned my forehead against the heavy wooden front door and pressed the bell. I let go, waited, and when I heard no sound inside, punched it again. There was still no response. With one last short burst on the bell, I pushed myself away from the door and sank down on the top step, heavy with fatigue.

At first I thought it was the passing headlights of a car, and shut my eyes to avoid the glare. Then I heard the dead bolt turn, and reaching for the railing above me I struggled to my feet.

Standing in the doorway, thick, hairy legs protruding below a threadbare flannel robe tied together with a cotton belt that did not match, Howard Flynn blinked into the harsh overhead light. He took one look at me and shook his head.

"How did you know it was me?" I asked as he shut the door behind us.

He turned on the light in the small entryway and looked at me from head to toe. "Why?" he asked with a shrug. "Because you're not wearing a tie?"

"What took you so long to answer the door?" I asked irritably as I followed him into the kitchen.

"I kept hoping whoever it was would go away." He paused and cleared his throat. "Actually, I was watching television and I didn't hear it at first," he confessed.

"How could you not hear that goddamn thing? It makes as much noise as an electrocution, for Christ sake," I grumbled.

"For a homeless guy, you're pretty damn pushy, aren't you? Sit down," he ordered. "I'll make you some coffee. You look like you could use it."

While Flynn carefully measured three level teaspoons of ground coffee into a paper filter, I waited at a small Formica table that looked onto a square atrium. A glass bowl of artificial fruit—yellow wax bananas, and red wax apples, and green and purple glass grapes—was right in the center where it always was. A bite mark on the side of the apple, left by the teeth of a disappointed child of a long forgotten friend, made all of it seem more real. Flynn poured water in the top of the coffeemaker and turned it on.

"That friend of mine—the psychologist—saw Danny." He stared into the glass pot, watching as first one drop, then another slowly formed and then fell, coating the glass bottom with a dark turgid liquid. "Turns out he isn't retarded after all—not in the usual sense, anyway. Fox thinks he's about twenty-three or -four. Can't be sure, exactly. Danny doesn't know. He lived somewhere—out in the country, near a river. Fox thinks it might have been somewhere down around Roseburg or Grants Pass."

The coffee kept dripping down, gradually increasing speed until it turned into a fine-flowing stream.

"His mother might have been retarded. She wasn't married—he didn't have a father that he knew—but there were always men around. He was abused, probably starting when he was just an infant: sexual things, physical things, mean, perverted, awful things. Fox thinks the burn marks weren't the half of it."

Turning around, Flynn put his hands on the counter behind him, looked at me, a grim expression on his face, and then stared down at the floor. "He never went to school; he never went anywhere. When he wasn't locked in a room he was chained like a dog in the backyard."

Flynn raised his eyes. "You can't really blame the mother. You ever know a girl like that when you were a kid, a girl who was a little slow, a little backward: a girl guys knew how to take advantage of? That's probably what you had here: A girl, young and retarded, who didn't have any parents of her own, finds herself pregnant, has the kid at home, lives from hand to mouth, becomes the punchboard for every lowlife in the county, and then one of these creeps starts getting his kicks with the kid."

Suddenly, from out of nowhere, an orange cat with a torn ear and a thick stump where its tail had once been bounded onto my lap and then onto the table. Like a boxer throwing a jab, Flynn flicked out his hand, grabbed the cat by the scruff of the neck, and sent it flying out of the room.

"Nomo isn't supposed to get on the table," he explained as he poured the coffee.

It was hard to know whether to be more astonished at how much speed Flynn still had in his hands or at the distance the cat had sailed before it landed, without so much as a whimper, somewhere down the hall.

"Nomo?" I asked.

Flynn handed me a mug of coffee and sat down on the other chair. "Yeah. Stands for Nomellini. You remember Leo Nomellini—played for the San Francisco 49ers back in the fifties? Leo 'The Lion' Nomellini?"

I did not remember, if I had ever known, but I was not surprised Flynn had.

"You named the cat after Leo Nomellini because he looks like a lion?"

Flynn rolled his eyes. "I named him after Nomellini because he's big and stupid."

It was the lawyer in me: Every answer was the invitation to a question. "How do you know Nomellini was big and stupid?"

"He was a defensive tackle," he explained patiently. "By definition he was big and stupid."

"Weren't you a defensive tackle?"

Flynn nodded. "Which means I know what I'm talking about," he said as he got to his feet.

I followed him down a short, narrow hallway to the smaller of the two bedrooms, the room which as long as I had known him had served as both a study and a guest room. A desk, a chair, a television set, and a beige sofa that made into a bed were the only furnishings. Turning off the television, Flynn sat down at the desk and thumbed through a stack of manila folders.

Flynn had loosened the cotton belt that held his robe together. Sitting on the wooden chair behind the desk that was really nothing more than a plain wooden door resting on cement blocks, the tattered ends of the robe lay in a heap on the rose-colored carpet. He was wearing a white T-shirt and a pair of blue and white striped boxer shorts underneath. The folds of skin around his eyes were thick and puffy, the way they are on the face of a fighter years after he has left the ring. His mouth moved silently as he read the names of the files through which he searched.

"I just had it here," he mumbled to himself. "Here it is," he said, as he pulled out a thin report, the pages of which were fastened together with a blue plastic paper clip, and handed it to me. "A lot of it is guesswork, but I don't think it's too far from right. The kid never went to school, never had a friend, never had anyone to talk to. He's not retarded, not in the clinical sense. There's nothing wrong with his mind. He's socially retarded; he's what you would expect to get if you locked a baby in a room and didn't let him out except to be mistreated for the first fourteen or fifteen years of his life. Except for one thing," Flynn said, shaking his head with a kind of wonder. "There's nothing vicious about him. He's an innocent. He's like a dog people keep kicking and he still comes back, hoping that maybe this time someone will treat him with a little kindness," he said, using the same analogy I had used when I tried to explain to Jennifer what the boy was like.

Flynn took a deep breath and, wearily, let it out. At the sound of it, I felt again my own fatigue. Sinking against the corner of the sofa, I let my feet slide out across the carpet until I caught sight of my own filthy, mud-encrusted shoes. "Sorry," I began to apologize as I sat up.

Lost in thought, Flynn did not hear me. My eye moved behind him to a photograph barely visible on the shelf behind his chair. Like the bowl of artificial fruit in the kitchen, the tarnished silver frame was always in the same spot.

"How old would he be now?" I asked in a voice that was more like a whisper.

He did not turn around, and I wondered if he ever looked at it anymore: that picture of the bright-eyed little boy held in the powerful arms of his young father.

A clumsy smile came and went and came again. "Twenty-nine last month. Hard to believe, isn't it: where all the time has gone?" His eyes looked past me into the distance. Then he got to his feet, tied the belt around his waist, and opened the closet door. "I've got some clothes you can wear. Why don't you take a shower, get cleaned up, and I'll drive you home. You don't want to show up looking like that," he said with a gentle laugh.

Halfway up the drive the porch light came on and Jennifer, wearing a knee-length cotton nightgown, dashed out and began to wave. The headlights swept past her as Flynn pulled up in front. Darting barefoot down the darkened steps, she threw herself into my arms as I got out of the car.

"I didn't think you'd be home for days." Standing on her tiptoes, her arms around my neck, she ran her hand over the side of my face. "You shaved."

"Say hello to Howard Flynn," I said, as I opened the back door of the car.

Her arms behind her back, Jennifer looked across the passenger seat. "Hello, Howard Flynn. Thank you for bringing my derelict home."

Reaching inside, I gathered up the thick bundle of clothing I had worn during my brief sojourn as one of the homeless. Out of the corner of my eye, I watched Flynn's face color slightly as he became formal and awkward, trying to be polite.

Dragging the bundle behind me, my arm around her waist, we walked up the steps to the porch and watched the lights of the car recede into the distance as Flynn drove down the drive and out the gate. Inside, Jennifer took the bundle from my hand, dropped it to the floor, and kissed me on the mouth. I gathered her up in my arms and climbed the stairs to the bedroom. She slid under the sheets and started teasing me about my borrowed oversize clothes, and then, after I had taken them off, she turned off the lamp.

We made love with a new intensity, and when it was over, and we lay together in the moonlight that splashed through the bedroom window, she put her hand in mine and touched my soul. "The only thing I want is to live with you and to die with you, live together, die together, just us, the way we said it would be. Remember?"

I remembered when we first said it, and I said it again, the same words, the same promises, but it was not the same. We had lived separate lives, and we knew that what we had promised before—that we could never survive apart—had been, not a lie, but something that had not been true. In the innocence of our youth we had believed love and death the only real alternatives, and had come to learn that life was neither so simple nor so kind.

Curling her arm around my neck, she held me as tight as she could. "Just love me, love me forever . . . please."

I put my arm around her and spread my fingers on the small of her back, and tried to relieve the tension that was running rigid through her. Her hard, sobbing breath began to slow down, and after a while I could barely feel her heart beating against me; and then, a little later, her hand let go of my neck and her arm slid down onto my shoulder. For a long time I watched her sleep, wondering about the way the most important things seem to come about by chance, and whether chance might be nothing more than a word we hide behind when we don't want to believe that everything has been decided by fate.

The next morning I found Jennifer dancing around the kitchen, humming to herself as she put dishes away with one hand and rinsed off a pot with the other. Both hands moving at once, she kissed me lightly on the cheek and ordered me to sit down at the table. I squinted at her through eyes still filled with sleep, staggered to the coffeemaker, and poured myself a cup. She watched with amused indulgence as I dragged myself over to the table and collapsed into a chair. Jennifer slid into the chair opposite, and with a pensive expression drank coffee from her cup. "Tell me about Howard Flynn," she said presently.

"Flynn? He's a private investigator. A long time ago he was a lawyer," I said, my gaze drifting across the kitchen to the windows that let in the yellow morning light.

"You told me once that he was disbarred because he came to court drunk and said some things he shouldn't have."

My eyes came back to her. She never seemed to forget anything, no matter what it was and no matter how long ago it might have been said.

"What happened to him?" she asked.

My gaze went back to the window, and I shook my head. "It's a terrible story," I said, reluctant to say more.

"You don't have to tell me if you don't want to."

"It isn't that," I said, as I began to stir the cup with a spoon. "It really is a terrible story, the kind that doesn't have an end."

"Does any story have an end?" Her voice was like a long slow breath that made you want to stay right where you were, listening to her talk. "Our story didn't."

I thought about what she said. "No," I remarked presently, "our story didn't end—it got better—but what happened to Flynn . . .

"Howard Flynn was a great athlete, one of the best high school football players anyone had ever seen. He was six foot three, two hundred sixty-five pounds, with a thick neck and a head like a barrel keg, and quick as a cat. Every college wanted him; everyone told him he'd be an all-American. He was, too, third-string all-American his sophomore year. But Flynn didn't play football because he loved it; he played it because he was good at it and because it paid his way through college. If he had come from a wealthy family, I don't think he would have played at all. Flynn wanted to be a lawyer—from the time he was a kid, that's what he wanted to do.

"He studied all the time, and almost never went out. Howard was a one-man wrecking crew on a football field, but around other people he was quiet, shy, always a gentleman. I don't know, but I'd be surprised if he'd ever had a date in high school. But now he was an all-American, and girls who would not have looked at him twice wanted to be with someone famous. There was one in particular: tiny, not more than five foot two, with flashing black eyes and a cute little smile. Her name was Yvonne Montero and they started going out. Everyone liked Flynn, and everyone thought it was great that he finally had a girl. It didn't matter that she had made it with half the guys in school. Flynn didn't know anything about that, and besides, they were just going out. No one thought it was serious, but of course it was serious. For the first and only time in his life, Howard was in love—the way I was in love with you.

"They got married the day after he graduated, and she probably started fooling around the day after that." I caught myself getting angry and took a deep breath. "To be fair, she worked while he went through law school. Three years later, he passed the bar and got a good job with a pretty good firm. A few months later, she had their baby, a boy, Howard Flynn, Jr. That was the happiest day of Howard Flynn's life—maybe the last really happy day he ever had—the day he first saw his son."

Locking my fingers together on top of my head, I stared out the window, rocking back and forth on the chair.

"What happened?" Jennifer asked, breaking my reverie.

"One day, about two years later, while Flynn was in court arguing a case, his wife was home in bed with another man, someone she had been sleeping with for more than a year. The boy, Howard's son, was asleep in his own room. He woke up and wandered into the living room, looking for his mother. The sliding glass door to the backyard had been left open. She was in the bedroom, making love, when it happened. She never heard her son fall into the pool, never heard him cry for help, never heard anything except the sounds she was making while she cheated on her husband.

"The boy drowned, and Howard died that day as well. He blamed himself. Odd, isn't it, that after what his wife had been doing, Howard would think it was his fault? He thought he should have known that it was too good to last. His wife was having sex with another man in their bed; their son drowns because of it; and Howard thinks that he should have known what she was going to do, and that he could have saved his only child if he had!"

"What about the mother, Howard's wife? Didn't she blame herself?"

"I don't think she was capable of blaming herself. She moved out right away. The last time Flynn saw her was at the funeral. Howard had made all the arrangements himself. He did everything himself. For a while—a few months—he kept to his old routine. He went to work every day and he did his job; he kept his grief to himself. Then something happened, some kind of delayed reaction, I guess. He started to drink and he didn't stop. And then Jeffries started in on him, ridiculing him, humiliating him in open court. Finally, he just said the hell with it and told Jeffries exactly what he thought. He did it drunk, but I think he would have done it sober, there was so much rage and hurt bottled up inside him. It wasn't a question whether he was going to explode, but when, and Jeffries was so incredibly easy to hate."

Jennifer pulled her knees up under her chin and wrapped her arms around them. "Is that why he has such strong feelings about this Danny? Because of what happened to his own boy?"

I did not understand at first, but then, searching her eyes, I began to grasp her meaning. "I hadn't thought of it," I admitted, "but I suppose you must be right. I'm sure he still blames himself; maybe he thinks he can make up for it a little if he can help someone else."

Turned down at the corners, her wide mouth looked like the smile of a brokenhearted child. "Maybe, in a strange way, he thinks this boy is his son. You told me he's a three-year-old in a grown-up's body. He's what Howard's son would be if he hadn't drowned, if he had just disappeared, and then, after all these years, been discovered." She looked at me through half-closed eyes. "We do that, don't we: imagine that someone we haven't seen in a long time hasn't really changed, not deep down inside, no matter how much older we both are?"

I wondered if she was talking about us, and as I watched a bittersweet expression form on her gentle face I felt a knot in my stomach, afraid I had done something to disappoint her, afraid that I had changed more than she had thought. Her gaze grew more distant and she pulled her knees tighter under her chin.

"Is everything all right?" I asked.

At first I did not think she had heard me, but then, a moment later, like someone clearing away the cobwebs, she batted her lashes twice and sat up. With a cheerful look in her eyes, she came around the table and sat in my lap, her arms wrapped around my neck. "I love you Joseph Antonelli, and I'll marry you whenever you want. Tomorrow, if you like."

She let go of my neck, and for a long time, the bare presence of a smile flickering across her fragile, vulnerable mouth, looked at me like someone peering at their own half-forgotten reflection. Without a word, without a sound, she gently rose and, taking me in her soft, naked hand, led me back upstairs.

Twenty-two

D r. Friedman was waiting for me. A nervous smile started on his mouth, failed, and then was just about to start again, when he let go of my hand and, glancing away, gestured toward the armless chair in front of the metal institutional desk.

"I was beginning to think you didn't want to see me," I said.

His ankle was crossed over his knee and his hands were clasped together in his lap. Repeatedly he clenched his teeth while his lashes beat rapidly over his eyes. I wondered if he had heard what I had said.

"Why do you want to see Elliott again?" he asked presently, his attention concentrated on the quick, abrupt movement of his thumbs.

He could have asked that question anytime during the last three weeks. Helen had tried to get him on the phone every day, and every day there had been some new excuse, some new reason why Dr. Friedman had not been able to return any of the calls that had been made.

"I don't care if I see Elliott or not." I turned over the fingers of my right hand and pretended to study my nails. "I came to see you."

His lashes stopped blinking. Slowly, he lifted his eyes. "You came to see me?"

I examined my nails more closely. "Yes, to see you." I closed my fingers into a fist and shoved it down next to my leg. "Do you remember a patient by the name of Jacob Whittaker?"

He turned the swivel chair and placed both hands on top of the desk. "You mean the patient who murdered the judge?"

"Yes—the judge, Calvin Jeffries: the judge who married Elliott Winston's wife. You remember: We talked about him when I was here before."

Tapping his fingers together, he gave me a look meant to suggest that he was far too busy to remember much of anything we might have discussed.

"You remember," I said, returning his look with one that said I did not believe him.

"Yes, of course. The name escaped me," he said, brushing it off. "What would you like to know about him? There isn't much I can tell you, I'm afraid. He wasn't one of my patients."

"Whose patient was he?"

"I don't know. I'd have to check."

"You didn't know him at all?"

"No, not directly. You have to understand, Mr. Antonelli. We have hundreds of patients, and we're constantly getting new ones."

I leaned forward and looked straight at him. "But you knew that he had escaped?"

"No, actually I didn't. You see, strictly speaking, he didn't escape. He was out on a pass and that time he didn't come back."

"That time? You mean he had been out before?"

Friedman seemed surprised that I had even asked. "Yes, of course. Whittaker had been here for years. He was quite stable— so long as he stayed on his medication. He was in the process of being transitioned back into the community." He hesitated before he added, "It had not been an entirely smooth transition. He had an apartment for a while, and a job washing dishes at a restaurant. But he didn't want to follow the rules. That was a couple of years ago. This time, when he was let out, it was to be for just a few days at a time, and, instead of allowing him to have his own apartment, he was put in a halfway house."

"What rules?" I asked. "What did he do that brought him back inside?"

He sank back in the chair and shrugged. "I don't really know. As I say, he wasn't my patient. I only know about this now because, after what happened, the case became the subject of a staff review."

"And?"

He raised his eyebrows. "And what?"

"What was the result of the staff review?"

"Everything had been done properly, based on the best evidence of his condition," he said, as he lowered his gaze.

"He was here because he murdered his father, if I recall correctly. And despite that, he's let out and murders—or I should say slaughters—a judge, and everything was done properly?"

Friedman sighed. "Look, Mr. Antonelli," he said, raising his eyes just far enough to cast an irritated sideways glance at me, "we do our best. I'll be the first to admit that our best isn't always good enough. But what would you have us do?"

Sitting up straight, he waved his hand at the window behind him. The bright clear light from the cloudless summer sky left a dull glow on the grimy dirt-covered glass.

"We try to make people well so they can live out there. We're not a prison, we're a hospital. Sometimes people are sicker than we think; sometimes they get better and then get sick again. It's awful what happened. But given the same diagnosis, the same course of treatment, the same results from the medication he was taking: Would I release a patient into a transition program? Yes, absolutely. Would I be completely confident he would not suffer some kind of relapse, have some kind of psychotic episode? No, I would not. I know that isn't very satisfying, but there you have it. That's what we do here. We treat the sick."

He started to sit back but thought of something else. "You defend people accused of crimes. Have you never gotten someone off and had him go out and commit another one? Have you never obtained an acquittal for a killer and had him kill someone else? Did that mean you did not do the same thing again: defend another person you knew might harm someone if you won your case and he was found not guilty?"

I was not in the mood to let him take comfort in a false analogy. "My job is to put on a defense; your job is to make sure people who are a danger to themselves or others can't hurt other people."

He knew he had struck a nerve, and that gave him sufficient pleasure not to contest the point. "I'm sure we both do the best we can." With a brief, professional smile, he asked, "You said something about another patient?"

I ignored him. "All right. He wasn't your patient. Did Elliott know him?"

"Whittaker? I don't know. He might have."

"He might have? Don't you know who your patients know in here and who they don't?"

Friedman lifted his chin and narrowed his eyes. "They might have known each other," he repeated. "There are hundreds of patients in the forensic ward. Besides, what's your point? What if they did know each other? It doesn't mean the same thing in here that it does out there," he said, nodding toward the windows and the world outside. "We have people in here who sleep in adjoining beds and never exchange a word. We have people in here who never speak. This is a mental hospital, Mr. Antonelli; it isn't a private sanatorium for wealthy, intelligent people who don't happen to feel very well," he said with a condescending glance.

"So because some of them can't talk, you don't take any notice of what any of them might be saying to each other?" I asked sharply. "For all you know they could be spending all their free time plotting the murder of half the people in Portland."

"Again, Mr. Antonelli, I think you've confused the state hospital with the state prison. We provide treatment and a decent, safe place to live to people suffering severe mental illness."

He pronounced each word of the official declaration of policy with an unquestioning assurance. It seemed to remind him of who he was, and of the great advantages he had over someone who lacked his training. He looked at me with a kind of tolerance and became, in his way, almost considerate.

"I owe you an apology, Mr. Antonelli. I know your office has been trying to schedule an appointment. It's just that I've had so much to do lately. And then, when your secretary called this morning and said you were on your way . . . I was a little annoyed—more with myself, you understand." He pressed his fingertips together and, putting me under his observant gaze, waited behind his professional mask.

"Has Elliott been out, the way Whittaker was—on a pass?"

Friedman shook his head. "No, never. Maybe someday, but— Why? You don't imagine he had something to do with the murder of the judge—Jeffries? Is that why you wanted to know if he knew Whittaker?" He shook his head again, this time more emphatically. "That's quite impossible."

"Why is it impossible? People have been known to convince someone else to do their killing for them. Why is it impossible? You don't know if he knew Whittaker or not, and if he did know him you certainly don't know what they talked about."

"It's impossible," he insisted, spreading his hands apart. "I know Elliott. I've worked with him for several years now. He barely remembers what happened to him. It was too traumatic."

"He remembers he wanted to kill me, and he remembers why."

"Yes, but he realizes he was sick and that what he thought then had little if any basis in reality. He doesn't blame anyone for what happened to him. He knows it's a disease. No, I'm afraid you're wrong," he said, watching me over the tips of his fingers as he again pressed them together. "And you've forgotten something. Even if after all this time he wanted to do something like this, what in the world could he ever have done to convince Whittaker to do it for him? These cases you talk about—aren't they usually cases in which someone does it for money, or out of some misguided sense of love? What did Elliott have to offer?" he asked with an irritating smile.

"Then you think it's just a coincidence?"

"Yes, why not? An unfortunate coincidence," he added with a dour look. "A mental patient takes the life of someone he doesn't know. Just because another mental patient—who may never have known the other one—happens to have known the victim some dozen years earlier, before he was a mental patient . . . It's quite a reach, isn't it?"

"Now you're forgetting something. There was another patient who escaped."

"What are you talking about? There hasn't been anyone since Whittaker. I can assure you of that, Mr. Antonelli." He saw the surprise register on my face. "Why? What made you think there was?"

He had to be wrong and I wondered if he was lying. "No one in the forensic ward has escaped? No one who might have been let out on a pass has failed to come back?" I stared at him, searching his eyes, trying to discover if there was something he was attempting to hide. If there was, he did not show it.

"No, as I told you: no one since Whittaker," he insisted. "I can assure you, we're even more conscious of our security precautions than we were before."

Pressing his lips into a brief, bureaucratic smile, he punctuated his decision that there was really nothing more to be said about it with a single, abrupt nod of his head. The next instant he was on his feet, moving with dispatch toward the door, where he flashed another grating smile and waited for me to come.

"I'm sorry I don't have more time. If you would like to see Elliott, I'll walk you over."

We went across the parking lot to the main building. A stoop-shouldered gray-haired man in a denim shirt trimmed the shrubbery below the first-floor windows with a pair of steel-bladed gardening shears. I raised my head and squinted into the light, looking up at the painted metal orb on the pole that stood atop the cupola. There was nothing there. The bird I had seen before had found another home.

Friedman was all business as we walked together down the broad central corridor, ignoring the few casual remarks I made as if he was too preoccupied with his own affairs to waste any more time than he had already. We got to the wire mesh screen that fenced off the area where Elliott was kept, and the doctor fumbled for his key.

"I'd like to see Elliott's file before I leave," I said as he slid open the gate. He stopped, both hands gripping the edge.

"That's impossible," he said, frowning. "Patient records are confidential. You know I can't let you look at them."

On the far side of the large day room, a group of patients were crowded together around a table next to a barred window. At the sound of Friedman's voice, Elliott Winston raised his head and looked around. He seemed to stiffen and draw into himself. Taking it as a cue, the others slunk away and, watching me with curious eyes, scattered to different parts of the room. Elliott stared straight ahead, peering into the distance, his pale features as rigid as ice.

It was the same look, or should I say the same mask, he had worn the first time I had come to see him. The question, which had only just begun to form in my mind, was whether when he wore it, he was lost behind it in a world of his own; or whether he used it to make you think he was not the whole time subjecting you to a scrutiny so close you would have flinched from it had it been more obvious and direct.

We stood next to the table, Elliott staring right past us. Friedman did not seem to know quite what to do. Finally, he cleared his throat and spoke Elliott's name. When there was no response, he placed his hand on Elliott's shoulder.

"Elliott, Mr. Antonelli is here to see you."

Without warning Elliott rose straight up from the chair and

with mechanical formality held out his hand. He did everything at right angles. There were no smooth, easy transitions from one movement to the next. It was like watching someone who had studied the manners of well-bred, elegant people, but who had never had a chance to make them his own, and turned them into an awkward parody when he tried to use them.

Excusing himself, Friedman left Elliott and me alone. On the other side of the ward, dressed all in white, the same black orderly who had been here before held a rolled-up magazine in his hand while he gazed absentmindedly at the flickering screen of a television set.

"I wasn't told you were coming," Elliott said as we sat down at the square wooden table. He was not wearing the tight-fitting suit and the throat-choking dress shirt and tie he had worn on my first visit. Like the other inmates, he was dressed in a white V-neck short-sleeve shirt and white drawstring trousers. I had taken the chair around the corner to his left. He settled a narrow-eyed glance on me and then looked past me. "Why are you here?" he asked.

"Judge Jeffries—Calvin Jeffries—was murdered—"

"You told me that when you were here before," he interjected. His hands were on the table, one on top of the other. He switched their position, and then, abruptly, as if they moved independently and were fighting over which should be on top, did it again. "You told me that before," he repeated, a look of impatience on his face.

"Murdered by someone in here," I said, finishing the sentence I had begun.

We were sitting so close I could see the thin folds of skin, bunched tightly together, at the outer edge of his eye. A smile started on the side of his mouth, crossed over, and vanished on the other. "Was it me?"

"No, I'm afraid it wasn't you."

A second smile made the same circuit as the first. "Damn! All the luck." His eyes seemed to taunt me, challenge me, dare me to figure out what was really going on in his mind.

"It was Jacob Whittaker. Did you know him?"

Elliott remained silent. There was nothing in his expression, nothing in his eyes, that gave me an answer to my question.

"You didn't know him, then?" I asked, watching him closely.

"Isn't that what I just didn't say?" His eyes glittered at his own grammatical joke, and then turned hard. "How would I know if I knew him? I'm an inmate in an insane asylum."

We were so close that when he spoke the air from his dead breath filled my nostrils. Placing my hand on his forearm, I moved closer still.

"That's right, Elliott, you're an inmate in an insane asylum. But you're not insane, are you? You never were. They twisted everything up—Jeffries and your wife. They pushed you as far as you could go: They made you crazy—not like the people who are supposed to be here—just enough to drive you over the edge. You had a breakdown, a nervous breakdown, but you weren't insane. You might not have known what you were doing when you came to my office waving that gun around, but you were not out of your mind. Remember when you were a lawyer? Remember the definition? A mental disease or defect: the inability to control your own actions, the inability to distinguish the difference between right and wrong. You weren't insane then, and you're not insane now."

He slipped his arm from underneath my hand, glanced at me, an amused expression on his face, and then looked away. He shook his head and began to laugh.

"And all this time I thought I was a mental patient. I must have been—what?—insane to have thought so." He scratched his chin and then put his finger between his teeth, gnawing at the edge of it where the skin covers the nail. Behind half-closed lids, his eyes darted from side to side.

"Do you think you're insane, Elliott?" I asked in an even tone. His eyes came to a rest, and he stopped chewing on his finger. After a deep breath he no longer seemed quite so agitated or distracted. A wry expression spread along his mouth.

"Dr. Friedman says it's so. Paranoid schizophrenia: signed, sealed, delivered—a certified nut case."

"I didn't ask you that. I asked what you thought." Pausing, I peered into his eyes, watching for a spark, a glimmer, some sign that he might decide to trust me. "Do you think you're insane?"

He raised his head and looked around at the patients lounging in different parts of the vast white room. "Does anyone think they're insane? It's an interesting question, isn't it? All of you out there think you're sane, but does that mean all of us in here think we're not? What difference does it make, anyway? All that counts is that you—I mean the people who put us here, the people in your world—think we aren't—sane, that is."

Our eyes were locked together. "Are you sure of that? Are you sure that's what they thought when they sent you here?"

Alert and expectant, he waited for an explanation, and I wondered if he needed one.

"I read the file, Elliott: the court file, the record, such as it is, of the case, your case, the one in which you were charged with attempted murder, the one in which you entered a plea of guilty but insane. Do you remember that? Do you remember entering that plea? Do you remember anything about that day at all?"

He stared at me with a stern expression, and then turned his head and looked past me. He held himself rigidly erect, the only movement the slight rustle of his thick mustache as the breath passed out of his wide nostrils.

"Do you remember your lawyer—the one Calvin Jeffries hired for you—Asa Bartram? You told me before you didn't know who the lawyer was who represented you. But you did know, didn't you? He was Jeffries's law partner; he took care of Jeffries's business. You had to have known that, and if you knew that, you had to know that Asa never practiced criminal law in his life!"

His eyes stayed fixed in that rigid forward stare, as if he could ignore me at will. Angrily, I jumped up from the chair and wheeled around into the one directly opposite him. With all the force I could summon, I brought my arm down on the table, and pushed my face as far toward him as I could.

"Asa Bartram was not a criminal lawyer, and you knew it. Jeffries had him take the case, and you knew that, too. What else did you know? What else was going on? What did they tell you was going to happen to you?"

The harsh severity of that unforgiving stare gave way to a look of almost amused disdain. "Asa was old then; he must be ancient now. Tell me, do they still let him leave his car under that NO PARKING sign in front of his building?"

The question was unimportant—trivial even—but whether it was a premonition, or just an instinct born of years of keeping my own counsel, I would not tell him. Besides, I was here to get answers, not give them.

"What did Jeffries tell you—that the fix was in? Did he tell you that you'd be sent here, to the hospital, and that you would be out in a few months?"

I could see Jeffries in my mind, giving assurances, making promises, and all of it with that confident sense of inevitability with which he regularly disguised his deceptions.

"Did he tell you that you didn't have anything to worry about—that he'd take care of everything?"

Elliott's gaze seemed to soften and draw inward. He sank into the chair and laced his fingers together. "I always trusted Calvin Jeffries," he said with a small, self-deprecating smile. "Even when I was in my right mind."

That was all he was going to say about it. I asked him about the psychiatric report, the one without which he could never have been committed in the first place. He claimed not to remember anything about it.

"Do you remember the doctor?"

"No," he said, tapping his thumbs together.

"His name?"

"No."

"Anything about him?"

"No."

"Where was it done?"

"I was in jail at the time."

"Was it done there?"

"I suppose."

"Are you sure there was one?"

He stopped what he was doing and raised his head. "You read the file."

"Part of it is under seal."

"Oh," he said with a show of indifference.

"I came here to see you, Elliott, because a second judge has been murdered. Did you know about it?"

His lifted his head and twisted it a quarter turn away. "Of course I know that. After all, I'm completely sane, aren't I? I know everything. What judge?"

"The judge who sent you here: Quincy Griswald. Remember him?"

He was watching me, waiting to see where I was going with this. Or was he perhaps testing me, seeing how far I could get without his help?

"Jeffries is murdered in the courthouse parking lot, stabbed to death by a patient who escaped from here. The police get an anonymous call telling them where they can find the killer. The killer confesses and then, that same night, smashes his brains out on the concrete floor of his jail cell." I was leaning forward, my weight on my arms, peering deep into Elliott's eyes. "There's no record he ever knew Jeffries. Maybe it's just a random act and it's only a coincidence he spent years in this place with you."

There was no reaction, nothing to betray what Elliott was thinking, if he was thinking anything at all.

"Then Quincy Griswald is murdered, murdered in the same place and in almost exactly the same way. Everyone thinks it's a copycat killer, but there's another anonymous call, and another arrest is made in the same place as the first one. Only this time they arrest the wrong man, someone who has the murder weapon because the real killer gave it to him. And the real killer, like the killer of Calvin Jeffries, is an escaped mental patient. Two murders, two killers, both of them escaped from here, and the only thing that links both the victims and the killers together is you, Elliott, just you.

"Jeffries took everything away from you, and Griswald helped him do it—that is the only thing that links them together, the only thing that supplies a motive for a double homicide. Neither killer had any connection with his victim. You're the one who would have wanted them dead, and you're the only one who could have put those two up to it."

His expression did not change. He sat there, the detached observer, perfectly content to listen, as if nothing I said had anything directly to do with him. I pushed back from the table and locked my hands around my upraised knee.

"I'm not sure how you managed it, but I must tell you," I said admiringly, "in all the years I've practiced law, it's the most ingenious thing I've ever seen. It isn't just a perfect crime. It's better than that. It's the perfect defense: You can't be held responsible for anything. You're insane, aren't you? The state says so. They can't turn around and say you're not: You're locked up in the hospital for the criminally insane."

Elliott listened intently, rubbing his index finger back and forth across his lower lip. "Why would I need that defense, or any other? What crimes would I have committed?"

I thought he must have forgotten one of the most basic principles of criminal responsibility. "Solicitation carries the same penalty as the crime solicited."

He raised his thick eyebrows. "Solicitation requires a specific request for a specific act." I looked at him, unsure of what he meant. "Besides," he went on, "these two killers you speak of were both escaped mental patients, correct? Then tell me: How do you go about soliciting someone insane to do anything?"

I had not thought of it, and with a flash of intuition, he saw it. He sat up and leaned forward. "Have you ever thought about how easily people are led to believe things that have no rational foundation at all—religion, for example—and not just this religion, or that religion, but all religions? Have you thought about the way some people believe the same thing is evil that other people believe is good? Or about the way some people are willing to die for what they believe, while other people think it's ludicrous, unless, of course, it is for what they believe in?"

The idea seemed to ignite something inside him. His eyes grew larger, more intense, and he sat straight up, once again rigid and erect, the veins throbbing in his neck. And then it happened, the same thing that had happened when I had been here before, that terrifying, inexplicable lapse into complete irrationality.

"Everyone has to believe . . . grieve . . . weave . . . heave . . . achieve . . ." He stopped, his eyes wide open, while his long lashes beat down over them, measuring the rhythm of his now silent speech. Then, as quickly as it had started, it was over. "What makes you think whoever killed Griswald was a patient here?" he asked, without any apparent awareness of what he had just been doing.

I had something else on my mind, something I wanted to leave him with. "Don't you think it would be difficult to accomplish something so ingenious and never have anyone know about it? Do you really think it would be enough to know that you had gotten away with a remarkable act of revenge when everyone else thought you were still either insane or the pathetic victim of someone much smarter?"

His head jerked up and his eyes narrowed. "Do you know why people seek revenge? It isn't to even the score, or to settle things once and for all; it isn't even to punish. It's to do the one thing everyone claims you can never do: change the past." His eyes flared open. "Yes, to change the past. You think that's impossible? You think you can never change the past?" He gritted his teeth, and in three spastic bursts pulled his lips back as far as they would go. "The past is the only thing you can change. Turn away from the perspective of the present, look ahead into the future, then look back and correct what the past will be. That's what revenge accomplishes. You can think of yourself as a victim because of what was done to you; or you can think of yourself in quite a different light because of what you did to them."

He cocked his head, like someone catching the sound of something far off in the distance. "If I were condemned to live my life over and over again, always the same thing, forever, what do you think I would want it to be? What Jeffries did to me, or—just for the sake of argument—what I did to him?"

"Just for the sake of argument?" I asked skeptically.

"For the sake of argument, because, again, what makes you think whoever killed Judge Griswald was a patient here?"

"Because it's the only way it could have happened."

"Ah, the only way if I was the one who somehow persuaded two different mental patients to commit two different murders. And tell me, my old friend, just who is this second murderer, this second patient you think I sent out into your world to extract this little measure of revenge?"

Friedman had denied that anyone after Whittaker had escaped, but I did not believe him.

"The history teacher, the one who does tricks with numbers, the one who slashed someone's throat in Portland because he thought he was in Vietnam—the one who asks permission to go to the bathroom."

He looked over my head, scanning the room. "You mean him?" he asked as I turned around to see where he was looking. On the other side of the room, the patient I was certain had escaped, the one I knew had killed Quincy Griswald and given Danny the knife, the one I was sure had drowned in the river, was standing next to the orderly, waiting to be taken to the bathroom.

Twenty-three

I drove directly from the state hospital to the downtown bridge where I had lived for a night and a day as one of the homeless, but I could not find him. The only witness I had to the identity, and even to the very existence, of the man who had given the knife to my innocent client had disappeared, moved on to some other temporary encampment, vanished into the vast migration that, right in front of our eyes, took place every night and every day. I had been so certain, so confident that I knew who had done it and why; and now, as I sat listening to the prosecution make its opening statement, I wondered if I knew anything at all.

Cassandra Loescher was clear, precise, every word so freighted with moral outrage that you might have thought the defendant had been charged with the murder of his mother rather than the killing of someone he never knew. I had heard the same thing a hundred times before and seen it in a dozen different dreams. Somewhere there had to be a dog-eared manual that described paragraph by paragraph what every prosecutor should say at the beginning of every homicide brought to trial. Everything followed a formula; every fact the prosecution was required to prove was fitted into place.

Dressed in a simple black dress, dark stockings, and black shoes, Loescher stood a few steps away from the jury box and, changing her tone, recited in a quiet, dignified voice the list of witnesses she intended to call and the testimony she expected each one of them to give.

"And when you've heard all the evidence," she said at the end, her brown eyes glowing with confidence, "I know you'll agree that the state has met its burden and that the guilt of John Smith has been proven beyond any reasonable doubt."

Sitting next to me, the defendant known to the world as John Smith played with his tie. He had never worn one before and every morning when the deputy sheriff brought him into the courtroom, I tied it around his neck. Clean-shaven, with a decent haircut, he looked like a perfectly normal young man, except for the way he sometimes let his mouth hang open or rolled his head from side to side. Shy, and even terrified around strangers, he was also, I think, curious about the proceedings that were going on around him. At first he would not look up from the table, but gradually, as he became used to his surroundings, and especially the twelve faces in the jury box, he began to lift his eyes. He watched Cassandra Loescher tell the jury why he should be convicted of murder and when she finished smiled at her as if she had just said something nice.

Loescher had held the courtroom for nearly an hour, and when she sat down there was a dim, dull shuffling sound as the spectators, crowded together on the hard wood benches, shifted position. Slouched in the chair, both index fingers pressed together on my mouth, I was still trying to decide exactly what I should say when I heard the voice of the judge call my name.

"Do you wish to make an opening statement?" Judge Bingham asked.

I looked over at the jury and searched their eyes. "Yes, your honor," I said as I got to my feet.

It had taken four days to pick a jury, and I had spent most of that time trying to convince them that they were there not to decide what had really happened the night Quincy Griswald was murdered, but whether the state had proven the guilt of the defendant beyond a reasonable doubt. I had done the same thing thousands of times before, persuading jurors to ignore their commonsense notions about what had probably happened and to insist on facts about which there could be no dispute before they considered convicting someone of a crime. But this time was different. It was going to take more than an insistence on reasonable doubt if I was going to have any chance to win.

Standing at the end of the jury box, I put one hand on the railing and pushed the other into my suit coat pocket. This jury was like all the others. Three of its members had graduated from college, and one or two had some training beyond the twelfth grade, but most of them had ended their formal education with high school. There were no doctors, no lawyers, no business executives, and no one who held any important public position. Four of the twelve were retired, and of the seven women, three were grandmothers. Though it was not the fair cross section of the community it was supposed to be, it was in another way the perfect mirror of who we are. These were people who wanted to do the right thing and were willing to follow the lead of whoever seemed to know what that might be. I began with a confession.

"During voir dire, when I had the chance to ask each of you questions, we spent a lot of time talking about reasonable doubt and what it meant. Ms. Loescher kept trying to suggest that it didn't mean you couldn't be left with at least some doubt, and I kept trying to convince you that you better not doubt it at all before you decide to convict someone of a crime. I've been doing this for much of my life now, and it never changes. We keep asking these same questions, keep trying to convince you what the words 'reasonable doubt' mean. Do you know why I do that?"

My eyes moved along the front row, from one juror to the next, until they came to rest on a young woman, Mary Ellen Conklin, sitting with her hands folded in her lap.

"Because I learned a long time ago that the best way to win was to convince jurors that their obligation was to decide—not if the defendant was guilty—but if the state had been able to prove it . . . beyond that famous reasonable doubt."

I looked away from the young mother of two and found a middle-aged Latino, Hector Picardo, in the back row.

"You're not here to decide the truth; you're here to decide whether what the state tells you is the truth, and not to take their word for it, either, but again, to prove it against the most stringent possible standard. I want juries that insist on that—the defendant has a right to have a jury that insists on that—and that's why I keep asking those questions about whether you think it's fair that the state has this incredibly difficult burden, fair that the prosecution has to prove its case and the defense doesn't have to prove anything."

I moved away from the railing, folded my arms across my chest, and stared down at the carpeted floor. Smiling to myself, I shook my head and then, a moment later, lifted my eyes and cast a sideways glance at the jury.

"The truth is: In most cases we couldn't prove anything if we had to, because, you see, in most cases the defendant is guilty." Out of the corner of my eye I saw the judge suddenly look up. "That's the reason defense lawyers always insist so strenuously that the whole burden of proof is on the prosecution; that's the reason why in more cases than I can remember I made certain the defendant never took the stand to testify in his own behalf."

Cassandra Loescher was sitting on the edge of her chair, ready to make an objection as soon as she figured out what there was to which she could object.

"We have this very famous jury instruction—Judge Bingham referred to it when you were first sworn in, I spent most of my time on voir dire talking about it—you can't convict anyone unless their guilt has been proven beyond a reasonable doubt. There is another jury instruction, one we did not talk about, but one that has to be given if the defense requests it."

I went back to the counsel table, opened the file folder that lay next to my yellow legal pad, and pulled out a single sheet of paper.

"Here," I said, waving it in my hand. "This is the jury instruction entitled 'Defendant Not Testifying.' It tells you that you may not comment on the failure of the defendant to testify, and that you may not in any way consider that fact in your deliberations. The judge is required to instruct you that it doesn't mean a thing. But the truth is, it means everything. It means that the defendant has something he doesn't want you to know. It doesn't necessarily mean he's guilty, it may only mean that he has done some bad things before: serious crimes, crimes reflecting dishonesty or a penchant for violence, things that would make a jury believe that because he had done it before, it was likely he had done it again.

"There are cases like this, where the defendant doesn't testify because, though he is innocent of this crime, he has the kind of criminal record that will make it almost impossible for anyone to believe he's telling the truth. But more often than not, when the defendant doesn't testify, it's because the defendant is guilty. The defendant did it, and because a lawyer cannot put someone on the stand he knows will commit perjury, and because the only truthful testimony the defendant can give is to confess to the crime, he doesn't testify at all. And then the jury is given this instruction," I said, lifting the single sheet of paper shoulder high before I let my hand fall down to my side. "No one can make the guilty testify against themselves," I went on, darting a glance at Cassandra Loescher. "And no one can stop the innocent from testifying about what they know."

She was out of the chair, raising her hand to attract the judge's attention. "Objection, your honor," she said without raising her voice beyond what was necessary to make herself heard. She was smart. It was too early in the game to show anger.

His hands clasped together under his chin, Bingham smiled politely. "Yes?"

"Instead of providing a preview of what he expects the evidence to show, Mr. Antonelli is attempting to characterize the credibility of the defendant."

He turned to me, the same civil smile on his face.

"I believe, your honor, that the jury is entitled to know the circumstances under which a witness is going to testify. For example, when an expert witness testifies, the qualifications of that expert—"

"Are elicited during the examination of the witness," Loescher interjected. "But he isn't talking about the qualifications of an expert in any event, your honor. He's attempting to bolster the credibility of a witness by invoking a jury instruction which, it seems obvious, has no application to this case."

That was exactly what I was trying to do, and we both knew it was too late to stop it. What she was trying to do instead was to let the jury know that I was not playing by the rules, and to let the judge know that even during an opening statement she was going to insist that the rules be enforced. She was no one's fool, and she would have been astonished had she known how grateful I was that she was not.

Bingham had heard enough. "Perhaps discussion of jury instructions should be left to closing argument," he said in that civil way of his that made every decision sound like a helpful suggestion.

I had not moved from the place where I had been standing when Loescher made her objection. Now I stepped forward, moving closer to the jury, and picked up where I had left off.

"The defendant in this case is going to testify, and he's going to tell you what he knows; though about all he knows is that he did not kill Quincy Griswald and that he has never harmed anyone in his life. He was living under the bridge—a bridge some of you may drive over every day to work—one of the homeless who wander around the city, picking up trash, things that other people throw away, things they can wear, things they can use, things they can trade for a little money or a little food. He was living under the bridge, homeless and alone, and someone gave him a knife—the knife that killed Quincy Griswald—and he took the knife and he kept it, and when the police came he told them it was his and he told them how he got it." I shrugged my shoulders. "They didn't believe him. Why should they? He was right where an anonymous caller had told them they would find the killer; he had the knife; and—let's be perfectly straight about this—they thought he was crazy."

I paused and, with both hands on the railing, leaned forward and searched the eyes of the jurors.

"When you hear him testify, you're going to think the same thing. He talks funny. His speech isn't always clear. Some of the words seem to take forever. He rolls his eyes and his mouth sometimes sags at the corner. I have even seen him drool a little."

I spun away and looked across at where he sat, watching me, his head tilted back, his mouth hanging half open, an eager, trusting expression in his pale eyes.

"But kill somebody?" I asked, turning back to the jury. "No, that's the last thing you're going to think him capable of. Not after you hear the things he was put through; not after you hear the scandalous, heart-wrenching tale of physical torture and sexual abuse to which he was subjected from the time he was an infant, an unwanted child no one, not even his mother, cared anything about or did anything to protect. No one ever did anything for him: They did not send him to school; they did not even give him an identity. There is no record of his birth; there is no record of him at all. He does not exist. He does not have a name."

I glanced at him over my shoulder and then looked back. "John Smith? That's the name he was given by the police when they arrested him and charged him with murder and discovered there was no record of his fingerprints. His real name is Danny. If he ever had a last name, Danny doesn't remember it, and because there was never any record made of it, he'll never know it. For all intents and purposes, Danny was born an orphan. It might have been better if he had never been born at all. No," I said, changing my mind, "it would have been better if the people who did these things to him had never been born."

Clinically and without emotion, I described a few of the things that had been done: the way he had been chained to his bed, the way his body had been covered with welts and burned with cigarettes.

"The prosecution will insist that these terrible things turned him into an animal without a conscience, someone who could kill without a reason. You can judge for yourself when you listen to him testify whether he is the vicious killer they claim, or one of the most harmless human beings you have ever seen."

Shoving my hands into my pants pockets, I began to pace back and forth in front of the jury box. Then, frowning, I stopped and looked up.

"They charged him with one murder. It doesn't make sense. They should have charged him with two."

The silence was complete; there was not a sound in the court-room. It was as if everyone was holding his breath, waiting to hear what came next.

"The defendant is charged with the murder of Quincy Griswald, but whoever killed Quincy Griswald killed once before. There were two murders, not one; two circuit court judges have been killed, not one. In nearly a hundred fifty years, no one has ever murdered a sitting judge, and now, in the space of just a few months, we have had two judges killed, and killed in exactly the same way. Calvin Jeffries, the presiding circuit court judge, was stabbed to death in the structure behind the courthouse where he parked his car. Quincy Griswald, who became the presiding circuit court judge when Jeffries died, was stabbed to death in the very same place. The defendant has been charged with the one, but not the other. Why? Because they know he did not have any-thing to do with the murder of Calvin Jeffries. But let me repeat again: Whoever is responsible for the death of Calvin Jeffries is responsible for the death of Quincy Griswald. John Smith—

Danny—did not kill Calvin Jeffries, and he did not kill Quincy Griswald."

I moved to the end of the jury box, next to the witness stand, and looked out over the packed courtroom, every eye on me, every face a study in concentration. In the very back, in the last row, Jennifer was watching, serious, intent, following every word.

"You remember the murder of Calvin Jeffries," I said, looking back at the jury. "It was all we read about, all we talked about. Everybody from the governor on down seemed to get involved in that case. Whatever the police did, it was never enough. We demanded results; we demanded an arrest; we demanded that the killer be brought to justice."

I stood still and stared across the counsel table to where Cassandra Loescher was taking notes. When I stopped talking, she raised her head, catching my gaze in her own.

"They never caught the person responsible for the murder of Calvin Jeffries; the police don't know who the killer is; the district attorney's office doesn't know who he is."

It took a moment before she realized what I was doing, and even then she could not quite believe it.

"Your honor," she said, as she sprang to her feet. "May counsel approach?"

I pretended outrage. "Your honor, this is the second time the prosecution has interrupted my opening statement. I didn't do that to Ms. Loescher—no matter what I thought of what she was saying!"

Bingham did not say a word. Instead, he gestured with his hand that he wanted a private conversation. He got up from his chair and stepped down on the side of the bench farthest from the jury.

"What is your objection, Ms. Loescher?" he asked. As always his tone was civil, but he could not completely disguise his irritation. He liked things to move smoothly, and already he could sense signs of trouble to come.

"He's making a patently false statement," Loescher insisted. "He knows as well as I do that what he said isn't true. The police made an arrest in the Jeffries case. The killer confessed. And it's more than that, your honor," she whispered forcefully. "He's trying to bring in the Jeffries case just to confuse the jury. That case doesn't have anything to do with this one."

Staring down at the floor as he listened, Bingham pinched the middle of his upper lip between his forefinger and thumb. When she was finished, he looked at me.

"I'm allowed to offer my own theory of the case, your honor—any theory that explains the facts of the case. Ms. Loescher should listen more carefully: I didn't say the police did not make an arrest, I said they never caught the person responsible." We were standing inches apart. I shifted my gaze and looked directly at her. "If you think they did—"

She was livid. She stared at the judge, who was again looking down at his shoes. "He knows I don't have a chance to offer rebuttal to his opening."

"Of course you do," I interjected. "It's called closing argument."

Bingham raised his head. "The defense has a right to offer an alternative theory. The prosecution has a right to offer any relevant evidence which contradicts that theory." He looked at me, then looked at her. "You're both fine attorneys. You've both done very well to this point." With a brief nod and an even briefer smile, he added, "Let's not let that change." It was as stern a warning as he knew how to give.

Loescher went back to her chair, and Bingham went back to the bench. "Mr. Antonelli," he said as he settled into place, "would you please continue."

I nodded at the judge and turned to the jury. "First Calvin Jeffries was murdered, then Quincy Griswald. Both of them were killed in the same way and both of them were killed in the same place. But why were they killed at all? And who would have had a reason to kill them both, not just Calvin Jeffries, but Quincy Griswald as well?"

With one hand on my hip, I rubbed the back of my neck. "That's the great difficulty in this case: trying to understand why anyone would want to kill Quincy Griswald. Everyone who ever knew him could understand why someone would want Calvin Jeffries dead: He was one of the worst people who ever lived."

It was instinct, pure and simple. If there had been time to think about it, she might have let it go. Whether it was her own sense of decency, or her belief about what the rules did and did not allow, Cassandra Loescher, acting on impulse, jumped to her feet.

"Objection, your honor."

This time he agreed with her. "Mr. Antonelli . . ."

Wheeling around, I glared defiance. "The character of Calvin Jeffries supplies the motive not only for his murder, but for the murder of the victim in this case. Everything I say about the late Judge Jeffries will be proven by the testimony of witnesses, your honor, witnesses the defense fully intends to call."

Pursing his lips, he tapped his fingers together. "Very well," he said presently. "But try to keep this within reasonable bounds."

It struck me as gratuitous, and I turned back to the jury, an incongruous smile on my face, amused at how angry it had made me. I respected Bingham as much as anyone on the bench, but he was as much a prisoner of convention as anyone else. We were not supposed to speak ill of the dead.

"I spoke ill of Judge Jeffries when he was alive," I explained to the jury. "I spoke ill of him to his face. He threw me in jail once because I told him during a trial exactly what I thought of him. I should probably not have done that. I may even have deserved what he did to me because of it. But whether I did or not, what Calvin Jeffries did to me was nothing compared to what he later did to someone I knew, someone I liked, someone I thought would eventually become one of the finest lawyers in the city. His name was Elliott Winston, and what Calvin Jeffries did to him was worse than murder.

"The law is the collective wisdom of the community, the attempt to live in accordance with the rules of reason, the effort to control our impulses and conduct ourselves as civilized human beings. No one carries a higher burden of responsibility than those men and women who put on black robes and apply the law without fear or favor to the people who come before them for judgment. It would be impossible to think of anyone who came to the bench with greater ability, or with a more brilliant mind, than Calvin Jeffries; and it would be impossible to think of anyone who less deserved to be called honorable. Calvin Jeffries was a disgrace. He cared nothing about the law; he cared nothing about justice. He cared only about power and how he could use it to get what he wanted. And what he wanted, ladies and gentlemen, wanted more than anything else, was the wife—and not just the wife—of Elliott Winston.

"Elliott was young, and bright, and hardworking and ambitious, with a wife he loved and two children he adored. He met Calvin Jeffries and was flattered at the attention he received. He became one of the judge's few friends, someone to whom Jeffries talked about the law, someone Jeffries wanted—or claimed he wanted—to help. Elliott trusted him completely, and he had no reason to doubt him when Jeffries told him things—things that were not true—about his wife. Elliott began to suspect his wife of infidelity, but it never occurred to him that she was being unfaithful with the man he revered, this man without children who treated him like a son.

"They worked on him, the two of them, his trusted friend and his trusted wife. They fed his suspicions, twisted his mind with false rumors and terrible lies until they drove him over the edge. Elliott was charged with attempted murder and was sent away, and while he was away, his wife divorced him and married the judge; and then the two of them together had him declared an unfit parent so the good Judge Jeffries could adopt Elliott's children and call them his own."

I put my hand on the railing and leaned closer to the jury. "And what does this have to do with John Smith, now on trial for murder? The judge who, acting on instructions from Calvin Jeffries, made certain Elliott Winston would be put in a place where he could not interfere with anything his former friend and former wife wanted to do, was Quincy Griswald."

I looked from one end of the jury box to the other. "Who do you think wanted both Calvin Jeffries and Quincy Griswald dead? Who do you think had a motive to kill them both? There is only one answer to that question, and it isn't John Smith," I said, shaking my head as I turned away and walked to the counsel table.

It was nearly four o'clock in the afternoon when I finished, and Judge Bingham decided to wait until morning before the first witness was called for the prosecution. The jury filed out of the courtroom and as the spectators behind us crowded into the aisle and shuffled a step at a time out the double-doors at the back, Cassandra Loescher waited patiently until it was quiet enough for the judge to hear.

"Yes," he said, a pleasant, if formal, smile on his face.

"Could we meet in chambers, your honor?" she asked, including me in her glance. "I have a matter for the court."

Judge Bingham's chambers consisted of a single narrow room. Two large windows took up most of the space on the wall behind his blond wood desk. There were no curtains and the venetian blinds were pulled all the way up. Light-colored bookshelves held the full collection of all the state court cases that had been the subject of an appellate opinion. On the opposite wall, next to the door that led to the clerk's office, a small, three-shelf credenza held a picture of his wife and pictures of the young families of his grown children. On the bottom shelf, out of view in the corner, was a tarnished bronze statue of a tennis player, racket raised overhead, a trophy from some long-forgotten country club tournament. In the corner behind his desk, where he could reach it without getting up, was a pewter-colored putter. Old and often used, the tape around the handle had begun to unravel.

Bingham removed his robe, hung it carefully on a hook behind the door, and put on his suit coat. He was not five foot nine, but he was of slight build, trim and fit, with a spring to his step, and looked taller. His hair was short and brushed close to his scalp. His face and hands had a clean, scrubbed look, and his teeth were straight and white. He was one of those people who could have slept in his suit and still looked neat and pressed the next morning.

He sat down and pulled first one and then the other shirt cuff into its proper position below his suit coat sleeve. He looked at Loescher and raised his eyebrows, waiting for what she had to say. Then, suddenly, he glanced across at me.

"Congratulations," he said with a slight inclination of his smooth forehead. "I only just heard about it." He turned to Loescher. "Mr. Antonelli is engaged to be married," he explained. "When is the wedding?" the judge asked pleasantly.

"In a few weeks," I replied. "As soon as the trial is over."

We barely knew each other, but Cassandra Loescher put her hand on my arm and with a huge grin immediately added her congratulations. Then, almost in the same breath, she went back to the business of trying to destroy me.

"Your honor," she said, the outlines of a smile still traceable on her mouth, "Mr. Antonelli has raised some issues during his opening statement that, quite frankly, the state did not antici-pate. For that reason, we find it necessary to ask leave to amend our witness list. Specifically, I want permission to call someone from the police department to testify regarding the results of their investigation into the murder of Judge Jeffries." She paused, and sat back in her chair. "We didn't intend to do this, your honor. It will certainly lengthen the time required to try this case. But after what happened in there today, I don't see that we have any choice."

Bingham nodded, and then turned to me. "I'm prepared to agree with that—unless you want to try and convince me other-wise."

"Who are you going to call?" I asked her.

She shrugged her shoulders. "One of the lead investigators. I don't know which one yet."

"It's fine with me, your honor," I said, trying to sound as indifferent as I could.

He looked at Loescher, then he looked at me. "Well," he said, standing up, "it seems like we're going to have an interesting few weeks."

The courtroom was empty. Danny had been taken back to his cell. I gathered up the notepads and the documents scattered over the table and slipped them into my briefcase. Gingerly, I lifted it up, hoping the restitched leather handle would hold. In the hallway outside, Howard Flynn was leaning against the wall, reading a section of the paper. When he saw me, he folded it up, shoved it into his coat pocket, and walked beside me toward the elevator.

"That was quite a performance. You think you can prove Elliott committed both murders?"

"Prove it? Of course not! All I want to do is get them to think he might have done it. Prove it? I wouldn't know where to start."

We rode the elevator to the first floor. As we went around the area where everyone who entered passed through metal detectors, a scuffle broke out. A gaunt, broad-shouldered man, with long dirty hair and a scraggly beard, dressed in the filthy clothes of the homeless, flailed away with his arm as two uniformed officers wrestled him to the ground.

"Let me in, let me in," he shouted hysterically, as they locked his arms together behind his back and managed to handcuff his wrists.

Outside, at the bottom of the courthouse steps, a grocery cart loaded with plastic bags and metal junk was lying on its side, the wheels still spinning. Someone said he had tried to get in, had been thrown out, and had then come crashing back through the door. No one seemed to know why. Flynn and I exchanged a look.

"Nothing," he said, twisting his mouth around. "Just a crazy."

I nodded halfheartedly. "Are you going to a meeting tonight?" I asked as we walked away.

"Yeah," he replied. A sly grin spread over his face. "Unless you'd rather go out and get drunk."

"Will Stewart be there?"

"He always is."

"You going to be at the bar afterward?"

"We always are." He looked at me out of the corner of his eye. "You going to be there?"

"You never know. I might."

Twenty-four

Jennifer was waiting for me when I got back to the office. Sitting in the chair opposite my desk, staring out the window, she did not hear me when I came in. I could see her lips barely moving, like the silent motions of a child beginning to grasp the meaning of an unfamiliar word. In the still half-light of the room I bent down and kissed her forehead just below the line made by the sweep of her soft fine hair. Her eyes stayed where they were, concentrating on something only she could see. Her mouth stopped moving, and she took my hand and pressed it against her cheek.

"Where's Helen?" I asked as I dropped my briefcase on top of the desk and fell into my chair. Exhausted, I put my hands behind my neck and slouched farther down.

Jennifer gave me a quizzical look, and then, as if she had only just understood, nodded quickly. "She had to run an errand. She'll be back in a minute. I answered the phone while she was gone," she said, her voice becoming more lively. She leaned forward, resting her hands on a large package she held in her lap. "Law offices of Joseph Antonelli," she said with marked formality. Alert and playful, she lifted her head. "Law offices of the soon to be married Joseph Antonelli," she said with a sly grin. "That was for anyone who called who was female and sounded young."

She was about to say something else, something she was already laughing about, when her hand shot to her temple, her eyes slammed shut, and a violent tremor shook her head. Before I had time to react, she raised her hand, forced a feeble smile, and carefully opened her eyes.

"I'm all right," she insisted. "It's just a headache. I get them once in a while," she explained. "It's okay now." She bit on her lip and her eyes opened wide, sorry she had made me worry.

"I bought you a present," she exclaimed excitedly, as if she had only just now remembered. She removed a gift-wrapped box from the large package she had been holding on her lap and handed it to me. "I hope you don't mind," she said as she watched me struggle with the ribbon. Her voice was quiet and subdued, but throbbing underneath it was the eager certainty that she had done exactly the right thing.

I think I knew what it was before I opened it, but I did not know how much it was going to mean to me until I saw it: a gleaming leather attaché case, my name inscribed on a small brass plate below the handle.

"I know you've had the other one a long time, but I thought . . ." Her voice started to fade into the vast obscurity of what might have been, but then she remembered—we both remembered—that nothing was going to make us regret our second chance.

We had an early dinner in town and when we got home she curled up with a book while I tried to outline the story I would attempt to tell through the state's own witnesses. The prosecution's case was entirely circumstantial, but if left unchallenged completely convincing. There would be testimony from the woman who first found the body, the two security guards she brought to the scene, the first police officer who arrived and took charge of the initial investigation, all of them describing what they saw and what they did. The coroner would testify that he had examined the body and determined that death had been caused by one or more wounds from a sharp instrument. Another police officer would tell the jury that the defendant had been found holding a knife that still had on it visible traces of blood. An expert on DNA would be called first to explain the procedure by which the blood on the knife was matched to the blood of the victim, and then with various charts and graphs calculate the nearly infinitesimal chance that it might have belonged to someone else.

"Do you remember T. E. Lawrence?" I asked Jennifer, stretched out on the sofa on the other side of the library, engrossed in a paperback novel. "*Seven Pillars of Wisdom.*"

She put the book down on her stomach and turned her head. "I remember T. S. Eliot. *Murder in the Cathedral.*"

"No, T. E. Lawrence, Lawrence of Arabia."

"I saw the movie. Why? Are you thinking of running away to the desert?"

"You know how you do something for a long time without quite knowing why, and then, all of a sudden, you finally figure it out? There are supposed to be two rules of cross-examination: Don't do it unless you have to, and never ask a question unless you already know the answer. I almost never follow the first and I frequently break the second. Years ago, I read *Seven Pillars of Wisdom*—it's a beautiful book, beautifully written—and I learned something I never forgot: The way to win is to turn the greatest strength of the opposition into its greatest weakness. The greatest strength of the Turkish army was a string of fortresses from which it controlled the Arab tribes. Lawrence went around blowing up railroad tracks and as many trains as he could. Then, while the Turks concentrated on how to keep open their supply lines, Lawrence and his Arab irregulars simply left them alone, prisoners in their own fortresses, and marched around them. It's the same thing on cross-examination: Let the other side concentrate on making the strength of their case stronger still, and while they're doing that, attack them in a way they haven't had time to think about."

Jennifer swung her legs over the side of the sofa and sat up. With her elbows on her knees she rested her chin on the heel of her hand.

"Do you work this hard on all your cases? You work past midnight every night and you're up every morning before six."

I closed the thick case file and shoved it to the side. "I'm worried about this case. I know the kid didn't do it. I can't afford to lose, and I've already made one mistake: I didn't bring in that homeless man, kept him safe somewhere, so I could produce him at trial and he could testify he saw someone give Danny the knife. I may have made another one today. The jury expects me to back up what I said about the same person being responsible for the death of both Jeffries and Griswald."

"And you don't think you can?"

"A lot depends on what I can do with Elliott." As I said it, I suddenly realized that it was really the other way around. "Or, rather, on what Elliott decides he wants to do with me."

Glancing at the clock, I remembered where I had to be. "I have to meet Flynn," I explained as I got to my feet.

I was in the hallway, throwing on my jacket, when I thought of it. "What did you say when I asked you about Lawrence?" The paperback dangling from her hand, Jennifer was leaning against the door to the library. "The T. S. Eliot book. *Murder in the Cathedral?*"

"Yes. Did you read it, too?"

"A long time ago," I said as I kissed her on my way out the door. Before it shut behind me, I leaned my head inside. "I promise I won't be late," I said with a mocking smile, meant to signal my abject surrender to married life and all its mundane formalities.

"I'll wait up," she replied with a smile of her own.

It was raining hard outside and I could barely see as I drove toward town. Water rushed through the gutters on the side of the street and splashed over the hood of the car at each low spot in the road. The lights of the city streaked the windshield with a multicolor blur, and the few pedestrians I could see on the sidewalks when I stopped at an intersection were vague black shadows that quickly vanished from view. The steady muffled drumbeat of the windshield wipers was the only sound I heard, that and the lonely, desolate noise of wave after wave of falling rain, sweeping down from the overburdened sky, as if it was the beginning of the rain that would fall forever until there was nothing left but water, endless water everywhere.

I parked down the street from the bar and bent the umbrella into the wind, holding my jacket close to my throat with my other hand as I struggled forward, a few steps at a time. Under the neon sign in front of the bar, I closed the umbrella and shook it out and tried to wipe my face dry with the back of my sleeve. Huddled on the pavement against the brick wall, a baseball cap shoved low on his forehead, a drunk rocked back and forth without any apparent awareness that it was raining, or even that it was night instead of day.

Inside, an old man with wrinkled hands and a solitary stare sat at the far end of the bar. A woman in her forties with black lacquered hair and dark red fingernails locked her high heel shoes on the bottom rung of the leather stool around the corner toward the middle. She watched in the mirror behind the bar while I made my way through the dim yellowish light toward the booth in the rear. The billiard balls were racked in the wooden triangle on the pool table, ready for anyone who wanted to play. Tired and bored, the bartender raised his eyes from a glass he was rubbing with a towel.

"A beer," I said over my shoulder as I slid into the booth next to Flynn.

They were slouched forward, nursing their coffee, Flynn and Stewart, grinning cynically while they watched each other through world-weary eyes.

"Guy comes into a bar and orders booze," Flynn said to Stewart. Then he looked at me and asked, "What kind of place do you think this is?"

My face was still wet and my shirt collar was soaked. Water ran down my neck.

"I get here too late to watch you throw somebody into a wall?"

He shook his head and shrugged. "It's still early."

The bartender brought a bottle of beer and a small, dirty glass. I took a short swig on the bottle, then put it down and looked at Stewart.

"I need a favor. I need you to testify." When he made no response, I reminded him what he had offered before. "You said if I did this, you'd help."

He remembered, and he had no intention of going back on his word. "But what can I testify to? I wasn't part of the investigation. I sat in when they questioned him because, like I told you before, I thought there might be some connection between the two murders."

"That's what I told the jury today: that there is a connection between the two murders, and that the same person responsible for the death of Jeffries is responsible for the death of Griswald."

"Howard was telling me about that. How are you going to prove it?" he asked.

"I don't have to prove it, I just have to show that it's possible," I replied, impatient to get back to my point. "I told them that the police didn't know who killed Jeffries and neither did the district attorney. Now Loescher has to bring in a witness to tell the jury that the police found the man who murdered Jeffries and that he confessed. She's going to call one of the lead investigators. It has to be you. I don't want you to testify for the defense; I want you to testify for the prosecution."

All his training, all his experience, everything he knew had taught him never to trust anything a defense lawyer said. His head snapped up and an ominous look came into his eyes. "Look," he warned, "if you think I'm going to—"

"Lie? I don't want you to lie," I insisted, as I bent forward and grabbed his arm. "I want you to tell the truth. You know: the truth, the whole truth, nothing but the truth."

"All right," he said, mollified, "but what difference does it make if it's me or one of the other people who headed up the investigation?"

I let go of his arm and sank against the wooden back of the booth. "All the difference in the world," I said after I took another drink from the brown beer bottle. "The question is: Can you arrange it so you're the one the prosecution calls?"

He thought about it for a moment, his head moving from side to side. "Yeah," he said finally. "There were three of us. I'll make sure I'm the only one available." He looked down at his hands, and then looked up at me. "Just so long as you understand: I'll answer any question they ask and I'll answer every one of them as truthfully as I know how."

"And I expect you to answer the questions I ask exactly the same way."

I took one more drink and then held the bottle in front of me, examining the label, before I put it down. "I'd love to stay here and drink great liquor and chase beautiful women," I said, nodding toward the woman at the bar with the red lipstick smeared across her mouth. "But I have to get home."

As I slid out of the booth, Flynn glanced at Stewart. "I didn't think it would ever happen, but Antonelli got himself engaged to be married."

I knew him scarcely better than I knew Cassandra Loescher, but just like her, he seemed genuinely pleased. "That's wonderful," he said as he stood up and shook my hand. "Congratulations."

I left them alone to finish their coffee and continue that long conversation, made up mainly of a companionable silence, by which they every night gave each other the encouragement to get through just one more day without a drink.

The wind that had lashed my face had stopped, and the rain, still heavy, fell straight down, surrounding the senses with a dull endless roar. The drunk on the sidewalk had fallen on his side, an empty pint of whiskey protruding from his coat pocket. I hesitated, then reached down and dragged him by the collar into the doorway under the neon sign. His eyes opened, and he looked at me, and then his head swung down onto his chest, and with water dripping off his cap and onto his face he started to snore.

I drove along the deserted streets and across the Morrison Street Bridge, wondering who was living under it tonight and where they went when they left, moving from one place to another, searching, I suppose, like the rest of us for something a little better, and finding, more often than not, something worse. A sense of the futility of it all started to close in on me. I picked up the car phone and called home, but when Jennifer did not answer by the third ring, I hung up, certain she had fallen asleep.

I was out of the city, driving along the tree-lined shore of the river, a few lights twinkling through the darkness. The rain began to let up, replaced by a murky gray drizzle. The headlights of a car appeared out of nowhere and a wave of water crashed against the windshield as it sped by. Then, as I left the river behind and followed the narrow lane that twisted through the hills and tunneled under the trees, everything was covered with the still, black solitude of a starless night.

I came around the corner, anxious to get home, and thought at first I was having the first real hallucination of my life. At the top of the knoll, at the end of the gated drive, the house looked like it had been set on fire. Every light in every room, upstairs, downstairs, must have been turned on. Then, as I tried to convince myself I was seeing things, I heard it, sweeping down across the dancing shadows on the rolling green grass lawn, the hard-beating, pulse-pounding music of a jazz piano player, his fingers flying, crashing, on the keys. When I reached the door, the music was deafening, and when I got inside I had to hold my hands over my ears.

Barefoot, wearing only a pink nightgown, Jennifer was pushing the vacuum cleaner across the living room rug, her head bobbing up and down in time with the music. I dashed to the CD player and turned it off. The noise of the vacuum cleaner filled the room and at first Jennifer did not seem to notice the difference. Then, she pulled up straight and looked around. A huge smile flashed on her face when she saw me standing there watching her. She switched off the vacuum cleaner.

"I thought I'd do a little housework while you were gone," she explained, holding the black cord in her hand as if she meant to continue. "I cleaned the bathroom; I cleaned the kitchen; and after I vacuum in here . . ." she said, looking past me toward the dining room.

"It's a little late to be doing this, isn't it?" I asked as gently as I could. I took the cord out of her hand and hung it over the handle. "Why don't we go to bed now."

Her eyes were wild with a kind of eager excitement, as if there was something she could not wait to tell me. She put her hand on the side of my face and then reached around my neck and rose up on her toes. "I'm so happy," she whispered in my ear. "I'm so glad we found each other again. I've never felt this good in my life." She let go of my neck and took hold of my hand. "Come on," she said, as she led me toward the stairs. "Let's go to bed.

"Carry me," she said as we got to the top of the stairs. "Make love to me," she said when we got to the bedroom door.

We tumbled down on the bed together, pulling and tearing at each other's clothes, and lost all separate sense of ourselves in the white-hot act of love. At the end, when there was nothing left of me, I collapsed in her warm, smooth arms and staring into the darkness drifted into a wordless dream that had neither a beginning nor an end.

I woke up with a start and thought I had overslept, but it was still dark. Pulling the covers over my shoulder, I turned on my side and reached out to put my arm around Jennifer. She was too far away, and I moved closer and reached again. My hand fell across her pillow and then down across the sheet. She was not there.

I found her downstairs in the library, her legs tucked under her, curled up at the same end of the sofa, reading the same paper-back novel she had been reading before. As soon as she heard me, she jumped to her feet.

"What time is it?" I asked, rubbing my eyes.

She was wide awake. "A little after three. I'm sorry. Did I wake you up? I tried to be quiet."

I cinched tighter the terry cloth robe and squinted at the clock on the fireplace mantel to see if it was really the middle of the night.

"I couldn't sleep," she said as she took my hand in both of hers.

For some reason, it struck me funny. "You couldn't sleep? After what we did? I slept like a dead man. When I woke up and it was all dark I thought at first I must have slept straight through the day."

We sat down next to each other on the sofa. An empty cup with a damp tea bag on the saucer was on the coffee table.

"Did you sleep at all?"

She was sitting on the edge of the sofa, wearing a blue silk robe, her hands in her lap. Her eyes darted around the room, staring first at one thing, then another. Her mouth twitched nervously at the corners and she started to rub her hands, stroking each finger in turn, over and over again.

"How long has this been going on?" I asked, suddenly alarmed. "You're not getting any sleep at all, are you?"

Biting on her lip, she grabbed my hand. "I'm all right," she insisted. Peering into my eyes, she tried to convince me it was true, but before she could say anything, she started to cry.

I tried to comfort her as best I could. "Everything is going to be all right. Nothing is going to happen to you," I promised.

She held me as tight as she could, her body tense and trembling, gasping for breath between her sobs. After a while her fingers loosened their grip around my neck and, laying her head on my shoulder, she started to breathe normally.

"Sorry," she said as she sat up and wiped away a tear. "I don't know why I did that. I feel fine, just fine."

"You don't have to lie to me about this," I told her. "There's something wrong, and we have to deal with it. You need to see a doctor."

I helped her up, and with my arm around her waist we climbed the stairs and went back to bed. She lay with her arm across my chest and her face next to my neck, and until the first rose-colored light of morning I held her while she slept, listening to her soft, peaceful breath, and never once closed my eyes.

Jennifer drove me to the courthouse a little before nine under a seamless blue sky. The streets in the city were jammed with cars and the sidewalks were crowded with brisk-walking men and women hurrying to work. The air was crisp and clean, filled with the sunlit smell of summer, and Mt. Hood, miles away, seemed to be just the other side of the river.

She passed the courthouse, turned the corner, and pulled over next to the park. Whatever had happened to her during the night had to have been an aberration brought on by sheer exhaustion. She was fine now; there was nothing wrong. She looked at me with that same mischievous self-confident sparkle in her eyes as she leaned back against the door, waiting for me to reach over and kiss her goodbye.

"You'll see the doctor today?" I reminded her as I started to get out.

She dismissed it as unimportant, but finally promised that she would. I stood watching her drive off, and found myself wondering if she really would. It was the first time she had ever told me anything I did not quite believe.

Twenty-five

The sound of his name still echoing in the hushed stillness of the crowded courtroom, Morris Bingham stepped quickly to the bench. Always pleasant, always polite, he glanced at me, and then at Cassandra Loescher. Neither the defense nor the prosecution had anything to bring before the court. A brief nod told his clerk she could bring in the jury.

While we waited, I turned to Danny and admired the way he looked, all dressed up in a dark blue suit and tie. "You're looking very sharp today, Danny," I assured him.

He sat with his shoulders hunched forward and his hands plunged between his legs. He looked at me with a bashful smile and took a deep breath. "Thank you," he said, letting it out.

Under the watchful gaze of several hundred strangers, the jury came in, wearing solemn faces and a dignified air, twelve normal people who seemed to have no hesitation about deciding whether someone else would live or die. Some of them stood waiting while the others squeezed past them to get to their places in the jury box. I looked down at the table and ran the palm of my hand over the smooth leather surface of the attaché case Jennifer had given me.

"It's very nice," said a voice on my right. "It looks brand-new,"

Cassandra Loescher said. She leaned closer. "I'll bet I know who got it for you."

The jury was seated and Bingham greeted them by reminding them where we had left off and what was coming next.

"Good morning, ladies and gentlemen. Yesterday, we finished with the opening statements. Let me remind you again that what the attorneys say in their opening statements is not evidence of anything. The only evidence you are to consider is evidence introduced by the testimony of witnesses. This morning, the prosecution will begin its case by calling its first witness. Ms. Loescher, who is the prosecutor in this case, will examine each witness she calls by asking that witness specific questions. This is called direct examination. When she has finished asking questions of her witness, Mr. Antonelli, the attorney for the defense, may, if he wishes, ask questions of his own. This is called cross-examination. At the end of the prosecution's case, the defense will have an opportunity to call witnesses of its own. The defense will then ask questions first and the prosecution will be allowed to cross-examine."

Pausing, he tilted his smallish round head slightly to the side in the attitude of someone about to impart something of particular importance.

"There will be a time—and you witnessed several occasions during opening statements—when an objection will be made either to a question that is asked or an answer that is given. These objections raise issues of law, issues which it is my responsibility to decide. Sometimes you will hear me sustain an objection; sometimes you will hear me overrule an objection. You should not assume that these rulings mean that I have in any way formed an opinion about the merits of this case one way or the other. You certainly must not assume that I have any feelings either of animosity or partiality toward either of the lawyers. Just because I disagree with an argument made by one lawyer or the other does not mean that I think he or she has the weaker case."

He let them consider the meaning of what he had said while

he arranged some papers he had brought with him. "Ms. Loescher," he asked, looking up, "is the prosecution ready to begin?"

She was wearing a blue print dress. Her hair was pulled up from behind her neck and stacked on top of her head. "Yes, your honor," she said as she rose straight up from her chair.

"You may call your first witness."

She turned her head toward the door at the back of the courtroom. "The prosecution calls Sharon Arnold."

In her early thirties, with long black hair and dark, flirtatious eyes, the first witness had worked as Quincy Griswald's judicial assistant for a little over four years. She had found his body in the parking structure, slumped against his car.

"How did you happen to be in the parking structure at that particular time?" Loescher asked in a calm, steady voice.

One leg crossed over the other, Sharon Arnold waited until Loescher's eyes left the jury and came around to her. "I didn't have my car that day. I left it at the dealer's that morning for servicing. Judge Griswald was giving me a ride."

With her hand on the railing of the jury box, Loescher tried to fill in the gap. "Were you going to meet him at his car?"

The question was met with a blank look. Then, when she realized what she had left out, she went on as if she had not forgotten a thing. "We left the office together, but when we reached the door to the outside, he asked me if I'd go back and get something he wanted to work on that night at home."

Quincy Griswald had not been the only judge to depend on his clerk to keep track of where everything was and to make certain everything was done on time. The clerks ran the courthouse, and after enough years doing it some of them knew more about the law than did the judges for whom they worked. It made sense that Griswald would ask her to go back for the court file he wanted: He would not have known where to look had he gone himself.

Loescher remained next to the jury box, at the end opposite the witness stand. Each time she asked a question, the faces of the jury turned toward her, and then, when she was finished, swung back to watch as Sharon Arnold gave her answer.

"And so you went back to the office to get the court file he had asked for. Approximately how long did it take from the time you left him at the doorway until you found him?"

She was used to deciding things quickly. "Just a few minutes," she answered immediately.

Without moving any closer to the witness, Loescher stepped away from the jury box until she was standing directly in front of her. "Please," she cautioned, "take your time. Try to be as precise as you can. When you say 'a few minutes,' how many minutes do you mean?"

While she worked for Quincy Griswald, Sharon Arnold had been in court as often as the judge, sitting below him on the opposite side of the bench from the witness stand, a model of administrative efficiency. She was not used to explaining herself to anyone, and she could not quite hide her annoyance.

"Well, I don't know—five minutes, ten minutes—something like that."

Loescher took two steps closer, raised her head, and gave the witness a glance that was like a warning shot across the bow. This was not Griswald's courtroom and she was a witness in a murder case, not a pampered judicial assistant who could make a lawyer's life miserable anytime she chose to do so.

"Please consider your answer carefully," she said, taking another step toward her. "Would you say it was closer to five minutes or ten?"

Arnold recrossed her legs and began to fidget with her hands. She sucked in the sides of her cheeks and struck a pensive pose.

"I had to go all the way back down the hallway to the elevator. I remember it took a long time to get there. Then the office door was locked of course, and I had to unlock that. The folder was in the file drawer of the judge's desk. Then I locked the door and . . . I suppose it must have been closer to ten minutes before

I got to the garage and found him, lying there, all that blood all over him . . ."

Now in control, Loescher moved back to her preferred position next to the jury and led her witness through the story she wanted her to tell. She had found Quincy Griswald bathed in blood and knew as soon as she saw him that he was dead. She dropped the file she had been sent back to get and ran screaming into the courthouse. Two uniformed security officers followed her back to the garage and the body she had been the first to find.

I was far more interested in what she had not seen than in what she had.

"Have you ever seen this man before?" I asked as soon as it was my turn to examine the witness. Smiling at Sharon Arnold, I stood behind Danny, my hand on his shoulder.

"No, I don't think so."

My hand fell away from his shoulder and I moved slowly to the front of the counsel table. Gripping the edge behind me, I leaned back against it, one foot crossed over the other.

"You didn't see him in the garage when you first found Judge Griswald?" I asked casually.

"No."

"You didn't see him anywhere in the garage when you went back there with the two officers?"

"No."

"You didn't see him anywhere in the courthouse, lurking around, when you were first leaving with Judge Griswald?"

"No."

Folding my arms across my chest, I stared down at my shoes. "You've never seen him before today, have you?" I asked, glancing at her from under my brow.

"No, I don't think so."

I lifted my head higher. "Can you think of anyone who would have wanted Judge Griswald dead?"

It was automatic, the other side of the insistence that we never

speak ill of the dead: the blind assurance that despite the fact
that someone killed them, no one could possibly have wanted it
to happen.

"No, of course not."

I raised my eyebrows, then lowered my head and walked the
few steps to the jury box.

"You're aware, are you not," I asked, turning suddenly toward
her, "that a lot of people—including Quincy Griswald—wanted
Calvin Jeffries dead?"

"Your honor!" Loescher shouted as she sprang from her chair.

I held up my hand before Bingham could open his mouth. "I'll
rephrase the question. You worked very closely with Judge
Griswald, didn't you?" I held her eyes in mine and refused to let
go.

"Yes, I did, for four years."

"And in the course of that time—working that close together—
you came to know quite a lot about him, didn't you?"

She did not hesitate. "Yes."

"And you knew quite a lot about the way he felt about other
people, including other judges, didn't you?"

Loescher was still on her feet, watching intently. Bingham had
both arms on the bench, peering down at the witness.

"Yes."

"And he didn't like Calvin Jeffries, did he? He didn't like him
one bit, did he?"

"Your honor?" Loescher insisted.

His eyes still on the witness, Bingham held up his hand. "No,
I'll allow it."

"No, he didn't like him." I started to ask the next question,
but she was not finished with her answer. "I think he was a little afraid of him, to tell you the truth."

"Afraid of him? In what way?"

"Intimidated might be a better way to put it. Judge Jeffries
seemed to have that effect on a lot of people."

"So he wasn't sorry, shall we say, when Calvin Jeffries was murdered?"

"Oh, I didn't say that," she replied, quick to correct the impression she was afraid she might have left.

"He wasn't grief-stricken when Calvin Jeffries was dead?"

She did not want to answer and was content to let her silence speak for itself.

Cassandra Loescher had sat down. She tapped the erasure end of a pencil while she watched, ready to object again.

"You worked for Judge Griswald a little more than four years, correct?"

"Yes."

"So you weren't with him twelve years ago when he handled a criminal case in which the defendant was Elliott Winston, were you?"

"Your honor—relevance?" Loescher inquired, turning up her hands.

"It's relevant to the defense's theory of the case, your honor," I said, as if that were any answer at all.

"And beyond the question of relevance, your honor," Loescher went on, "it's beyond the scope of direct examination."

Bingham looked at me. "Your honor, the prosecution established the employment connection between the witness and the victim. I'm simply exploring the scope of the relationship."

"Then please do it as quickly as possible and then move on to something else."

"During the time you did work for him," I asked her, "did you ever hear him mention the name Elliott Winston?"

She thought about it for a moment. "No, I don't recall that he did."

"You're sure?"

"Was he the one who Judge Jeffries's wife was married to?"

"Yes, that's right."

A knowing smile crept over her mouth. "He did say something once, but not about him, not directly, that is. He was angry with

Judge Jeffries about something. I don't know what. And he said he wondered if Jeffries's wife would have married him if she'd known he was as crazy as her first husband was. That's when I think he used that name—Elliott Winston."

"So he thought Elliott Winston was crazy?"

She shrugged. "I don't know. I assumed it was just a figure of speech."

I had no more questions, and Cassandra Loescher had nothing she wanted to ask on redirect. Sharon Arnold was excused and the prosecution called its next witness, one of the security guards who had gone with her back to where Griswald's body had first been discovered. Short and to the point, his testimony added little to what had already been said. Certain he was dead, but afraid to touch the body, Arnold had left it to the guard to check for a pulse. The second guard followed the first and except to ask them each whether they had seen the defendant at the scene, I did not bother to cross-examine either one of them. Loescher ended the first day of testimony by calling the police photographer who had taken pictures of the body. Over my objection, the photos were entered into evidence and the jury was shown the graphic obscenities of a violent death.

Quincy Griswald, whose eyes had so often filled with anger, and whose mouth had so often been twisted with rage, had a look on his face of puzzled innocence, as if he could not understand why anyone would want to bring him harm. I looked at that picture a long time before I gave it back to the clerk. All the years that had left their mark on his deep-lined features seemed at the moment of death to have faded away, and all the disappointments of his life vanished with them. He looked almost young again.

The next morning, Loescher called the coroner, who described the cause of death, and then called Detective Kevin Crowley, who had been in charge of the investigation. I was becoming more and more impressed with the way Loescher did her job. Each witness was called in a perfectly calculated, completely logical sequence, their testimony part of a story told according to a strict chronology. She would ask the same question three differ-ent ways if it was the only way to make the details clear. And she wanted more than to describe it to the jurors. She wanted them to know what it was like to discover someone you knew stabbed to death; she wanted them to know what it was like for the victim in that instant when he knew he was about to die.

Wearing a dark brown dress and flat shoes, she stood in front of the jury, patient and attentive, listening as Detective Crowley reported how the police had apprehended the suspected killer.

"He had the knife in his hand when you found him?"

Short and stocky, with small quick-moving eyes, Crowley was a little too eager to answer. "Yes," he said before she had quite finished.

"I'm sorry," she said without any apparent irritation. "What was your answer?"

This time he waited. "Yes."

"What did you do with the knife after you removed it from the defendant's possession?"

"I put it inside a plastic bag, sealed it, and tagged it."

Loescher had gone to the table in front of the clerk, where she picked up a large clear plastic bag containing a kitchen knife with a black wooden handle and a six-inch blade. She handed it to the witness.

"Is this the bag?"

"Yes."

"And is that the tag you mentioned?"

He held it up and examined it closely. "Yes, that's my mark."

"What did you do with it then?"

"I placed it in the evidence room at police headquarters and then had it sent to the police crime lab."

"And what was the reason it was sent to the crime lab?"

"To examine it for fingerprints and to have it examined for DNA evidence."

"We'll have testimony later about the fingerprints that were found on the weapon as well as the results of the DNA testing,"

Loescher remarked as she returned to her place next to the jury box. "But let me ask you, Detective Crowley, what further steps were taken in the investigation after you learned whose finger-prints were on the handle and whose blood was on the blade?"

He glanced at the plastic bag and the knife inside it. "We closed the investigation," he said, looking up.

Loescher cast a meaningful glance at the jury, and then, turning back to the witness, said, "Thank you, Detective Crowley. No further questions."

"When you began the investigation," I asked as I rose from my chair at the start of cross-examination, "were you not struck by the similarities between the murder of Quincy Griswald and the murder of Calvin Jeffries?"

"I wasn't involved in the Jeffries investigation."

I stared hard at him. "That wasn't my question, detective. And, by the way," I added almost as an aside, "if you weren't involved in that investigation, you were the only police officer in the state who wasn't. Let me repeat: When you began this investigation weren't you struck by the similarities between the two murders?"

"There were some similarities," he allowed. He sat forward, spread his legs, and rested his hands on his knees. As I began to pace back and forth in front of the counsel table, he followed me with his eyes.

"They were both circuit court judges, correct?"

"Yes."

"They were both killed near their cars in the structure where they both parked?"

"Yes."

"They were both stabbed to death?"

"Yes."

"Then tell me, Detective Crowley, as the lead investigator in this case, what investigation did the police make into the possible connection between the two murders? Let me be even more specific." I stopped pacing and raised my head. "What effort was made to determine whether there was anyone—perhaps someone they had both sentenced to prison—who might have had a motive to want both of them dead?"

"The Jeffries case had already been solved. There was no connection. There could not have been."

"In other words," I asked impatiently, "you couldn't conduct an investigation into that possibility because you assumed it didn't exist?"

"Objection," Loescher interjected before he could answer. "That's an assertion, not a question."

Bingham considered it. "Perhaps you could rephrase the question, Mr. Antonelli."

"You testified a moment ago that you weren't involved in the Jeffries investigation, correct?"

"Yes, that's right."

"So your knowledge of it—your knowledge of what really happened—is at best secondhand, correct?"

"I suppose," he replied, watching me with sullen eyes.

I turned until I was facing the jury and the witness was on my right. "There's another similarity, isn't there? In both cases the police were told where to find the person who supposedly committed the crime. Isn't that true, Detective Crowley?"

"We were given information from an outside source—yes."

I kept looking at the jury. A thin smile flashed across my mouth. "'An outside source.' You mean an anonymous phone call, don't you, Detective Crowley?"

"Yes, we received a call."

"An anonymous call," I said as I turned to face him. "An anonymous call in which the caller in both instances sought to disguise his voice, isn't that true?"

He tried to turn it back on me. "The caller wanted to remain anonymous."

I ignored it. "And don't you think it a little strange that both times—in these two cases in which you assume there was no connection between the murders—the police were told they could find the killer in the very same place, a homeless camp under the Morrison Street Bridge?"

He jumped at it. "You forget: The killer in the first case confessed and then killed himself. He couldn't have had anything to do with the second case, could he?"

With a bored expression, I shook my head and dismissed it with a cursory wave of my hand. "Move to strike, your honor. The answer is nonresponsive. Besides that," I added with a glance at Loescher, "it's nothing but hearsay."

Bingham instructed the jury to pretend they had never heard what they were not very likely to forget. With no more questions to ask, I sat down and waited for Loescher to call the next witness for the prosecution.

With a drooping gray mustache and disheveled gray hair, Rudolph Blensley looked more like an aging professor of mathematics than he did a police detective. Loescher first established his credentials as a fingerprint expert and then asked him whose fingerprints he had found on the knife that had been taken from the defendant.

"The only fingerprints found on the weapon," he replied, "matched the fingerprints of the defendant, John Smith."

Blensley was suffering from a cold, and his words came out muffled and garbled. When Loescher sat down, he removed a large white handkerchief from his side coat pocket and blew his nose. He put the handkerchief in his pocket and with the back of his hand tried to wipe his red, runny eyes.

"Would you like some water?" I asked. We had been in court together before, and he had always answered my questions in the same straightforward manner he answered those asked by the prosecution. "Summer colds are the worst," I remarked while he took a drink.

When he was finished, he settled back in the witness chair and waited.

"The fingerprints you found belong to the defendant, known as John Smith, is that correct?"

"Yes."

"Do you know, by the way, whether there were any fingerprints on file for John Smith, or were you given them by the police after they had taken him into custody?"

He saw where I was going. "You mean, did we take prints from the knife and then run them to find out who they belonged to, or did we compare them to the ones we had for the defendant? We compared them to the set we were given—the ones that belong to the defendant."

"I see. In other words, this was not an investigation in which you used the fingerprints taken from a weapon to find out who among all the millions of people out there who have their fingerprints on file might have held the knife in their hand and used it as a murder weapon?"

"That's correct," he said, reaching for his handkerchief.

I waited while he blew his nose and when he finished asked him if he wanted more water.

"I'm fine, thanks."

"If you had not been given a set of his fingerprints," I asked, pointing at the defendant, "would you have been able to identify him as the person whose prints were on the knife?"

He coughed into his hand. "No," he said finally. "There are no prints of his on file."

"Isn't it true, Detective Blensley, that everyone arrested for a crime—even a misdemeanor—has their fingerprints taken?"

"Yes, that's true."

"And those fingerprints are kept on file?"

"Yes."

"So what you're saying is that the defendant in this case has never before—not once—been arrested for a crime, any crime, isn't that right?"

He lifted his arms and turned up his palms. "All I can say is what I said before: His fingerprints weren't on file."

I went back to the counsel table and stood next to my chair.

"Your honor, may the witness please be shown state's exhibit number 106?"

The clerk handed the detective the clear plastic bag containing the knife.

"I won't ask you to take it out and test it, but just looking at it, does the blade seem to have been filed sharp? In other words, does it have an edge on it?"

"No, it doesn't have an edge."

"In fact, wouldn't you say it appears rather dull?"

He nodded, and waited.

"Of course even a dull knife can be used to stab someone, can't it?"

He nodded again, and I had to remind him to answer out loud. "Yes."

"Now, if you would, look at the handle. Does it look to you—the way it looked to me—worn, faded, a knife that has been used a lot?"

"Yes, I'd say so."

"In other words, from everything you observe, you would have to say, wouldn't you, that this is a rather old knife—certainly not a new one?"

"I would agree with that," he said, sniffing into his handkerchief.

"Probably used by lots of different people from the time it was first sold, wouldn't you think?"

"Yes, I would imagine."

"And yet, if I heard you right, the only fingerprints you found on the knife belonged to the defendant. All those people—dozens, perhaps hundreds—used this knife and you only found one person's prints. Doesn't that suggest something to you, Detective Blensley?"

He hesitated, not certain what I meant. I drew myself up, and with a sense of urgency in my voice, asked, "Doesn't it suggest to you that whoever had that knife before it came into the possession of the defendant must have wiped it clean?"

He started to answer, but I cut him off. "Doesn't it suggest to you that whoever had the knife before didn't want anyone to know? And why do you think whoever that was wouldn't want anyone to know that he had held that knife—that knife that the prosecution tells us was used to murder Quincy Griswald—unless it was because he was the one who murdered him?"

Loescher was on her feet, shouting her objection. "Nothing further, your honor," I said as I started to sit down.

I was back on my feet before I had touched the chair. "There is one more thing, your honor."

Loescher looked at me, her mouth still open. Bingham looked at me, his mouth still shut.

"Detective Blensley, the fingerprints you found—the fingerprints that belong to the defendant—can you tell us if they were put there before Quincy Griswald was murdered?"

He shook his head. "No, there is no way to know that."

"In other words, they could just as easily have been put there sometime after Quincy Griswald was murdered, correct?"

"Yes, that's true."

Twenty-six

The prosecution began the third day of testimony with Dr. Friedrich Zoeller, head of the laboratory that had conducted the DNA testing on the blood residue found on the knife. Tall and thin, with prominent cheekbones and deep-set eyes, he slouched on the witness chair, one leg dangling over the other, one arm sticking straight out to the side. With astonishing rapidity he rattled off facts and figures and did it with such confidence that it was almost impossible to think he might be wrong. From nine-thirty in the morning until the court recessed for lunch a few minutes after twelve, Dr. Zoeller lectured the jury on the nature of DNA and the absolute certainty that the blood from the knife belonged to Quincy Griswald and to no one else.

Cassandra Loescher treated him with a deference she had not shown anyone else. Zoeller was not just an expert witness, he was a scientist, and science, she seemed to say with every respectful question she asked, was the one thing no one could question. The testimony of the state's witness that the knife found on the defendant, the knife that had only his fingerprints on it, had been used to murder Quincy Griswald was something only a fool could doubt.

Standing in front of the charts and graphs that had been carefully arranged on two large easels between the jury box and the witness stand, I studied for a moment the brightly colored, neatly labeled exhibits. With my hands clasped behind my back I moved to the far end of the jury box.

"I'm afraid I'm just a lawyer, Dr. Zoeller," I said, watching the faces of the jury. "Earlier we heard testimony from someone about fingerprints. If I followed what you were saying, DNA is the same kind of thing. Is that right?"

He seldom moved from the languid position he had assumed when he first took the stand. His head rolled onto his shoulders and he looked at me down his nose.

"In a manner of speaking," he replied with an indulgent smile. "The difference is that fingerprints are just what the word suggests: the surface skin of the tips of the fingers. DNA, on the other hand—as I tried to explain—can be taken from virtually any part of the body: skin, blood, hair, bodily fluids—the saliva inside the mouth, for example."

"No, I'm sorry," I said, flapping my hands in the air. "I understand that. What I want to be clear about is this: DNA, like fingerprints, is unique to every individual—no two people have the same fingerprints or the same DNA. Is that right?"

"Yes, that's right," he said, flashing that same patronizing smile. "With the exception of identical twins."

I smiled back. "Tell me, Dr. Zoeller, do identical twins have the same fingerprints?"

He blinked. The smile disappeared, and the hand that had been dangling in the air gripped the arm of the chair as he started to sit up.

"I don't think so," he replied cautiously.

"You don't think so?" I asked, still smiling. "You don't know?"

"No, I don't believe they would be the same," he said, becoming a shade more pale.

I dismissed it as a matter of no great consequence. "Fingerprints aren't your specialty. You're an expert on DNA."

He seemed relieved. "Yes, that's right."

"Then tell me this. You gave us an extraordinarily clear account of the way this works. The genetic code you described, made up of billions of very specific directions—is it all right to put it like that?"

He was sitting straight up, following every word. "Yes, that's a fair way of putting it."

"It's like a vast, enormously complicated computer program, isn't it?"

"Yes, that's a good analogy."

I stopped and looked at the jury. "It's a miracle, isn't it?"

"Yes, I suppose one could say—"

"A miracle that science has now proven the existence of God?"

"No, I don't think you can say—"

"But you said it, didn't you? You said it was like a computer program. Every program has a programmer, someone who designed it, doesn't it?"

"Yes, but—"

"Do you know of any computer program more intricate and complex than the genetic code?"

"No, but—"

"You're a scientist, Dr. Zoeller. Would it be reasonable—would it be rational—to assume that less complex systems can only come into being by design, but more complex systems come into being by chance?"

He sat back, a condescending smile on his mouth. "Or millions of years of evolution."

"Which is chance plus duration," I said with a dismissive glance. "Now, Dr. Zoeller, however the genetic code was first written, you were able to establish that the blood on the knife was the blood of the victim in this case because the DNA in one sample matched the DNA in the other, correct?"

"Yes." He gestured toward one of the charts left on the easel.

"I see that. You showed how the pattern of horizontal marks which represents the DNA taken from the body of the victim matches the marks which represent the DNA taken from the blood left on the knife. And because each of the marks in these two samples match each other, we can be confident that they belong to the same person, correct?"

"Yes, that's absolutely correct."

"We can be confident, in other words, that they have a common origin?"

He seemed amused at the way I was struggling to understand something which to his well-trained mind was self-evident. "Yes, they have a common origin; they belong to the same person. As I said, they're identical."

"So we can all be confident—with scientific certainty—that if two things are in all important respects the same, they're identical and have the same origin?"

"Yes, yes of course," he replied, relaxed and self-assured.

"Even two murders?" I asked innocently as I turned toward the jury on my way back to the counsel table.

Loescher shot an angry glance at me as she got to her feet and, eager to show everyone just how wrong I was, almost shouted out the name of the prosecution's next witness. "The state calls Detective Jack Stewart."

Though long since abandoned by even the most senior members of the department, Stewart still adhered to a formal dress code. Perhaps he remembered the time when he made his first appearance in a courtroom, a uniformed patrol officer, testifying in front of a jury in which every woman wore a dress and every man wore a tie; perhaps, living alone and close to retirement, he just needed an excuse to put on a suit.

Cassandra Loescher was wearing one as well, a dark-striped tailored suit that fit her perfectly. It was new and it was expensive, and more than the way she looked, it changed the way she felt. She held her chin just a little higher and her shoulders just a little straighter than she had before. When she turned on her heel, there was a bit more confidence in her step and a kind of hard sparkle in her eye. While Stewart took the oath, she stood with one hand on her arm, stroking her sleeve.

After a few quick questions established Stewart's rank and experience, Loescher moved directly to the only issue left, the utterly absurd suggestion that the defendant could not have killed Quincy Griswald because whoever killed him had killed Calvin Jeffries as well. Her hand still on her sleeve, she tapped her fingers, impatient of the necessity of having to prove what everyone already knew.

"You were the lead investigator in the case involving the murder of Judge Calvin Jeffries?"

"I was one of them," Stewart explained.

She pivoted a quarter turn. Facing the jury, she asked, "And was an arrest made in that case?"

"Yes, there was. Jacob Whittaker was charged with the murder of Judge Jeffries."

"And would you please tell the jury," she said as she plucked lint from her sleeve and brushed it away, "did the person you arrested confess to the crime?"

There was no response from the witness. Loescher glanced up. "Detective?"

"He made a confession. That's true."

It was not as emphatic, nor as immediate, as she would have liked, but when he finally gave it, the answer was clear enough. One more question and there would be no more room for doubt, and that slight hesitation in his voice would be all but forgotten, a momentary lapse of memory, the sort of thing that happens to witnesses all the time.

She settled her eyes on the jury, a confident smile on her lips. "And tell us, Detective Stewart, what did the confessed killer of Calvin Jeffries do after he confessed?"

"That evening he was found dead in his cell."

The smile froze on her face. Her eyes flared as she turned on him. "You mean he committed suicide, don't you?"

"That was the official finding, that's correct," Stewart replied without expression.

She looked at him, trying to figure out why he did not answer her questions the way he was supposed to, instead of insisting on all these unnecessary distinctions. He was a police officer, not a lawyer, and while he was not supposed to lie, neither was he supposed to make the truth more difficult to grasp.

"Just to sum up, then. There was an arrest, there was a confession, and the man who confessed, it was officially decided, then took his own life. One last question, Detective Stewart. After the arrest, after the confession, after the suicide, what happened to the investigation? Did it continue, or was it closed?"

"It was closed," he replied.

Loescher looked at the jury. "The killer was caught, and the killer confessed, and the case was closed." She sat down, and then, as if she had just remembered, glanced up at the bench. "No further questions, your honor."

I stood up so fast I had to catch the chair from falling over. "We've met before, haven't we, Detective Stewart?" I asked, laughing at myself as I stumbled free of the chair.

He did not hesitate. "Yes, we have."

Loescher's head came up, and she looked at him and then at me.

"You've been a witness for the prosecution in several trials in which I've been the attorney for the defense, isn't that correct?" I asked as I straightened the chair and moved away from the table.

"Yes, that's correct," he said.

Loescher looked back at the legal pad on which she had begun to scribble a note to herself.

"Jacob Whittaker—the man who was arrested, the man who confessed, the man found dead in his cell—how did you know where to find him?"

"An anonymous phone call."

"And where did this anonymous caller say the killer could be found?"

"Under the bridge."

"That's the Morrison Street Bridge, correct?"

"Yes, that's right."

"And that's where he was found—under the Morrison Street Bridge—living as one of the homeless?"

"Yes."

"How do you imagine the caller—this anonymous caller—knew who the killer was and where he could be found?"

Stewart shook his head. "I don't really know."

"Did Whittaker have any idea who the informant might have been?"

With an audible sigh, Loescher stood up. "Your honor, I fail to see the relevance of any of this."

Judge Bingham looked at me, waiting.

"I'm trying to establish a pattern, your honor. In both cases an anonymous caller informed the police where they could find the alleged killer, and both times it was in the same place. I'm trying to find out who could have had this information about both murders."

Loescher stretched out her hands. "It's simply a coincidence. The detective has already established by his testimony that the killer of Calvin Jeffries could not possibly have had anything to do with the murder of Quincy Griswald." She darted a glance at the jury. "Being dead and all."

"You'll address yourself to the court," Bingham snapped. "Now, Mr. Antonelli," he went on in his usual tone, "are you about finished with this line of inquiry?"

"Almost, your honor." I turned back to the witness. "Did Whittaker know anything about the informant?"

Stewart tilted his head, pursed his lips, and shut his eyes into long thin slits. "I don't know if he did or not. But if he did, he didn't tell us."

"When he was arrested and brought in, you assumed he was one of the homeless, didn't you?"

"Yes, I did."

"Tell me, Detective Stewart, did you discover before or after you closed the investigation into the murder of Calvin Jeffries that the man who confessed to his killing was a mental patient at the state hospital?"

The courtroom erupted, and for the first time in the trial Bingham had to use his gavel to quiet the crowd. The public had never been told that Jeffries's killer had been an escaped mental patient. From the look on Loescher's face, she had not been told either.

"Whittaker was arrested, confessed, and died, all in the same day," Stewart explained when the courtroom became quiet. "We did not know who he was, or what he was, until his fingerprints came back a few days later."

I went after him as if we were old adversaries instead of recent friends.

"You were in the room when he confessed and you didn't notice anything strange about him? He struck you as a completely normal, a completely sane individual?"

Even if I had been acting in anger, it would have had no effect: Stewart was unflappable. "There were things about him that didn't seem normal."

"Such as?"

"The way he kept repeating the same phrase over and over again when I asked him why he did it. He kept saying, 'I really can't say.' At first I thought he meant he didn't know, that he couldn't explain why he had done it. Then, gradually, I began to believe that he knew, but that for some reason he couldn't, or wouldn't, talk about it."

I stood completely still. "That he wasn't allowed to talk about it?"

Stewart was not going to be led into saying something he did not believe. "That he knew why he had done it, but that he wasn't going to tell us. Why he wouldn't tell us is a question I can't answer. I just don't know."

"But it struck you as odd that someone would confess to a murder—tell you he'd done it—but refuse to tell you why?"

"Yes, it struck me as odd," he agreed.

That was all I would need: the admission by the state's own witness—the lead investigator in the murder of Calvin Jeffries—that there was something odd, something not quite right about the confession of the killer. It gave me the opening to argue that there was a reason to doubt that the person responsible for Jeffries's death had ever been found, and that there was a reason to believe that the two murders were connected. Loescher, too smart not to see it too, closed it with a few well-phrased questions on redirect.

"You just testified that Jacob Whittaker confessed to killing Calvin Jeffries, but would not tell you why he did it," she asked as she rose from her chair.

Stewart nodded. "Yes."

She stood at the table, resting the fingertips of her left hand on top of it. "Mr. Antonelli asked you if you agreed that this was—I believe the word he used was 'odd'—correct?"

"Yes."

She indulged herself in one of those smug little smiles that the smartest girl in class used to have when she knew the answer and, worse yet, knew you did not. "But Mr. Antonelli also asked you if you knew that Jacob Whittaker was a mental patient. In your experience, Detective Stewart, would it be unusual for a mental patient to do things or say things that the rest of us would consider odd?"

"No," he agreed.

She raised her chin, the smile replaced by a look of earnest conviction. "You were the lead investigator in that case. Just tell us: Do you have any doubt—any doubt whatsoever—that Jacob Whittaker is the person who murdered Judge Jeffries?"

Without a moment's hesitation, Stewart replied, "No, no doubt at all."

Turning toward the jury Loescher repeated the question for effect. "No doubt at all?"

Bingham, sitting sideways to the bench, looked up from something he was reading in his lap. "Recross?"

"Detective Stewart," I said as I got to my feet, "why are you so certain that Jacob Whittaker killed Judge Jeffries? People have been known to confess to things they didn't do, haven't they?"

"Yes, but in this case Whittaker knew things about the murder—details—that weren't released to the public."

"What details, Detective Stewart?"

"Judge Jeffries was not just stabbed to death: The killer disemboweled him."

"Gutted him?"

"Yes."

"And when Whittaker told you this, his account was both clear and convincing?"

"Yes."

"He wasn't ranting, or raving, or doing any of those other 'odd' things we tend to associate with lunatics?"

"No, he wasn't doing any of that."

"You discovered that Whittaker was a mental patient. Why was he a mental patient? Was he there because of a civil commitment or a criminal commitment?"

"Whittaker had been found incompetent to stand trial for a crime he committed."

I walked toward the jury box. "And what crime was that, Detective Stewart?" I asked, my head bent down, my hands locked behind my back.

"Murder."

I could feel it, the inaudible gasp, the tension that gripped the room at the knowledge that the killer of Calvin Jeffries had killed before. I did not look up.

"And who did he murder, Detective Stewart?"

"His father."

I slowly raised my head. "His father? With a knife?"

"No, he beat him to death with his bare hands."

"Why did he do it?"

Stewart was leaning forward, his elbows braced on the arms of the witness chair. His head moved from side to side. "There was a long history of abuse. His father was a drunk, and he made a habit of beating up his wife—Whittaker's mother. Finally, something snapped, I guess, and he literally went out of his mind."

"So he had a motive?"

"Yes."

"What motive did he have to kill Jeffries?"

Stewart shook his head and shrugged. "I don't know."

"Well, did he know Jeffries?"

"No."

"Was Jeffries the judge who sent him to the state hospital?"

"No."

"It's true, isn't it, Detective Stewart, that you weren't able to find any connection at all between Whittaker and the man he killed?"

"No, we didn't."

"And there was no other obvious motive either, was there?"

"No."

He looked at me, a quizzical expression on his face.

"It wasn't a robbery, was it?"

"No."

"Nothing was taken from Judge Jeffries, was there?"

"No."

"So it wasn't a robbery, it wasn't revenge; he did not even know him and without any motive just decides to lie in wait for him and kill him in a particularly gruesome manner. But, of course, he was a mental patient—insane—and that explains everything, doesn't it?" I asked rhetorically, glaring across at Cassandra Loescher.

"Where was he a mental patient, Detective Stewart?"

He seemed surprised by the question. "The Oregon State Hospital."

"He had been there more than ten years, hadn't he?"

"I believe so."

"In the forensic ward of the state hospital, where the criminally insane are kept, correct?"

"Yes."

"Isn't that the same place where Elliott Winston has been kept for the last twelve years?"

"Objection!" Loescher protested before he could answer. "There's been no foundation established to demonstrate that the witness would have direct knowledge of this."

"Withdraw the question, your honor." I stood at the end of the jury box, my arms folded across my chest. "Now, Detective Stewart, you've testified that you have no doubt at all that Jacob Whittaker was the person who murdered Judge Jeffries, but you also testified that you thought there was something odd about his confession. I don't need to remind you that you're under oath, Detective Stewart, but I want you to think carefully about your answer to this question. When he was telling you—repeating it over and over again—that he couldn't say when you asked him why he had done it, did you believe then that there was something else going on, that there was in fact a reason why he had killed this man he did not know and had never met?"

"Yes, I thought that was a possibility."

"And when Quincy Griswald was killed, did you think there might be some connection—some possible connection—between the two murders, even though the second one could not have been committed by the man who committed the first?"

"The two murders were almost identical."

"Almost?"

"Yes. Both victims were stabbed, but only the first one was disemboweled."

"But with that exception, they were identical?"

"Yes, but that exception seemed at first to argue against any connection. It was the one important detail that had never been released to the public. Because of that, I assumed the second was some kind of copycat killing."

"At first?"

"Yes. I began to wonder more about it when I learned of the way the arrest was made and where it was made: the anonymous phone call, the homeless man living under the same bridge. It was hard to believe there wasn't some connection."

"Did you do anything to pursue this suspicion?"

"When they brought in the suspect . . ." He paused and nodded toward the counsel table. Danny was sitting with his head sunk down on his chest, half asleep. "I sat in on the interview."

"You weren't part of the investigation?"

"No."

I glanced over at Danny and then looked back at Stewart. "Did he confess?"

"No. We didn't talk to him very long. He was filthy and he had to be cleaned up. But, no, he didn't confess."

I made my way from the jury box to the chair where Danny was just starting to pay attention and stood behind him, my hands on his shoulders.

"Ms. Loescher asked if you had any doubt whether Jacob Whittaker killed Calvin Jeffries. You sat in on the police interview of the defendant. Do you have any doubt about his guilt?"

Stewart had been around for years. He knew there was something wrong with the question. More by instinct than design, he gave the prosecution time to object.

He did not have to wait long. Loescher's arm shot into the air with such force it seemed to pull the rest of her along with it.

"Your honor!" she shouted, banging her hand down on the table. "This goes beyond anything—!"

Bingham seemed almost amused by her outburst. "You wish to make an objection, Ms. Loescher?"

She looked at him, her mouth hanging open, and blinked. "Yes, your honor," she said, quite calm. "The question calls for speculation."

"The prosecution asked this witness his opinion of the guilt of the person charged with the murder of Judge Jeffries," I responded. "That opened the door to an inquiry of this same witness about his opinion of the guilt or innocence of the defendant in this case."

Bingham politely disagreed. "I'm afraid I don't see it quite that way, Mr. Antonelli. The witness was the lead investigator in the first case. He was asked his opinion based on that investigation. And no objection was made to that question," he added, letting me know that he would not, given a proper objection, have allowed that one either. "You're asking him to give an opinion on a case in which he was not involved. For that reason the objection must be sustained."

"I'll rephrase the question, your honor," I said as I started to turn back to Stewart. "It doesn't matter how he phrases it, your honor. The question can't be asked."

"She's right, Mr. Antonelli."

"I'll limit myself to what Detective Stewart observed."

"Just so you don't elicit any opinion regarding the ultimate issue," Bingham insisted.

"Yes, your honor. I promise I won't ask the witness what he really thinks."

"Your honor!" Loescher cried.

Bingham held up his hand, then leaned back in his chair and began to tap his fingers together, a stern expression clouding his brow. Presently, he sat forward and the seldom disturbed civil smile returned to his clean, straight mouth.

"I really never expected that sort of thing from you."

I could have ignored and almost enjoyed the angry shouting of one of the many intemperate, self-important judges who take pleasure in the pain they can inflict on the lawyers who practice in front of them. This hurt, all the more because he was right. It was a cheap trick that never worked.

"I apologize, your honor. That was inexcusable."

He kept his gaze on me a moment longer, then looked at the jury.

"Sometimes, in the course of a trial, things are said that shouldn't be said and that the person who says them immediately regrets. This is particularly true in a case like this one where something very serious is at issue. Mr. Antonelli said something which I'm going to ask you to ignore and which I know he wishes he had not said. I want you to understand this very clearly. Detective Stewart was asked if he had an opinion about the guilt or innocence of the defendant. I don't know if he does or not; I do know that it doesn't matter if he does. Opinions don't count: Facts, and only facts, count. Detective Stewart, like any other witness, may testify about things he knows—that is to say, facts about which he has knowledge. The conclusions which are to be drawn from whatever facts are established during this trial, including whatever facts Detective Stewart has to offer, are to be drawn, not by the witnesses themselves, certainly not by the lawyers, and not by me. That job is for you, the jury, and only for you. Therefore, I now instruct you that you are to ignore what Mr. Antonelli said, and you are not to infer from it, either that the witness believes the defendant to be innocent of the charge of murder or guilty of that charge. Do you understand?"

When the twelve of them nodded dutifully in unison, Bingham's eyes came back around to me. "You may continue."

It did not hurt if the jury thought I was zealous; it would be the end of me as a lawyer if they thought I was too chastened to keep fighting. It was the judge's courtroom, but it was my case.

"You were present during the police interview of the defendant, correct?"

"Yes, I was."

"When he was asked a question, did he look away?"

"No."

"Did he fidget nervously with his hands?"

"No."

"Did he spend a lot of time thinking about his answers before he gave them?"

"No."

"Did he do anything at all that, based on your experience, you could label as an indication of deception?"

"No."

"He denied he killed Quincy Griswald?"

"Yes, he did."

"Did you believe him?"

"Your honor—!" Loescher cried.

"Mr. Antonelli," Bingham began.

"Withdrawn," I announced with a wave of my hand as I left the witness and headed back for my chair.

Twenty-seven

A s soon as I saw him I started to smile. Howard Flynn had
on his best suit, the one he wore to weddings and to funer-
als and to any other formal event to which he was on occasion
invited. It was the only suit I had ever seen him wear, and so far
as I knew, the only suit he owned. There was not a wrinkle anywhere on the dark blue coat and the matching pants were creased
tight down the front. With a starched white shirt and burnished
black shoes, a solid gray silk tie and a breast pocket handkerchief
to match, he looked like the prosperous and successful attorney
he should have been. It was not hard to figure out why he had
gone to so much trouble.

"It's nice to see you, Howard," Jennifer said as she held out
her hand.

Flynn was standing at the table, clutching a white linen napkin. "It's nice to see you, Jennifer," he said, gently taking her
hand in his thick fingers.

"I'm sorry we're late," she said as he pulled a chair out for her.
"It's my fault. It took me a little longer to get ready than it should
have."

It was a rare performance, one I would not have missed for
anything. Flynn had not only been on time, he had actually ar-

rived a little early. To make sure we got a good table, he explained as if it were the kind of thing he did all the time or something he would have done had he been dining alone with me.

The waiter, a balding middle-aged man with round, chubby cheeks and a small, thoughtful mouth, brought menus. Jennifer ordered a glass of wine and Flynn asked for a Diet Coke.

"And what would you like?" the waiter asked, glancing at me over the top of his notepad.

"Scotch and soda." Jennifer darted a worried glance at me. "It's all right," I assured her. "I'm just going to have one." Then I realized that was not what concerned her. "Howard doesn't mind."

His face reddened slightly when he told her it did not bother him at all. "Just as long as he doesn't enjoy it too much," he added, trying to put her at ease.

The waiter brought our drinks and took our order. Stirring the ice, I remembered the last time we had come here, the two of us, that Saturday night she had to go home early, the night I called Flynn to get me out of the bar. As I sipped on the drink, I watched them chatting amiably, and knew that whatever else happened I could always count on them both. I was glad they liked each other, though I would have been surprised if they had not.

While they talked, I started thinking about the case, or rather the case, which had taken over my life, pushed its way back into my mind. I had left the courtroom quickly, jubilant about what I had been able to achieve during the cross-examination of Stewart. It was the vanity of performance, and the farther away I got from the courtroom, the less impressive it became. What had I actually accomplished? An agreement that there was something odd about the mental patient who murdered Calvin Jeffries and something unusual about the similarities of the two crimes. I had raised questions, but I had not supplied any answers, at least none I could prove.

"I'm going to lead with the psychologist tomorrow," I said out loud. Jennifer and Flynn stopped their conversation and looked at me. "Then I'm putting Danny on the stand." I sat with my hands in my lap, the chair pushed back from the table far enough so I could cross one leg over the other. "You think he can handle it? You see him every day, talk to him . . ."

Jennifer looked at Flynn, then back at me, a question in her eyes.

"Howard goes to see him at the jail every day after court. He tries to explain to him what happened that day and what's going to happen next."

"I see," she said, looking at Flynn with a new sense of appreciation.

"I try to talk to him in court when I have the chance, but he just looks at me with those trusting eyes of his, and smiles, or says yes or no, but not much else. I don't think he knows half the time what I'm talking about."

"He knows more than you think," Flynn replied as the waiter began to serve dinner.

"All I'm going to ask him is what his name is, how old he is, who gave him the knife, and did he kill Griswald. He'll understand those questions?"

"We've been over it a dozen times," Flynn reminded me.

I was irritable, impatient, and I knew it. "Sorry."

Jennifer's hand slid onto my wrist and then along my arm. "You're going to win," she said with an encouraging smile.

I peered into her eyes for a moment and then shook my head. "You're about to find out what a fraud I really am. I hate this work. I hate doing this. I hate not being able to think about anything except what I have to do to win. God, I hate it when they're innocent."

She had an instinct for the essential. "Would you like it better if that boy was actually guilty?"

"No," I said with a sigh. "But it would make things a lot easier."

Flynn put down his fork. "Did you ever think that maybe the problem is that it's actually been a little too easy?"

"No," I said, raising my eyebrows. "I have to confess that's one thought I haven't had."

He was serious. Moving his plate aside, he put his forearms on the edge of the table and bent forward. "If Elliott Winston is really behind both murders, why didn't he make it more difficult? Why did he make it so easy?" He folded his broad, light-haired fingers together. "Why do everything the same way—not just the way Jeffries and Griswald were both killed—why the same anonymous call, the same place each time as the location where the killer could be found?" He pulled back his head as if to get a better look at me. "Why did he want them found? Why would he want Jacob Whittaker to confess? Why would he want anyone to know that Whittaker was a mental patient locked up in the same hospital? He might just as well have signed his name."

Jennifer had stopped eating. "But you're missing something," she blurted.

Startled, Flynn sat up and, perhaps not even aware he was doing it, smiled at her as she tried to apologize.

"I'm sorry." She laughed, embarrassed, holding up her hand. "That just came out."

"What did Howard miss?" I asked.

"You," she said, her eyes glittering. "You're the only one who knew—no, you're the only one who could have known of the connections. There are two of them, aren't there?" she asked, looking at Flynn and then back at me. "The one between Elliott Winston and Whittaker, and the one between him and the two murdered judges. And if you didn't know about the second connection, the first would have no meaning at all, would it? And who besides you would have had any reason ever to look for it?"

Nodding, I looked at Flynn. "What do you think?"

"I think it will be good for you to be married to someone so much smarter than you are."

Jennifer got up from the table and put her hand on Flynn's shoulder to keep him from getting up as well. "I won't be long," she said as she picked up her purse.

"She's right, you know," I said as soon as Jennifer had left. "I agree with what you said: If Elliott really is behind all this, he put a signature to both crimes, but there's no reason to think he wanted anyone to know it was his signature."

As I listened to myself I wondered if I really believed it. The last time I had seen Elliott had I not taunted him with the impotence of doing something that no one will ever know you've done? Was I now simply resisting the possibility that I had been wrong and that he had somehow foreseen how it would all work out while I was still struggling to understand how he had done it in the first place?

Flynn moved his jaw from side to side and then bobbed his head back and forth. He draped one arm over the corner of his chair, crossed his ankle over his knee and held it there with his hand.

"This guy has been sitting there for twelve years. Whether he's crazy or not: You think he hasn't thought through every angle of this? Consider that for a minute: twelve years before he does anything. Maybe it took him that long before he found someone like Whittaker, before he found whoever killed Griswald—maybe it took that long to talk them into it—but after twelve years he still wants his revenge."

There was something left unspoken. "Wants his revenge?" I asked. "You think he wants more than Jeffries and Griswald?"

He did not answer, not directly. "Jennifer was right: You're the only one who could have made the connection between Whittaker and Elliott, but there are a few other people who could make the connection between Elliott and the two judges."

I could think of at least two others. "His wife," I said. "And Asa."

"Right. Now, if he was ready to have Quincy Griswald murdered when all the judge did was preside over the hearing that sent him to the state hospital, what about the lawyer that was supposed to look out for him?—and what about the wife who betrayed him? Twelve years he's waited. Do you think he's going to forget about them? Do you think that just maybe he wants them to see the connection between the first two murders so they can worry about when it's going to happen to them?"

"But they wouldn't have figured it out," I objected. "Neither Asa nor Elliott's wife. They wouldn't have had any reason to think it was anything more than a terrible coincidence—if they thought about it at all. Jennifer's right. I'm the one who put it together. I brought out the fact that Whittaker was a mental patient. I'm the one who accused Elliott of being behind both murders."

"Which may be exactly what Elliott wanted you to do."

Before I could express any doubt, a doubt about which I was myself not quite certain, Flynn shook his head and slid closer to the table. "Look, we know two things, don't we? He left a trail you were able to follow."

"But how could he know I'd follow it?" I interjected. "How could he have known that I'd get involved? How could he have known I'd end up defending the kid who got charged with the murder?"

Flynn's rust-colored eyebrows lifted up and he clicked his teeth. "The first killer confesses and then kills himself. The second killer does what?—gives the murder weapon to someone else and disappears."

"Thrown in the river," I reminded him.

He shrugged it off. "Doesn't matter. The point is he gives up the weapon. And remember," he added, again raising his eyebrows, "he first wipes it clean so only the kid's prints will be found on it. Why?"

I tried to sound more skeptical than I felt. "So someone innocent will be charged and I'd take the case?"

The more Flynn talked, the more certain he was that he was right. He swept over my halfhearted objection. "He waited twelve years to have Jeffries killed; he only waits a couple months to have Griswald murdered."

He said it as if it explained everything; I was not sure it explained anything.

"In twelve years he doesn't have a visitor he's willing to see. In twelve years you don't try to see him, and then, after all that time, Jeffries is murdered and you show up. He knows you've been thinking about it, all of it, the way anyone would: what he had been like when you first knew him, the way you brought him into the firm, the kind of man and the kind of lawyer you thought he was going to be. We all think about that, don't we?—the way things could have been and the way they didn't turn out. He knows you've been thinking about Jeffries, too—what an evil bastard he was and the terrible things he did to people."

Flynn took a long drink from his water glass and looked around at the well-dressed couples having a quiet dinner on a weekday night, the kind of people who were used to good food and did not think twice about what it cost. How many nights, I wondered, had Elliott Winston stared at the blank wall of his asylum cell and driven himself a little more crazy thinking about his beautiful young wife having dinner with Calvin Jeffries in a place like this?

"He knows all this," Flynn went on, "and what does he do with it? He tells you what they did to him—Jeffries and his wife—how they made him crazy with jealousy and how he almost killed you because of it. He lets you know—doesn't he?—that he has every reason in the world to hate them both. And then what happens—after your visit? Griswald is killed in exactly the same way as Jeffries. He knows you'll think about it; he knows that sooner or later you'll figure it out. And he knows something about you. Don't forget that. He knows he can trust you and he knows you won't let an innocent man be convicted."

"Trust me? What makes you think that?"

A wry smile creased his mouth. "He shot you, didn't he? No," he said when I started to protest, "I mean it. He tried to kill you, and you told him that you don't believe he really meant it. Besides that, he knows you think you're in some way responsible for what Jeffries did to him."

Jennifer had not yet come back to the table. I turned around and looked across the dining room toward the hallway in front that led to the rest rooms.

"There's something else," Flynn said as I searched for a sign of Jennifer. "If the Griswald murder wasn't enough—if that didn't tell you what was going on—there was always Asa Bartram. There would not have been any doubt then that they were all connected."

I spun back around. "I'm calling Asa as a witness. I haven't told him why. But we better warn him about this. Asa is old. He may not have heard about what happened in court, and I doubt he put the two murders together on his own. First thing in the morning would you call his office? Talk to Jonah Micronitis. He'll know what to do," I said, looking over my shoulder, expecting at any moment to see Jennifer.

"You said there were two things we knew," I said. "The first: that he left a trail we could follow. What's the second?" I asked, wondering what was taking Jennifer so long.

Flynn sat still, staring at his hands. "For the first time in twelve years Elliott Winston is going to get out of the state hospital," he said, slowly raising his eyes.

"To testify in court," I added.

Flynn cocked his head. "If he gets to court."

"His wife?" I asked as I got up from my chair. "Do you think that's what he wanted all along—to get out so he could . . . ?"

"Because she's the one person he wants to kill himself?" Flynn wondered aloud, one thought leading to another, each more sinister in its ultimate implications.

"I'll be back in a minute," I explained, thinking about two things at once. "I just want to check on Jennifer."

There was no one in the hallway near the rest room. I knocked on the door to the women's room. There was no answer. I knocked again, this time more insistent, but there was still no response.

"Excuse me," I heard someone say behind me. A woman with gray, silver-tinted hair was looking at me with annoyance, waiting for me to get out of her way.

I apologized but did not move away from the door. "I'm a little worried about my fiancée," I explained to her. "Would you mind seeing if she's all right?"

The annoyance vanished. "Of course," she said. "I won't be a moment," she promised as I stepped aside and she pushed open the door.

"Oh, my God!" I heard her shout, the sound muffled by the door that had swung shut behind her. I nearly knocked her over as I bolted inside. Behind her, curled up on the white tile floor, Jennifer had her arms wrapped around herself, clutching hard as her body shuddered in violent convulsions. Her mouth was shut tight, her teeth clenched with such force that the color had drained out of her face. Her eyes were fixed on the wall in a rigid, deathlike stare. I got down on my knees next to her and pulled her into my arms, rocking her back and forth, telling her she was all right. When she finally turned her head and looked at me, she tried to pull away, to fight me, and I held her with all my strength to keep her from hitting me or hurting herself.

"It's all right," I repeated over and over again. She stopped resisting, and a moment later I felt her go limp.

"Is there anything I can do?" asked an anxious voice.

I had forgotten the woman. She was still there, watching, terrified, too decent to leave. "There's a man at our table: heavyset, reddish wavy hair, dark blue suit. Would you ask him to come?"

She hesitated, wringing her hands. "Should I call an ambulance, a doctor?"

Jennifer was breathing quietly now and all I could think about was the quickest way to get her home. "No," I told the woman. "She'll be fine. It's nothing serious. If you'll just get my friend. His name is Howard Flynn."

"Do you think you can get up?" I whispered when the woman had left.

Pale and exhausted, Jennifer looked at me with quiet, curious eyes as if I was a stranger she instinctively knew she could trust. With my help she slowly struggled to her feet. Holding her, I bent down and picked up her purse.

Flynn arrived as I opened the door. He turned white when he saw her. "Home or the hospital?" he asked as I lifted her into my arms.

I was not sure anymore. I wanted to say home, but now it seemed like some place far away. Flynn read the answer in my eyes.

"Lay her down in the back seat," he said as he held the car door open. "You better get in with her," he added as he went round to the driver's side.

He drove carefully, trying to keep the ride as smooth as possible, while I held her head in my lap, mumbling words the sound of which seemed to soothe her. Once, just before we got there, she grasped my hand and held it tight against the side of her face. From the moment I found her on the bathroom floor she had not spoken a word or opened her mouth to try.

The emergency room of the hospital was nearly deserted. A large Hispanic woman looked up with a start as I burst in shouting for help. A thin, agile nurse and a thick-armed orderly took Jennifer from my arms, put her into a wheelchair, and whisked her through a set of swinging double doors. I signed everything the admitting nurse put in front of me, and without listening to what I was saying, answered every question she asked while I kept my eye fixed on the green doors behind which Jennifer had disappeared.

Forty-five minutes after we arrived—forty-five minutes of anger and fear and strange discordant thoughts whose only connection was that they all had something to do with the woman I had known all my life and hardly knew at all—the doors opened and a young doctor with a surgical mask draped around his neck and a thin file folder under his arm called my name. I followed him through the door and down the corridor. There was a smell of disinfectant in the air, and for an instant I remembered the hospital where as a small boy I had followed my father on rounds. The doctor led me to an empty examination room and shut the door behind us. I sat on a molded plastic chair wedged between a stainless steel sink and a color diagram of the human circulatory system pinned to the wall.

"Has this happened before?" he asked. It was ten-thirty at night, but his voice made it seem like three o'clock in the morning. I knew what that was like: to work so long that you forget what it was like to be tired.

"No," I replied. "Maybe," I added. "I don't really know."

He looked at the chart, and then put it down on the corner of the examining table. "I know you already went over this with the admitting nurse, but, if you would, tell me what happened."

I described what I had seen when I found her, and he asked if there was anything else I could tell him.

"Jennifer is a manic-depressive. She was hospitalized once—a long time ago. So far as I know, she hasn't had any trouble—any serious trouble—with it since."

"She's on medication?"

"Yes."

"Lithium?"

"Yes."

"Does she take her medication regularly?"

"Yes, I . . . I think so."

"Do you know exactly when she was hospitalized, or how long?"

"About seven years ago, I think. And I think she was there for about six months. I'm not sure," I replied, hanging my head.

I felt his hand on my shoulder. "It's all right," he said. "We'll get her records. It shouldn't take more than a few days."

I raised my head. "A few days?"

"She is going to have to stay here for a while."

"A few days?"

"Hopefully, it won't be any longer than that," he said. "But I'm afraid I can't really say for sure. We'll have to run some tests."

I was getting confused and I was getting angry. "Look, you're a doctor. What's wrong with her?"

"I don't know yet. She's had some kind of seizure, some kind of episode."

It seemed a strange word to use. "Episode?"

"I'm an emergency room physician, Mr. Antonelli. I'm not a specialist in psychiatric medicine. What I do know is this: Manic-depression is caused by a chemical imbalance in the brain."

It was a condition, he went on to tell me, that could be there for years, without any symptoms, and then, suddenly, with just a slight alteration in the body's chemistry, everything changed. Usually it happened only once, and then, with the right treatment, the balance was restored and the patient lived a normal life. But sometimes it happened more than once, sometimes after a long interval. No one could tell when it might happen and no one yet knew why.

I heard what he said and I understood it, but it seemed to come from somewhere far away and to be directed to someone other than me. All I could think about was Jennifer.

"Can I see her?" I asked before he was quite through.

"Yes, of course," he said as I got to my feet. "She's asleep. She's been given a sedative. But, yes, of course you can see her."

We walked down the corridor to the last room at the end. Behind a white curtain pulled to separate her bed from the empty one next to it, Jennifer was lying with her head on a pillow. An IV was connected to her arm.

"We have some very good people in psychiatric medicine. She'll have the best of care," the doctor said as he slipped her file underneath that of the next patient he had to see.

I stood next to the metal hospital bed and looked down at Jennifer's gentle face. In the dim light of the room the tiny lines at the corners of her eyes became invisible and her skin was as smooth and fair as the first time I saw her, a pretty girl I never stopped thinking was the most beautiful woman I had ever seen. I stood there for a long time, looking down at her while she slept, talking to her in my mind, telling her what I felt, telling her what she already knew. I would have stayed there longer, stayed there until they made me leave, but Flynn was waiting, worrying about what had happened to us both.

"Is she going to be all right?" he asked as he caught up with me and we walked together out of the hospital.

"She's going to be fine," I said, staring straight ahead, wondering as I tried to wipe the tears away when I had first begun to cry.

Twenty-eight

I had the strange sensation of spinning rapidly in the same place, taking everything in, unmoved and unaffected by what I saw and what I heard, the invisible observer of everything around me. For the first time, I knew what it was to be like Danny, and maybe Elliott Winston as well: alone and apart, forced out of the world, the last link severed, no hope left of a normal life. I could hear Morris Bingham talking to me from the bench; I could see the twelve men and women in the jury box, solemn and attentive, turning their eyes to me, waiting for my response, all of them—judge and jury and everyone else in that crowded courtroom—concentrating on someone who was sitting where I was but who was not really me. I waited, like everyone else, to see what I would do, and then, like everyone else, looked to see what the judge would say when I said nothing.

"Mr. Antonelli, does the defense wish to call a witness?" he asked, repeating with the same civil smile the same question he had asked before.

Is this what it was like to go out of your mind: to be aware—acutely, intensely aware—of everything going on all around you, struck by how strange are all the things you always took for granted, astonished at the infinite complications of even the most seemingly simple things? Words, for example: breathe air in to stay alive; breathe it out to make sounds that explain to yourself and maybe others as well why you should keep doing it. Is this what it was like, locked up inside yourself, seeing things with a clarity you never had before, and then, when you try to explain it—describe what you've seen—discover you have forgotten how to talk?

"Yes, your honor," I heard myself say, surprised to find myself standing up. "The defense calls Dr. Clifford Fox."

The tan suit coat he wore was a little too wide for his shoulders, and his pants were bunched up in front at his belt. His gray hair curled up over his collar at the back of his neck. He spoke very softly and chose his words with care. He had the tolerant habit of someone who spent much of his time with children. I asked him all the usual questions about his training and experience and, thinking about Jennifer, paid almost no attention to what he said.

"And have you had occasion to examine the defendant in this case, known as John Smith?" I asked, opening the file that held his report.

"Yes, I have."

I closed the file. "And?"

Fox leaned forward, resting his elbows on the wooden arms of the witness chair. "And?"

"Yes. What did you find? What can you tell us about John Smith?" I pushed back from the counsel table far enough to cross my legs. I put my hands in my lap and began to tap my fingers together.

"Where would you like me to begin?"

I was watching my foot swing back and forth and I did not hear his question.

"Mr. Antonelli?"

"Yes, your honor?" I replied, looking up at Judge Bingham. He seemed to be worried about something.

"The witness asked you where you wanted him to begin. Are you all right, Mr. Antonelli?"

"Of course, your honor," I said, sliding my leg off my knee as I turned to Fox. "Just begin at the beginning, doctor," I said. I crossed the other leg and began to move that foot back and forth.

Fox had just begun to say something. "Your honor," I interrupted, abruptly rising from my chair. "Could we have a short recess?" Before he could answer, I turned away and walked quickly out of the courtroom.

I moved down the hallway, picking up speed with every step I took, banging my fist on the wall, swearing under my breath, wondering why I could not find a telephone. Just as I turned the corner at the end of the hall, I felt a hand on my shoulder and then another one under my arm as someone shoved me through the door to the men's room. It was Howard Flynn and he could barely control himself.

"What are you doing in there?" he yelled as he turned me around. His eyes were bulging and his face was burning red. "Don't do this! I know what you're going through, damn it! But you can't do this!" His chest heaved with each short, hard breath he took. "You want to end up like I did: a drunk who spends the rest of his life regretting it? You think that will make everything all right?" he jeered. "You're not doing Jennifer any good! You're not doing that kid in there any good! You're not doing yourself any good!" he shouted in my face.

I did not want to hear it. Turning away, I bent over a basin and threw water on my face. "I have to find a phone," I said as I dried my face with a paper towel. "I have to call the hospital."

"Look, damn it," he said, struggling to contain himself, "you're in the middle of a murder trial. You have a witness on the stand. You can't go walking in and out of the courtroom like you've got more important things to do somewhere else."

I wheeled around. "I have to call the hospital," I repeated, glaring at him. "I shouldn't have left there last night. I should be there now, not here."

"What about the kid? What's going to happen to him?"

"I don't care what happens to him! Don't you understand? I don't care! I only care what happens to her. I should be there now."

"Let the doctors do their job, and you do yours!" he insisted. "You can't do anything for her by sitting around the hospital."

"I have to be there!"

"No, you don't."

"Yes, I do. Maybe if you'd been there with your wife," I screamed, taunting him, "instead of spending all your time try-ing to be a lawyer . . . !"

The anger, the frustration, all the nameless fear that had boiled up inside me, blinding me to everything except what I felt, van-ished in an instant and I realized what an awful, unspeakable thing I had done. I reached for his arm, but he pulled away.

"I didn't mean that," I said, shaking my head at how easily I had fallen into a state of mind in which the worst thing I could ever have said to him had become a weapon I was only too eager to use.

"I'm really sorry," I said. "I didn't mean it."

The color in his face had returned to normal. He sniffed a cou-ple of times and cleared his throat. "You better straighten your tie," he said. His voice was quiet, subdued. "I shouldn't have grabbed you like that."

He bent his head, biting the inside of his lip. When he looked up, he searched my eyes. "There's nothing worse than living with the thought that you could have saved somebody and you didn't. Don't let that happen to you."

I turned back to the mirror and adjusted my tie. "I'll see you in court."

The door swung shut behind him, and I gripped the sink with both hands and hung my head and tried to convince myself that there was some excuse for what I had done. I turned on the faucet, threw some more water on my face, and then pulled another paper towel from the metal dispenser. Flynn had ignored my apology and felt sorry for me that I had done something that made me feel I had to make one. It was a measure of his strength, and a measure of my weakness.

When I returned to the courtroom, I stood at the corner of the counsel table, waited until Judge Bingham brought court back into session, and before the echo of his voice had finished fading away began to ask my first question.

"Tell us, Dr. Fox: Is the defendant retarded or in any other way mentally deficient?"

"No, Danny—that's the name he was given, whether by his mother or someone else I don't know—is not retarded. He has an intelligence in the normal range, but precisely where in that range, I can't say for sure."

"Why can't you say for sure?"

"Because he can't read, and because he has a very limited vocabulary, and because he knows next to nothing about numbers. I could not run all of the tests I would normally do with a child."

"But Danny isn't a child, is he?" I looked across to where Danny was sitting. He was grinning at Dr. Fox, waving at him whenever he caught his eye. "He's a full-grown adult."

"Physically, yes; mentally, he's a child, a very young child. A very innocent child, I might add."

Cassandra Loescher rose from her chair ready to object, thought better of it, and sat down.

"Would you explain that last remark, Dr. Fox? What do you mean: a very innocent child?"

There was something inherently kind about Clifford Fox, something that flickered unceasingly from beneath the shadows of his melancholy eyes. No matter how often he had been deceived and disappointed by what they became as adults, he could always find something to hope for in children. He smiled at me.

"Did you ever read *Robinson Crusoe* as a boy?"

I thought he was going to describe Danny as isolated and alone, without skill or training. "But Robinson Crusoe was a well-educated man, with a knowledge of all the principles of modern science at his disposal. Danny can't read."

"No, Mr. Antonelli. He's not like Robinson Crusoe; he's like Friday. He has no education, but he isn't for that reason stupid, and he knows how to survive in the situation in which he finds himself. Reverse it: not Robinson Crusoe on the island, Friday in London, and you have something close to what I mean."

He had my attention, and more importantly, that of the jury. Clifford Fox was a marvel of sense and intuition who had listened to the murmurs of a childlike heart and turned them into a blood-chilling account of human indifference and utter depravity. More even than the story he told, the innocence of the manner in which he told it concentrated your mind. You could almost see the burning cigarettes shoved against Danny's pale skin; you would have sworn you could hear at least the echoes of his screams, until you learned that the screaming only made them want to do it more. Then you heard the silence, and the silence itself became unendurable.

Asking questions, moving him first in one direction, then another, I kept Fox on the stand until he had told the jury everything he had managed to put together from the long hours he had spent talking quietly with the strange young man who sat next to me accused of murder. When he described the way Danny had been kept a prisoner, shackled to a metal frame bed, soiled in his own feces, or chained to a stake in the backyard and made to sleep outside in the dirt and cold, jurors wiped their eyes or used a handkerchief to blow their nose. If the trial had ended right then, that jury would have returned a unanimous verdict of not guilty before they had reached the door to the jury room. I asked one last question.

"Dr. Fox, based on your examination, is the defendant, in your professional opinion, capable of an act of murder?"

It called for a conclusion, an opinion about the ultimate issue in the case. I expected an objection, but Loescher did not rise to make one. Resting her chin on her folded hands, she watched the witness and tried to pretend that she had heard nothing new and that she was as certain of what she was doing as she had been before. I expected a one-word answer, but I did not get that either.

Shifting his weight to his other hip, Dr. Fox crossed his legs and leaned against the arm of the witness chair. "Not if you mean a planned, premeditated act of violence in which he deliberately set out to kill another human being."

I tried to save it. "That is the definition of murder. Thank you, Dr. Fox," I said as I sat down.

Fox had been on the stand answering my questions for three hours; in fifteen minutes Loescher managed to undo much of what I had managed to accomplish. Her first question played off my last.

"In other words, Dr. Fox, there are circumstances in which the defendant would be capable of an act of violence, correct?"

Fox raised his eyebrows the way he did at the end of every question, a signal that he was about to answer. "There are circumstances in which all of us are capable of acts of violence."

With her arms folded in front of her, Loescher moved closer to the witness stand, a slightly amused expression on her mouth. "Self-defense, for example? To protect himself from harm—or what he perceived to be a threat of harm?"

The eyebrows went up again. "Yes, of course. As I say—"

"So it would be your opinion, would it not, that if the defendant was somewhere he should not have been—a parking structure, for example—and were surprised there, thought that someone was going to harm him, he could in those circumstances commit an act of violence?"

"It's possible, but—"

"According to your testimony," she went on before he could finish, "the defendant was subjected to physical torture, sexual abuse, things worse than any of us have ever had to imagine, isn't that correct?"

"Yes, there is no question—"

"And isn't it also true, Dr. Fox, that people who are abused as children frequently engage in acts of abuse themselves? And isn't it also true, Dr. Fox, that children who are subjected to the kind of violence you've described here today become not only capable of violence but turn out to be almost incapable of anything else?"

Fox held his ground. "Not this kind of violence," he replied, sitting straight up. He shuddered with disgust. "No, that isn't the way someone reacts to that kind of torture. Besides, you forget—"

"Dr. Fox, let me ask you—"

"Objection, your honor." I was on my feet, pointing angrily at Loescher. "She didn't let the witness finish his answer."

Bingham looked at Loescher. Loescher looked at the witness. The witness looked at Bingham. "You may finish what you started to say," said the judge.

"I was going to say two things. First, the reaction to the kind of long-term, systematic torture to which the defendant was subjected is fear, not aggression. Second, his feelings of weakness and vulnerability were intensified by his isolation. You have to remember: This is someone who has never been to school, never been around other children, around other people except the ones who abused him."

Cardinal Richelieu said that give him any seven sentences a man had ever uttered and he could have him condemned; Loescher could have done it with five. She took Fox's answer as if it was what she had wanted to hear all along.

"I see," she said, raising her eyebrows in turn. "He was isolated, ignorant and vulnerable and afraid. Correct?"

"Yes," he replied without hesitation. "Exactly."

Peering down at her midnight blue high heel shoes, that same irritating amused expression returned to her mouth. "Exactly," she repeated, savoring the word as if it had a value only she understood. "And when you say vulnerable, you mean, don't you, someone easily taken advantage of, someone without the ability to

distinguish between those who mean him well and those who
mean him ill?"

"Yes, absolutely."

She looked down again and repeated this word as well. "And
because he was never around other children, because he's never
been around other people, he would be more eager to please someone he thought might be a friend, someone he thought he could
trust, someone he thought wouldn't hurt him?"

"Yes, without question."

"Without question," she repeated, moving one shoe slightly
ahead of the other. "So, if Mr. Antonelli is right—if there is someone behind both the murder of Judge Jeffries and Judge Griswald,
someone able to convince others to do the killing for him—someone as vulnerable, as susceptible to suggestion as the defendant
would be the perfect candidate, would he not?"

"No, you don't—"

Whirling away, she jabbed her finger toward the defendant and
talked right over the witness. "He could have killed Judge Griswald
because he was caught doing something he shouldn't have done,
or he could have killed him because someone told him to, or he
could have killed him for a thousand other strange reasons and
there is nothing in your training, your experience, or your psychological evaluation of the defendant that can tell us otherwise,
is there?" she demanded.

Fox waited until he was sure she was done. "I'm not sure Danny
could kill anyone, even in self-defense."

She rounded on him, staring hard as she drew herself up to
her full height. "You didn't say that at the beginning. Would you
like to have the court reporter read back your testimony—the
part where you said there were circumstances in which everyone
is capable of violence?"

"'Acts of violence,'" I corrected without rising from my chair.

Loescher looked at me, a blank expression on her face, then
looked up at the bench.

"An 'act of violence' suggests a single, perhaps unique, event;

'capable of violence' suggests a disposition. Dr. Fox said 'acts of violence,' your honor. Perhaps Ms. Loescher would like the court reporter to read it back to her," I said, parrying her false smile with one of my own.

She had made her point, and I had made mine; she moved immediately to something else. "You never saw John Smith—the defendant—until some time after he was brought into custody, correct?"

"Yes, that's correct."

"When you first saw him, he was clean-shaven, with short hair like he has now, wearing clean clothing, correct?"

"Yes."

"Are you aware of what he looked like when he was first brought in? Are you aware that he had long greasy hair, a long, filthy beard, with rags for clothing and cardboard stuffed into his shoes because the soles were falling off?"

"That's my understanding."

"Is it also your understanding that his body was covered with vermin, that there was lice in his hair, as well as other places; that he was so infested, so filthy, that his clothes had to be cut off and he had to be deloused—fumigated? Isn't it true, Dr. Fox, that the defendant—who sits here today in a navy blue suit and tie, looking like a young professional—was living like an animal?"

Fox nodded sadly. "That's my understanding, yes."

"Like an animal," she repeated, casting a sidelong glance toward the jury as she returned to her place at the counsel table.

It was one of the most effective cross-examinations I had ever seen, and it changed everything. I had planned to call the defendant as the next witness for the defense. It was all supposed to be very straightforward. The psychologist would provide a sketch of what Danny's life had been like, and then, with Danny on the stand, the jurors could see for themselves how timid and harmless he really was and how eager to please. But Loescher had used the words of my own witness to show that precisely that vulnerability, that eagerness to please, could have led him to kill in exactly the way I had suggested. She had done to me what I had tried to do to her: taken the strength of my case and turned it into what now seemed a weakness. She was good—far better than I had imagined—and I was in trouble, serious trouble. The only thing I was sure of was that I could not afford to let her subject Danny to that kind of withering cross-examination. If I called him at all, it would be at the very end, the last witness for the defense, and only then if I had no other choice.

"Your honor," I said, rising from my chair as I weighed all this in my mind, "the defense calls Asa Bartram."

Wearing an expensively tailored double-breasted gray pin-stripe suit, Jonah Micronitis stepped inside the courtroom, took a careful look around, and then went back outside. A moment later, the doors opened again and with Micronitis right behind him, Asa Bartram started up the aisle. Micronitis caught my eye, nodded, and pushed his way into a seat in the first row. He turned around and faced the back, his small head moving from side to side, keeping a watch on everyone, ready for the first sign of trouble.

"Mr. Bartram," I began, "you've been a lawyer for how many years?"

He cocked his head and tugged on a shank of his snow white hair. A good-natured smile creased his craggy face and his pale blue eyes twinkled. "More years than I want to remember."

"More than forty?"

"Yes."

"What kind of law have you practiced during that time: civil or criminal?"

"Mainly civil."

"When you say civil, do you mean civil litigation, personal injury cases, that sort of thing?" I asked as I stood behind the counsel table.

"No, not really. I did some of that early on, but my practice is more of what you might call business law: real estate, commercial transactions."

"And when you said 'mainly civil' did you mean to imply that you also did some criminal work?"

"Only at the very beginning. When you're just starting out," he said with a nostalgic smile, "you pretty much do everything."

I edged my way toward the front of the table. "When is the last time you took a case—civil or criminal—to trial?"

"As I say, my practice is largely a business—"

"The last time?" I insisted.

He really did not know. "Thirty years or so, I guess."

"When was the last time you handled a criminal case—not whether you took it to trial, Mr. Bartram—the last time you represented someone charged with a crime?"

He shrugged. "I suppose about the same: thirty years or so."

I took a step toward him. "But didn't you represent Elliott Winston twelve years ago on a charge of attempted murder?"

He planted both feet on the floor, wrapped each of his large, heavily veined hands around the ends of the arms of the chair, and wagged his head. "No, that's not exactly right. I only agreed to represent him for the purpose of a hearing. I never agreed to be his lawyer."

I took another step closer. "I don't think I understand. You represented him at a hearing, but you did not agree to be his lawyer?"

Bending forward, he laced his fingers together and pressed his thumbs. "There wasn't going to be anything else, just the hearing. Everybody knew he was going to be sent to the state hospital. The hearing was just a formality, but there had to be one and he had to have a lawyer. I did it as a favor."

"A favor to Elliott Winston?"

"No," he replied, shaking his head.

"A favor to his wife?"

He looked at me, beginning for the first time to suspect that I was after something beyond the mere fact that Elliott Winston had been declared insane in a duly constituted judicial proceeding.

"No, not his wife."

"A favor to Calvin Jeffries?" I asked, one foot on the step below the witness stand. "You did it as a favor to the judge—because he asked you to—isn't that true?"

"Yes. Calvin—I mean Judge Jeffries—asked me to."

"He wasn't the judge in the case though, was he?"

"No, he wasn't."

"Do you remember who the judge was in that case?"

"Yes. Quincy Griswald."

"At the time this happened, Calvin Jeffries was the presiding circuit court judge, wasn't he?"

"Yes."

"And in those days, the office of the presiding circuit court judge was in charge of assigning cases, wasn't it?"

"Yes, I believe that was how it was done then."

"In other words, the fact that Judge Griswald and not some other judge had the case was no accident, was it?"

He looked at me, wondering how far I was going to go.

"Let's save ourselves some time, Mr. Bartram. This case—this hearing on the question of whether Elliott Winston was insane so a plea of guilty but insane could be admitted—this case was fixed, wasn't it?"

"Fixed?" he blustered. "No, of course not! What do you mean— fixed?"

"You say you did this as a favor to Calvin Jeffries. Why did he ask you, instead of any one of a hundred other attorneys, any one of whom by your own admission was far more experienced in the criminal law? Why do you think he did that? Because he knew he could always trust you—his former law partner and the man who continued to take care of his financial dealings—to do what you were asked without asking any questions?"

Before he could answer, Loescher objected: "Your honor, he's attacking his own witness."

"Let me rephrase the question," I said without taking my eyes off the witness. "When you were asked to do this, what reason were you given?"

"Calvin—Judge Jeffries—told me that there was no question Winston had gone out of his mind, and that he needed to be in the hospital where he could get help."

"And just why was he so concerned with what might happen to Elliott Winston as opposed to any other defendant?"

"Winston was a young lawyer, and Judge Jeffries had become quite fond of him."

"Fond of his wife, too, wasn't he?"

"Fond of both of them," he replied.

Taking a step back, I looked over at the jury. "She eventually divorced Elliott Winston and married him, didn't she?"

"Yes."

"As a matter of fact, she and Judge Jeffries had been having an affair for some time before Elliott Winston was accused of a crime, weren't they?"

"I don't know," he replied with a lawyer's caution.

"As a matter of fact, they—Judge Jeffries and Elliott Winston's wife—gave him every reason to suspect she was having an affair, but having it with someone else, didn't they?"

"I don't know anything about that," he insisted.

"As a matter of fact," I went on, my eyes still on the jury, "they made him so convinced of it—drove him so crazy with the thought of it—that he was charged with attempting to murder the man they made him think she was sleeping with, didn't they?"

"I don't know why he thought what he did."

I stopped and turned around until we were face-to-face. "But you must have some idea. There must have been something about it in the psychiatric report, some explanation of why he did what he did?"

Asa wearily shook his head. "It was a long time ago."

"So long ago that you've forgotten the name of the victim? That certainly must have been mentioned in the report."

"No," he replied with a faint smile. "I certainly remember that."

"Tell us who it was," I said, turning back to the jury. "Who did Elliott Winston think was sleeping with his wife? Who did Elliott Winston attempt to murder?"

"You. Joseph Antonelli. You're the one he tried to kill."

"Yes," I said, wheeling around. "That's what he was accused of: attempted murder. Would it surprise you to know I never thought he really intended to kill me? I don't think he would have fired the gun if I hadn't tried to take it away from him. But tell us, Mr. Bartram—because you read it—what did the psychiatric report say about that? What did it say about what he thought he was doing, what he really intended to do?"

Asa turned up the palms of his hands. "As I told you: It was such a long time ago. I'm sorry, but I just don't remember now."

I walked quickly to the counsel table, opened a file folder, and ran my finger down a typed list.

"Would the clerk please hand the witness what has been marked defense exhibit 109?"

The clerk found the exhibit, a large manila envelope, and brought it to the witness.

"Would you please open that and remove the file folder inside." When he had done what I asked, he looked up. "Now would you open the file and tell us what it is."

It was the court file in the case of *State v. Elliott Winston*, the file that contained the official record of the proceedings that led to the official determination that Elliott Winston was insane and should be committed to the state hospital for a period not to exceed the maximum sentence which he could have been made to serve in the state prison.

"Would you please take out of the file the psychiatric report which formed the basis for the court's finding."

Asa fumbled through the documents until he found it. He held up another, smaller, manila envelope. "It's under seal."

"Open it."

"Your honor!" Loescher protested. "It's under seal. It can't be opened."

"It can be opened if the court so orders, your honor. And there is no reason not to. This is a murder trial, and whether or not that report should have been under seal in the first place, keeping it there doesn't serve to protect the vital interests of anyone."

Bingham considered it for a moment and then agreed.

"Go ahead," I told Asa. "Open it."

He hesitated, and he kept hesitating. "Here," I said, ripping it out of his hand. I tore it open and pulled out a typed document, stapled at the corner. I shoved it in front of his face. "Read it. Read it out loud. Read the report that was used to find Elliott Winston insane."

He would not look at it, and I read it for him. It was the daily court docket, dated the day Elliott Winston had his hearing. There had never been a psychiatric report. There had never been a psychiatric evaluation. Elliott Winston had been adjudicated insane for no other reason than because Calvin Jeffries had wanted it that way.

Twenty-nine

"What would you have done if there had been a psychiatric evaluation?" Howard Flynn wanted to know, surprised and a little troubled by the chance I had taken. "You couldn't have known they never did one."

I watched out the passenger-side window the river and the mountain fall farther away as we drove up the hill to the hospital. Scattered across the blue high-arching sky, great billowing clouds had turned the color of copper dust; down below in the city, reflected off the glass-walled buildings, the late afternoon sun painted everything behind it a black-edged gold as it ran reluctantly ahead, chased by the soft summer night.

"I'm sorry about what I said. It was unforgivable," I said, looking across at Flynn.

He kept his eyes on the curving road, the only response a slight change in the way he tilted his head, a gesture meant to let me know that it was not important.

"I knew what was inside," I remarked as the car approached the front of the hospital.

"How could you know that?"

"I read the file."

He brought the car to a stop. "That part was under seal."

"It's just a little adhesive," I said as I gathered up my attaché case, the one Jennifer had given me, and opened the door.

"Then you just resealed it?" He shook his head at the sheer simplicity of it.

"It was hard to believe that even Jeffries would go that far," I explained. "I had to be sure." I ran my finger along the letters of my name, engraved on the narrow brass plate, as I thought about what had happened in court and what had happened twelve years before. "Makes you wonder," I said, looking at Flynn as I started to get out, "which of them was really insane."

I had to wait a long time to see the doctors, and I stayed with Jennifer until I was told I had to leave, but Flynn was still there, sitting on a bench, smoking a cigarette. I asked him if he had another, and without a word he reached inside his sport coat pocket and pulled out a crumpled pack. The smoke caught halfway down my throat and made me cough. I let the cigarette tumble from between my fingers and crushed it out with the heel of my shoe.

"They're still running tests," I reported, trying to sound encouraged. "More tomorrow."

Flynn took one last drag on his cigarette, stomped it out with his foot, and stood up.

"Why don't I take you home. You need to get some sleep. You've been running on nothing but nervous energy."

I did not want to go home; I was afraid to go home. All night the night before I had been chased by ghosts of my own invention, maddening thoughts about what I could have done to stop all this from happening. I had not slept at all and had not even tried.

"Listen, why don't we get something to eat," I suggested as we walked to where he had parked the car. "There are some things we need to talk about—to get ready for tomorrow."

He knew it was not true, but he went along with it as if it was. We had a sandwich and a bowl of soup in a diner I had never heard of, and when he offered to take me by the house to get a change of clothes and spend the night at his place I accepted with an eagerness that surprised even myself. First we stopped at the jail.

"I told Danny I'd come by," Flynn explained as we waited for the jailer to open the metal door. "If I didn't show up, he might start to wonder if he could trust me."

I sat next to him every day in court, and except when I wanted by some gesture, some apparent word of encouragement, to convince the jury I believed in his innocence, barely noticed he was there. He had neither the mannerisms of a child, nor the idiosyncrasies of an adult; his face had none of the physical features that reveal the character, the essential lines of what we are: He was a blank page on which nothing permanent had yet been written.

We did not stay long.

"Just came by to say hello," Flynn said cheerfully when he was brought in.

Danny greeted him with a drowsy smile. "Hello, Howard."

Flynn smiled back. "Just had dinner, didn't you?"

"It was good," he replied as he turned to me. "Hello, Mr. Antonelli. Do I get dressed up again tomorrow?"

"Want a different tie?"

He seemed alarmed, and I realized he thought it meant having to give up the one he had. "Then you'll have two you can choose from."

He brightened immediately. "Sure. I'd like that."

When we left the jail and drove through the city to Flynn's apartment, it was almost completely dark. Under the blue-black sky, a scarlet haze hung low on the horizon, the last light till morning.

Flynn made up a bed for me on the bulky tattered sofa in his makeshift study, while I stood in the doorway, glancing furtively at the aging picture of his long-dead son.

"I really am sorry about what I said."

Holding a pillow under his chin, he tugged on the dull white pillowcase. "I know you are," he grunted. "Let it go. Things get said. They don't mean anything."

He gave the pillowcase one last pull. "There, that should do it," he said, plopping it into place at the far end of the couch. A wry grin spread across his broad, heavy mouth. "What did you expect: a mint on your pillow?"

I followed him back into the kitchen. The cat heard us coming and, before Flynn could grab him, jumped off the table and ran for cover.

"Stupid cat won't give up: thinks there has to be something to eat in that bowl," he growled, nodding toward the wax fruit and glass grapes.

Things I had forgotten that yesterday seemed important started to come back into focus. "You must have called Asa's office. That's why Jonah came to court with him," I said as we sat down at the gray Formica table.

"Strange little bastard," Flynn observed. "When I told him Bartram's life might be in danger, he laughed. Said he thought you were nuts. Swear to God—that's what he said. He wasn't happy about the subpoena. He didn't think you had any business taking up the old man's time to come over and testify that he'd made a court appearance for some screwball a dozen years ago."

"That sounds like him. I wonder what he thinks now, after he heard what good old Asa helped Jeffries do." I remembered the other call I'd asked him to make. "Did you reach Jeffries's widow?"

"There was no answer," he replied. "I left a message, but she never called back. Maybe she's out of town."

"She better be back by morning," I said, stretching my arms. "She's my next witness."

Flynn got up to get a bottle of milk out of the refrigerator. "What are you going to ask her?"

I asked her a question a gentleman would never ask; I got an answer no lady would ever give.

"Tell me, Mrs. Jeffries," I asked the next morning as soon as she had been sworn in as a witness, "did you and I ever sleep together?"

Jean Jeffries was not a young woman anymore, but in a gray jacket and an ankle-length skirt she was, if anything, more beautiful than when I had first met her, years before, the wife of Elliott Winston. Even then she had been a little too sure of herself.

"Why?" she asked with a taunting glance. "Don't you remember?"

Standing at the corner of the counsel table, I stared back at her. "I'm sure I would have, Mrs. Jeffries. I take it your answer is no. Which brings me to my next question. Why did your husband—your first husband—think we had?"

"Because he was a very sick man. You of all people should know that, Mr. Antonelli. He tried to kill you, didn't he?"

"So there was no basis in reality for his belief that you were having an affair?"

"No, of course not."

"But he was so convinced of it, so convinced you were having an affair with me, that he tried to kill me?"

"Apparently."

"Because he was crazy?"

"He was sick."

"Isn't it true, Mrs. Jeffries," I asked, searching her eyes, "that the reason Elliott thought we were having an affair is because Calvin Jeffries told him we were?"

"No, of course not. Calvin wouldn't have—"

"And isn't it true, Mrs. Jeffries, that he did that because he wanted to keep him from finding out that you were actually having an affair with him?" I asked with a scathing glance.

She sat on the edge of the witness chair, her hands held rigid in her lap, her long-lashed eyes flashing, speechless anger the only answer she could give.

I walked toward the jury, my arms folded, my eyes lowered, trying to get myself back under control. "How often did you visit your husband when he was first sent to the state hospital?" I asked quietly. There was no answer, and still staring down at the floor I repeated the question.

"I didn't visit him there," she said, clearing her throat.

"I'm not sure everyone could hear that. Would you please say it again?"

"I didn't visit him there," she said more loudly, and more irritably.

"And your children—Elliott's children—how often have they been to visit their father in the twelve years he has been locked up in that place?"

My head bowed, I listened to the silence and felt something of the loneliness Elliott must have known. Then I felt something else and turned on Jeffries's wife with a rage I barely recognized as my own.

"You never allowed them to see their father, did you? You were afraid of what might happen—afraid of what he might tell them—weren't you?"

Her hands, clutched tight together, began to tremble. "I was afraid of what he might do! I'm still afraid of what he might do!"

"Afraid he might harm you?—harm your children?"

"Yes."

"Because he's threatened you?—written letters threatening you?"

"Yes."

"Because of what you and Calvin Jeffries did to him?"

"We did nothing to him," she insisted.

"You never went to see him, you divorced him, you married Calvin Jeffries, and then the two of you took away his children so Calvin Jeffries could adopt them and call them his own, but," I added, glaring at her, "you can say 'we did nothing to him'? You did everything to him, and you know it, and you know what he's done because of it, don't you? He's managed to kill your husband, hasn't he? And you know who he's coming after next, don't you?"

Loescher was screaming an objection, trying to make herself

heard over the bedlam that had broken out as the courtroom exploded in noise and confusion.

"You knew that Calvin Jeffries fixed it so that Elliott would be sent to the state hospital, didn't you?" I shouted while Bingham was trying to quiet the courtroom.

"Calvin did it for me," she shouted back. "I didn't want Elliott to go to prison!"

All the noise had stopped as everyone suddenly turned to hear what she said. Her voice reverberated off the silent square walls of the courtroom and then slowly faded away. I stood a few feet from her, my hands in my pockets, and watched as her head sank down between her shoulders and she began to rub her hands together.

"So you both knew—you and Calvin Jeffries—that Elliott didn't need to go to the state hospital, because you knew—didn't you?— that he was never really insane."

She lifted her head and stopped rubbing her hands. "No, that's not what I meant. What I meant to say was that—"

Waving my hand in the air, I turned away, cutting her off before she could finish. "No more questions of this witness, your honor."

I had shown anger and contempt; Loescher made a show of boredom and indifference. She got to her feet, managing to make even that seem an effort, then shook her head and sighed. Facing the witness with an apologetic smile, she asked two or three questions designed to underscore the fact that the widow of Judge Jeffries had no knowledge about either the defendant or the murder of Quincy Griswald. Then, when she was finished, she looked at me with a puzzled expression and shook her head again, as if she was trying to understand what in the world I thought I was doing wasting the jury's time like this. Smiling smugly to herself, she sat down.

There were only two witnesses left to call, unless I decided finally to call the defendant himself. One of them was waiting in the hall; the other one was supposedly on his way to the court-house. I wondered if Elliott Winston would ever actually arrive.

"The defense calls Dr. Melvin Friedman," I announced before the wife of Calvin Jeffries had reached the door at the back of the courtroom. If the name of her former husband's doctor meant anything to her, she did not show it. With her head held high she opened the door and let herself out, as certain as she had ever been that every eye was still on her.

With an armload of file folders, Dr. Friedman, a nervous twitch at the corner of his mouth, pushed through the gate in the rail-ing at the front of the courtroom. In doubt what to do with the documents he carried, he looked up at the judge. Bingham smiled, nodded to his clerk, waited until she had relieved Friedman of his burden, and smiled again.

"Dr. Friedman," I asked, "you're here under subpoena, correct?"

He tugged on the lapel of his lightweight tan sports jacket, then straightened his slacks. "Yes, that's correct," he said, pulling his shirt cuff.

"You were also served with a subpoena duces tecum, requiring that you produce certain documents in court today. Do you have those documents with you?"

"Yes. The clerk has them," he replied, pulling on the other cuff.

"There is a patient at the state hospital by the name of Chester MacArthur?"

"Yes."

"Do you have his file with you?"

"That was one of the ones I was told to bring."

The clerk, at my instruction, handed him the file.

"Chester MacArthur was a high school history teacher who thought he was a soldier in Vietnam, and he murdered a man—an insurance salesman, I believe—who was walking to his car in a parking structure because MacArthur thought he was Vietcong. Am I right, Dr. Friedman?"

Clutching the file on his lap, Friedman agreed.

"He hid in the garage, waiting, and then slashed his throat with a knife, didn't he?"

"Yes, that's right."

Leaning against the front edge of the table, I pointed toward the file he was holding. "Can you tell us if during his incarceration in the state hospital Chester MacArthur has ever been let out?"

He did not need to check; he had already done it—checked and no doubt double-checked—after I obtained a court order compelling him to show me what was in MacArthur's file.

"During a period of eight months he participated in a standard community release program. This is part of a supervised effort to help patients make the transition back into society," he explained to the jury.

"How often was he let out under this program?"

"Patients are let out three days every other week at the beginning, gradually increasing to a week at a time, sometimes longer, depending on how well they adjust to life outside."

"MacArthur is no longer in that program, is he?"

"No. He found it too difficult. He didn't think he was ready yet."

I told Dr. Friedman the date on which Quincy Griswald had been killed. "Chester MacArthur was out then, wasn't he?"

Opening the file, Friedman fumbled through the pages. "Yes, he was." He held his finger on the page as he looked up. "He was out for two weeks that time."

"It was the last time, wasn't it?"

"Yes, that's right, it was, but—"

"This release program: Isn't that the same program Jacob Whittaker was on?" Friedman seemed to hesitate. "You were asked to bring that file as well. If you need to consult it, I'll have the clerk give it to you."

"No, that's right," he said, nodding abruptly. "It was the same program."

THE JUDGMENT ⬧ 393

"Only Jacob Whittaker didn't come back, did he? He murdered Calvin Jeffries and then killed himself, didn't he?"

Pressing his lips together, Friedman looked down at his hands. "I'm afraid so." His head bounced up. "But there's no reason to think that Chester MacArthur did the same thing."

"They were both in the forensic ward of the state hospital, weren't they? And both of them had killed before, hadn't they?" Before he could respond, I added, "And both of them were there with Elliott Winston, weren't they?"

"We have hundreds of patients in the forensic ward, many of them in that transition program we were just discussing."

"What is Chester MacArthur's middle name, Dr. Friedman?"

"William."

"Does anyone ever call him Billy?"

It seemed to surprise him that I knew. "Yes. It's the name he prefers. He doesn't like the name Chester. He thinks it's too formal. His father insisted on always calling him that. He associates it with authority."

"Elliott Winston calls him Chester, doesn't he?"

Friedman shrugged. "You may be right. I really don't know."

"You don't know? I see. Well, tell us this: How long does someone have to be a patient at the state hospital before they become eligible for this release program we were talking about?"

He wanted to make it sound as safe as he could. "Quite a long time. A patient would have to be very near the end of the time for which he had been committed, and even then only if he was not considered a danger to others. Unfortunately," he added, deciding to bring it up before I did, "in the case of Jacob Whittaker a mistake was made. When you're dealing with the human mind you're dealing with something that is always going to be something of a mystery."

Pushing away from the table, I closed the distance between us until I was just a step away. "But it's not such a mystery that you don't routinely decide which people are sane and which are not, is it?"

"I meant the individual case, trying to decide precisely what is wrong with someone who isn't sane, and what can be done to help them."

"Elliott Winston: What is precisely wrong with him?"

Knitting his brow, Friedman slowly nodded. "Paranoid schizophrenia."

"Are you sure? Are you absolutely sure of that?" I asked, staring hard at him. "Whatever may or may not be wrong with Elliott Winston, Dr. Friedman, he's different from the other patients at the state hospital, isn't he?"

"In what way?"

"More intelligent."

"He's quite intelligent, that's true," he answered cautiously.

"Quite intelligent? This isn't a staff meeting, Dr. Friedman. This isn't some academic seminar on abnormal psychology. This is a court of law, and you're under oath. Elliott Winston is more intelligent than any patient you have, isn't he?"

"Yes, he is."

"And he's the most interesting case you have, isn't he?"

"Well, I don't know if I can . . . But, yes, he's an extremely interesting case."

"Within that group—that collection of mentally disturbed people—some of them would no doubt be particularly susceptible to suggestion, wouldn't they? Made to believe that certain things were true, even though they weren't; made to believe it the same way we believe in certain things, the things we're willing to die for?"

He tried to dismiss it. "Well, I think that's going a little far."

"Do you? You've read about Islamic Fundamentalists who blow themselves up in a terrorist attack. Would you describe that as the act of a completely sane man?"

"No, of course not."

"What about a Russian Communist who confessed to a crime he did not commit because he was convinced it was the only way he had left to serve the Communist cause? Insane?"

"Yes, I'd certainly say so," he replied, nodding his head nervously.

"An American soldier who throws himself on a live grenade to save the lives of other soldiers: insane?"

"Well, no, that's completely different," he said, shifting uneasily in the witness chair.

"You treat the mentally ill. Through therapy, through medication, you try to establish—reestablish—some stability, some structure to the way they think, correct?"

"Yes, that's what we try to do."

"And isn't an important part of that properly functioning mental structure what I think you call a coherent belief system?"

"Yes, that's true."

"If I could make you believe the world is flat, you probably wouldn't be going on any very long boat trips, would you?"

"No, probably not," he admitted, as he began to relax.

"And if I convinced you that Calvin Jeffries, or Quincy Griswald, was the worst human being alive and that you would never be safe until the one or the other was dead, that might give you a reason to kill, wouldn't it?"

I was finished with him, but Cassandra Loescher knew right where to begin. With an impish grin, she looked first at Friedman, and then at the jury. "Is the world flat, Dr. Friedman?"

"No," he said, relieved to be talking to someone sane.

"And is there anything Mr. Antonelli could do to convince you that it is?" He was certain I could not. "Are there many patients in the forensic ward of the state hospital who believe the earth is flat?"

"Not too many."

"So there are limits to how far even a person with Mr. Antonelli's fevered imagination could convince someone of something that wasn't true?"

I could have objected, but I let it pass. There was one question I had left to ask.

"Tell us, Dr. Friedman," I asked on redirect. "Is there a telephone in the ward, one that a patient could use to call out?"

"There's a pay phone. Patients can use it if they have permission."

"Do you have another witness?" Bingham asked after Friedman was excused.

"Yes, your honor. The defense intends to call Elliott Winston."

Bingham looked at the clock on the back wall of the courtroom and then motioned for Loescher and me to approach.

"Do you know if he's here yet?" he asked me at the side of the bench. "The hospital called just before we started this morning and said they had just left. He should be here by now."

I did not know why they had not arrived, and I did not want to talk about what I was afraid might have happened.

"It's almost noon anyway," Bingham observed, making up his mind what he was going to do. "We'll recess for lunch and start again at one-thirty. He certainly should be here by then."

He was about to let us go, then thought of something else. "Is this going to be it? Is he your last witness?"

I was not ready to make a final decision. "Unless I call the defendant."

"Understood," he replied. "How long do you think this witness is going to take? Can you finish with him today?"

"That shouldn't be a problem," I assured him.

"Then if you don't call the defendant . . ." He looked at Loescher. "Any rebuttal witnesses? I won't hold you to it," he added when she appeared reluctant to answer.

"I don't think so," she said.

"Then we could have this to the jury before the end of the day tomorrow. Good."

With a brief explanation that the defense would call its next witness after lunch, Bingham gave the jury the admonitions they had now heard a dozen different times and excused them until court reconvened at one-thirty.

*   *   *

As soon as the jury was gone, all I wanted to do was to get away from the courthouse and from anyone who might want to ask me about the trial. More than anything, I wanted to be left alone. Something was going to happen and I did not know what it was. All I knew was that waiting for me on the other side of the next hour and a half was the strangest witness and the most important courtroom examination of my life.

Unless Elliott Winston did not come at all. Where was he, and what was taking so long? As I walked across the dark-shaded park on my way to the privacy and solitude of my own office, I began to think about what it must have been like for him, being driven here to the city where he had lived, to the courthouse where he had practiced law. I tried to imagine what was going through his head, let out of the hospital for the first time, that dismal, desolate place that had become the only world he knew, revisiting his life twelve years after it had been taken away from him. He would notice the way the city had changed, the way it had spread out over the other side of the river, the way the buildings downtown crowded out the light. More vivid than anything that was actually in front of his eyes, he would see the face of his wife, the way she looked the last time he had seen her, young and beautiful, cold and duplicitous, the mother of his children, the whore of the man he had trusted, the man he had revered. How could he not want to kill her?

A woman I did not know was waiting in the outer office. I was too preoccupied to notice much about her except that she had a soft round face and open, friendly eyes. Helen grabbed the stack of accumulated telephone messages and caught up with me as I dropped into the leather chair behind my desk. When she saw the look in my eye, she changed her mind.

"These can wait," she said as she sat down on the front edge of the armchair across from me. "You need to get some rest," she went on with a worried smile.

"Who is that?" I asked, motioning toward the doorway. "I can't see anyone now. I have to be back in court in an hour. I don't have the time, and even if I did . . ."

Helen had the expression of someone who does not know what to do. "Her name is Mrs. Lewis. She's been here for an hour. She said she knew you a long time ago and she just wanted to say hello."

"I don't know her," I said honestly.

"She seems like a very nice person. She's visiting a friend of hers and saw your name in the paper and just wanted to say hello. I'm sure she doesn't want more than a few minutes."

If I didn't do it, Helen was going to have to get rid of her, and for all her hard surface toughness, Helen hated to be rude.

I relented, and began to regret it as soon as Mrs. Lewis appeared in the doorway and I got a clear look at her. I had never seen her in my life. I was certain of it.

"What can I do for you, Mrs. Lewis?" I asked in a perfunctory tone.

She smiled a little, then she smiled a little more. "There's no reason for you to remember me, Mr. Antonelli. It was years ago. You helped my mother once, and when I read your name in the paper—this trial you're in—I thought it was about time I said thanks. You helped me, too."

I turned up my hands, embarrassed that I did not remember her or her mother.

"You defended my mother when she was charged with the same thing my father was doing to me. My mother was Janet Larkin."

I forgot all about the trial and about Elliott Winston. "You're Janet Larkin's daughter?" I asked, astonished.

"Amy," she reminded me. "Amy Lewis now." She laughed a husky, full-throated laugh. "Amy Lewis for going on quite a while."

"You're married?" I asked with a kind of stupid surprise, as if it had happened just last week and I should somehow have known.

"Two children," she added with a certain matronly pride.

I leaned back in my chair and looked at her, shaking my head at how perfectly normal, how wonderfully well adjusted she seemed to be. "I used to worry about you. I wondered what was going to happen to you . . . after everything."

A shadow crossed over her eyes, a hint of the secret I had once forced her to share with a courtroom full of strangers, and I wondered if it was a secret she had shared with anyone since. I did not ask.

"I've had a very good life," she said.

Her smile was muted now, and for a while she did not say anything more. She let her eyes roam around the room, past the shelves filled with law books and the windows that gave a view of the city and the river and beyond that of the mountain that somehow gave a sense of permanence to all the transitory things that happened below it.

"It might not have been such a good life if you hadn't saved my mother. She died two years ago, and I think I only started to realize then how much I owed her, and how much she went through because of me."

"What happened to . . . ?"

"My father? I don't know. After the trial I never saw him again. He moved away—somewhere—I don't know."

"And your brother?"

A faraway look came into her eyes. "It wasn't true, you know: what he said about my mother. Poor Gerald. It was all he could think to do; the only way he thought he could get us all back together." Her gaze came back into focus. "That was the worst part of all of it. He knew it was a lie, but he could never bring himself to admit it, and the longer he denied it, the more real it became for him until I think he actually believed it must have been true."

Amy Larkin Lewis looked at me with the candid eyes of a woman who had learned more painfully than most that the past is never really gone. "Sometimes I think it was my fault; then I remember how young I was. It doesn't seem fair, does it? That Gerald and my mother should have ended up paying the price for what my father did to me."

It was not fair, but then, it was hard to think of many things that were.

We stood up and said goodbye. She noticed the photograph on the credenza, a picture of Jennifer and me, taken just a few weeks before. "Your wife? She's very beautiful."

There was no reason to correct her assumption. "Yes, she is. I've known her since we were kids. The strange thing is," I remarked as I walked her to the door, "that even though there were long periods of time when I didn't remember her, I know now that even then I was still in love with her."

I told her how glad I was she had come and watched her for a moment as she walked down the hallway to the elevator. When I closed the door and turned around, Helen was holding the phone, her hand cupped over the receiver, waiting.

"It's the hospital," she explained. "The doctor wants to talk to you."

Thirty

I was at the courthouse a half hour early. An old man with sharp-edged shoulders and a sunken chest hobbled into the court-room ahead of me, a newspaper folded under his arm. He sat on the aisle in the last row, just inside the door. He was a fairly frequent visitor, sometimes the only spectator in the routine trials no one remembered the moment they were over. I had never known his name, but I had been told that he had spent a long life as a lawyer and did not know what to do with himself after he retired.

"Interesting case," he remarked as I went past him.

I kept going, pretending not to hear, but then, perhaps because I felt something—a memory of something that had not yet happened to me—I stopped and turned around.

"You were a lawyer, weren't you?" I asked, trying to seem interested.

His gray wispy eyebrows uncovered clear, fully lucent eyes. "Until I was seventy-five, when a cabal of notorious and incompetent doctors conspired to deprive me of the only reason I had left to live." With a bony finger he tapped his chest. "Heart," he explained. "That was ten years ago," he said. "I think the doctors are all dead now."

He got to his feet and leaned on the bench in front of him. "Now I just come and watch. I like trials. Every one of them is a different story; every one of them has an ending and you find out what happened."

He was eager to talk to someone, another lawyer, someone who knew what he meant.

"Life isn't like that. You don't know when it's going to end, and you don't know what's going to happen. In the trial, you know if you've won or if you lost. How do you ever know that outside a courtroom?"

A troubled expression in his eyes, he thought about his own question. Then, pulling himself up, he patted my arm. "Better get ready," he said with an encouraging smile. "Interesting trial," he added as I turned away and walked to the front of the otherwise empty courtroom.

From my chair at the counsel table I glanced back over my shoulder, but the old man was lost in his newspaper, reading perhaps the obituaries of just a few of the people he had managed to outlive. He was right in what he had said: Trials were stories, stories about other people's lives, told in a way that made each part fit with every other, as if they had from the very beginning followed a single design and had come at the end to form a single, coherent whole. That is what I was: a storyteller who made sense out of the lives of other people and could not make any sense out of his own. I was the storyteller who had no story of his own to tell.

The door at the back of the courtroom squeaked open and I heard the sound of shuffling feet as someone else found a place on the spectator benches. A few minutes later the door opened again. It was Harper Bryce, notebook in hand, getting ready to jot down anything he thought essential for the story he was going to write for the readers of tomorrow morning's paper. Five minutes later, at twenty past one, the first juror, careful not to glance in my direction, made her way to the jury room. The bailiff, an amiable deputy sheriff with a gray mustache, caught up with her and opened the door. The courtroom began to fill up, and the court reporter, getting ready for the afternoon, put a new spool of paper into her machine.

My mind was a blank, and I felt nothing, not even a vague curiosity about what was going to happen. I listened to the sounds made by the courtroom as it gradually came back to life, and the only thought I had was that like the old man who sat watching somewhere behind me this was what my life had always been and would always be, the endless repetition of one trial, one story, over and over again.

The courtroom was full, and the last juror had returned. The defendant had been brought in and put in the chair next to me. Cassandra Loescher was sitting at the other end of the long, mahogany table, busily making notes to herself. The clerk, a generous-hearted woman waiting for retirement, took the place she had filled for the last twenty years. Everyone was where they were supposed to be. Like an old soldier, the bailiff drew himself up straight and tall and then issued the only command he knew.

"All rise," he said. Before the words were out of his mouth, everyone was on their feet, waiting while Morris Bingham, eyes straight ahead, walked to the bench. Calvin Jeffries had walked that way as well, never looking around, but he had moved more quickly, like someone always in a hurry, trying to do two things at once.

Bingham nodded at the jury. "Good afternoon," he said in his pleasant, muted-tone voice.

"Is the defense ready to call its next witness, Mr. Antonelli?" he asked, turning his attention to me.

"Yes, your honor," I said as I stood up. "The defense calls Elliott Winston."

I stared at the double doors at the back of the courtroom, wondering if they would open and whether, if they did, Elliott Winston would walk through them. I waited, and I kept waiting, but there was nothing, not a sound. He had escaped, just as I had thought he would, and was perhaps right now alone in the elevator, on his way up to where the woman he hated had lived with the man he had killed. I turned around, ready to explain that my witness was missing and that in his absence the defense would now call the defendant himself.

"Your honor," I began, but Bingham was looking over my head. "I believe your witness has just arrived, Mr. Antonelli."

Elliott Winston stood just inside the door while one of the two well-muscled orderlies who accompanied him removed the handcuffs that pinned his wrists behind his back. Elliott was dressed exactly the same way he had been the first time I saw him at the hospital: the threadbare suit that fit too tight, the frayed white shirt held together at the throat by the knot of the same off-center tie. The two orderlies leaned against the back wall while Elliott, rubbing his wrists, walked up the aisle with slow, methodical steps, gazing intently from side to side. His eyes never stopped moving, not when the clerk administered the oath, not when he first sat down on the witness chair. It was as if he was trying to impress on his mind the lasting image of every visible square inch of that courtroom and everything and everyone who was in it.

"Would you please state your name and spell your last for the record," I asked.

He looked at me, but just for an instant, and then, with a flash of impatience, commenced another circuit of the room. When his eyes came back around they settled not on me, but on Cassandra Loescher.

"You're the prosecutor in this case?" he asked, bending slightly toward her.

Startled at first, she quickly changed her expression to one of annoyance and looked to the bench for help.

"Mr. Winston," Judge Bingham informed him in a quiet but firm voice, "witnesses answer the questions directed to them; they don't ask them. But, yes, Ms. Loescher is the prosecutor in this case. Now please, answer the question Mr. Antonelli asked you. Please state your full name and spell your last for the record."

Elliott sat stiff and straight, an imperious look on his face. He treated Bingham's request like the suggestion of a servant: something he might listen to but would under no circumstances acknowledge. He turned to me, propped his right elbow on the arm of the chair, placed his thumb under the side of his chin, and set both his index and his middle fingers against his cheekbone. A thought raced through his mind and left behind it a smile that darted over his mouth.

"My name is Elliott Lowell Winston," he said finally, and then slowly spelled the last.

I glanced down at the file that lay open on the table.

"I believe the next question is 'How are you employed?'"

My head snapped up. The smile on his face, meant to appear officious, could not quite hide a certain sentimentality nor completely mask a kind of nostalgia.

"I'm not employed. I'm a member of the leisure class, which, as you know, is always, one way or the other, supported at state expense."

"You're an inmate at the state hospital."

"That's what I just said."

"How long have you been there?" I asked as I closed the file.

"Twelve years, five months, three weeks, four days," he said, in a harsh, almost brutal voice. He seemed to be proud of it, and ready to defy anyone who thought to disagree.

I worked my way along the back of the table, passing the defendant—poor, mystified Danny, who seemed amazed by this strange creature on the witness chair; passing Cassandra Loescher, who, despite herself, could not keep her eyes off Elliott Winston.

"Twelve years, five months, three weeks, four days," I repeated aloud to myself as I paused at the far side of the counsel table and looked back across the oblique angle to the witness stand. "How have you survived it all these years, knowing there was nothing wrong with you, nothing so serious that it could not have been cured with a little rest and a little weekly counseling with a good psychologist?"

He made no reply, and I could sense that he wondered what I knew.

"We know all about it, Elliott." I leaned back against the front of the table and clasped my hands together. "We know that Calvin Jeffries arranged to have you sent to the state hospital; we know you were sent there without a psychiatric evaluation. And we know why he did it. We know he wanted you out of the way— in a place where you could not do anything about it when he took your wife and took your children. What we don't know is when you first figured it out, first understood that you weren't going to be there for just a few months. That's what he promised you, wasn't it? That you'd go to the hospital and with the same kind of influence he used to get you there, get you out again, didn't he?"

Dark with rage, his eyes burrowed into me. "I always knew I could trust the honorable Judge Jeffries!"

"When did you first understand that you had been deceived, that you weren't going to be getting out of the hospital, not for twenty years or more?"

His hand came down from the side of his face and rested on his knee. He bent forward, his back still straight, a half smile, more enigmatic than any look I had ever seen, slashed across his face.

"I understood it the first time I saw him look at my wife; I didn't know I understood it until I had been in the hospital for nearly half a year." Not without a certain satisfaction, he noted the puzzled expression on my face. "When I realized she was never going to come to see me; when I was sent a copy of her divorce decree; when I was served with a notice that my rights as a parent were being terminated; when I found out that she had married Jeffries and they were going to give my children his name. When I realized what they had done to me, then I saw everything in a different light. Looks, words, gestures took on a whole new meaning. The way they kissed each other when we said goodbye, the way he touched her—things I thought showed how fond he was of her—now showed me, when I remembered them, how much they wanted each other, how hard it was for them to keep their hands off each other." His mouth curled down in disdain. "I discovered, you see, that the past was not what I had thought it was. They changed it," he added, as he moved his hand from his knee to the arm of the chair and again sat straight up.

"And what did you do then, when you realized that you had been betrayed?"

His eyes were cold, hard, mocking. "I thought about it." He paused and inclined his head slightly to the side. "Does that surprise you? That I thought about it?" He shrugged his shoulders and threw up his hands. "What else was I going to do?" He leaned forward again and with a riveting glance suddenly beat his open hand on the wooden arm of the chair. "What else could I do?" he shouted. "I'd been declared insane—I was living in an asylum, for God's sake—what else was I going to do but think about it? That's all I've done for twelve years—think about it!"

"About what they had done to you?"

"Yes."

"About what you were going to do to them?" I asked, trying to goad him into an admission I could use.

His head, rigid and erect, began to shudder and his eyes flashed with contempt. Then it stopped. "I thought about a lot of things," he said, the only expression left a smile so small I could barely see it just under his mustache at the corner of his mouth. "It did occur to me, I must admit," he said, his voice hoarse and guttural, "that by having me declared insane they had also conferred upon me absolute immunity for any otherwise criminal acts I might care to commit."

For the first time since he had taken the stand, he turned his head and looked at the jury. "I was a lawyer once," he explained with a polite smile that was so close to the way Judge Bingham habitually acknowledged their presence, I wondered if it was deliberate.

He seemed to forget what he had wanted to say. "Gave you absolute immunity," I reminded him.

"Yes," he said, his eyes coming back around to me. "As you can imagine, with that thought I began to imagine all sorts of things. I was insane—the state said so—and no one would ever be able to hold me responsible for anything I did." A shrewd glint came into his eyes. "In that sense—and maybe not just in that sense—I was like Calvin Jeffries, wasn't I? Above, or at least outside, the law. Isn't that what everyone wants? To do anything they want and not have to face any consequences for it?"

Pausing, he started to look around the courtroom again. "Do you still like doing this?" he asked, a pensive expression on his face. "Being a lawyer, trying cases in court? I should have listened to you when you tried to warn me about Jeffries," he said, biting his lip while his eyes flared open. His mind was starting to wander back to the beginning of what had happened to him. "This was always where I wanted to end up," he said, looking at me as he narrowed his eyes and shook his head. "In court, trying to convince a jury that I was right."

He seemed to draw into himself. I moved down the length of the counsel table and stood at the end of it, closest both to the jury box and the witness stand. I pointed at Danny.

"Elliott," I said quietly, "you've never seen him before, have you?"

He did not hear me, or if he did, he chose not to answer. Whatever was going on in his tortured mind, he was now a prisoner to it. His eyes grew larger and even more intense, his neck bulged, and his shirt collar, too tight as it was, cut into his throat and his face turned red.

"Insanity confers immunity, but immunity is irrelevant when it is a question of self-defense," he said, the words tumbling rapidly out of his mouth. "You're entitled to take another's life when they're trying to take yours, aren't you?" he asked, challenging me to disagree.

"Do you know him? Have you ever seen him before?" I asked insistently, pointing again at Danny.

Elliott glanced at the defendant, then looked back at me. "No, I've never seen him before," he said impatiently. "It would be self-defense, wouldn't it?"

"No," I replied, keeping my voice low. "It could not be self-defense. No one tried to kill you. But even if they had, it was twelve years ago."

It was an odd sensation. For a moment I thought we were repeating a conversation we had had before, one of the hundreds we had had when he was an associate in the firm and we talked about the criminal law and the various and sometimes inventive defenses that could be raised to a charge of murder.

"Self-defense has to be contemporaneous with the attack. Otherwise there's nothing to defend against. You can't just take the life of someone who injured you at some point in the past. That's nothing more than revenge."

He could barely wait for me to finish. "Are you sure?" he asked, his eyes ablaze. "What if, as soon as he was attacked, he started to defend himself—but moved slowly. What if," he continued, thrusting his head forward, "the attack itself went on—day after day—for years? What if someone was crushing the life out of him, strangling him, a little tighter all the time, with the thought of what he was doing with his wife, with his children? And then, years after it started, he finally makes it stop. Are you so certain that would not be self-defense?"

I refused to concede anything. "No, it isn't self-defense and you know it. You're talking about the way you felt, about the effect of what Calvin Jeffries did to you. It wasn't self-defense, because it was too late—far too late—to prevent him from doing what he did, and because you can't change the past. All you could do was try to take your revenge. And that's what you did, wasn't it, Elliott?"

He was beside himself. "Can't change the past? Don't you understand anything? The past is the only thing you can change!"

His eyes were growing wider and his voice was becoming louder, more violent, with every word he spoke. He was close to going completely over the edge. I had to get him to admit what he had done now or it was going to be too late. I took a step toward him.

"You thought by having Calvin Jeffries killed, by having Quincy Griswald killed, you could change the past?"

"Of course!" he insisted. "They changed my past, didn't they?" His eyes darted toward the jury. "My wife—the woman I loved— became the woman who betrayed me. My children—the children I loved—became the children who forgot me. Don't you see? My past was that of a man who was loved; it became that of a man who was hated and abandoned."

His head jerked back around until he was again staring straight at me. "Can't change the past? What would my past be now if I had just lived all those years in the asylum, a patient in the hospital for the criminally insane? What would you see, looking back on my life? A lunatic. And what would you have seen," he asked, bristling, "when you looked back at the life of Jeffries and Griswald and the mother of my children? Whatever you would have seen, it isn't what you see now, is it? Can't change the past? They did it to me, and I did it to them. They tried to write the history of my life, but I wrote theirs instead!" he shouted, rising from the chair.

The judge exchanged a quick, worried glance with the bailiff, who immediately started to move toward the witness stand.

"It's all right, Elliott," I said, trying to calm him as I moved another step forward. The bailiff looked at me, then looked at the judge. Bingham hesitated, then held up his hand to let him know he could stop.

I was not through with Elliott yet. There was something more I had to have.

"How did you do it? How did you get Jacob Whittaker to kill Jeffries? How did you get Chester—Billy—to kill Griswald? How did you talk them into doing it?"

He looked at me like I was a fool. "I gave them something to live for. I gave them something to die for. I gave them something to believe in."

"What did you give them to believe in, Elliott? What did they believe in so much they were willing to kill for it?"

"They believed that evil really exists, that evil people really exist, and that if you don't stop them they'll keep doing evil things." He paused and a smile crept across his mouth. "They're insane, remember?"

Our eyes were locked together. I took another step toward him. We were now not more than an arm's length apart.

"You admit you ordered them to kill Jeffries and Griswald?"

He laughed. "Ordered them? I didn't order anyone to do anything. We had a trial, just like you're having now." He looked around the courtroom. "Or perhaps more like the court proceeding they held when they had me committed. I made my case the way any good lawyer would: I was clear, logical, and persuasive, just the way you are. And then, at the end of it, they reached a verdict, and after they reached a verdict they passed sentence. They carried it out. I had nothing to do with it."

His eyes glittered with self-satisfaction, but he was not finished yet. There was something more he wanted to say, something important.

"So you see," he began, "I did change the past."

That is when it happened, that dreadful, pathetic beating together of same-sounding words, worse—far worse—than when I had heard it before.

"I did change the past . . . last . . . fast . . . mast." The words came in short staccato bursts, faster and faster. He began to choke, and he tore at his collar, pulling it away from his throat as if that was what was blocking his breath. His eyes bulging, he tugged at his collar harder and harder as he staggered off the witness chair, stumbled and started to fall. I caught him with both hands and as I fell back under his weight the bailiff rushed in to help.

He must have dreamed about it, seen it in his sleep, gone over it a thousand times in his mind, planning every motion of his hands, every movement of his feet, until it had all become as instinctive as a dance. I was right there, holding him, trying to help him, and I never saw it happen. Suddenly, I was clutching at nothing and Elliott was standing free, waving the bailiff's gun.

"Quiet!" he demanded as the courtroom dissolved into chaos. "Quiet!" he shouted again, but panic had taken over. People who had come to watch were trying to hide, throwing themselves onto the floor between the benches, some on top of others who had gotten there first. Elliott aimed the gun toward the back and fired off a round. Everyone froze.

"Now," he said, holding the gun steady, "I want everyone to listen to me very carefully." His voice was surprisingly calm. "Very slowly, and starting with the first row, I want everyone to leave—everyone sitting out there," he said, nodding toward the spectators' benches. "Now," he said. "Very slowly, just like you were leaving church after a wedding or a funeral. One row at a time."

They did as he told them, one row at a time, looking back at him, afraid he might change his mind before they got out the door. When they were all gone, he turned to the twelve terrified people in the jury box. Gesturing with the gun, he ordered them into the jury room.

"You go with them," he said, nodding at both the court clerk and the court reporter.

When they were out of the room, he turned to the bailiff and ordered him to take the defendant back to the jail.

"Go with him, Danny," I said when he appeared reluctant to leave me alone.

There were only three of us left: Bingham, Loescher, and me—the judge, the prosecutor, and the defense attorney.

Elliott moved across the front of the courtroom and leaned against the empty jury box, the gun dangling down from his hand. "Shall we bring the jury back in and have a trial of our own?" Elliott asked, looking at Loescher. "Or do you think I've adequately prosecuted the case against Calvin Jeffries and my wife?"

Cassandra Loescher was one of the few who had not panicked when Elliott began brandishing the gun. She had risen straight to her feet and stayed there, glaring at him as if he had offered an insult instead of a threat to her life. She refused to answer, and when he repeated the question her only response was to look at him with even greater contempt.

Her silence made him angry and I tried to get his attention.

"What do you want, Elliott?" I asked, taking a tentative first step in his direction. He warned me away with his eyes.

"You can't get out of here," I told him, trying to sound calm and self-assured. "And even if you could, what then? Would you go kill your wife? Is that what this was all about—to get out of the hospital so you could kill her yourself?"

"Kill her?" he exclaimed feverishly. "I don't want her to die; I want her to live forever. I told you all before," he cried, as he waved the gun in the air, a dark, menacing look in his eyes. "I came to court to make the record, the record of what happened, the way you do when you want to appeal a case you should never have lost. Kill her? I want her to live knowing that everyone knows what she is and what she did!"

I was too angry, too tired, too worn out by everything that had happened to feel any fear.

"Then why are you doing this? You made your record—you changed the past. Everyone knows. What else is left to do?"

His eyes were on fire. "To finish what I started twelve years ago."

"What you started . . . ?"

"When I came to your office that day, when I was going to . . ."

Then I knew, not just what he was going to do, but what he had always intended to do, and in a strange way it made sense.

"Don't," I said reflexively, but I knew there was nothing I could do, nothing that was going to make him change his mind. It was too late. It had always been too late.

He pointed the gun right at me. "It's time for you both to go,"

he said, glancing up at the judge and then across to the prosecutor.

Loescher turned to go, but Bingham refused to leave. "It's my
courtroom," he insisted.

Elliott seemed surprised. "Jeffries would already be out the door,"
he remarked. He looked at me to see if I agreed and then looked
back at Bingham. Stretching his arm straight, until the gun was
as close to my head as it would go, he asked him again to leave.

"I would be very grateful if you would go." He said it with a
kind of respect, the way he must once have thought every judge
was supposed to be addressed.

Bingham, still reluctant, looked at me.

"It's all right," I assured him. "I'll be fine. You better go."

We were alone, and Elliott took a position in front of the
bench, just below where Bingham had been sitting. Gesturing
with the gun, he had me move to the far end of the counsel
table, closest to the empty jury box and farthest from the double
doors at the back. We stood like that, facing each other, and for
what seemed like forever did not say anything at all. Everything
in that quietest courtroom was now so quiet I could have sworn
I could hear the thoughts that were passing through Elliott Winston's mind.

"There's no reason to do this, Elliott."

He looked up at the clock. "Four forty-four. We'll wait one
more minute: four forty-five."

I stood there, helpless, staring at the barrel of the revolver, and
from somewhere deep in my subconscious recalled the story Anatoly Chicherin had told me about Dostoyevsky waiting in front
of a firing squad, waiting for the order to fire, knowing with absolute certainty it would be the last word he would ever hear.

"Don't do it," I begged. "What happened twelve years ago was
an accident. It wasn't a crime."

For an instant he looked like the Elliott Winston I had known
at the beginning, the bright, eager young man with the wife he

loved and the children he adored, his whole life in front of him, certain that nothing bad would ever happen.

He shook his head. "It wasn't a crime?" He smiled. "It wasn't what I intended."

I heard the clock strike four forty-five. "Don't," I begged again.

The gunshot exploded in my ear, and then there was nothing but silence, silence everywhere. Then I heard it: the sound of feet running, rushing, and the sound of voices, a huge, animal roar, and then the sound of the door at the back of the court- room behind me crashing open.

I looked up just in time to see Elliott, tranquil and unafraid, smile at me as he lowered the gun which he had just fired into the air.

"Don't," I begged again, turning toward the door as the police began their assault. No one heard me, but it would have done no good if they had. The sound of that single gunshot had been the signal for Elliott's own execution. He lay there, at the base of the bench, his eyes open, blood trickling past that strange smile that was still on his mouth.

Two police officers tried to help me out of the courtroom.

"Elliott Winston didn't come to my office to kill me," I told them. "He came to kill himself. This time he let someone else do it for him."

The two officers exchanged a glance. Neither one of them had any idea what I was talking about.

Thirty-one

Though I had told her all about it before, I told her again, trying to remember everything just the way it had happened.

"Bingham meant it when he said it was his courtroom," I said as the Porsche moved easily through a wide sweeping turn. Jennifer's eyes were fastened on the road. Her hair flew back behind her as we picked up speed.

"He had everyone back in court the next morning. 'Mr. Antonelli,' he said, 'do you have any other witnesses you wish to call?'

"'No, your honor,' I replied. 'The defense rests.'

"Then he looked at Cassandra Loescher. 'Does the prosecution have any rebuttal witnesses it wishes to call?'

"She shook her head. 'No, your honor.'

"He turned back to me. 'Does the defense have any motions it wishes to make at this time?'

"'Yes, your honor. The defense moves for a directed verdict of acquittal.'

"Bingham looked at Loescher the way he does when it's your turn to say something.

"'The prosecution does not object,' she said with a slight nod.

"That was it, all of it. Five minutes and it was over. Bingham thanked the jury and told them that while he did not think any of them would ever forget what had happened, he hoped they would also remember that justice had been done and an innocent man had been set free."

We raced down a straight stretch of road, the engine screaming, and Jennifer lifted her head and smiled as the wind rushed past us.

I kept on talking. "Sometimes I think about Elliott and the things that happened to him and the things he did."

Sinking low behind us, the October sun turned the fields and the vineyards and the orchards brown and orange, dark green and black, the last colors of autumn before the winter rains turned everything a damp, dismal gray.

"Sometimes I think about those people out there, the ones who live under the bridges, the ones who don't have anywhere to call home. Sometimes I wonder if they're everywhere, all the time, but we only take notice of them at night, because that's when we're most vulnerable and most afraid. Sometimes I wonder if there are any more of them out there, ones that Elliott knew in the hospital."

After a while I stopped talking, and just watched the road in front of us, glancing across every so often at the face that had haunted me all my life, glad we were once again together.

"There was one good thing that came out of this. Danny won't be homeless anymore. You were right about Howard Flynn, when you said he thought of Danny as his son. Howard took him in, gave him a home."

It was getting dark, and we had been gone all afternoon. Jennifer was tired. I helped her out of the car and held her by the arm as we walked to the door. The light was on inside.

"Good evening, Mr. Antonelli. Did Jennifer enjoy the drive?" the nurse asked as I let go of her arm. "See you next week?" she asked with a kindhearted smile.

"Of course," I replied. I watched them walk down the corridor together, hoping until they disappeared around the corner that

Jennifer would look back, remember finally who I was, and call my name.

Outside, in the cool night air, I opened the door to the Porsche and then, before I got in, glanced down the street toward the opposite end of the three-story brick building and remembered the first time I had come here, to the state hospital, to see Elliott Winston.

I drove through the darkness on my way back to Portland. To keep my mind off Jennifer, I turned on the radio and a few minutes later, after the music stopped, I heard the news. Asa Bartram had been killed, stabbed to death outside his office, in the street next to his car.

RUMBLE, YOUNG MAN, RUMBLE

RUMBLE, YOUNG MAN, RUMBLE

BENJAMIN CAVELL

F
CAVE

ALFRED A. KNOPF　　NEW YORK 2003

Library of Congress Cataloging-in-Publication Data
Cavell, Benjamin.
Rumble, young man, rumble / Benjamin Cavell.— 1st ed.
p.   cm.
ISBN 0-375-41464-9 (alk. paper)
1. Young men—Fiction.   I. Title.

PS3603.A9 R8 2003
813'.6—dc21   2002027525

Manufactured in the United States of America
First Edition

TO MY MOTHER AND FATHER

THE HANDS CAN'T HIT WHAT THE EYES CAN'T SEE.
FLOAT LIKE A BUTTERFLY, STING LIKE A BEE.
RUMBLE, YOUNG MAN, RUMBLE.

—Bundini

CONTENTS

RUMBLE, YOUNG MAN, RUMBLE

BALLS,
BALLS,
BALLS

On Thursday, a man comes into the store and asks me how to kill his wife. I know, because it's my business to know, that what he really wants to ask is how to kill his wife and not get caught.

The man wears a short-sleeved button-down shirt and dark blue Dockers. His face is cratered with acne scars. It looks like the surface of the moon. I know without being told that this man works at one of the tech firms that have sprung up in the last year or so all along the road from Albany. He has never lifted a weight in his life. He has probably never been in a fight. He has never even been paintballing. But for some reason I feel sorry for this poor, bony fool and so I ask him whether he has a gas furnace.

I explain how to drill a hole in the main line that will allow a tiny stream of gas to trickle into his basement. The emission is so gradual that his wife is unlikely to notice. This is less detectable than disabling the pilot light on a gas stove. Also, it's more controllable than blocking the return-air vents and filling the house with carbon monoxide. Then I tell him that he'll need a spark.

The spark can come from anything. The static electricity

of shoes scuffing a rug, the momentary discharge from the flipping of a light switch, the red power light on a clock radio that usually clicks on when the alarm sounds, a lightbulb that has been filled with gasoline and then screwed back into the socket—each can become a trigger that will *turn out all the lights*, if he knows what I mean. He does. He buys the Taskmaster Tool Kit (Deluxe Set), $179.99 on sale.

In the afternoon, I tell a nineteen-year-old in a fatigue jacket how to make napalm from gasoline and frozen orange juice concentrate (just mix equal parts—diet cola and gasoline works also) and then he buys a superthin Maxi-Grip C-series folding knife ($124.99)—which can be concealed in a boot or even inside a shirt collar for easy access—and a telescoping graphite police baton ($64.95). I tell him two stories about my time in the SEALs and show him my tattoo of Freddie the Frogman and then sell him *The Mercenary's Guide to Urban Survival* ($19.99, paperback), and he leaves smiling and even salutes me, almost dropping his new baton.

The tattoo is temporary (I got a whole box of them two years ago at a novelty shop in Jersey City) and I've never been in the Navy. I've never even been farther than Philadelphia. And I can't swim.

My name is Logan Bryant. I sell sporting goods.

Actually, I sell sporting goods, hardware, athletic equipment, patio furniture, barbecue grills and hobby literature.

But don't get me wrong: I'm not just some wanna-be. Truth is, I *could* have been a SEAL if I'd ever bothered to learn to swim. I hold at least a green belt in several fighting disciplines and am nearly a black belt in Thai kickboxing (I just haven't had time to take the test). I am the uncontested star of what is generally acknowledged to be the fourth-best paintball team in the tristate area. (We were scheduled to compete for the national title on ESPN2 but were scratched at the last second. Politics.) I have a full collection of green and brown face paint in various shades. I was All-Conference at middle linebacker my junior year of high school and would have been All-State or maybe even Honorable Mention All-America the next year if I hadn't quit. I used to have subscriptions to *Soldier of Fortune* and *Guns and Ammo* until Barry told me that no one reads those anymore. Also, I am confident in my willingness to take the life of another human being.

And I can almost bench-press three eighty-five.

Barry arrives as Lou and I are totaling Thursday's receipts. Lou nods to him and Barry swaggers around a standing rack of catcher's mitts and ducks under the counter. Barry is wearing a lime-green New York Jets warm-up jacket.

"The average American," I am telling Lou, "has an IQ around seventy-three. At that level of intellect, even basic functioning requires considerable effort. Decisions that you or I would consider simple border on impossible for Joe Citizen. That's why people are so easily swayed by celebrity pitchmen and Oprah Winfrey and demonstrations of the new-and-improved Spic and Span. That's why a presidential candidate can give the same speech over and over—they're all talking to five-year-olds. People are just like children."

"But all people *were* children at one point," Lou says.

"So?"

"So, if they're children now, what were they then?"

I sigh. "I'm trying to illustrate a point."

"And what is that?"

"What is what?"

"The *point*, guy, the *point*."

"My point is that people, for the most part, have no understanding of the realities of the world. That's why it's so easy for guys like you and me to get ahead."

Lou finishes with his receipts and lays them down on the counter in a neat stack. "Isn't that the same point you made on Monday?"

"No," I say, exasperated. "My point on Monday was that college degrees are meaningless and that the only useful intelligence is street smarts. And that guys like you and me should really be running this country—and *would* be if we had little pieces of paper that said we'd gone to Princeton. Also, my point on Monday was based on the figure they released over the weekend, which put the average national IQ around seventy-six. In light of the most recent data, the conclusions must be even more extreme."

"And who," Lou says, "is compiling this data?"

I stare at him. "What do you mean? It's a study."

"By who?" He smiles. "Who's 'they'?"

Before I can answer, Barry says, "Do you doubt what he's saying, Louie?"

Lou shrugs. "I just don't know if people are so dumb."

"Don't *know*," Barry says. "Look around you, man. We have the corrupt, liberal media. We have unchecked and unquestioned federal power. We have suppression of the First *and* Second Amendments, babies being murdered, kids' shows that promote homosexuality, twenty-four-hour music videos, political correctness, celebrity magazines that promote homosexuality, celebrity talk shows, school shootings, celebrity profiles, celebrity political campaigns, celebrity fund-raisers for homosexual causes. This country is in the midst of a moral, racial, political, economic, social, sexual, military, environmental, educational, moral, fiscal, ethical, moral, class-based, moral crisis. We have forgotten our morality. We need a leader with *character*, who can provide moral stewardship and protect our kids from nudity and foul language and violence in the media and from entertainment with a homosexual agenda and who will institute a foreign policy to keep the ragheads in check *and* who has the compassion necessary to phase out the welfare system that lets *fifty million* unwed, teenage black mothers live lazily in the veritable lap of luxury by sucking on the overtaxed teat of real, hardworking Americans. Instead, we get these goddamn midwestern smooth talkers, chosen—by *fifty-three percent* of voters according to the most recent statistics—on the basis of *height,* for Chrissake. And you don't know if people are dumb?"

I watch Lou triumphantly.

"That's quite a speech," he says.

"Damn right," Barry says. "I always have one ready for you goddamn bleeding hearts."

Lou frowns. "Are you sure there are fifty million black girls on welfare?"

"Sure I'm sure," Barry tells him.

I'm tired of losing," Barry says.

"At paintball?" I say.

"That's right."

"We don't lose too often."

"Often enough."

We're at our gym, which is called Size, and Barry and I are taking turns on the leg press. He is wearing a tan leather weight belt to support his lower back. I pull the pin out of the weight stack—it was at two hundred, the weight Barry uses—and slide it into the hole marked four twenty-five.

There are only a few sluts in the weight room, stretching on the mats in the corner or else working on the lat pulldown, all of them dressed in spandex and string-strapped tank tops. I wait until a few of them are done with their various sets and then I lie back on the red-padded machine and set my feet shoulder width on the dimpled metal plate and push hard against it. The rack I am on slides away from the unmoving metal plate, and next to me four hundred twenty-five pounds of Bodysmith Nautilus weights creak upward in a quivering pile.

I can't see anything but the white plaster of the ceiling, but I know the sluts must be looking. Even if they hadn't already noticed me, the sound would have gotten their attention.

The ideal weight-lifting sound is never very loud. If you scream, you look like you're trying too hard. The sound should combine the moan of sex with a muted angry roar. It should grow louder with each repetition, ending at about the same volume as a normal speaking voice.

When I am finished with the set, I sit up with my legs hanging off the edge of the machine and blot my face with a towel, looking out the side of my eye at one of the wall-size mirrors, inspecting the veins on my arms and the bulges of my chest and shoulders under the T-shirt.

I stand and Barry lies down for his next set.

"I've decided to bring in an expert," he says.

"What kind of expert?"

"You know—an operator, a specialist, a mechanic."

"Like a mercenary?"

He glances around us to see if anyone heard and motions for me to lean toward him, and when I do, says, "Like a mercenary."

I keep my breathing normal. "Where's he from?"

Barry smiles, our faces still close together, and says, "Israel, I think."

"Why Israel?"

"Because they're experienced."

I groan. "But they don't even *lift*. He probably has skinny little arms."

Barry stares at me.

"Also," I say, "what does some *yid* have to teach me about being hard?"

"He might know more about it than you think. And don't say 'yid.' "

"Sorry, but this all comes as quite a shock."

"He'll be here for our morning session on Saturday."

He waves for me to move away from him and starts his set.

In the locker room, after we shower, Barry and I examine each other's bodies and give constructive criticism. I know this sounds bad, but I just want to assure everyone that I'm not a fag. In fact, I would hate fags except that I read somewhere that hating fags meant you were a fag yourself. So I don't hate them. I'm just not one. Really.

My apartment looks onto a grassless soccer field and the abandoned hulk of a paper mill and then onto the bright gray surface of Route 90, stretched out between banks of rust-colored trees, separated from the soccer field by a chain-link fence.

I turn on the television and slouch, sore-limbed, on the sofa. I drink a ready-mixed vanilla Met-Rx. The light from the television flickers across my face as I prepare the hypodermic and line up the bottles of pills—Dianabol, Nolvadex, Maxibolin, creatine phosphate. After I swallow the pills, I give myself the injection of B-12 and, so that doesn't keep me up all night, follow it with two Seconal capsules the color of velvet-red cherries. I take four chalk-white zinc pills to keep the steroids from putting zits on my back and then I lie back and watch the bright gray screen.

The champion has teased hair and a sequined dress. She sings "I'm Still Here." She is seven years old. She would like to thank God and her parents. She smiles all the time. The judges give her three and a half stars.

The challenger is an eleven-year-old boy with blond hair that flops over the sides of his head. He smiles wider than the girl. He sings "Yankee Doodle Dandy," marching energetically in place. Suddenly, I have a vision of this boy in fifteen years, bruised, crying, track marks all along his arms. He is curled in a ball on the floor grabbing at the ankles of a V-bodied stud in leather pants. The big stud is saying, "It's over, Julian. It's . . . over."

The judges give the challenger two and three-quarters stars.

The Seconals take hold and I am drifting and my chin sags to touch my chest. My eyelids droop closed and then pop open and droop closed again and do this over and over until finally they do not open anymore and I am asleep and the television is saying, "Kill, kill, kill."

On Friday morning a blond slut in a purple tank top comes into the store and asks me about recumbent stationary bicycles. I am wearing a dark blue T-shirt with the Navy SEAL crest over the heart and UNITED STATES NAVY SEAL TEAMS across the back in white. The sleeves hug my biceps. My jeans are dark and boot-cut (I never wear a taper). My boots are tan Timberlands ($59.99 with the staff discount).

The slut stares at me hungrily. I lift up my T-shirt, using the bottom to wipe some imaginary grime from underneath my eye, showing her the cobblestone abs and the striations of the obliques.

"Are you an athlete?" she asks.

"I'm captain of the store paintball team."

"Are you any good?"

"Bill Cookston said I was almost the best he ever saw. He said I could make any team I wanted, including Shockwave."

"What's that?"

"You've never heard of Shockwave? They're only the winningest team in the *history* of the World Cup of paintball."

"So, were you guys ever in that tournament on ESPN?" she says.

I snort. "ESPN."

"I thought those guys were the best."

"That's what a lot of people think," I say. "But for the serious MilSim competitor, that stuff is a sellout. It dilutes the purity of the sport."

"What's MilSim?"

I look at her for a few seconds and then say, "Military Simulation. What do you think we're talking about?"

"I thought it was called war games."

I can feel the muscles tighten in my shoulders. "It's not a game."

"Sorry."

"Don't worry about it," I say, teeth clenched.

To calm myself, I put my hand on the seat of the Ergometer 9000 with optional heart-rate monitor and reading rack ($1,499.95).

"The recumbent feature," I say carefully, "is particularly important if there will be any men riding the unit. Studies have shown that the upright models tend to promote impotence."

"How do they do that?"

"Excuse me?"

"Promote impotence. The upright bicycles. How do they do it?"

"Well . . . I believe it has something to do with"—I look around for Lou, but I don't see him anywhere—"with the ah . . . the heat of the testicle walls."

Stevie is the only other salesman on the floor. He is showing a Merry Men compound bow ($334.99) to a fat-body in jungle camouflage complete with bush hat. I catch Stevie's eye and he says something to the fat-body and walks toward me. The fat-body lays down the bow and begins fingering various arrowheads and stroking his thick mustache.

"Hello," Stevie says when he reaches us.

"Hello," the slut says. She is looking at Stevie with the same expression she had when I showed her my stomach.

Stevie is taller than I am, but thin, and I wonder whether I am misreading her reaction.

"I was just explaining how upright bicycles cause impotence by overheating the testicle walls," I say.

"Well," Stevie says, smiling at me, "of course, that's part of it. Also, the pressure restricts blood flow and damages the soft tissue."

He walks the slut toward the displays of upright bicycles.

When erect, my cock is nine and a half inches long and as thick as some men's wrists. A year ago, Stevie started working at the store and I heard from some slut we both know that he was packing almost eleven. Since then I have been seriously considering the experimental penile-enlargement surgery, which has been performed (I understand) with great success by two doctors in Sweden.

On the way into Champagne Dreams, the bar we go to on Friday nights, Barry points out two men in suits standing on the corner and tells me that they could be from the secret police.

I say, "This country doesn't have any secret police." I frown. "At least, I've never heard of any."

Barry shakes his head. "Why do you think they call them *secret*?"

Inside, the place glows blue and orange from neon signs that hang outside the windows. The room is full of sluts dressed to show their belly buttons and the narrow strip of skin between their inflated breasts.

"I could never fuck a girl with a tit job," Lou says.

"I don't care if she's had a tit job," I say, "as long as she *looks* like she's had one. And not one of these cut-rate three-grand hack jobs where you can still see the scar. I'm talking about seven thousand *per*."

Ken, who is the fifth member of our paintball team and the only one who doesn't work at the store, is sitting in a horseshoe-shaped corner booth with two brunette sluts. We all slide into the booth, the sluts crowding closer to Ken to make room.

The slut sitting next to Barry looks at the gold that glitters on each of his fingers (including the thumb) and at his platinum necklace, which she probably thinks is silver, and asks him what he does for a living.

"I own a store called Balls, Balls, Balls," Barry says.

"On the highway? 'Everything for the New American Sportsman,' or something like that?"

"That's the one."

"And what about the rest of you?" the other slut says.

"They work for me," Barry says. "Except for Ken. But he used to."

"So you're the boss," she says.

Later, Barry and I will take turns fucking these sluts. We'll tie them up. We'll beat them with phone cords and Spiritbreaker riding crops (two for $79.50). But now I just smile at them and then I go to the bar.

Waiting for the drinks, I talk to Samson Taylor, who is the largest man I know. He is slumped, sullen, close to the surface of the bar. In the dimness the features of his face are nearly indistinguishable. He is a gray-haired, mahogany mountain.

"How many years you play, again?" I ask him.

"Five," he says, his eyes closed.

"All in Minnesota?"

"Yeah."

"So, why'd you stop so early?"

He sighs. "Can we not talk about this right now?"

"Sure, sure. Whatever you want. I heard it was drugs."

"You shouldn't believe everything you hear."

"What do you mean?"

He shrugs.

"Barry's bringing in a professional," I say, "to help with our training. He gets here in the morning. I'm worried that Jew fuck is trying to phase me out of the team. I practically *built* that team for him. You think they'd be fourth-best without me? The fuck they would. None of those bitches has my skills."

He puts one of his enormous hands on my forearm and I almost jerk away. I stare at the hand, imagining that I can smell the blackness rising from it.

"You're my friend, right?" he asks.

"Of course."

"Then leave me alone a while."

"Okay. Leave you alone. No problem. Done and *done.*"

He removes his hand from my arm and I take a deep breath.

"I knew you'd understand," he says. "You're the only one who understands."

The bartender brings my drinks and pours two more shots for Samson, who does not open his eyes but smiles slightly when he hears the shots set down in front of him. A tear dribbles down his cheek.

I walk back to the booth, thinking that Samson Taylor is not as tough as I thought.

I am nervous that my cock shrinks too much when it's limp. I read once that black guys don't actually have larger dicks, it's just that they grow less, so they walk around bigger.

Sometimes I even wonder whether I am really as good as I think, whether all the sluts who have screamed my name and begged for more, more, more weren't in it for the sex but were trying to attach themselves to my rising star. I have heard that, sooner or later, all great men have that worry.

One slut I used to know—I think her name was Laura— told me when I broke up with her that I was selfish in bed.

I said, "I tried to give you everything I have. You're just not deep enough."

I drive Ken and Stevie to practice on Saturday morning in my black Pathfinder, which I got for *well* under the list price from some Panamanians Barry knows. I have the tuner set to National Public Radio. The host of the show says, "We're talking America's foreign policy woes. Do you have the solution? Our lines are open."

Sitting in the passenger seat, Ken says, "How can you take this crap?"

I say, "I need to have the information."

"This isn't information, it's opinion."

I wave him off. "It's not my fault if you don't care about being educated."

"But they're all so self-satisfied."

"It's a small price to pay."

He shakes his head. "Carl Kassel can kiss Ken's crevice."

" 'Crack,' " Stevie says from the backseat.

"What?"

"Use 'crack.' It's funnier."

"There's nothing funny about using crack."

"I mean instead of 'crevice.' "

Ken turns around in his seat to look at him. "Just say no, guy."

The practice site is a replica of a few blocks from Beirut circa 1985, contained inside an immense warehouse that is owned by a paintball-organizing company called Marked for Dead. When we arrive, all of us dressed in gray-and-white urban-camouflage jumpsuits, Barry is there already, standing next to a full-scale model of a bombed schoolhouse. He is with Lou and a man I don't recognize. My heart is thumping fast. My face has begun to sweat.

When we reach them, Barry introduces us to the new man, whose name is Jack.

"Jack what?" Ken says.

"Just Jack," Barry tells him.

"Like Madonna," Stevie says.

Jack smiles. "That's right."

He is my height and twenty pounds lighter, which is considerably larger than I imagined. Even so, I doubt he can bench-press three-fifteen. But he *is* thick through the shoulders and awfully cut, the veins in his arms raised like seams. I get a view of him in profile and, I have to admit, he doesn't look too kikey. His nose is short and broad. His head is shaved almost to the scalp. His skin is as dark as mine. I wonder where he does his tanning.

He is wearing a light blue short-sleeved flannel shirt and beige pants, which are made from a horrible, coarse-looking material but which, as far as I can see, do not taper. His shoes are low-top boots that are probably not *half* as expensive as my Timberlands (if I had paid full price), although they might be more durable.

"How old are you?" I ask him.

"Thirty."

"Mmm," I say, "I would have guessed older. But still, thirty might be a little old for this business. Killing, as I'm sure you know, is young men's work."

"I'll be all right."

"Your English is pretty good."

He looks at me for a moment. "I'm from Pittsburgh."

"Barry said you were from Israel."

He shrugs. "I worked there for a while."

"What did you do before that?"

"I was in the Navy."

"Doing what?" Stevie asks.

Jack shrugs again. "Let's just say I wasn't a sailor."

My face is suddenly hot. I sit down on the charred remains of a swing set and lean my head down, pretending to retie my boots, hoping that no one will notice.

Jack makes us run laps around the inside of the warehouse to warm up. He keeps us running for forty minutes. When we stop, I open my duffel bag. Sweat stings my eyes. I take out my goggles, which are made by V-Shock. I put on the goggles and then take out the face mask (also by V-Shock). Jack looks at the mask.

"What are you putting on a mask for?" he says. "This is paint*ball*, not paint*pussy*. Not paint*ovary*. I see why you guys never win."

I open my mouth, but I can't make a sound, so I begin setting up my weapon, which is a Hicap 180-round front-loader with Trimount sight rail and TF90 reflex sight, all from Gods of War. I walk to the high-pressure air pump behind the jagged ruins of a small apartment building and fill the gun's tank (I *never* use carbon dioxide for propulsion).

When I come back, Jack is checking the sight of a pistol that looks like a Beretta automatic.

"Who makes that?" I say. "Spyder? Hardboilers? Gods of War? Bloodsports?"

"No," he says.

"Who then? It looks so real."

He glances up at me. "It *is* real."

Somebody once told me that the average man experiences his greatest rate of hair loss at age twenty-three, so for the last five years (since my twenty-first birthday) I have been using Rogaine (Maximum Strength formula) twice a day, every day. I haven't detected any sign of fallout.

• • •

Sitting on the sofa Saturday night after practice, too tired to move, waiting for the Seconals to kick in, I hear one of the square-jawed network anchormen say that the average American now has an IQ of seventy-one. He starts a story about the stock market and then interrupts himself for breaking news: the national IQ has dropped below sixty. This has resulted in record sell-offs. While he is telling me this, the IQ drops to fifty-three, then to forty-seven. As I succumb to the Seconals, the number continues to plummet. By the time I am completely surrounded by blackness, it is approaching twenty.

For Sunday's practice, we are simulating night fighting. All the windows are covered with blackout blankets. The ceiling of the warehouse is a glowing map of stars with a perfectly rounded moon in the center. The bomb-cratered buildings of our Beirut are lit dimly with recessed floor lights and dull floodlights that line the edges of the course. We sit on broken seesaws in the playground beside the schoolhouse, waiting for our eyes to adjust to the gloom.

"He's not such hot shit," I am whispering to Lou. "It's not like he was in Vietnam or anything. All he's done is ran a lot and swam a lot, and jumped out of some planes. Big deal. I've sky-dived; you've sky-dived."

"I don't know," Lou says. "He seems to know what he's doing."

"He *can't* be better than I am."

We practice house-to-house assaults. Door kicking, Jack calls it. Cardboard silhouettes pop up to confront us as we enter some of the ruined houses and we pepper the targets with small yellow blotches. Occasionally we shoot each other.

We break after finishing each block. During the second-to-last break, all of us lying on the floor of a gutted, roofless mosque, Jack sits next to me and looks at the false sky.

"You have anything you want to say to me, Logan?"

I feel the muscles behind my testicles contract, but I keep my voice as normal as I can and say, "I've been wondering how much combat experience you've had."

"Ah," he says.

"Because I personally don't like someone passing themselves off as some kind of expert when they don't have the *credentials*. Playing soldier in California doesn't do much for me. I mean, being able to swim don't make you a dolphin."

"Mmm," Jack says, nodding. He reaches into the front pocket of his tan windbreaker and comes out with a crumpled pack of Pall Mall unfiltereds.

I smile at him, little chills of relief running along my spine. "You know, everything I've read says that commandos shouldn't smoke. Especially in the dark. Ruins the night vision."

He ignores me, lighting one of the cigarettes and sucking on it until the tip glows orange.

"Don't feel bad that you didn't know," I say, dizzy from the chills. "You've probably never been on long patrol."

He takes the cigarette out of his mouth and looks at me and then presses the burning end to the back of his hand and holds it there as we listen to the quiet sizzling. His expression does not change.

"Jesus Christ," Stevie says.

I feel the circular exterior wall of the mosque begin spinning around us. The stars twinkle like strobe lights. Gray smoke floats from under the edges of the cigarette. Ken and Barry have their hands held against their eyes.

Jack stares at me all the time, not blinking, grinding the flaming tip into his hand. My chills have disappeared. My mouth is hanging open. And then I feel nothing. I cannot move. All I can do is watch the gleaming coal of the cigarette reflected in Jack's eyes.

• • •

can't remember anything else until we are sitting in our booth at Champagne Dreams. Jack is there, laughing with Lou and Stevie. They are talking about Bosnia. I lean my mouth close to Ken's ear. "*Lots* of guys can put cigarettes out on their hands," I whisper.

"Not lots," Ken whispers back.

"I must've seen it in a hundred movies."

"That's *movies*, guy. Can *you* do it?"

"I think so," I say.

Ken shakes his head and turns away from me. I walk to the bar, dazed.

Samson Taylor is in his usual seat, a line of empty shot glasses in front of him. I sit down next to him.

"I thought about what you said," he tells me.

"Yes," I say.

"About the expert. I don't think it's a real challenge to you. I mean, you know Sugar Ray Robinson was a better fighter than the guys who trained him."

"What are you talking about?"

"Sometimes the guy with the knowledge isn't the guy with the skills."

I look at the sluts around the room and wonder how many people know what happened with the cigarette.

"You know," I say to Samson Taylor, "you really are a silly nigger."

"What?" He is blinking, trying to focus his eyes.

"You," I say. "Are. A. Silly. Nigger."

"I don't understand."

"What's to understand?"

"You're my friend."

"Bullshit. I'm not friends with silly-nigger winos. No wonder your kids won't see you. I wouldn't either."

There are tears running down his cheeks. "No," he says. "No, no, no, no."

"What do you mean, no?"

"You're my friend. My friend."

"Wrong, nigger. I'm better than you." I look around the bar. "I'm better than all these stinking people. I'm the kind of man who knows how to get ahead. You're nobody. That's why somebody else gets to fuck your wife every night."

He groans.

"Do you wonder about it?" I say. "You must. You must wonder if she likes it, if she makes different noises with him than she did with you. Maybe that's why she left—you couldn't make her scream."

His groan turns into a growl and then into a roar, and his tree-trunk arm comes around, much faster than I was expecting, and knocks me off the stool and onto the floor. He stands over me, his bulk blocking out everything else. He picks up the stool to smash on my head and I brace for it and then there is someone on his back, who I think might be Stevie, and there is someone else hanging from one of his arms. Then there is confusion and bodies flying through the air above my head and then there is a moment of calm and I see that Samson has thrown off everybody and lifted the stool again and I can only see one other person, who is standing behind Samson and to the side and has one arm extended with a handgun on the end of it. The gun is pointed at Samson's temple, but he does not notice. We are frozen like that.

Then Samson screams again and hurls the stool against a wall and runs out of the bar. I can hear him roaring in the street. I sit up.

Jack is standing above me, his arm still extended, the pistol held steadily in his hand, sighting down the barrel just like the textbooks teach.

"He could have killed me," I say.

He nods.

"Why didn't you put him down?" I say.

"I don't know."

"Well, I guess you *better* fucking know. This is my *life*."

He lowers his arm and shakes his head. "I *wanted* to fire," he says. "I was all ready." He shakes his head again. "Hunting scuds, we always tried to avoid everybody. Never had to shoot. Not in Somalia, either."

I hear sirens in the distance.

Jack kneels beside me. His mouth is inches from my face. "I never killed anybody," he whispers. "But I *could*. I'm sure I could."

ALL THE NIGHTS
OF THE WORLD

n the car, snowflakes floating against the
windshield and then melting in the defrost
and streaking the glass like tears, Chris
tells me how nervous she is. I make the turn. My hands are
cold against the steering wheel. "Why should you be nervous?" I say.

"This is *my* audition," she says.

I glance over. She is huddled inside her coat. She has my
jacket wrapped around her legs and her hat pulled down low
over her ears. The only part of her I see is her nose, peeking
from under the mass of clothing, windburn red and tiny and
perfect. She is sitting on her hands.

"Is that what you think?" I say. I turn back to the road.

We drive in silence for a while.

Chris says, "Is he going to like me?"

"I told you before," I say.

"Tell me again," she says and I do.

As I am making the turn onto the street that runs in front
of the restaurant, Chris says, "Am I going to like him?"

I laugh. "Everybody likes him," I say. "He's a star."

We pull into the parking lot. I ease into a space near the

entrance. I turn off the engine. Then we sit, not moving, the car clicking, and before we open the doors I tell Chris how much I love her and she nuzzles my shoulder.

My father is never late.
He is already at the table when we enter the room. Several of the waiters have recognized him. They are gathered around him excitedly. He is telling a joke. When my father finishes the joke, the waiters laugh too loudly. He half-smiles and picks up his glass of water and drains it. The glass disappears in his fist.

The room is red-carpeted and dark-walled and is filled with men who have never torn off another man's ear. The men are soft and pink-faced. They sit separated from their dates by cream-colored tablecloths. The dates are young models with skeletal fingers and long legs or middle-aged wives with faces like marble floors.

The maître d' leads us to the table. When he sees us, my father stands and steps past the group of waiters. He throws his arms around me and claps me on the back. I am drowning in Old Spice and the familiar smell from his shirt. I am shocked, as I always am, by the size of him. He steps away from me and looks at Chris.

"You must be Christina," he says. He leans down very far to kiss her delicately on the cheek.

The waiters are nervous with my father standing. They disperse quickly.

Without all the coats wrapped around her, Chris seems very small. The men in the room notice her, as they always do. I watch my father notice them noticing.

I pull out Chris's chair for her and we sit.

The menus are leather-bound. They do not list prices.

"What *is* this place?" I say.

"First class," my father says. "It's first class."

Chris reaches into her purse and brings out a black jewelry box. She hands it to my father. "Happy birthday," she says.

He opens the box and peers inside.

"It's a tie clasp," I say.

He begins to nod and then catches himself. He picks up the tie clasp. In his hand it looks like a toothpick.

"Chris made it," I say.

He smiles at her. "It's wonderful," he says.

Chris smiles back at him.

A waiter slides in to take our drink orders. When he's gone, I say, "How was the flight?"

My father shrugs. "Made it in before the storm."

"I suppose we should have come down," I say.

"Please," he says. "I had to fly so much when I was playing, I could practically *pilot* one of those things."

The waiter returns with the drinks.

"Should we order?" I say.

"We're waiting for Don," my father tells me.

"Will you tell one of your stories?" Chris asks him.

"What do you want to hear?"

"I'm not sure. I don't know much about sports."

"Me neither," he says and they laugh. He begins to tell her about Bobby Layne jumping into the pool at the Hyatt in Philadelphia from his window on the third floor, but he stops and looks at the front of the room. When I look, Don Erskine is standing beside the maître d'.

The maître d' walks toward the table. Don Erskine lumbers after him. He is almost as tall as my father and not quite as thick through the shoulders. In front of him he carries a hard-fat gut like a swollen hot-water bottle.

We introduce Don to Chris. He shakes her hand and glances at me. He sits across from me and says, "I hate the winters in this city."

"Move," my father says.

"Play nice. It's your birthday."

The waiter comes back with a gray-haired man in a white dinner jacket. This is the owner. I know it before he tells us. The collar of his shirt is open. The skin of his chest is the same unnatural tan color as his face.

The owner puts his hand on my father's shoulder and says, "I just want you all to know what an honor it is to have you dining with us this evening."

"Glad to be here," my father tells him.

"Does anyone need recommendations? We have some five-pound lobsters. Just got them this morning. Watched them get unloaded myself. Also, I hope you will do me the courtesy of being my guests."

"That would be fine," my father says. "Thank you."

"After your meal, perhaps we could take a picture together for the wall."

"Why not?"

"I'd like to bring my son over to meet you. If he's going to run this place, he's got to learn how to treat our special guests."

"We'll help you break him in."

We order the food. The waiter and the owner disappear.

Chris says, "You never finished your story."

Don Erskine says, "What story?"

"Bobby Layne at the Hyatt," my father tells him.

"That's a good one."

"I'm always telling stories," my father says. "I want somebody to tell me a story for a change. I want Chris to tell me the story of her life."

"That's not so easy," she says.

"It's easier than you think. There are only tiny parts of it that anyone wants to hear."

"Where should I begin?"

"Tell what you do for a living."

"He hasn't told you?"

"He doesn't tell me much."

"I'm a dancer."

"Ballet?"

"I'm with a jazz company."

"I don't know anything about jazz dancing," my father says.

The waiter brings the salads.

When Chris is in the ladies' room, Don Erskine says, "A shiksa?"

"I'm not exactly Jackie Mason," I tell him.

He nods. "But you're not Pat Boone, either."

"He never liked the Catholic girls," my father says.

"Jesus Christ, Pop," I say, "you haven't been inside a church in twenty years."

"First of all, you're too young to remember what I did twenty years ago. Second, not going to church doesn't make me not a Catholic. Sure as hell doesn't make me a WASP."

He eats a bite of his steak.

"You going to marry this girl?" Don Erskine says.

"It's a little early for that. She only just met the old man."

"So what?"

"So he'll charm her for me. Then I won't have to marry her."

"Careful. Your old man might not be as glamorous as you think." Don smiles. "Anyway, answer me seriously."

"Seriously, I don't know."

"What's to know?"

"What if I don't love her?"

"Don't marry her."

"I mean, what if it turns out I don't?"

"It never *turns out*. Either you do or you don't. When you're under the covers in the dark, either you're the only two people on earth or you aren't."

"That's not much."

"That's all there is."

"That's all you need," my father says. His face is a picture of solemnity.

We look at him for a moment. Then I say, "How lyrical of you."

He can't hold it. His lips force their way up at the sides and he smiles and then he laughs with his head thrown back.

"Jesus," Don Erskine says. "I'm just trying to give your son a little fatherly advice."

My father's eyes are shining. He says, "If the earth moves then she's the one? That's not advice, that's pillow talk. The only romantic advice you need is give her an enema before you fuck her in the ass. That and abs. Girls like abs. Don't let yourself go the way Don has."

"Fuck you, you prick. It's part of the aging process."

"I weigh thirty pounds less today than I did the day I quit playing."

"Different metabolisms," Don mutters.

My father pours himself more wine. He looks at me. "I assume you inherited your father's cock. That'll keep a woman better than any ring."

"Comes a time when a woman needs you to settle down," Don says.

"If you're poking her in the kidneys every night, she'll deal with the uncertainties."

"So why'd you get married?"

My father looks at him. "I don't have bastard kids."

Don shakes his head. "Never take romantic counsel from a man who can't invite his ex-wife to his fiftieth birthday."

When the owner brings his son over, my father tells them about the night he broke Mike Webster's nose. The owner's son is tall, nearly my height. The top of his head would be even with my father's chin. He has blow-dried hair and caps on his teeth. He smiles as often as possible.

My father tells about reaching under Webster's face mask and grabbing and tearing and how he felt the bone give and how the blood poured as though someone had turned on a faucet. He tells about the sound that Webster made and how he clawed at my father's hand and pulled the index finger out of its socket and bent it back so far that it touched the back of the hand. My father shows them the crooked finger.

The owner and his son are very happy. My father tells them about thumbing Gene Upshaw in the Adam's apple and how Upshaw went down on his hands and knees and vomited. The other men from the Raiders' line were insane with rage. They tried to get even on every play. Finally Art Shell stomped my father in the groin near the end of the third quarter and he pissed blood for a week.

I examine Chris's face while my father speaks. I expect her to be excited or disgusted. She only looks sad.

"You know," the owner says, "my son was a halfback in college."

"Mine, too," my father says.

"Where?" the son asks and I tell him.

My father says, "Nobody your age knows how to play ball."

"There are a few," Don Erskine says.

"Maybe," my father allows. "Who's that boy they have now—the one with hands the size of pie plates?"

"I don't think you can say 'boy,' " I tell him.

"You can't say anything these days."

The waiter brings coffee and the dessert cart. After he leaves, my father says, "I'm twenty-five years old in every story I tell."

"We're famous for playing a little boys' game," Don tells him.

"You're not really *famous.*"

Don smiles. "No, I suppose not."

"I'm not complaining, you understand. It keeps me fed. They put my name on the letterhead and give me an office and a partner's salary, and all I have to do is sit around and tell war stories. I haven't really worked in fifteen years."

"Wonderful," Chris says.

I clear my throat. "We need to think about going. It's only supposed to get worse out there."

"All right," my father says. "I still have to give the jock sniffer his picture. Don'll drive me to the hotel."

We stand. Chris kisses my father and Don Erskine.

In the coatroom, I say, "Every time I see the way he affects people, I feel like I'm going to be a failure."

Chris turns around and looks at me. "That's the dumbest thing you've ever said."

Before I can ask what she means, the girl is back with our coats and then my father has come up behind us and put an arm around each of us and is walking us to the parking lot. I decide to ask her on the way home, but by the time we are in the car I have forgotten what it is I was going to ask.

C hris is so cold when we get back to my apartment that she is unable to speak. Her teeth chatter wildly. She strips off her clothes and throws herself onto my bed. She wraps the blankets close around her.

I undress more slowly and fold my clothes and then fold hers and lay them all at the foot of the bed. I turn on the stereo with the volume low. I light an orange candle that smells like ginger tea.

Chris is still shivering when I climb in next to her. She has bedclothes clutched against her chin. I slide down under the covers and blow warm breath on her body. I take each of her feet between my hands and rub it hard until the sole loses its iciness. Then Chris turns on her side and I emerge from under the bedding, dripping sweat. I wrap myself around her and breathe hot against the back of her neck.

She stops shaking. Her breathing slows. I go back under the sheets and kiss my way down her back. She squirms slightly each time I press my lips against her. When I reach her underwear, I kiss along the waistband and then gently turn her over onto her back. I kiss the front of her panties and the soft outlines of what is underneath. She moans.

When I come up again, we are both breathing deeply. She pushes her mouth against mine very hard.

"I think you impressed my father," I say in a voice I don't recognize.

"It wasn't him I was trying to impress."

We push our mouths together again and then we lie together. Light from the candle flickers over us. Snow falls past my window in bloated flakes. Below, the street bustles silently.

We lie like that a long time.

KILLING TIME

Ray sits with his eyes half closed and does not look at the girls. The girls look the way they always look. They sit across the room all in a row on the banquette, whispering to each other, giggling, staring at our table. We order a second round and Milt Bailey says, "Maybe I should go show those three a little piece of Philadelphia."

Davey Manzelli says, "A very little piece," and we laugh. Dave's face looks like a boiled dinner.

"Fuck you, Garlic," Milt Bailey says.

"Up your ass, you jungle-bunny fairy."

Frank Patterson, the bodyguard, sits beside Ray and does not watch the girls, either. He is wearing a white suit. He leans far back in his chair. The only parts of him that move are his eyes.

"What time is it?" Davey asks.

"Eleven-thirty," Milt tells him.

"You sparring in the morning, Ray-Ray?"

Ray shrugs without looking up. "Ask Sunshine."

"Well?" Davey says.

"Well, what?" I say.

"Are you sparring in the morning or not?"

"Fuck should I know? It's up to Doc. I'm not the trainer."

"Well, Doc ain't here. I think maybe we ought to call it a night."

"Hey, Dave," I say, "I already have a mother. And a wife."

"Hey, fuck you, Mike. I'm just trying to be the voice of reason. These niggers would stay out all fucking night. Can't even hardly tell time."

"Why are you in such a rush?" I ask him. "The new *Playgirl* just come out?"

Ray smiles for the first time. "Hey, Dave," he says, "did you suck cock before Dannemora or did the spade sodomites make you into a bitch and one day you discovered you liked it?"

Dave smiles slightly. "It was Folsom, and who you calling a spade?"

Ray brightens further. "You mean the pot and the kettle? Well, get one thing straight: I ain't no spade, Daddy. I'm a high-yellow, gold-colored African prince with a cock that hangs to my knees."

Dave says, "Doesn't it get in the way when you *drop* to your knees?" and we laugh and Ray reaches across the table and musses Dave's hair and Dave slaps his hand away.

"**Y**ou're Ray Martin," the girl says.

"That's right," he tells her.

"We think you're the sexiest. Except for Oscar De La Hoya."

Ray nods. "Fuck Oscar De La Hoya."

The girl smiles nervously.

"Who's your friend?" one of the other girls says.

"That's Mike Larkin."

"Are you a fighter too?" she asks.

"Not anymore," I tell her.

The third girl is brunette and prettier than the others. She wears a black wrap skirt that clings to her hips. She smells like a peach. "Don't you worry about your face?" she says.

Ray laughs. "It's not much to begin with."

"Doesn't it hurt when you get hit?" one of the others asks. "Whenever I hit my head—getting out of a car, or whatever—I always want to cry."

"Not Ray," I tell her. "Ray didn't even cry when the doctor slapped him on the ass. They thought he was stillborn."

Ray's smile fades, but does not disappear. He says, "Mike is so tough he doesn't even have to throw punches. He just *scares* them to death."

"Would it hurt if I hit you?" asks one of the girls who is not the pretty girl.

"Depends," Ray says. He looks only at the pretty one.

She smiles. "On what?"

"On what you hit me with."

"What about with my fist?"

"Try it on Mike first."

Her eyes are wide. "Can I?"

"He doesn't mind."

When Ray takes the two girls into the men's room with him, I am alone with the pretty one and I ask her why she didn't go.

"I'm no groupie," she says.

"Of course not."

"What's that for?"

"Sorry. Sometimes this gets me down."

"This happens often?"

"Fight week is nasty," I tell her.

"So why are you here?"

"Because I'm his friend."

We are silent for a while. I sip my drink.

She says, "Have you known him a long time?"

"Ten years."

"How did you meet?"

"We used to fight sometimes in the amateurs."

"Who won?"

"We split pretty even."

"What about now?"

"What do you mean?"

"Could you beat him now?"

Across the room, Ray has reappeared, smiling hard, one of the girls on each arm. When she sees them, the pretty girl shakes her head.

"I'm glad you didn't go with them," I tell her.

On the street, mist makes the lights stretch out long. Frank Patterson sits beside me while I drive. The Navigator rides high in front like a motorboat.

"You guys won't say anything to Doc?" Ray says.

We are silent.

"Come on," he says. "The whole worry is the legs, right? Well, I was sitting the whole time. I made them do all the work. All I had to do was stay hard. I didn't even move the hips."

I listen to the breathing sound our tires make against the wet pavement.

"Fuck this," Ray says. "Who's the fucking champ here, anyway?"

"You are," Davey says.

"So I must be doing something right. If clean living won titles, Mike would be champ. Hey, Frank, you're on my side, aren't you?"

Frank shifts in his seat.

"Well, then fuck you too," Ray screams. "You want to shut me up, you big fuck? I don't care that you're Man-Mountain Dean. You think you can whup me?"

"No, Ray," Frank mumbles.

"What's that?"

"No," he says. "I can't."

• • •

We lie in the twin beds with the lights out, staring at the ceiling, unable to sleep. We listen to the cars passing and to the sounds from the sidewalk outside the casino. Ray says, "These beds make me feel like we're at camp."

"You never went to camp," I say. "Besides, they don't sleep two to a room there. They sleep in cabins with lines of beds. Like a barracks."

"All right. College, then."

"You never went to college, either."

"Fuck you, man."

After a while I say, "You want to play cards?"

"I don't have the energy. I wish we could just sleep."

"I miss my wife," I say.

"Mikey," he says some time later.

"Yeah."

"I don't know if I can take it."

"Just two more days," I tell him.

Ray walks into the gym from the lobby wearing track pants and a white T-shirt with a gold lion's head in the center. He sits on a folding chair at the gray plastic table next to the ring and Davey comes over and sits across from him. They do not speak. Ray puts his right hand on the table, palm down, and Davey lifts it gently and begins wrapping it in a light-brown cloth bandage.

"We on colored-people time this morning?" Doc says from across the room.

Ray shakes his head. "Too early for bullshit, Doc."

"Sorry. I thought we were training for a fight."

"Nobody else has to spar the day before."

"What if, for a little while, I was the trainer and you were the fighter?"

Ray shrugs.

When Ray is finished having his hands wrapped, I put in

my mouthpiece and strap on the headgear and check my cup.
I slide on the pillowy sparring gloves and mount the portable
metal steps and duck through the ropes and into the ring.
The chinstrap from the headgear is chafing and I try to adjust
it by rubbing it with my shoulder. Davey helps Ray into his
gloves and then Ray climbs into the ring and stands in front
of me.

"Light," Doc tells us. "Light."

"Careful of the face," Ray says through his mouthpiece.
"Press conference tonight."

We circle. Ray hops easily from foot to foot. I stalk,
crouched low, forcing him into the corner, narrowing his
angles of escape, cutting off the ring. I throw a short combination to his body, pulling the punches so that they thud
harmlessly against his belly and his pulled-in forearms.
He counters by hammering a left hook behind my ear. He
bobs once and then throws an uppercut into my ribs. He slips
my next few punches. He works his way out of the corner
with jab-jab-hook. I hook him as he weaves past me and
he counters with a right hand over the top that lands on
the bridge of my nose and makes white flashbulbs explode
in my head. I shake the haze away and I can see again and
now the flashbulbs are like furry white bees that dart around
the edges of my vision. I bully Ray into a corner again and
he brings his right leg even with his left and squares his
shoulders and pounds uppercuts just above my belt. I pound
him back. I lean my head against his shoulder and weave
with him. I watch the muscles in his chest to know when
he's punching. He works his way out this time with a seven-
punch combination to my head. The punches are so fast that
the sound of them runs together. As he dances away, I throw
a big, looping hook at him that misses terribly. He winks
at me.

Doc lets us go for fifteen minutes before he rings the bell.

· · ·

The first two Mexicans come in and stand by the entrance, working hard to look tough. After a few seconds, Bennie Suarez sweeps in behind them. And then comes Pachanga, flanked by one of his brothers and a kid with a mean-looking puckered pink scar running along his jaw. Pachanga is wide-shouldered and shorter than Bennie Suarez. Bennie is thin and careful in his movements. He spots us and oozes toward the table. Pachanga follows. The four Mexicans move with Pachanga.

"Good evening, Raymond," Bennie says.

Pachanga looks only at Ray. Pachanga's brother and the first two Mexicans glower at each of us in turn. Davey glowers back. The kid with the scar looks only at Frank Patterson. Frank seems about to fall asleep.

"You been working on your accent there, *vato*?" Ray says to Bennie Suarez.

"I am making an effort at assimilation," he says.

Ray snorts. "Wearing a mink shirt?"

Bennie shrugs. "I forgive myself a few little eccentricities."

"You just buy one of those word-a-day calendars?" I say.

"There's nothing wrong with sounding educated."

"Maybe you ought to teach your boy a little something," I say. "How long's he been here and he still can't speak the language? People are starting to think he's retarded."

Bennie half-smiles. "He knows what he needs to know."

"Doesn't take too much education for 'No mas,' " Ray says.

There is grumbling from the Mexicans. Pachanga raises his hand.

"I haven't quit yet," he says quietly.

"He hasn't *queeeet*," Davey says.

Pachanga does not look at him.

"Maybe," Ray says. "But you're at middleweight now, *cabrón*. I ain't no hundred-thirty-five-pound spic."

"You going to say that to the cameras?" Bennie asks.

Ray smiles. "You using an interpreter?"

"Of course."

"Too bad. Throws off my timing."

"All apologies."

A blue-jacketed hotel security guard comes through the double doors and says, "Five minutes."

Bennie says, "Time to get mean."

Ray says, "You tell your boy, he pulls any shit today and I'll ruin him for you."

The Mexicans head for the exit from which they will enter when the reporters are seated. When they are almost to the side door, Pachanga stops and turns around. "You piss blood tomorrow, *mayate*," he says.

Ray blows him a kiss.

"He *peeees* blood," I say.

We are already on the stage when the reporters are let in. Milt Bailey and Bennie Suarez are standing behind us with the promoters and the head of the commission, in front of the white sheet dotted with Budweiser crests that hangs at the back of the platform. When the reporters are seated, Pachanga enters behind Cleveland Henderson, his trainer. They are followed closely by Pachanga's brother and the kid with the scar. Cleveland Henderson sits next to Doc at the center of the table. Pachanga flops into the chair beside him, calm and brown and tough. Ray leans forward and grins at Pachanga. Pachanga pretends not to notice. He keeps staring straight ahead.

The reporters begin asking questions.

"How do you feel?" they say.

Pachanga mumbles into the microphone. The interpreter says, "I am an Aztec warrior. I have heart. I fight no matter how I feel."

"How's the eye?" they say.

"I am an Aztec warrior. I feel no pain."

"The bell hasn't rung yet," Ray says and everyone laughs.

"How long will the fight go?" they ask Pachanga.

"If he faces me like a man and does not run, the fight will be very short. If he runs like a rabbit, we will be there longer."

"I have no question that I will win," the interpreter says. "I am an Aztec warrior."

When it's Ray's turn, he says, "I've been in with Hopkins. I've been in with Jones. Who's *he* been in with?"

Ray says, "I'm not an idiot. I'm not going to bang with him. But I'm not planning on doing much running. He's used to guys standing in front of him. I don't do that. I can't see him being able to find me."

Ray says, "As far as that rabbit business, ask him about it after the sixth when he can't breathe and I'm still bouncing. I don't like watching these clumsy guys fight. It's not artistic. Makes me feel like a thug."

Ray says, "Sure, he has a chance—there's always a *chance*. But if you're asking me where to put your money, I'd have to think that's easy." He smiles. "When you're at a bullfight, you don't bet on the bull."

They are weighed on a black balance scale. The head of the commission slides the weights along the beam and calls out the numbers. The cameras chatter and flash. Pachanga wears sunglasses. Ray smiles and flexes his biceps.

Afterward, they pose together for the photographers. They face each other, hands up, trying to look bored.

The morning of the fight, we eat pancakes and eggs in our suite. We watch television. We do not answer the phone. Ray drinks as much water as he can handle. We play rummy and don't keep score.

At noon Ray eats two bananas and two hard-boiled eggs.

When he's finished with the second egg, he says, "You pissed at me?"

"Don't break your concentration," I say.

"You want me to apologize 'cause I'm better than you?"

I am silent.

"You don't have nothing you want to say?" he says. "I can look in your eyes and see what you're thinking. Why don't you grow some balls and tell me?"

"Careful, Ray."

"Careful of what? If you was my friend you'd tell me what you thought. But you get *paid* to be my friend, so you have to shut up and take what I give you. I throw my punch a little faster than you throw yours and it lands a little harder and that means you spend your life with your tongue in my ass. What do you think of that?"

"I think fight week is a tough week."

"Yeah, it's *my* tough week."

"Fine," I say.

It is hot in the locker room under the arena. Ray dances between us over the cement floor and throws combinations in the air. Sweat pours off him. He is dressed in gray sweatpants and his ring shoes. The noise of the crowd breaks in above our heads. The walls shake with the force.

When Ray stops shadowboxing, he stands shuffling his feet, unable to keep still. Davey sits on a high stool in front of him and massages the sweat into his chest and shoulders.

"I'm ready," Ray says.

"Goddamn right," Milt Bailey tells him.

"Bring that motherfucker," Ray says, his voice rising.

"He don't even belong in the same ring with you. He's never been in with anybody serious."

"He hits like a bitch."

"He can't break popcorn."

"I'm gonna take that motherfucker *out*."

"It's your ring, baby. It's *your* ring."

Milt is almost screaming now. Ray, his eyes wild from the tension, pulls himself away from Davey and begins flying around the room again and throwing bombs with both hands.

Milt screams at him as he throws. "There ain't nobody else, baby. They can't *see* you. He'll be lucky to make it through the first."

One of the security guards appears in the doorway. Thunder from the crowd pours in behind him. He shouts over the roar, "You boys ready to exchange trainers? They want to wrap Pachanga."

Doc is sitting on one of the benches in front of the banks of lockers. He glances up and nods.

"I'll go," I tell him.

He nods again.

The security guard motions into the hallway. Cleveland Henderson glides past him. Cleveland Henderson is small and caramel-colored. His fists are the size of grapefruits.

"Doc," he says. "Ray."

"Cleve," Doc says.

Ray sits on the high stool in front of Dave Manzelli. I walk toward the door.

"Your boy looks a little edgy," Cleveland Henderson tells me as I pass him.

"You know how he gets," I say.

The security guard leads me down the hallway. We pass lines of event staff and cameramen with laminated cards hanging from chains around their necks. We pass ring-card girls in sequined bikinis craning their necks for a glimpse of the crowd.

The Mexicans are gathered outside the dressing room, near the entrance to the tunnel. The kid with the scar slouches elaborately against one of the walls and looks fierce.

Inside the room, Pachanga sits on a padded table, staring at the floor. His brother sits next to him on a wooden chair. The inspector from the commission is the only other person in the room. In the corner, an immense radio blasts Tito Puente. Pachanga's brother nods at me and does not speak. He begins wrapping Pachanga's hands with white gauze.

Pachanga does not move. When the hands are wrapped, I inspect them. I check the knuckles for lumps. The inspector takes the gloves out of his bag and sets them on the table. The brother puts the gloves on Pachanga and laces them and covers the laces with tape. I examine the gloves and the covered laces. I pull a fat marker from my pocket and write "M. Larkin" over the tape on each wrist.

As I leave, the brother nods again and still does not speak. Pachanga is still staring at the floor.

Ray is standing in the center of the room when I get back. He is stripped down to his shorts. The sweat on his body gleams. Davey is on his knees in front of him, retying the laces of the ring shoes.

"How'd he look?" Ray asks me.

"Scared," I tell him. He nods.

Cleveland Henderson chuckles.

Ray jerks his head at me. I cross the room and lean in close to him.

"Thanks, Mikey," he says.

I look at him.

He lays a gloved hand on my shoulder.

Dave finishes with the shoes. Ray takes his hand from my shoulder and then he is weaving again. He uses the back of his forearm to wipe the sweat from his eyes.

"How we gonna do it?" he shouts at Milt Bailey.

"Limb from limb!" Milt Bailey shouts back.

"All night long!" Milt Bailey shouts.

Cleveland Henderson watches them peacefully, half-smiling. The rest of us stand back and let Ray get himself ready.

EVOLUTION

PART ONE: SEX

On our first date, Heather Gordon orders the Maryland crab cakes with red-pepper polenta and when I walk her home she asks me to take her to bed. On our second date, she has portabello and endive salad followed by veal tenderloin with poblano chiles and we make love on the swing set of an empty playground. On our third date, she tells me she is going to marry me.

For our one-month anniversary, Heather lights candles all around my bedroom and strips me naked and walks me to the bathtub, which is filled with warm water and rose petals. After three months, she takes me to Paris for the weekend. When we have been dating for six months, she asks me to kill her father.

. . .

"**T**he first thing we have to do," Kelly says when I tell him, "is cross over."

"Cross over," I say.

"Cross over the line between the good people and the bad people."

"There's a line?"

"Sure," he says. "Actually, there are several. We'll cross them in stages. We'll work slowly. We'll keep upping the ante."

"Did you get this from a book?"

He shakes his head. "No books. This is about personal experience. We must walk the path."

"The path."

"The path to emotional detachment."

"Are you making this up?"

He shakes his head again. "It's in all the latest literature."

I stare at him. "I thought you said no books."

He frowns. "From now *on*," he says.

We are sitting on the sofa in our apartment watching Kelly's high-definition television, which is shaped like a fish tank. The picture is so sharp that it reveals the individual pores in human faces.

Kelly says, "Everything's going cerebral these days. If we want to resist that trend, we have to master the physical world. If we want to be masters of the physical world, we have to know about life and death."

"Kel," I say, "are you sure you want to do this?"

He looks at me in silence for a while. Then he says, "This is what we've been waiting for."

The room is cavernous and blue-carpeted and honey-combed with tiny cubicles. The analysts sit in the cubicles between eighty and a hundred hours each week. The traders come in at eight-thirty and leave at five.

A green digital stock ticker rushes along the edges of the ceiling.

Kelly and I are sitting in brown leather armchairs outside a glass-walled conference room. Inside the conference room is a long cherry table with a podium at one end.

A kid about our age wearing Ferragamo lace-ups strolls past the analysts and pours himself a cup of coffee from the cart next to us.

Kelly says, "You have to come all the way over here every time you want coffee?"

The kid shrugs. "Can't put it on the trading floor. Someone would crash into it."

"You a trader?" Kelly says.

"Apprentice. You the boys from Merrill?"

Kelly shakes his head.

"We work for a start-up," I say.

The kid frowns. "But you're wearing suits."

"We're in new investment."

"You're here to pitch us?"

"Something like that," Kelly says.

The kid nods. "You guys have one of those cute tech names where you change the first couple letters of an existing word? Like Verizon. Or Cinergy."

"We're called eVolution," I tell him.

"Small ee, big vee?"

"That's right."

He smiles. "So what does it do?"

"The small ee, big vee?"

"The *company*."

I look around the room at analysts hunched over keyboards and at traders in shirtsleeves shouting into telephones. "I really don't know," I tell him.

· · ·

You can open a car door without a slimjim by bending a hanger into a squared hook and inserting it between the window and the weather stripping and using it to catch the lock rod. Sometimes you can open the door by using a key from the same manufacturer.

It is possible to hot-wire the car from the inside, but to do this you need to remove the ignition mechanism and complete the circuit manually. This risks severe electric shock. It also damages the car.

It is better to pop the hood and run a wire from the positive side of the battery to the positive side of the coil wire. The coil wire is red. Use a pair of pliers to hold the starter solenoid to the positive battery cable. This fires the engine. To unlock the wheel, insert a screwdriver into the steering column and use it to push the locking pin away from the wheel.

Kelly says, before you can kill you have to know what it is like to die.

Before you can know what it is like to die, he says, you have to know what it is to live.

"Do you know the life span of the common housefly?" he asks me.

"One day."

"One day," he says. "Twenty-four hours in which to pack all his loving and hating and living and dying."

I say, "I don't think a housefly does much loving and hating."

I change the channel on the high-definition television. The news is running a feature on school shootings.

Kelly sighs. "You're missing the point."

I shrug. "His life isn't short if he doesn't know it's short."

Kelly frowns and wrinkles his forehead and then says, "He only gets one sunrise and one sunset."

"And you only get a few thousand."

"Hopefully more than a *few*."

"Even so," I say.

Kelly nods. "Even so."

We are in a taxi. The driver wears a green knit hat and loafers with no socks. He has a stick of incense burning on the dashboard, which makes the air smell and taste like hot soap. I am sitting in the middle, between Kelly and my boss. My boss wears a linen suit. His tan is perfectly even.

Looking out the window at skyscrapers like enormous gray wafers, I say, "I don't understand my job."

My boss says, "What's to understand?"

"Shouldn't we bring a programmer with us?"

"Didn't I explain this to you last week?"

My scalp itches. I say, "It's just that I've been thinking some more about it and I figure it couldn't hurt to have an expert along."

My boss sighs. I look at Kelly. He is shaking his head. My boss says, "Our investors didn't grow up covered with zits."

"Excuse me?" I say.

"These people made their money the old-fashioned way— they inherited it. And they'll *never* give it away to some fruitcake in clear-framed glasses who wears his jeans two sizes too small. The key is charm, not knowledge. You were born for this."

Kelly is smiling at me. I ignore him. "But what if they ask me"—I lean close to my boss and whisper—"*technical* questions?"

"Do they ever?"

"They *could*."

He rolls his eyes. "Make something *up*. We're *salesmen*, for Chrissake."

"What are we selling? We don't make anything."

He looks at me. "We make *money*, kid. I sell experience. Kelly sells cool. You sell cheekbones and green eyes and leading-rusher-in-Ivy-League-history."

"Second-leading."

"My mistake," he says.

"It's just," I say, "that I don't know anything about computers."

He shakes his head. "This isn't about *computers*. Do you think Rockefeller knew anything about oil? Do you think Carnegie knew anything about steel? All you have to know is what people want and how to tell them they want it from you."

"But what if you don't know what people want?"

He shrugs. "Then you have to know how to tell them what they want."

When you die violently, your bowels let go. It's called involuntary-sphincter-release response and it means that you spew all the foul waste from inside you, more than you ever imagined possible.

Kelly says the next step after crossing over is the planning phase.

Really, he says, the two steps are simultaneous.

I am sitting in our living room, listening to the steam heat, and Kelly is telling me that evolution means the extinction of the weak.

"Every human and animal characteristic is the result of random genetic mutation."

"Yes," I say.

"Think of the creatures who lived before certain features developed. Think of the ones whose mutations failed to increase their fitness."

I close my eyes and picture ancient sea creatures with

squat bodies and tails like embryonic alligators', bobbing on the tide, near powerless with their shrunken fins, watching one of their fellows crawl out of the surf and onto the beach. He will go on to populate the world. The rest will be prey for prehistoric sharks or else will have descendants who will be less and less suited to the sea and will eventually drown as infants or occasionally flop their way onto the sand. I wonder whether these creatures know that they are the footnotes of history while their friend on the beach is the ancestor of an entire planet. I think of all the animals not selected for a place on the ark. I think of the thieves crucified next to Jesus.

"Eyelids," Kelly says.

I open my eyes. "What?"

"Eyelids are the result of random genetic mutation."

"Yes," I say.

"You have to be able to imagine how it felt before eyelids. If you looked at the sky during the day, your retinas would burn. You'd have to walk with your face pressed into the ground, dirt in your mouth all the time. You'd have to sleep with your eyes open."

"Yes," I say.

Kelly nods. "You need to be able to imagine the time before tear ducts."

Heather's father leaves his office between six-eighteen and six-fifty-one, Monday through Friday. On Saturday and Sunday he works noon to five. It takes him between four and seven minutes to make his way down to the garage, depending on the elevators. He drives a black Lexus sedan.

There ought to be two men in bland suits who drive Heather's father to and from work and sit all day behind Plexiglas in the hallway outside his office and shadow him wherever he goes.

This would make for more of an operation.

In that case, we might use a pipe bomb. We might use an incendiary device underneath the backseat. We might use a sniper. If the bodyguards blocked sight lines to the subject whenever they were out in the open (as they should), we might use the sniper to take out the bodyguards and use a chase man to go after the subject if he broke and ran. Of course, it is better to snipe in two-man teams. And neither of us knows how to use a rifle.

I am pressing my face into Heather's neck and smelling her perfume and her shampoo and the soap she uses, which is goat's milk and honey and costs twenty dollars a bar. Even through all of that, I can still catch the scent of her skin.

Heather is wearing a pair of my boxer shorts and a T-shirt from the gym I go to, which is called Advance.

We are watching *2001* on my DVD player.

I stop nuzzling Heather's neck and sit back into the sofa with my legs extended in front of me. Heather rests her head on my chest. The light from the television twinkles all around us.

"It's less than two thousand years since the fall of the Roman Empire."

"Is that right?" Heather says.

"That's right," I say. "Less than two thousand years after chariot races, we have airplanes and space shuttles and movie-theater popcorn."

"Amazing."

She shifts the position of her body and nestles into my chest.

I say, "We weren't even the same *species* until about twenty thousand years ago. Before that we were Cro-Magnons."

"Fascinating," Heather murmurs. Her breathing is becoming deep and slow.

"Until recently, we were carrying clubs and living in caves."

She is silent.

I watch the television. Keir Dullea has just shut down the supercomputer. This is immediately before the part I don't understand, in which he imagines himself sitting in a room that looks like the smoking room from the world's fanciest mental hospital and then sees himself as an old man and a fetus.

I say, "Kelly and I are making preparations."

Heather stirs for a moment and then relaxes back onto me. "Mmm," she says sleepily. "Preparations for what?"

"Never mind," I say. "It's all right if you don't want to talk about it."

Kelly says, "You're the bastard who gave measles to the Yanomami." He is talking to the waiter, whom he has just accused of sneezing over his Parmesan-and-onion tartlet. "These people lived in isolation for hundreds of years and then you goddamn sociobiologists and you save-the-rain-forest fairies came in and gave them a measles vaccine, except that there *were* no measles in the rain forest until you brought them. And when the vaccine made some of the people sick, you refused them treatment on the grounds that you wanted to study a society completely free from outside influence."

The waiter is trying to figure out whether Kelly is making fun of him. The men sitting next to Kelly are laughing. One of them says, "This guy is a card. A goddamn *card*."

The other one nods and says, "The genuine article."

Kelly says, "Do you have any *idea* how many germs live in the mucus inside your nose?"

We are in a restaurant called Neoterra in which each of the tables has a different shape than the others and none of them is round. Our table is shaped like a lima bean or like a slug writhing to death under a blanket of salt.

The men we are eating with all wear suspenders and Kenneth Cole glasses and have their sideburns trimmed every other day. There are five of these men. They are venture capitalists. I cannot remember any of their names, so I have assigned names to them at random. When I cannot remember the name that I have assigned, I say the first name I can think of. They do not seem to notice.

One of the men next to Kelly is saying, "The plain ones are always the most suggestible. The pretty ones tend to be too uppity and the ugly ones are too wary. The plain ones are up for what*ever.*"

Kelly says, "How do you know who's pretty and who's ugly?"

The man says, "You *look.*"

"But how do you assign categories? Certain features make you feel physical attraction, but these features are different from culture to culture and even, sometimes, from person to person. It is a selection-based instinct to want to combine your genes with the genes of someone physically attractive, in order that you will have attractive offspring whose appearance will make them more likely to have reproductive success. Of course, you have a chicken-and-egg problem there. Also, that does not account for differences of opinion."

The man stares at him.

Kelly says, "Do you ever try to imagine the time before dilating pupils?"

When I open my eyes, the man to my right is speaking earnestly to my boss. He is asking to see the business plan.

My boss shifts in his chair.

"You do *have* a business plan," the man says.

My boss clears his throat. "Of course we have a plan," he says. "But we're not planning to be captains of industry. This isn't industry. We're not planning to be the world's leading distributor of butt plugs. We're sure as *hell* not planning to build the world's best shuffleboard Web site so that some Daddy Warbucks can stroll up and pat us on the head and pay us twenty-five million to split twenty-four ways, so we can buy a town house and a Benz and some pussy and live god-damn upper-middle-class. Upper-middle-class means *dick*. Fuck the suburbs. Fuck commuting. Fuck neighbors. Our plan here is to be rich enough not to *have* neighbors. To be able to stand in front of your house and turn around in a circle and own everything you see. Not season tickets, not even courtside. I'm talking about owning your own team. No Internet millionaires here. Fuck that, too. I'm talking about Internet *billionaires*. What we're offering you is the opportunity to be part of that."

The man to my left, whom I have decided (I think) to refer to as Gill, looks at me and says, "So, you played halfback at Princeton?"

"Not Princeton," I tell him.

"Of course not," he says. "How tall are you? Six feet?"

"Why not?"

"You weigh around two hundred?"

"One-ninety."

He smiles. "What's your forty time?"

"My forty time."

He nods.

"I don't know these days."

He frowns.

"I'm not really an athlete anymore," I explain.

"Hmm," Gill says.

We drink in silence for a while. Suddenly Gill looks at me. I lean back toward him.

Gill says, "What's your body-fat percentage?"

. . .

We are standing at the urinals in the bathroom at Neoterra and Kelly is saying, "The difference between assault and aggravated assault is mostly about the severity of the injuries."

I say, "How bad does it have to be to be aggravated?"

"It's subjective."

We zip up. The urinals flush automatically when we walk away.

We hold our hands under the faucets, waiting for the sink to recognize that we are not just dust particles blowing in front of the electric eye.

Kelly says, "Last night I was reading about the human botfly."

"I thought you said no books."

He nods. "I think we're going to have to forget that rule."

"I already did," I tell him.

The water begins to spray from our faucets.

He glances at me. "When?"

"From the beginning."

"Why didn't you tell me?"

I shrug. "I don't care much about it. As long as we don't say no movies."

"Of course not," he says. "That would ruin everything."

"The human botfly," I remind him.

"Right, right. Anyway, when it bites you, it raises a bump like a mosquito bite. Except that the fly has burrowed its way into your arm and the bump is covering it. It incubates for a while until it gets hungry and then it begins to consume you. You can feel it eating its way up your arm."

We take our hands from under the faucet and the water stops. We stand with our hands under the nozzles of the hand dryers.

Kelly says, "There are tiny parasitic worms that can live

in drinking water. Once they're inside you, they gather in sores on your legs. The only way to get rid of them is to immerse them in water and allow them to flow out of the hole they'll open in your skin."

They are laughing when they leave the club and weaving as they walk. Both of them wear white baseball caps emblazoned with the letters of their fraternity.

Kelly says, "Are you ready for this?"

I nod.

"Deep breaths," he says. "Try to swallow."

I nod again.

The frat boys do not notice us until they are only a few feet away. Then they stop.

Kelly is wearing a long black overcoat and leather gloves with lead studs sewn into the knuckles on the inside. He says, "You boys sure you're all right to drive? You look a little under the weather."

The frat boys are silent.

Kelly says, "Is this your car?"

"Yeah," one of them says.

"This a Corvette?"

The frat boy snorts. "Try Lamborghini."

"Ah."

He narrows his eyes. "You fuck with the alarm or something?"

Kelly smiles. "Now why would you think that?"

"Should be going off with you sitting on the hood."

"Well," Kelly says, "we're not as heavy as we look. The camera adds ten pounds." He laughs.

The frat boy says, "If you get off the car by yourselves, we'll give you a running start." He spreads his hands, palms up. He is thick through the chest and shoulders. His friend is taller than he is and wide.

Kelly slides off the car onto his feet. The frat boy smiles and turns his head to glance at his friend and when he turns back Kelly throws a straight right hand into the middle of his face. The gloved fist makes a dull-hollow slapping sound when it lands, followed immediately by the crunch of the nose breaking, and the frat boy's head disappears in red mist and then he has fallen to his knees. His friend is staring, openmouthed, and does not notice me standing up off the hood. He is reaching for Kelly when I kick him in the groin as hard as I can. He crumples next to the other one. And then we are on top of them.

I take the big one, who is curled into a ball with his hands cupped between his legs. He is dry-heaving. White lines of saliva hang from his chin. I kick him a few times in his kidneys and he rolls onto his back and I stomp his forearm with the heel of my boot and I am pretty sure I feel bones breaking. He screams. I kick him in the stomach and listen to him gasp as the air rushes out of him. Now he has no breath to scream and he is gagging. I drop onto his chest and, as I do this, I bring my elbow straight down into his mouth and feel the teeth give. He brings his arms up to cover his face and I punch the broken forearm. He screams again. When he moves the forearm, I drive my fists into him over and over. The skin splits along his eyebrows and forehead and cheekbones and blood seeps through the cracks like lava. Sweat is rolling down my face, plastering my hair to my forehead. I feel like crying.

Kelly says, "Enough."

I stand up and look at the big frat boy at my feet. His wrist is bent at a terrible angle. His mouth looks like a tomato with ripped skin. There are teeth sticking through his upper lip.

I look at Kelly, who is also standing. "Wallets?" I say, my chest heaving.

Kelly shakes his head. "This is assault, not robbery."

"Two birds, one stone?"

He chews his bottom lip and considers this. "Fuck it," he says. He reaches inside his frat boy's jacket and pulls out his wallet. The frat boy groans. Kelly kicks him in the ribs.

"We taking the car?" I say.

"No," Kelly says. He looks at the frat boy below him. "Don't take it too hard, fellas," he says. "We've just grown past you. You're the giraffes whose necks never stretched." He pulls off his gloves. "You're the elephants with short noses."

I think we're ready for the next level," Kelly says. I glance at him. The streetlights we pass turn his face ghostly white and run the shadow of the windshield wipers along his profile. I massage the fingers of my left hand against the knuckles of my right, which are scraped bloody and have already begun to swell.

"What's the next level?" I say.

Kelly turns his head slightly so that the wiper shadow now flows over his face asymmetrically, making a jagged line on his nose. He is smiling enough for me to see the tips of his teeth.

"It's time to shoot somebody," he says.

Heather is wearing a red dress with no back. The dress is longer on one side than the other. On the short side, it rises almost above her hip.

The skin on Heather's thighs is the color of butterscotch.

We are standing under an enormous crystal chandelier that hangs over a crimson staircase. Everywhere I look, there are men in tuxedoes. Heather has the fingers of her left hand laced through the fingers of my right.

The poster next to the theater door shows two immense eyes and, above that, the word "Gatsby" in white letters.

Heather is talking to Cynthia Lowell-Wellington and

Vanessa Mather Coppedge Bryson, who are jammed up against us by the crush of people. Cynthia's boyfriend, who is taller than I am and has a dimpled chin, looms on my left, just behind Cynthia. I am fairly certain that he was on the crew team at Brown, but it is possible that he was on the lacrosse team at Penn. He shakes my hand at every opportunity.

For dinner, Heather had the New Orleans–style catfish with chipotle dipping sauce.

She is saying, "If you're going to use a bronzing agent of *any* kind, you *have* to couple it with a good moisturizer."

Cynthia says, "Should I be looking for one with sunblock in it?"

"I suppose it couldn't hurt. But really, you should be keeping yourself out of the sun completely. That's what the bronzer is for."

Vanessa leans toward Heather and says, "So, do you put it *every*where?"

Heather nods. "No white should show."

I say, "Can you picture the time before melanin?"

Heather raises herself on the balls of her feet and kisses the side of my mouth.

The mob surges all around us, moving with tiny shuffling steps.

We are sitting in a private box on the left side above the orchestra. The house lights are down and the women onstage are singing to each other and staring into the audience. According to the program, they are singing in English, but it is impossible to understand them and my attention is focused on the seat backs of the row in front of us where a thin digital screen shows a scrolling transcription of the lyrics.

Heather is sucking my thumb.

Next to me, Cynthia's boyfriend, Clay Harrison Adams, whispers, "When's your IPO?"

I say, "We're not trying to be the world's leading distributor of butt plugs."

He says, "Oh."

The stage is darker now and the women are gone. They have been replaced by a dancing mob and bright-colored balloons. In the background a tiny green light is flashing.

Suddenly I have the urge to climb on top of my seat and throw my head back and scream. I have this urge every time I go to the theater. I believe it is a similar instinct to the one I have to turn on the engine of my car when the mechanic has his hand inside it. Or the impulse I feel on subway platforms to push the man next to me in front of the oncoming train. Or when I imagine swerving my car into a group of pedestrians and feeling the dull cracks of their heads against my windshield and gazing at the wet smears of their blood. Or when I think of diving through the plate glass of the Rainbow Room at Rockefeller Center and plunging, back arched, head up, gleaming shards of glass falling all around me, into the middle of the herd of ice-skaters circling sixty-seven stories below.

Clay says, "Johnson and Johnson?"

"What?" I say, turning to him.

"The butt plugs. Leading distributor."

I sigh. "I don't *know*, guy."

"Oh," he says.

I think about throwing him over our balcony and watching him drop, arms and legs windmilling, into the front row.

With all these impulses, there is the idea stage, then the imagination stage, then the spine-tingle, adrenaline-shot, testicle-clench moment when you *know* that you are actually going to do whatever it is.

But you never do.

• • •

During intermission Heather and I get on one of the mirror-walled elevators and ride it until we are alone. She pushes the Run-Stop button. A voice comes over the intercom asking if everything is all right. Heather begins unbuttoning my shirt. The voice from the intercom says that if the elevator does not begin moving in the next five minutes it will call the fire department. Heather licks my chest. I put my arms around her. The voice tells us not to panic.

Heather pulls away from me and takes two steps backward, smiling slightly, and presses herself against the brass handrail. As she leans onto the handrail, her dress drifts up and I can see the thin black string of her panties. I move close to her and she kisses me hard and runs her hand along the back of my neck and along my shoulder and down my arm and then she takes my hand and puts it gently between her legs. Her underwear is already moist. I grab hold of it and pull so that the narrow strip rubs against her. She gasps. I slide my hand under the wet fabric and touch the soft, slick skin and then I ease my middle finger inside her. She tips her head back and moans. I suck on the skin of her neck. Her perfume has a bitter taste.

She says, "Oh my God."

I kneel down in front of her and grip the backs of her thighs and pull her close to me, resting my head just below her ribs.

She strokes my hair. "How much do you want me?" she whispers.

I groan against her stomach.

Back in my seat, I can smell Heather on my fingers and I can taste her when I lick my lips.

In front of us, dozens of miniature chandeliers hang on long cords from the ceiling. In the hallways behind us, the lights flash off and on and an usher closes the door to our box. The cords begin to retract and the chandeliers float toward the high ceiling.

Heather whispers, "What's wrong with you lately?"

"What do you mean?"

"You've been even more distant than usual."

I say, "I've been walking the path to emotional detachment."

She frowns. "This is Kelly's idea?"

I nod. "We're working in stages."

She opens her mouth to say something else, but the two women are singing again. They are slumped in lawn chairs. They wear straw hats and white dresses. They draw out a single note so long that I have to take a deep breath in sympathy. The urge to scream washes over me again.

The words click by in white block letters on the digital screen in front of me. IT'S HOT, says the screen. IT'S HOT.

PART TWO: VIOLENCE

The man by the door is wearing a beige turtleneck and a leather jacket. He leans us against the wall and frisks us quickly.

Kelly says, "Won't you at least buy me dinner first?"

The man sighs. "Haven't heard that one yet this week."

Dexter is sitting in the far corner on a hydraulic chair that looks like a life raft. The man cutting his hair wears a long white shirt that says MECCA across the chest. The room smells of cocoa butter. The floor is covered with hair.

The man beside Dexter is almost as thick as he is and has

a big jagged scar along his jaw. He wears a cream-colored suit and a silk shirt.

The only other man in the barbershop lounges on a leather sofa in the corner opposite Dexter. His entire body seems frozen, including his eyes, which are locked on mine.

Dexter raises his head and looks at me in the mirror. "Looking good, baby," he says.

I smile. "You remember Kelly?"

He shrugs. "Why not?"

"Good to see you again," Kelly says.

Dexter grunts. He jerks his head toward the window. "That your new whip?"

"Yeah."

"Whip?" Kelly whispers.

"Car," I tell him.

Dexter whistles. "Fuckin' ay. You niggers must be *flush.*"

"We can't complain," I say.

"I thought you were supposed to call me before you went public."

"We will."

He frowns. "So how come you niggers are rolling Bill Gates–style all of a sudden?"

I look around at the bodyguards. "You think you have enough security?"

"Can't be too careful."

"I don't remember anyone ever taking a shot at Butkus."

Dexter grins. "He wasn't a Nubian king."

"All right, I don't remember anyone taking a shot at Willie Lanier."

"That was a different era. It's all haters out there these days. Can't stand to see a brother living the dream."

"Is *that* what you're doing?"

Dexter's barber opens a drawer in the counter in front of him and changes the guard on his clippers.

Dexter says, "You watch me in the Pro Bowl?"

I nod.

He says, "They've never seen anything like me."

The barber removes the guard from his clippers and carefully shapes Dexter's sideburns. He unsnaps Dexter's maroon smock and passes the razor over the back of his neck. He pours alcohol onto a cotton ball and runs it around Dexter's hairline. He douses him with talcum powder.

Dexter says, "That's enough. Don't give me any of that Afro-Sheen shit."

The barber nods.

Dexter shrugs out of his smock and stands. He is an inch or two taller than I am. He is wearing a white knit tank top. His body is like a clenched fist.

"Shame the way you're letting yourself go," I say.

Dexter snorts. He takes a fat wad of bills from his pocket, peels one off the top, and hands it to the barber.

The man in the corner is moving now. He is on his feet and coming toward us. I can't remember seeing him stand up.

Dexter says, "This is Wilton."

"Wilton?" I say.

Dexter smiles. "Him a yardie, y'know."

"What?" Kelly says.

"He's Jamaican," I say.

Wilton looks at Dexter. "That accent's a little Harry Belafonte."

Dexter says, "So are you."

Wilton is wearing gray wool slacks and a black ribbed turtleneck sweater.

Dexter says, "These are the boys I told you about."

Wilton nods. He does not move to shake our hands.

I say, "Dexter tells me you used to work for Mike Tyson."

He shrugs.

"You know what we're working on?"

He shrugs again.

"We're trying to reach the next stage in our development."

Wilton stares at me.

Kelly says, "For most mammals, grooming is a sign of affection. That's why I cut my own hair."

Wilton is saying, "You'd be amazed how long it takes some guys to die."

I say, "Doesn't it depend on where they get hit?"

"Not always."

We are at an outdoor shooting range, lying on our stomachs beside green T-shaped shooting benches, facing white-and-black silhouette targets set up in front of a stone wall. I am leaning on my elbows on the concrete apron, sighting down the barrel of a rifle that looks like it is made out of Legos.

I say, "I wish these things still looked like they used to."

"Why?"

"It would make me feel more real."

Wilton says, "Draw down center body mass on everybody. No head shots."

"What about bulletproof vests?"

"That's just movie shit."

"*Some*one must wear them."

"Sure. But they'll still be incapacitated if they take one in the chest, provided you have enough stopping power. Even with body armor, a heavy load can break ribs and collapse lungs."

I squint through the aperture and place my crosshairs on the center of the target.

"Raise your aim four inches at two hundred yards, ten inches at three hundred."

"Why?" I turn my head to look at him.

"Gravity," he says.

"What do I do past three hundred?"

"You miss."

I nod.

Wilton says, "How you know Dexter?"

"We went to high school together."

"You play ball with him?"

"Sure."

He frowns. "I thought he was from Cleveland."

"So?"

"So, you don't look too Cleveland to me."

I shrug, gently so as not to lose my target picture. "Near Cleveland."

"Shaker Heights?"

"Something like that."

He smiles. "Always knew that motherfucker was wanna-be hard."

"Don't need to be from the ghetto to be hard."

"It helps." He looks at Kelly, who is on his stomach fifty feet to my right, sighting down the barrel of his Lego rifle. "What about the ofay?"

"Why is he an ofay and I'm not?"

He shrugs. "Ain't just about skin color."

"Mmm," I say. "We lived together in college."

Wilton nods. "He's a fuckin' fruit loop."

Sometimes, particularly when you can anticipate the precise location of your target, it is preferable to snipe at a near-flat trajectory. For countersniping, because you cannot predict your target's whereabouts and because the target will likely be concealing himself from anyone on the ground, it is vital to occupy the highest position possible.

In close quarters, the pistol is ideal because of its conceal-ability and ease of use. However, its effectiveness drops sharply as range increases. It is very difficult to be accurate with a pistol at distances greater than fifty feet. Past a hundred, it is almost impossible.

• • •

My boss is riding in the cart in front of us with a man from Goldman who has skin like tapioca. We all wear green sweaters and brown-and-white spikes.

Kelly is driving our cart, bouncing over ruts in the dirt path. The air tastes like the dirt thrown up by the other cart. Kelly is saying, "Why doesn't he have an accent?"

"He told me he lost it."

"He talks like a goddamn Yalie."

"He's self-educated."

Kelly snorts. "You *must* know what that means."

"What?"

"Anytime a Nubian says he's self-educated, ten to one he was reading with his ass to the wall."

"Prison?"

He nods. "Probably has one of those correspondence diplomas."

"That's not fair."

He glances at me. "You two have been getting awful close lately."

"He's been *teaching* me."

"I hope you're not losing perspective."

"Perspective on what?" I say.

"Just make sure you keep in mind what it is we're doing."

The cart in front of us stops dustily. Kelly pulls in behind it. We sit off to the side on a wooden bench while the man from Goldman sets himself over the tee.

Kelly says, "In gorilla societies, each adult male has his own position in the hierarchy. You don't look directly at anyone higher than you. Eye contact indicates provocation for all primates. No one looks at the alpha male, unless they are ready to challenge for his position. If you look him in the eye before you're ready for him, he will tear your limbs off."

• • •

I am sitting in the backseat, between Heather and her father. We are on the way to the opening of an art gallery called Cave Paintings. Heather is gazing out the window.

Her father is my size with big hands. He has a thin white scar under his right eye. I am trying not to look at him.

He is saying, "Sometimes we would wait all night and not see anyone. Some nights we would all see movement on the road and we would blow the claymores and launch flares and pour fire into the tree line and when we walked down, we wouldn't find anything except the craters we'd made."

I say, "How'd they get away?"

"Who?"

"Whoever was on the road."

He looks at me. "There *wasn't* anybody on the road. We imagined it."

"You all imagined the same thing?"

"The visions are contagious. One guy points at what he sees and you make yourself see it, too."

"So, after a while, why didn't you stop believing something was there?"

"Because sometimes something *was* there."

"What were those nights like?"

He shakes his head. "You don't want to hear about *those* nights."

"Sure I do."

He says, "Later on, I was with Recon and we did less search-and-destroy, but we still had visions."

"Does it give you nightmares?"

"Nightmares?"

"Because you hated it so much."

He frowns. "Did I say that?"

"I just assumed. I thought everybody hated it."

He says, "It was the happiest time of my life."

· · ·

We are sitting in a rented van at the curb across the street from Heather's father's office building and Kelly says, "What about knives?"

Wilton looks at him. "This ain't *West Side Story.*"

"It's just that I thought we were supposed to learn these things in stages."

"You niggers want to learn knives, you can do it on your own time."

Wilton is shielding his eyes from the sun and staring up at the building, which looks like a giant milk carton. He says, "Next time we're doing reconnaissance, you ought to bring a jacket."

Kelly says, "Why not just keep the heat on?"

Wilton says, "Three guys sitting by the curb all day in a car with the motor running might as well hang out a sign that says STAKEOUT."

"Why are we here at all? We already know his schedule."

"*You* already know it. I want to see it for myself."

"You don't trust us?"

Wilton shakes his head. "You can't learn this stuff from books."

"And you've learned it through experience."

"That's right."

"So when we have the experience we'll be as good as you."

Wilton shifts his eyes to look at Kelly. He says, "You can't have a late start."

Armor-piercing or KTW rounds can puncture steel doors and pass through bulletproof vests. Their drawback is that they make neat, surgical wounds.

Full-metal-jacketed rounds also have a better penetration value than standard loads, but they are less streamlined than the armor piercers and cause more tissue damage.

Hollowpoints carry low penetration values but expand on impact. This is also true for dum-dums.

You can create a hollowpoint effect by cutting cross-shaped grooves into the tips of your cartridges. On impact, the round will flatten out along the grooves, disintegrating muscle and bone. (Note: Handmade loads may tend to jam an automatic.)

I am kneeling by an open window on the ninth floor of the Ritz, looking past the Public Garden at Beacon Street, and Wilton says, "Blue suit with the grocery bag."

"Got it," says Kelly.

"Why him?" I say.

"I don't know," Wilton says. "Easily identifiable."

Kelly says, "It doesn't pay to stand out."

They are on their feet next to me, binoculars held to their faces. I open and close my hands against the rifle and blink my eyes and watch through the scope as the man scratches his neck, magnified ten times.

"I don't know if I can," I say.

Wilton sighs. "This is what you said you wanted."

"I know. I just wasn't expecting him to be so *alive*."

Kelly says, "I'll do it."

"Wait your turn," Wilton says.

The man stops walking and checks his watch.

I say, "Won't they be able to tell where the shots came from?"

"Who's 'they'?"

"I don't know. Somebody."

"Unlikely. The flash isn't too apparent in daylight."

"What about the sound?"

"It'll echo off the buildings. It'll seem to come from everywhere."

"What if somebody sees us?"

"The chances of that increase with every second you don't take the shot."

The man is whistling now. I steady the crosshairs on the top button of his suit jacket. I close my eyes and imagine the way his face will look when the bullet hits him and the noises he'll make and the way his body will come apart. I wonder whether he will drop the groceries. I open my eyes.

Wilton says, "Deep breaths. Squeeze, don't pull."

The man smiles suddenly and switches his grocery bag to the other arm. A young girl with blond hair runs into the sight picture. The man bends down and scoops her up with his free hand and spins her around in a circle. She kisses him on the cheek.

I draw back from the scope and lay the rifle on the windowsill and stand up. I shake my head. "Not in front of his daughter."

Kelly looks at me. "The fuck you care?"

"She'll never recover."

"Nobody recovers from anything. Your experiences shape who you are. You have a chance to be the defining influence in this girl's life."

I don't say anything.

"If you're so worried about it," he says, "maybe we should do her too."

"No," I say. "I won't do that."

He groans. "Have Wilton do it."

"The girl can't die."

"She can and she will. The only question is when."

"Not today."

"What difference does it make? Today, tomorrow, eighty years from now. She won't be in a position to care."

"But in eighty years, when she feels it coming, she'll be able to look at all the things she did. Now she could only think of what she didn't do."

"So what if this girl has an unpleasant last few minutes in which she imagines the life she didn't live? It'll probably be better when she imagines it than it would have been to live it. It'll be better than remembering all the things she could never quite do. Besides, it's only a few minutes at the end. And if you hit her right, she won't even have that. Like flipping off a light switch."

Wilton turns to look at him. "I don't wash anybody for free."

"We'll pay you," Kelly says.

On the street below us, the man has put the girl down and is holding her hand. Holding the girl's other hand is a pretty blond woman in a blue cardigan.

Wilton turns back to the window. The family is moving away from us. They round the corner onto Charles Street.

I say, "They'll go home tonight like they do every night and they'll never know that they just lived through the most important moments of their lives. They don't even know we exist."

Kelly says, "Goldfish have thirty-second memories. Everything that happened more than thirty seconds ago is erased to make room for the new things. That means that at the very end, when they look back, they've been dying their whole lives."

Wilton grunts. When Kelly shoots him, his body clenches and he half turns from the waist, head rigid, pupils crammed to the sides of his eyes, trying to look at Kelly behind him. Then he sags against the glass, blood spraying from the big exit wound in his chest. The sound of the handgun is much softer than I am expecting. It is the dry crack of a twig snapping over and over.

"Sorry about that," Kelly tells me.

"You're crazy," I say quietly.

He smiles. "I doubt it. It's just that I've developed a more complete understanding of our situation."

"Do you understand that Dexter's other boys will be looking for us now? Along with God-knows-who-else."

He shrugs. "I hope you see why it was necessary."

I stare at him.

He stands very close to Wilton, who is gurgling. "It's

all perfectly natural. Today we're selecting for people who draw their guns on time." He smiles. "We're selecting against surly tarbabies who don't know how to watch their mouths."

We are sitting on long sofas in the dark-maple locker room at the Harvard Club and my boss is saying, "If poor people were as smart as rich people, they'd be rich by now."

The man next to him is soft everywhere and colors his hair red-brown. He netted eleven million dollars last year. He chuckles.

My boss says, "Every generation of a family has a chance to hit it big. If they keep missing, after a while you have to assume that something's wrong with the genes."

The carpet is blood-colored. The walls of the locker room are covered with lacquered plaques that show vertical columns of men's names. Kelly and I have our legs stuck out in front of us and crossed at the ankles. We are wearing white Izod shirts and gray shorts. We have long-handled rackets laid across our laps.

The television that hangs from the ceiling of the locker room shows a pretty blond woman with straight teeth and a gray-haired man, also with straight teeth, sitting at a curved desk in front of Corinthian columns and windows that show false sky. At the bottom of the screen, stock prices churn by in a blue strip.

Kelly whispers, "Ancient chieftains developed efficient methods of agriculture so that they could throw banquets to show their power."

"What?" I say.

"It wasn't to better provide for their people. For that, the old methods were sufficient."

I stare at him.

"Technology develops not to advance the species but to consolidate the power of individuals."

"Listen," I say, "I don't have any idea what you're talking about."

"I'm talking about the death of emotion and the sublimation of desire."

"I thought the death of emotion was what we wanted. I thought you said we were walking the path to emotional detachment."

He nods. "Yes. I've come to reexamine our position. At the beginning I thought we were working to evolve into things capable of murder. I thought we were trying to divorce mind from body. I thought we were trying to resist going cerebral." He sighs. "I realized recently that our problem is that we had already *gone* cerebral. We had already separated mind and body. We've been denying our instincts. For human beings to be able to kill, they don't need to evolve, they need to regress. All these computer-geek faggots live in the world of the cerebral and they've probably never been in a fight. They can't fight, they can't fuck, they have no physical *presence.* You and I have been trying to regain our instinctive behaviors. We're trying to get back to basics."

"But my instinct was to feel sorry for those frat boys and for the guy I was supposed to shoot."

"You're making the mistake of classifying compassion as a human emotion. Really, your natural instincts are to do what's best for yourself and to eliminate anything that challenges your success. You do for you, I do for me, everyone does for themselves, shake it all up and the cream rises to the top. It's mathematics."

"How can you tell me what my instincts are?"

"Because human behavior has been completely dissected. The genome is mapped. There are no more secrets."

My boss is smoothing a terry-cloth headband over his hairline. He looks at the man next to him, who is still chuckling. My boss says, "Take the Gettys, for example."

The pretty blond anchorwoman looks into the camera and

says something, but I can't hear it because the sound on the television has been muted. Her words appear in a black closed-caption box below her. The black box says, "Now, the day's headlines."

I ignore the first two stories, both of which include videotape of rolling tanks. When the third story begins, a graphic appears over the anchorwoman's shoulder featuring a painting of the Ritz-Carlton Hotel splattered with enormous puddles of blood. Written over this painting in white block letters are the words "Ritz Murder."

Kelly says, "Normally they don't make so much fuss over a shine killing."

My boss says, "Location, location, location."

The man sitting with him says, "Such a waste."

Kelly says, "We don't know if it's a waste. It's not like this was some kid on the honor roll. Maybe this was just a big, mean dog who ran into a bigger, meaner dog. These things happen."

The man turns to look at him.

"Do you know any of the men on the walls?" I say quickly.

"Sure," he says. "Most of them."

"That must be hard."

He turns away from Kelly to look at me. "What must be hard?"

"To lose so many friends."

"Lose?"

"In the war."

He shakes his head. "The war dead are in the lobby, kid. These are the trustees."

"Oh," I say.

Kelly leans close to me and whispers, "Human beings have come to treat death differently than other animals do. When lions get too old, they lose their place in the pride and are forced to wander, scavenging for food, unable to hunt, until eventually they die of starvation or disease or they become immobilized by starvation or disease and are then eaten alive by hyenas. When sharks are injured, other sharks come from miles around and tear them to pieces. Human beings are the only species that tries to prolong life artificially after the subject has outlived his usefulness. We are the only creatures that mourn our dead."

"Elephants," I say.

"Elephants?"

"Elephants mourn their dead."

"That's impossible," he tells me.

We are standing in Dexter's living room, surrounded by Persian rugs and sliding glass doors and a glass-topped coffee table dusted with cocaine residue. The residue is smeared into white streaks. On the floor beside the table are three long-stemmed champagne glasses and a metal ice bucket.

On the other side of the glass doors are the floodlit patio and the swimming pool and the hot tub, both of which have underwater lights, and past all that are evergreen-covered hills that loom black in the darkness.

Dexter is in the hot tub with one of the girls. The other girl, naked and brown and smooth and gleaming, is standing on the edge of the pool and swaying in time to faint music. They are all laughing. I can't tell where the music is coming from.

Kelly motions toward the glass doors. He is dressed entirely in black. His face is covered in greasepaint.

"What if they hear?" I whisper.

"They won't," he whispers back. "And, even so, if they look back at the house they'll be looking from the light into the dark."

"It's not really *dark* in here."

"Dark enough."

I slide one of the doors open. It hisses on its runner. I freeze. Dexter and the girls keep laughing. I slip through the opening and onto the slate of the patio. Kelly follows me. We move slowly, crouched low, careful to keep our footfalls silent.

The dancing girl sees us first. She stops swaying and opens her mouth. Kelly shows her his gun. She does not speak.

I kneel down behind Dexter and press the barrel of my automatic into the back of his neck. His body shudders and tenses. The girl next to him gasps. She has long hair and skin the color of coffee ice cream.

I say, "Where are the roughnecks?"

"We're the only ones here," Dexter says. His voice is very steady.

"Bullshit," Kelly says.

"I swear to God."

Kelly says, "If you're lying, I'm going to slice your eyeballs open with a razor."

"I'm not lying."

"After that, I'm going to pour gasoline into your eye sockets and pull off your fingernails one by one. Then I'm going to tie your hand to the side of this pool and mash it with a cinder block. Then I'm going to take a pair of garden shears and cut your tongue in half while it's still in your mouth."

The girl in the hot tub starts to cry.

Kelly turns to her. "Is he lying?"

She shakes her head.

Kelly says, "If he is, I'm going to do the same thing to you."

She sobs more loudly. She keeps shaking her head.

Kelly looks at me. "I believe it."

I stand and walk around in front of Dexter. "It's me," I say.

He squints at my face. "Jesus Christ," he says. "You almost made me piss myself."

Kelly says, "Don't think I didn't mean what I said."

Dexter says, "What do you want?"

"We need to talk," I tell him.

Dexter is sitting on the black leather sofa in his living room and wearing a white robe that pulls very tight across his shoulders. I am seated facing him on a ceramic barstool that I dragged in from the kitchen. Kelly is on the other side of the room, leaning on a mantelpiece. The girls are upstairs in the windowless walk-in closet in Dexter's bedroom. We slid a heavy bureau in front of the closet door. We balanced a mirror between the bureau and the door. Kelly told the girls that if we heard the mirror break he was going to come upstairs and pull out their teeth with pliers and shove straightened coat hangers into their ear canals to rupture the drums.

"Where'd the hitters go?" I ask Dexter.

He says, "Wilton's disappeared. They're trying to find him."

"They have any ideas?"

He shrugs. "Not that I know of."

I glance at Kelly. He shakes his head.

"I don't believe you," I say to Dexter.

"I can't help that."

Kelly says, "The next time you lie, I'm going to shoot you in the hip. Won't be too many more Pro Bowls after that."

"Tell us," I say.

Dexter says, "They think maybe you two clipped him."

"You try to talk them out of that?"

"I tried. They weren't sure anyway."

"They have a theory?"

"They think Wilton's that thing at the Ritz."

"I thought that guy couldn't be identified."

He looks at me carefully. "Yeah, somebody put some caps

in his face. Blew out his teeth and everything. Also, they took his wallet and cut off the tips of his fingers."

"So what makes them think it's Wilton?"

"It's just a guess right now. That's why you're still walking."

"How long before it's not just a guess?"

"Who knows? Depends what they find."

"Any chance you can get them off of us?"

He shakes his head. "They're looking for payback. I can't call them off."

"What are they doing now?"

"They're checking you out."

"Any prediction about what their conclusion will be?"

"Again," he says, "it depends."

"On what?"

He stares at me. "On what you've done."

"What's your instinct?"

"These guys are pros. They'll put this together in their sleep. They'll take just enough time to be certain." He takes a breath. "Then, Kelly goes for sure. I tried to tell them that *you* couldn't have been involved. They'll spend a little while thinking about that."

"And then?"

"And then I figure you go too."

"Unless?"

He shrugs. "Unless you're gone to somewhere they can't find you."

"Or they aren't good enough," Kelly says.

"They're good enough," Dexter tells him.

"Wilton wasn't."

We are silent for a while.

Dexter says, "I'll try to warn you."

"Why would you do that?" Kelly says.

Dexter jerks his head at me. "He's my friend. It isn't fair for him to get burned just because of the company he keeps."

"You're so sure it was me?"

"Sure enough."

Kelly smiles. "Then how do you know I won't do you too?"

"Because I'm your early-warning system."

"How can you warn us when you don't know where they are?"

"They still check in." He frowns. "That reminds me—how'd you get past the alarm?"

Kelly's smile widens. "I think you may need a new one," he says.

H eather comes out of the dressing room wearing blue jeans made from some kind of stretch material. She lifts the bottom of her sweater, showing a narrow strip of belly. The jeans ride low on her hips.

"What do you think?" she says.

"Great," I say.

"That's what you always say."

"I always mean it."

She examines herself in a long mirror on the wall.

"I like them," she says. "You can wear them with a blouse. You can wear them with a halter."

"You're sexy," I tell her.

She turns her head toward me and smiles. "You're sweet."

The walls of the store are lined with light brown shelves. Most of the shelves hold scented candles and kitchenware and lamps with rice-paper shades. The shelves in back hold thirty-dollar T-shirts.

Heather walks to the narrow doorframe of the dressing room and leans her head inside. She pulls her head out and says, "Still empty."

She takes my hand and leads me into a pine-smelling corridor lined with stalls. The door of one of the stalls is hanging open and Heather pulls me inside. She closes the door behind us and throws the bolt. Her jacket is lying on the gray bench in the corner. Her shoes are on the floor under the bench. Each wall, including the back of the door, is completely covered by a mirror. The mirrors reflect each other's reflections. We are surrounded by infinite versions of ourselves that extend as far as we can see in every direction. We can see ourselves from every angle.

Heather runs her tongue along the edge of my ear. She puts her palm between my legs. I feel myself stirring against the zipper of my pants. I grip her shoulders and gently push her away. She frowns at me.

I say, "I'm sorry if my behavior has been strange lately."

"I hadn't noticed."

"I've been under a lot of pressure."

"Work?"

"Not really. I've been dealing with some personal issues."

She presses me down onto the gray bench and sits across my knees with her arms around my neck. "Like what?" she says.

"Oh, I don't know. I've been working on my development."

"As a person?"

"Sort of."

She strokes my hair. "I want to get married."

"I know. You told me after our third date."

"I mean I want to get married soon. I want to take care of you. I want you to take care of me."

"I don't have *anything*," I tell her. "At least let's wait and see what happens with the company."

"I don't like waiting. Besides, my father is practically *made* of money."

"I don't want your father to take care of us."

"No," she says, "neither do I."

• • •

Kelly's sketch has wide eyes and too much nose. Mine is a cross between Errol Flynn without the mustache and Paul Bunyan without the beard. The sketches are superimposed side by side on the blue-sky background behind the pretty blond anchorwoman with the stock ticker flowing beneath her.

We are sitting on the sofa in our living room.

Kelly says, "I don't like her as much on the HDTV. She wears too much makeup."

"Everyone wears makeup on television."

"She has bumps on her face. She looks like a pickle."

The anchor is talking to a brunette with thin lips who is standing in front of the Ritz in the rain, looking concerned. The anchor also looks concerned.

I say, "Aren't you a little bit worried?"

"About the sketches? You can't tell it's us unless you know what you're looking for. Even then, they're kind of a stretch. They made me look like Groucho, for Chrissake."

"Maybe we ought to lay low. Get out of the apartment. *Some*thing."

"Forget it. Those pictures could be almost anybody. The cops aren't gonna find us with these descriptions unless they're already onto us."

"And what about Dexter's boys?"

"The Jamaicans?"

"How do you know they're Jamaicans?"

He shrugs. "Wilton was."

"Fine, then," I say. "What about the Jamaicans?"

He sighs. "The important thing is for us to stay on-mission."

"On-mission?"

"Heather's old man."

"Are you serious?"

"We have to finish what we started."

The back of my neck is hot. "I'm not sure about that."

"You don't have to be sure. I'm telling you it's going to be done."

"I think I may have made some kind of mistake."

"Trust me," Kelly says. "This is best for everybody. This is what you said you wanted."

"I think I've changed my mind."

Kelly nods.

The sketches are gone. The anchorwoman is smiling now.

Kelly stands up from the couch and walks to the door.

"Where are you going?" I say.

He opens the door and walks into the hallway. I listen to the door click shut behind him. I turn back to the television.

When the phone rings an hour later, I pick it up immediately. "Kel?" I say.

There is no answer.

"Where are you?" I say.

I hear the ticking of the open line.

I say, "Just come back and we can talk about it."

I hold the receiver against my ear and listen to buzzing static and then Dexter's voice says, "They're coming."

PART THREE: CLIMAX

"You don't look good," my boss says.

"I had to get a hotel room last night."

He half-smiles. "You have a fight with your boyfriend?"

"We're having some work done," I say.

We are looking out the big window of the Credit Suisse

luxury box at the Fleet Center, squinting at tiny players on a tiny floor hundreds of feet below us. It is almost impossible to tell what they are doing. When we want to see the game, we watch wide-screen televisions in the corners of the room.

My boss says, "I was trying to reach you. I called the cell phone."

"It didn't get reception in the hotel."

"You need to be available to me twenty-four hours. Where's Princess Grace?"

"He's not here?"

My boss shakes his head. "If you two want a job where you don't have to come in on Sundays, go work at the post office."

"I *am* in," I say.

A young trader is screaming at one of the televisions. His friends sit in front of the television in leather armchairs, Frisbeeing paper plates at the screen.

My boss says, "Any of these guys would kill for your job."

The skin on my face feels very tight. "So would I."

I imagine throwing my boss through the tinted window and watching him plummet into the middle of the court. I can see the stain of him spreading on the bleached wood.

My boss says, "Let's see some of that."

I pull my gun from inside my coat and touch the barrel to his eyebrow. "Open your mouth," I say.

"What?"

I hit him in the forehead with the side of the gun. He steps back. Blood trickles down his face.

"Get on your knees," I say.

He does.

"Open your mouth."

The traders have stopped making noise. I know that people around the room are looking at us. No one moves. My boss opens his mouth.

"Wider," I say.

I shove my gun deep into his mouth. It clatters against his teeth.

I say, "You're going to have to learn how to treat people."
He nods. He is shivering.

I say loudly, "You're a ridiculous man. You don't even understand your job. I don't know who put you in charge. I'm younger than you, I'm better than you. I don't even need this gun. I could kill you with my *hands*."

A dark patch has appeared on my boss's light gray trousers. There are tears running down his face.

I say, "You don't have the balls for this kind of work."

I take my gun out of his mouth.

Everyone stares at me uncertainly. A few of the traders applaud.

"Thank you," I say.

My boss is slumped on the floor, moaning. I smile at the room. I put my gun away and give one last wave and then walk quickly to the door.

I say, "If I see this door open while I'm still in the hallway, I'm going to come back and choose two of you at random and shoot you in the balls."

When the elevator opens, it is full of security guards. They have their guns drawn.

I say, "There's some maniac in there with a gun. He has baggies of nitroglycerin taped all over his body. He said he would detonate if he heard anyone trying to come in. If you shoot him, the whole place might go up. Can you imagine what that would be like? You'd spend days sifting through body parts. You'd have to make piles of limbs. Can you imagine an enormous pile of severed arms?"

One of the security guards says, "Get behind us."

They push past me and fan out around the entrance to the luxury box. One of them puts a finger to his lips and leans his ear against the door.

I step inside their elevator and press Lobby.

Standing on the sidewalk next to the Fleet Center, listening to the sirens approaching, I take out my cell phone and call Heather.

I say, "How soon can you be at South Station?"

"Is this a joke?" she says.

"It's not a joke. I'm leaving. Will you go with me?"

"Yes."

I cross Causeway Street. "How soon?"

"Do I have time to pack?"

"No."

"Half hour," she says.

I push the End button and put the phone back in my pocket and look over my shoulder at the Fleet Center and at the squad cars pulling up in front and that is when I see the Jamaicans.

They are on the other side of the street, half a block behind me, watching the cops pile out of their cars. One of the Jamaicans is tall and wide. The other is the one who frisked us at the barbershop. They are moving at the same speed I am. They turn away from the cops and toward me and I snap my head back around, but I am almost certain they saw me see them. I keep walking, sweat dripping down my back, feeling them behind me.

I cross Merrimac Street.

I glance over my shoulder. The Jamaicans are still matching their speed to mine. They are maintaining the same distance.

At Cambridge Street, I reach the corner just as the DON'T WALK sign stops blinking and I slow down and almost stop and then suddenly I dash into the street and hear squealing brakes and slide over the hood of a moving taxi and hear horns screaming behind me and then I am on the other side, running.

Heather's father stands up to meet me. His office is lined with black shelves that hold crystal eggs and lacquered cigar boxes.

"How did you know I'd be here?" he says.

"What do you mean?"

"It's Sunday."

"Oh." I run my tongue along the backs of my teeth. "Heather must have told me."

He looks at me. "Must have," he says.

I take a deep breath. "I need your help." I glance out the window. "By the flower cart."

Heather's father walks to the window and gazes down at the street. "Who are they?" he says.

"I don't know exactly."

"They're pros."

"Yes."

"How'd you make them?"

"I don't know. They just sort of appeared across the street from me."

"I mean, how'd they let you see them?"

"I was looking for them. I knew they were coming."

He shakes his head. "Shouldn't matter."

"But why would they want me to spot them?"

He shrugs. "Maybe they wanted to see whether you'd run. Maybe they figure only a guilty man runs."

We are silent for a while.

Seven stories below us, the big Jamaican crosses the street and walks along the sidewalk and around the far side of the building.

"Why don't they follow me in?" I say.

"They don't know which floor you're on. Also, they'd be worried about the building's security force. And they don't want to trap themselves in case things go south. If they take you in the open, they have escape routes and it's easier for them to avoid the cops. They'll cover the exits and wait to reacquire."

"You learned all this in Vietnam?"

"It's textbook," he says. He lifts his telephone receiver.

"What are you doing?"

"Cops."

I shake my head.

He puts down the receiver. "Sounds like you have something to tell me."

I don't say anything.

He steps away from the window and takes his key ring from his pants pocket and unlocks the top drawer of his desk. He brings out a heavy automatic. He pulls back on the slide and checks the cylinder.

"You keep it *loaded*?" I say.

"Doesn't do much good when it's not." He puts the gun in the waistband of his pants. "You carrying?"

I show him the pistol inside my jacket.

"You any good with that?"

I shrug.

"Who put these guys on you?"

I shrug again.

"This have anything to do with that fairy you hang around with?"

"You mean Kelly?"

"How many fairies you know?"

"But Kelly's just cool."

He snorts. "For a catamite."

"No," I say. "It's his *job*. Kelly sells cool. I sell cheekbones."

He looks at me. "I don't know what the fuck you're talking about. I don't much care. All I want to know is why there are two hard guys waiting for you outside my building."

"It's kind of a long story."

"Give me the broad strokes."

"They think Kelly took out a friend of theirs."

"Did he?"

I stare at him.

Heather's father nods. "I guess that's not too surprising."

"Will you help me?"

He frowns. "You ever do any wet work?"

I take a breath. "Not really."

"Stay close to me. When it happens, hold low and put your man down. Nothing fancy. Keep shooting until he drops."

I am having trouble breathing. "Are we going now?"

He shakes his head. "We'll wait until the game breaks. The more confusion, the better."

When it's time, Heather's father says, "Get yourself frosty. They won't go easy."

"You can tell that by watching them stand on a street corner?"

"That's right," he says. He taps his middle finger against the handle of the gun in his waistband. "Let's go have a little roughhouse."

In the lobby we fall in step with a group of gray-suited corporate lawyers and pass with them through the enormous revolving door. Outside, the street is seething. The sidewalk in front of us is a sea of bobbing heads. We move with the crowd.

I am peering over the people around me, watching the Jamaican leaning against his flower cart on the opposite sidewalk. He is staring into the crowd, trying to keep sight of the door. Heather's father is directly in front of me, crouched slightly, also watching the Jamaican.

Heather's father glances at me over his shoulder. He says, "Cross at the corner. We'll take him as soon as we hit the other side."

I nod. Everything seems far away. I no longer feel shoulders jostling against mine. I no longer feel feet scraping the backs of my heels.

I imagine what would happen if a V-shaped flight of F-4s passed over us and dropped flaming orange sheets of napalm. I see the commuters around me turn black in the heat. I see their melting faces. I imagine an earthquake in which the skyscrapers above us disintegrate into a concrete avalanche. I imagine a world without skyscrapers where we would huddle close together and wait for lions or saber-toothed cats to charge us from the underbrush. We would scatter, lungs burning, tingling-hot all over from the adrenaline burst, and the lions would go after the youngest or the sickest or the weakest and they would bring him down with airborne strikes that break his legs and they would rip him apart.

I imagine meteor showers.

We are almost to the corner when I see Kelly. He is in a second-story window across the street. I do not see his rifle. He nods to me.

I lean toward Heather's father. "We may have a problem," I say.

"You mean your boy in the window?" he says. He does not turn around.

"You saw him."

"When we got out here."

"Why didn't you say anything?"

"I didn't know it was an issue."

"He may not be a friendly," I say.

"Is he a hostile?"

"Possibly."

He turns his head now. "Is there something you're not telling me?"

We have reached the corner.

I say, "I believe there's been a series of misunderstandings and misinterpretations."

"Leading to what?"

"Kelly is probably going to try to kill you."

He stares at me. "Why would he do that?"

I don't say anything.

Heather's father says, "Because you told him to?"

The light changes and we begin moving across the street.

"I've recently come to reexamine some things," I say.

When Kelly appears next to me, Heather's father is still on his knees. The smaller Jamaican is lying next to the flower cart. There is a hole in the center of his face. His cheeks are caved in toward it. The big Jamaican is on the ground next to us. On the ground next to him are the white and gray and blue-veined coils of his guts. He has been cut nearly in half by the exit wound from Kelly's hollowpoint. His face is smooth and unmarked. His eyes are wide open.

Kelly says, "Let's get what we came for."

"I don't think this is what Heather wants."

"Sure it is. You said so."

"I know that. I think I made it up."

"That's crazy."

"Yes," I say.

He shrugs. "I suppose it doesn't much matter. It was never really about her."

"What was it about?"

"Getting back to nature."

Heather's father says, "You don't have to do this."

Kelly draws his pistol. "Don't flatter yourself. It was never really about you either."

I say, "You've already made your progress. You don't need this."

"We need to finish what we started."

I shake my head. "You're being too literal."

"It's what separates us from the animals."

"I thought what separated us from the animals was that we know we're going to die."

"What separates us from the animals," he says, "is our ability to ask what separates us from the animals." He aims his pistol. Heather's father closes his eyes. "The danger," Kelly says, "is to become all talk and no action."

I close my eyes before I fire—holding low, squeezing-not-pulling—so I do not see Kelly's face when the bullet hits him. I imagine him looking at me with enormous, shocked eyes and reaching out his hand and taking a shaky step toward me and I fire again and again with my eyes closed until I hear his body fall.

He is still alive. He sounds like he is trying to clear his

throat. I imagine the way he looks on the ground, flopping like a landed fish, drowning in the air.

I turn away before I open my eyes.

Heather's father is leaning against me. We are shuffling along Purchase Street, trying to seem casual. I have draped my jacket over him to hide his shoulder. Taking the jacket off revealed my gun harness, so I unstrapped it and threw it in a garbage can on Federal Street. I have the pistol in my pants pocket.

There are sirens everywhere now. The cruisers are stuck in the traffic from the Central Artery construction site. The sidewalk is full of people who do not know what has happened. We are lost in the crowd again.

Heather's father drags himself along, stepping as lightly as he can so as not to jostle his shoulder. We do not speak.

Heather is sitting in her Mercedes with the line of taxis in front of South Station.

She says, "Get in."

I open the back door and help her father inside and slide in next to him. Heather pulls away from the curb.

Her father says, "Where are we going?"

"What is he doing here?" Heather says. "What's wrong with him?"

"It's sort of a long story," I tell her. "We can't go home."

"No," her father agrees.

"We need to get out of the city for a while."

"What if they shut it down?"

"The whole city?"

"They could."

"But they don't even know what to look for. They don't know what we're driving."

"Chancy," he says.

• • •

Heather's father closes his eyes and leans against the back of the seat. We creep onto the bridge beside the Children's Museum and sit in the steaming line of stopped cars.

Heather's father is taking deep breaths.

Heather turns her head toward me. "Do it," she says.

"Do what?" I say.

"Kill him."

I feel the inside of the car begin to spin. I open my mouth but no sound comes out.

"What's wrong?" Heather says.

"I thought I imagined it."

"Imagined what?"

"That you asked for this."

"Why would you think that? This is what you wanted."

"*Me?*"

"You said you wanted to take care of me."

"I do."

"Then he's served his purpose."

"So he has to die?"

"You want me, you want money. He has both. I want a man who doesn't *ask* for everything. I want a man who *takes.*"

"Are you sure you want this?"

"Really, I want it for you. I want you to feel like you can be the man in my life."

I rub my neck.

"I'm establishing my independence," she says.

Heather's father says, "You must know she's crazy." His eyes are still closed.

"Shut up," Heather says. She turns back to me. "Kill him."

"I don't know," I say.

Heather's father says, "This can't be the first time you've seen it. She used to sprinkle detergent in the birdfeeder."

"Do it," Heather tells me, "so we can start our new life."

Her father says, "She was thirteen the first time she tried to kill me."

"Why don't you stake out some territory for yourself?" Heather asks me. "Be a man. Get in the *game*, for Chrissake. You can't let people walk all over you. Let's break free. Let's set out on our own."

"Let's," I say.

"Do it, then."

"Why can't we just leave?"

She says, "We have to cut all our ties."

Her father says, "In an hour she'll love me again. She'll blame you for killing me. Every day you'll be wondering who she's going to ask to do *you*. Indecision, kid. It's what separates man from the animals."

"Regret," I say.

"That too."

I take a deep breath and unlock my door.

"Where will you go?" Heather says. "I thought you were on the run."

"I'll have to think of something."

"You're nothing," she sneers. "You always need someone else to do your work. Maybe I'll get Kelly to do it. I'm sure *he* has the balls. Maybe I'll even throw a little pussy his way."

"Good luck with that," I say. "Today we've been selecting against silk-suit thrill killers."

As I am opening the door, I hear Heather say, "I don't need you anymore."

"I love you," her father says. "I want to help you." His voice cracks.

I close the door and leave them there.

Walking back along the bridge, I imagine the beginning of the universe.

THE ART
OF THE
POSSIBLE

You date pretty, brown-haired, apple-cheeked girls who will seem like virgins even after they have children. You stay away from drugs. You drink just enough not to stand out. You use football to get yourself to school, but not to pay for it (your school doesn't give athletic scholarships)—for that you take out loans and get work-study jobs hauling trash and sweeping floors. Your hair is cut short, but not *too* short. You work for various campus political organizations—all of which are liberal, but not *too* liberal.

You are handsome, but not *too* handsome. You are tall, but not *too* tall.

After college, from which you graduate one year early, you go straight to law school and then to the state attorney's office and you establish residency in a district with a congressman who you have heard is about to make a run for the Senate and when he does you run for his seat. And you win it. Election day is two weeks after your twenty-eighth birthday.

You're going to make a name for yourself championing the common man. You're going to get on the Judiciary Committee during your second term. You are not going to cave to big business. You are going to be a senator. You will keep all of

your promises; you will never sacrifice your ideals for political gain. You will be president by the time you're forty.

You are going to do some good.

You are pretty sure it's Wednesday, but it might be
Monday, and you're dressed in a navy overcoat
and black oxfords and you are striding, strong-jawed, project-
ing quiet confidence, along the edge of a vacant lot in the
center of your district where a construction crew is breaking
ground for a low-rise affordable-housing complex. You are
walking with the contractor, both of you wearing bright orange hard hats, leading a phalanx of reporters. Really, the
phalanx is one longhaired photographer and a beat reporter
from the city paper with coffee stains on his shirt.

You are wondering when your father will call.

Later, you will be interviewed at a local television station
with a blue bedsheet hanging behind you for background.
You will talk about the new housing complex and the economic boon that it will be for your district. You will talk
about your commitment to your constituents.

You will be forthright.

The reporter waddles up from behind you and says, "How
much longer are we staying?"

On your other side, the contractor is still talking about his
building plans. He does not seem to notice the interruption.

You give the reporter the medium smile with just a hint of
teeth and incline your head toward him for increased intimacy and say, "Until you have what you need."

He snorts. "You think I need to walk around a goddamn
parking lot to write this shit? I could have written it sitting
on the toilet."

Your smile widens just a bit and you chuckle and give the
reporter a look that tells him that you acknowledge the
ridiculousness of the situation and that you regret any incon-
venience it has caused him—you feel his *pain*—but that

simultaneously you feel the grave burden of your responsibility to the people you represent. You are a servant of the people. You are the voice of the people.

You could tell him about Betty Friedkin, who is seventy-eight years old (a proud American senior, you would call her) and living on her Social Security and who has trusted you to stand up for her against those Washington fat cats; you could tell him about Jamir Winslow, twenty-nine-year-old African American father of four (*proud* African American father), who is worried about his recent trouble with the state police and wants you to get behind the new federal civil rights bill, which contains strong language against racial profiling, that the fat cats are trying to block; you could tell him about Angela Martinez (proud Latin American—no, you think, that's not quite right, but you don't like the sound of "Hispanic American" and you don't think you've ever heard "Latin American American," although it would seem to make sense—mother of an indeterminate number of children), who wants you to clean up the water and the air and the streets and television—also, you think she wants you to stand up to the fat cats in Washington, but you can't be sure because you've never actually met her. You haven't actually met *any* of these people, but you have been *fully* briefed. You've got your hand on the pulse. You are willing to go the extra mile.

You give one hundred and ten percent.

Wes has been talking to the longhaired photographer, but when he saw the reporter come up alongside you he crept forward so that now he is hovering just over your left shoulder. He says to the reporter, "All I'm thinking about is the single-malt I left in the car. I'm hoping we can kill it on the ride back."

The reporter smiles at him and fades back to walk beside the photographer.

You lean close to Wes and say, "Why aren't you wearing a hard hat?"

"They're just for the pictures," he whispers. He looks at the sky. You follow his eyes. He says, "They haven't started building. There's nothing to fall on you."

Wes is not a bodyguard, but he has a big semiautomatic pistol slung under his left arm. You are not sure that he would be able to use it if the moment arose. Still, you are comforted knowing it's there. Although you very rarely think about the possibility of assassination.

Theo, your security man, trails the group, not smiling. He looks like he could be distantly related to you.

You pass a drugstore on the way to the car. You shake hands with a few people who are wandering in or out. You clap some shoulders. A gray-haired man in a plaid shirt tells you that he met your father once.

"They don't make them like that anymore," the man says. "He'd always shoot you straight."

"Yes," you say.

The car is a black Lincoln Navigator. You have had a row of seats added where the trunk used to be. You have had the original backseat turned around so that the two rows face each other. You sit next to the reporter while the photographer sits across from you snapping pictures. Theo drives. Wes sits beside him, half turned, leaning on the back of his seat, listening to everything you say.

Today is Wednesday (you saw the front page of a newspaper on the rack outside the drugstore before you got into the car). In two weeks, you will be thirty years old. You have not slept in six days.

After the television interview, you lock yourself in a canary-yellow stall in the station's men's room and chew a small handful of pearl-colored Benzedrine tablets. You sit on the closed lid of the toilet and press your palms against your forehead. Your throat is raw.

You hear footsteps in the hallway. You hear the sigh of the air spring on top of the bathroom door and then the footsteps are inside the room. They scrape along the tiles. A shadow appears outside the door of your stall.

Wes's voice says, "You all right?"

You are silent.

Wes says, "Maybe you ought to lie down for a while."

You look up at the closed door. You listen to Wes breathing.

He says, "I have something for you."

The outlines of the door are very clear.

You say, "Any good?"

"Do I ever let you down?"

You smile slightly. "Where is she?"

"In the hallway."

You groan. "I don't know if I can stand up."

"Don't worry," Wes says. "I'll bring her."

The shadow disappears and you hear the footsteps again and the sigh of the door and then the footsteps are in the hallway, getting softer. The footsteps stop and after a few seconds they are replaced by the harsh clacking of high heels. You reach out and unlock the stall door and listen to the high heels clattering into the room.

The girl who pushes open the door of your stall is dirty-blond and smooth-faced. She has wide hips and a narrow waist. She is wearing a gray skirt.

She says, "You were great."

You blink at her. "I haven't touched you."

"The interview."

"You saw it?"

"You were on after my weather report."

You frown. "I thought I knew the . . . ah . . . the meteorologist here."

She nods. "Veronica. She's in Peoria now. And I'm a weather girl."

"What?"

"I'm not a meteorologist."

"Right. Sorry about that."

"It doesn't matter." She smiles. "You know, since I got here I've wanted to meet you."

"I'm a rookie congressman. How do you even know who I am?"

"I like politics. Also, I've always been interested in your father."

"Oh."

She steps into the stall and closes the door behind her.

"What's your name?" you say. Your voice is hoarse.

"Annie."

She reaches behind her and slides the bolt.

You say, "It's good to meet you, Annie." You have to stop yourself from moving to shake her hand.

She says, "Just relax."

She kneels in front of you and smooths her skirt over her thighs and you lean your head back against the wall over the toilet. She is unzipping your fly and you think about speaking on the Senate floor and the way you'll thunder and the way you'll look on television (although it'll mostly be C-Span). You try to imagine what it is you'll be thundering about, but Annie has pulled your pants down low on your hips. She is unbuttoning the fly of your boxer shorts and now you can see yourself in the Rose Garden and you can see yourself in the White House press room, looking stern (the commentators will say that you have gravitas), and you can see yourself during the State of the Union getting a standing ovation from the *entire* audience (*both sides* of the aisle, *across* party lines—you are a *uniter*). You can see a black-and-white photograph of yourself as you stare out the window of the Oval Office, dressed in your shirtsleeves, contemplative, concerned, stoic. Annie has opened the fly of your boxer shorts and reached in and pulled you out and you watch her head begin to bob up and down. And then you don't think about anything at all.

You are at a horseshoe-shaped booth at the back of the diner and Wes is funneling people toward you a few at a time. You are using the medium smile with open mouth. You had your teeth whitened at the beginning of the campaign season.

Every time you shake, you grip the top of the other person's forearm with your left hand. You are giving casual intimacy. You are jovial. You have seven jokes that you are telling in sequence. Three of them are self-deprecating. (These show that your power has not gone to your head.) Four of them are about the president. (These show that you cannot be intimidated.) You have two dirty jokes that you do not tell as part of the sequence. You tell these only to old white men. You lean close to them and whisper. Sometimes, after the punch line, you slap the men lightly on the chest with the back of your hand.

You say, "I'm running for reelection as your representative in Congress. I want to go on fighting for you against the special interests and the Washington fat cats. I sure would appreciate your support."

You like this last sentence. It sounds like something your father would say.

The Benzedrine is washing over you in waves. Your eyes are wide open. You imagine that you can hear lobster-shaped microbes crawling through the fluid in your brain.

You watch the pink glow of the sunset through the long windows at the front of the room.

Wes comes over to the booth and says, "That's enough."

"Are we leaving?"

He nods. "We're taking the act out into the street. We'll catch some of the rush-hour crowd."

Wes nods to Theo, who has been standing in the corner watching your table. Theo pulls himself off the wall and leads you out. You wave at everyone who looks at you as you walk to the door. You shake hands with the people who are close enough.

Wes whispers, "Harrison."

You say loudly to the man behind the counter, "Mr. Harrison, I wish you'd give me the recipe for that apple pie. The wife keeps asking for it."

Harrison, who has a pasty-white bald head dotted with liver spots, smiles and shakes his head. "Trade secret."

You look at the people around you and say, "Looks like I'm sleeping on the couch tonight."

There is laughter. At the door, you turn back toward the room and give thumbs-up with your right hand held high above your head (thumbs-up with your hand held low is a cliché). You keep your arm slightly bent to make the gesture less formal.

On the street, you use the high-intensity smile. You do a lot of waving. People stream past you. Wes talks to the people who are waiting to talk to you. Wes is also using the high-intensity smile.

A woman with deep wrinkles creasing her cheeks, hair bleached blond, says that she never heard your father tell a lie.

"He was genuine," she says.

"Yes," you say.

"He could charm the panties off a nun." She laughs. It sounds like choking. "He was honest, though. An honest man."

She moves past you down the street.

During a lull, when the three of you are alone, Theo says, "Green jacket."

"What about him?" Wes says.

"He hasn't moved since we came out here. He keeps trying not to let me catch him looking at us."

"What do you think?"

"Don't know yet."

You glance at the man they're talking about. He is dressed in a fatigue jacket. He is probably in his mid-forties (proud forty-year-old American veteran). He is leaning against the side of a Laundromat on the opposite sidewalk. While you are watching, a girl in a tight gray skirt suit passes the Laundromat. Her hair is brown and flows around her face. You watch her as she moves down the street.

"You see that?" Theo says.

"The girl?" Wes says.

"He didn't look at her."

"Maybe he's a fag."

"Homosexual," you say automatically.

Theo nods, not looking away from the man in the green jacket. "Maybe."

"Homosexual American," you mutter. "*Proud* homosexual American veteran."

Theo says, "Start going for the car. Don't rush."

Wes puts a hand on your back to guide you. Theo keeps his body between you and the man across the street. You are still waving. Your smile does not falter.

Green Jacket is moving. He is walking parallel to you on the opposite sidewalk.

Wes says, "Can we make the car?"

"Maybe," Theo says.

When Green Jacket begins to cross the street, you are not more than fifty feet from the Navigator.

Theo says, "Go."

Wes takes hold of the back of your suit and starts running, pushing you in front of him. You look over your shoulder and watch Theo move to intercept Green Jacket. They come together in the center of the street. Theo grabs the man's wrist and spins him around. Theo kicks out Green Jacket's legs and knocks him facedown onto the pavement and falls on top of him. People on the sidewalk have stopped to observe the action. Some of them watch Wes hustle you past them.

As Wes opens the sliding door of the Navigator and shoves you in, you give the bent-arm thumbs-up. The sky is dark.

Through the tinted back window, you watch Theo stand and pick Green Jacket up from the asphalt. Green Jacket looks angry. He is yelling. Theo says something to him. He stops yelling and turns to walk away. The onlookers begin moving again.

"Shit," Wes says.

"You'd rather it was a hit?"

He shrugs. "It would have gotten us some press."

Theo opens the driver's door and slips in behind the wheel. He starts the engine and pulls away from the curb. He says, "Guy was planning to spit on you."

Wes says, "You frisk him?"

Theo glances at him. "Of course." He turns back to the road. "He was clean."

"He gonna sue us?" Wes says.

"Doubtful."

"Why doubtful?"

Theo shrugs. "He doesn't even know who we are."

"What the fuck are you *talking* about? You just said he was ready to spit on us."

"On *him*," Theo says, jerking his head back at you. "But he doesn't know who he is. Just figures he's *somebody*."

"Jesus Christ."

"Guy's a fuckin' loony tune, you ask me. Plus he was shit-faced. At *least*. Probably won't even remember it in the morning."

"Homeless?"

"We didn't get that far, but it wouldn't surprise me."

Wes shakes his head. "Sooner or later, every wack job wants to be Oswald."

You say, "Doesn't he know about my antipoverty program?"

"He didn't seem too enfranchised."

You shrug. "At least we won't be losing his vote."

Wes says, "We need to get you some sleep."

You imagine tiny decomposers devouring the old skin cells on Wes's face. If you watch him long enough without looking away, you can see him gradually dying.

Your wife is sitting on the sofa in the living room when you get home. She is reading a newspaper. She does not look up at you. You cross the room and lean down and kiss the cold skin of her cheek.

She says, "Your father's coming over."

"Jesus," you say. "Tonight?"

She nods. "He called an hour ago."

"Why didn't you call the cell phone?"

"I didn't want to interrupt. Besides, I was getting the house picked up."

"Where's Ashley?"

"In her room. Maria's getting her ready." She looks up at you now. "How was it?" She has her hair tucked behind her ears. She is wearing a green skirt and a white V-neck sweater. She looks like she has no pores in her face. She photographs extremely well.

You take a deep breath. Then you give her the medium smile with the left corner of your mouth curled up, which she finds charming. She smiles back at you. You bend down and kiss her on the mouth. You give her the open-lipped kiss with no tongue.

She says, "You look tired. I thought you only had to go this hard the first time. Doesn't the incumbent get to rest?"

You say, "The more I win by this time, the more attractive it makes me as a Senate candidate two years from now. That's what we're campaigning for."

"Is it really going to happen?"

"Yes. Are you ready for it?"

"I was born for it."

"That's true."

She folds the newspaper and lays it down next to her and stands up. "I'm going to put on some perfume." She walks out of the room. Her walk is graceful and elegant and sexy enough to be feminine but gives no hint of her ever taking her clothes off or of there being anything between her legs or of the sounds she makes when you run your tongue around her nipples.

The Benzedrine is wearing off. The speed crash is making your body feel unbearably heavy. You walk as though you're underwater.

You call the cell phone from the phone in the hallway. Wes picks up on the second ring.

"My father's on his way over here," you say.

"He going to endorse us?"

"I don't know. I didn't talk to him."

Wes pauses. "Is something wrong?"

You hold the receiver in your right hand and use the index and middle fingers of your left hand to pinch the bridge of your nose. "I'm just a little worn out."

He says, "I'll be back there in two minutes."

"No," you say. "It's better if it's just the two of us."

Your father says, "You look like shit."

"Thanks, Pop."

"Are you sleeping?"

You shrug.

You are standing in the oak-doored vestibule of your house. Your father is on the stone porch at the top of the stone steps. His bodyguards are standing at the bottom of the steps next to a black Mercedes sedan.

Your father is thick-lipped and taller than you. His shoulders are very wide. He is wearing a tan raincoat and a brown fedora that covers his bald spot.

You say, "Aren't you going to come in?"

He slides past you into the house. In the entrance hall, your wife is standing with your daughter, Ashley, both of them facing the door and giving the high-medium smile with teeth.

You lock the door. You close your eyes and wait for the dizziness to pass.

When you come into the entrance hall, your father is leaning down toward Ashley.

"Put your hand out," he is saying.

She does.

He reaches into his coat and brings out his key ring and hands it to her. "There you go," he says.

Ashley giggles. She is wearing a flowered dress and white stockings and black shoes with gold buckles. She has blond hair and brown eyes.

He frowns. "Isn't that what you wanted?"

Ashley shakes her head.

He takes the keys back from her. He straightens up and makes a big show of patting his various pockets. "I don't know what else I can give you." He reaches into his coat again. "The only other things I have are these." He brings out a handful of caramels wrapped in gold paper.

Ashley claps.

"You want *these*?"

She nods.

"How old are you now?" your father asks her.

"Almost five."

"How close?"

She stares at her hands for a few seconds, her mouth moving. Then she turns and whispers loudly to your wife, "Mommy, how long until I'm five?"

"Two months," your wife says.

Ashley turns back to your father. "Two months."

He scowls. "Well, I guess we'll give it to you. Put your hand out."

He crouches down again and counts five caramels into her hand and puts the rest into his pocket.

"What do you say?" your wife says.

"Thank you, Grampa," Ashley says. "I love you." She kisses him on the cheek. He hugs her.

He stands up and hugs your wife. He kisses her on the cheek.

"I'm glad to see you," she says. She looks down at Ashley. "Time to say good night."

Ashley shakes her head. The high-medium smile has disappeared.

Your wife says, "Don't make your grandfather think you don't have any manners."

Ashley shakes her head again.

You say, "Getting enough sleep is important, especially for little girls. I knew a girl in high school named Emily Thomas who never slept more than four hours a night. She had to drop out. Now she's got three kids and no husband. She's a drain on our country's overextended welfare system. With these new fat-cat welfare-reform bills she may lose her only source of income."

They are all staring at you.

You say, "We don't need any more Emily Thomases."

Your father turns back to Ashley and says, "I thought you were almost five. Five-year-olds don't throw tantrums when it's time for bed."

She nods.

"Maria," your wife calls over her shoulder.

Maria appears wearing blue jeans and a gray sweater.

Your wife says, "Bedtime."

Your father says, "Good to see you again, Maria."

Maria says, "It's good to see you again, Governor."

"I'm not the governor anymore."

She frowns. "I thought you kept the title for life."

"You do, but it's a little embarrassing. It's like a woman keeping her husband's name after they're divorced."

Maria smiles. She takes hold of Ashley's hand and they walk to the stairs.

Your wife says, "I'm going to bed also."

She kisses your father again.

"They're dropping like flies," he says.

When the two of you are alone, you say, "Should we sit down?"

He shakes his head. "I'm not staying."

You give him the medium smile. "All business."

"Shouldn't I be?"

You shrug. "I am."

He nods. "Why didn't you ask for my endorsement last time?"

"I wanted to break in on my own."

"And now that you're in, all the pride is gone?"

Your eyelids are sagging. "It seems more expedient this way."

He says, "I liked that you wanted to do it by yourself. I respected your not wanting me to campaign for you. I respected your not wanting me to pay for your school."

"I don't care about respect anymore."

"What's happening to you?"

You look into his eyes. You are earnest and determined. Your head feels packed in cotton. You say, "My dreams are coming true."

Your father looks at you for a long moment. "I'm sorry," he says.

When he's gone, you sit on the bright white tile floor of your bathroom feeling your stomach churn. You listen to the buzzing of the fluorescent light over the sink. You wonder whether you should have spent some time in the army.

You kneel in front of the toilet and feel the nausea all over you, but you do not vomit. You grip the black porcelain sides of the bowl and stare at your reflection in the water. Your face is blurred by tiny ripples. You have dark purple fatigue bruises under your eyes. Your skin is pale. Still, you recognize the face. This surprises you somehow.

Behind you, in the hallway outside the bathroom, the wooden floor is creaking. The creaking comes closer and closer and then stops and you hear the muted slaps of bare feet on the bathroom tile. Then the footsteps stop and there is only the hum of the lightbulb.

Your wife says, "Aren't you coming to bed?"

You can imagine her face—mouth closed, eyebrows drawn together with concern, eyes wide with urgency and love. In the outside corner of one of her eyes, there might even be the beginnings of a tear.

You do not turn around. "Soon," you say.

"Please come with me."

You can imagine her eyes closing with sadness.

"Soon," you say again.

"At least look at me," she says. She is using the loving tone with a hint of pleading.

You close the lid of the toilet in front of you. You take a deep breath and push yourself up with your arms and turn around and sit on the closed lid.

Your wife is dressed in her white nightgown. The curves of her body make gray shadows in the fabric. Her face is almost as you pictured it, although she is using sadder eyes than you imagined. As soon as you are looking at her, she allows one of the tears to trickle out and along her cheekbone and past the corner of her mouth.

"I love you," she says. She sighs. Her cheeks draw up toward her forehead and she makes more tears that collect at the bottoms of her eyes, ready to spill.

You frown. You say, "Careful not to give too much too soon. Always try for the slow build. Also, it's better to err on the side of understatement."

She sniffs. "What?"

"Real emotion makes people nervous. It's important to reflect quiet calm. Ideally, you should be sitting down behind a big desk. It makes you look powerful but stable. It's vital to stay placid. Passion is too Mussolini."

She is silent.

"We've talked about this," you say.

"I know," she says. She pushes out a few more tears that leave wet streaks on her face.

"If you weren't ready for this, you should have said something earlier."

She is really pouring on the tears now. "But I thought things would still be the same between *us.*"

You spread your arms wide and give her the welcoming smile. "They are," you say.

BLUE YONDER

The girl sat at one of the outdoor tables with a much younger girl who looked like her in miniature. They both had blond hair and enormous round eyes. The little girl wore a flowered sundress and sat as tall as she could, straining upward, her chin barely clearing the tabletop. The older girl wore a white blouse and high-heeled sandals and a black skirt that hung below her knees. She sat leaning forward, with her elbows on the table and one soft, smooth, tanned calf draped over the other. Her hair was gathered in back and held together with a silver clip. Her sunglasses had tortoise-shell frames and she wore them pushed back high on her forehead.

When the waiter brought my coffee, I motioned him close to me and said, "Do you know that girl?"

The waiter, whose name was Ricky and who spoke English with extreme care, said, "No, mister."

"She's never been here before?"

"No, mister," Ricky said. "I have not seen her."

I nodded. "Tell me your real name, Ricky."

"You don't want to know."

"Tell me anyway."

He told me.

"You're right," I said.

He smiled. "Will you eat?"

I shook my head and he took away my menu.

I did not want to be caught watching the girls, so I only glanced at them occasionally and the rest of the time I watched the people moving into the Public Garden. The sky was steel blue and cloudless. The street was all couples and families, and businessmen who walked side by side very fast. There was a group of boys trying to climb the statue of Washington. Washington sat rigid in his saddle while the boys grabbed at his boots and at the horse's neck.

The older girl was speaking on a cell phone now and I stared at her for a while and then I forced myself to turn back to the park and I noticed Lucien walking on the other side of the street. He was whistling in that nervous way he had and, although I couldn't hear it, I thought that the tune was probably from *Threepenny Opera* because that was almost always what he whistled. When he saw me, he stopped whistling and dashed across the lanes of traffic, between the speeding cars.

"Mr. Tolstoy, I presume," he said when he reached me, his chest heaving.

"Mr. De Quincey," I said.

He frowned. "No, no. All wrong. I haven't had any opium since I was seventeen and even then I could take it or leave it. Also, he was never a painter."

"Sorry," I said. "Short notice."

He flopped into the chair across from me.

"Mr. Basquiat would be better. Or perhaps Mr. Cézanne."

"They certainly would be."

Ricky appeared beside us. "It has been a long time, Mr. Lucien," he said.

Lucien smiled and spoke to him in French.

"Only English, please," Ricky said.

"You'll get rusty," Lucien warned him.

"No one speaks French back home," Ricky said. "Only the government."

Lucien shrugged. "I'll have an espresso then, Ricky—or is that too much Italian for you?"

"Don't be angry, Mr. Lucien. I'm only trying to improve myself."

"I know. I'm sorry, Ricky, I shouldn't be that way. Bring me an espresso, please."

Ricky walked back inside. Lucien said, "Are you working?"

"Some," I told him.

"I have been finding excuses to stay away from the studio. I despise it."

"The studio or finding the excuses?"

"Both."

Far down the street, a construction crew was repaving part of the sidewalk. The men in the crew wore orange vests. Their trucks poured gray exhaust. We could hear the faint, high-pitched beeps that the cement mixer made as it was backed into position, its cylinder turning lazily.

"In with the new," Lucien said.

Ricky brought Lucien's espresso and disappeared again.

"When did you leave the hospital?"

He smiled. "You've been thinking about how to ask me."

"Yes."

"You shouldn't worry so much. It ages you."

"You were released?"

"It's voluntary, anyway," he said.

"I thought it was only voluntary checking in."

"If your money's the right color, anything you do is voluntary."

"That's bullshit," I said.

He waved his hand dismissively. "Whatever it is, there's no point talking about it."

I looked at him for a while, not saying anything, and then he reached into his shirt and brought out a long, cream-colored cigarette.

I shook my head. "Can't do that here."

"I forgot," he said, and put the cigarette back inside his shirt. He sighed. "This really is a terrible city."

"Why are you here?" I asked him.

"Are we philosophers now?" he said.

I stared at him.

He shook his head. "So serious," he said. "You mean, why am I here and not in New York?"

"I mean, if you're leaving the hospital why come back *here*?"

"Too much New York. Even a month is too much. Also, there are no artists here."

"There are some."

"Some," he agreed. "But you can avoid them." He sipped at his espresso. "Why are *you* here?"

"Where would I go?" I took a deep breath. "So why no artists?"

He shrugged. "It seems lately as though the world is full of talentless men who suffer all the responsibility of possessing a really major talent."

"Why do you care about the deluded?"

"Because there is no difference between the way they think about what they do and the way I think about what I do."

"So?"

"So what is there to separate me from them?"

"The work."

He smiled without meaning it. "But I am judging my work and they are judging theirs and we are coming to the same conclusions and what if I am one of the deluded and everyone is laughing behind my back."

"No one's laughing."

"I used to think that if you knew when you woke up every morning that you were supposed to do a certain thing and you thought that you could be great at it then you *could* be great at it. But it isn't true."

"No," I agreed.

"Well, I don't want to wake up one day when I'm fifty and realize that I'm only a decent painter."

"There are worse things to be than a decent painter."

"Not if you are a decent painter who thought he was going to be a great painter." He looked at the sky. "I won't be a failure."

He lowered his eyes. "I had to agree to work with a doctor here," he said. "I mean, for them to let me leave I had to let them palm me off on somebody."

"You don't have to talk about it."

He put up his hand to stop me. "I gave you as my emergency contact. I hope that's all right. You're the only person I know who's still here."

"You know plenty of people."

"I am *acquainted* with plenty of people. I barely *know* anyone."

"Of course it's all right," I said.

"Jack," he said, "tell me I'm going to be a great painter."

"You will."

He grinned. "I wonder whether you would lie to me if we were talking about writing."

I drank some of my coffee, which was cool now, and looked at Washington. Lucien sipped at his espresso again and put it down and looked around and that was when he noticed the girls for the first time. He looked back at me.

"You see this?" he said.

"Since before you got here."

"What have you been doing about it?"

I shrugged. "I get too nervous talking to women I don't know. Especially when they look like that."

"My God," he said. "How old are you now?"

"Twenty-four."

He sighed. "You're squandering your youth."

"I don't think you have the right to talk about my youth. You're not even six months older than me."

He smiled. "But I am an old man."

"Well, why don't you gather yourself then—while you still may—and go over?"

"No," he said. "Why don't *we* go over?"

The girls were more beautiful the closer we got. When we reached their table, they looked up at us with their immense eyes and for a moment I could see nothing but the eyes of the older one and the way a few loose strands of her hair hung forward into her face. My heart was beating fast, as I had known it would, and I was afraid to speak because I wasn't sure whether I could catch my breath.

Then Lucien said, to the little girl, "Excuse me, madam, but you appear to have something in your ear."

The girls stared at him.

"Allow me," he said and reached behind the little one's head and when he pulled his hand back he was holding a quarter.

"I believe this is yours," he said to her.

She held out her palm and he dropped the coin into it.

"Very nice," the older girl said.

Lucien shook his head. "That's nothing. Now, if you want to see *real* talent—" He reached behind the little girl's head again and again brought out a quarter, but this time he put it in his mouth and bit down on it and then he was holding half a quarter with jagged teeth marks along its edge. The girls looked on, openmouthed. Lucien blew hard on the torn quarter in his hand and then suddenly it was whole again. The little girl gasped. The older girl applauded.

"Will you sit down?" she said.

I pulled over two chairs from the neighboring table and we sat. We introduced ourselves.

Kate, the older girl, said, "Where did you learn that?"

Lucien shrugged. "Around."

The little girl, whose name was Nina, looked at Lucien and said, "Where are you from?"

He smiled. "Where do you think I'm from?"

She frowned. "England?"

"Close," he said. "I'm from Denmark. Do you know where that is?"

She shook her head.

"Why aren't you tall and blond and pale?" Kate asked him.

"Good genes."

"You don't have much of an accent."

"I have enough," he said.

"So, how do you know each other?"

"We went to school together."

"Where?"

He told her.

"So," she said, "are you bankers or lawyers or trying to rule the world?"

"Trying to *make* the world."

"Lucien's a painter," I said.

"Is he good?" she asked me.

"He is good," I said.

"Jack is a writer," Lucien told her, "and even if you never see him again, you'll tell your grandchildren about the day you met him."

She looked at me.

Ricky came over and we ordered another round. The girls were both drinking orange juice.

"So," Lucien said, "are you two sisters?"

"I'm her aunt," Kate said.

Lucien watched the cars as they passed and said, "Don't they sound like the ocean?"

"What do you mean?" Kate asked him.

"The tires," he said.

"I thought painters were supposed to *see* differently," I said, "not *hear* differently."

"It just occurred to me," he said.

"I think I see what you mean," Kate told him.

The crew was finished with the sidewalk and had moved into the street. The cement mixer had been pulled away and replaced by a dump truck that was pouring hot tar. The men were spreading the tar before the paving truck came through with its enormous roller.

Nina tugged at my shirt. "Are you strong?" she asked me.

"Why?" I said.

"You look strong."

"So do you."

She nodded vigorously. "I am. I can even beat most of the boys in my grade at arm wrestling."

"Well, then, I know who to call when somebody's giving me a hard time."

She giggled.

"So what have you been doing this afternoon?" I asked her.

"We were shopping with my mother but she was taking too long."

"Is she meeting you here?" Lucien asked.

"No," Kate said. "We're spending the afternoon together."

"We should all go somewhere."

She smiled. "Where should we go?"

"I don't know," he said. "Where do people go?"

"We could ride the swan boats," I said.

"Wonderful," Lucien said. "*That's* what people do. I just don't have a sense of them lately. I'm only doing abstracts and landscapes now; no more portraits."

Nina turned to her aunt and said, "Can we?"

"I suppose so," Kate said.

We signaled to Ricky for the check.

"If I *were* painting portraits," Lucien said to the girls, "I would use both of you as subjects." They smiled. "And Jack, too," he said, turning to me. "Of course, Jack. It should be against the law for someone to be so talented *and* look like that. God ought to choose one gift or the other."

"It doesn't bother *me*," Kate said.

Lucien smiled. His eyes were bright. "You know," he said, "maybe it would be better if just the three of you went. There are some things I really should get done."

He stood.

"Are you sure?" I said.

"Sure, sure." He ran two fingers around the tiny bald spot on the back of his head. "You know, when my hair starts really thinning I'm going to shave it all off. I hope I won't look like a cancer patient." He clapped a hand on my shoulder. "Value your youth, young Tolstoy."

He kissed each of the girls on the hand and saluted us and then walked down the street in the same direction he had been heading when he had first seen me. We were quiet as we watched him get smaller and smaller and pass the construction site where the new-poured tar was flat and steaming. He turned the corner and passed out of sight and that was the last time I saw him until the night I was called to identify him. And when the sheet was pulled back I could hardly recognize him because of what the pistol had done when he fired it inside his mouth.

We stayed at the table for a while before we went to the swan boats. We laughed about things I can't remember. Kate kept touching my forearm. We listened to cars that sounded like the ocean.

THE DEATH OF COOL

Any of the people you pass on the street could pretend to trip and stumble into you and sorry sorry my mistake pour a glass full of cyanide onto your bare forearm. They could push you into traffic. They could swerve their cars into you. They could pull out a nine-millimeter Browning automatic or a snub-nosed thirty-eight or a twelve-gauge Remington shotgun with the buttstock filed down and the barrel chopped to let it fit inside a holster and do you wild wild West. They could shoulder you inside the sliding door of a waiting van and take you blindfolded to an abandoned warehouse and lock you in a coffin full of rats.

From the roof of any skyscraper, someone could be sprinkling pennies that the acceleration during the drop will turn into bullets raining on the sidewalk. Someone could smash a jar of hantavirus on the tracks at one of the downtown subway stops and let the trains carry the death from station to station. Any of the people stepping onto the bus you're riding could have bricks of plastic explosive taped to their chest. They could have covered the explosive with nails and bolts for shrapnel.

You are at their mercy. You are alive because they want

you alive or because they do not care whether you live or because they do not notice you.

You walk with your eyes down. You try to stay under the radar.

You depend on the kindness of strangers.

I lock my door. I take a breath. I speed-walk along the hallway of my building and almost make the stairs before I have to turn around. Back outside my apartment, I check the door and then sprint away from it toward the stairway and this time I get as far as the second-floor landing. I go back and check the door again. I rattle the knob so that I hear the bolt clicking against the inside of the locking mechanism. I take another breath.

I say to the empty hallway, "It's locked."

I go through versions of this routine every morning. You can never be too careful.

I hit the street and start walking.

Any time you slide into the backseat of a taxi, the driver could seal the doors and windows with a button on the dash and trap you inside a Plexiglas cage. After that, you're his. He could pump in chlorine gas through vents in the floor. He could take you to a car compactor. He could point you at the harbor and use a rock to hold down the accelerator. He could let in thousands of inch-long driver ants that would take less than fifteen minutes to strip all your flesh and turn you into a pile of dry white bones.

Public transportation is even worse.

Three days ago, the man waiting next to me on the subway platform got pushed in front of the train. He ended up facing me. The side of the train had pinned him against the side of the platform. Most of his upper body was sticking out of the gap.

The train doors were still closed. Passengers were crammed against all the windows, trying to see what had happened. I thought how strange it was, given the nature of my work and how many dead bodies I'd seen, that I'd never actually watched anyone die.

Then the man blinked.

My mouth opened. No sound came out.

The man said, "It doesn't hurt."

I knelt down beside him.

"I know I'm dying," he said.

A wide-eyed transit cop appeared above us.

The man said, "There's so much to do."

The transit cop said, "Do you have any family we can call?"

The man was silent.

My eyes burned. I said, "You don't have anything to worry about. Obviously, they'll receive the accidental death and dismemberment bonus."

The transit cop said, "If you tell us how to reach them, we can bring them here to say good-bye."

My vision blurred. I said, "If they can show you were on your way to work, they may have a claim on the benefit for death due to homicide while the policyholder is actively engaged in his or her employment. Generally, it's intended for soldiers and policemen, but there's a case pending in Nevada that's trying to get the morning commute included under the legal definition of the workday. They'll want to watch for that decision."

The man was looking around frantically. Now all he kept saying was, "Did anyone see who pushed me?"

I said, "Of course, if they could get this classified as business travel they'd make out like bandits. I admit that's kind of a long shot."

Another cop appeared. He was taller than the transit cop. He had thick pink forearms.

The big cop said, "I have a couple witnesses who say they got a pretty good look at the guy."

The man's eyes widened. "What was he like? Was he tall?

Was he thin? What was he wearing? Did he have a mustache?" He lowered his voice. "Was he black?"

The cop sighed. "Seems like he was just some homeless guy. Some nobody."

"But he can't be," the man said. "He *can't* be."

The EMTs arrived. One of them gave the man a sedative and the cop motioned me away.

"Did you see anything?" he asked.

"I just felt him get shoved past me and then someone started screaming."

"Doesn't matter. I'm sure you wouldn't have recognized the guy." He shook his head. "Must be weird knowing you got killed by someone nobody knows."

"There's no chance he'll make it?"

He shook his head again. "He's all smashed up and twisted around under there. The train's holding his guts in. As soon as we pull it away, his organs will all whoosh out. I've seen it before. It happens sometimes with the push victims. They're trying to stop their momentum so they fall closer to the platform. Every so often they get stuck. The suicides usually jump out pretty far and the impact breaks them like an egg."

I grind my teeth against my tongue. "So if we just left the train there and closed the station we could keep him alive indefinitely. But we're going to let him die so as not to delay rush hour."

The cop stared at me. "He can't live like that for more than a few hours. And it's important to end it before the shock wears off."

My hands were shaking. I couldn't stop them. "So he's finished."

The cop nodded. "Whenever I ride the train, I make sure to stand against the wall while it pulls in. I don't let anybody get behind me." He frowned. "Of course, that doesn't protect you from a bomber or some loony who wants to stick an ice pick in your throat. But I guess you can't worry about *everything.*"

. . .

My office is on the fifty-fifth floor and for the last few days, since that morning in the subway, I have been taking the stairs. There's no limit to what they could do to your elevator.

I step out of the stairwell, and after nine hundred seventy-two eight-inch risers I'm barely even sweating. Your best weapon is your physical condition. An army is only as good as its feet. Even before a few days ago, I would never have let myself go.

The receptionist smiles as I pass her. She has curly brown hair and enormous breasts that don't sag. A few years ago, when I was still in college, I would have taken her home and dripped maple syrup all over her and stroked her belly button with a feather. Now, before I did that I would have to perform a full background check—call the IRS, lift her fingerprints from the phone receiver and run them through the FBI database. If the only things you know about somebody are what they've told you, then you don't know anything.

My boss is half-sitting on my desk, sipping his coffee. I never drink coffee. An army marches on its stomach.

My phone is ringing. My boss picks it up. "Claims," he says.

He listens. Then he says, "You want Sales. It's three-five-eight-oh . . . Same exchange . . . That's right."

He puts the phone down and looks at me. "Did you walk up again?"

I don't say anything.

He sighs. "Didn't we have this conversation yesterday?"

"It's not like the stairs are so much better. Someone could always just block the fire doors and drop in a handful of nerve-gas pellets."

"I'm not sure I understand."

"Someone could place charges that would destroy the support structure and send you plummeting all the way down through parking levels and sub-basements until you melt against the damp cement floor at the bottom."

"But what are the *chances* of that?"

"Not too high," I say. "But they exist. Last year, triggered stairway collapses were responsible for fifty percent of homicides by indoor dropping."

"Those are just numbers."

"Life is numbers."

He nods. "But in order to get *through* life, you need to accept small possibilities of catastrophe. That's risk management."

"What about risk elimination?"

"There's no such thing." He frowns. "I suppose you could shut yourself in your apartment and have someone slide your food under the door."

"I've thought of that," I tell him. "You'd still have to worry about poison in the food and about rocket attacks or aerial bombardment. Besides, what's the point of living unless you can find a way to be in the world? I'm not going to let them close me out of my life."

"Who?" he says.

"But I'm also not a sap. I'm not going to ride their goddamn *elevator*." I move closer to him. "You know that old myth about jumping just before the thing hits? It's bullshit."

He stares at me.

"For one thing, how would you know the right moment to jump? Even if there were windows, the timing would be almost impossible. Also, in a frictionless system the elevator would be falling at exactly the same rate you are. You wouldn't be able to generate any force against the floor. And even if you managed to jump, you'd probably just smack against the ceiling and then ping-pong around while the whole thing collapses from the impact and crushes you. It wouldn't do you much good."

My boss stands up off of my desk. He shakes his head. "Have it your way," he says.

· · ·

I rina Christina Molesky, widow of recently deceased policyholder Alexander I. Molesky, sole beneficiary of a term-life package with an after-tax value approaching three and a half million dollars, does not offer me anything to eat. She doesn't have the Honduran housekeeper, who keeps flitting around us while we sit at the glass-topped kitchen table, brew me a cup of tea. She doesn't tell her to bring out a pitcher of ice water.

Instead she says, "I already told everything to police."

"I understand that," I say.

"Now I have to tell everything again."

"Your husband had an abnormal amount of insurance for a man of his age and medical history. That, coupled with the nature of his death, raises a red flag."

"I do not see red flag."

"A suspicion."

"What suspicion?"

Alexander Molesky, thirty-eight-year-old male nonsmoker with a benign preexisting respiratory condition caused by prolonged childhood exposure to coal dust while working in mines in the Ukraine, father of two, had been president and cofounder of the Mad Russians Car Repair and Limousine Service as well as co-owner of an electronics store, a road-paving company and two junk and demolition yards until Saturday night, when he was found facedown in a gravel parking lot with a plastic bag over his head and both his thumbs missing. The total of his annual life insurance premiums had been twenty-seven thousand dollars.

I'm keeping close track of the maid with my peripheral vision because as soon as I look away she might dash forward and hit me with a syringe full of Dilaudid. They would let me flail around for a while until I passed out. Then they would drag me over to the oven. They would remove the racks. They would wrestle me inside and lock the door and set the dial to Self-Clean.

I say, "It's a long-standing principle of common law that

no one will be permitted to take advantage of his or her own iniquity."

"I am not seeing you."

"It's my job to make sure no one benefits from doing wrong."

She is biting her lip. "Why you're telling me this?"

I take a breath. "Any potential beneficiary who intentionally causes the death of the decedent will be denied the insurance to which he or she might otherwise be entitled."

"You think I murder my husband?"

I shrug. "Twelve percent of male homicide victims in the United States last year were murdered by or at the behest of their wives or domestic partners."

She stares at me.

I say, "For women that number is more like seventy-eight percent."

Her eyes leak tiny tears.

"This isn't personal," I tell her. "Look at the numbers."

"Numbers say I kill my husband?"

"Not necessarily. But you *could* have."

It's not the dying that bothers me. Everybody does that and, mostly, it's not as bad as you think. Some people just drop dead. (This is usually attributed to SCF, sudden cardiac failure, which accounted for 48.7 percent of last year's heart-disease deaths.) But when you're murdered, another person has become your God. They have forced you to bow down to them. And you'll never get even.

Maybe your waitress has ground up glass into your orange juice. Maybe your roommate will toss a plugged-in toaster into the bath with you. Maybe your wife has pumped up the water pressure in your house so when you turn the knob the showerhead howitzers through your skull. She'll fuck your best friend on the floor of your living room, rolling around on piles of money from your annuity payments. She'll spread rumors about you and talk about how she loved you in spite of your shortcomings.

She'll laugh.

I meet Sadie in the lobby of the Four Seasons and, as far as I can tell, I wasn't followed. During the walk over, I doubled back on my route twice. I boarded a city bus and, just as the doors were about to close, I jumped back down to the sidewalk. I went inside a Japanese restaurant and then darted through the swinging door into the kitchen and past white-jacketed sushi chefs who didn't even have time to turn around before I was through the emergency exit and out into an alley.

Sadie is wearing a short gray skirt. She has her sunglasses pushed up on top of her head. She is talking into a cell phone. When I reach her, she gives me a silent kiss and keeps talking into the phone. She smells like honey.

The bellhops stare at Sadie as they move around us. Hotel guests in chinos and short-sleeved polo shirts sneak peeks at her when their wives aren't watching. When we move into the bar, young lawyers with loosened ties glance over and then laugh together.

Any of them who wants her badly enough could follow me into the men's room and slide a three-inch blade into the space between the top of my spine and the bottom of my skull. If he used the right implement, the wound would hardly bleed. He could arrange me on one of the toilets with my feet on the floor and my pants around my ankles. Then he could lock the stall door and slither out through the gap at the bottom. No one would find me for hours.

We sit at a table near the door.

I say, "Somewhere in this room there's probably a guy who can outfight me. He could make me beg for my life."

Sadie looks up at me. "Let me call you back," she says into the phone.

I sweep my eyes around the room. "I'm tired of letting the law protect me. I'm tired of hiding behind the skirts of some cop. I'm tired of trusting in the other guy's morality." I shake my head. "There's no guarantee in that, anyway."

She gives me big eyes. "Baby," she says, "I don't know what you're talking about."

"I'm talking about self-reliance. I'm talking about the State of Nature. I'm talking about, if some guy can own me like that, how can you want me more than him?"

"I'm nervous about what this job is doing to you."

"You're supposed to love me, forsaking all others."

She takes a deep breath. "I think maybe it's time for a change."

"Either you're lying to me, or you're going against the order of things."

"Why don't you think about going to work for your father?"

"We talked about that," I say.

"You know you'll end up there sooner or later."

I am silent.

"Or, forget about your father," she says. "I'm sure one of your college friends would be happy to get you in at Goldman or Bear Stearns or Morgan."

"This isn't about where I *work*."

She takes a breath. "Is this because you're nervous about moving in with me?"

"I just want to know I can protect you."

She smiles. "That's sweet."

"Also, what if you're not who you say you are?"

"What?"

"I mean, obviously I've met your parents and I've seen where you allegedly grew up, but what if it's all a show? What if you're all just acting? What if everybody's in on it but me?"

Sadie's eyes are wet. She says, "There's something wrong with you."

"I used to have a dream where I was walking on a street somewhere and suddenly everyone turned toward me and started stalking me like zombies. The entire world was zombies, except for me. They were pouring out from everywhere to join the chase. I ducked down alleys. I raced through backyards and even through houses. At night, I broke into this skyscraper and hid under a desk on one of the high floors while helicopters shined spotlights in the windows."

"I think you need to talk to somebody."

I nod. "I think you might be right."

A waiter materializes to take our drink orders.

Monroe Grady says, "I hope you're not here about the Molesky thing. It's a gangland killing. A fucking infant could read this one."

I shake my head.

"What, then?" he says.

I don't say anything.

He sighs. "How long have we known each other?"

"A while," I tell him. "Four years?"

"And haven't I always shot you straight?"

"I think so."

"And don't you trust me?"

"That's an awfully complicated question."

He chews his bottom lip.

After a long time, I say, "I'm interested in learning how to defend myself."

"Those self-defense classes are mostly for girls."

"I'm looking for something . . . a little more serious."

He steeples his hands in front of him and taps his index fingers together. "How serious?"

"All the way."

We are at Monroe's desk in the middle of the homicide

unit, surrounded by cops who might all turn on me at once and throw me inside one of the soundproofed interrogation rooms. They could line the doors and windows with watertight tape and then flood the place. They could watch through the two-way mirror as the water rises and I start to panic. They could turn on the hidden microphones and listen to me drowning.

Monroe says, "Are you sure this isn't about the Molesky thing?"

"What do you mean?"

"I mean, are you here because you're worried about getting mixed up with those people?"

"Everybody's mixed up with everybody."

"But these Russian guys are dangerous."

"Everyone's dangerous. Besides, they're Ukrainian."

He rolls his eyes. "Whatever. It's all ex-KGB hardcases. They're worse than the Colombians."

I shrug.

"That doesn't worry you?"

"No more than anything else."

"Then I don't understand what you're asking me."

"I guess I'm looking for general rules."

"Safety rules?" he says. "Well, for one thing, you're always safer in a public place."

"But not *completely* safe."

He spreads his hands. "I don't know if completely safe is possible. You piss off the wrong guy and he decides to grease you no matter what the consequences to himself, there's not a lot to do."

"But you can make it hard on him."

"Sometimes the most you can do is give yourself a chance." He takes a breath. "But that's the rare case. Mostly, with a few simple precautions you give yourself the upper hand." He leans toward me. "First," he says, "be certain you're seeing all the angles. Once you know where the danger might come from, you can take steps to protect yourself. Always have an emergency plan."

I nod. "Well," I say, "I suppose the key is not to let them get control of you in the first place. Once they have you locked in the room and they start pumping the water, it's already too late."

He leans back away from me. "The water?"

I nod again. "Obviously it would be tough to smuggle anything through the metal detectors. It would be better to lift a service revolver from inside somebody's desk."

"Wait," he says. "I'm not following."

"You'd need to be set to go as soon as the situation starts to deteriorate. You'd have to get through the room as quickly as possible. Once you stopped moving, they would call the SWAT team and then you'd be forced to take hostages. After that, it's only a matter of time."

He is staring at me. "I think you may have misunderstood."

"You'd talk to the negotiator for a while and you'd make demands and he would stall and they would talk you out or wait you out or they'd decide you weren't going to crack and they'd roll flash-bang grenades in through the air vents and they'd make a three-point entry with assault-team members dressed in black jumpsuits. When they have resources like that," I say, "you can't afford to let them get coordinated."

Monroe is shaking his head. "You came here for my advice. My advice is just make sure you're aware of your surroundings. Be ready for anything."

"Don't be a victim," I murmur.

I used to sleep with an aluminum baseball bat beside my bed. Saturday afternoon, I replace it with a Smith & Wesson riot shotgun. I set the police lock on the front door. The police lock is an iron bar that sticks into a hole in the floor. To get past it, they'd need to take the door apart. They could use a sledgehammer. They could use a blowtorch. Either of those takes time. If they used a shaped charge to blow the door off its hinges, the lock might still hold.

Each of my windows is alarmed. I have installed motion detectors on the fire escape.

I will hear them coming.

In a perfect world, I would install security cameras in the hallways and the stairwell and in the street facing in every direction. I would have an antiaircraft battery on the roof. Every night, in a perfect world, I would booby-trap the living room windows with white phosphorous grenades. I couldn't do this to the windows in my bedroom because I would be too close to the blast area and a detonation would inciner-ate me.

Late Saturday afternoon, someone pushes my buzzer. I stare at the intercom for a long time before I press the Talk button and whisper, "Who is it?"

I press the Listen button.

Sadie's voice says, "It's me."

I buzz her in and wait with my eye against the peephole. I watch her appear at the top of the stairs and come toward me. I look for any sign of movement behind her. She reaches my door and knocks. I keep watching the stairway. She knocks again.

"Let me in," she says.

I undo the police lock and open the door and pull her inside and slam the door closed and reset the police lock and jam my eye back against the peephole. The hallway is still empty. I turn around. Today Sadie smells like gardenias.

"We need to talk," she says.

I say, "Every time I have to talk into the intercom, it gives away my position."

"I think we should see about getting you some help."

"How would you know you could trust them?"

"I've gotten some recommendations."

"I looked into it myself. I'm afraid it's hopeless."

Her face relaxes. "That's great that you've been looking. I thought you were going to say there wasn't a problem."

"Of *course*, I understand there's a problem." I shake my head. "Most of the available guys are Africans or South Americans who just drift from revolution to revolution and pretty much sell themselves to the highest bidder or attach themselves to the side that happens to be winning at any given moment. They have substandard training and suspect loyalty."

Past my window over Sadie's shoulder, the sun is setting. The sky burns pink and orange. Beside her, the television flashes and hums.

I say, "The English guys are mostly ex-SAS, so they obviously have the training, but they're prohibitively expensive. Also, they might have their own agendas. Same goes for the Americans. The fact is, it's a disreputable business that sometimes attracts disreputable people. You could get some crazed Nazi who's waiting for you to fall asleep so he can go to work on you with a chain saw. It's not worth the risk. There's too many freaks out there."

Sadie is silent.

Beside her, the anchorman shuffles his papers. He looks up from his desk. Normally, he says, a particle accelerator is built in a straight line.

Sadie steps toward me and touches my cheek. She is crying.

Speeding up the particle to any substantial velocity requires a great distance.

She pulls herself close to me and gazes up with wet eyes. "I love you," she says.

Because the largest particle accelerators are not even two miles long, their maximum velocity is low.

She says, "I want you to know that I'm not going to abandon you."

A cyclotron or synchrotron solves the distance problem by

moving the particle around in a circle over and over. This may one day allow a particle to achieve velocities approaching the speed of light.

She strokes my face. "I wish you could tell me that you'll snap out of it soon and everything will be all right."

But some theorists predict that accelerating a particle to such an extent will produce enough energy to create a small black hole.

Sadie says, "I'm so worried."

The anchorman pauses. He sets his jaw and looks stoic. The prospect of such an outcome, he says, would give the experiment a tiny but real possibility of destroying the Earth.

Monday morning, I bring a gun to the office because I'm ready. I'm ready if one of my former coworkers bursts in with an automatic rifle and starts executing secretaries. I'm ready if one of the custodians comes after me with the ax from the wall-mounted fire safety kit. I'm ready if the lobby explodes and flames shoot through the elevator shafts and the stairwells fill with black smoke. In that case I would go out the window.

Velcroed to the underside of my desk is a LALO, fast-open, base-jumping parachute rig. In thirty seconds, I can be strapped in and running full-out toward the floor-to-ceiling glass of the north wall. While I run, I will put a few slugs through the center pane to weaken it and then I will cover my face with my forearms and smash through into the sky.

My boss is sitting in my chair when I come back from the men's room. As I approach, I start fiddling with the zipper on my pants. It doesn't fool him. He says, "How many times have you washed your hands today?"

"I'm not sure."

"Try to understand my position."

I nod.

"I need you to be able to take care of yourself. I need to know that I can rely on you."

I nod again.

He leans back in my chair. "Do you remember what I said to you when I offered you this job?"

"You said you were worried I would be bored."

"Is that what's happening?"

"No."

"Do you feel you're having some sort of breakdown?"

"I'm questioning my assumptions."

If he makes a move, I can use my first shot to shatter his kneecap. Even the worst tough guy can't take that smiling. Probably my boss would drop his coffee and crumple to the floor. I would stand and walk around my desk and put the next shot straight into the top of his head.

"How's the Molesky thing?"

"Not bad. I'm meeting with his partners this afternoon."

"You think that's necessary?"

"They called me. They want to meet in some park down by the waterfront."

"And you think that's safe?"

"I'll be careful."

He nods. "I suppose you're right. It's just, they seem so unsavory. Why have contact with them if you don't have to?"

"I won't live in fear," I tell him.

One of them has a pasty-white chemotherapy complexion and steel-wool chest hair. The other is young and dark. They wear thick gold chains and silk shirts with the necks wide open.

They are sitting together on a green bench with cement feet. They are surrounded by trees. Looming behind them over the trees is the Mad Russians Car Repair and Limousine Service garage. It is the only building I can see.

The paler one stands to meet me. He slaps his hand against one of the trees. "To protect from parabolic microphone," he says. He puts out his hand. "I am Victor." We shake. "This is Michael." Victor leans toward me. "Michael, he don't speak English so good like me." Victor sucks on his teeth. "They frisk you already, yes?"

"Yes."

"I know they did. Otherwise you would have not get through. We own this park. They use metal detector, too?"

"Yes."

"Maybe you think we too careful?"

"No."

"Well," he says, "everybody is careful about something. Some man want to know all the time where is their woman. Some people afraid to drive car. I have a friend he don't like to fly because he don't understand how plane stay up. He is all the time waiting to fall, waiting to fall." He shrugs. "Me, I like fly."

"Me, too."

"Please sit down," he says.

I sit.

"Look down at your chest."

On my chest is a small dot of red light, the size of a pencil eraser.

"You know what this is?" he says.

"Yes," I tell him.

"You not scared?"

"Not really."

"How come you not scared? Because you know I am businessman so probably I don't kill you?"

I shake my head.

He smiles. "Because maybe you think you are like Superman?" He beats a fist against his chest. "You think bullet no hurt if it hit you?"

"No," I say. "It would hurt."

"So why you not scared?"

"Because there could always be a rifle pointed at me. Why should it be scarier just because I can see it?"

He says something in Russian. Michael says something back.

Victor turns back to me. "We think you are maybe very brave man."

I shrug.

He says, "I hope you not offended by rifle. Is necessary these days. These days, you frisk somebody, he still have bomb in his shoe and he blow himself up with you. Is crazy."

"Maybe he has packets of Sarin gas in his tooth fillings."

Victor holds up his hand. "So please you don't make sudden move because rifle always there. Because I don't know if you crazy."

"I'm not crazy," I say.

He takes a breath. "Is difficult way to live. People think is difficult in Russia, but in Russia you don't have to be scared of badman because you know why? Because is businessman. He want something. You give him, then probably you okay. But you find man who say I kill you because I enjoy or because God tell me, then you have crazy man and you can't say what he do and what he don't do."

At night it is completely dark in this spot. You can see stars that you never see from anywhere else in the city. They look like glowing powder. I know this because I was gazing at the sky last night while I duct-taped handguns to the underside of each of these benches. I had to put one on each because I didn't know where I'd be sitting.

Victor says, "And these crazy man is everywhere now. Okay, maybe not so much here. A few, but maybe not so much. Yes. Okay. But we has business all over the world. We go Africa. We go Uzbekistan. Sometimes Pakistan."

Packed into the dirt around the cement feet of each bench is enough C-4 to take the thing out of the ground and send pieces of its occupants flying all over. I have radio detonators hidden in the heels of my boots.

"Okay," Victor says, "so maybe we decide don't go, is too dangerous. You need protect yourself. But also you need take advantage of opportunity. Maybe everybody else scared to go so you go and you beat competitors and nothing bad happen. So maybe is good thing world is dangerous place because is easy to get success if you know how to be brave."

Somewhere on the ground behind me, covered with leaves, I have a 7.62 mm Dragunov SVD rifle with a forty-magnification starlight night scope. The rifle is fully assembled and wrapped in an oilcloth.

Victor is looking at me. "You are afraid of these man I mention?"

I shrug.

"You should be," he says. "If you Russian, if you American, they want kill you. I go Afghanistan when I am young man and I see these people crazy. And now they kill you when you go in restaurant or when you fly on plane or when you at work. But sometimes, you so worried about people like this you can't see how dangerous is the people right in front of you."

If it starts to break down, I will roll over the back of my bench and crouch behind its cement foundation. I will have to move very quickly and roll at an angle so as to ruin the sniper's aim. In the same motion, I will cover my ears and touch off the C-4 under Victor and Michael's bench. The cement will shield me from the concussion. The smoke from the explosion will blind the sniper. I will grab the pistol from under my bench to use against the bodyguards who will converge on me. I will pull the rifle out of the leaves and sling it across my chest in case, at some point, I have to take out the sniper.

I will have to remember to keep moving. If I hole up, they might send in dogs to find me.

"Is this why you asked me here?" I say.

"You know why I ask you here. I ask you here to talk about Sasha's murder."

"What about it?"

Victor smiles. "You meet Irina? She is very beautiful, no?"

"She's all right."

"And you meet also her maid? So, on night that Sasha disappear, this maid see him leave house with a man she know is old friend of Mrs. Molesky. She say she seen this man many times. He come to house, sometimes to see Sasha and they drink tea together and they make chess and they friends. So, okay. But also, she say, this man come sometimes when Sasha away. He come to see Mrs. Molesky, but she don't know what they do together. Maybe they also drink tea. Okay, so, but this maid she don't like go to police because maybe they make trouble for her because maybe she is not really citizen. So, I wasn't always citizen, but I take test and I say she could do same thing and then she don't have to be scared. But for now, I tell her, we wait to tell police and first I go find this man and I ask him if maybe he know something about what happen to Sasha."

He clears his throat. "So, we find him and we ask and he say he don't know nothing. And I say but you was with him on the night he get killed and maybe you see something and then he don't want to say. So we ask him again and he still don't want to say."

He says something in Russian. Michael smiles.

"So, we ask again and this time we really ask and this time he tell us. He say, he love Irina and she decide she want him to kill Sasha and pretend is some kind of gangster who kill him. Some kind of Marlon Brando. Okay, so he find this other man to help him and they take Sasha and they kill him and then they cut off thumbs and they put him in parking lot and they wait for police to find and say, Marlon Brando do this."

He spreads his hands. "So, we go and find other man and we tell him say if it's true and he don't want to say either. But then we ask him until he do say and it's true."

When he finishes, we are silent for a while.

"Why did you want to tell me this?"

He nods. "Here we come to this part: I want to know who get this money if Irina do not."

"Probably it would be split evenly among the children."

He nods.

"Of course, before I make that determination, I'll have to talk to Mrs. Molesky again."

He smiles. "Maybe she no be there when you go."

I don't say anything.

He says, "I like you. You are brave man. You are young. I hope you don't have to tell police what I just say about Mrs. Molesky."

"I like you, too. I'm glad you didn't push things too far."

He frowns. "I think maybe I don't follow you. I just want to make sure everything okay about Irina."

I sigh. "Are you the beneficiary of her life insurance?"

He narrows his eyes. "I don't think so."

I nod. "Then it's really not my business."

There is a tiny but real possibility that tomorrow will be the beginning of the revolution. If the system collapses, you will be ready to fill the void and prevent the slide into anarchy. You will assign jobs and ration food and gasoline and establish a command-and-control structure. You will provide for basic needs. You will build the whole world from the ground up. You will be king.

Of course, you hope none of this will be necessary.

Of course you hope that.

HIGHWAY

Eddie would not stop staring at the radio. He said that the V of the metal antennae reminded him of a girl with her legs spread. The radio sat on a narrow shelf above the grill. The man working the grill was so big that he was blocking Eddie's view. Eddie leaned forward in his chair and stretched his neck, trying to get a better angle. Carl reached across the table and snapped his fingers next to Eddie's face.

Eddie drew himself upright, startled. "Hey," he said. "What'd you do that for?"

"You're embarrassing me," Carl said.

"I was just having fun."

"You were acting like a goddamn retard."

Eddie's eyes narrowed. "I ain't no retard."

"Well, that's what everybody in here thinks now, watching you carry on like that."

"They don't think that," Eddie said.

"Have it your way. I thought you wanted to be normal."

"I do."

"Well, I'm just trying to help you."

"I know. I just forgot."

Carl shook his head. "Sometimes I don't know why I bother. Maybe I should leave it alone."

"No, please."

"Some people just don't want to change. I don't have to stay where I'm not appreciated."

"Please," Eddie said, reaching out to touch Carl's forearm. "Please, I'll be better."

Eddie and Carl sat by the door at a blue Formica table. Beside them was the high window that ran the length of the front wall of the diner. On the other side of the window was the parking lot and the white sun and the black line of the highway that disappeared, flat and uncurving, into the distance in both directions.

The waitresses wore blue dresses and white aprons. The three of them sat together at the far end of the room. They were the only other people in the diner. One of the waitresses was thin and old and hard. One of them was fat and old and hard. The third had smooth skin and dark blond hair that fell to her shoulders. When Carl put down his menu, the third waitress slid out of her chair. She swayed her hips slightly as she walked.

She stood beside the table and smiled at Carl. "What can I get you?" she asked him.

"What's good here?" Carl asked.

She shrugged. "It's all good."

He grunted. "That's quite a boy you have behind the counter."

"Luther?" the waitress said. "He's just like a big teddy bear."

"That so?" Carl said.

"He's the best cook we've had since I got here."

"When was that?"

"Two years ago."

He nodded. "And before that you were captain of the second-best cheer squad in the state."

"Third-best." She stared at him. "How'd you know that?"

Carl said, "We'll both have orange juice and coffee with cream—sugar in one—and I'll have the Denver omelet and he'll have the scrambled eggs and sausage and a side of French toast."

The waitress said, "How'd you know about the cheer-leading?"

"His eye-cue is one sixty-three," Eddie told her. "That means he's a genius."

She smiled at Eddie. "Where'd they test you?" she asked Carl. "Army?"

"Something like that," he said.

"Where were you stationed?"

Carl frowned. "All over."

"My brother's at Fort Leavenworth. You ever get up there?"

"Time to time."

"What were you doing you had to move around so much?"

"I'm not really supposed to talk about it," he told her.

"Mysterious," she said.

He stared at her.

"My name is Celia."

"That's beautiful."

"Thank you." She stared at him again. "Don't you have a name?"

Eddie glanced at him.

"My name is George," Carl said.

"And your friend?"

"Steve," he said before Eddie could answer.

"Nice to meet you both," she said.

When the waitress was gone, Eddie said, "I don't even *like* the name Steve."

Carl said, "I almost called you Lenny."

"I don't understand. Why's that funny?"

"Never mind."

Eddie scowled. "Hey, I didn't know you was in the army."

Carl ignored him. He was remembering the way it felt to run over the groundhogs or rabbits or even the occasional coyotes that tried to dash across the road in front of his car. He would swerve toward them, leading them slightly, hoping to get them just at the bottom of the spine. If he hit them right, he would crush their back legs and then he could watch in the rearview mirror as they poured blood, scrambling to stand. Sometimes, if the road was empty, he would pull to the side and sit on the hood and listen to the sounds the animal made as it tried to drag itself away. Sometimes he would stand over it on the hot black asphalt and spit in its fear-widened eyes or grind his heel on its mangled legs. But none of that was as good as the feeling just before the hit when he saw the thing disappear under the bumper and waited for the thump of the tire going over and maybe the ringing of the head against the underside of the car.

He watched Celia as she moved behind the counter and gave their orders to the enormous cook.

"You think she liked you?" Eddie said.

"Sure."

"You going to try her?"

"I don't know."

Celia brought the orange juice and coffee. Carl watched the muscles in her legs. When she was next to him again, he examined her soft, hairless arms.

"Who gets the sugar?" she asked.

Carl pointed at Eddie. Celia set down their drinks.

"You must like it here," Carl said to her.

"Why do you say that?"

"Just a sense I get."

She nodded. "I love that everybody who comes in here is going somewhere."

"Makes you feel full of possibilities."

"It makes me feel like there are all these worlds around me that I'm not a part of."

"Makes you feel bigger and smaller at the same time."

She looked at him and did not say anything.

"Why don't *you* ever go?" Carl asked her.

"Where would I go?"

"Anywhere."

"You can't just go *any*where."

"We are," Carl said.

"You don't know where you're going?"

He shook his head. "We're just going."

Eddie was shifting restlessly in his chair.

Carl said, "You got a jukebox in here?"

Celia shook her head. "Just Luther's radio."

Eddie frowned. "It ain't even turned *on*."

Celia said, "I'll see if he can find some music for you."

She walked away from them and spoke to the cook. He nodded at her and turned on the radio. It was tuned to a blues station.

"That all right?" the cook said.

"It's all right," Eddie told him.

Eddie closed his eyes. His shoulders slumped forward slightly and he did not look quite so big.

The song ended and the station went to a newsbreak. When the lead story began, Eddie's eyes popped open and he said, "Turn that up."

Carl looked at him quickly. Luther glanced over his shoulder at them and turned up the volume on the radio. The announcer said what he had been saying all morning.

One of the old waitresses said, "I read where the cops think it might be the same fellas who set that girl on fire in Pennsylvania."

The other said, "I heard they raped the girls after they was dead."

"I heard they made the boy watch them do it."

"I heard he was still alive when they cut his thing off."

"Hell in a handbasket," the first one said.

Luther said, "Order up, Celia."

Celia brought their food on three plates. She had Eddie's

French toast balanced in the crook of her left arm. When she had put down the plates, she said, "I always told my mother I wanted it to make the news when I died."

Eddie looked up at her.

Carl said, "By the time that happens it won't do you much good."

"But it's how you know you were important," she said.

"But you don't want it like that," he said. He nodded at the radio.

"No," she said, "not like that."

She pulled a ketchup bottle from inside her apron and set it on the table. "I just want to be remembered."

"Those folks will be remembered." He nodded at the radio again. "Their names are on the front page of half the papers in the country."

She shuddered. "I don't think it's worth it."

Carl thought he saw Luther glance at him again. The newsbreak ended. Eddie poured a lake of ketchup in the center of his eggs and laid down neat lines of maple syrup on his French toast and began to eat.

When Celia was sitting at her table again, Carl stood and walked to the counter. Eddie was so concentrated on his food that he did not look up. Carl climbed onto one of the red swivel-top stools. Luther was spooning lard onto the grill from a white bucket.

Carl looked both ways to make sure there was no one near him. "You ever do any Lewisburg time?" he said quietly.

Luther did not turn around. "What makes you think I done time?" His voice was very soft.

Carl snorted.

Luther spread the lard with his spatula. He nodded. "No," he said. "Never Lewisburg."

"These people know?"

Luther glanced at the waitresses. "These people don't know nothing," he said.

"Luther your real name?"

Luther did not say anything.

"You know why I want to talk to you?" Carl asked him.

"I suppose I do."

"Eddie give it away with the radio?"

Luther shrugged. "A lot of things give it away."

"Yeah," Carl said. "Anyway, it appears we have a problem."

"Maybe."

"You know how to play Helen Keller?"

Luther nodded.

"So maybe we finish here and get back on the road and keep driving and you keep flipping your pancakes and the people here keep knowing nothing about nothing."

"I can live with that," Luther said. "But you have to leave the girl."

"What do you care about her?"

Luther shook his head. "She don't deserve that."

Carl glanced at Celia, who was pretending not to look at him. "What if I say no?" he said.

Luther turned around, the spatula still in his hand. He looked even bigger from the front. "Then you're right. We do have a problem."

"You think you can put us both down?"

"I think we can find out."

Carl stood up and walked back to the table. Eddie was still working through his eggs. Carl sat down across from him and poured ketchup beside his omelet. They ate in silence for a while.

When the state police car rolled off the highway and into the parking lot, Carl reached across the table and touched Eddie's hand. Eddie looked up and saw the car. He continued to eat, but more slowly.

Carl leaned back and unzipped his jacket and let his right hand fall into his lap.

The cops wore campaign hats with wide brims and powder-blue shirts with short sleeves. The first one in was short and thick with blond hair cut very close on the sides of his head. His partner was almost as tall as Eddie. The partner had brown hair and dimples.

The cops walked to the counter and did not sit. The short one said, "How you doing, Big Luther?"

Luther said, "Yourself?"

"Can't complain," the cop said. "I'll have an egg sandwich."

The tall cop said, "Make it two."

Luther went back to the grill.

The short cop swaggered toward the waitresses. The tall one leaned against the counter and looked at Carl and Eddie. Carl was picking at his omelet with his left hand so he could keep the right one in his lap.

"How you boys doing?" the cop said.

Carl smiled at him.

The cop said, "You from around here?"

Carl shook his head. "San Diego."

The cop frowned. "You don't look too San Diego."

Carl said, "What do you want me to do?"

The short cop was looking at them now.

"Where you fellas going?" the tall cop said.

Eddie put down his fork.

Carl said, "There some kind of problem?"

The tall cop said, "You been watching the news?"

"We've been on the road."

"From San Diego."

"That's right."

"That your Ford in the parking lot?"

"Yeah."

"How come you don't got California plates?"

"My sister's car."

The tall cop smiled. "You got all the right answers, don't you?"

Carl said, "We do something wrong?"

"I don't know," the tall cop said. "Did you?"

Eddie's hand was under the table.

Carl could feel the muscles tightening in his stomach.

Luther said, "Two egg sandwiches." He was holding a brown paper bag dotted with dark blotches of grease.

The tall cop paid him and took the bag without looking away from Carl and Eddie.

Luther said, "These boys been in here last night, too. I think they stayed at the Super 8. No way they could be the ones done them folks up north. They wouldn't have time for the drive."

"That's true," the cop said. He stood up from the counter. "You got a kind of a smart mouth," he said to Carl.

The short cop fell in behind him, looking mean.

Carl watched them through the window as they got back into the cruiser.

"Will they run the license?" Eddie asked him.

"They might. If they do, they'll probably wait until they're out of sight."

"Should we go?"

Carl waved to Celia. She came over.

"Are you done?" she asked.

He nodded. She took the check pad from the pocket of her apron and tore off the top slip. She put it on the table and kept her hand on top of it. She was smiling. She said, "I didn't know you were in here last night."

Carl was looking at Luther, but he was bent over the grill again with his back turned. Carl took a long breath and shifted his look to Celia. "I think you might make the news tonight."

Her smile wavered. "Why do you think that?"

"Because you've been talking to me."

The smile returned. "A girl talking to you isn't news."

Carl said, "Sometimes you make the news for being dead; sometimes you make the news for being alive."

She waited but he did not say anything more and she turned and took the dishes behind the counter.

In the parking lot Carl knelt in front of the Ford, holding his screwdriver. Eddie stood behind him, blocking the view from inside the diner. Carl removed the license plate and replaced it with one from the set he had stolen at the last rest stop. Then he and Eddie walked around to the back of the car and did the same with the rear license.

Carl pulled out of the parking lot and onto the on-ramp and merged with the traffic, which was heavier now than it had been when they pulled off. There were cars all around them. In the Ford, with the new plates, they looked just like everybody else.

THE ROPES

For the first day or so, even when I had visitors the doctors kept my room in velvet darkness and sometimes I couldn't tell whether I was awake. When I was sure I was awake, I wouldn't remember ever having slept. There were no clocks in my room. I had tried once to check the time on the digital watch one of the nurses had left on my bedside table, but the green light from the watch's face burned like a welding torch in the center of my brain.

It hurt to talk. Most of the time it hurt to open my eyes. I lay on my back and watched the glowing shapes that floated through my vision.

I couldn't remember the fight. The last thing I remembered was walking along the concrete aisle with the crowd screaming all around me. Spotlights made the ring rise up in front of me like a blue island in a sea of black. I wasn't sure how much to trust my memory, because the scene would always end just before I started up the stairs to the apron and it would always be followed by the same dream. In the dream, I was lashed to cliffs that overlooked the ocean. The dream was just as vivid as the memory. I could feel the waves crashing below me while gulls pecked at my heart.

I remembered bits and pieces of the day that led up to the fight. It had started out well for me. In the early morning, I had made love to a pretty green-eyed girl whose grandfather's great-grandfather had, indirectly, given orders to mine. Hers was Ulysses Grant. Mine, Thomas J. Folsom, had been with the Irish Brigade at Fredericksburg. It would have been more fiendish—or at least more interesting—if her grandfather's great-grandfather had (indirectly) killed mine. But Thomas Folsom was not even scratched at Fredericksburg. The Irish Brigade, however, took almost fifty percent casualties in a charge on the stone wall at Marye's Heights. The Union Army came at the wall in waves all afternoon. Before each charge the men would draw up wills and leave them with Headquarters Company. By the end of the day, they had lost more than seven thousand men in front of that wall. They never took it. I took Christina Grant-Stevenson at her parents' house in her childhood bedroom under a thumbnail moon.

A fter three days I could keep my eyes open most of the time and one of the nurses cracked the blinds in front of my window to let in a gray trickle of sunlight. The headache was constant. My eyes leaked. Everything I could see was blurred and doubled and squashed together. I had jumbled pictures of my mother sitting beside my bed and sometimes of my father sitting with her, but those scenes could have taken place fifteen minutes ago or fifteen years ago and I wouldn't have known the difference.

• • •

Toward the end of the week, the headache would go away for long stretches and I would feel almost clear again. I could eat a little. I could lift myself out of bed. I could walk some, but my balance still hadn't come back and when I went anywhere I had to hold myself up with my hands against the wall.

I was sitting up in bed when Connelly came in. He wore a white track suit with green trim. He was holding a tweed watch cap in his hands and mashing it nervously. My mother closed the book she was reading and stood. She looked too long at Pete Connelly. Then she turned to me.

"I'm going to the cafeteria to find your stepfather," she said.

Connelly nodded to her as she passed him. She didn't acknowledge it.

He chewed his lip.

"You want to sit?" I said.

He sat in the chair my mother had left.

"Congratulations," I said. "I hear you took the whole thing."

He shrugged.

"You trying for the Olympics next?"

He shook his head. "Turning pro." He squinted at me. "Your face don't look too bad."

"I guess not," I said.

"They have to pack your nose?"

"No."

"That's good. You ever have that?"

I shook my head.

"I've had my nose broke three times," Connelly said, "and it never hurts getting broke like it does when they pack it. They cram the gauze in so tight it makes your eyes swell up like a frog's. You feel like your head's gonna pop."

"Glad I missed it."

He nodded and then swiveled his head to look around the room. "You're a college boy, right?"

"That's right."

"Don't see too many college boys in Open class. Not at the finals, anyway."

"I won the Novice two years ago."

He stopped examining the room and looked back at me. "Novice ain't Open," he said. "Ain't even hardly the same sport." He took a breath. "You good in college?"

"Yeah."

"That ain't the same sport, either."

"No," I agreed.

"How many years you have left?"

"I graduated a month ago."

"Congratulations," he said.

"Thank you."

"You fight light-heavy there, too?"

"The last three years. As a freshman I fought middle."

"That musta been tough for you to make. You ain't built like a middle." He took a breath. "But you ain't really tall enough for light-heavy, either. You got kind of a tweener build. What's your walk-around?"

"One-eighty, one-eighty-one."

He gave a little whistle. "Goddamn. I'm walking around at one-eighty-eight before breakfast and buck-ass naked. Guy I beat in the local finals in Houston said he dropped down from one-ninety-four. I can't believe you made it past regionals."

"Thanks."

"I didn't mean it like that."

"Never mind," I said. "I know how you meant it."

We were silent for a while.

Then Connelly said, "When they carried you out, I thought you was dead for sure. You wasn't moving or anything. They put one of those orange boards under your head. Your arms was all floppy."

"I'm not dead," I said. I didn't know what else to say.

Connelly said, "If you really had been dead, I don't know if I woulda been able to fight anymore. I was in a neutral corner when they started working on you, so I was by myself, and I felt alone like I never felt before. I felt like the worst person in the world."

"It wasn't your fault."

He narrowed his eyes. "They told me you didn't remember what happened."

"My mother told me about it. Someone has a video."

"You gonna watch it?"

"I don't know."

He nodded. "Anyway, it don't matter if it was my fault. It still woulda been me that killed you." He took a breath. "For a couple hours, I tried to blame you. I said you was just a fool college boy and you had no business here if you wasn't prepared and you couldn't protect yourself. But the truth is if you're here you had to earn your way here and anybody can get hit wrong and so maybe it's nobody's fault. But it's hard to make yourself believe that."

"No one would have blamed you if I'd died."

"Your mother blames me anyway."

"She's my mother."

Connelly looked through the open blinds at the parking lot below my window. "What do the doctors say?"

"They don't understand this stuff too well. They say once the swelling goes down in my brain, I'll probably get everything back all the way. Motor skills, memory, stuff like that. But now that I've had one like this, I'm much more likely to have another. Or even one of the kind that you never come all the way back from. So I have to take it easy for a while and after that I can live a normal life. But no more boxing."

He looked away from the window and stared at me. "I'm sorry," he said.

"I was pretty much done anyway. I would've liked to take

a shot at the Olympics, but that was probably just college-boy fantasy." I took a breath. "I couldn't beat those guys," I said.

He didn't say anything.

My mother sat next to my bed, reading one of her mysteries. I watched her with my eyes slitted, keeping my breathing slow and regular, careful not to move. After a while, without looking up, she said, "Some girl named Christina came to see you a few times while you were coming out of it. Do you remember?"

"No."

"She seems sweet."

"They all seem that way. It doesn't mean much."

"You don't really believe that. You're just saying it because you like the way it sounds."

"How does it sound?" I said.

"Like your father."

She still wasn't looking at me. She kept turning the pages of her book.

"Have you heard from him?" I said finally.

Now she looked at me. "He called when he read about it in the paper."

"What did he say?"

"He asked how you were."

"What did you tell him?"

"I told him how you were."

"Did you tell Hal he called?" Hal was my stepfather.

She smiled. "Don't change the subject."

"You still want to talk about Christina? I went to school with her. She's from around here."

"You know her well?"

"Not really."

My mother sighed. "That's not an awfully safe way to behave these days."

"I'm careful."

"Apparently not."

"I meant . . . during."

She made a face. "I knew what you meant. Are you going to call her to tell her you're all right?"

"Can we not talk about this?" I said.

"Fine."

She went back to her book. I closed my eyes. We didn't say anything else until my stepfather came into the room much later.

"Hal," I said.

"Alex," he said.

He moved to shake my hand and then reconsidered and stood uncertainly next to my bed. My mother stood and kissed him on the cheek.

"I spoke to the doctor," he said. "They're a little concerned about you flying. Something about the pressure change."

"So, where does that leave us?" I said.

"Well, I was thinking maybe we should just drive."

"To New York? That's two thousand miles."

"I know that." He glanced at my mother. "We could make an adventure out of it. We'd stay in some fun hotel each night. It shouldn't take us more than four days."

"I'm fine to fly."

"Alex," my mother said, "if it's not safe it's not safe."

"What's the danger? A little headache? I can make my own decisions. I'm twenty-one years old."

"Not quite."

I sent them back to their hotel. Then I packed my suitcase and stood it against the wall. A young dark-haired nurse brought my dinner. When she was gone, I called Christina at her parents' house to tell her I was leaving. She didn't seem surprised.

· · ·

After a week in New York, I still wasn't sleeping. My appetite came and went. Car-horn blasts made my heart flip-flop and set off fireworks in my head.

Some nights I would leave Hal's apartment after dinner and walk to Madison Avenue and watch all the people hurrying out together or, if it was late, watch the couples hurrying home together. I would walk into the park, which would be almost deserted, and then walk across to the West Side, praying for someone to jump out in front of me and put up his fists and dare me forward. There would be no neutral corners. There would be no mandatory eight counts. I would put this man on the ground and then stomp him until my bootprints showed on his chest. Thick blood would ooze from his ears. If I were still angry enough, I might lift him up by his hair and smack his face again and again into the pavement until his skull opened and poured gray-yellow brains.

One night, on Amsterdam in the high seventies, I watched a homeless man steal a pair of shoes from an outdoor display. I could have taken two steps to my left and gotten in front of him, but he was mean drunk or mean crazy, or both, and as he passed I could smell his antiseptic, old-sweat, hospital smell, which made me very sad. I didn't move. He jogged away with the shoes clutched against his stomach like a baby.

Walker, my stepbrother, came over from his mother's place in the West Village to take me to a movie.

We sat on the aisle. I used a sip of Walker's soda to wash down one of the codeine-laced Tylenols the doctor had prescribed because the tiniest sounds were like hammers beating against my eardrums. My senses had become so acute that I imagined my blood had been replaced with liquid amphetamines. I was very aware of the warm bodies around me and the way the whole theater smelled like hot butter. I could feel armies of microbes covering all of us and scuttling in huge columns along the cement floor. Walker, who was tall and handsome like his father, slouched in his seat and told me about the end of his sophomore year and how drunk he had gotten. He told me about the summer internship he had just begun at his father's law firm.

He said, "After I graduate, I'll probably put in a couple years as a trader. Your quality of life is really a lot better there than it is as an analyst. The danger is that you get tracked differently and you might not be able to move up as high. But after those two years I'll go to law school. Definitely on the West Coast. Probably Stanford. Again, it's a quality-of-life decision. After that I'll make a determination about which firm to work for, based on opportunity for advancement as well as quality-of-life considerations. Also, I've already started paying into a retirement fund. If you start paying when you're eighteen, by the time you're sixty-five it's like winning the lottery."

"What about the writing?"

He nodded. "I almost forgot. Being a trader will also leave me some time to write on the side. I mean, you only really need to be in the office while the market's open. You also have to entertain clients in the evenings, but I'm sure I'll still find some time. Anyway, I'll give myself those two years to make it with the writing and if that doesn't pan out I'll still have done some serious résumé building." He shook a few M&Ms into his hand and tossed them into his open mouth. "I'm pretty sure it'll work out. I mean, sometimes I take passages from *Gatsby* and make little corrections that any editor in the world would tell you are improvements. I'm not saying it's not a great book, I'm just saying there are some things I do differently that are just objectively better. I've been wanting to talk to you about that." He sipped his soda. "What about you? Do you know what you're gonna do now?"

"No," I said.

During the movie, whenever I felt the nausea coming I just closed my eyes and pressed my palms against my ears and mostly I was all right. Afterward, Walker took me to a party at his girlfriend's parents' duplex on Park Avenue. Bass from the stereo shook the floor. The air tasted like beer and sweat. I sat in an armchair and talked to a girl who had just finished her junior year at Dartmouth. We had to shout to hear each other over the music.

She was saying, "I just don't know if people realize how fucking good *The Waste Land* is. I mean, they say they know, but it's just so fucking good."

"Yes," I yelled at her, "it's very good."

"It's like Picasso. Or *Middlemarch*. Everybody always tells you how good they are. But they're really, *really* good. It's amazing."

"Are you studying English?"

She nodded. "I think maybe I'd like to be a writer. I keep meaning to be disciplined about it."

"That sounds like a good idea."

"I'm going to Tahiti this summer. I'm going to see some of the places Gauguin painted. I spent last semester in France. I visited his house. He's another one. Do you realize how good he was? How fucking *good*?"

"I think so," I told her.

When I came home, my mother was reading in the living room. I sat down next to her and turned on the television. The television was showing baseball highlights.

"Did you have fun?" my mother asked.

I shrugged.

"It was nice of Walker to want to take you out. It was his idea, you know?"

I took a breath. "I've been thinking I might go visit Dad for a while."

She was silent for a long time. Then she said, "Fine."

"Do you want to talk about it?"

"I told you it's fine. I think it's a good idea."

"I'm happy to talk about it if you want to."

"I'm trying to read," she said.

The bus went along Central Park West past buildings that looked like stretched-out Renaissance palaces—the Dakota, the San Remo, the Beresford—until the park ended and then across and uptown through East Harlem and then onto the raised highway into the Bronx. We passed over dull garages and bodegas with bright signs and the bombed-out skeletons of old warehouses. We passed boarded-up apartment houses and enormous political campaign banners and billboards that carried advertisements for the state lottery and for an amusement park and for a newsmagazine show.

The man next to me had his clothes packed into gray garbage bags that he had stuffed into the roof racks. Two rows in front of us, a baby was crying. When we got out onto the highway, the driver started the movie, which played on tiny screens mounted on the ceiling. I pressed my face against the air-conditioned glass of the window and tried to sleep.

During the layover in Boston, I went into the station men's room and splashed water in my eyes and rubbed at the sleep creases in my face.

In Boston, the baby and the man with the garbage bags got off and were replaced by young couples with straight teeth and matching luggage sets. We drove out of Boston and into the country for a while and then across the bridge to the Cape. We drove through narrow streets between clapboard houses and down to the dock, where the bus sighed to a stop.

The ferry was already docked when I stepped down off the bus. I went inside the Steamship Authority building and bought my ticket. I walked through the back door and up the ramp to the gangplank, which creaked in the wind, and across onto the ferry.

I sat outside on one of the white benches near the bow and waited for the cars to load. Some of the cars were delivery trucks. Some were old and dented. But mostly they were Mercedes and BMWs with new finishes that gleamed in the sun. When the cars were loaded, their passengers pulled themselves up the metal stairs to the deck. Most of them were families dressed in white polo shirts and no socks. As we pulled away, I looked over my shoulder and watched the low wooden houses of Woods Hole shrink into the shoreline and then watched the shoreline shrink into the ocean. Then I turned around and watched the water rushing past.

Gulls flew with the ferry. Sometimes one would land on one of the masts. He would sit for a while and then fly away and start circling again and another gull would take his place.

Two of the truck drivers stepped out of the snack bar in the middle of the upper deck and stood together by the railing. They spoke to each other quietly and laughed and spit into the water.

My father was waiting in the parking lot at Vineyard Haven. He was standing beside his truck, talking to the men who would direct the unloading of the cars. They were all smiling. Behind them the sun was setting. When he saw me, my father stopped smiling and nodded. He said something to the men. They glanced in my direction.

My father came toward me. He was wearing old blue jeans and a short-sleeved khaki dress shirt. He hugged me and I stood holding my bags, not sure whether to put them down.

He stepped back. "You feel all right?" he said.

"Sure."

"How was the trip?"

"Long."

He nodded. He took the bags out of my hands and walked back toward the car.

The night my father had his retina detached by Earnie Shavers in front of a full house at Madison Square Garden, he weighed one hundred ninety-seven pounds. Now he was at least twenty pounds over that. But he carried it well.

"He caught me with a lucky right hand at the end of the fourth," my father would say when he told the story. "The doctor stopped it between rounds. Shavers had dynamite in both hands. I once heard an old fighter say every time Joe Louis hit him with a jab it felt like he was smashing a light-bulb against his face. Well, Shavers didn't have Louis's jab, but when he landed that steam-shovel right it felt like all the lights in Yankee Stadium just got cracked against my skull. It was like a fire alarm going off inside my head. He had the best straight right I ever saw. Foreman had thunder in his right, but he didn't really throw it straight. Besides, I was never in with Foreman. I would put Shavers's right up there with Dempsey's or Louis's or Marciano's. Of course, I was never in with them, either. Anyway, Shavers had big-league power. But he had kind of a soft chin. If he hadn't caught me with that lucky right, who knows?" My father would pause here and look around at his audience long enough for them to take in his ruined nose and the drooping muscles around his left eye. "If the fight had gone on, maybe I would've been able to hurt him." He would smile. "If I'd done that, he would've killed me."

He slid my bags behind the backseat and hopped up into the truck. I climbed into the passenger seat. My father started the engine. As we pulled out of the parking lot, he gave the men on the dock a little mock salute.

"How long you planning to stay?" my father said.

"I'm not really sure." I looked at him. "That okay?"

"Of course it's okay," he said.

We were driving along the two-way road that curved

through the middle of the island. The houses were all set
back in the trees. They were invisible from the road.

"How you fixed for money?" my father said. "You want
me to get you on with Dave Mayhew? Or Billy Sanders's
crew?"

"Maybe. See if Billy can use another roofer."

My father frowned. "You sure? I could ask Billy to let
you drive one of the trucks and do some light carpentry or
something."

"I'll make a lot more roofing. Plus I'll get a tan."

"We can talk about it later. Maybe you'll take it easy for a
couple weeks just to humor the old man."

"I've *been* taking it easy."

He made the turn onto North Road. "How's your mother?"

"She's fine."

"She say anything when you told her you were leaving?"

"Not really."

He chuckled. "I'll bet she can't understand why you'd ever
want to come back here. She couldn't stand it. When we
moved out here, she thought I was a big shot just 'cause I'd
seen some money. She thought we were gonna get invited to
cocktail parties. Thought she was gonna be chairwoman of
the Chilmark sewing circle. But you can't buy your way into
that."

"I guess not."

He nodded. "It ain't like as soon as you put a little cash
together you get invited down the Cape with Ethel Kennedy.
It don't work that way."

"No," I agreed.

"It don't really bother me, you understand. I mean, at the
beginning I felt bad for your mother." He grunted. "But she
wised up quick, boy. You better believe she wised up."

"Maybe we shouldn't talk about her."

He shrugged. "Whatever you want."

"You tell anybody I was coming in?"

"I told Charlie McClure. He'll tell Tommy."

"Tommy still living at home?"

He nodded. "So's Luke Hanlan. Tommy and Luke're working for Billy these days."

We turned off the main road onto one of the dirt roads into the woods. The truck bounced over the ruts, just clearing the trees on both sides. We took a few turns and then suddenly the trees opened up into a clearing and there was my father's house. We parked on the gravel in front. Behind the house was a huge yard with a swimming pool and a hot tub. Past that, the trees closed in again like a wall.

"The truck looks funny parked in front of this place," I said.

My father smiled. "I know," he said. "It looks like the caretaker's truck."

In his sweltering office outside Oak Bluffs, Billy Sanders said, "I'd pay you just like I pay all the other carpenters. Obviously it's not like the roofers, but your old man says you might still be having some problems with your balance and I can't be responsible for that. Also, there's a few things we have to get straight. For one, you wear long pants and steel-toes on my jobs. I know some of the other guys are lax about that but that's not my problem. Also, I ever catch you stoned, you're gone right there. That kind of shit puts everyone at risk. If I have to, I'll start piss-testing everybody twice a month."

"I can live with that," I told him.

"I'll bet you can."

He started me at a tiny reshingling job in Oak Bluffs. In the course of that first morning, I discovered that the shock that traveled up my arm every time I swung my hammer made me feel like my eyes were bleeding. The second time I puked, Billy sent me home.

The rest of the day I lay on my father's couch, popping codeines and watching television. I imagined what it might be like to unscrew my head and crack open my skull and use steel wool to scrape the bruises off of my steaming brains.

The next day Billy sent me to Boston with Tommy McClure to pick up a load of Italian marble. On the ferry on the way back to the island, we ran into a pair of Sun Transport drivers. They sat with us at one of the indoor tables.

"How come Sanders didn't get us to move that stuff around for you?" one of them said. "He doesn't like his jobs done right?"

"He didn't want it to end up on the floor of some bathhouse," Tommy said.

"There you go," the other one said.

"There I do go," Tommy said.

"Who's your friend?" the first driver said. "I ain't seen him around."

"He's Galahad Kincaid, the famous race-car driver. He's here on his honeymoon."

"I'm the man who shot Liberty Valance," I said.

The first driver sighed. "You gonna tell us who he is?"

"Sure," Tommy said. "He's Alexander Folsom, the famous prizefighter."

The driver rolled his eyes.

"No, really. He's the kid who almost got killed at the Golden Gloves. It was on the news. You musta seen it."

The first driver stared at me. "That really you?"

I shrugged.

He said, "Didn't your father go the distance with Jerry Cooney?"

"Quarry," I said.

"What?"

"It was Jerry Quarry."

He nodded. Then he glanced at his friend. "Must be tough," he said, "being Ron Jeremy when your old man's Johnny Wad."

I shrugged again. "I don't really think about it much. Besides," I said, "your wife doesn't seem to feel the difference." All four of us laughed at that. The first driver pounded me on the shoulder. The other passengers didn't look at us.

When the announcement came over the loudspeaker, we walked down inside the cargo bay and sat in the truck while the ferry was brought into its slip. The cars were unloaded one row at a time. When it was our turn, I drove across the ramp and out of the parking lot and through the intersection at Five Corners.

When we got to Edgartown, Tommy said, "Slow, now. I sometimes miss the driveway."

I slowed the truck. We passed a deer-crossing sign.

"On the left," Tommy said.

I eased the truck onto the dirt path through the woods and drove straight until the trees opened onto an overgrown field. The road curved around to an iron gate in the middle of a tall hedge. I stopped in front of the gate and Tommy jumped down and unlatched the gate and swung it open. I drove through. He closed the gate and jumped back up beside me. We were on a cement driveway in the middle of an enormous lawn. The lawn slanted up gradually to the edge of a cliff and behind that was the ocean. Just in front of the edge of the cliff was the biggest house I had ever seen. A few hundred feet away from the house was another house maybe half its size. Scaffolding covered the smaller house like vines.

Tommy said, "You're not gonna believe this place, kid."

The big house was five stories tall and had a huge deck in back facing the ocean. From the front of the house, you could see an immense piece of the island. You could see other houses built into the cliffs and long empty private beaches and huge fields filled with grazing cows. But you couldn't see any of the cars passing on the road below. The view of the road was blocked by the hedge and the trees.

Billy waved us over and we began unloading the boxes of eighteen-by-eighteen-inch filled-travertine tiles and straining to lay them softly on the dolly. When the dolly was full, we rolled it up the ramp and into the foyer of the smaller house. The walls of the foyer had already been painted linen white. We rolled the dolly across the plywood subfloor of the foyer and into the living room and stacked the boxes against the wall.

As we were loading another set of boxes onto the dolly, a new-looking Lexus SUV came through the iron gate and along the driveway and pulled up in front of the big house, spraying gravel. I used my forearm to wipe the dust and sweat out of my eyes.

Tommy glanced at me and didn't say anything.

The girl who got out of the SUV had dark brown hair that fell to her shoulders. She wore sunglasses and gray knit shorts and a yellow tank top. Her legs were tan all the way down past her ankles.

The hammering on the roof stopped. Billy Sanders was standing near the entrance to the smaller house, by the base of the scaffold. He pretended not to notice any of it. The girl walked up the stone steps and into the house. The hammering started again.

"Jesus Christ," Tommy murmured. "Jesus, my good Christ."

I shrugged. "Plenty around like her."

He snorted. "Not around me."

"She's too short for you. Also, girls like that don't age well. They shrivel up like raisins. They end up having to buy new faces every few years."

"Just once I want to know what it's like to be with a girl like that."

"It's like being with any girl."

He shook his head. "I'll bet her pussy tastes like peaches and cream."

"Vinegar," I said.

"You're a cynic," Tommy told me.

Billy Sanders shuffled over to us. "How's your head?" he asked me.

"Fine as long as I stay out of the sun."

"What do you think happened yesterday?"

"I'm not sure. Good days and bad days."

He nodded. "Any time you need a break, just say so." He scratched his chin. "No need to be a hero."

There were never fights on the island. It did not have the seamy side of Gloucester or Provincetown, where every so often two fishermen would carve each other into jigsaw puzzles outside some waterfront bar. In those places, especially during the off-season, there would be times when one of the fishing boats would chug back into the harbor one man short. The crew would tell stories of freak squalls and rogue waves taller than the mast. As far as they could figure, the lost man must have been washed overboard in the dark. It was impossible to investigate cases like that. As long as the crew kept telling the same story, the event joined the legend of the place and the name of the vanished man joined a list on a monument in the town square built to honor locals lost at sea. Most of the time, of course, the story was true. But once in a while the thing would smell wrong and everyone would know it and nothing would ever be done about it but the feeling of it would hang over everything like a fog. In a place like that, you could feel the violence in your sweat.

The island was not that way. There was alcoholism in the local population and there were lean winters as in any summer town, but the place was not threatening. This was a source of disappointment for me during the days I spent imagining how I would meet the girl from the big house in Edgartown. I wanted to pull her out from the middle of a brawl between Portuguese fishermen. I wanted to save her from a mob of drunken sailors. I wanted to discover her being harassed by a giant longshoreman and step between them and push her behind me.

The longshoreman would grin like a crocodile. He would swing at me with a fist the size of a cinder block. I would step to the side and let him stumble past me and hit him on the ear with the heel of my hand, which was what my father had taught me to do if I ever had to fight without gloves. He would come at me again and I would step inside his next punch and bring my elbow straight down on the bridge of his nose. Blood would pour like a dam had broken. Then his knife would be out. I would keep my eyes locked on the knife hand. When he slashed, I would suck myself up away from the blade. We would circle for a while. He would be tired by now because he was so big. Eventually, he would move too slowly with the knife and I would grab his wrist and pull myself toward him and thumb him hard in the Adam's apple. That would be the end of it. The knife would clatter to the pavement and he would sink to his knees. I would take the girl's hand and walk down the street with her, leaving the enormous longshoreman on the ground behind us, holding his neck with both hands, trying to grunt the pain away.

It didn't happen like that. What happened was that I ran into Thatcher Harrison at the supermarket in Vineyard Haven.

I was with my father. He was leaning forward on the handlebars of his shopping cart, pushing it absently in front of him. We were in the freezer section.

My father was saying, "Get a couple of the family-size lasagnas. We're almost out. Also, get the big pack of chicken cutlets and that ice cream you like."

Thatcher came around the corner at the far end of the

aisle. He didn't notice me. He was talking to a young girl who kept trying to climb into his cart. When he came close, I said his name and he jerked his head toward me. Then he smiled. "Alex," he said.

We shook hands. I introduced him to my father. He introduced the girl, who turned out to be his sister.

"How long are you here?" he asked me.

"Not sure."

"Don't you have to get back to start your job?"

"No job," I said.

He gave me the phone number at his parents' house on the island. I gave him my father's number. We said good-bye and they moved past us down the aisle.

"He lived on the floor below me," I told my father.

"Looks like a frat boy," he said.

"Not his fault."

"Also, what kind of name is Thatcher?"

"He's all right," I said.

My father shrugged. "Have it your way."

That night, while my father and I were eating canned beef stew and instant biscuits, sitting on the couch in the living room so that we could watch the baseball game, Thatcher called to invite me to a party.

Two-tenths of a mile after the sign for East Chop, I passed the stone wall and the cluster of mailboxes that Thatcher had used as landmarks in his directions. At the light blue mailbox, I turned onto the dirt road into the woods. The road curved around to the right and then I could hear the music. When the trees opened, I saw the ocean and the glow from the fire. The flat stretch of sand in front of the dunes was filled with cars. I parked my father's truck off the road next to a green Land Rover. I walked between the parked cars toward the fire.

Open coolers full of ice and beer rested on the sand at the

foot of the dunes. The big stereo sat next to them on a lawn chair. In front of the stereo, down toward the water, was the bonfire. People were strewn all over, dancing or lying on blankets in the sand or drinking and talking in tight circles.

I walked down one of the dunes and took a beer from the cooler. The flickering of the fire made my stomach churn. My vision blurred. I felt as though I was on the pitching deck of a ship. I sat down in the sand and held the cold, sweating beer can against my forehead.

Thatcher sat down next to me. He was wearing jeans and a blue dress shirt with the sleeves rolled up. He had a navy sweater tied around his shoulders. "I was hoping you'd come," he said.

"This your party?"

"Not really. Some friends of mine own this beach."

"How nice for them."

"Isn't it?" He smiled. "You want to come let me introduce you around?"

"Give me a second."

"You still recovering from that thing?"

"I hope so. I'm still feeling it, anyway."

"Must be rough."

I shrugged. "I'm used to it now. It's part of my day-to-day. If it went away, I think I might actually miss it."

He looked at me. "You really believe that?"

"I don't know. Maybe I just said it."

We sat and drank together. The light from the fire played tricks with my vision and when I first saw her I thought it was my imagination. It would have been easy, through the heat shimmer, to have seen her face on another girl. I stared for a while. The face didn't change.

"Who's that?" I said.

Thatcher squinted into the firelight. "Which one?"

"In the white sweater. Talking now. Just touched the elbow of the girl next to her."

"Jamie Mitchell."

"What's funny?"

He shook his head. "Nothing."

"That bad?"

"You up to another beating?"

"For her?"

He shrugged. "I'll take you over."

We stood. I brushed the sand off my jeans. Jamie Mitchell was standing with several other people. They were close enough to the fire that I could feel the heat on my skin as we walked toward her. When we arrived, the group stopped talking and looked at us.

"This is Alex," Thatcher said. "We went to college together."

The people in the circle introduced themselves. A kid with curly hair and a shell necklace said, "Where are you staying on the island?"

"My father has a house near Menemsha," I told him.

"What does he do?"

"As little as possible."

I looked around the circle and paused too long when I came to Jamie. I lowered my eyes. My heart was beating so hard I thought it might choke me.

"I love your sweater," she said.

I was wearing an old gray cable-knit sweater of my father's. "I think it's called a fisherman's sweater," I said.

She nodded. "I've never seen one like it."

The curly-haired kid said, "It's like the kind Picasso used to wear."

"Those were striped," someone said.

"I mean the *style*," the kid said.

"Also, Picasso's were more jerseys than sweaters. I think they were Cuban or something."

"I don't know about Cuban," someone else said and then the conversation was away from me.

Jamie moved over so that she was standing next to me. "I know you," she said.

"That's not impossible."

"You're working on my fiancé's house."

"Your fiancé," I said.

"Well, it's not really *his*. It's his family's."

I didn't say anything.

"You look like an athlete," she said.

"So do lots of people," I said.

"He's a boxer," Thatcher said.

"Not anymore," I said.

Thatcher turned to me. "You didn't tell me that."

I shrugged.

"What happened?" Jamie asked me.

"I got hurt."

"Were you a good boxer?"

"Yes."

"Could you have been a professional?" she said.

"Anyone can be a professional. All you have to do is pass the physical."

"Could you have been a champion?"

"No."

"Could you have come close?"

"No."

"I thought you were good."

"I am."

"I don't think I could ever hit anybody," she said.

"Almost everybody thinks that before they do it." I took a breath. "When I was five years old, my father brought me home a tiny pair of gloves. He showed me how to put them on and lace them up and make sure they were tight enough. Then he got down on his knees in front of me and told me to hit him."

Jamie's eyes were wide. "Did you?"

"Not at first. I just stared at him. Then he said, 'Hit me. You won't kill me.'"

"So you hit him."

I nodded. "All you need to learn is that you can hit him

and he can hit you and that it might hurt but you're not going
to kill each other."

"Except sometimes," she said.

I nodded again. "Except sometimes."

The next day was Sunday and the hours stretched
out like a desert. I went down into my father's
basement and lifted his weights for a while. When I was
done, I went running. I ran through the headache. The sun
was heavy on my shoulders. My breath came in gasps and
moans. Cramps seared my chest. When I got back, I walked
back and forth along the porch with my hands on my hips.
My throat felt raw. I coughed a few times and spit into the
bushes.

I sat on the couch and thought about how I didn't have
anything. The thought didn't give me any of the delicious
self-pity thrill I was expecting. My father wandered downstairs from his bedroom. He flopped down across from me in
his armchair.

"Why wasn't I a better fighter?" I said after a while.

He stared at me. "I didn't think you cared too much about
that."

"Sometimes I wanted it so badly I thought I'd go crazy."

"Maybe you just want it now that you can't do it anymore."

"Why didn't you ever come watch me?"

He shrugged. "Who needs to watch two middle-class college boys fight? Fighting's what you do when you can't think
what else to do. Middle-class boys always have something
else. They don't need it enough to be good at it."

"What about Ali?"

"Ali's *black* middle class."

"That makes no difference to me."

"I'll bet it makes a difference to him."

I chewed my lip. "Anyway," I said, "why didn't you come
watch me just because I was your son?"

He shifted his weight, which made the chair creak. "I don't need to watch my son try to be a thug."

"Then why did you teach me at all?"

"I also didn't want you to be one of those lily rich boys who doesn't know how to take care of himself. But there's a long way between that and being able to handle the real bangers."

"The guys I saw at the Gloves weren't bunnies."

He nodded. "Look what they did to you," he said.

I didn't call Thatcher Harrison for her phone number or to ask him to arrange another meeting. I didn't go to work every day at the house in Edgartown praying for her to show up. I was happy not to be seeing her again. I was happy during the bright mornings and the hot, lazy afternoons and I was very happy at night when I would lie in bed and dream I had been washed overboard and dragged away by the tide.

Thursday evening, my father and I met Billy Sanders and Dave Mayhew at the bar in Oak Bluffs. We sat at a table by the window. We all ordered beer.

The waitress squinted at my driver's license when I gave it to her. "Happy birthday," she said. She gave the license back to me.

"I remember my twenty-one," Dave Mayhew said when the waitress had gone.

"I don't," Billy Sanders said.

"I was with two girls at once," Dave said. "It was the only time."

"How much that cost you?" Billy said.

"Didn't cost me nothing."

"Like hell. You're not Sinatra."

Dave smiled. "My old man paid."

"Nice of him," my father said.

"I thought so."

"That the plan for tonight?" Billy said. "I could give him tomorrow off if he's having trouble walking."

"Having trouble walking anyway," I said.

"That's true. Good thing your father's got friends in high places."

"Like who?" Dave said.

Billy ignored him. "Otherwise you'd be out of luck. We don't really need a gimp on the job. Especially not one who can only work every other day." Billy had been drinking before he came to meet us. I hadn't noticed it until now.

"Go a little easy," my father told him.

"It's his birthday. Didn't you always take some on your birthday?"

"Sometimes. But that doesn't mean he has to."

This time when I saw her I was sure I was imagining it. We were on our third round of beers. I was looking across the street through the fading light and really it could have been almost anybody with the right body. She was with another girl. They were waiting in line outside the old wooden building that held the carousel. I watched them until they were out of sight inside the building.

When I turned back to the table, Dave Mayhew was smiling. So was my father.

Billy said, "That wouldn't be the girl who's marrying Greg Cunningham, would it?"

"How do you know I wasn't looking at the other one?"

He stared at me. "It *was* her, wasn't it?"

"It might have been," I admitted.

He shook his head.

"Your problem," I said, "is you've got no imagination."

He frowned.

My father said, "I spent my twenty-first birthday in jail."

We looked at him. He wasn't smiling anymore.

Dave said, "You never told me that."

My father shrugged. "It's not much of a story."

"Was it about a girl?"

"Why would you ask that?"

"I don't know. It seems as likely as anything else."

My father nodded. "But it wasn't jailbait and it wasn't any kind of restraining-order business."

"No," Dave said, "it wouldn't be that."

"As far as the cops were concerned, it wasn't about her at all. For them it was about her husband and whether he was gonna die."

"He come close?"

"Pretty close. He stayed in the coma almost three days."

"Rich man?"

"Rich man's son."

"He hit you first?"

"He didn't hit me at all. But he *swung* first."

"I suppose you told them that."

"Sure. But I had turned pro by then. My lawyer said it was the same as if he'd thrown a punch at me and I had pulled out a gun and shot him."

"What'd they want you to do?"

"Not use my hands, I guess. Maybe if I'd have just kicked him I would have been all right."

"You would have had to take off your shoes," Billy said. "Otherwise, the legal issue is still the same."

"I'm not sure he would have been willing to wait for that. He seemed quite anxious to get at me. Anyway, it wasn't really my hands that did the damage. It was the curb that got him on the way down. The cops didn't think too much of that distinction."

"Hard to blame the curb," Dave said. "It was just standing there."

"So was I," my father said. He sighed. "To be honest, I probably should have thought about the curb, but I hadn't fought outside a ring since I was fifteen. I forgot that on the street when they go down they don't just hit the canvas."

"Canvas can still hurt them if they hit wrong."

"Not like pavement." My father sipped his beer. "I was pretty dumb back then. You know, the thing that bothered me most in the lockup wasn't wondering how long I might be there or how I was gonna feel if he died. What really got under my skin was that the other prisoners didn't know who I was."

"You mean because if they'd known who you were they'd have left you alone?"

"They left me alone anyway. Everybody there was pre-trial. They were all on best behavior. I just wanted them to know who I was. I wanted them to know we might have come from the same kind of place but I was somebody now. I wasn't like them."

Dave frowned. "You were young."

"Yeah."

"If you went to jail now, they'd know you," I said.

My father shook his head. "No, they still wouldn't. But it wouldn't matter to me so much."

"Smart man," Billy said.

My father took a deep breath. Then he smiled. "Handsome, too," he said. "Rare for a white pug these days."

Dave smiled back at him and nodded. "After the fifties, the white guys got pretty unfortunate. Faces like chew toys and clumsy and no class."

"There were still some," I said. I was happy to be talking about something else.

"Some," Dave said. "But mostly they were like that Chuck what'shisname that knocked down Ali."

"Wepner," my father said.

Dave nodded again. "Wepner."

Billy said, "Why haven't I heard of him if he knocked down Ali?"

"Ali didn't stay down," Dave told him.

"Sometimes they won't," my father said. "It can be awfully discouraging."

"Right after the knockdown, Wepner was in the neutral corner and he leaned out and said to his manager, 'Start the car. We're going to the bank. We're millionaires.' "

"Premature," my father said.

Dave grinned. "The manager said, 'You might want to turn around before we start counting our money, 'cause he just got up. And he looks pissed.' "

"He was, too. He knocked Wepner out of the ring."

"Not all the way. But he took him apart. After the ref called it, Wepner almost couldn't make it back to his corner."

"At least he didn't make any excuses."

"Like Liston did. Neither of them could stay in with Ali, though."

My father shrugged. "Neither could most people."

We drank. I watched the carousel building. When Jamie and the girl with her appeared in the doorway, I pushed my chair back and said, "I have to go."

My father looked at me. "Where?"

I stood. "Thanks for the beers. I'll find my own way back."

"What should I tell your mother when she calls to say happy birthday?"

"Tell her I'll call her when I get back if it's not too late."

He waved his hand. "I'll let the machine answer," he said.

I was across the street and standing in front of her before I realized I didn't have anything to say. The other girl was staring at me.

Jamie smiled. "Hello," she said.

I felt her voice in my stomach. "I don't know if you remember me."

"Don't be silly."

I gestured toward the bar. "I was having a drink with my father," I explained. "I saw you out the window."

"Is that him on the left?"

"That's right."

She nodded. She turned to the other girl. "Stephanie Durham. Alex"—she turned back to me—"I forget your last name."

"Folsom."

I shook Stephanie's hand.

"I'm about to take Stephanie home," Jamie said. "You probably need to get back."

"Not really. I was feeling a little strange in there. Like my head was full of paint."

"Alex was injured in the ring," she told Stephanie. "He's a boxer."

"Really?" Stephanie said.

"No," I said, "but I used to be."

"Well," Jamie said, "would you want to take a ride? Stephanie lives in Chilmark."

"Maybe."

"The air might be good for you. If I stop in Menemsha, would you walk out on the jetty with me?"

"I don't see why not. It's down the road from my father's house."

She smiled. "It's my favorite place in the world."

We drove on the road that twisted along the north side of the island. There were forests on both sides and the road had been cut in between. It was easy to imagine the island before the road was here. It was easy to imagine the time when the seas were frozen and the island was lifted by glaciers the size of countries and laid down again and lifted again and laid down until the ice melted. It was easy to imagine the time before that when dinosaurs grazed over the ground where the yacht club now stands and stomped giant footprints into the private beaches.

We dropped Stephanie and got back on the road into Menemsha. We parked at my father's house and walked down toward the water. The sky was dark now. The air was full of mosquitoes.

"Your father was a boxer, too?" Jamie asked.

"You mean, because of his face?"

"Yes."

I nodded. "He was a boxer."

"Was he born here?"

I shook my head. "East Boston."

"When did he come?"

"When he stopped boxing."

"He brought your mother?"

"And me, but I was just a baby."

"And you lived here year-round?"

"Until she left him."

We walked along a fence past a yard with several dogs tied up inside it. The dogs turned their heads with us as we passed them.

Jamie said, "You graduated with Thatcher?"

"That's right."

"Do you know what you're going to do now?"

"I don't like to talk about it."

"What do you mean?"

"I don't like a lot of talk about plans. Most things you either do or you don't do. It doesn't help much either way to talk about it."

"I agree. Let's not talk about it."

"It doesn't leave much to talk about."

We passed Larsen's, the fish market, which was dark inside. The air tasted like salt. This close to the beach, there were no more mosquitoes. We walked through the parking lot beside the dock. We walked onto the sandy part of the parking lot and then up onto the sand and then onto the huge square stones that had been crammed together to make the jetty. We walked all the way out to the rusted light tower. In front of us we could see the blue light of the buoy and hear its bell ringing as the waves jostled it. In the darkness the water was like the top sheet on an enormous bed.

"I used to come here when I was a little girl," Jamie said.

"Pretty far from Edgartown."

"My family's house is out near Gay Head. I go to Edgartown to visit Gregory."

"I haven't seen you there lately."

"He usually only comes up on the weekends. He works during the week."

"Doing what?"

"Banking."

"Where?"

"New York."

"I meant, which bank?"

"Oh. Does it matter?"

I smiled. "Probably not. How did you meet him?"

"Our parents are friends. I've known him forever."

"How long have you been engaged?"

"A year."

I scraped my teeth against my lip. "I've never known anyone my age who was getting married."

"It's not so rare."

"I was shocked when you told me."

"Didn't you see my ring?" she said. "It's as big as the Ritz."

"I don't usually notice things like that."

We were silent for a while.

"We could talk about boxing. I've always wanted to know about it."

I shook my head. "No good."

"You shouldn't look at me that way," she said.

"What way?"

"You know."

"It's too dark for you to see how I'm looking at anything."

"There's a moon," she said.

"So you drove me all the way out here just because you felt sorry about my poor head?"

"Don't be mean. I'd like to be your friend."

"A girl like you is drowning in friends. What's one more or less?"

The air was cold off the ocean. Jamie was hugging herself to stay warm. "I like you," she said. "You're more interesting than most of the people I know."

I wanted to lean over and kiss her and smell her hair and carry her back to the house and lay her down on my bed and feel how warm she was. But I didn't know how to do any of that.

Some time later, I walked her back to her car and watched her drive away.

When the phone rang the next evening, I knew it wouldn't be her. Still, I wasn't surprised when I lifted the receiver and heard her voice.

"Thatcher gave me your number."

"Yes," I said.

"Can I come see you?"

"Of course."

"Right now?"

"If you want."

"You don't want me to?"

I listened to the ticking silence.

"I really do want to be your friend. I think maybe you got the wrong idea last night."

"Did I?" I said.

I strained to hear her breathing.

"I'm used to getting everything I want," she said after a long time. "I've never had to resist my impulses."

I didn't know what to feel. Until then, I had never quite believed any of it was true. "So why not just never see me again? Why make it hard on yourself?"

"Exposure is the only cure, I think. Anyway, it's a good test. Resisting temptation is part of what it means to be an adult."

"I don't know what it means to be an adult."

"Can I come over there?"

"Yes," I said.

I went into the living room to wait. I couldn't sit still. I paced in front of the window. Every time I heard a car engine I held my breath. My father sat in his armchair and shook his head.

When Jamie's SUV pulled into the driveway, my father said, "You're on your own." He dragged himself out of his chair and shuffled up the stairs to his bedroom.

She walked quickly toward the house with the light fading behind her. She was wearing a flowered sundress and white canvas sneakers. I met her at the door.

"Do you want to come in?"

"Come out," she said. "It's so beautiful."

We walked to the far end of my father's lawn without speaking. Next to us, the pool was steaming.

"Do you want to go swimming?" I said.

"It's a little cold for that."

"It's heated."

"Even so."

I imagined for a moment that the sound of the crickets was really the sound of the trees' breathing.

"Doesn't your fiancé usually come in on the weekends?"

"They were having weather problems in New York."

"He flies," I said.

"Of course."

"Of course."

She looked away from me. "I want you to teach me to fight."

"You know, sometimes I feel like that's all anybody ever wants to talk to me about."

"It's interesting," she said. "It's also safe. Anyway, I don't want to talk about it, I want you to teach me."

"Now?"

"Why not?"

I took a breath. "I haven't really been practicing."

"But you didn't forget how." She sighed. "You can't live your whole life treating yourself like you're made of china."

I ran my tongue over my bottom lip. "Make a fist," I said. She smiled.

"Keep your thumb bent and down to the side. If you keep it straight out like that you'll break it." I walked around behind her. "Now, keep your right hand locked against your jaw. Keep the left up too, but out in front of you and turned out a little. Keep your elbows in tight to your body. When you punch, you start and end in this position. Don't pull your hands back or drop them down before you throw and don't leave them stuck out for show after they land. You get back to this position as quick as you can. Make sure you're off balance as little as possible. Make sure your legs never cross. Keep your chin down. Always be ready. When you punch, explode from your legs and through your shoulder and throw your fist straight out like a bullet out of a gun."

She tried that a few times.

"You have to step into your punches," I said.

"That feels unnatural."

"As you get better, the step gets smaller. When you're good, the step is so small you almost can't see it."

"So why learn it this way?"

"At the beginning you have to take a real step to learn how to throw with your weight behind it."

She frowned.

"My father used to say imagine there's a ditch in front of you filled with alligators. Every time you punch, you have to think about stepping over the ditch."

She sighed. "When do I get to fight *you*?"

"I'm not sure you're ready for that."

"I thought you said you'd teach me."

"Not in one night. Where's your patience?"

"I don't have much." She turned toward me. "Come on. Tell me how you'd fight you. If you were me."

I looked at her. Then I said, "You'll want to stay inside to take away my reach advantage."

"What's 'inside'?" she asked.

"Inside just means close to me."

"So I have to stay close to you."

I felt the tingle along my spine. "Right," I said. "But first you have to *get* inside."

"How?"

I shrugged. "There's no one way. Mostly, you have to be willing to pay the price. I'll be trying to keep you off me by jabbing, which holds you at the proper range for my overhand right. Some people say jab a jabber, which means your job would be to counter with your own jab and use that to cover you so you can get close to me. Another way would be to just bull in under my jab. You'd have to eat a few if you did that, but probably you'd have to eat a few no matter what. Anyway, once you're inside you'll have to crowd me so I can't create enough distance between us to use my right hand and so you can keep us fighting inside where the shorter fighter has an advantage because it's easier for him to work to his opponent's body."

"Her," she said.

"What?"

"Easier for *her*."

I smiled. "If you can stay inside against a tall opponent, there's a chance he'll just fold, because the really tall guys usually aren't effective close in."

"You're not all that tall. You're not even six feet."

"Tall enough. Taller than you, anyway. But, unfortunately for you, my left hook is my best punch, which means I'm more dangerous inside than out. The only way to give yourself a chance is to try to beat me to the punch and throw your own left hook inside mine. If yours lands first and hits me as I'm putting my body into mine, then you'll be using my own power against me."

"Kind of like jab a jabber."

"Kind of," I said.

We walked back to the house with our bodies very close to each other but not touching. When we hugged good-bye at the door, she wouldn't let go. I looked at her.

"One of your eyes is smaller than the other," she said.

"I realize that."

"It's not noticeable unless you're really close and really looking."

"Yes."

She was looking up at me with big eyes.

Much later, when my headaches were gone and the summer had ended and Jamie's wedding was coming like a train, my days would blend together. I woke up. I ate. I worked. I lay in bed with Jamie and pulled the covers over us and the hours didn't pass and the world disappeared. I slept. At the end of every day there would be a moment when I thought I couldn't take it.

"You can't marry him," I would say then. "I love you."

"It's not that easy," Jamie would say.

"It should be," I would tell her.

But that night, in my father's living room, I didn't know about any of that. I said, "I'm going to kiss you."

"All right," Jamie said.

"Unless you tell me not to, I'm going to kiss you."

"Yes."

"Do you want me to?"

"Yes. You know I do."

I kissed her with my hands around her waist. She had one hand on the back of my neck. When we took a breath, I leaned back and looked at her face. I moved in again and kissed her again and then we were tearing at each other like animals. I was happy and desperate and delirious and frustrated all at once. Still, some part of me was very calm.

I took her to bed.

"Talk to me," she whispered after a while.

I pressed my lips against her ear, burying my face in her hair. "It's mine," I growled.

She gasped and pulled herself toward me even harder.

"It's mine," I told her.

"It's yours," she said between breaths.

My teeth were clenched. "It's always mine."

She held herself against me so that her back wasn't touching the bed. "Oh, my God," she said.

I licked her ear.

"Oh, my God," she said. "I'm coming."

She moved her hips against me. I felt the wave rising inside me, so I closed my eyes and thought about pain. Jamie's arms tightened around my neck.

"I'm coming," she said.

I felt the wave rising again. I imagined smoldering cities that bled rivers of refugees with burnt-paper skin hanging off them like rags. I pulled my head back out of Jamie's hair and opened my eyes to make sure she was still there. Her eyes were shut. Her lips shook like she was about to cry.

"I'm coming," she said. "I'm still coming."

This is real, I thought. But, really, it didn't matter.

A NOTE ABOUT THE AUTHOR

Benjamin Cavell attended Harvard College, where he was a boxer and an editor for The Harvard Crimson. Rumble, Young Man, Rumble *is his first book.*

A NOTE ON THE TYPE

*The text of this book was composed in Trump Mediæval.
Designed by Professor Georg Trump (1896–1985) in the mid-
1950s, Trump Mediæval was cut and cast by the C. E. Weber
Type Foundry of Stuttgart, Germany. The roman letter forms
are based on classical prototypes, but Professor Trump has
imbued them with his own unmistakable style. The italic
letter forms, unlike those of so many other typefaces, are
closely related to their roman counterparts. The result is
a truly contemporary type, notable for both its
legibility and its versatility.*

Composed by Creative Graphics, Allentown, Pennsylvania

Printed and bound by R. R. Donnelley & Sons, Harrisonburg, Virginia

Designed by Iris Weinstein